The Devil Chasers

Book I

In the Beginning

K.L. Hopkins

Tate Publishing, LLC

"The Devil Chasers" by K. L. Hopkins

Published in the United States of America
by Tate Publishing, LLC
127 East Trade Center Terrace
Mustang, OK 73064
(888) 361–9473

ISBN: 1–9331489–7-7

DEDICATION

To God, the Father of all spirits, who has delivered us
from the power of darkness
To Jesus, the Alpha and Omega,
the beginning and the end
To the Anointed all powerful One,
in whom are hidden all the treasures of wisdom
and knowledge
And to the Joshua generation, the called out ones,
coming with Jesus in great power
and dominion
to execute judgment
on the kingdom of darkness.

For by Jesus all things were created
that are in heaven and that are on earth,
visible and invisible.
whether thrones or dominions
or principalities or powers.
All things were created through Him and for Him.
And He is before all things,
and in Him all things consist.
And He is the head of the body,
who is the beginning,
the firstborn from the dead,
that in all things
He may have the preeminence.

Colossians 1:15–18

The Devil Chasers

In the Beginning

The wind gently blew over the trees skimming their tops like a glider. The familiar dance of the air currents surrounding the globe was undisturbed by the speed of light motions occurring in the secret places. Two separate movements unrelated to each other were taking place in the same space, but only one was aware of the other.

The dark side of the planet earth was only slightly illuminated because the moon was exposed as a sliver in the atmosphere. The stars were partly blocked by clouds moving with the wind. The piercing of the earth's dimension from deep space was faster than human detection. To the naked eye it seemed quiet, but to the trained spiritual eye the many movements indicated an organized military exercise.

Dwellers on earth lived in three dimensions, unaware of the spiritual maneuvers occurring in the many dimensions surrounding their existence. Most humans who entered the cycle of night, the side of earth concealed from the sun, spent that time sleeping, allowing their body the rest it required. To the rational, natural mind, whether it was night or day, the spiritual dimension was hidden. Even though a spiritual army was on assignment to protect a race of beings who categorically denied their existence, they were unmoved by unbelief because they had their orders. They were ministering spirits sent forth as a flame of fire defending the inhabitants on earth against the kingdom of darkness.

The invisible mysterious beings in white surrounded a two story mansion. Their orders were to protect the family inside from the many attacks perpetrated against them by the dark ones. Encamped around the property line, they stood shoulder to shoulder enforcing strict security measures. The latest communication put them on high alert status; they were preparing for the Anointed One.

The heavenlies shook and trembled at His coming. He came as a thief in the night, transported dimensionally with the darkness under His feet. Penetrating the night with His glory, He made the darkness His secret place. He moved with the swiftness of a gazelle and wore the cloak of humility, the secret weapon of invisibility.

He was the Son of the morning and the light of the world. All things existed by the Word of His power. Darkness was exposed by the brightness of His coming. Unable to comprehend His ways, the dark ones could not stop Him. With an unquenchable vengeance the darkness hated the light. They vainly plotted to destroy Him and all He had illuminated, but He who sat in the heavens laughed. Their attempts were futile.

Splitting dimensions and time, the light, like the sun shining in its strength, arrived and the ministering spirits bowed announcing His entry to those inside the home. The faithful witness, the firstborn from the dead, the ruler over the kings of the earth, the One who is and who was and who is to come, the Almighty passed through the front door.

CHAPTER 1

Joshua Paul Knight woke up suddenly.

In the corner of his room a small ball of light appeared. Strangely, instead of being fearful, a warm feeling of peace enveloped him. Curious about the light, he sat up in his bed and studied it. The light grew increasingly intense as it turned round and round and a form of a man materialized.

Joshua shielded his eyes from the light's brilliancy. The man appearing before him had glowing white hair and beautiful gold piercing eyes. Looking directly into the intense beams of radiant light was almost impossible, but an irresistible desire flooded him, drawing his spirit like a moth toward the light. Almost simultaneously a sensation of indescribable peace and joy entered him and instantly he felt free from his soul. It was the most powerful feeling that he had ever experienced in his young life.

He was released from all fear.

A voice from the light spoke to him. "Joshua, you are called to manifest My word to your generation."

Jesus! How he knew it was Jesus speaking to him he had no idea, but he received instant knowledge of that fact and he knew that he knew. Countless times he heard Jesus speak with his spiritual ears, but he had never heard His voice with his natural ears, until now. Every cell in his body and every thought in his mind and every vowel or syllable he had ever learned were shouting JESUS inside him.

Joshua dreamed about meeting the Lord many times. Only, in his dream, the meeting was in heaven and not his bedroom. He had carefully rehearsed all the things he wanted to ask Jesus, but he couldn't remember one of his questions. His mind seemed blank and his throat was dry. The light radiating from the form suddenly ceased and the man Jesus appeared before him. A warm golden glow surrounded him.

"I have come in answer to your prayer."

He nodded his head, wondering why he didn't say something.

Joshua had been praying about leaving the Christian high school that he was attending, but his parents had major concerns. Even though he loved his friends and respected his parents' judgment, he could not ignore the feeling in his gut every time he had contact with any teenagers outside of the church. His parents, with an increasing number of Christians, believed that the spirit of anti-Christ was controlling the public school system in America. By having removed prayer, the Ten Commandments and the Bible out of the schools, students were open targets for satan and his kingdom of darkness who hated God.

From experience, Joshua knew that many people chose not to believe that an evil invisible being, known as satan throughout the ages and who Jesus proclaimed to be the father of lies, existed. He agreed with his parents that satan manipulated politicians and the courts by establishing the doctrine of separation of church and state. He understood statistics revealed that the success of the public school system since the mid-sixties had declined dramatically. He speculated that unbelieving teachers and administrators could have a problem with his religious beliefs, especially his belief in their perceived imaginary character, the devil, but Joshua was willing to take that chance.

All these things that concerned his parents were the very things that compelled him to attend public school, especially after the Holy Spirit opened his eyes to see into the spirit realm. He had gone to a public school basketball game with a friend from church and during half-time the Holy Spirit gave him an open vision sitting in the bleachers. His immediate reaction was one of repulsion and wonder if he was just imagining the terrible scene before him. Moving around, he realized that he was in full control of all his senses.

He saw all kinds of creepy, ugly distorted looking evil beings hanging around humans and attached to them. With shock he saw them using humans as toilets. Black spiders, monkeys, bats and all kinds of grotesque creatures were literally harassing and torturing people all around him. The Lord even opened his nose to smell how disgusting the demonic spirits smelled. He was totally horrified at what he saw and after that experience he could not eat or sleep peacefully for a week. At the time, he wasn't sure why the Lord let him see things happening to the people sitting around him, but his life was forever changed.

He kept thinking over and over if only they knew the truth about satan, then he was sure that kids his age would denounce all ties and bondages with the devil. If only they knew that Jesus Christ, the Word made flesh, had already defeated these horrible creatures from hell, then they would never listen to satan's lies. He wanted to shout to everyone in that gymnasium that Jesus was the all powerful One.

If only was all he thought about day and night. It was frustrating to know the truth and not know a way to share it with his generation.

"The young people of your generation will overcome God's enemy,"

Jesus told him. "I have come to reveal the Father's plan for you at this time. This is the beginning of your assignment on earth."

Joshua's spirit leaped inside him.

"Revival will start in America with the youth. The ones that satan is trying to destroy and kill, God is going to turn them around and use them against the kingdom of darkness."

Joshua knew of several prophets of God that had predicted a great revival in America that would start with the youth. It certainly didn't look like that was possible with his generation. It seemed to him that satan was winning the battle over the minds of teenagers through the American public school system and media arena. He thought about the way satan seduced teenagers daily through movies, magazines, radio and TV programs dealing with sex, teen idols, rock stars, drugs, sports, image and money; all of it without the benefit of knowing the God who created them.

He was talking to the Lord once after his open vision at the basketball game . . .

. . ."Global wars with horrible acts are being perpetrated against mankind daily," Joshua quoted an article from a very liberal newspaper in America. He folded the paper setting it aside. "Yeah and the majority of humans do not have a clue of what is going on and who is causing it!"

The Lord answered him. *Satan may have won a few battles, but he hasn't won the war.*

"What about Columbine?" Joshua opened the newspaper again to show it to the Lord. "According to the press, killing at schools is the latest catastrophe confronting America." He was mad. "Satan is literally trying to get rid of the generation that You said is going to be the fire to ignite the biggest revival this world has ever known, but look how he is killing teenagers and getting away with it?! Look at what the press is saying about the whole thing! They think that it is kids killing kids, but You and I both know that it is really satan killing kids!" He pointed to the article and looked over his shoulder as if the Lord was literally standing behind him.

Your generation will learn from Columbine.

"Satan killed those kids and it makes me mad!"

Satan is killing a lot of people. It makes Me mad too!

Joshua waded up the newspaper into a ball and shot it at the wastepaper basket by his desk. "The thing I hate the most is when the kingdom of darkness convinces Christians that You somehow planned or willed those Christians kids to be killed!"

I hate it too!

"Lord, I have to do something!" Joshua stood and started walking the floor in his bedroom. "I want to expose the devil to the kids that attend public school."

The Lord listened to his words.

"I want to chase all the devils out of every school in my city!" He stopped pacing thinking about what he just said. "Not just here! I want to chase devils out of every public school in the whole U.S.!" . . .

. . . It had been almost two years now since his conversation with the Lord and the fire inside him that started that fateful day after the killing of several teenagers burned with an intensity level that seemed unquenchable.

Jesus watched Joshua get absorbed in the passion the Father put in his heart. He smiled as Joshua got out of his bed and went around Him to his desk and back again, almost as if He wasn't even physically in his bedroom. His reaction was proving that the Father's plan was going to be fulfilled through him.

Sitting on the edge of his bed, he looked up at Jesus. "What's the plan?" Thinking about the seemingly impossible situation he asked, "How can my generation overcome when the political structure is so set against them hearing, reading or knowing anything about You through Your Word?"

The Father is going to turn around what the devil has done and double it back in blessing on this generation of believers. What satan has meant for evil against My young people, God means it for good.

I can hear what you are thinking! Oh wow! I not only have to watch every word I say, but every word I think!

Out of the mind the mouth speaks, Jesus reminded him.

It's different having You here in the natural realm. I don't usually talk to someone who knows everything that I have ever thought or said. Joshua was so use to imaging the Lord in heaven, not on earth. "I mean, You know I talk to You all the time, but not face to face."

"I know what you are saying. My body needs to start imaging Me on earth NOW every day. This is our Father's time." *I am come for the Father's purpose on earth now. Not yesterday, not tomorrow, but now.*

Wow! It is really awesome that I can hear Your thoughts!

Our Father has many ways of communicating. He is unlimited in every resource. Jesus continued directing his thoughts into Joshua's mind. *Thoughts are words in the spiritual realm. On earth, thoughts are building blocks for the words that come out of your mouth.*

Joshua's natural mind reasoned. *Wouldn't it be great if we could read each other's minds here on earth?*

"No," Jesus spoke plainly. "You would not want to read the thoughts of an evil mind."

A scripture from Proverbs came into his mind; *the thoughts of an evil man were evil continually.* It was inconceivable how God could put up with all evil thoughts from people all over the world at the same time. "How can God stand hearing evil thoughts?"

"He doesn't listen to everything that is said. He listens to His Words that are spoken."

Joshua wrote exactly what Jesus said. "I know that you know what I say every day because Your Word says that You are the High Priest over my confession."

Suddenly, Joshua realized that the glow from Jesus had disappeared as the chair he was sitting on moved closer to his bed. His hair was now a golden brown and his eyes reflected a blue-green sea color. He was wearing a beige color robe with a gold belt and sandals.

When he locked eyes with Jesus' he was no longer interested in His physical appearance or the thousands of questions he wanted to ask Him. The feeling of freedom from the curse of this world was awesome, but the unconditional knowledge of love from Him was beyond words. Joshua thought about the deep-seated need inside every human being that craves and desires love and acceptance above all else. That need was instantly fulfilled in the presence of Jesus.

Jesus.

Just thinking and talking with Him created an atmosphere of peace that was beyond human comprehension. It was like Joshua entered a time warp and everything in the room blacked out as he focused totally on Jesus. Love filled his heart and overflowed into his mind and body. He had read about people who had had an encounter with Jesus and they said His eyes looked like pools of love. He wondered what they meant, but now he knew exactly.

"I love everyone. I died for every soul. Every man, woman and child that has ever been born on this earth, was on my mind when I went to the cross. But I don't want you to stop at the cross; I want you to start with My defeat of the kingdom of darkness. Your generation needs to learn how to live for Me. This is the Father's time and today is the day of knowledge that will keep My body from being destroyed. Begin your calling by organizing a phone ministry."

"I've been thinking about . . ." The voice of Jesus stopped Joshua's thoughts. He cleared his throat and said in a lower tone, "Phones?"

That was exactly what he was thinking. Almost every teenager owns their own personal cell phone. Ministries with telephone prayer lines were usually answered by adults. Phones were the communication link between most teenagers, but not necessarily between teens and adults. He was thinking that maybe a phone line with Christian teenagers answering would encourage more young people to seek help from Christians their own age.

"I gave you that idea."

"I get so many ideas. Once in awhile I wonder if it is my idea or if it might be from you . . . or . . ."

"Is that your confession?" The Lord interrupted his words.

Joshua lowered his head smiling. The Lord caught him and they both knew it. "No. I've been confessing John 10:3, 'To him the doorkeeper opens, and the sheep hear his voice. He calls His own sheep by name and leads them out. And when he brings out his own sheep, he goes before them. The sheep follow Him, for they know His voice.'"

"Continue confessing My Word. I will bring it to pass. The Holy Spirit's job is to remind you of the Word you have studied. Your job is to read, hear, memorize and meditate. Take your thoughts about God and His Word with your voice and speak to your generation. They will listen. This is our Father's pre-set time. Tell them about My Father's everlasting love and Covenant with His children who will hear and obey His voice. He loves everybody and He is not willing that ANY should perish."

Jesus stopped talking as the Holy Spirit communicated a message to Joshua.

God is a Spirit who is a Father that has a great desire for sons and daughters; children. God is a Father. God is a Mother. God is love. God has a great desire for children. God loves His Family. God yearns and desires a personal relationship with His children. Jesus, My Son, opened the door and is the door for My Family to be with Me for eternity!

Joshua heard the message with his spiritual ears. It felt like every cell vibrated in his body with an outpouring of love from God and that love responded to the voice of the Holy Spirit. Each word sounded like a perfect melody playing inside him and he was one with the song of God.

"The Father's love is greater than the power of darkness. It is written that love covers a multitude of sins."

Many scriptures about God's love filled Joshua's mind almost faster than he could think. *God is love. Jesus is the Word made flesh. As the Father loved Me, I also have loved you. Abide in My love. If you keep My commandments, you will abide in My love, just as I have kept My Father's commandments and abide in His love. Greater love has no one than this, that to lay down one's life for his friends. These things I command you, that you love one another. For God so loved the world that He gave . . .*

"Love is the most powerful force in our universe."

Joshua, feeling the power of that force, wanted to fall to the ground and bow in total worship to Jesus. Keeping his flesh from reacting to such an intense level of love from Jesus was extremely difficult. He concentrated his thoughts on God's mercy and grace since he was amazed that he was hearing the audible voice of Jesus and looking at His face.

"I feel so . . ." He interrupted himself realizing that his feelings were bound to flesh and in the presence of the physical form of the pure love of God with all knowledge, wisdom and understanding, feelings are worthless. Knowing God's Word kept Joshua from surrendering to the weak, fainting feeling that threatened to overwhelm him. "Lord . . ." He demanded his flesh to obey him. "You have revealed in Your Word that we should seek Your wisdom and desire understanding with all our heart and strength."

He couldn't stop talking.

"Wisdom is the principal thing. Not natural wisdom, but God's wisdom through the written Word. That is the most important thing in life. Exalting the Word of God is the wisdom of God and wisdom protects and delivers to Christians a crown of glory. You are the Word of God . . ."

"Joshua, your flesh is driving you now."

"What?" The Lord's words stopped him.

"Your flesh is talking."

Joshua felt the blood drain from his face. He was so embarrassed that his flesh was talking so much when it should have been silent and listening. Saying the words "I'm sorry" that came into his mind would have only compounded his mistake because that would have been fleshly sorrow.

"Tell your generation that *I am coming!*" Jesus understood the feelings that Joshua was experiencing.

"I don't understand. Tell Christians or unbelievers? Doesn't everybody know about Your coming?" The question in his mind caused him to forget about his embarrassment. "I mean every Christian that I know talks about Your return."

"No, they don't know. Tell them over the phone that I am coming."

Maybe I don't understand what Jesus is saying. "I mean, are you talking about the rapture?" Joshua reached for the yellow pad and pen from his bed and wrote down what Jesus just said underscoring the statement with a question mark.

Jesus leaned forward. "What you call the rapture is a coronation celebration and dinner uniting the members of My body who live in heaven and on earth. It is going to take place in Our Father's house."

"A dinner?" He had never heard the rapture called a dinner before.

"Yes. The angels are preparing it now. The people of the world are not ready from My coming; they are not accepting my invitation."

But his thinking still hadn't connected to what Jesus was talking about. "Am I missing something? Why won't Your own people accept an invitation to dinner?"

"This celebration is for My body of believers filled with both Jew and Gentiles made new into one new man."

Joshua inserted, "You are the head and we are the body."

"Yes, we are one new man. When a human accepts the Covenant I made with the Father through the sacrifice of My body, then he or she becomes one with Me. We are a new creation."

You just repeated what You said, so that means it is very important, he thought as he underlined it in his notes.

"Our Father is pleased when He is believed through His written Word."

Without faith, it is impossible to please Him. Faith comes by hearing the Word of God. Joshua couldn't count the times that he had meditated the written Word of God after he discovered that the Greek verb for hearing was an action word that meant to hear over and over again.

"You have to believe what I say, not what you see. Faith is the only way to please our Father. My people don't know that I am coming to invite them."

Now he was really confused. Joshua couldn't count the sermons he had heard teaching about the rapture of the church before the tribulation and that Jesus was coming soon. His parents believed that the rapture would take place before Jesus came back to earth to set up His Kingdom. They told Joshua that since scripture supported many different appointed times of transfiguration or rapture, they might as well use their faith and go with the first load.

That made sense to Joshua.

"You are coming." He repeated it again beginning the process of meditation over the specific Words of Jesus. "Lord, I believe that You are coming."

"I know, but I am coming now."

"I have this feeling that I am missing something."

"Separate traditions from your mind. Meditate on what I am telling you, understanding will come."

One question still lingered in his mind. "Why is it called 'rapture' if it is a dinner?"

"Rapture is the name of the way of departure not the name of the event. Early Christians gave it that name."

"What does Father God call it?" Joshua asked.

"A royal coronation to crown Me King of kings and Lord of lords. It is dinner celebration with His family and assignments will be given out to My body, His children so that We can rule the earth."

"Is everybody invited?"

"Everyone," Jesus answered.

"Some believe that this event is automatic if you are a Christian. There are books that say every Christian will go up in the rapture, even all children under the age of accountability and all unborn babies."

Joshua was really asking Jesus to reveal His thoughts on something he had been thinking seriously about for a couple of years now. Every Christian fiction writer he had read used the standard seventies rapture scenario; people disappearing and leaving neatly folded clothes behind, children and even babies disappearing from pregnant ladies, cars crashing, airplanes falling from the skies with total chaos reining on earth.

"It's hard for me to believe that God could be the author of such confusion on earth after the rapture."

"Our Father is not the author of confusion."

"The whole scenario of destruction and chaos after the rapture represents a picture of God as a cold, heartless, harsh being throwing lightening spears at people on earth from somewhere in outer space."

"Joshua, I have a special note of thanks from our Father. He is pleased that you have chosen to believe that He is a God of love and that you choose to believe that everything good is from Him and that everything bad is from the devil." Jesus knew that Joshua didn't know that the ultimate test of a prophet is to be able to discern between good and evil. "You have never been mad at God when bad things happen."

Once again Joshua's heart leaped inside of him.

Jesus liked the way Joshua was thinking about Father God. When He was on earth, His disciples didn't know what to think about their Father in heaven. Countless times they asked Him "what did He look like" or "how do we pray to Him?" All their questions revealed that they knew nothing about their Creator.

"Our Father wants to communicate with His children, not destroy or hurt them, especially those who don't believe in Him. What is the purpose of any of His creation being lost for eternity? How could the Creator get any pleasure in death?"

Joshua had spent many hours meditating on those exact questions. He had come to the conclusion that a good and righteous God even with justice would get no pleasure out of destruction or death.

Jesus changed the subject knowing that Joshua had many questions he wanted to ask of Him. "Nothing is automatic on earth because of the influence of the kingdom of darkness and wicked men. As long as the enemy controls the heavenlies surrounding earth, he is working to keep My people blocked from the windows of heaven."

"Then we are really responsible for the timing of the rapture?"

Jesus liked the path way of his thoughts. "Remember, I am coming for a body that is perfect, without spot and wrinkle."

"That's another difficult scripture to visualize."

"Nothing is too difficult for our Father."

"Hmm . . . '*All things are possible to him who believes.*'" His mom raised him on that scripture. "My mom and dad said that the only way to live on this earth is by faith through Your Word. They have taught me to make confession of the Word over every situation in life. It's the Word that cleanses us, so it must be the Word that is going to make us perfect."

"Your parents are wise."

Doctrines of men have divided Your body, not made it one.

"You are right; doctrines do not have the power to make My body perfect. The father of lies has taught mankind his system of operation under the law of sin and death."

"Many of Your followers still relate more to the old person they were than the new person that they are now. What will happen to those who are left behind?"

"He has made provision for all people, even those who do not accept His invitation for that special occasion."

"I'm not going to miss it!" Joshua couldn't subdue his enthusiasm.

"Continue to study My Word and meditate the scriptures. My coming is in My Book. It is important for you to understand your calling. It is your generation that will be the channel for the Holy Spirit to fulfill Our Father's plans for a great harvest at the end of the age. Remember, the enemy knows that God has chosen and ordained the youth to carry the message of the gospel to the ends of the earth."

Repent, for the Kingdom of God is at hand. The message of the good news entered his mind. He understood that the message of the Kingdom of God was God's way of being right and doing right. His mind was thoroughly trained in God's predestined purpose that sent His Son anointed with power to destroy the works of the devil. Joshua had meditated many hours about the only way to God was through Jesus Christ crucified, dead three days and risen from the grave with a new spirit and body. "I will obey You, Jesus."

"Satan's kingdom is busy destroying My Father's works. My body should be destroying his evil works. I left this earth under the jurisdiction of My body, not the kingdom of darkness. In the time that is left, he will strike the young people with death and destruction as never before."

Joshua felt like he was getting combat orders.

"Your job is to teach young people My Word and how to fight the devil. Take My authority and push back the enemy until he is completely subdued and under My feet. Tell them I love them and that I am coming."

He stood and said, "Yes, Sir!"

Jesus put his hands on Joshua's shoulders. "I ordained you before you were born for this time." He touched Joshua's head. "From this moment on, you will operate in several manifestations from the Holy Spirit and visions will be part of your anointing."

When the Lord touched him, an electrical current went all over his body and a very warm feeling enveloped him; he felt like fainting. He forced himself to continue standing because a soldier at attention does not fall over. He looked up at Jesus and smiled. He wondered if this is what it felt like to be drunk.

The Holy Spirit spoke to his heart. *You are drunk and under the influence of Me!*

Joshua's spirit leaped once again like so many times since Jesus materialized in His glorified body to visit with him.

"Go, be My voice and my witness and tell them that I am coming."

"Yes Sir!"

"And Joshua remember what your mother says to you every time you leave her: you are a winner, not a loser, the head and not the tail, above only and not beneath, a son of God, seed of Abraham, joint-heir with Me. You are blessed coming in and going out, no weapon formed against you will prosper and you can do all things through Me because of the Holy Spirit inside you who gives you strength."

Jesus walked back into the light that appeared in the corner of his bedroom and disappeared. As fast as the light first appeared, suddenly it was gone and he was alone.

The glow of the Lord's presence lingered. He looked around the room sensing an almost surreal atmosphere surrounding him. His nightstand light was still on, but everything else was dark again. Sitting at his desk, he closed his eyes thinking how awesome it was to know that Jesus sat in his chair.

He prayed, "Lord, you said the steps of a righteous man are ordered by You. You said to seek first Your kingdom and Your righteousness. Father, in the Name of Jesus, I ask you to guide me with the Spirit of wisdom and understanding in the next steps I am to take in forming this ministry according to Your will. Thank You that You said You would never leave me or forsake me. I am totally confident in Your ability."

Joshua began writing furiously. Every word had to be written exactly as Jesus said. Later, he would meditate and study on each word and find scriptures to support them . . .

. . . Laying his pen down, Joshua stood and inhaled deeply to breathe in the beautiful presence of the Lord. His room smelled like a fresh bouquet of flowers. It reminded him of the first time he smelled a sweet aroma in his room. Wondering where it was coming from, the Lord told him that He was that fragrance.

In the Word of God, he found that Jesus was the lily of the valley and the rose of Sharon. Fragrance emitting from God was delightfully pleasant. Joshua hoped the smell would stay forever. He got back in bed and pulled the covers over him, wondering if he would be able to sleep.

Not realizing that throughout the rest of the night he occasionally released an outburst of laughter, he slept like a baby.

CHAPTER 2

That night in the heavenly regions above earth and in the Lord's space station, Michael the Archangel began to organize the angels that would be appointed to the ministry that Joshua was starting on earth. The army of angels in their white gleaming attire of shirts and trousers was standing at attention in the Hall of Faithfulness waiting for their orders. It was the beginning of what was being called the Knight Campaign.

"Kientay, I'm putting you in charge of helping Joshua locate the members that will be the foundation of this ministry." Michael informed him, standing taller than the other warring angels and a foot taller than most guardian angels. He was wearing a white shirt with a huge golden belt at his waist and white trousers. His copper color skin glowed from being in the presence of the Lord and his hair matched the color of the golden shoes on his feet.

Kientay, guardian angel of Joshua, was filled with delight! He wore a brown v-necked shirt with laces and brown trousers. On earth he liked to wear clothes that looked like his charge, Joshua, but in honor of the invitation to the warring angels' headquarters in the heavenlies, he wore one of the warring angel's official outfits.

His exuberance was overflowing. "When Joshua was born, I knew instantly that he was a special baby. It was almost like the night when Lord Jesus was born! Glory to God on the Highest!" He could hardly contain his emotions. At the mention of His blessed name the angels fell to the ground and worshiped the Son of God.

Michael stood. "Be careful Kientay! Do not let the Adamic human emotions carry you away! This is a big assignment for a human as young as Joshua; he is still in need of a lot of tutoring. You must follow your training and refuse to be distracted with emotions."

"I pray that the Almighty would never allow the Adamic emotions to control me!" Just the thought of the Adamic nature controlling one of God's angels was repulsive to all the faithful angels that still lived under the authority of the Almighty's Kingdom.

Kientay instantly reigned in his emotions. He didn't want to start out on the wrong foot with Michael, since it was a privilege to be given a personal assignment from the top commander of the division of warring angels.

"The Knight campaign will be the catalyst for revival with the youth of America. I hope you understand how important it is that Joshua be successful in forming this ministry."

"Yes, sir!"

"Humans are notorious for catching their vision and then letting it slip out of their hands," Michael reminded him.

"Oh, but General, sir, Joshua's parents have been preparing him for this time ever since he was born. They have taught him the Anointed One's Words day and night. He is ready for the battle."

"I read his file from the heavenly archives. The Almighty is pleased with his training. When the enemy finds out about him, he will spare nothing to try to destroy him."

"I believe that Joshua and his parents will be victorious over anything the enemy plans against them. There are no seeds of death in them." Kientay was more than confident that the devil would find nothing in them.

"They meditate and confess Psalm 91?" Another angel asked.

"Yes. Everyday they declare that 'no weapon formed against them will prosper in the name of Jesus.' And they plead the Blood of Jesus and apply it to their home, cars and physical body every day. They know that a spiritual war is taking place on earth."

"It is a rare human that wakes up every morning realizing that he is fighting a spiritual war," another angel spoke.

The Holy Spirit's voice sounded from His headquarters on earth as the angels bowed their faces to the ground.

A war is taking place on planet earth. Satan and his angels of darkness are fighting the Lord Jesus and His angels of light over the fate of this planet and man. Untold numbers of My warring angels are stationed on earth fighting daily for the protection and deliverance of the human race against the forces of evil. It is a war that My angels are thoroughly and skillfully trained to fight and it is a war that will take on a new dimension seeing these are the last days.

It is a war between good and evil. It is the war that the Lord God has declared before the beginning of time that His Son and His body has won. It is a war that will result in the kingdom of darkness being totally banished from earth and the full restoration of the original earth that We created. There is a predestined end that will prove unequivocally that good is triumphant over evil, and We will recover all that We lost.

Kientay decided to fly home on the back of a white horse instead of taking the angel transport system. A multitude of thoughts entertained his mind as he took his time enjoying God's creation. *War on earth is hell, but partnered with God, war is victory,* he thought as he viewed earth coming within his powerful eyesight. He eagerly awaited the total conquest of the kingdom of darkness by the body of the Anointed One and the liberation of God's creation. He thought about the groaning and longsuffering of creation waiting for the revealing of the sons of God that would deliver them from the bondage of corruption and how glorious it was going to be.

Praise the Lord! He couldn't help but shout out loud as he entered earth's atmosphere cloaked from the enemy. Joshua was one of the called one's Enoch prophesied that would come with ten thousands of His saints, to execute judgment on all, and to convict all who were ungodly among them of all their ungodly deeds which they had committed in an ungodly way. Joshua was one of the called out ones that will fight in the heavenlies with Jesus before His second coming.

The stars were twinkling and singing of the glories of God. He especially was delighted in the singing of the morning stars that signaled another beautiful day of creation that the Lord had made. Their sounds declared the glory of God and His righteousness. Kientay stopped in mid-air to allow the sweet music to minister to his ears. It was sad that the inhabitants of earth were blocked from hearing because of the covering of the curse. Like all God's angels, he hated the evil that allowed the curse entrance to the earth.

Thinking of evil reminded him that soon the skies above Joshua's house would host numerous beings both good and evil in a very powerful conflict. The lord of darkness may have already picked up the fact that the Lord God Jehovah would be establishing another stronghold in Jesus' Name.

As Kientay neared the Knight house, he knew that a good solid foundation of prayer was the only way for Joshua to begin his ministry. He smiled as he thought about the blessed parents that God had given Joshua. Dan and Vicki Knight were great spiritual praying parents. He was so excited that he would be seeing some action. It was hard for angels, especially Kientay, to have to sit on the sidelines of a human assignment that does not understand that natural earth life is engulfed in a spiritual war.

He landed on the roof and waved at the warring angels surrounding the Knight home. The prayer covering that was coming from the Knight family was the reason so many angels had been dispatched for the family's protection. He descended from the roof and touched ground by one of the angels. "What is the status of the hedge of protection?"

A warring angel walked forward. "There is no entrance into this house. The prayers with faith give us more than adequate power to defeat the principalities and powers surrounding the area."

"Have you ever been assigned to a human family that tries to fight spiritual problems with natural weapons?" Kientay wondered.

The warring angels looked at one another. One spoke out. "Is that possible?"

Kientay looked surprised. "Where have you been for the last two thousand years?"

"We are a special warring force assigned to General Michael."

"Hmm. No wonder you don't know about God's children trying to use natural weapons against spiritual problems."

"What happens?"

"You have to stand down no matter what the situation is because you are bound."

"No!" They both said together.

Several angels gathered around and spoke in their angelic tongue. One called out to Kientay as he walked toward the house. "Do you know why we have been assigned to the young human?"

He turned around smiling. "Yes. He is a mighty man of valor and the Lord is with him!"

Kientay entered the house and walked up the stairs to Joshua's bedroom. Vicki walked passed him as he stepped aside to watch her. The day that they could communicate with humans in the natural realm would be awesome. Soon, angels from heaven and humans on earth would be working side by side, but for now angels on earth were the only ones that had knowledge of several dimensions.

He continued to the top of the stairs thinking about how the good angels walk in perfect harmony with the Holy Spirit. They were filled with His presence and kept well informed on the works of the enemy.

Walking through the door into Joshua's bedroom, he was so glad that his young charge joined the war effort with him through the spiritual force of faith. Even though Joshua could not see Kientay, he used his spiritual eyes with faith to fight the kingdom of darkness. He stood behind Joshua watching him write down notes over the Bible.

His faith is growing by leaps and bounds as Joshua exercises his spiritual senses. The angels are going to love working for this family, thought Kientay. *Faith is released several times a day around this house so the enemy has no defense against their Word based faith.*

Praise the Lord! Glory to God! He shouted over and over again jumping up and down. "Finally," he spoke out loud, "a human child who loves God with all his heart and soul!"

Joshua turned around thinking he heard someone speak out loud in his room.

Walking around the room, Kientay didn't realize that he disturbed his young charge. *While kids his age played sports and spent much time with their computers, games, videos, movies and music, he spent his time seeking the Lord through study of the Bible and praying. Most angels are bound and bored, but not me!* He was jumping up and down all around Joshua's room. *Thank you Lord! Thank you Lord! Thank you Lord!*

"What's up Kientay?" asked Kara, Vicki's guardian angel, as she walked through the wall from Joshua's parents' bedroom.

He was trying to contain himself, but he could not do it any longer. He grabbed Kara and danced ballroom style, twirled her around as she tripped over his feet, and they both landed on the bed.

"Oh! Sometimes you are too strange! Do you even remember that you are a guardian angel?" Kara brushed off her white robe and straightened her gold belt that had twisted around her waist. "Do you?" She asked indignantly.

He ignored her choosing to watch Joshua.

She was still wearing her heaven clothes, since she had been visiting other angels about the coming change of events. On earth Kientay and she both liked to wear the clothes that human teenagers wear. Instantly she transformed her attire into her usual jeans and t-shirt by thinking about it.

"I know my Creator, and I know who I am," Kientay reminded her. "Joshua just had a visit from the Lord and I have personally talked with Michael about his calling."

"Kientay, haven't you realized by now that some of the other guardian angels here on earth and some angels in heaven are talking about you?"

She used a tone of human frustration to indicate her feelings about his emotional outbursts. He had been the main topic of conversations in heaven more than once with her angelic friends. She loved her visits to heaven, but she disliked having to answer their inquiries about Kientay.

"Why bother talking to the angels who still live in heaven about humans on earth? Kara, you know that the angels in heaven still wonder about the humans God created. You can't explain a human who is living on earth to them so why try? They only live with humans in heaven without their flesh body and we both know that you can't even compare the two states."

He was right. It was hard to explain to a heaven bound angel what it is like protecting humans on earth, but in heaven she tried to justify Kientay's actions anyway, even though she was also concerned about his seemingly human emotional break downs. "That's beside the point!" She didn't want to let him off the hook that easy. Guardian angels were trained with strict protocol. "It is imperative that we are calm in all situations. Our instructions . . ."

Kientay held up his hand. "I am thoroughly versed in the Covenant between God the Father and Jesus and the laws that govern earth. I have been assigned to earth since the beginning of time. I know that we are the administrators of the Covenant between God and humans. I know that we are ordained as official ministers to the heirs of salvation. I know that some humans would call us babysitters and some tutors, but those who understand the war against good and evil would call us guardians of the secret place."

"That sounds great, but how many humans even know what the secret place is?" Kara wanted him to be realistic instead of idealistic.

"Whether they understand what the secret place is or not is irrelevant to you or me. We are still honored guardians over the recipients of the secret place."

She stared at him. It was hard to make a point with him since she had only been a guardian angel for a few hundred years. She still guarded her heart when it came to attachment to her charges, but it was getting more difficult with each passing year not to become emotionally involved with her assignment.

"I'm surprised at you Kara." He went over to the window to look through the blinds to the angels guarding the Knight estate. "We worship the Lord God first and then we have the honor of being a guardian over a human who is in continual conflict with the forces of darkness. What if you were assigned to another human besides Vicki? Hmm? Maybe one that does not recognize Jesus as the Messiah?"

"I know what you are going to say next," she said sitting down on Joshua's bed. She tried to justify her position as she walked over to look at what Joshua was writing. "But soon we will all be living together and . . ."

"Then it will be different." He often interrupted Kara. "The curse will no longer be here with all the little pesky evil demons interfering with human emotions and will. No explanations will be necessary then."

It was his continual interruptions that gave her opportunity to connect with the human emotion of frustration, but then she had learned how to not let that emotion control her.

Kientay moved next to Kara who was still standing behind Joshua as he finished writing at his desk. He moved to put his hand on Joshua's shoulder. "We see and hear the attacks of evil against them daily. How can we not be affected by the continual onslaught that they endure on earth?"

Kara had to admit that he was right. Many times she had to turn away so she wouldn't see the attack of an evil spirit against her charge. "Waiting for permission to protect them is extremely hard. Especially when they could just speak the words from their own mouth and receive the Covenant protection ordered from God the Father."

"Now you are walking down the path of my thoughts. Since thoughts and words govern the actions that we can take on earth and most humans are ignorant of that fact, I can not be less than thrilled that we are assigned to the Knight family!" He raised his hands rejoicing thinking that he finally got through to Kara. "You know what I am saying is true."

"I know that you know we are bound to the Laws of God that reign over the earth and our human assignments."

"I know you, Kara, you act tough, but there are times that you would stop the harassing and torture if you could."

He was right, but she wouldn't admit it to him. "It is very hard not to want to interfere, but we have our orders and accordingly that is our mission on earth. Only those angels that are trained and trusted by the Lord completely merit a chance to guard a human being and I do not want to jeopardize my assignment."

"You have already demonstrated your choice to obey the Lord since the rebellion. You are a loyal angel who chose to be obedient and willing to resist the temptation of Lucifer." Kientay thought about a close friend of his who joined about a third of the heavenly host who were deceived by Lucifer and were kicked out of heaven.

She didn't want to think about the War of the Rebellion. "I trust in the love of God and the Holy Spirit's ability to protect and lead God's children. He is an excellent communicator and has never abandoned the human race." She defended her position as she sat down on Joshua's bed again.

"Jesus said that He would not leave his children orphans and He didn't. We are proof that He loves His family since we are working with the Holy Spirit protecting them. I don't think the Holy Spirit minds my emotional outbursts occasionally."

"Then what are we talking about? God is a perfect planner. The Holy Spirit is a perfect communicator. Satan would never be allowed to put one over on the Lord and sneak anything behind His back that He didn't know about. You and I both know that the Trinity is never late and They provide all the needs and wants of His family who trust in Them completely."

Now this was the Kara he liked to be around. "I agree. The problem is not with God it is always with the human. Most Christians do not develop a hearing ear to receive the warning that the Holy Spirit is trying to communicate to them before an evil attack. After being assigned to so many humans with dull ears, I am happy to have a human with a hearing ear. Kara, admit to me that you have feelings toward humans who don't know the Lord and the others who know the Lord, but do not know His Word."

"I will admit that I hate it when humans are at the mercy of the kingdom of darkness and they don't know how to protect themselves."

He had her on a roll. "How do you feel about protecting the Knights since we have permission to interfere in evil plots and intentions against them?"

She knew where Kientay was headed with this. "Okay, you want me to say that I am excited and have *happy* emotions because we can interfere with demonic will on their behalf and you are right."

"Yes!" He leaned over to give her a high five.

"Now see what you are doing. That is totally a human adolescent emotional expression."

Kientay ignored her and followed Joshua into his walk-in closet.

She went over to look at Joshua's notebook. "The Teacher has already informed me about his calling. The Lord is visiting Vicki in a dream and giving her a commission to form the prayer group with the mothers of the members Joshua is going to recruit."

He exited the closet. "Vicki knows how to apply His Blood for the covering they will need. She has been a great mother, preparing Joshua for this special assignment with her prayers and teaching of the Lord's Word. Joshua is the perfect one to receive this call."

Kientay was walking all around Joshua's room. With every excited thought, his body lifted a couple of inches off the ground. "Do you remember the first time Joshua ever stomped the devil's head?"

"Sure. You remind me at least a couple of times every day!" Kara rolled her eyes.

Joshua turned off his desk lamp and went over to his bed to lie down. They adjusted their angel night vision.

He ignored her. "He was so cute with his curly blond hair and very blue eyes. Vicki and Dan . . ."

"Kientay, I was there remember?"

Kara moved above the bed, hovering in the air, as Joshua straightened his covers and got back in bed. She didn't like knowing when a human walked through her spirit body; it was like she could feel something even though she didn't.

"Wasn't he cute during their devotional prayer time? There he was stomping the ground as hard as he could over and over with his little feet and his mom said, 'Joshua, what are you doing?'"

Joshua turned off the light by his bed and quickly went back to sleep. They could see through the veil of darkness that blacked out Joshua's vision.

"I'm stomping the debil's head!" They both said it out loud together laughing.

"That is probably why Joshua received this commission, he's not afraid of the devil," Kara said.

"Remember the time that Dan parked his car in front of the bar?"

Kara smiled recalling that Joshua wanted to go inside the bar. She remembered it vividly.

"How old was he?" Kientay asked.

"Let's see . . . I remember he was sitting in Vicki's lap, I think he had just turned four earth years."

"He said, 'Mama, I want to go in there.' She said, 'Oh no honey! You don't want to go in there, the devil is in there.'"

Kara laughed. "That's when Joshua said . . ."

They both chorused the answer, "'I'm not afraid of the debil!'"

"He certainly isn't like most young male adolescent humans," Kara laughed with him. She was excited about Vicki's teaching Joshua about the Lord. Abraham taught his children and the Lord called him a friend of His.

"Truly Kara, except for those who are in the same position I was, no angel can really understand a carnal human, especially a carnal Christian human."

"Kientay, just remember that you are not alone. All guardian angels have experienced flesh-centered, non-Bible reading, non-praying, baby Christians before." She moved over to sit with Kientay on the floor facing Joshua's bed. He loved to watch him sleep at night. She put her hand on his shoulder. "This is a celebration for all of us." She looked around the house wondering why Matthan, Dan's guardian angel wasn't with them.

He read her thoughts. "He is on special assignment."

Kientay and little Joshua had become close from the start of his assignment until Joshua lost his ability to see him. "I loved talking to Joshua when he was a baby."

"It is so heartbreaking that humans can't see us or talk to us like it was in the garden of eden before sin." Kara said softly. "When did Joshua lose his ability to see us?"

"Uh, I think he was about four years old."

"Do you think Joshua might remember us?"

"I don't know since normally by the age of five, the world's system infiltrates a child's soul and destroys all knowledge of us and the Lord who created all things, but Joshua is an abnormal child."

"Remember how Vicki or Dan would come into the room and we would be playing with him and he would be standing in his crib laughing and pointing at us?" Kara asked.

"Of course I do." He remembered Vicki looking over at the empty corner and she told Dan that Joshua was talking to his guardian angels. "What a blessed mother!" Kientay materialized his sword and raised it to the ceiling and yelled, "Yahoo! Praise the Lord, were going to kick some major . . ."

"Kientay! Put your sword away! What are you doing?" Kara immediately stood to reach for him to pull him back to the floor. He was levitating again. "Shush! Do you want to call attention to the demons flying around in the heavenlies before we are ready? You know that they are constantly looking for open doors into human homes so that they can cause mischief."

He ignored her.

"Why can't you understand that emotional outbursts at the wrong time are dangerous?"

Kientay breathed deeply. The hard line emotionless angel returned. He gave her a look that said she knew why. He was tired of answering the same question from her.

"We are different than humans," she said insistently. "I should not have to constantly remind you!"

He wished the more compassionate Kara would return. "You are talking and thinking like an angelic warrior and they really don't share the same light that we do about humans."

Not again, thought Kara. *First it was the angels in heaven and now it is the warring angels*. "I will not discuss this again with you tonight."

Kara left Joshua's bedroom and floated outside about roof-line level to watch the warring angels stand in their circle of protection around the Knights' home. She sat on the roof.

Kientay followed her.

"I like this assignment, Kientay, and I don't want to be reassigned."

He gasped at her as he put his hand over his angelic heart. "The Lord would not take you away from Vicki. Not even death will do that."

Once assigned to a true believer, the assignment could last throughout eternity. "I am as pleased as you are with your assignment. I love Vicki, but I still believe in angel protocol. Faith pleases God and to protect and prosper His children who walk in faith gives great pleasure to the Lord . . ."

"We are blessed," Kientay interrupted her as he sat down next to her. "But not all angels who personally work with humans have any reason at all to develop any emotions for their charges."

She looked up at the open sky filled with stars. Once again, she couldn't argue with his reasoning. Even though strong emotions were sometimes seen as a lack of faith among the angels, it was those angels who were pretty much bored with their assignments that seemed not to have any emotions at all. "Kientay, please remember that human emotions are . . ."

He shook his head and interrupted her again. "Uh, no. You said this conversation is over. Besides, not all emotions are tied to the Adamic nature, only those that have not been crucified."

Now she breathed deeply. He was beginning to wear her down.

She noticed that the warring angels were starting to take notice of them. "Let's go back into Joshua's room."

They descended through the roof and saw that Joshua was smiling and laughing in his sleep. "Oh, he must be thinking about Jesus," Kientay rejoiced.

"Please listen to me just this one last time and I will not speak of this matter again." She rethought what she just said. "Well, at least I will not speak of this again tonight. Emotions should never take the place of obedience. I know that for us human emotions are infectious and hard to resist especially from the Knight family, but don't jeopardize this assignment for us."

"I promise you, I will not jeopardize this assignment for us, but you have to admit Kara that all angels share a new emotional stirring about the signs of the time; especially the ones that live in heaven."

Her latest visit to heaven proved that Kientay was right. Heaven had always been a lively place to be, with all the construction of mansions, the city of paradise that moved from hell to heaven, the city of faith growing daily and the preparation for the big coronation celebration dinner. But this time she recognized that heaven was different; there was an atmosphere of expectancy that permeated every being.

"You know that time is running out on planet earth. It is now or never for the saints of God to make the move on the kingdom of darkness. Praise the Lord! The time is now and Joshua is making his move!"

Once again he couldn't contain himself. Kientay stood up and shouted and danced all around the room.

Several warring angels appeared in the room with them.

Kara held up her hand. "Everything is alright."

"We saw you leave the house and we wondered if a demonic spirit slipped by us and you were engaged in battle." One of the angels answered.

She stared at Kientay. "We were rejoicing and praising the Lord for our new promotion."

The extremely tall warring angels looked at each other with a knowing look and returned their swords to the sheath at their side. Kientay was responsible for all the commotion they had heard.

"If you need anything, we are ready."

They disappeared from the room. Being assigned to the Knight family they were used to seeing the guardian angels in emotional discussions, but tonight they were also feeling the supernatural and natural emotional atmosphere surrounding the house. After all, Jesus had personally visited Joshua in his room and they could feel how the Lord's presence stirred the heavenlies. They really understood his emotional outburst this time.

Praise the Lord! Kientay couldn't help thinking and saying this phrase over and over. *Praise the Lord! Praise the Lord! Praise the Lord!*

‡ ‡ ‡

Vicki Knight sat up in her bed and looked around the room. Her dream was so real that she thought Jesus was in the room with her. She looked for her note pad and pen to write the words that the Lord spoke to her. The presence of the Lord was so strong all around her that her skin tingled. It was easy to remember His words since they were still playing over and over in her mind.

Vicki, I have called Joshua to take My voice to his generation. His calling is to minister to his peers with My Word and prayers and teach them how to fight the devil. This phone ministry will free many from the chains of bondage.

In the night vision, she was standing before the throne of God and Jesus was standing at the Father's side wearing a white robe and a gold belt with gold shoes. His hair was brown and she remembered thinking that He didn't have a beard like she had seen in so many pictures. His eyes could melt a mountain full of ice.

She could see a form of a man sitting on a great golden throne. Angels were flying around a cloud of glory shouting "Glory!" over and over. A rainbow of colors surrounded the glory and Vicki saw hands resting on the arms of the throne. When he moved his finger, a great wind caused one of the angels to break formation and fly to the side of the great arena. A song of praise came out of the angel's mouth as his face registered the joy of being "touched" by the Almighty God.

Jesus stepped out from the side of the Lord and walked down the steps to face Vicki. She saw herself bow down to her knees in front of Him. A power of love instantly enveloped her. His Words sounded like the gentle flow of water soothing her soul.

Form a prayer group that will meet daily during the week to provide a prayer covering for his ministry. The enemy will launch powerful attacks against him. My Word will be planted in the hearts of many young people. Joshua will prevail because of your prayers.

Waking as the dream ended, she looked over at Dan, wondering if she should wake him. It was an hour before his alarm would go off. Deciding to let Dan sleep, Vicki went down stairs to the library. Her heart was still pumping fast with excitement as she wrote every word that Jesus said exactly the way he said it.

For several weeks now she had sensed that a major change was going to take place in their lives. Dan agreed with her and they both decided to give extra minutes of prayer daily to keep their spirit and mind sensitive to the voice of the Holy Spirit.

When Joshua started fasting and seeking the Lord for his ministry, she didn't think they would have to wait long. She was right. This was the night she had been praying for and believing the Lord for her son; his call into the ministry.

CHAPTER 3

"Mom, don't make me anything. I can't eat. Where's Dad?" Joshua smelled the food all the way upstairs in his bedroom as he was getting ready for school.

"He had to be at work early." Turning around from the stove, Vicki saw a glow of light surrounding her son's face. "You've been with the Lord."

He sat down at the table. "How do you always know these things?"

"Because I talk to the same Lord that you do and besides, your face is glowing. What did He tell you?"

"I'm supposed to organize a phone ministry manned with teens. You know, teens helping teens. I had some ideas, but I wasn't sure if it was the Holy Spirit giving me those ideas or . . ." He stopped himself from repeating his wrong thinking. "I didn't realize that this call was so important that I would get a personal visit from the Lord. Go figure." He was still in awe from seeing the Lord.

She was standing by the stove in her robe. "Joshua, there's nothing to figure out about Jesus visiting you. How many kids your age have devoted their life to prayer and reading the Bible like you? Maybe," she stopped scrambling the eggs and thought about what she was going to say to him, "well, maybe He wants you to know how serious your ideas are." She shook the wooden fork at him, forgetting about the eggs. "You better give them priority. The Lord doesn't make personal visits that often." She turned around to stir the eggs just before they were about to burn.

"Mom, have you and Dad prayed about me changing schools?"

"Yes, but we still don't have a release yet."

"You know that the public schools are an open field for evangelizing and you know that according to the Supreme Court it is only open to the teens themselves. Adult evangelizing is not allowed on school campuses." He wasn't telling his mom something she didn't already know; he was just reminding her.

"And you know that we are praying for us to make the right decision. And you know," she emphasized his words, "that we want to know the mind of the Lord before we decide." Vicki flipped a pancake over while she was talking to Joshua.

She made a commitment to the Lord not to let any of her children get bored with life because they were Christians. Observing some families in their congregation, she was convinced that they were losing their children because the things of the world seemed far more exciting that the things of the Lord. She didn't think that was right at all. She just hadn't planned to wait almost 10 years for Joshua and that he would be their only child. Vicki set the scrambled eggs and pancakes in front of Joshua. "What's the first step of your plan?"

"Prayer."

She poured him a glass of orange juice and sat down with him. "Good choice. Why can't you start at your school, especially since you know a couple of very committed and dedicated Christians?"

"You know that I am thinking about Kellie. She's has a great relationship with the Lord." He picked up the glass of juice and drank it down in one gulp.

"She would be a great choice. Who else?" She was so full of joy on the inside, but she knew that he didn't like for her to display an abundance of emotions. It seemed to her that boys like to act cool and sometimes try to resist emotionalism, so she held back her desire to act like a silly female around him. But she knew that there were times that he could be as emotional as any female; he just wouldn't admit it.

"I don't know. I haven't prayed yet. I may include some of my friends, but I still need contacts with unbelievers. So don't think I don't know what you just did. See you after school." Joshua kissed his mom on the cheek and ran out the door.

"Joshua, wait a minute!" Vicki couldn't resist asking him as she stood to stop him.

"Mom, I told you I wasn't hungry!" He yelled back into the kitchen as he grabbed his roller blades and helmet out of the garage.

She followed him to the porch where he sat down to put on his skates. It was hard not to resist asking him the obvious question. "What did Jesus look like?"

He looked up and smiled at her. *Got you!* "I knew you were going to ask." He figured that was the first thing everyone would ask him.

"Well, I wasn't going to ask, because I thought you would tell me. But since you didn't tell me, what did He look like?" She couldn't remember what Jesus looked like in her dream. His appearance was hazy in her mind, almost, like Jesus didn't have a face.

"His eyes were so . . . I don't know . . . and His smile was . . . you know . . . He was wearing a dress kind of thing with a gold belt and brown hair. He was about . . . uh . . . Dad's height, maybe a little shorter and He looked like a man."

He stood, grabbed his backpack and visibly took a breath. His mom was always asking him female questions that didn't matter to him that much. "Bye."

"But . . ." Vicki hated it when Dan or Joshua wouldn't give her good descriptions of situations or total words from telephone conversations. They just didn't know how to keep a woman informed on what was happening.

He started skating off when she remembered she hadn't declared her usual scriptures over him. "Joshua," she shouted at him, "you are a winner, not a loser, the head and not the tail, above only and not beneath, the son of God, seed of Abraham, joint heir with Jesus, you are blessed coming in and going out, no weapon formed against you will prosper and you can do all things through Jesus because of the Holy Spirit inside you who gives you strength!"

"Thanks mom, see ya later!" He waved at her. Her goodbye speech took on a whole new meaning since Jesus repeated it to him. It was something she said to him whenever he left the house as long as he could remember. Something until today that he had let become a ritual; but not anymore.

‡ ‡ ‡

Hovering over the Knights' house, but not too close, was the demon spirit metraloas. He was a medium sized demon, about seven feet tall, with dark green leather-like skin. He had spikes around his head, with red eyes and brown rotten looking teeth. At one time he had a long tail, but satan got mad at him once and cut it off. He looked like a large flying lizard dinosaur. He was of the many demons created by satan called androids. His classification was powers and his job description was watcher.

His assignment was to observe and appoint demon androids from the class of principalities to terrorize and victimize the Knight family. But unfortunately for him, the Knights were tough Christians to crack. He cursed the day he received them as assignments. He failed at every sinister plot or evil devise he could think of to come against them. Not one fleshly weapon or temptation had worked.

They are a very weird family, he thought. He had never known of a human family whose favorite pastime was studying the Word of God and praying together. During the days that he could get close enough to see what they were doing inside their house, he saw that they watched very little secular TV. He was sick to death of observing them praying and talking about the Word of God. She even had the Word posted in pictures all over the walls of the house.

But all that was nothing compared to the day that Vicki learned how to apply the Blood of Jesus and confess the Word in her prayers. She became one of those word of faith freaks and his life has been a literal nightmare ever since.

Everyday he would watch her as she daily applied the Blood of Jesus by speaking scriptures out of her mouth and every day the angels would literally cover all entrances to their house with the Blood of Jesus. They came in several groups carrying their golden buckets filled with His Blood and applied it to the door posts of the Knight's two story home, all their cars and their bodies. It was so terrible that he wanted to puke.

The first time she prayed with the Blood, metraloas tried to get inside the house and the Blood burned him so bad that he left for weeks. And on top of everything else, he had to endure the prayer ritual continually day in and day out. She never missed a day. He hated this assignment with a passion. Not one other demon in the neighborhood had to watch Christian humans who actually practiced what they believed.

It was no secret that the Holy Spirit visited their house almost daily; so he developed a routine of leaving his base every morning and not coming back until the glory glow wore off. It covered the Knights' house like a cloud. Many times metraloas had to fight other spirits when he returned to his base. Most of the local neighborhood demons made fun of him and ridiculed him at every opportunity. While they were wreaking all kinds of evil tricks and having a great time torturing their assigned families, he could only watch and dream.

Returning to his base, metraloas thought he heard something from the Knight house. His eyes zoomed in on the house. Something was up. In the past few weeks he could see lightning-like streaks out of the sides of his eyes indicating angelic activity picking up around their house.

Once again, he hovered high in the skies over the Knight house. It was embarrassing how high he had to fly over the force field that protected their house. He cursed the hedge of protection hoping that holes would appear in it like Job's did in the Old Testament. He was beginning to believe that the master lucked out when he discovered that Job's protection had been weakened by his own mouth. Metraloas wasn't as lucky as other demonic androids since only faith-filled words came out of the Knight family's mouths.

He spewed out blasphemies and cursing just thinking about them.

Flying as close as he could to the house, he couldn't detect any spiritual movements. The wind was gently blowing, but it did not register on his spiritual instruments as actions of any angelic beings. The deviations in the air currents seemed to be natural. Sometimes angelic activity was hard to detect, because they had the ability to operate in several dimensions that demonic androids could not enter. But he had been specially trained to watch for suspicious changes in the atmosphere surrounding any believers.

This is sure beginning to look like one of those suspicious atmosphere changes, he thought. His old run-down demonic bones were feeling a spiritual weather change and depression was moving in like a cloud over his assignment. The handwriting was on the wall and it was time to call a retreat, but he couldn't convince anyone to believe him.

Returning to his post, he decided he was seeing things. Only the usual circle of warring angels surrounded their house. If there were any speed of light movements from other warring angels, they were masked from his detection sensors.

Another boring day seemed to loom before him.

Suddenly from the corner of his eye, he saw a tall warring angel, with massive wings, holding an enormous sword for just a split second or two above the Knight's house.

That's no mirage!

He was shocked at the size of the angel he saw briefly. Only big operations merited an angel of that caliber. Of course, he couldn't be sure it was a warring angel, but a streak of light that size revealed something was going on.

Shoot! Cursing because he was going to have to check out this new development, he slowly moved from his base. He had no choice now because of a direct command stating upon suspected discovery of any powerful warring angel, further investigation was necessary. He hated having to get closer to a division of warring angels fortified with the strength from the Knights' prayers.

Sighing heavily, in his mind he reviewed the rule of discovery; *IF any Christian family started praying and receiving help from a division of angels other than guardian angels, especially the powerful and special class of warring-type angels, then the area supervisor, usually a ruler of darkness, was to be notified immediately.* He slowly rethought what he saw. *It probably was a figment of my imagination,* he concluded.

A demonic bat, who had been trying to befriend him for the last few weeks, flew over and sat next to him on the twisted oak limb. "Did you see that streak of light?"

Metraloas ignored him.

"It's none of my business, but shouldn't you alert the specially trained demonic force to combat those warring angels before they build their fortress?"

Inwardly he was seething that a lower-level demon was telling him what to do. "You're right; it is none of your business."

"Are you really going to defy a direct order?"

BAM! He punched the bat and knocked him out of the tree. "You think you need to tell me how to do my assignment?"

The bat shifted into a large black gargoyle and flapped his crooked wings. "I am your only friend and you dare to hit me?" He flew within inches of his face.

Metraloas retreated, shocked at the bat's ability to shape-shift into a powerful-looking gargoyle. "You are right. I reacted out of frustration and anger. I can't seem to ditch this — assignment." He cursed. "Everything bad always happens to me." He poured on the "whoa is me" pity talk so the demon's anger would be appeased.

The bat rematerialized and sat next to metraloas to his perch. "Have you tried to speak words of doubt and fear over them?" For some reason he liked metraloas and felt sorry for him.

He nodded his head yes.

"Did you try the dynamic duo?"

"Do you think I am stupid? The android pig can only hunt and rout out the newly planted seeds of the Word of God in a baby Christian. A young Christian lacks knowledge of the Word of God."

"What about the pig's follower, the flying dinosaur with its huge long claws and . . ."

"I told you the Word of God was already planted deep into their spirits and even the blades that began to show were too hard for the demonic pterosaurs to pull out."

"Ptero . . . what?" the bat asked.

"The flying dinosaur is not a dinosaur; it's a demonic winged lizard . . . you know the dynamic duo?" Metraloas wondered just how much training the stupid android got before he was assigned on earth. "The roots of the Word of God in the Knight family have grown farther than the roots of the common fig tree."

"You're kidding me!" He was a little irked at the old android revealing all his knowledge about facts on earth. The bat didn't know about half of the things metraloas was talking about.

Metraloas didn't respond.

"I know that God designed the human spirit to react to words like good ground where seeds are planted, but I thought they could easily be plucked out like natural seeds," the bat replied very curious about this Christian family. He had never seen or heard of a family like them, but then he hadn't been on earth very long.

"Believe me when I say that the Knights are weird. I have never seen humans live like they do in all my existence on this earth. They have defied every trick, every trial and every temptation that I brought against them. And they are not baby Christians!"

"It's been my experience that most Christians give up the Word of God when trials and tribulations come their way."

"Not this family. They have genuinely accepted Jesus as their Savior and they know that they have power to cast out demons. But worse than that, they believe they have power over the prince of darkness."

"Are you serious?" The bat couldn't believe what metraloas was saying. "That's impossible!"

"Stick around me long enough and you will see what I'm talking about with your own eyes."

"What are you going to do?"

He sighed as he zeroed his zoom lens on his target. "Nothing."

"Are you crazy! You have to get closer and report what's going on!"

"I made detailed records outlining all the activities of the Knight family from the very beginning. I don't think that my supervisor, chemah, has read one of the reports I gave him. You know how the master hates any android that allows Christians to develop their faith and learn how to release the power of God. I made three copies of the report and hid two of them."

"We are servants of the prince of darkness and of the powers of the air," the bat argued with him. "The master's power will take care of you!"

"Do I look like they care about me?" He turned around and showed him his shortened tail. It was all black on the end. "The master did that to me. He cut my tail in half with a sword and then hacked the tail into pieces and burned them with fire when he pointed his long index finger at them."

"What did you do?"

"I went to hell and refused to go back to this assignment on earth."

"Uh, wrong move."

Metraloas wanted to slap him. "No kidding?" He said sarcastically. His plan was to cover his backside and get back into hell where he wanted to be assigned until the end of the kingdom of darkness. "I want to be in hell at the end of this age and our kingdom."

The bat covered his ears with his wings. "I refuse to listen to your doom and gloom. The master says that we are going to defeat the Kingdom of God and I believe him!"

Metraloas ignored his rebuke. "Maybe we are as deceived as we deceive humans."

The bat cussed him vehemently. "Obviously, you are in a self-destruct mode and the master will be forced to terminate you."

Metraloas stood and unfurled his wings stretching them wide as he took off. He sighed and thought he might as well take another look just in case.

A demonic crow flew over and hit him on the back of his head. "Have you decided to admit that you are a miserable failure?"

Metraloas turned and saw the bat shake his head and silently mouth widely that it wasn't him. Metraloas released fire from his mouth trying to burn the crow. He hated it when they hit him in the head. "Go to hell you old crow!"

The crow mocked him and shouted, "You go!" as he flew out of the range of the fire.

Metraloas rubbed his head and flew back to his perch. He cursed. "I know that the Word of God causes the spirit of the Christian to grow and mature, but they were mature before I was even assigned to them!"

"Since we were told during training to stay away from Christians who have knowledge of their power over us, who was responsible for allowing them to mature?"

"They should have assigned an angel from the class of spiritual powers of the heavenlies to this family." He ignored his questions.

"That would be one powerful spirit for just one small human family. But I still don't understand why someone hasn't paid the price for their failure before you were assigned. We were taught that the key to keep a Christian from becoming mature is to strike hard and fast with trials and tribulations before the Word has time to form any roots in the human's spirit."

Metraloas took offense. "I'm not stupid! I may have been around for thousands of years. You didn't exist when the master learned about defeating the followers of Jesus three hundred years after . . ."

"Don't say it!" The bat covered his ears screaming and hissing loudly as he flew away from the oak limb. He didn't want to hear about satan's defeat in hell three days after Jesus was crucified. "You know we have been warned not to talk about that time!"

"You mean when Jesus defeated the master in hell?"

The bat screamed curses at him. "You said it anyway!" He silently mumbled to himself as he flew off the branch, "I must have been crazy to befriend you!"

Metraloas ignored his last comment. "I know that a non-germinating seed is a dead seed, but the Knights have never let go of the Word of God because of tribulation or trials," metraloas turned his head thinking he saw another streak of light. "The hard and fast rule no longer applies to them."

"Did you know the watcher that was assigned before you?" The bat slowly turned around.

"No. He was destroyed during a battle between the warring angels and the warriors of darkness."

"I've only been around a few weeks, but I wouldn't want your assignment!"

There it was again! Like a blink of the eye, a light flashed before him. Metraloas quickly moved his head to see what looked like a couple of new warrior angels arriving at the Knight's house. Swooping down from his perch, he realized that if special warriors were being assembled around the house, then he would have to write a report and submit it to chemah before he could get reassigned. He flew as close as he could to the house.

BAM! Hit from behind by one of the warring angels guarding the house, he went into a spiraling roll, over and over. Stretching out a wing he grabbed a tree limb and pulled himself into the tree trunk.

SPLAT! He slid down the tree and fell to the ground. Sitting up right, he shook his head and cursed.

Standing, he bent over to inspect his spirit body to see if anything was damaged. Cursing, he wondered why he didn't even see the angel coming toward him as he adjusted his bent wings.

The other demonic androids in his neighborhood saw the warring angel a mile away. They roared with laughter. "I wouldn't get up if I were you, metraloas the moron!" An evil spirit in the form of a rat laughed mocking him.

"What a loser!"

"Have some respect for your elders!" His bat friend flew over to help him in the form of the large gargoyle. "I don't know why they treat you like they do." He used his huge wings to wipe off his short dinosaur tail. "After all, we're supposed to be on the same side."

"You haven't been assembled long enough for your android heart to get that hard and calloused."

"Didn't I read in the Bible that Jesus said that a house divided against itself can't stand?"

"Are they still teaching you Jesus' Words?" metraloas asked as the large gargoyle followed him back to his fortress.

"Yes. We have to know a lot of the teachings of Jesus. We memorize several scriptures that we can twist around to confuse them. The older and wiser demon spirits have taught us their doctrines that will undermine the Christian's faith and cause them to be ineffective as a witness for Jesus."

"I don't believe that Jesus is God or even became a God, but it is true about the fighting and bickering that goes on between us. It seems like the prince of darkness is losing the battle for souls because we can't focus on our assignments. The *house* is crumbling."

He put his smaller bat wing over metraloas' mouth, "Shhh! Do you want someone to hear you and report you?" He quickly looked all around to see if hearing ears were flying to the nearest gateway to hell.

"You don't know the differences in the master's kingdom. I know because I was one of the first androids before Jesus. I know what it was like before and after He was born on earth. We had very few defeats before that day in hell . . ."

"There is a prime directive that says we are NOT to talk about defeat in any way, shape or form! Violation can result in termination!" The bat shook from the tips of his claws to the top of his head.

Metraloas saw how afraid he was and backed down. "I'm not staying here and taking any more physical or mental abuse!" He grabbed some personal belongings, shut the window and door, and after he placed the "no trespassing" sign on the door, he left. He had enough of the neighborhood demons humiliating and cursing him.

"Hey! Wait for me!" The bat flew behind him.

Metraloas stopped just before they entered the black spiral tornado-like gateway to hell. "Are you sure you want to go to the dark place of despair, the regions of the damned in utter hopelessness, the realm of the desperately wicked, the terror of human souls, the fun center of torture, and the place I love and long for?" His diabolic laugh replaced his stoic face.

Maybe that was what the bat liked so much about the big fat ugly dinosaur facing him, his overly dramatic mannerisms. He didn't know whether to slap him or hug him sometimes. It made him wonder how he had made it all those thousands of years without being destroyed. He moved to the back of metraloas' hard leather skin and clung to him so that they could descend into the prison of damned souls together.

"I just want to go to hell with you!"

Suddenly, metraloas saw Joshua Knight out of the corner of his eye. Taking off like a bat out of hell, he turned away from the tunnel.

The bat held onto his back for his life. "What the——!" He screamed cursing.

"Hold on!" . . .

. . . Rollerblading down the driveway and through the gates, Joshua began his daily ritual of quoting scriptures out loud. "Greater is He in me, than he that is in the world!" Flying down the sidewalk on his roller blades and beating his chest like Tarzan he said, "I am a chosen generation, a royal priesthood, a holy nation, a special person!"

A squeal of breaks and a horn blast went completely unnoticed by Joshua.

"Watch out Knight, you stupid jerk!" Justin Walker, his neighbor, hit the brakes and skidded on his driveway to avoid making Joshua flat like the pancake he didn't eat.

He hit his steering wheel, made a bad gesture at him with his finger and cussed him out . . .

. . . Metraloas observed Joshua skating fast down the block in front of the Walker's house at the same time he saw Justin driving out of driveway. Suddenly, it occurred to him that an opportunity was presenting itself. Immediately he spoke to the demon controlling the driver of the car traveling down the Walker driveway. "Kill him! Speed up the car and crush the life out of that . . ."

Flying fast toward the scene, he cursed Joshua hoping a spirit of death could take over. But faster than the speed of light, warring angels surrounded the car and used their swords to block the accelerator being pressed by the demon. One of the angels picked up Justin's leg and applied the brake.

Kientay stood between the car and Joshua. A battle raged around the car as other demons appeared to help the few who surrounded and were inside of Justin. Green android blood was spurting out of the demons and flowing everywhere.

Angels were declaring the words of Dan and Vicki, who daily proclaimed, "No weapon formed against Joshua will prosper!"

This is awesome, thought the bat as he flew off metraloas' back to watch.

Kientay pulled out his sword and cut off the head of the demon that was trying to make the car speed up and run over Joshua. "How dare you try to kill a child of God! He is a member of the royal priesthood and don't you ever forget it!" He stabbed another demon that came out of Justin who was trying to attack Joshua.

The angels gathered around Kientay as the remaining demons took off running to save their lives.

"It looks like this one won't be reassembled," Kientay remarked as he observed the android disintegrate into a gooey green glob at his feet. A flame of fire appeared over the green liquid and burned the remains of the android into ashes. The ashes scattered and disappeared by the wind.

"Another android bites the dust!" The angels laughed.

Kientay thanked the warring angels and watched them as they returned to guarding the perimeter of the Knights' house. It was then that he realized that Joshua was already a block away, not realizing that a battle had just taken place around him. A couple of warring angels joined him as they flew over the head of Joshua keeping up with him and watching for another attack . . .

. . . Moving his mirror, Justin looked to see if the sudden stop disturbed his hair. He stared with baby blue eyes into the mirror and ran his fingers through the long strands of blond hair. Every time he looked into the mirror, he thought about all the girls that loved everything about him, especially his hair. *With these looks and this hair, I can get any girl I want.*

Looking into the mirror several times a day was a habit that evolved into a ritual. Justin had a bad case of being stuck on himself. It didn't help his character development that the girls had drooled over him and told him how cool he was ever since he first entered school. His rich dad warned him that girls would pursue him because of money, but Justin believed it was his great looks that attracted them.

His dad owned a bank that would, of course, one day be his, so he didn't feel like he had to prepare himself for working. And since he really didn't have to worry about his grades, or think much about his future, he spent his time thinking about women.

Justin floored his accelerator as he saw Joshua skating down the sidewalk. *What a jerk*! He cussed him out again adding to the thousands of times he had bad-mouthed him in the past. As far as he was concerned, his younger neighbor was a nerd. He hated Joshua and bullied him at every opportunity he could. It was a good thing that Joshua attended a private Christian school. Even though he was older and bigger, he would have looked for opportunities to beat up on him.

Joshua had learned to ignore Justin. He came to the conclusion that it was a spirit of anti-Christ that was coming against him through Justin. Every time he accidentally met his neighbor, he thought about the scriptures that taught him that he didn't 'wrestle with flesh and blood, but with principalities, powers and rulers of darkness in the world.' He was satisfied how the Bible explained the intense hatred that Justin felt about him. Jesus said the people would hate His followers since they hated Him, so it was easy to forgive Justin since Joshua understood that he was just a puppet in the hands of a devil.

He thought about their obvious physical differences. While Justin's muscular body put him in the category of a male model, Joshua's appearance put him in the category or everyone's kid brother. He always wore a baseball cap to cover his short, curly and very thick head of light brown hair. Being a little above average height and a little thin for his age wasn't a plus or a minus for him. Most of the girls were as tall as he was, especially since he was only a freshman. He did have one quality that all the boys envied in him: all the girls liked to talk to him since he was a good listener.

Justin slowed his new Corvette and drove along side of Joshua as he skated down the sidewalk unaffected by Justin's previous cussing. The visit from Jesus transported his mind into the supernatural realm. He never did see that he was almost run over by Justin.

Joshua turned his head to his left side just in time to see Justin repeat the obscene gesture he missed earlier. Flooring his accelerator Justin beat him to the end of the block and pulled over to the curb at the corner. He tried to stop when he realized that Justin was blocking him from crossing the street.

BAM!

It was too late and he thudded into the side of his car. Justin cussed him out and jumped out of his car to see if there was any damage. The passenger door was slightly crushed. Another round of not so nice words came from his mouth. "I can't believe you, Knight! You idiot!" He rubbed his hand over the dent. "You are going to pay for this!"

"What did I do?"

A spirit of anger inside of Justin took over him. His facial expression and eyes revealed a total anger melt down and a potential loss of control. The urge to hit Joshua was strong. He put his fist close to Joshua's face.

Joshua kept his mouth shut. From experience he realized that talking back to Justin just made things worse.

"Defend yourself!"

Joshua looked into the eyes that were burning with hatred toward him. It didn't surprise him that the demon influencing Justin hated him. "I know that you are a Christian, Justin, because you told me when I first moved into the neighborhood that you accepted Jesus at Vacation Bible School."

Instantly, Justin thought of that day six years ago when he walked over to watch the building crews construct the large house next to his parents' property. His old man was furious that a house was being built so close to their acreage. "Yeah, my dad said that the neighborhood would never be the same when your family moved next door to us and he was right. You're a freak of nature, Knight."

Joshua's expression didn't change. He wasn't afraid of him even though Justin tried to make him afraid several times in the past.

The spirits inside Justin hated it when they couldn't see fear in Joshua's eyes no matter what they made come out of Justin's mouth. He released a couple of curse words. "You're not afraid of me, even now that I have you cornered. You don't have enough brains to be afraid of me!"

"God hasn't given me the spirit of fear, but power, love and a sound mind."

Justin cursed again. "Stop quoting the Bible to me you little . . ." He called him a bad name. The spirit of anger moved him to an emotional feeling to hit Joshua. "Do you know how stupid you would sound to the guys I hang around? No kid that I know studies the Bible and quotes scriptures like you do!"

Hearing his words, Joshua knew in his heart that was the real reason why the demons stirred Justin to hate him with such an intense hatred. He didn't hide the fact that he walked, talked, breathed, ate and slept the Word of God. His parents taught him at a young age that there is a direct correlation between how much time you spend meditating God's Word and the power in a Christian's life. Joshua wanted to manifest God's Word in signs and wonders with great power so than other teenagers desired to know about Jesus. He wasn't going to change the pathway he chose just to please Justin.

Justin sighed heavily. The last few times that he tried to get into a physical fight with the jerk, he wouldn't talk with him. "Defend yourself, you fool!"

Scriptures flowed through Joshua's mind like a river. *A fool's voice is known by his many words. Do not speak in the hearing of a fool, for he will despise the wisdom of your words. Make no friendship with an angry man, and with a furious man do not go. A fool's mouth is his destruction and his lips are the snare of his soul. A fool's lips enter into contention, and his mouth calls for blows. Fools die for lack of wisdom. Hatred stirs up strife, but love covers all sins.*

"I'm talking to you Knight!" Justin shouted at him. It was like he blanked out for a few seconds. "Oh——!" He cussed him again and decided to hit him even if he wouldn't defend himself.

"I love you Justin," Joshua blurted out.

"What!" Justin lowered his fist, pausing long enough to allow a spirit of peace to bind a spirit of anger. He bent over as he realized the desire to punch Joshua's lights out escaped from him like air out of a tire. He shook his head and silently said an expletive to himself. He looked up and said, "You did it again."

"Hatred stirs up strife, but love covers all sins. I can't fight you Justin. It's not in me," he replied truthfully.

Standing straight, another spirit took over his mouth. "Are you trying to tell me that you are gay?"

"No. I'm telling you that Jesus' words are in me and that is why I say what I do. I know that your parents worship the Lord in another congregation, but we are all Christians. I don't judge you or your parents because you don't believe like my parents believe. And if you don't want to go to your congregation, then that's between you and the Lord."

"Man, I hate it when you do this," Justin lowered his head deflated. He couldn't find any fault in Joshua so he didn't have a reason to hit him. He looked over at his car and saw the dent in it. Even that didn't anger him anymore. Turning back he saw a police car drive up with his lights flashing.

"I think you're parked in a no parking zone. I'll pay to get your car fixed."

"Is everything alright boys?" An officer asked getting out of the car.

"Go to school. I'll talk to the officer."

Joshua loved it when a spirit from the Lord overtook a spirit from the kingdom of darkness and that evil spirit could no longer influence the human. Justin didn't even sound like the same person.

He thought about Jesus saying that the world would know that he was His disciple by the love that he had for another person. That is why he couldn't understand how Christians who got mad at one another did not realize that they were in violation of the words of Jesus.

I love Justin. Joshua smiled thinking about the words that came out of his mouth. Jesus was the one talking, not him. In himself he could never say something like that out loud to another boy. *Take that devil!*

"Praise the Lord!" He shouted out loud and continued rollerblading down the street headed for the church school.

CHAPTER 4

Flying back to the roof of his house, metraloas watched Joshua rollerblade down the sidewalk unharmed. He threw his stuff on the ground and started kicking it all over the place. Every time he thought he had a chance to do someone harm from the Knight family, it backfired on him.

The bat tried to stop him. “What are you doing?”

Slowly he turned around and raised the demonic bow and arrow that materialized into his hands and aimed it into the backside of one of the demons that was running from the fight in front of the Walker’s driveway. He was furious at their failure in attempting to kill Joshua.

The vulture he hit with an arrow screamed and turned to see how many warring angels were chasing them. He was shocked to see that it was the dirty low-down scum of the earth metraloas himself. He immediately changed his direction and furiously charged toward him. “What do you think you are doing, you fool?”

“You better run!” The bat yelled at metraloas as he led the way back to his fortress in the oak tree.

The hurt vulture whistled for the other vultures that were still flying in the opposite direction of him. Shouting out for revenge, he led the charge that rammed into metraloas full force, pushing him off the top of his base in the oak tree. They were kicking and hitting him ferociously on the ground.

The bat flew around them trying to find a way that he could help metraloas. Finally he screamed out to the power of arbitration, declaring a right of defense.

An invisible power pulled the gang of vulture demons off metraloas and broke up the fight. They squared off facing one another with fierce hatred glaring from their red-hot eyes.

“What right do you have in invoking the code of defense? We were trying to help you.” The biggest vulture turned into a fierce, fire-breathing dragon. He was ready to pounce on metraloas once their rebuttal was heard and noted by the spirit of arbitration.

Another demon cut in between the two. “He’s right you stupid android!

You have no right to retribution."

"I called you to kill Joshua! But you bungling idiots failed!" metraloas was ready to hurl fire at them.

"The demon who failed was terminated, you fool. You have no right to inflict pain. The human was not our assignment!"

"You know that this action was a shot in the dark!" A black vulture protested.

The spirit of arbitration materialized in the form of a gigantic black cloud hovering over them. It was his job to keep demonic androids from destroying each other. "Demons! Return to your assignments!"

"Watch your back metraloas! I will repay you for your attack on my body." The demon vowed revenge as he disappeared.

Metraloas fell to his knees and grabbed a handful of dirt. He threw it after them and let his head hit the ground as he pounded it over and over cursing and screaming. "I almost did it!" He cursed again. "I was almost freed from the torment of this assignment!"

Arbitration watched his emotional outbursts. "Give it a rest, metraloas. I may not be able to save you next time."

"Who cares?" He raised his head and glared into the black cloud surrounding his tree. "You don't understand how close I was to ending this nightmare!"

"I understand your frustration, but I didn't think you were so ignorant to attack other demons more powerful than you." The spirit of arbitration had saved metraloas more than once.

"They are cowards! If they would have stayed and fought we would have won!"

"No. You are making bad decisions. If they had stayed those warring angels would have destroyed them. Do you need your eyes adjusted?"

Metraloas refused to answer him.

"I order you to report to your division leader at once!"

He disappeared instantly.

Once Joshua arrived at school, he immediately started looking for Kellie Todd, a short, good looking junior. Being in a predominantly all female household with two sisters, she adopted Joshua as her little brother. And since Joshua was an only child, he adopted Kellie as his sister; a very pretty sister. She was one of those girls you would rather date than be considered a brother to, but Joshua rarely thought about dating and he would never jeopardize his relationship with her.

Kellie looked like an American Indian. With her clear complexion and dark brown eyes, she almost looked like one of those china dolls you could put on display or show off to other guys at school.

Actually, Joshua rarely thought of her as a girl, except when she dressed up and let her long dark brown hair down. It wasn't her looks that qualified her as a close friend; it was her love for the Word of God. She was the only person he knew that read the Bible almost as much as he did and since she spent a lot of time with the Lord, they had a lot in common. He knew he could trust her with his vision.

"Kellie!"

"Hi Joshua. What's up?"

He leaned against the locker next to hers out of breath. "I've got something to tell you."

"What?" She couldn't discern whether it was good or bad.

"I can't tell you here. I need to talk to you alone. When can we get together?"

She closed her locker door and started walking toward her first class. "Let's get permission to leave the building for lunch."

"It needs to be somewhere very private. No one can hear what I've got to tell you. See you later."

Now she was really curious. That was the worse thing you could do to a girl. She turned around and grabbed his arm, catching him off balance. "Hey!" She wasn't going to let him get away that easy. "It must be important, can't you tell me real quick?"

"No!" He said trying to keep from falling. The bell rang. "Gotta go!" His class was the other direction and in another building. He pulled his arm free with the arm of his sweater flapping behind him as he took off running down the hall.

She yelled at him. "Is it good or bad news?" At least he could have the decency of not letting her suffer with curiosity for three and half hours before lunch.

Joshua turned around running backwards. "It's great news!"

"Meet me at my car," Kellie yelled back.

‡ ‡ ‡

While Joshua was at school, Vicki began her daily time with the Lord praising and worshiping before she started her day.

"Lord, I thank you for Your faithfulness. Great is Your Name and greatly to be praised. I will bless You, Lord, at all times. Your praise shall continually be in my mouth. I will magnify the Lord and exalt His name!" She said as she bowed before the Lord.

After confessing scriptures, she praised the Lord with singing and music. It helped her to get her mind and spirit in agreement with the Spirit of the Lord.

"I will love you, O Lord, my strength. The Lord is my rock, and my fortress, and deliverer; my God, my strength, in whom I will trust; my buckler, and the horn of my salvation, and my high tower. I will call upon the Lord, who is worthy to be praised; so shall I be saved from my enemies." She walked the floor with her arms up and her voice singing and speaking praises . . .

. . . Kara and all the angels assigned to the Knight family started praising, worshiping and dancing with her. They rejoiced whenever Vicki began worshipping the Lord, because she didn't stop praying until the Holy Spirit descended and His presence was revealed. Then the angels spent the rest of Vicki's time with the Lord face flat on the ground. They did not move until she was finished . . .

. . . Soon Vicki was ending her prayers, "Father, I apply the Blood of Jesus as a circle around this house. As Moses applied the blood of a lamb to the doorway of his house, I do the same by declaring faith in the Blood that Your Son Jesus shed on the cross. I apply the Blood of the Lamb on my husband Dan, and on our son Joshua. I apply His Blood to our cars and all our possessions."

Standing, she talked directly to the kingdom of darkness.

"Demons, remove your presence from my husband, my son, my home and all my possessions. The Knight family belongs to Jesus and His Blood annihilated sin in our lives. We no longer belong to you, we belong to Jesus and God is our Father!"

She raised her hands to praise the Lord. "Father, thank You for the gifts that You have given to my family. Thank You for blessing my family with all spiritual blessings in all places! I love You Lord. Help me to worship You with all my heart, my soul, and my body. Amen." . . .

. . . The angels stood in the middle of Vicki's bedroom and stretched in the new spiritual strength they received from her time with the Lord. It was always a spiritual charge to be in the presence of the precious Holy Spirit.

"Oh my!" Kara stretched her arms over her head. "If humans could only know how great that feels to us when they spend time with the Lord in prayer and praise."

"I know," replied Kientay cherishing the renewing of their spirit from the Word of God coming out of Vicki's mouth.

Matthan, a logical mathematical thinker like his charge, Dan, added, "In my opinion, the secret place was the greatest truth that God hid from the kingdom of darkness."

The angels loved to worship the Lord with the children of God.

"Those humans who don't know the authority they have from the word of God are so pathetic," Kara remarked. "If only they could all know the truth and really see with their spiritual eyes the demons that daily torment them."

"I still have a hard time understanding human thinking," added Matthan. "How can some humans believe their ancestors were apes?"

"Have you heard the latest?" Kientay asked. "I heard a Christian scientist on the Christian network talk about the latest findings in this world system."

"What?" Kara asked.

"The newest missing link is a rat. An illustrator took three small bones and created a prehistoric imagined long-nosed rat. And from that, some scientist commissioned a statue named Morgie at the Smithsonian Institute in Washington D.C. The statue is the height of small children so that they can rub their 'ancestor.'"

"You've got to be kidding!" Kara exclaimed like a human.

Kientay smiled at her response. "No. Angels never kid." He couldn't help rubbing it in, because she rarely gave him the opportunity and he couldn't ever remember hearing her use that adolescent human phrase.

Matthan said shaking his head, "It makes you wonder how low satan is going to drive this evolution thing with the human race. I can't believe that any human that can look into a mirror would swallow such garbage."

Now Kientay laughed as they stared at him. "Don't you get it? Rat . . . garbage? Matthan made a joke."

They didn't laugh. "I don't find anything humorous about the theory of evolution," Matthan replied seriously. "Satan is destroying the image of God through distortion of the true creation story."

"Kientay, I don't think jesting about the image of God is proper," Kara told him.

"Forgive me if I offended you Matthan, but I don't think the Lord minds a little laughter over the ridiculous theories about creation. You need to relax and think about how funny it is that some humans really believe that they came from an animal."

Kara pointed out, "The father of lies found a human that accepted any thought that came into his mind. That's why humans have a theory about the beginning that proves their understanding is darkened because of the ignorance that is in them and the blindness of their hearts."

"They were alienated from the life of God walking in the futility of their mind because of Lucifer," Matthan said.

"Satan. His name is no longer Lucifer, its satan, the father of lies," Kientay insisted.

"Satan loves to mock human beings because they were created in God's image," Matthan reminded them.

"Don't forget that satan vowed to destroy the works of God's hands," Kientay added.

"It is the ultimate expression of pride to believe one created one's self!" Matthan indignantly replied.

"Even satan knows that he didn't evolve," Kientay laughed.

Vicki went into the bathroom to shower and dress, so the group of angels in her bedroom stepped out into the hall through the wall.

"You have to have help from a religious person to ignore Genesis Chapter One," Matthan replied as he walked through the wall.

Kientay laughed again. "That's considered humorous by humans."

Matthan looked surprised. "It is?"

He decided not to explain it to Matthan. Some human language escaped angel understanding.

"Some humans behave like monkeys and apes," Kara reasoned with a laughing smile trying to see it Kientay's way.

Now Kientay wanted to be serious. "Listen," he interrupted, "we need to concentrate on this new assignment the Holy Spirit has given us. We cannot let down our guard. As soon as the kingdom of darkness is made aware of Joshua's assignment, the rulers will send out reinforcements against our charges."

"I heard through certain angels that you were promoted to work with Michael and the warring angels on this special assignment," Matthan commented to Kientay.

"There is nothing like the graceline," Kara smiled.

"I have been given a promotion." Kientay didn't respond with wild emotion. He was practicing acting like an angel with higher authority.

"Vicki has been asked by the Lord to start an intercessory prayer group for this new ministry," Kara told them.

"This sounds big." Even Matthan started to feel the excitement. "So Joshua is starting his ministry. He is very young, but he has a very responsible human father to help him."

"His first direction from the Lord is to find others to join him in his vision. When he finds them, they will be the foundation of this operation and then we will have extra responsibilities as guardian angels," explained Kientay.

"What is the name of this operation?" asked Matthan.

"The Knight Campaign. Our first order is to keep the kingdom of darkness clueless and the devil's forces scattered and confused about this operation until it has a solid foundation and the communication links are established," Kientay said.

"Clueless?" Matthan didn't know exactly what he meant.

"He means," Kara explained, "even though they see a lot of movement, they don't know what's going on."

"We all know what demons will do as soon as they smell an anointed human . . ."

Kara interrupted Kientay. "Powerful evil spirits will be called on to drive the Word out of their heart by cutting roots and not allowing the fruits of the Holy Spirit to grow."

"Not this time," Kientay declared.

"He will fail with his efforts to stop this ministry," Matthan and Kientay said together.

"In all the years that Dan and Vicki have prayed for Joshua's ministry they have never fainted or lost heart," Kara added.

"Most important, they were consistent," Matthan said.

"I expect Michael to give us his best agents from his division of warring angels. Let's find our charges and . . . wait a minute . . ." Kientay paused as they received a message from headquarters.

Special warrior angels are being assigned to each member of the Knight family. The headquarters of the special angelic covert operations will be located at the Knights' house. The angel, Chroni, has been assigned as the messenger between Michael and the angels on the Operation Knight assignment. Kientay is Chroni's assistant.

‡ ‡ ‡

Metraloas flew off in the direction of a tunnel leading him to the dark underworld to find his division leader and beg to be reassigned. He hated his job on earth. He hated humans and he hated daylight. He stopped at the entrance when he heard the bat calling after him.

Landing on metraloas' back again, he was panting hard. "I thought you might go to this tunnel."

"Why do you want to be with me?" he asked the bat.

"You've been around for a few thousands years. I've only been active a few weeks. I want to learn everything I can from you."

"Why?" He entered the tunnel and slowly floated down to the dusty floor of hell eyeing him suspiciously.

"How many androids do you know are as old as you and are still alive?"

"Okay, I see your point." He breathed deep as he smelled the familiar horrible odor that had been home to him for thousands of earth years before he was assigned topside. Passing the dark gray evil spirits embedded in the walls of the tunnel, he once again had to endure more laughter at his failure.

"Back again metraloas, murderer of mothers? That is but one, Vicki Knight, mother who has brought you to nothing in the kingdom of darkness. Ha! Ha! Ha!"

"Shut up!" metraloas put his hands over his ears trying to stop their words as he descended deeper and deeper unto the pit of hell.

"We will not fail the prince of death when we are released!" They jeered at him. "We will succeed on earth when our time comes!" They laughed sarcastically, hissing with thousands of snake like voices piercing his ears.

"What is their problem?" the bat questioned.

"They've been chained by the master until their appointed time."

"Why?"

"They almost cost the master his kingdom on earth during Noah's time before the great flood."

"The great flood?"

"Don't listen to him. He knows nothing about our story. He is a liar. We never disobeyed satan," a fallen angel disputed the words of metraloas.

Metraloas ignored them. He knew that they were growing impatient waiting for the days of tribulation on the surface before they could be released. "They were responsible for exceedingly great wickedness in the hearts of men and women. The Christian God from heaven came down to earth and saw that the thoughts of all humans were only evil continually."

"So?"

"Legend says that this earth was created by the Christian God, who is good. The evil thoughts and words of man caused the core of earth to erupt and it almost destroyed everything."

"Shut up, metraloas! What do you know about it?" An embedded spirit exploded. "You weren't even on earth then!"

He stopped in mid-air and breathed fire into his face. "I was in hell riding out the great molten fire hurricanes that wiped out everything!" They were still building the prison cells for the souls that were dying on earth. "I know plenty about what went on then! All our work was destroyed in a few seconds by the internal core exploding! I will never forget having to re-dig thousands and thousands of pits!"

They loved the fire that cleansed them. "Ahhh! Do it again! That felt so good!"

The bat could barely breathe. It was his first time back into hell since his training. "I forgot how this heat can take your breath away." As they continued their descent the embedded spirits kept cursing them. "Why are they so hateful?"

"You don't know the half of their abilities. The master couldn't take a chance that they might destroy the earth again and that's why they are chained to the walls of the tunnels into hell." metraloas laughed, "They also terrorize humans who have just died and come into hell, especially those who don't believe in hell."

"Why is he going to release them?"

"Well, it's my guess that he is going to use them to wipe out the Jewish Nation, Israel, and all the Jews. The master hates the Jews."

"Why?"

They landed at the gate of hell. "You ask too many questions."

"Just give me the quick version," the bat pleaded with him.

"Read the book of Hebrews. Abraham is the father of the Jews. He was the first man on earth to develop his faith that defeated the power of fear. Have you ever been to the pits?"

"No."

Metraloas smiled. "You will like the pits." As he walked along the corridor, demon spirits of all sizes and grotesques shapes were passing them. Most of them growled and hissed at one another.

"I don't understand all this animosity that exists between androids."

Metraloas sighed. "You may be more trouble than you're worth. Don't they tell you anything when you get off the assembly line?"

"There's not a lot of time. The birth rate in the third world countries is still climbing faster that the rulers can provide androids," the bat explained. "And I hear that hell is enlarging itself daily beyond all future projections." They passed through another tunnel floor as dead bodies fell all around them.

Weaving through the demon spirits in charge of chaining the dead humans, metraloas tried to explain the way of the kingdom of darkness. "Evil spirits are jealous of one another and hate each other almost as much as they hate humans and indulge in constant conflict."

"I've noticed."

"The master takes great pleasure in the rivalries and jealousies that exist between all evil spirits, evil angels and demonic androids as long as it doesn't interfere with our human assignment."

"Okay."

Metraloas stopped first at the left leg of hell, the place of the pits. "Two things keep the kingdom of darkness from destroying one another; the rewards that the master dangles out in front of us and the policing action by the spirit of arbitration."

"Where does that spirit reside," the bat asked.

"He exists in another dimension. He is invisible in our spiritual realm."

Hmmm. He was learning a lot of things from the older android.

"As you've already noticed, we androids viciously compete with one another over the rewards that the rulers promise to give to those who are successful. Did they tell you what you will get if you are successful?"

"A bigger demon just told us to go to the surface and do many evil things. Like break up homes and destroy families and seduce weak Christians and mislead and deceive as many as we can. He said that we would receive our reward when we return."

"No wonder you're asking so many questions." He was looking for his supervisor while talking to the bat. "They didn't train you right."

"I knew that I would need a mentor, but unfortunately they've been hard to find."

"The rulers give power, wealth and a humanoid body to the androids who complete their assignments on earth. Several humans delivered at the gate of hell could procure a beautiful humanoid body of your choice, male or female. Power, wealth, and a beautiful body: what else is needed to live the good life on earth?"

"What is so great about a human body?"

"Without a human body, you can't enjoy the pleasures of earth."

As far as the eye could see, pits of fire dotted the landscape. A deceased human was in the middle of each pit swimming in hot boiling fire. The screams were music to his ears. Metraloas focused his special vision to zoom in on individual pits. He knew this was chemah's favorite place to visit when he was in hell.

The bat flew next to him as he walked through the pits. "What does he look like?"

"At first glance, he looks like just another demonic android. But he is in fact a member of the spiritual hosts in the heavenlies."

"You're kidding me!"

"One thing you've got to learn, batty, is no one ever kids in hell."

"Batty?"

"Yes. You're driving me batty with all your questions! I assume you don't have a name yet."

"No, just a number off the assembly line. Now what about chemah your supervisor?"

"There is a myth circulating from the Christians on earth that the prince of death, our master satan, caused a rebellion on the planet heaven. The gossip is that chemah's form was severely altered in the war of rebellion. The angels who followed satan in his rebellion against their Creator, were kicked out of heaven and forever banished from their home," he answered, walking around the pits, keeping his eyes open for chemah.

"I know that the spirits that reside in the heavenlies are not like us."

Metraloas laughed at his comment. "Our master, lord of the kingdom of darkness, designed us, but rumor has it that the God of the Christians created our master and the host of wicked spirits in the heavenlies."

"And the difference is . . ."

"The difference is that when we battle the angels of God we can be destroyed, but the angels that came from God can never be terminated. And neither can the higher evil spirits in the master's kingdom."

"It seems like the higher spirits could have come from the Christian's God."

"Now you're getting smart. The myth continues to say that one-third of all the angels from heaven chose to follow satan. I've heard gossip that several evil angels have condemned themselves for listening to satan's promises."

His eyes widened. "They would dare come against the master?" He couldn't believe what his ears just heard.

"Things started falling apart after Jesus defeated . . ." he was whispering as he looked around to see if any demon spirit was listening. "Jesus defeated the master and showed every evil spirit in hell that Jesus is the supreme Master. Many know that satan deceived them just like he tries to deceive all humans. I think most rulers know that they have no choice now but to follow the master and try to reverse the prophesied end."

"What prophesy?"

"I can't tell you here. Satan blamed everything on the Second Person of the Trinity, the Word of God, as the perpetrator and inventor of their sufferings." metraloas wouldn't tell him that he was beginning to believe that satan was as deceived as the dead humans who were prisoners of hell. "There he is!" He finally spotted his supervisor.

Chemah was at least two or three feet taller than metraloas. He was ugly and fierce looking. At the end of his right arm was a torch-like claw that sprayed fire instead of the hand he lost in the war of rebellion. He had long red hair, yellow eyes and yellow teeth. He dyed his hair to match his burnt red skin after the war. He enjoyed the fact that he was so ugly looking, even though he could change his appearance at will. In this form, he could torment humans with the fear of his appearance along with physical torture.

"Watch him. Many humans have fallen to his torment on earth and in hell. The left leg of hell is my favorite place to be. I love the way brimstone is embedded in the sides of the pits and glows like red-hot coals of fire."

He pointed out that in every pit there was a lost soul who had no idea that hell even existed until they arrived all chained up in a bundle and delivered into the pit. "Watch the fire. It begins at the bottom of the pit and sweeps upward and covers the lost soul in flames."

The screams were ear shattering. Desperately trying to climb out of the pit, just as the soul was about to be successful the fire swarmed over him or her and plunged them back into the pit of despair.

Metraloas laughed. "Look how much enjoyment chemah receives from torturing those pathetic looking humans."

Numerous evil, hideous-looking creatures flew over the souls in hell and added torment to their permanent stay. "I helped to construct a lot of these pits that you see." He pointed to the vast land of hundreds of thousands of pits. "I liked my job of overseer of the pits of hell."

"Why did you leave?"

"Some demon told me that I would have more fun on the surface." He turned around and saw that chemah was gone. "Guard, have you seen chemah?" metraloas grabbed the demonic snake's throat walking back to the entrance to the left leg of hell.

"He was here earlier having a little fun with these pitiful, poor excuses for souls, before reporting to the master," he choked out.

A look of fear entered his eyes.

"Why you are so afraid of the master?"

"I heard that he is replacing older androids with newer models. I'm as old as they get. Besides he gets his kicks out of pain, disembodiment and total extermination." Releasing the snake, he walked down the corridor leading to long winding steps down to a large open floor where the heart of hell was located.

"This is satan's special place of torment for those souls that willingly served him on earth."

"He tortures humans who served him on earth?"

"Yes. Isn't that ironic? Imagine believing that the master would actually give humans a part of his kingdom? They are the most gullible and stupid creations I think I've ever been around. Even I know when a spirit is lying to me or not."

"You do?"

"Yes. It's easy, just look into the eyes. Eyes are the windows of the soul," metraloas boasted.

"Look into my eyes." The bat flew in front of his face and stopped forcing metraloas to stop before he ran into him.

He swatted the bat out of his way. "I don't have to look into your eyes. You're easy to know." He thought he was too ignorant to lie.

He spotted chemah, having fun with the fire that spewed from the end of his right arm, burning someone inside the fun circle. Hiding behind the stands of cheering evil spirits, metraloas tried to get chemah's attention as he flew back and forth over the arena.

"Chemah," he called out in a whisper darting his eyes to the right and left as chemah flew over the stands. "I need to talk to you."

He tried to communicate to him through the system of mental spirit telepathy. Batty opened his mouth about to ask him a question when metraloas told him to be quiet. "Rulers of darkness have their own communication system different from the graveline. All messages that are transferred and received within the kingdom of darkness can be intercepted at any time by satan."

"What are you doing here, you miserable excuse for a demon?" chemah swooped low and let a blast from his arm extension heat up a soul trying desperately to get away from him. The blast added heat and pain, if that was possible, since the soul was chained over the top of a kettle of fire and dipped up and down in it.

Satan let out a blood-curdling sound. Metraloas pointed to the human in the center of the arena. "See that human?"

"The one with the black gown and long black hair?"

"Yes. She is going into the kettle next." It was especially ironic for him to watch. "When she lived on earth, a demon drove her to boil humans alive in a kettle of hot, boiling water."

With one last swoop and fire spraying everywhere, chemah landed next to metraloas and clutched his neck with his claw like hand. Digging hard into his leather skin and breathing fire into his face, he said, "This better be good, because I will personally throw you into the abyss for disturbing my fun."

The bat quickly moved away from metraloas so that chemah wouldn't attack him. He made a mental note that this android had developed a mental problem because of the physical and mental attacks on earth and in hell.

It was imperative that metraloas be reassigned to the pits in hell since he didn't think that he could overcome the Knight family or his eventual termination from a ruler of darkness. Obviously, at the moment, it did not seem to him that chemah would be willing to reassign him, especially in view of the fact that he was choking the life out of him.

Releasing him, metraloas fell to the floor of hell with a thud.

CHAPTER 5

Kellie and Joshua drove to a park near the school to talk in private. Joshua prayed that the Lord would give him the right words so that she would understand his experience. Very few Christians have seen the Lord in person.

"Kellie, did you hear me?"

"I heard you Josh. That is so cool! I would love to see Jesus!"

"I think if you don't see Him its better."

"You can say that after what you've just experienced?"

"Don't you remember what Jesus said when Thomas had to touch him before he would believe? All Christians remember him as 'doubting' Thomas. Jesus said, 'be not faithless, but believing, Thomas because you have seen me, you believe, blessed are they that have not seen me, but yet they believe.' There is a special reward for those who have never seen Jesus and yet believe in Him."

"I never thought of it like that before." *He did it again.* "You always give me a different way of thinking about scriptures," she said. He had the ability to see the Words of Jesus in ways she had never thought about before. Most of the boys she knew were so immature, especially freshmen, but not Joshua. "How do you do it? Just when I think I have something figured out, you blow it away."

Joshua shrugged his shoulders.

Kellie sat on top of the table. "So, who are you going to pick to be in this club?"

"It's not a club, it's a ministry. How about you?"

"Me?" She put her hand up to her chest and acted surprised. Secretly, she was wondering if he would think of asking her.

"Yes."

"Me? You really want me?" She looked down into his eyes.

He was sitting on the bench looking up at her. "You don't have to tell me now, you can pray about it."

"Are you kidding?" She put her hand on his shoulder. "I mean, you saw Jesus in the flesh."

"Glorified body," he interrupted.

"Whatever. How can you ask me that?"

"Don't make a big deal about it."

"You're the only person I know that has seen the Lord in person and you think I have to pray about it? Where do I sign?"

"Hey, I just got my commission early this morning. I don't even have a name for the ministry yet."

"Jesus appeared as a light?"

"Yes. Like a ball or an orb. It was rotating and glowing. Before he stepped out of the light, He talked to me."

"That is too awesome. How can He be light and have a flesh body?"

"I wasn't surprised that He appeared as light, because John said that God is light. But I don't know how He is both. I'm going to pray about the name for the ministry after school."

"You know my mom is on this new thing now, after she prays she says she really enjoys putting the kingdom of darkness under her feet by quoting scriptures. Maybe the name should be like some kind of devil-kicking club."

"Ministry. Think of it as a ministry not a club."

She nodded her head. "Something like the movie *Ghostbusters* . . ."

"No, we don't want to copy anything the world does."

Kellie playfully slapped his arm. "Joshua Knight, I was just kidding."

Joshua did not kid, joke or jest like some teenagers did. He didn't believe in it. "You know what most Christians think about anything connected to satan."

"I really don't know that much about it."

"Talking about the devil seems to paralyze some Christians. My parents were once asked to leave a certain congregation because they learned how to take authority over satan during prayer."

"You never told me about that. Which one?"

He gave her that look that said he couldn't believe she asked that question. He might tell her about a situation, but he would never tell her names. "It was a long time ago. I wasn't born yet. My mom told me that she started directly addressing satan after her prayers and some of the members didn't like it. They stopped the weekly prayer meeting with some lame excuse. She thinks they stopped the prayer meetings because once she told satan to get his hands off her pastor when they were laying hands on him and praying for him. She thinks he got offended."

"Who, satan or the pastor?"

Joshua laughed. "Probably both, but she doesn't hold it against the pastor. She told me that he was ignorant of the devises of the kingdom of darkness."

Kellie leaned over putting both her arms on her legs and putting her hands together. "I heard a rumor about you."

"Now what?"

"Are you thinking about leaving our school?"

"Yes."

"Why?" She jerked her head up to look into his eyes.

"Because I think the Lord wants me to attend a public high school."

"You?"

"Yes."

"Josh, you will never make it in public school."

He didn't answer her. That very thought bothered him. But "never" was a word that he didn't think about much, especially when he felt that the Holy Spirit was directing him.

"What about your calling?"

"I think the change will work with my calling, not against it."

"Don't you think this ministry should be operated within the church?"

"No. The purpose of this ministry is to destroy the works of the devil and give glory to God."

"Isn't that what all church outreaches are suppose to do?"

"Yes, but the Lord wants me to teach kids like us how to fight demons and train them in the Word of God. That means I will need a place to openly address that issue without being worried about offending members of a congregation. You know some of the teens that I want to minister to are not welcome at some congregations."

"We have a lot of open-minded people at our church when it comes to breaking traditions."

"I really don't care what people are going to think about me, especially religious people, but I think we will need a congregation that openly fights the kingdom of darkness and will support us while we are training fighters."

"Have you considered my church?"

"I've thought about it, but that's my dad's department."

"Wow! I am so excited." Kellie really wanted to be a part of his calling. She hopped off the picnic table. "I'm ready."

"Maybe you better think about it before you commit yourself. I'm serious about fighting demons for souls. We will be attacked."

"I know, but I'm not afraid of them. Look, the kingdom of darkness is going to try and destroy us whether we do this or not," Kellie sat down on the bench next to him. "I'm tired of hearing about evil works in public schools and feeling like it's a hopeless fight. I think about this all the time. I want to know that I'm doing something about the bad stuff that is happening to kids our age." She looked directly into his eyes. "What do we do next?"

"We need to find a few more Christians who think like us and get started."

Looking at her watch, she jumped up and grabbed his hand. "Joshua, we're late!" Pulling him off the bench she ran toward her car.

Sitting in Kellie's car, Joshua thought about other members. "Kellie, come over to my house tonight. We can pray together for other members to join our ministry and you can help me think of our name."

"Sure. Can I bring someone that might be a perfect fit?"

"Hannah?" He knew that she was her best friend even though she didn't go to their school.

"I know that she acts like a ditzy blonde sometimes, but she really does love the Lord."

"How much does she know about the Word of God?"

"She knows the Lord and His Word."

"It will be very important that all members of my team know the elementary principles of the scriptures."

"She knows a lot more than she lets on. And Joshua, there were a couple of times when I couldn't find a scripture in the Bible she knew exactly where to find it." As she turned into the school parking lot, she had to ask him one more time, "Now, tell me what Jesus looked like again."

It was evident to him why Eve was the first one who tasted the tree of the knowledge of good and evil.

‡ ‡ ‡

The telephone rang as Vicki finished some of her late morning chores.

"Hello?"

"Is this Vicki Knight speaking?"

"Yes."

"This is Ruth Pearson. I was talking to a mutual friend of ours, Kathy Todd . . ." she paused to let Vicki acknowledge that she knew who she was talking about.

"Kathy and I have been friends for many years."

"We were talking earlier and she told me that you were thinking about putting together a prayer group for our children in school?"

"Yes. I have been praying about putting together a prayer team that will meet at my house daily during the week. The Lord has directed my son to start a phone ministry for young people."

Ruth was delighted. She felt a real leading of the Lord to pray and teach the youth of their church and in the community.

"I have a great passion for young people!"

"You have a teenager."

Ruth laughed. "How did you guess?"

"I think the word passion tipped me off," Vicki laughed back with her. "Seriously, my husband Dan and I are interceding that the Lord will send a new move of His Spirit to our city."

"Praise the Lord! So are we. My husband David and I have a great desire for the youth to know the Lord of all power and authority. I have to confess. Kathy told me that I sounded a lot like you. She said that we would get along because of our mutual love of the Word of God and our commitment to prayer. I don't mind meeting new prayer partners." Ruth was looking for a soul mate that she could pray with. *The wife of a pastor needs all the praying friends she can find,* she thought.

"Kathy has given us a couple of your husband's tapes and we love his preaching."

"Have you ever been to our church?" Ruth asked.

"Just to hear a special speaker, but I think we need to get together."

"How about tomorrow for lunch?" Ruth replied.

"Great. Where would you like to meet?"

"I love that soup and sandwich restaurant at the mall downtown."

"So do I."

Vicki asked, "Do you want to meet around 11:00, before the lunch crowd?"

"I think that would be perfect," answered Ruth.

"See you tomorrow."

Joshua was so glad to be home from school. He ran up the stairs to his bedroom to be alone with the Lord. All day long he couldn't concentrate on anything his teachers were saying.

"Lord," he prayed, "I need some ideas, some great big ideas, for this ministry. I need a name. I need other partners." When the Lord personally came to him, he couldn't think of anything to ask Him. Now he had a hundred questions and many needs.

"Thank You that the Holy Spirit is my Guide and Teacher. I need your wisdom for this ministry . . ." Suddenly he remembered something. *Forgive me, Lord, I forgot to enter Your gates with thanksgiving and Your courts with praise.*

Joshua raised his hands walking back and forth in his room praying. "Oh Lord! I want to thank You for salvation obtained through Your shed Blood on the cross. What a plan, to redeem us by the Blood of the perfect Lamb,

Jesus."

In a matter of seconds, because of his pattern of praise and worship, his spirit, soul and body began to flow in the spirit of worship. "Praise Your name! Praise Your name! Praise the Name of the Lord!"

His parents taught him how to worship the Lord as he allowed his spirit freedom after declaring the Word out loud. His mom told him since he was a toddler that singing and dancing was a way that they worshipped the Lord. A feeling of dancing before the Lord came upon him and he began to sing and dance. In the privacy of his own bedroom he was completely free of all self-awareness around other people.

"Thank You Lord for Your plan of salvation! Thank you Jesus that rulers of darkness had no idea about Your plan. They did not know that they were crucifying the Lord of glory. Praise Your name! It was hidden from them. Paul said the rulers of this world would not have crucified Jesus if they would have known about Your plan."

The scriptures began to overflow from the inside of him.

"Thank You, Father, for sending Jesus! Jesus You are the one! You defeated and paraded the devil all through hell. You chased him and caught him. You took the keys from him. Now instead of one Devil Chaser, evil spirits have to contend with millions of devil chasers that will enforce your victory in hell over the devil! Thank you, Lord!"

From his whole heart, Joshua was praising the Lord.

"Thank you, Lord, that I am one of Your devil chasers. I will chase satan with . . ." Joshua was so caught up in his prayers that it took a few minutes for him to suddenly realize that he was saying something that he never heard himself pray before. He stopped walking and listened to what he just said. "Devil Chasers?"

Wait a minute, wasn't that what Kellie said, 'a devil-kicking' name?

"That's the name for this ministry!" With his spirit jumping up and down inside him, Joshua realized the Holy Spirit answered his prayer while he was praising and worshipping the Lord. "Praise the Lord!" He shouted over and over. "The Devil Chasers! This ministry is going to chase devils!"

While Joshua prayed, Kientay organized the warring angels outside the Knights' house. A legion of warrior angels assigned to reinforce the hedge of protection surrounding the house stood shoulder-to-shoulder. The headquarters was assembled under the cloud of the anointing. Even though it was hidden from the watchers of the kingdom of darkness, they knew something was up. The neighborhood was buzzing.

The demon spirits who lived in the vicinity of the Knights' house were aware of the fortress that the Knights lived under, but they had never sensed this much activity before. Looking toward metraloas' base, they saw that he was gone. But because it wasn't their assignment, it was none of their business.

"Try to stay hidden as much as possible," instructed Kientay. "We don't want to attract too much attention and raise the suspicion of metraloas."

Even though Kientay hadn't seen the demonic android, he had an angel assigned to find him. It was imperative to know exactly where metraloas was at all times. "No evil spirit breaks through our hedge of protection, unless someone in the family opens the door to an evil spirit without realizing it," he continued.

A newly assigned angel spoke out. "How do you know if one of the humans allowed them in?"

"The demon will let you know that they have the right of entry," Kientay told him. "Of course challenge the demon, because they may be lying. As soon as you hear anyone in the Knight family exercise their Covenant rights, then you can cast the demon spirit out immediately."

"Do we have to wait for confirmation from the Holy Spirit?" a warring angel asked.

"No," Kientay explained. "This family has passed many tests that give us the right to attack before the demons can even plan an offensive. Usually the Knights are very careful of the words they use and the thoughts that they think, so demons seldom get into their house. But occasionally a word or thought sneaks by them, so it is always best to be ready. Metraloas, android from the class of powers, is assigned to them now."

Another new warrior angel raised his hand. "Does he look like a fat dinosaur?"

"Yes."

"I was forced to attack him because he was trying to sneak around the hedge of protection. I think he suspects something is going on now. I saw him limping off to one of the gateways to hell with a demonic bat flying after him."

"He probably had to make a personal report to his division leader," reasoned Kientay. "No problem. You did an excellent job protecting the Knights' property."

The angel sentry replied. "It is easy to guard the Knight family because they constantly command all evil spirits to stay away from their property with the authority of the Word and the Blood of Jesus."

"No doubt the neighborhood demons have noticed the bigger and stronger warring angels taking their place around the house," reported another angel assigned as a guard.

"Watch for another attempt from metraloas. We need time to construct the communication tower."

"Yes, sir. You will get your time."

An angel directly under Michael's command, Chroni, appeared from heaven. He was around seven feet tall with the muscular look of a Roman soldier. His brown tunic with a v-neck shape neck line, revealed a hairy chest with curly brown hair touching his shoulders. The angels in the house noticed his arrival. It was obvious that this assignment was important in God's plans for the end time.

"I have been with the Lord of Hosts. You need to position yourself now! Chemah is coming with metraloas from one of the gateways to hell. The Holy Spirit will provide cover from His command center."

As he spoke the words of the Lord, a cloaking device was engaged that caused them to be invisible from the evil spirits . . .

. . . Four fierce, evil looking eyes flashed intensely from metraloas' station in the oak tree. Scanning every inch of landscape surrounding the house with their x-ray vision, they could see nothing.

Metraloas' eyes were darting back and forth all around the Knights' one acre property. He couldn't get his zoom-in focus lens to work. He was seeing men like trees. "I tell you chemah, there's something going on."

"How can you tell with that . . . that glory cloud covering the house? My x-ray super vision can't penetrate that light! Unbelievable!" He readjusted his vision to see if he could pierce through the glory cloud and light. Chemah cursed. "It even covers most of the trees, bushes and the sky all around it! There could be an army of God's angels under that cover and we would never know it!" He spit out angrily with a harsh tone of frustration.

"Then they must be establishing a communication link . . ."

"Don't go there!" Chemah cursed the Knights. He cursed metraloas. He cursed every thing he could think of. "I curse the day that God created me!"

Batty observed that metraloas didn't tell chemah the whole truth of the situation.

He continued ranting and raving. "They may even be establishing a command headquarters!" Chemah viewed the position of metraloas with disgust. He spit on the ground. "Look where we are! How in satan's name can you do your job from this distance? You're a loser metraloas."

He began to dematerialize. *I think I should turn you over to satan and wash my hands of you!*

"Why didn't you tell him," batty asked as he flew over and sat in chemah's vacated spot.

"Didn't you hear him? He doesn't want the facts. He wouldn't know the truth if it hit him in the butt! Which is exactly what I want to do every time I see his face!"

"Uh, I wouldn't do that if I were you."

"He is already thinking of ways to cast blame on someone else and I'm just a pawn for him. He's going to get rid of me." He laughed.

"What's so funny?"

"He's so occupied with devising a plan that he hasn't even realized that I can read his thoughts."

"You can?"

"Yes."

"How did you develop that power?"

Metraloas felt a sick feeling in his stomach. For some reason he felt like he just made the biggest mistake of his existence. No one knew that he had the ability to cloak his thoughts and now the stupid bat knows his secret. "Don't you have something you're supposed to do?"

"No." Can't I stay with you?"

Metraloas turned around to go back into his house. He wasn't sure if he should trust the bat or not.

"You can stay."

CHAPTER 6

Driving her red, 1965 Ford Mustang into the Knights' driveway, Kellie prayed she had not mistaken the Holy Spirit's prompting to invite Mose and Hannah. She unbuckled her seat belt, opened her car door and stood. Bending over to grab her purse from behind the driver's seat, she pushed back her long dark brown hair and waited for her passengers to get out of the car. Her petite 5'2" body was a perfect fit for her car.

"Hey!" Joshua opened the front door and greeted the three young people.

Kellie turned to her guests and introduced them, "Joshua, you know Mose Pearson and Hannah Coyle."

"Hey!" Joshua stuck out his right hand to Mose.

"Hey!" Mose tried to maneuver one of his special handshakes but Joshua didn't know the moves. For some strange reason, he was nervous and wasn't acting like himself. Lowering his hand, he realized how awkward the situation looked and he felt stupid.

"I invited Mose too. I hope you don't mind," she explained as they walked into his house.

"Sure." Joshua withdrew his hand hoping Mose wasn't embarrassed. "Mose is the preacher's son at the church you attend and I've seen Hannah with you before."

"Hey!" Hannah put out her hand.

Joshua had seen her before, but never this close.

"I'm not your typical blonde, trust me." Hannah saw his look.

Anticipating a great beginning, he invited everyone into his family room.

As they seated themselves on the sofas that surrounded the huge rock fireplace, Joshua immediately started to question them. "I don't know what Kellie has told you, but I have a mission from Jesus to form a special ministry for teenagers. What do you know about fighting the kingdom of darkness?"

"Well . . ." Mose and Hannah started talking at the same time.

"You first," Mose pointed to Hannah.

"No, you first," Hannah insisted.

"Well, bro," Mose replied, "I dunno when I was saved, but my mama fed me by speaking in tongues and she do speak in tongues!" Inside, Mose felt like crawling into a hole.

Kellie couldn't believe it. She had never heard Mose talk like that before.

"She do?" Hannah said wondering if he realized that he just used bad grammar.

She do? He was shocked. *Why did I say that?*

"Fed you by speaking in tongues?" Joshua was totally clueless to what Mose was talking about.

"Let me start over. I don't know what got into me, but I can speak as white as you . . ."

Joshua held up his hand. "I don't think in terms of black or white."

Oh brother! Kellie thought as she lowered her head in her hands. W*hat a disaster! Mose is talking like a black hood person or something and Joshua is talking like a grown up adult and both didn't sound like themselves.*

It was hard for Mose to be comfortable in this house. Looking at the huge fireplace, he felt like he was in a ski resort. There were large, over-stuffed wine colored leather chairs. The sofa they were sitting on was a plaid yellow, navy and wine conversational grouping. Some of the paintings in the room looked they were originals. The ceiling was at least 20 or 25 feet high with windows from top to bottom at the end of the room. It was a little over-whelming.

"Kellie has told me a lot about you. Man, I messed up. I never talk like that!"

"I'm no one special."

"Not special?" Hannah interrupted him. "You've seen Jesus and . . ."

Joshua turned his head to look squarely at Kellie.

"I was hoping you wouldn't mind if I told them."

"I really don't want a lot of people to know about my visitation."

"Hey," Mose raised his hand and crossed his heart with the other. "I promise not to tell."

"Me too!" Hannah added as she crossed her heart. "If I lie, I hope I . . ."

"Noooo . . . don't say it!" Kellie raised her voice. *Please, don't say that around Joshua!*

Maybe Kellie missed the leading of the Holy Spirit, Joshua thought.

"What I was trying to tell you is that my mom prayed in the spirit with my dad over me since the first day she knew she was pregnant. Her prayers scare the devil. She's a real prayer warrior," Mose explained.

"She sounds like my mom," Joshua said feeling like maybe the awkwardness was broken now.

Kellie felt the break in the uneasiness and let out a breath of relief. Mose was known at his school for clowning around and joking but not for talking like he just did. She looked at Joshua's face to see if she could tell what he was thinking. He was smiling, so she let out her breath quietly. She figured that once Joshua really got to know Mose they could become real close friends.

"My mom is really into the Word of God." Mose was the son of Pastor David and Ruth Pearson. His short stature and super skinny frame helped him develop the ability to make kids laugh. When he got nervous or anxious, he talked a lot, but he was serious about his relationship with the Lord. He knew his Bible and how to pray.

Kellie told Joshua that Mose wasn't like some preacher's kids that pretended to be saved at church, but acted like the devil when they weren't around their parents. His relationship with the Lord was genuine. She knew how important that was to Joshua.

"Where do you go to school?" He asked Mose.

"Lincoln High."

Joshua nodded his head.

I bet he's wondering why I don't go to Lincoln High Christian School, he thought as he continued surveying the family room. *This house is the bomb!*

It was hard not to stereotype Joshua as a spoiled rich kid but that was as bad as white kids stereotyping black kids as poor. Though, he had to admit that he jumped at the chance to see the inside of the house when Kellie invited him. It looked like one of those mansions on the hilltop that Christians sang about a long time ago. Although he lived in a two-story house, it wasn't as big as Joshua's house and it wasn't located in a famous neighborhood that was known for extreme wealth.

There was an awkward silence. "I forgot my manners. Would anyone like something to drink?"

"Sure!" Hannah was always thirsty or hungry.

"Mose?"

You don't want anything from this rich kid.

"Shut up devil!" He whispered.

"What did you want?" Joshua asked.

"What?"

"A drink," Kellie reminded him.

You probably couldn't even name the kind of drinks he could offer.

"I bind you demon!" Mose whispered to himself.

"Mose, they don't drink wine," Hannah gasped.

"What?"

"Didn't you say something about wine?"

"No, girl, what's wrong with you?"

"Me? You're the one that's talking so weird!"

He grimaced because she was right. He was flat nervous and blowing it big time. If he didn't get himself under control fast, he would start talking too much.

"Mose?" Kellie stared at him wondering where his mind went.

"I'm cool."

Kellie then looked at Joshua. "I'll go get some water from the fridge." She knew where to go because many times she had been studying with Joshua and they would stop for a break and get a snack. She walked down a couple of halls and into the kitchen and got a couple of cool bottles of water from the refrigerator. "Lord, I sure hope you have this under control, because I sure don't." She talked out loud to herself.

Joshua looked at Hannah waiting for her to drink down some of her water. After a minute or two, they all were staring at her.

"What?" She looked down to see if she drooled or something.

"Hannah, Joshua wants to know a little about your background," Kellie reminded her.

"Oh yeah, sure."

Hannah ran her fingers through her long blond hair as she stood to talk. Model tall and slender, she wore an orange mini dress with huge yellow daisies. A little out of style, she loved the revival of the seventy's clothes a couple of years ago, but disliked the latest fashions.

"I was raised in the Catholic church . . ."

Kellie interrupted her. "Hannah, you aren't giving a speech at school. Sit down so we don't have to stretch our necks."

"Sure." Hannah sat back down on the couch. She ran her hand over the fabric. "I love the feel of this sofa." She crossed her legs and leaned back on one of the fluffy yellow velvet pillows.

Joshua covered his eyes.

"Don't worry. I always wear gym shorts under these short dresses."

Joshua blushed.

Mose laughed, "You'll get used to her. She's acts like an air-head. You know the blonde thing."

"I do not! Anyways, back to what I was saying before I was rudely interrupted. I still attend a Catholic church occasionally with my parents, but my grandmother received the Holy Spirit and spoke in other tongues watching Christian TV. She used to baby sit me when I was little and we watched TV together. I was baptized in the Holy Spirit when I was . . ."

"If you don't stop her she will tell you *everything* about her life," Mose interrupted her.

"I will not!"

Kellie looked at her watch. "Maybe we better cut this short."

"That's not fair! Mose got to talk for a long time." Hannah wanted to give him a disgusted look, but decided she better not.

"Joshua, I think you can tell them what you told me. I'm sure the Lord put them in my heart to be part of your team." *At least I thought so before they started talking.*

"Kellie, you interrupted me." Hannah paused.

Kellie breathed out loud noticeably.

"I'm waiting. What do we say?" Hannah crossed her arms looking at her.

"I'm sorry. Now can you hurry?" Allowing another frustrated breath to escape her lips, now she was positive that she hadn't heard from the Lord.

"I just want to tell Joshua that I am excited that you invited me to your house and that you have a gorgeous family room."

Kellie rolled her eyes.

Hannah ignored Kellie's obvious attitude. "And that I love Jesus with all my heart and it's my desire to give him all of my life. Thank you very much."

"Uh, I would like to add that I feel the same as Hannah, that is, about Jesus. And please don't hold it against me, you know, how stupid I sounded," Mose asked apologetically.

This is the first team to work with you in your ministry. Joshua heard the Holy Spirit speak in his spirit.

He decided to share his visit from the Lord since Kellie already told them a few things about it. Both Mose and Hannah thought the visit was cool and believed him when he said that he saw the Lord. His testimony broke the ice between them totally.

"Get outta here! This is so awesome that I can touch someone who has seen Jesus! Wait until my Grandma hears this," exclaimed Hannah as she reached out to touch Joshua.

Joshua tried to down play his experience. "A lot of people saw the Lord in the Old and New Testament." He didn't want them to make a big deal out of him seeing the Lord.

"Cool." Mose liked the sound of this ministry.

"Like . . ." Hannah was excited. "Like, Joshua in the Old Testament saw the Lord, at least, some scholars think it was the Lord. Personally, I think it could have been an angel, like, Michael or something. Like, he had a big commission from the Lord and he had to follow Moses, example. Did you have to take your shoes off?"

"My shoes?" That went over Joshua's head until he remembered about the Joshua in the Bible and his encounter with the Angel of the Lord. "I didn't have any shoes on, I was in bed."

"Ignore her Joshua. She's famous for her off-the-wall comments," explained Kellie.

Hannah glared at Kellie. "To hear you talk, Joshua wouldn't know that we are best friends." Many times she excused Kellie's behavior because she was the big sister to two little sisters and that tended to make Kellie act bossy to her at times.

Kellie ignored her last comment. She really was Hannah's best friend, but at that moment she wished that Hannah would drop the dumb blonde act.

"Did Jesus tell you anything special?" Mose asked.

"I wrote everything down that He said." He reached over to get his notebook and Bible off the coffee table. "He told me three times to tell everyone that He was coming."

"I don't get it." Kellie asked. "Doesn't everyone know that Jesus is supposed to come back and get us?"

"Yeah, like, now?" Hannah added. "You know, now that we are already way past the year 2000?"

"Man, remember all the hype about Y2K?" Mose laughed.

"Do you mean everyone in the world or every Christian?" Kellie asked Mose.

"I didn't mean everybody on earth," Mose replied almost with an attitude.

"Yeah, like don't most Christians know about the rapture?" Hannah asked.

"Jesus didn't tell me that He was coming to get us or take us away. He just said that He is coming soon."

"I don't get it either." Hannah looked at Joshua with a puzzled look. "Every Christian knows that Jesus is coming."

"What do you think Jesus meant?" Mose asked.

"I think that I need to do a word study on coming and then meditate on it before I can give you an opinion," Joshua answered him, picking up his Bible.

"That's cool." Mose respected his answer. *Some people try to give the answer to a Bible question every time instead of saying they needed to study on the subject*, he thought. *I think I'm going to like this guy.*

"Uh, like, you think Jesus would tell you something, like, where do UFOs come from or something. You know, like, tell you something that you don't know." Hannah was thinking out loud. "Like, where did demons come from?"

Kellie rolled her eyes again. She couldn't believe her ears. *How many 'like' words can she put in one sentence?*

"One thing I do know, when you're looking at the Man who is God, you don't tell Him what to tell you," Joshua pointed out.

"Maybe this is something, like, we don't know but assume like we do know. You know, like, maybe it's something I think I know, but like, I really don't know." Hannah wasn't letting the subject drop.

"Huh?" They all said together. She lost them.

"I think you're right Joshua. Whatever Jesus tells you, you sure don't say something, like, 'tell me something I don't know' with an attitude. That would be like, a dumb thing to do."

Kellie shook her head. "Hannah, why don't you drop the 'like' word? That is so nineties!"

Joshua changed the subject. "I got a name for this ministry while I was praying this afternoon. The Devil Chasers."

"Word! That is awesome!" Mose declared.

"Did the Lord really give you that name?" Hannah wondered out loud.

"How are we going to chase devils?" asked Kellie.

"Yeah, like, we're not going to get weird are we?" asked Hannah.

Mose started singing, "Who-you-gonna-call, the Devil Chasers" to the tune of *Ghostbusters*.

"Talk about old, wasn't that movie made back in the eighties?" asked Hannah.

"I know a lot of trivia," Mose explained.

Hannah protested, "Well, we can't do that, my mom would make me quit."

"Do what?" Kellie asked.

"Chase devils!"

"Even my mother might have a problem with me chasing devils," Kellie agreed with Hannah.

"We're not going to get suits and guns and stupid stuff like the movie, are we?" Hannah put her hand to her head like she was really upset and stood. "I look terrible in space-like suits!"

Kellie jumped up and grabbed Hannah and shook her. "Will you forget about what we are going to wear! Who cares?"

"The Mickey Mouse Club had these cute little hats with ears . . ." Hannah kept on talking even though the others weren't really listening and her voice sounded wobbly with all the shaking. She hit at Kellie's hands to get her to stop.

They all started talking at once. The conversations were shooting back and forth faster than Joshua could hear and he thought he had made a big mistake and missed hearing the voice of the Lord. *Lord, did I hear you correctly?*

These are the ones I have chosen. The Lord answered him.

Inside him a spirit of peace took over. He knew without a doubt that he had heard from the Lord. He interrupted all of them, raised his hands, put his lips together and whistled. "Quiet! Please."

Hannah grabbed her ears and fell back on the couch. Mose and Kellie stopped fussing with one another and instantly shut up.

Joshua moved to the edge of the leather chair. "I didn't mean to whistle so loud. I need to share with you why the Lord told me to start this ministry."

Once he had everyone's undivided attention, he continued. "You guys know that I go to the private Christian school with Kellie, but I have a burden for young people our own age and, well, I feel like I need to go to the public school so that I could witness to those who don't know Jesus."

"That's why I attend Lincoln High," Mose added. "I mean, to be honest, I was raised in the public school system and now that my parents can afford to send me to a private school, I feel like I need to stay to be a witness."

"Me too. But really my dad isn't a Christian and he wouldn't let me attend a private Christian school anyway," Hannah said.

"Uh," Mose hesitated, "not that it really matters, but just so you will know for future reference, we don't call ourselves young people, only adults at church say that."

"Yeah and, like, they are way older," Hannah added.

"It does really matter," Kellie corrected Mose. "Kids at your school can be cruel."

Mose gave her a puzzled look. *As if she would know!* "They will cut you to pieces if you talk that way."

Hannah defended Mose. "Joshua uses a lot of adult words."

"Uh, what they are saying, is that you might have a hard time blending in with some of the kids at school," Kellie tried to be a little kinder.

"Might?" Mose couldn't believe his ears. "How about throwing a lamb to hungry lions?"

"That's a little extreme," Kellie said.

Mose shook his head. "No it's not. Public school is going to be a shock to Joshua."

"Your probably right, Mose, but the Holy Spirit gave me a vision about kids our age getting pushed into hell."

"Yeah, like they are getting deceived by the father of lies," Hannah agreed with him.

"Demons don't care how young or innocent a human is."

"We hear you brother," Mose said, "but those kids at our school that are influenced by demons are mean. They won't give you any mercy no matter how much you care for them."

"I'm afraid I agree with Mose," Hannah added.

Kellie cringed when she heard Hannah use a fear word, but Joshua ignored it. He figured now was not the time to point out how the word "afraid" was connected to the spirit of fear.

When Joshua didn't say anything, Kellie apologized to Hannah. "I've been a little worried about Joshua's reaction to my inviting you guys to his house. I guess a spirit of fear has been messing with my head."

Joshua was glad that she was able to discern that her worry was connected to the spirit of fear. "Don't be concerned about bringing Mose and Hannah, I believe that God wanted them to be here with us," he told Kellie. "When I look at the young . . . uh, teenagers in the world, I see them being herded down a wide path that leads to destruction."

"Word! Were you dreaming?" asked Mose.

"No, it was an open vision, a scene in my head. Almost like watching TV. The fire was red hot, like molten lava. The people in the back are pushing the ones in front. When they finally wake up and realize where they are headed, it's too late. The edge of this mountain overlooks the red-hot lake of fire."

Mose's eyes widened again. "No offense, but I don't ever want to see a vision of hell!"

"It's in Revelation," Kellie told him. "John saw the sea and hell give up the dead for the white throne judgment. Then death and hell were cast into the lake of fire."

"At the ledge the people frantically try to turn around, but they can't and the crowd behind them pushes them into the fire. It's impossible for them to turn back, even though they start screaming and fighting with all their strength and might. They are trapped. It's too late! They are burned and tormented for all eternity!"

Hannah gasped and covered her mouth with her hand.

"I have a heavy burden for young . . . uh, teenagers. They are playing with the kingdom of darkness with drugs and drinking and they don't even know it."

"Oh, that's not even the latest one . . ." Her voice started out strong and then progressively got softer as she looked at Kellie. "The cool thing with a lot of kids I know is joining Wicca.

"Wicca?" Joshua asked.

"Yeah, a lot of girls think it is good witchcraft," Hannah explained.

Kellie's eyes started misting. "Joshua, kids get pushed into the lake of fire not knowing that Jesus is the only way out of hell, right?"

He nodded his head yes. "It seemed like they woke up just before they were going to be pushed into this lake of fire and when they turned around and started fighting with all their might to escape, it was too late."

"How can God allow that to happen," Kellie couldn't stop the tears.

"He is not responsible. We are."

"Us?" Mose asked.

"But Joshua, they are the ones that listen to death rock and then think nothing of killing their family, friends and even themselves," shuttered Hannah.

"Hannah." Mose motioned his eyes and head towards Kellie.

"Well, they do. When I walk down the halls of our school, I am always wondering if the kids around me are going to hell. Now I have this lake of fire picture in my mind. Everyone I see I'm gonna wonder if demons are gonna take them to hell when they die!"

"Joshua, do you mind me calling you Josh instead of Joshua?"

"No, but my mom might. She only calls me Joshua. She tells everyone that if she wanted me to be called Josh, she would have named me Josh. But I don't really care. Kellie calls me Josh occasionally. What does Mose stand for?"

"Moses."

"Your parents really named you Moses?" he asked with a smile breaking through the somber mood.

"Yeah, they really did."

"I'm serious Joshua, you have no idea what it is like to go to school with kids who dress in black and wear skulls on their fingers and nails in their ears and . . ."

"She's right, Joshua," Kellie finally agreed with Hannah.

"My goal is to reach the lost and to teach Christian teenagers how to fight demons and expose the kingdom of darkness to those who have been blinded." He didn't deliberately ignore them, but he had heard the same objections before. "This is what we can do. We print up cards that say something like this." He handed them a paper that said:

THE DEVIL CHASERS

HAVE BIBLE: WILL TRAVEL

We deal with fear, unbelief,

doubt and sickness

DEVILS AND DEMONS HAVE TO FLEE!

"Wait a minute! Joshua, you really are serious about naming this ministry the Devil Chasers?" asked Kellie as she passed the paper to Mose and

Hannah.

"Sure, it's something I've been thinking and praying about for a long time. A phone line for teens answered by us; teenagers who know God's word. Seriously dedicated, committed teenagers that know the heart of God and whose hearts are filled with God's Word and His love!"

Hannah got excited. "People like you who know how to pray and believe for any situation the caller would face!"

"Cool! Kids who know how to fight the kingdom of darkness!" shouted Mose. "That's a cool slogan. You got it off an old TV show, right."

"What?"

"You know it was from a television show back in the fifties. It was called *Paladin* or something like that."

"I've never seen the show."

"Trust me," Kellie told them, "He hardly ever watches TV or movies."

"It's still cool."

"Will you join me in the ministry of the Devil Chasers?"

"Sure!" Hannah was excited.

"You want me even though I totally blew your first impression of me?" Mose asked.

"Mose, I want what the Lord wants. He already told me that you are to be a part of this ministry."

"Cool!" Mose shouted. "This is an answer to prayer!"

Joshua's mother came into the room. "Joshua, forgive me for interrupting, but it is late, and I was wondering about curfews?"

Kellie jumped off the sofa after looking at her watch. "I can't believe that we have been talking so long."

"I'm surprised my mom didn't call," Mose said.

"Well actually, your mom did call about an hour ago. I told her that you were still busy talking. You probably better call her."

"Mom, I need to introduce you to Mose and Hannah. This is my mom, Vicki Knight. This is Mose . . ."

"Mose, I'm having lunch with your mother tomorrow."

"This is Hannah, Kellie's best friend."

"Hi, Hannah. I'm sure glad to meet you, both of you."

"I know we still have a lot to discuss Joshua, but I need to get home," Kellie said. "Why don't we get together this Saturday? That will give us more time so that we can pray together."

"Great. Let's pray before we leave," Joshua said as he stood to hold hands and form a circle. "Lord, You are God, who made heaven and earth and the sea, and all that is in them. Grant to us, Your servants that we might speak Your Word with boldness, by stretching out Your hand to heal. We are believers. We preach the gospel to every creature. Signs and wonders follow us. In Jesus' Name we cast out demons. We speak with new tongues. We take up serpents. If we drink anything deadly, it will not hurt us. We lay hands on the sick, and they recover."

The rest of the group agreed with his prayer in lower voices as Joshua prayed.

"Thank You, Lord, that You will confirm Your word through signs and wonders. You said Your word would not return to You void. We say that You are our refuge, our rock, our fortress and our deliverer. We put all our trust in You. We call upon You now Lord and ask for the anointing to destroy the works of the devil."

"Amen."

CHAPTER 7

That night while the Knight family slept, Chroni called a meeting in the living room with all the guardian angels and special warring angels assigned to the humans involved in the Knight campaign. They were crammed into the room along the walls, in and around the ceiling, on the floor and sitting on the furniture. Every space was filled with the ranking angels assigned with their divisions to the newly formed ministry of Joshua's.

"We have our official name now. We will be known as the angels of The Devil Chasers."

"As Mose says constantly, Word!" exclaimed Malcolm, the guardian angel over Mose.

An angel in the back of the room spoke up. "Are these kids that bold to publicly announce that they are going to chase devils?"

"The spirit of boldness is an anointing over Joshua," Kientay told them.

"I heard him talk with fellow members forming this ministry; he spoke with wisdom and authority with the Word of God," a warring angel informed those around him.

"He is most definitely a different human," another said.

"He might even be able to keep us busy!" A few angels wondered about an adolescent human able to keep so many angels busy with the work of the Lord.

"As a teenager, Joshua has walked in the Word of God and proven his knowledge and understanding given to him through the Holy Spirit," Kientay assured them.

"He has some awesome shoes to fill. Some of us who were involved with the Israelite campaign to conquer Canaan will remember what the Old Testament Joshua went through," another angel said.

"That's why so many of you warring angels have been assigned to this campaign. The prayers of the Knight family will keep you very busy." Chroni added, "Learn the words that are spoken by this generation; words, as always on earth, will be a very important part of this ministry."

"Has this young Joshua gone through his wilderness?" Malcolm asked.

Kientay responded, "He was home schooled and separated from the world's system for the first 12 years of his life. Then his parents enrolled him in a private Christian school, which he is attending at the present time. But now the Lord is calling him to attend the public school system and . . ."

"Excuse me," Malcolm interrupted him, "but are you counting the first years of life as his wilderness experience?"

"Yes, but let me explain. Even though Joshua hasn't been tested by the kingdom of darkness yet, he has been trained like John the Baptist."

"How do you know he will turn to the Word when trials and temptations come his way?"

"I . . ."

Another angel interrupted, "Or will he turn away from the Word, like so many other young humans?"

Several angels started to openly discuss the situation.

"I am the guardian angel of Joshua Knight. I have heard his words and I have listened to his prayers. He confesses the scriptures and prays according to the Word. When trials and temptations come his way, he will run to the Word!"

All the angels stopped talking as Kientay spoke so forcefully.

"Words are the ammunition for our weapons," Michael said as he walked through the wall to join the meeting with his assistant angel. "Joshua's file is filled with voice of the Lord coming forth from his mouth. He will accomplish the will of the Father."

"How many teenage believers do you think will want to be known as a devil chaser?" asked Matthan.

"You would be surprised. This generation knows more about the kingdom of darkness than any other generation in the history of man," Michael informed them.

"But many only know about the kingdom of darkness from lies filled with half-truths." An angel from the back of the room spoke.

Agreeing with him, many of the angels began to talk among themselves.

"How many times have we been bored with the watered-down version of the gathering of the saints?" Another angel asked.

"Look at the world's temptation through the media sources."

Several guardian angels defended some of the older Christians on earth. "How can the older generation compete for the hearts of their young?"

"Past generations faced the same thing," one pointed out. "But they did it with the manifestation of the power of the God through His Word."

The angels talked among themselves, agreeing with the last comment made. Warring angels were usually very disciplined about showing any emotions. Kientay was surprised to hear all the concerns.

"What about those who won't take action against the kingdom of darkness because of fear of reprisal?"

"We all agree that fear has stopped them from preaching the cross, the Blood of Jesus and operating in signs and wonders; when the pressure is applied will the Devil Chasers cave in?"

"The older generation has allowed demons to kill, steal and destroy their young, because they allowed the name of Jesus to be taken out of their politics, their business, and their schools; how will they accept this ministry?"

"They refuse to get in agreement over baptism, how will they get in agreement over fighting the kingdom of darkness?"

A muscular ten-foot angel walked through the wall of the living room. "I was told by Captain Gabriel to attend this meeting for reassignment. I am curious to know the answer to that question."

"We know that the time is getting closer to equalization. Michael, we desire a true work for the Lord God. Many of us have been disappointed with the prevailing thoughts and actions among the Lord's children. With Joshua being so young . . ."

Angels all over the room began talking among themselves again. It would seem as though the angels were complaining, but they had legitimate questions about this new assignment. They were eager to be actively warring against the forces of darkness and not one of God's angels wanted to be idle in these last days.

Another angel stood to speak. "My previous assignment was a ministry on the front line of a lengthy battle. My human charges denied their Covenant rights and when they actively engaged the enemy, they received many blows through death and sickness. How will this child's ministry compare?"

Michael understood what they were thinking. "In the past many of the Lord's angels have been bored with the humans they were guarding and protecting. Instead of fighting and driving back the evil from their charges, most of you had to sit around while His children would whine, cry, plead and beg. But we need to put that all behind us now and look to the prophetic utterances of the Lord's voice. This is a new age!"

Chroni agreed with the general of the Lord's armies. "We know exactly how vexed Moses got in his spirit when the children of Israel constantly complained and whined against the Lord and didn't believe what God told them to do. We do not want to be guilty of complaining and whining against the Lord's children."

Everyone was quiet.

"I agree with Chroni," Gabriel appeared in their midst. "This is the age of grace. We cannot forget how much the Father loves His creation. He wants to flood His people with revelation knowledge, but their hearts and minds need to be enlarged to receive all the things that God wants to bring to pass through His children before the next coming of Jesus."

"Michael," a lower angel bowed waiting to be acknowledged.

"Speak."

"I think I can speak for many of us who are waiting for the next coming of the Lord in the heavenlies to fight with satan and his kingdom of darkness."

Many agreed. "We don't want to miss that fight in the heavenlies!"

Another angel raised his hand. "It is obvious to us that the believers on earth are looking for their removal from earth instead of the war that God has prophesied in Revelation."

All the angels quietly waited for Michael to respond. "It is true that many in the body of the Anointed One do not have knowledge of the war in the heavenlies that is soon to take place, but the Lord has hidden mysteries that will be revealed to turn the hearts of the fathers to the children and the hearts of the children to the fathers."

"What does the Lord want us to do?" one of the recording angels quietly asked.

"If the Lord God will not call things that are as they are, then we, His angels, will not call things that are as they are! We will speak what the Lord commands us to say and do," Michael commanded.

Kientay looked around the room and was not surprised to see how quickly the angel troops got into line. Every eye was directed to Michael. He was the highest ranking angel in attendance and one of the few members of the inner circle of God's personal angels. If anyone had the answer, it was Michael.

Kientay stood to talk. "May I answer them, sir?"

Michael nodded his head.

"I was assigned to Joshua before he was conceived. The Lord God Almighty, praise His blessed Name, told me that Joshua would be a mighty man of valor and save many young people from the pit of hell. His parents gave him to the Lord before he was born, but they did not abandon him to grow up by himself. They took responsibility by imparting generational blessings over him and have seeded a love of the Word into him before he was born. They did it consistently. This teenage boy is full of the Word and his spirit is strong, because he has grown in the wisdom and knowledge of God."

The angels were listening intently.

"You will see. This ministry is a special one in the heart of The Almighty. Joshua reminds me of King David."

The warring angel's ears perked up when he compared Joshua to King David.

"He knows how to fight the Lord's enemies. When this ministry gets started we will need a thousand times more angels than this. And every angel here will receive a special thanks award from the Lord personally." Kientay stepped out on a limb, but the words came out of his mouth before he could stop them.

Michael was surprised at Kientay's boldness. "In Kientay's exuberance, he has committed the Lord to . . ." Michael received a message from the Holy Spirit that interrupted his next statement. "It seems that Kientay has just given us a good example of 'calling those things which do not exist as though they do.' The Lord agrees with his statement and He will be giving out special awards with those assigned to the Knight campaign."

He again stopped to listen to the Holy Spirit.

"We are entering the first wave of the mighty anointing of God that is going to cover this earth like a tidal wave. Believe me when I say that you are stepping into the water with your toes, but soon you will be over your heads in wave after wave of the greatest Holy Spirit move of the Heavenly Father that this earth has ever seen!"

Michael received more words from the Holy Spirit. "The Lord God Almighty has a plan even though it seems like this generation is lost. God is not willing for the people of earth to miss the coming of His Son, and since they are not ready He has told me that a mighty sign in the heavens is coming before that great day of the Lord. It is coming soon and it will prepare the way of the Lord and all the inhabitants of the earth will know it is a sign from God Himself."

"Praise the Lord!" Everyone stood and shouted.

Michael waited for the angels to become quiet. "Do not forget the way the Lord remembers the older generation." The angels stood at attention as Michael gave a slight reprimand. "Each and every tear shed, each and every prayer spoken . . ." He walked back and forth among them. "God has been collecting *all* tears. *All* prayers and they are in storage waiting to be poured out during the greatest campaign that has ever been deployed over earth in the heavenlies. These end time warriors will be blessed to harvest the seeds of every child of God from Adam until the last one born. The wrath of God is the tears of *all* saints! The wrath of God is the prayers from *all* saints! It is not just the young people that will accomplish the greatest move of God throughout eternity, the war in the heavenlies! It will be *all* God's children from *all* time that will receive blessings and benefits from this spiritual war."

No one moved.

"Is everyone clear?"

"Yes, sir!" The angels shouted in one accord.

"Now you can praise Almighty God!"

‡ ‡ ‡

The bat waited for metraloas to fall asleep before he left the tree and flew to his special hiding place, an apartment in the higher priced district of the city. Walking through the outside wall into his bedroom, he shape-shifted into a male model. He hated having to spend so much time watching metraloas, but the master wanted to know if the android had evolved and how he did it.

Sensing a chilling change in the atmosphere of his bedroom, the android turned around and saw satan had materialized next to his full-length triple mirror sitting in his golden chair. Dressed in white, the light almost blinded him.

"What have you learned?"

"You were correct," the android said as he placed the shirt from his closet onto his bed. "He has evolved since he was invented."

Satan leaned forward, "What new processes have formed?"

"He just told me that he can block his thinking from chemah and he can read his mind."

Satan cursed. "Did he tell you how he has attained those abilities?"

"No, he clammed up. I think he thought it was a mistake that he told me."

"Can he read your mind?"

"No, I don't think so. He arrogantly told me that he could look into the eyes and tell if a being was lying or not as he was intently looking into my eyes! I was lying to him at the time."

Satan stood and cursed again. "I need to know how he did it. Metraloas is one of the oldest surviving androids that still exist."

The android picked out a sleek pair of black pants. He checked his body and thought it would be wise to take a shower. His flesh closely resembled human flesh and it needed a lot of care and attention.

"Where are you going?" satan stopped pacing.

"I'm going dancing and looking for female companionship."

"What is metraloas doing?"

"His circuits needed a rest. He's sleeping."

"What about his assignment?"

"I don't know much about the Knights, but I know that he thinks that they are a hopeless cause. He says that he wants to be reassigned to hell because he knows that JC is going to defeat you."

Satan released a string of curse words. "I'll kill him!"

"He even started to talk about the war of rebellion."

"I have given a prime directive that prohibits any talk about that time."

"I guess he has decided to ignore your commands."

"Did he say what is going on between him and chemah?"

"He thinks chemah is a fool."

"What!" satan was astounded. "How can an android think that about a powerful fallen angel?"

"Maybe he is dangerous," the android said as he gathered his underclothes to go into the bathroom.

Satan grabbed his arm and yelled at him. "Sit down!" He resisted the urge to inflict physical pain on his own android spy. "Listen to me. When I leave, then you can continue your plans for tonight. I need to know how metraloas has developed these powers on his own. I do not want androids that have more power than I gave them. Do you understand?"

He looked at his master with a blank stare. "Sure, I was made to serve you and do your every command." He sat docile. "I don't know how he is doing what he says he can do, because he is a very stupid android."

"Why do you say that?"

"He named me Batty."

Satan stared at him and then busted up laughing. Calming down he looked at the android with an evil eye. "You better report to me as soon as you find out anything and don't you think that you can receive more power than I give you. I destroy those that think on their own!" Immediately satan disappeared.

The android slowly stood and took his things into the bathroom slamming the door.

‡ ‡ ‡

Kientay wiped his forehead. When he thought about what he said about the special rewards given out by Jesus, he couldn't believe he had said it without knowing for sure that it was the Holy Spirit speaking.

"How many warring angels from the first rank will He assign to the family?" asked Matthan.

"I am one," said Natsar, suddenly appearing through the wall.

"I am another," added Milchamah following after him.

"Oh praise the Lord!" Matthan rejoiced with a big smile.

Standing before the guardian angels were famous warring angels known among all the host of heaven. Natsar and Milchamah were high in authority and power under Michael. Those in attendance gave thanks to the Holy Spirit that powerful angels were assigned to Joshua's ministry. They raised their hands, floated about two feet above the floor and praised the Lord in their angel tongues.

Then Natsar, whose name meant to guard, protect and maintain, flexed his wings and stretched his nose upward. "I can smell the heavenly aroma of the Holy One. Breathing the anointing gives us such strength on earth!"

Milchamah, whose name meant warrior, shouted, "We will have many victories! I smell the victory! The prayers from this room are glorious! As long as they continue they will give us great strength and covering for any attack that is directed at them."

"The special team of prayer warriors will be contacted soon," Michael informed them. "They will begin their prayers immediately. All angels of the families of this group are to stay out of the enemies sightings until the communication link is established between heaven and earth."

"What about the three new members' angels?" asked Chroni. "Are you here?"

Three angels stood in the back of the room. "We are."

Michael continued the meeting. "It is your duty to learn all about the Knight family, each guardian angel and each of the first three chosen by the Almighty to help Joshua fulfill this call."

Chroni stood and unrolled a scroll reading the names of the Devil Chasers. "The names of the Devil Chasers are Kellie Todd and her angel, Marisa; Mose Pearson and his angel, Malcolm; Hannah Coyle and her angel, Chloe; and Kientay is the guardian angel over Joshua Knight."

Michael looked at each section of angels. "You all are familiar with the scenario. When the kingdom of darkness becomes aware of the great loss they will experience by the anointed hands of the Devil Chasers, they will arise with fury."

"It looks like it won't matter what will be released against Joshua Knight's ministry," an angel from the back of the room spoke.

"Amen," another angel raised his sword.

"We need to know which one of the four in this core group is the weakest link for the enemy to attack first," Chroni said.

Chloe raised her hand. "That would be my charge, Hannah. Strife exists between Hannah's parents. Her father has not been born again yet. The mother is a newborn. Many evil spirits are at work in their home. I have been bound by all the curses that are spoken in that house. My power over the enemy is mocked among the evil demonic androids who run freely in the Coyle family."

"The Almighty has already put things in order for her protection. The word is being spoken over Hannah and her family. You will be feeling a renewed strength," assured Michael. "The Teacher is adding His assurance, that situation will change soon."

"It's been a long time since I've smelled such heavenly words going up to the Throne room." Natsar was talking about the heavenly presence of God's Word that permeated the rooms of the Knights' home. "We will strike the enemy before they know what hit them and scatter them!"

Michael spoke to the division of warring angels. "Scatter the enemy and keep them away from the Devil Chasers headquarters."

The warring angels were huge in stature and fierce looking, covered with white armor that reflected the anointing of the Holy Spirit. The armor was made of a metal unknown on earth and it was able to absorb the prayers from the bowls of heaven when they are poured out to earth.

Natsar raised his hand and his sword appeared glowing. "This sword has been in the heat of several battles and my armor radiates with the intense yellow-white heat from the anointing. With the prayers and words from the Devil Chasers, the enemy will be scattered and kept in the state of confusion and derision!"

"The forces of evil have no defense against the power of the anointing through the prayers of the Devil Chasers," Kientay said.

"I believe the first four members already have a good foundation on the rock of the Word." Chroni observed them together during the meeting in Joshua's house and was impressed with their unity.

"Rulers of darkness will gather their forces and plan a counter strike in the heavenlies," said Milchamah. "They won't give up until we make them through the written Word of God."

Natsar folded his wings as they disappeared. "We will be ready to crush any assigned division from the army of darkness against the Knight campaign."

"I am second in command under the Lord of Hosts, as Michael told you. I will have my headquarters in eden. Kientay is next in command with his headquarters here. All other angels assume normal ranks and divisions awarded you before this campaign," Chroni commanded them.

Michael ended their meeting with some basic reminders. "It will be very important for us to oversee the operation of the intercessory prayers and the ministry of welfare over your charges. The Holy Spirit will lead many to pray constantly and it will be our job to intercept any interference from the enemy. We will keep the forces of darkness scattered and ignorant until the communication links have been established."

A shout of praise with jubilee spontaneously erupted from the room.

"The Lord has seen great and mighty battles between the forces of darkness and the Devil Chasers. They will overcome. Joshua Knight is a mighty man of valor with prosperity and success. As with Joshua of old, he is a strong and courageous human. We will have good success because he meditates day and night in the Word of God. The Lord God is with him and His angelic army will also go with him. Now, everyone report to your divisional commander. You are dismissed."

Michael dematerialized upon receiving a call from heaven.

CHAPTER 8

Chemah materialized in front of the oak tree and saw that metraloas was sleeping. Immediately he thought about knocking him out of the tree, but then had a better idea deciding to investigate on his own. Walking over to the Knights' property he stopped just in front of one of the warring angels. Not saying anything, he walked a couple of feet in front of the guarding angels following their line surrounding the property.

Michael started to leave the property when he saw chemah materialize outside the line of defense surrounding the property belonging to Dan and Vicki. He alerted the Holy Spirit who was currently in His tactical room in the city of eden. The Holy Spirit told him to stay to observe what chemah was doing.

Chemah walked up to one of the warring angels. "Will you talk to me or are you going to act like the guards of Buckingham Palace?"

The warring angel stood motionless and did not acknowledge his presence. He heard through the graceline that Michael was standing close by in a dimension that chemah could not discern his presence.

"I wonder what is going on in that house." He turned to the side to continue walking and inspecting the angelic wall just to make sure that there wasn't a breech that would give him access.

"You wouldn't be willing to let me have a peek now would you?" he said softly. He noticed that the house looked dark with the inhabitants asleep. But he had this feeling that an angelic meeting was taking place inside.

He walked completely around the house not finding one hole in the hedge of protection. "Now isn't that interesting. Not one hole for access? What human family is perfect on earth? Let's see, maybe Jesus has been born again . . . again?" chemah laughed at his words. "That's it! Jesus has come back to earth and Mr. and Mrs. God live in this house with their god-like son!"

Chemah bent over with laughter. "Look at me, I'm a comic!"

Michael relayed the words that chemah was saying to the Lord of hosts. *What would You like for me to do, Lord?* He asked.

Just ignore him, the Lord replied. *He is on a fishing expedition and he thinks he is funny. The Lord God has set a special time for him in the Knights' house. He will get his wish to get inside the house.*

Michael relayed the orders of the Holy Spirit to the guards and continued on his journey back to heaven. The angels were on high alert and knew that the Holy Spirit would warn them of a pending attack if and when chemah made up his mind about what he was going to do.

Chemah stopped walking and talking. It was obvious that he wasn't going to crack one of the angelic guards and it was also obvious that the fortress set around the Knights' house was impenetrable. He dematerialized and beamed to his spaceship docked above the city. It was time for him to rest and reevaluate the next move he needed to take against the Kingdom of God.

He needed a plan to penetrate the Knights' fortress.

"Kientay," Chroni sat behind Dan's desk. "The Lord has told me that you are to make contact with Joshua. He is to be made aware of the angelic help on his side. I want you to remind him how important confession of the scriptures will be in the foundation of this ministry. He needs to be prepared for the attacks that will come against him with great wrath. Especially when satan finds out Joshua had a personal visit from the Lord."

Kientay's heart started beating with anticipation at the thought of talking to Joshua again as he pulled up a chair close to the desk to listen to Chroni. "I know that the family is well equipped to fight any battles the devil directs against them."

Chroni raised his eyebrows, "Is Joshua aware of the demonic plant attached to his mind?"

Kientay wanted to explain, "No, but . . ."

"What is the status?"

"There are no roots. It cannot form roots because of the Word Joshua quotes daily."

"Why has he not taken authority over the doubts coming against his mind?" Chroni asked.

"He is quoting scripture, but he did not subject the first thought of doubt to the authority of Jesus. So, it gained entrance into his brain, but it has not grown. Since he hasn't taken authority over the thought, I have not had the opportunity to cut out the demonic implant." Kientay was glad that Chroni gave him a chance to explain the situation. It was not like Joshua to allow doubts to get inside his mind, let alone linger for awhile. "I will be ready when he recognizes that a doubt has gained entrance into his mind."

Natsar was standing behind to the right hand side of Chroni. He raised his sword and caused his wings to appear so he could fly to Joshua's bedroom and take care of the problem immediately, especially since he was quoting scripture. "Let me at the demonic scumbag! I'll cut him into pieces!"

"No!" Chroni put his hand on his sword. "You know the android implant has to be denied access by the human first. If Joshua does not resist him, then we are bound by his lack of thoughtlessness."

Natsar put his sword away. "It's frustrating when we are stopped by a demon's rights."

"It's not the demon's right; it's the human not demanding his rights!" Kientay corrected him.

Natsar wondered about Joshua's guardian angel, since he was bold enough to correct him. "Satan demanded that all humans be tested like Adam and Eve, so by default demons have a right to test them."

"Well," Kientay backed down. "I don't like to let a demon spirit believe he has any rights at all, especially when the foundation of that right is based on deception and lies."

"I can agree with that statement," Natsar said. "Sometimes I do feel bound like some human policeman having to 'read a person his rights' even though they caught the perpetrator red-handed stealing or killing!"

"Thank the Lord, we are not bound by human laws," Kara said.

"No, but we are bound by the Blood Covenant between the Lord God and Jesus the Anointed One," Chroni added.

"And to activate that Blood Covenant they have to declare their rights," Kientay reminded them.

Kara and Matthan exclaimed together. "We know! They have to say it out of their mouth." They looked at the other angels. "We go over this together every earth day."

"God is not mocked. His Word will not return to Him void. Joshua is watering the seed of God's Word planted in his heart. I have always taken care of all demonic implants assigned to his mind." Kientay directed his comments to Natsar. "I appreciate that you have been assigned to help the Devil Chasers team, but I have a need to take care of this particular demonic implant personally."

"Remember, we are bound to the law of binding and losing." Chroni quoted Matthew 16:19 reminding them of their duty as an angel. "'And I will give you the keys of the kingdom of heaven, and whatever you bind on earth will be bound in heaven, and whatever you loose on earth will be loosed in heaven.' We can only bind what they bind and loose what they loose."

"Hail, Jesus, King of kings!" Kientay proclaimed, "He has defeated death!"

They bowed and took a moment in time to give praise to the Lord

Jesus.

"Lord," Chroni led their prayer, "We thank you that we were appointed by You to worship Jesus first and then to minister to the heirs of salvation: men and women who have accepted the work of the cross and make Jesus the Lord of their life."

"Amen," agreed every angel in the room.

"We know that there are two laws that govern the earth, the law of sin and death and the law of life in Christ Jesus," Chroni told them. "Remember just because we have that knowledge does not give us the right to enforce those laws. Humans have the rights and privilege to enforce the laws over this planet. And we know that it is the mouth of a human that decides which law he is under."

"It is regrettable that the recognized version of the scriptures has translated the Greek word *ourano* as heaven instead of heavenlies, the sky and space above the planet earth," Kara said.

"I don't understand why some Christians believe that Jesus meant God's planet when he taught them the law of loosing and binding," Kientay said. "Nothing needs to be bound on our planet heaven."

"They don't know about the war that occurred on our planet that expelled all disobedient angels," Matthan said. "Only those who meditate His Word can understand the battle that is raging over the souls of men."

"Those who know how to bind the forces of darkness and loose us on earth to fight are the humans that speak sweet words to my ears." Natsar rejoiced raising his sword once more.

A couple of angels agreed. "Who enjoys guarding a human who is ignorant of the forces of darkness?"

Natsar loved the fight against the host of wicked angels who had exalted themselves against God and His creation in the heavenlies that was loaded with unseen space stations surrounding earth. "I can't wait for the day that God's Word will wipe out all rebellious angels that have invaded earth and prey on ignorant humans who know nothing of their existence."

"Imagine how some of the Lord's children are going to feel when they understand that they could have pulled down strongholds during spiritual warfare . . ."

"Shame, uh, excuse me. I interrupted you, Kara. But for a moment they are going to experience the shame of not understanding what the Word has already provided for them before they departed from earth."

"I agree with you, Kientay," she said. "They are going to be so disappointed that they missed out subduing the enemy while they still lived in their flesh body."

"That's just it," Kientay added. "Never again will they ever be able to experience the joy of defeating the enemy like they could have while they lived on earth in a flesh body!"

Natsar nodded his head. "Having a part in the Lord's angelic army in spacecrafts surrounding earth in the heavenlies is better than watching those Hollywood movies like *Star Wars*."

"Wait until they find out that the Lord has a multitude of different modes of transportations that are journeying between heaven and earth," Milchamah said.

Natsar eyes glared. "Demons have told most teens that when they get to hell that they are going to party all the time. Instead of fast cars and fast girls, they are going to find themselves chained to a lonely cell enduring extreme torture."

"What a shock it is going to be when human eyes are open to the real supernatural world that surrounds their natural world," Kara said.

"What a shock to find out that hell is a reality not just a cuss word that they can use at a whim," Kientay said.

Chroni interrupted everyone. "We are way off our meeting subject."

Natsar received a message from the Holy Spirit and opened a link for all of the angels to hear.

I have many angels who fight against the spiritual hosts of wickedness in the heavenlies with Michael, Gabriel and the Lord of Hosts in the war that occurred on our planet heaven. It was a great victory to expel them from the Father's home. The Special Forces of the Lord use weapons that are dimensional. No human can fight these high evil spirits without aid from the Holy Spirit, because they are hidden in a dimension that human eyes can't detect. Even earth's science fiction stories have never dreamed of the advanced technologies that angels use to keep the enemy under the feet of Jesus and His body. You are My ministering spirits, sent to guide and protect during this most difficult time of the history of earth. You will be successful.

They raised their silver glistening and translucent swords to the Father in heaven and shouted after hearing Words from the Holy Spirit. Several humans on earth who practice using their spiritual senses picked up that message from the Lord.

"Victory will be so sweet!" Natsar shouted. "Praise the Lord!"

"What if we could take every Christian on a tour of heaven so they could get a better understanding of the spiritual realm and its many dimensions?" Kientay was dreaming.

"Let's not get carried away, the Lord's Kingdom is powered by faith and not what you can see. The Lord knows the inside and outside of the human heart. It is imperative that they learn how to develop the force of faith inside them before they see with their spiritual eyes," Chroni said.

"But many won't believe until they see," Kara pointed out.

"Jesus said that even if they see with their physical eyes, they won't believe," Chroni reminded her.

"What is the phrase they use?" Milchamah asked.

"Seeing is believing," Kientay told him.

"That is the difference in this campaign from other campaigns that you have fought." Kientay informed Milchamah and Natsar. "The Knight family recognizes that a war is taking place around them. They know that we are bound to the law of binding and losing. They know that the Lord's Kingdom is empowered by faith and not by sight."

"The Lord knows that the fleshly body is made of dust and is weak," Kara reminded them. "He is giving them time to disconnect from their flesh nature and connect to their new spiritual nature."

"And the enemy knows precisely where to attack that weak spot," replied Chroni.

"I can witness to the fact that Dan and Vicki have raised him on the Word. He walks by faith and not be sight." Now Kara was showing a little emotion.

"What if satan petitions the Lord to test Joshua now?" Chroni asked. He was curious to know if he could handle the pressure.

"He will past any test that the rulers of darkness devise against him!" Kientay was quick to defend Joshua.

Natsar raised his eyebrows.

"Forget about the demonic implant. It will be taken care of soon."

Matthan added his witness. "He is speaking a fact. Joshua Knight is a believer in the Word of God and has a passion for revelation knowledge. He knows how to deal with the demon that is causing him to doubt when he discovers him."

Kientay thought about all the prayers Dan and Vicki had prayed over Joshua like Jesus prayed for Peter. "When satan desired to sift Peter, the Lord prayed for him. Joshua has a praying mother and father. I am confident that the kingdom of darkness will not find an open door into their house."

"The greater the prayers released in faith, the greater the victories," exclaimed Natsar.

"Amen!" they all agreed.

Chloe was hesitant about interrupting, but she was wondering about her charge Hannah. "What about Hannah's family? Her mother was just recently baptized into the body of Christ and her father has a spirit of alcohol. Many generation spirits are living in the home and their bodies."

"You know, that is the most unbelievable thing about born again humans. They get a new spirit and they are new creations in the Kingdom of God," Marisa commented. "But they think like dead spirits."

Kara agreed with her. "They enter into the Covenant between the Father and the Son and they have the Spirit of God in them. They are entitled to the Holy One's Name, Jesus' Blood, and written Word, yet a lot of them allow demon spirits to dominate them and live in their flesh."

"Hannah and her mom have not had the spiritual training that Joshua received," Chloe pointed out.

"I agree with you that humans are sometimes hard to understand, but it is not our place to understand humans. Our job is to execute the Covenant whenever they speak it out of their mouth," Chroni said.

"Joshua has knowledge of that truth." He knew that they were all thinking about the demonic implant in Joshua's brain. "It is only a matter of time now before Joshua executes his authority."

Talking directly to Chloe, Chroni repeated what he told her earlier, "The Lord has not forgotten the Coyle family. You will know of His plans soon."

Chloe was so glad to receive a word from the Lord. She never doubted the wisdom of the Lord and never would. She was proud that she was an angel counted among those who stayed faithful to the Father.

Looking upward, Chroni said, "I am a witness to the Word spoken from the Knight family in the throne room. They have a powerful bowl of prayers that will be ready to be poured out on earth in His timing. The Teacher has prepared them for His coming."

They were all thanking Him once again for this assignment.

"All of heaven is in silent awe as the Father demands quiet to give His full attention to His Words coming out of His children's mouth," Chroni declared. "He gets great pleasure when they take their authority over the enemy!"

The angels were in wonder and amazement of the treatment that man received from the Father. They could not understand why humans didn't take advantage of their position in the Anointed Jesus. *Those who have confessed that Jesus is Lord over them are heirs to His inheritance and all His power,* the guardian angels were thinking.

"Father God has appointed us angels on earth as administrators of the Covenant. Do not forget your mission, guardian angels!" Chroni reminded them. "God says faith comes by hearing and hearing the Word, so I will remind you over and over about the laws of God."

Natsar pointed his sword toward heaven. "We are ministers of the fire of God, the Anointing upon the Word of God. We are here on earth as a guarantee with the Holy Spirit to enforce the Word of God coming out of their mouth with believing faith. No devil in hell can escape the wrath of an angel executing the Word he hears a believer speak!"

Chroni told them, "It is good that we review the laws that govern earth so that every angel is reminded of his duty."

Natsar lifted his sword. "Let's not forget that we are not totally unaffected by the kingdom of darkness that permeates this earth's atmosphere. I think we should have taken care of the fallen angels before they were allowed to come to this beautiful planet."

Chroni could not believe his ears. "Natsar some words should not be said. The Almighty knew exactly what Lucifer was going to do before He created him. It is not our place to make statements like that or to even question the Almighty of His infinite wisdom and understanding!"

"Forever forgive me! I don't know why I said what I did. My opinion counts as nothing when compared to the Almighty Creator!" Natsar completely bowed to the ground.

The Holy Spirit came into the room and hovered over Natsar. He was cleansing him of any unrighteous thoughts.

All angels bowed and worshiped Him in His presence.

Then the Holy Spirit materialized before them and spoke in the angel's language.

There is a war taking place on planet earth. It is a war of good against evil. It is a war that will soon end and the Lord Almighty God will reign triumphant with all His children throughout eternity! If the Father wills to let His family know of certain secrets from the beginning of Creation, then so be it. If not, then so be it. Whatever the Father chooses to allow you to know, it will be for your highest good. He will spend eternity revealing His love for His family and all His creation.

Be still and know that the Almighty is God and it is He that wills to do His good pleasure for your pleasure. It is He that has made you and created you so that you will have the pleasure of searching the depths of His infinite love throughout eternity!

The Holy Spirit left the meeting and all those with the privilege of hearing Him speak in person were silent for a long time. Later, the angels rejoiced at His words and gave the Lord all the glory and praise.

Kientay was the last angel to leave the library with Kara. Walking upstairs, thoughts of their meeting lingered in his mind. He stopped in the hall outside Joshua's room to talk to her. "It's not their fault that they do not know about the billions of angels on earth warring against the kingdom of darkness and protecting them."

"I know," she said looking through the wall at Joshua sound asleep. "Because of their lack of knowledge of the battle raging over their souls, many of them provoke us by speaking wrong words and thinking wrong thoughts, but we've got to stop thinking about that. Our hands are tied because of the negative and idle false words that immobilize us. It is not our fault nor is it God's fault." Kara put her hand on his shoulder.

Kientay eyes misted. "The same words give power to demons. They are empowering them with their own words. Oh, when will the rest of His body wake up so they can unite with the ministries that are working on earth?"

Kara touched Kientay's arm. "You heard the words from the Holy Spirit. We are not without hope! We are the overcomers! Stop thinking about words of doubt and unbelief and especially thinking about how tied and powerless some of the guardian angels are here on earth. We've got to think positive, looking to the end of the age and the great thousand year reign of Jesus on this earth."

Kientay walked through the door into Joshua's room and sat on his bed, gazing down at his charge. The child had never provoked him. In fact, a bond of love had developed between them beyond Kientay's wildest dreams. Joshua's love of God and every Word that proceeded from God's mouth generated a force of faith that he had never before experienced with a human.

Kara followed him. "I know that you have developed a strong love bond between you and Joshua, but even with all the angelic hosts that protect and guide humans on earth, nothing compares to the protection and love of the Holy Spirit who lives in them spiritually and has made His home here on earth with them. He lives in them."

"I know that it's the Holy Spirit that gives us hope for the children of this world," Kientay said. "He will never leave them, never lie to them, and always lead them to God's salvation; Jesus."

The Holy Spirit called them to His headquarters, discerning that Kientay and Kara needed a rest from their earthly duties.

CHAPTER 9

Jeffrey Stanton walked into the office of Lincoln Christian School and greeted the secretaries. He was the youth minister of one of the city's largest charismatic churches.

Turning to his right he went over to the wall with letter boxes and reached into the cubby hole labeled *Principal.* Since his appointment over two years ago, the school had reached an all time high of 1,003 students from pre-kindergarten to high school. Successfully doubling the attendance was an accomplishment that was sure to guarantee an appointment of head pastor at his own church in the near future.

"Good morning, Pastor Jeff," Marilyn Stewart greeted the tall, dark, handsome and single mid-twenties minister.

Turning to walk into his office, one of the two secretaries for the church, Ann Haley approached him. "How are you doing this morning?"

He looked up to see the short, stout, about twenty pounds overweight, single red-head that had been trying to hint at a relationship beyond his personal secretary for about the last 16 months. "I'm fine, just fine."

She followed him into his office. He sat behind his desk flipping through all his mail. Sitting down in one of the two chairs facing his desk, she began to explain that maybe his day wouldn't be as fine as he thought.

"Oh?" He looked up at her. "What's up?"

"Well," she looked behind her and got up to close the door of his office. She had just turned 30, but she told everybody that she was in her late twenties; since it really wasn't their business how old she was anyway.

"Leave it open a crack, please." He reminded her of the head pastor's rule because he didn't want any rumors started from his office and then filter through the church. Jeff went back to sorting his mail, opening the more important letters and tossing out the advertisements.

"I just don't want anyone to hear the latest rumor that I heard."

"Really, Ann, I'm not sure I want to hear any office gossip." It was still beyond his understanding how two of the biggest gossips in the church could end up as secretaries. They knew a lot of confidential things and it seemed that within a few weeks so did the rest of the congregation.

"You'll want to hear this, I'm positive." She closed her mouth and waited.

He opened one of his letters. Realizing she wasn't talking, he looked at her. "Alright, what did you hear?"

"I was told that Joshua Knight is going to leave our school."

Jeffrey let the letter drop from his hand. "Who told you?"

"Well, I promised not to mention any names, but I've heard that if he leaves, he might influence others to leave with him."

She knew that he was building the church school to build his resume for future opportunities. They all knew that the Knights were very influential, meaning rich and big donors for the school. It would be a very heavy blow if the Knights were to quit the school and if others left because of them. It could hurt the future of the church and certain reputations.

"I don't think that rumor has any truth in it at all."

"Well, my source assures me that Joshua wants to attend public school and that his parents are praying about it."

"Why would he want to leave our school?"

"She, I mean, uh, my source, said that they didn't know why, but that his mind was made up and that he may quit before the semester even ends."

"That's silly. Why would he want to move before Christmas break?"

Quickly, he assessed the lost of revenue if Joshua moved before the year was out. It cost about $2,000.00 a month to attend the school, but the Knights gave enough money monthly to pay for two more students.

Oh man, I wonder if they are thinking about leaving our church?

She stood up. "It makes you wonder if they are going to leave our church."

He hated it when it seemed that she could read his mind.

She opened the door. "I think it was a couple of weeks ago, but they were absent one Sunday. They could have been visiting another church. Marilyn said that she drove by their house and their cars were in the driveway. Makes you wonder, doesn't it?"

It makes me know what a busybody you are.

She closed his door behind her. She wasn't blind to his obvious lack of interest in her socially and neither was any one in the office or school staff oblivious. That was the hard part. Going day after day to work and seeing Jeffrey was getting to her. She might be a little heavy and five years older than him, but he wouldn't even give her a chance. She just knew that the Lord spoke to her and told her that Jeffrey was the one for her, but he wasn't giving the Lord a chance to tell him.

Sitting back down in her chair, she turned around and told Marilyn what just took place. "He says he doesn't believe me, but you should have seen the look on his face."

Marilyn thought she detected a little satisfaction in the tone of Ann's voice. She acted sometimes like a woman scorned. Being the older one and married, even though her husband wasn't a Christian, she didn't think that Pastor Jeff would ever look at Ann with romantic interest. As far as she was concerned Ann was blind and being very unrealistic. He was the kind of man that needed a woman that would compliment his physical looks and be an asset for his future plans. That left Ann out, because she was definitely not a fit. Everyone else that she talked with in the church agreed with her, but they all felt sorry for Ann, so no one told her their true feelings about the situation.

"You act like you're happy about telling Pastor Jeff what you heard."

"Well, of course, I wouldn't want anything to happen to our church school, but Pastor Jeff is a different matter." She looked around the office to make sure no one was listening to her. "You will never convince me that he is really concerned about our church or school."

"You don't have to remind me. I know what you think about Pastor Jeff . . ."

She looked up to see Jeff cross the office to knock on the office door of the senior Pastor Benjamin Baker. Glancing at her watch she mouthed quietly, "Just what I thought, under five minutes and straight to Pastor Baker's office!"

"What did you expect him to do? Especially since you purposely wanted to panic him."

"Well, mister high and mighty deserves a trip back to reality."

Marilyn shook her head and turned back to her desk. *Someone in this office needs a reality trip and it's not Pastor Jeff.*

"Good morning Jeff. Come on in."

Jeff shut the door and sat down facing the desk of Pastor Ben. "Can I take a few minutes?"

"Sure," Pastor Ben said as he wondered why the stressed look on his assistant pastor's face.

"I heard some distressing news."

"From Ann or Marilyn?"

"Can't you guess?"

"Ann," he smiled knowing of the secretary's obvious interest in the bachelor facing him.

"Correct." He leaned back and tried to relax. "I may have to leave this church because of that woman."

Pastor Ben dropped his smile, "Don't kid about the subject of your leaving."

"She really is annoying."

He stood walked around his desk and slapped Jeff's back. Putting his hand on his shoulder, he chuckled at him "Surely one woman couldn't push you out of God's will."

"If anyone could she could!"

"What did she tell you?" Pastor Ben changed the subject. They could talk all morning about Ann, but he would rather know about the latest gossip that will probably go around his church.

"She said that Dan and Vicki Knight are thinking about leaving the church and taking Joshua out of our school."

"What?" Pastor Ben walked back around his desk and looked Jeff straight in his eyes. "She said what?"

"From a reliable source, she heard that the Knights are leaving."

Sitting down on the edge of his desk he shook his head. "I can't believe that the Knights would leave this church."

"I know exactly what you're thinking." Jeff leaned back in his chair and crossed his legs. He wondered who would be the first to voice their true concerns.

"Dan is an elder and a member of the board. Vicki teaches Sunday school and is one of the leaders of the woman's ministry and Joshua, why he is already preaching and teaching the youth. No, I don't think that rumor is true." He walked back behind his desk and sat down.

"Joshua told me that he thinks the Lord is leading him into the beginning of a ministry."

Pastor leaned forward. "What ministry?"

"A ministry that will deal with the youth outside the church."

"Dan and I have talked about Joshua in the ministry. Besides you and I both know that he can't operate a ministry outside the church!"

"Well, for some reason, I think what she told me is true. And if it is true, I've figured out how much the church school will lose if the Knights leave."

"How much?" Pastor Ben leaned back in his chair waiting for the amount in dollars and cents.

"Around $6,000 a month in revenue and an untold amount in volunteer hours."

Pastor Ben did a quick mental sweep of the church ledger that he saw last week. A few months ago he made it a point of telling the congregation that he never kept track of who gives tithes and how much. But then he felt guilty about not being a good steward of the churches finances and decided to look at the monthly giving record. It would be a serious blow to their monthly budget if they left his church.

"Did she say why they were leaving?"

"No, uh, I think I was so shocked that my brain froze."

Many different scenarios passed through Pastor Ben's head as he weighed some of the reasons that people leave churches. He tried to remember if any of his sermons might have been offensive to them. He knew that they watched Christian television all the time and supported many various ministries other than the church.

Once, after he first accepted the pastorate, he asked the members of the church to give a one year commitment of sole support for their mortgage and not give financial support to any outside ministries. The next day, Dan told him very directly that the Lord was the only person who could tell him where his tithes and giving were to go. If he insisted on a one year commitment then he and his family would have to quit the church. He quickly told Dan that he would pray about it and get back with him.

Once Dan left, he asked Marilyn to bring the church books into his office. After reviewing their giving record he didn't have to pray about recanting his plea. The very next Sunday he asked the church members to forgive his enthusiasm and told them that by faith he believed that the Lord would provide the funds for the mortgage. Fourteen months later, they were debt free and had been ever since even with the church school.

"Why do you believe Ann this time?" Pastor Ben rubbed his forehead.

"Well, I've just had this feeling that Joshua is dissatisfied about something. I don't think he tells me everything. You know we're not bosom buddies."

That fact really bothered Jeff. He has always been very intimidated that Joshua was so knowledgeable about the Bible. He couldn't even count the times that Joshua had pointed out a mistake from the scriptures in one of his sermons. He didn't even bother checking them out any more, since Joshua had never made a mistake quoting a verse or even knowing where a verse is located in the Bible to his knowledge.

"If this rumor is true, it could seriously jeopardize many outreaches of this church to the community and to our members."

Jeff nodded his head. It was exactly as he thought; the Knights were needed for the operation of their church.

Your salary could even be in jeopardy!

After the last thought, Jeff felt a check in his spirit, but he brushed it off. Even though the thought of his salary being in jeopardy was ridiculous, he never bound it to keep it out of his mind . . .

. . . The black spider demon jumped from the outside of Jeff's mind into the inside penetrating his skull. He screamed out to the division of mind-binding spirits hollering that he made it. Winding down and around the neuron networks, he looked for a pathway that he could bury himself and start the process of making a nest for his eggs to grow in Jeff's brain.

He communicated with his division noting that other demons of worry, concern, and doubt had many nests growing in his mind. The root of fear had the biggest network of tentacles reaching out to Jeff's spirit. Seeds were growing in the ground of his spirit unchecked.

Traveling to an area of his brain that was untouched by previous demonic plants, the black spider buried himself spinning a chemical web at the base of a neuron cell so that he could lay his eggs. Soon babies would hatch to help him build a perverted network of thoughts linked to the kingdom of darkness.

Success was eminent and another Christian pastor's brain would be full of demonic spiders weaving webs of lies insuring the master's control over him . . .

. . ."What are you going to do?" Jeff asked as he leaned forward, feeling a little dizzy in his head waiting for a plan from his boss. The senior pastor was a man full of ideas.

"I'm not going to panic until I talk to Dan." Pastor Ben picked up the phone and punched in Dan's office numbers.

Jeff stood and suddenly felt a sharp pain in his head like the start of a migraine headache. "Let me know what he says."

Pastor Ben nodded his head at Jeff as Dan's secretary answered the phone.

‡ ‡ ‡

"Hey? Is something up?" Kellie wondered about the look on Joshua's face as they met before school started.

"I just wanted to be sure we're doing the right thing," replied Joshua. A spirit of doubt was bugging him again.

Kellie gave him the I-don't-know-what-you're-talking-about-look as they sat down in a deserted section of the library.

"You know, Mose and Hannah."

Kellie wasn't sure that she understood. "I prayed Josh. I know you are praying. My parents are praying, your parents are praying. I think the Lord would have told us by now if Hannah and Mose weren't the right ones."

"I think you're right, but we *need* to know that we are on the right path."

She recognized the look of anxiety, but was shocked to see it come over Joshua. "Are you having second thoughts?"

Yeah and three and four and . . . "No. I mean, I know what the Lord wants me to do. I just want to make His decisions, not mine."

Kellie looked at Joshua, still confused. *Maybe it's just nervous jitters; after all he is only a freshman. And it has only been a few weeks since school has started. High school could be intimidating when you are a freshman.*

"Joshua, you know the Word of God better than anybody I know. You know the voice of the Lord. Better yet, you know the Word so that you can test any spirit that speaks to you. God picked the right guy. Remember Moses came up with many reasons why God was picking the wrong person. Don't be like Moses and doubt your ability to do what he has asked you to do!"

"I know, but . . . wait a minute? Wrong person?"

"Not Mose from last night, Moses from the Bible!" Kellie laughed. "No buts about it!" She leaned over and took a hold of his arms. "I know what we are doing is gonna stretch us, but it is a good idea. The phone is a major part of our lives." Kellie could relate to that comment. "Everywhere you look kids have cell phones. You can't even have a decent conversation with somebody without a phone beeping somewhere."

Joshua smiled. She should know. Many times he had tried to call Kellie and discuss something he learned from the Bible and her line was busy.

"Now, what is our next move?" asked Kellie. She looked intently into his eyes thinking how strange he was acting. It just wasn't like him to have doubts after he made up his mind.

"We're waiting on my mom and dad now. You know that our mothers are meeting tomorrow to start the intercessory prayer group. Mom got a couple of extra women from other congregations to pray with them. Dad has called the phone company and scheduled the installation of the phone lines . . ."

He was talking to her about the Devil Chasers but he was totally void of excitement. Kellie loved Joshua like a brother. She wanted him to know that she supported him totally, but she couldn't handle him being like this. "What's up?"

He hesitated telling her. "There is something I haven't told you."

"What?"

"You know when the Lord visited me?"

Kellie nodded her head.

"Before He came, I was having doubts about hearing His voice."

"You, question the Lord?"

"I get so many ideas in my head, and well, I started questioning if it was me or the Lord or the devil. The next thing I knew the whole thing got out of control. I actually felt fear for the first time in my life!"

"You fear?" That thought just didn't register with her. "No way!"

"Yes, I actually had a thought that maybe I wasn't hearing the right voice. To hear a voice and then doubt that I really heard the Lord's voice or not has never happened to me before."

"What?!"

"You know if you start doubting whether the voice your hearing is the Lord's or not, you could open a whole can of worms with that kind of confusion."

"Yeah and I know who the big worm is!" Taking her Bible out of her backpack, she decided to take action, "Remember what the Lord said in John 10:4, 5?"

"But that's just it! I quote that scripture to myself, to the devil, to the angels, to the Lord, to anybody and to everybody that will listen, everyday."

"Hey, don't freak out on me."

Joshua inhaled and let the air out of his lungs slowly. "I never freak, okay?" The spirit of irritation made a move over Joshua. He was feeling the tug in his mind.

"No, it's not okay! You're the one that taught me to never stop confessing the Word until your mountain has moved."

"You don't understand . . ."

She interrupted him. "I'm trying to."

"Before the Lord left my room, He, uh, He touched me and imparted gifts to me!"

"So?" Kellie prayed. *Lord, what is wrong? Why can't I understand why Joshua is so upset? I need your help Holy Spirit.*

"I thought that I would be different after Jesus touched me."

The Holy Spirit gave Kellie discernment in her spirit and then transferred it to her mind. "You think that just because Jesus touched you in person that you would never again have an attack from a demon spirit?"

The words she said cut to his heart. "Well, when you put it like that I guess that is exactly what I was thinking."

"Just because Jesus visited you doesn't mean that you have been removed from this planet. Hey, earth to Joshua? Knock, knock, knock!" She rapped her fist lightly on the side of his head. "If you think that having a doubt means that Jesus didn't have the power to change you, then your thinking is wrong. All it proves is that you're being attacked by a spirit of doubt."

That was it. Joshua immediately recognized not only a spirit of doubt was attacking him, but also he was allowing this attack by not taking authority over the doubt thoughts coming against his mind. *Man, how could I be so slow?*

"This is a direct attack from the devil. Remember what you taught me? You can't combat thoughts with thoughts! Joshua, you are a sheep of the Lord. Talk to yourself and say, 'I know the Lord's voice. I will not listen to the voice of strangers.' Have you been doing that?"

He realized that he had been allowing a spirit of doubt to talk to him. "I didn't take authority over a doubt that came against my mind."

"Yeah! You messed up. Somehow it is comforting to know that Joshua Knight isn't perfect."

"Me perfect? You're kidding, right?"

"Joshua, for someone who knows God's Word as much as you do, the only way to stop you would be to put doubt in your mind." *Kidding? Joshua used the word kidding? Man, a demon's been messin' with his mind!* "Kick that demon out of your mind before it transfers to your spirit! You told me that the angels can't bind demons unless we first bind them."

"You are so right! I haven't attacked this like I should."

"I don't have to tell you that without faith it is impossible to please God, do I?"

"I know, I know! Keep on telling me!"

"Joshua Knight! Jesus said that you know His voice. You either believe His Word, or you don't."

"I know . . . I know . . . tell me again."

"I'm going to do something better than that." She took him by the hand and led him behind a bookshelf in the corner. Moving closer to him she said, "Evil thoughts cease and desist from attacking Joshua. Demons, you can't have his mind. He belongs to Jesus!"

With a subdued calm voice he prayed after her. "Lord, forgive me for allowing that thought to stay in my mind and play with my thought life. I agree with Kellie. I listen and hear Jesus' voice. I flee from the voice of strangers. I will not listen to demon thoughts. I submit myself to the voice of the Lord. I resist you in the name of Jesus. Mind-binding spirits, you have to flee! Now!"

"I agree!" She opened her eyes looking into Joshua's eyes. "Mind-binding spirits?"

"I saw them in an open vision once. They look like little tiny black spiders. They weave webs throughout the neuron cells in our brain."

"Gross!"

"I actually found several scriptures in the Old Testament that talk about them."

"Really?"

The bell rang and Kellie realized that she was going to be late for the first time in her life. But it was worth it . . .

. . . Kientay and Marisa were listening intently to the conversation between Kellie and Joshua.

"Come on, Joshua, say it . . . come on!" Kientay was cheering him on.

Since the first time the demonic implant attached himself to the outside of Joshua's brain, he wanted to cut him up in pieces. But Joshua didn't bind the little dot that wasn't bigger than a microchip. That shocked him. It was a little tiny thought that deceived Joshua, but Kientay couldn't do anything about it until Joshua resisted the demonic implant.

Just one tiny thought. *Was that the Lord's voice?* Joshua actually repeated the words without thinking of binding them with scripture. Kientay wanted to flatten the pest as soon as possible. The ugly demon spirit even reared his ugly head once he found a place in Joshua's brain and laughed at Kientay. He determined to make him pay for that little indiscretion of annoying him once Joshua realized what was going on in his head.

Immediately, when Kellie took authority over the evil spirit responsible for bothering Joshua, Kientay pulled out his sword to hack him into pieces. Before he could use his sword, the demonic implant let out a squeak, came out of Joshua's brain, and took off running. Kientay flew after him.

"Finally! I had to endure his presence long enough!" proclaimed Kientay coming back into the school hallway after chasing the demon.

"Those little demonic implants are a nuisance!" declared Marisa. "Did you get him?"

"Yes, it's like stepping on potato chips." He picked up his foot and looked at the green gunk on the sole of his shoe. "The crunching sound is satisfying. If humans would only resist the thoughts from those evil things, their lives would be a lot easier."

"You think *you* would know about a demonic android implant in the form of a spider if you didn't have spiritual eyes?" Marisa asked.

"There are a lot of things in this natural world that humans can't see but they understand them."

"Like what?" Marisa watched Kellie go into the school office.

"Electricity. It only takes one touch and *ZAP!* They recognize that it exists and they use caution whenever they are around it. Most of them don't understand how it works, but they use its power anyway. All they have to do is recognize that any thought that deals with doubt, unbelief, or fear is from the kingdom of darkness."

"You have a point." Marisa saw a few evil spirits scamper into the office behind Kellie. She took her sword out of her sheath. It appeared for her before she even thought about needing it.

"Besides that, when humans get to heaven, 2 Corinthians 10:5 will be their judge. No human who let a thought, a demonic mind implant from a demon, get into their mind will be able to say that they didn't know about them."

"You're right, especially here in America where they can freely read His Book."

Marisa started moving toward the school office. The office door opened and Kellie walked out. A spray of light beams momentarily blinded their eyes. Two ten foot tall angels materialized on both sides of Kellie as she came out of the office. They stopped to clean the green android blood off their swords.

Kientay quoted the Word smiling, "Casting down arguments and every high thing that exalts itself against the knowledge of God, bringing every thought into captivity to the obedience of Christ."

Thank you very much. Marisa smiled at the warring angels who just protected Kellie.

They communicated that they would always surround each Devil Chaser and would be ready to materialize from their dimension when needed.

"And being ready to punish all disobedience when your obedience is fulfilled, which is just what I did as soon as Joshua said the Word." Kientay finished quoting the scripture and laughed at the demon spirits scurrying out of the way of the huge angels walking with Kellie down the hall to her class.

They slowly disappeared into the dimension that hid them from all demonic demons.

"Joshua is very good at quoting God's Word, just like Kellie," Marisa said. "Why did it take him so long to take authority over that thought?"

"He was confused about the origins of the thought."

"You mean Joshua didn't know that thoughts come from two sources; the Father of light or the father of darkness?"

"He knows, but he allowed himself to be confused and a demon suggested that he didn't know for sure which thought was God's or the devil's or his."

"That certainly would cause confusion."

"Confusion causes indecision which interferes with the Lord's plans and pursuits," Kientay told her.

"Evil spirits are very clever at making humans think that evil thoughts are a result of human thinking," Marisa said.

"It would be so easy for them if they would just understand that thoughts come from two sources: God or satan." Kientay saw Joshua enter his class. "He knows now."

"Yes," she commented. "You either think and talk like God or you think and talk like the devil."

"It is still the same war as it was in the beginning: good against evil."

Chroni appeared before Kientay and Marisa. "Praise be to the Lord God and the Lord's blessings be upon you."

"Kellie just took authority over the little demon implant that was harassing Joshua," Marisa informed him.

"The Holy Spirit is pleased with her obedience. Recording angels are writing her good deed in her file now and depositing credit into her account as we speak," Chroni reported as he received the information from the angelic graceline. "It is important that Joshua realizes he has to take control over every thought and every thing that exalts itself against the Word of God, especially in his ministry."

"Knowing Joshua, he has already made a mental note of the incident."

"The Almighty desires a meeting with you, Kientay. He has a special message for you to deliver to Joshua."

"Do you know what he is going to say?" asked Kientay.

"Michael told me that Jehovah God discussed the message of the prophet Malachi with him recently. The Almighty has an overwhelming desire to reach the rebellious children. Before the coming of the war in the heavenlies, He will turn the hearts of the fathers to the children and the hearts of the children to their fathers."

Kientay's heart leaped inside of him. "I believe that the Lord will use this ministry to enlist satan's army of humans and convert them into His army!"

"You were right when you said that this was a very important ministry," Chroni reported to them. "I heard the Lord call this generation of young people the Joshua Generation."

Kientay let out a war hoop. "I knew it, I knew it! The Lord told Vicki and Dan to name their unborn son, Joshua. Praise the name of the Lord. He is a great planner!"

They all fell to the ground and worshipped the Lord.

Marisa had tears in her eyes. The heart of the Father and His love touched her. "Oh, the depth of the love that the Lord God Almighty has for His creation, His children."

"He is coming to wipe the curse from the face of the earth," Chroni declared.

"The Devil Chasers will awaken this generation for the next move of the Lord," Kientay declared.

CHAPTER 10

Vicki looked across the table at the beautiful black woman, Ruth Pearson, facing her. They had only been visiting for an hour or so, but it seemed like they had known each other forever. She placed her napkin in the empty soup bowl and breathed deeply. "I love the smell of the bread in this place," she said.

Ruth finished the last bite of her sandwich and grabbed her napkin as a combination of mayonnaise and mustard dripped down the side of her chin. "Excuse me," she muttered under the napkin.

"Oh don't even think about it." Vicki looked down at her blouse and commented as she brushed off crumbs, "I always manage to get something on me when I eat. I'm surprised that my blouse is clean."

"This is a great restaurant to meet for lunch," Ruth said.

"Well, I've got to tell you. For some reason it's like I've known you forever."

"I have the same thought. Have you ever heard of kindred spirits?"

"Yes, but I've never experienced it before," Vicki said. "You think that's what is happening to us?"

"Maybe," Ruth hesitated before asking more personal and direct questions.

"What do you want to know?"

Ruth smiled, "How did you know that I want to ask you something personal?"

"That kindred spirit thing," she laughed

"I know from some of your comments that you are a woman of faith. How have you survived in a mainline denomination?"

"At first it was hard, but I think we've been accepted better than the average couple because of our money and my husband's position."

"At least you're honest about it."

"Oh, we have to be to know who our real enemies are. I remember going to a couple of faith movement conventions; Dan was in court and couldn't come with me and I tried to find someone from church to go with me." Vicki smiled thinking about the reactions she received. “Some people thought I was going to a cult-type meeting and others were shocked that I even watched Christian TV.”

“You know, I’m still shocked at how many Christians do not watch Christian television today.”

Vicki nodded her head. “Imagine what it was like 25 years ago.”

“How long have you been a member of your church?”

“Twenty years.”

“That’s a long time.”

“You’re wondering if we are thinking about changing churches.”

Ruth laughed again. “You’re reading my mind.”

“We’re not church hoppers, but we feel that God is moving us into a new phase of ministry.”

“Do you feel it’s connected with Joshua’s calling?” Ruth moved back as a waitress removed their empty plates

“Can I get you ladies anything else?”

Vicki picked up her glass and said, “I would like some more tea, please.” She waited until the waitress left to answer Ruth’s question. “Joshua wants to quit attending our church’s Christian school.”

“That’s what Mose told us last night when he got home late from your house.”

“Joshua was home schooled until the sixth grade. He’s just a freshman and has never been around kids at a public school. He . . . well, he’s just different. There are many Christian kids that he doesn’t relate to very well. I can’t imagine how he will relate to secular kids.”

“I think I know what you’re talking about. Our two children are very much home bodies and . . .” She was interrupted by the waitress returning with their drinks. “ . . . they talk about Jesus and the Word of God a lot.”

Vicki nodded her head. “Being into the Word as much as he is separates him from other teens and, well, he doesn’t talk like other kids. He wants to obey God and has asked us to pray.”

“What has the Lord said about it?”

“Nothing, but I’m wondering if my emotions are blocking my ears from hearing the Holy Spirit. I think I’m being a carnal mama.”

“I really appreciate your truthfulness. I mean, you judge yourself.”

Vicki’s face changed to a very serious look. “I try. I know that I will eventually move out of the way, but I have this feeling that the Lord is going to shake a lot of things around me.”

“What about your church?”

“We sense a stirring inside us to move.”

Suddenly, it dawned on Ruth that maybe Vicki might think that she had been trying to proselyte her. "I hope you don't think . . ."

"Don't worry. I know you're not trying to get us to move to your church."

"Well, that's not to say we wouldn't be excited if you decided to visit us, but we also know that Jesus directs his body according to his will, not according to our will."

Vicki was very encouraged by what she was hearing. She looked at her watch and realized that they had been at the restaurant for over two hours. "Oh my goodness! We better leave a big tip for this waitress."

"Oh dear, I have to pick up my daughter in less than an hour!"

"You are coming to the meeting tomorrow, right?"

"Yes! I wouldn't miss it. I was wondering . . . would you mind if I brought my mother? She is a prayer warrior."

"Of course! We will need a lot of prayer to cover this ministry." Vicki stood and picked up their bill.

"Mose told me the name of the ministry."

"Dan and I don't know what to think about them being called the Devil Chasers." They walked toward the cashier. "We are almost certain we will need to attend another church."

"I can't imagine why?" They both gave each other a look that said they knew exactly why that name would bother some church people. "The next time we meet, I'll tell you about some of our denominational experiences."

Laughing together, Vicki opened her purse to get her wallet.

"Let me pay for . . ."

"Oh, no! This is my treat. I wanted to talk to you and get to know you and I am paying!"

"But I want to get the blessing for buying your lunch," Ruth insisted.

"You can get the next lunch."

Driving away, Vicki waved at Ruth. It was a good feeling to make a God connection. She knew that God was going to make some big changes in her life, and those changes would probably bring some sorrow and pain, but they would also bring new friends and new adventures.

It was time for her to submit to God's next season for the Knight family.

Dan reached for his phone to return the call from Pastor Ben late in the afternoon. "Hi Marilyn, this is Dan Knight, is Pastor Ben in?"

"Yes, I will transfer you."

"Hello, Dan."

"Pastor Ben, I am so sorry that I couldn't talk with you this morning."

"Think nothing of it."

"I have a court case that is taking all my time."

"Well, then I will cut to the chase and tell you what someone told me."

"It's not gossip is it?"

"Now Dan, I know how you feel about gossip, but . . ."

"Did you know that when a 'but' comes after a statement, it means that you can forget about everything you just said before the but?"

Pastor Ben cleared his throat. He continued talking to him, choosing to ignore his comment. "I have been told that you are thinking about taking Joshua out of school and quitting the church. Is there any truth to this rumor that will soon be circulating our church family?"

Dan sat back in his chair feeling as if a blast of wind had just hit him. He took a few seconds to reply.

Pastor Ben did not like the hesitation he sensed from Dan. Maybe there was truth in this rumor. It had been his experience that almost all gossip was wrapped up in some truth. A deep churning pain hit the pit of his stomach. He pulled out one of his desk drawers and reached for a pink antacid pill.

"Pastor, I think that this is a question that I would like to discuss with you in person and not over the phone. We have talked to no one about Joshua leaving the school nor have we talked about leaving the church."

"So, I can relax because this was a false rumor."

Dan hesitated again. "All I'm saying is that we are seeking the will of God for the direction that He is taking our family."

Pastor Ben began to feel nauseated; like he was going to throw up the pill that he had just swallowed and anything else in his stomach. Ever since he met the Knights and realized how wealthy they were, he had a fear that they would leave the church. Besides the fact that he didn't believe in television evangelists, he had a sneaking hunch that they were sending hundreds of dollars of support to outside ministries. The false doctrines didn't bother him near as much as the financial support. Without people like the Knights, TV ministries would fail.

"Has anyone said or done anything lately to offend you?"

That's exactly what Dan didn't want the Pastor to think. "Ben, you should know me by now. I don't get offended and if that was the case I would have already come to you and talked to you directly about any offense."

The words of Jesus came into the Pastor's mind. *If your brother sins against you go and tell him his fault between you and him alone. If he hears you, you have gained your brother. But if he will not hear, take with you one or two more, that by the mouth of two or three witnesses every word may be established. And if he refuses to hear them, tell it to the church, let him be to you like a heathen and a tax collector.*

"You know that I would strictly adhere to the instructions that Jesus gave us in Matthew 18:15–17. If you offended me I would come to you first. I don't know where this gossip got started, but I believe that it has no foundation from my family."

Dan's secretary came to the door and motioned to him by pointing to her watch.

"Pastor Ben, I have a client waiting for me. Please let me talk with Vicki and then I will call you for a meeting."

"I sure hope that you realize what a devastating blow your leaving this church would cause. The consequences of such a move . . ."

Dan interrupted him. "Thank you for your call. Goodbye."

Pastor Ben hung up the phone and put his hand over his stomach. The churning was getting worse. He didn't want to think about it right now. He just wanted to go home and go to bed.

Dan opened the front door of his home. He laid his briefcase on the table in the entry and looked for someone to greet him. "Vicki . . . Joshua, anyone home?"

His six-foot two slender frame reflected back at him in the foyer mirror. Stopping he pulled in close to look at his eyes to see if they revealed how tired he felt. His full head of brown hair was cut like the latest fashion from a male magazine. Part spikes were definitely not his choice, but Joshua convinced him that he needed to keep his hair style current. He ran his hand through his hair and thought surely it was time for this look to change. In his business as a lawyer, appearance was everything. He wore the fashionable suits, ties, shoes and accessories; not because he particularly cared about that stuff, but the world which he worked did.

Glancing at his watch he saw that he was earlier getting home than he had been lately. He shared a law firm with two other Christian partners and they were busy all the time. The case he was working on at the moment was a big one. A business owned by a Jewish man was getting sued for not printing what the owner considered pornographic literature. The guy was claiming he was being discriminated against because he was gay.

The law was confusing when a person's personal rights conflicted with another's religious and moral rights. It was easy to get emotionally involved with the situation, especially when it was Dan's view that the new discriminatory laws opened the door to a lot of frivolous law suits. People were sued if they wouldn't rent apartments to unmarried people or gays. It was just plain crazy. It was a time in the history of America that the judicial system was still the greatest in all the earth, but it was showing signs of running amuck and dangerously out of control. He and his law partners had discussed the situation numerous times in the past few years.

Of course the rulers of darkness were aware of the Christian money and time they were wasting by having this kind of legislation passed. It upset Dan that ungodly men who didn't fear God or man were tearing up the justice system of America with their ungodly laws. God assured Dan that He was placing godly men into the system right under the princes of darkness' nose. He told him that he was taking over the politics and politicians of America. Dan could hardly wait.

Vicki entered the large foyer of their several thousand square foot home, and greeted him with a hug. Her day had gone exceptionally good and she couldn't wait to tell him about her meeting with Ruth Pearson. "What is wrong?"

Dan smiled as he hung his coat in a hallway closet just beyond the foyer. Vicki could always tell when something was up with him.

"Let's go into the kitchen."

"This must be serious if I have to wait for the kitchen."

The kitchen was situated all the way in the back of their home, facing a view of the lake outside and a wonderful garden and swimming pool overlooking a few acres of immaculate lawn. It was evident to anyone who had personal contact with the Knights that they were very wealthy. Although they didn't start out rich, the Lord had blessed them with several businesses that were very prosperous. For ten years they prospered in every area, but one; having a baby.

And then God blessed them with Joshua.

"Should I call Joshua to a family meeting?" Vicki asked.

"Is he home?"

"Yes, he is in his bedroom I believe." She started to dial up his number on her cell phone when Dan stopped her.

"Let's talk about this first before we include him."

Entering the kitchen, Dan led her to the bay window with the breakfast nook and round table. The bay windows let in the light with a spectacular view of the setting sun. It was one of his favorite places to sit, but they had several seating arrangements they could choose; seating by the kitchen fireplace, a bar that separated the working kitchen from the casual table and hutch and a kitchen island with a couple of bar stools.

Vicki stopped at the six-burner commercial stainless steel gas stove to put on some water for herbal tea. She loved to drink a healthy mix of green tea and herbs for their natural healing power. Dan had become a gourmet cook as a stress relief from his career, and they both appreciated God's natural plants that provided nutrients for their body.

Vicki's motto was to live happy, healthy and holy.

"What's going on?" she asked as she slid next to him on the built-in window seat.

Dan looked out at the lake in the distance. "You know, this spot never fails to remind me of God's goodness to us."

"Jesus is good," Vicki agreed with him.

"All the time . . . Pastor Ben called me this morning."

"Oh?"

"He heard a rumor that we are thinking of withdrawing Joshua from school and that we are leaving the church."

"What? From whom?"

"He didn't say."

"We've never told anyone about our conversations this past year."

"Not only that, we've never officially discussed leaving the church with one another," Dan added.

"Have you heard from the Lord about Joshua?" Vicki stood to get the whistling tea pot from the stove and make their tea. "Wait, this doesn't make any sense. We haven't even officially discussed what Joshua has asked us to pray about." She faced Dan with her hands on her hips.

"I know."

She finished making their tea and returned to the table. "Are you thinking what I'm thinking?"

Dan nodded his head. "Demons are mixed up in this."

"How else would anybody know except . . ."

"What's to eat?" Joshua entered the kitchen.

"Joshua." They said together.

"What?" He sat down with them.

"We've encountered a situation that involves a personal family circumstance," Dan tried to explain even though he hadn't had time to pray or meditate about it first.

"What situation?"

"School," Dan replied.

"Oh great, you've heard from the Lord!"

"Uh, not exactly," Vicki answered.

Joshua was perplexed. "What's up?"

"Pastor Ben told me that a rumor is going around the church about us. I wanted to pray about this with your mother before . . ."

"If I knew what is going on, I could pray too!"

Joshua leaned forward on the table looking intently into his parent's eyes after they informed him of the rumors. "Is it true?"

"We were wondering if you talked to anyone about leaving school." Dan asked directly.

He put his hand on his chest. "Me?"

"We haven't told anyone." Vickie said.

"So you just assume that it had to be me?" The tone in his voice started to change.

"Now don't get offended. We were just wondering where this rumor might have originated," Dan said.

"Dad, I promise you that I have never shared my idea about attending public school . . . oh, wait a minute." The Holy Spirit brought a scene to his mind. "I did talk to Kellie about the Lord leading me to attend public school day before yesterday."

Vicki nodded her head. "Kellie told her mother, her mother could have told her Grandmother, who knows one or two key people who told Marilyn. And I know Marilyn would have told Ann, who would have definitely told Pastor Jeff, who then would have directly gone to Pastor Ben . . . okay that's how it probably went."

"Mom, it was only two days ago, how in the world could it have gotten that far?"

"Gossip is like wild fire. It hardly ever starts with the intent on being gossip. You know what James said," Vicki reminded him.

"Yes, that 'the tongue is a fire, a world of iniquity. The tongue is so set among our members that it defiles the whole body, and sets on fire the course of nature' . . . straight to hell if not stopped. But I don't think Kellie deliberately set out to gossip!"

"I don't think she did either. It's like someone who throws a blown-out match out of his car window and doesn't think that the heat still in the match could catch the grass on fire," Vicki said.

"It looks like I started a forest fire."

"Don't lose any sleep over it, son," Dan told him, "Things have a way of working out if we let the Lord handle them."

"I never said a word about leaving the church." Joshua scanned his memory trying to remember if anything was said last night about that subject. "I'm almost positive that I didn't say a thing about the church." He felt a check in his spirit. "Wait, I'm going to have to retract that statement. I told Kellie that we would probably need a different church for this new ministry. I remember telling her that I didn't think that the people at our church could deal with our ministry. Then she asked me if I would consider going to her church."

"Son, what were you thinking? You've never even discussed this with me or your Mom."

"Dad, you won't let me talk to you. Every time I've asked Mom, she brushes me off with saying she hasn't heard from the Lord yet. I've waited several months now and inside me the desire to attend public school is getting stronger, not weaker."

"Joshua, that's my fault. I realized today that I've been pushing this to the back of my mind because as your mom, I don't want to see you in any situation that will cause you harm."

"Jesus said that people will hate us because they hated Him first."

"I know . . . I know . . . I've allowed my carnal nature to override my spiritual nature."

"Okay, I think we can officially open this topic up to a family discussion," Dan picked up his cup and gently hit the table like a judge's gavel.

"Can we fix dinner while we discuss this?" Joshua rubbed his tummy as it let out a huge growl.

Vicki stood and went to the refrigerator. "I made some vegetable soup yesterday for a couple of nights." She got out a big pot and put it on the stove. "I had a feeling that we might be having several family discussions in the next week or so." She stayed in the preparation part of the kitchen to put together their dinner. "Go ahead, start without me."

"Dad, I feel that the Lord wants me to attend public school. I know that it won't be easy, because I know how the world thinks about Jesus and I'll probably have a rough time of it . . ."

"Is that your confession?" Vicki asked.

"No, it's not Mom," he said trying to keep his emotions under control. "It's just realistic thinking. Even Jesus said that in the world we would have tribulation . . ."

"You don't have to go walking into the tribulation just because Jesus said that you will have . . ."

"He also added that we are not to be afraid, because He has already overcome the world," Joshua interrupted his Mom.

"That's true," she acknowledged as she cut a loaf of bread up into slices.

"I believe that the Lord wants me attend public school."

"How do you know?" Dan asked.

"It seems right to me every time I think about it. I dream about it. I just know that the Lord is dealing with me. And Dad, it's not like this just came up yesterday. I've been meditating about this for months now . . . maybe even two years."

"I think your mom and I both realize that the Lord is calling you into a new phase of your life and obviously we have to take this seriously."

"What about our church?"

"I know you might not want to hear me say this, but we need to pray about this first, before we make a decision."

"What does your inner man think about it?" Joshua asked.

Dan hesitated, and then decided against telling him. "When I hear from the Lord, you will be the second one to know."

‡ ‡ ‡

After dinner, Joshua went back to his room to study and work on his plan of action. Dan and Vicki retired to their favorite family room.

"What are you going to say to Pastor Ben?"

"Well," Dan sat down in his favorite overstuffed leather chair and pushed it back into a reclining position, "how about telling him the truth."

"You mean tell him that the Lord is telling Joshua to attend a public school?" Vicki sat in her favorite chenille lounger across from him and the fireplace. "He will never believe that."

"Hmm . . . you've got a point." Dan closed his eyes.

"Dan Knight! Don't you dare go to sleep on me! We need to know what we are going to tell Pastor Ben."

"Vicki, I've been talking all day and now almost all night with Joshua. I would like a few minutes of peace and quiet please."

She held her tongue. It took her several years of marriage to understand that usually Dan needed some downtime from the stress of work and being out in the world when he first came home. What amazed her was the fact that he really didn't like to talk all that much and his profession required that he talk a lot. And the thing that he had to make himself learn to do, facing a jury, was now the thing that he did best. He was a man of few words. Not like her, she liked to talk a lot.

Suddenly, their intercom system buzzed revealing that someone was at their front gate wanting entrance into their driveway. Dan's eyes stayed closed. She knew that meant he was already fast asleep. It was a personal joke between them that he could fall asleep before his head hit the pillow.

Going over to the far wall of the family room she pushed the button and talked into the speaker. "Yes?"

"This is Pastor Ben, may I come in?"

Reluctantly, she pressed the button that would open the gate. "Dan . . . DAN!" she shouted a little louder.

His eyes popped open. "What?"

"Pastor Ben is driving up our driveway now."

"What?" His eyes looked very red, indicating how deep he had already been into a sleep pattern. "You let him in?"

"Well, I couldn't very well tell him to go away."

Dan rubbed his hand through his hair and got up. "I told him that we would meet with him later." He followed Vicki down the hall.

Vicki opened the front door.

Pastor Ben extended his hand. "I hope you will forgive my intrusion."

Well, at least he called it what it was, Vicki thought.

Dan walked up behind her. "Pastor, I thought we were going to call you."

"I know . . . I know." He walked into the foyer. "I just couldn't go to sleep without talking to you personally." He extended his hand to Dan.

"Let's go into the living room." Vicki led him into their formal living area. She didn't want to be in a very comfortable room so that the meeting wouldn't last very long.

He sat down on the formal couch as Dan and Vicki sat in the very formal Queen Anne chairs. It didn't get past him that Vicki chose the stuffy formal room for them to talk. Pastor Ben looked around at the luxurious room decorated in white, off whites and gold with shinny brass, crystal and glass; he refused to be intimidated by his surroundings. Sitting on the white satin brocade couch, he wondered what it would be like to be as wealthy as the Knights. Before he surrendered to preach the gospel, he knew that he probably would have to give up the "riches" of this world. He believed that money was the root of all evil and now this experience was beginning to confirm what he always thought.

"You know why I am here. I want to hear it from your mouth what you are going to do about the school and Joshua." He was really more concerned about their church attendance, but he thought he would start with the school situation.

Dan hesitated again. He should have completely discussed this with Vicki before he fell asleep. He glanced at her and saw the "you-should-have-

move to the public school system."

"But, how do you know for sure that it is the Lord that is talking to him?" Pastor Ben could not believe that Joshua had heard from God.

"Ben, we do not take a move like this lightly. We have given this a lot of time and prayer."

"Besides," Vicki added, "we trust Joshua's relationship with the Lord."

"But don't you remember when it was prophesied that we were to start the church school?"

"We were both at church that Sunday, Pastor. We still believe in the church school."

"But Dan, if you allow Joshua to quit our school and go into the public school system, many church members will believe that you no longer support our school."

"People are always going to believe whatever they choose," Vicki replied.

"You know that removing Joshua may cause many others to remove their children."

Dan let out his breath slowly. "Ben, I know that some of the members of the church will not understand what we are doing, but I cannot let that stop us from being obedient to God."

"Of course, I don't want you to disobey God. I just want you to be sure that it is God."

Vicki was beginning to think that this conversation was going in the opposite direction that they wanted it to go.

"We will pray about how to tell the church or even if we should tell them, but we are going to withdraw Joshua from school at the end of the week."

"I can't change your mind, can I?"

"No."

"Can I be honest with you?"

Dan looked into his eyes intently. "I wouldn't have it any other way."

"I think you are making a mistake and I just pray that it doesn't harm Joshua."

"What are you saying?" Dan was hoping he wasn't saying what he heard him say.

"I don't believe that it is God's will for Joshua to leave the church school."

Dan stood. "There's really nothing else we can say."

Pastor Ben stood. "Don't do this Dan."

Vicki stayed seated and prayed under her breath as her heart started beating faster.

"What about the money that you are giving to the school and the support of two other students?"

"Is money what this is all about?"

"Dan, you know as well as I do that money makes the world go round."

Vicki lowered her head shaking it. *That's exactly what we would expect someone from the world to say. And it's the last thing he should say to Dan,* she thought.

"No, I really don't believe that. I believe the Lord makes the world go round."

Ben blushed. He forgot how Dan and Vicki always spiritualize everything. "We need money for our school to operate. Very few Christian schools are in the black like we are and you and I both know that is largely because of your support. If you leave my, uh, our church, we will have serious financial concerns."

"If God tells us to leave, then God will provide the funds for His church, not me, not you and not any one person."

No one moved.

Vicki wondered if he was going to ask the question he really wanted to know.

"Thank you for coming over, but you should have waited for me to call you." Dan moved to the large double French doors and went through them pausing for Pastor Ben to follow.

Well, that was straight to the point, Vicki thought as she stood to walk him to the front door.

"Please forgive me for coming without calling first." Pastor Ben stopped after a few steps, turned to Vicki and saw Dan walking the other direction down the hallway. "Vicki, are you leaving the church?"

"Whatever the Lord tells Dan, I will support him."

"Aren't you concerned about Joshua's ability to relate to the kids in a public school?"

"I've learned to turn all my cares over to Jesus."

"Good night, Vicki." As he walked out to his parked car he shook his head thinking what a waste of time that had been. It was frustrating that the Knights always talked about the Lord or His Word. Even as a pastor of one of the biggest churches in their city, he didn't talk or think about Jesus constantly like they did.

What he feared was finally coming to past. The Knights were jumping off the deep end into the Word of faith movement. And there was nothing he could do about it.

CHAPTER 11

Vicki Knight sat in the largest living room of her house and looked at the ladies sitting around her. Vicki was a tall light brunette with medium hair to her shoulders. Her hair was straight and curled under with a few wisps of bangs. She dressed modestly in a blue a-line linen dress that matched perfectly with her blue eyes and shoes. Having been raised in a pastor's home, this was a scene from one of her childhood days. Many times she helped serve tea and cookies to the women's group from her father's congregation; only the house and circumstances were very different.

She turned her head to answer a question from her best friend, Kathy Todd, Kellie's mother. Kathy, raised in a Christian home, had married her high school sweetheart, Mark. Her frosted short curly blond hair and small petite frame did not adequately represent her spiritual strength; she looked like a giant in the spiritual realm and in the heavenlies she was known as a fearless prayer warrior. The two of them together were greatly feared by the kingdom of darkness.

Kathy was sitting next to Mose's mother, Ruth Pearson, and his grandmother, RubyMae White. Ruth was very knowledgeable about the Bible. Dan and Vicki visited their church once, but planned to visit again. After meeting with Ruth for lunch the other day, Vicki was sure that the Lord had ordained that a special relationship would develop between them.

Ruth believed that her husband David and she would become close friends with Dan and Vicki after their luncheon the other day. They had prayed and asked God to give them favor with a white couple. David, the pastor of an independent Christian church,desired a racially-mixed congregation. He received great pleasure destroying religious traditions and bigotry. But Ruth was adamant that they not talk to them about joining their congregation. She wanted to be sure that the Lord was leading Dan and Vicki to attend their church for His will and not other reasons.

The obvious reasons were apparent as she scanned the exceptionally large living area and the showcase home that she had been invited to this morning; wealth was the theme of this household. She heard that the Knights were rich, but this had to be what people refer to as "filthy" rich, except there was nothing filthy about this house. *What church wouldn't covet members that are as rich as the Knight family?* she thought. *No way! Not you, girl! Don't even let that thought touch a hair on your head!*

RubyMae leaned over and whispered in her daughter's ear, "Wouldn't you love to have Vicki as a member of our church?"

"Mother!" Ruth said with a lowered voice. It was hard enough fighting her own flesh; she didn't need help from her mother.

"You know you were thinking about it!" She replied.

Ruth tried to ignore her mother's words, but she was right, her flesh was thinking about the financial gain the Knights' membership would bring to their church.

Vicki looked over at Ruth dressed elegantly in a coral linen suit and her hair up in a French twist with curls on top. The color was beautiful on her. A great love had already developed in her heart for Ruth. In Vicki's spirit, she felt that Mose was an excellent choice from the Lord as a part of Joshua's ministry. She was sure that their newly formed friendship was a special blessing from the Lord.

Mose's grandmother, a large woman, arranged her salt and pepper hair in a bun and laughed with a hearty, jovial laugh. Even though she was an elderly person, teenagers loved her immediately. She would adopt any young person she met and put them under her wing of authority in prayer. Vicki sensed the prayer-warrior power around her.

Hannah's mother, Sheila Coyle, was a soft-spoken shorthaired brunette. She sat by herself listening to the women talk while she sipped her tea. The women were all strangers to her. Sheila wanted to get to know the mothers of her daughter's friends and she wanted to develop some Christian friends. Her mother told her about Jesus from watching Christian television. Sheila and her mother had visited many churches, but were still looking for a church home when they got this call from Vicki.

Looking at the last two women sitting in chairs at the end of the couch, Vicki was glad that the Lord put them on her heart. They were very skilled in intercessory prayer. She had met Evie Danson and Joan LittleFeather when their church held a citywide prayer telethon. Evie, a short, over-weight widow was laughing and telling the ladies about her grandchildren.

Joan stood to take the tea pitcher in the kitchen and refill it. Her tall graceful dark figure and long jet-black hair gave a hint of being an American Indian. Evie and Joan were the only single females in the group. Joan was called by the Lord to minister full time as a prayer warrior. She was very interested in Joshua's calling.

Vicki waited for Joan to return from the kitchen to start the meeting. She placed her teacup on the marble table in front of her and cleared her throat. "I think everyone has met each other, so I'd like to get started. I explained briefly over the phone about my calling to organize this prayer group."

The ladies set their cups down and listened with interest to Vicki telling them about her dream and Joshua's visit with Jesus. They seemed to receive her testimony with an open mind, believing the Lord visited both of them.

"Kellie, my daughter, is so excited with the vision the Lord has given to Joshua. She can't wait to get started," Kathy commented.

"I've prayed over every person Joshua has contacted. Joshua wants young people who really know the Lord and has a deep desire to win souls for Jesus." Vicki's eyes scanned every eye in the room. "I want each of you to make sure you understand the Lord's instructions, if you decide to join the prayer group. The Lord is asking for a total commitment."

"Vicki, are you going to teach us how to pray?" Sheila asked hesitantly.

"Yes. The Lord has given me specific instructions on how we are to pray. You will be given a sheet with scripture verses and names of the young people who phone the Devil Chasers." She started handing out the sheet with scripture verses.

"What a great name. Where did it come from?" asked Joan.

"Joshua was praying and heard that name in his spirit," Vicki answered.

"It doesn't sound like he is afraid of the devil," commented RubyMae.

"How do you think the name is going to be received?" asked Ruth.

"Those whose minds who are connected to the mind of the Lord and know the heart of God, will not be offended," Vicki answered her as she sat down in the chair facing the group of women.

"The Lord showed me that this generation of young people is going to wipe the devil and his kingdom completely off earth just like He did in [illegible]

"Mother!" Ruth was shocked.

"What . . . does *butt* offend you? Honey, when it comes to the devil, he doesn't have a behind, he has a *butt*!" laughed RubyMae.

All the ladies laughed at her comment.

"You know, I would never let Kellie say butt when she was little, bu[t] [illegible] ." Kathy laughed. "Since I've learned how to kick satan's [butt] [illegible] having fun doing it!"

"Amen, sister! That snake better get out of my way, especially if he puts his hands on my grandchildren!" exclaimed RubyMae.

"I have to agree with my mother, even though that sounds rather crude."

"Crude? With that rude dude?" RubyMae shook her hand at her. "No way!"

It was very apparent that RubyMae was not restrained with any social protocols. It irritated Ruth sometimes, but Vicki loved her personality instantly.

"It is very important that we pray in agreement when we pray." Vicki tried to get the subject back on discussing prayer.

"How long are we going to pray?" asked Joan.

"The Lord wants us to block out three to four hours every morning, Monday through Friday," answered Vicki.

"I don't know if I can pray that long," remarked Sheila in a tentative voice.

"I know how you feel, I use to think that way," Vicki explained. "But since I've learned how to pray, I've had to make myself stop praying. I told the Lord one day, someone has to take care of the daily household commitments."

"Honey, the Lord can send an angel to wash my dishes and do my ironing, any day!" declared Ruth.

"I'll amen that!" agreed Kathy as the other women laughed in agreement.

"You are always free to leave at anytime. But I believe we must set a minimum limit of one hour. We will be providing the necessary covering for a ministry that is going to enrage the devil when his works are destroyed among our young people."

"The most important thing we need to remember is to be Spirit-led in everything we do," Vicki said.

"When are we getting started?" asked Ruth.

"We are going to discuss procedure today and begin praying tomorrow. The Devil Chaser's phone line will be connected next week. That will give us time to establish a cover of protection over them before they officially get started. Are there any other questions?" asked Vicki.

The ladies all looked at one another and shook their heads no, except Sheila.

"First, I want to thank you for responding to the call of the Lord. This is a high honor to stand in the gap and pray for another person. That is what an intercessor does."

Joan interrupted Vicki. She noticed the hesitation on Sheila's part. "Maybe you better explain first why we need to pray."

"That's a good idea. Praying is how we get things done on earth. We pray and the Lord answers with the power and anointing that changes people and situations. John Wesley once made the comment that, 'God is limited by our prayer life. He can do nothing for humanity unless someone asks Him,'" explained Vicki.

"Why is that?" asked Sheila.

"The Bible tells us that God owns the world, but He gave it to the children of men," Vicki said.

"I've always heard that God was in control," commented Sheila.

"Vicki, do you mind if I answer?" Ruth asked.

"No, feel free to talk as the Lord directs you."

"My husband is a pastor. He tells people that ask him that question that if God is the one ruling, then He sure is making a mess of things!"

All the women nodded their heads in agreement.

"I've never though of it like that, but He must have allowed satan to be here."

"No. He didn't allow satan to live on earth, Adam did," Vicki said.

"God has always been blamed for all the bad things that happen on this planet!" Ruth declared.

"Most people think that if it's bad it's God and if it's good it's God. It's easy to accept the good things as being from God, but the bad . . ." RubyMae started shaking her head. "Oh no! Now don't you go blaming the works of the devil on my Jesus!"

Vicki quoted from the book of James. "Every good gift and every perfect gift is from above, and comes down from the Father of lights."

"Amen! The opposite of that statement is that every bad and imperfect gift is from below," Ruth interjected.

"It comes from the father of darkness," Vicki said.

"Do you think that everything that happens bad in this world is from the devil?" Sheila was confused.

"Yes," Everyone said at the same time.

"How can evil exist without God allowing it?" Sheila asked.

"The Bible gives you the answer," Vicki explained. "God has never created any beings to be puppets. He gave dominion or total control of earth to Adam in the garden."

"Yeah and every foul thing that creeps on the earth," RubyMae pointed out. "And satan is the foulest!"

"Amen!" A couple of the ladies said with laughter.

"Adam allowed satan to enter our earth with the curse when he disobeyed God," Ruth interjected.

"The devil is the curse that has invaded our planet. He is all that is bad, evil and wicked. He created the sin that caused spiritual death in men and women," Vicki said looking at Sheila.

Sheila thought of world catastrophes that are reported and how almost always God's name was yoked with the disasters. The insurance business has even named them acts of God.

"We know from God's Word that we don't fight flesh and blood, but the forces of darkness. Every television and radio station broadcasts the news resulting from the curse of the knowledge of evil. The works of demons bombard the human mind daily. You don't have to convince one human that lives on this planet that earth has some serious problems. Everybody knows it," Vicki taught.

"People recognize evil but they sure don't recognize who is the root cause of the evil," Ruth said.

"When you study God's nature you will find that He can only do good. Death has no part in life. John says that God is life. God can't kill you even if he wanted to," Vicki answered her.

"Now honey, you know you better be careful. You are stepping on some sacred cows," laughed RubyMae.

"Sacred what?" asked Sheila.

"Sacred cows. She is talking about traditions and interpretations that some Christians believe are scriptural," explained Vicki.

Sheila didn't know about Biblical doctrine. "An evil angel named satan is responsible for man's violent nature and all the bad things that happen on earth?"

"Yes and no . . ." Vicki started to explain.

Ruth interrupted. "He is the father of sin and the one who rebelled against God. Excuse me for interrupting . . ."

"That's okay. Satan is the father of lies, but Adam gave him permission to enter the world by not casting him out of the garden. God owns the earth, but he gave it to man. Let's say that He is the owner and we are the landlords. When Adam didn't kick satan out of the garden and disobeyed God, he lost his covering from the Father. Satan became man's stepfather," Vicki stated.

"God can't do anything unless somebody down here asks Him to do it, because He's not like the devil who forced his presence into our world," added Ruth. "After we sinned, he demanded that all men be put in the underworld prison called hell."

"That's pretty good," interjected Evie. "I've never heard satan called a stepfather before."

"He's sure not my father!" RubyMae proclaimed.

"Wait a minute, girls, I think we are way ahead of Sheila," Ruth observed her face. She looked lost.

"Well, it certainly sounds better to blame satan than to blame God, because before I accepted Jesus into my life, it really bothered me that children die of starvation and war in the third world countries. I never could understand why God could allow such suffering," Sheila explained.

"I used to think the same way. Then I found out that God isn't responsible for people dying of hunger, we are," Vicki told her.

Ruth answered, "Jesus has a simple answer to the problems in our world. If children are hungry, feed them."

"If they are naked, clothe them," RubyMae added.

"If they are sick, lay hands on them and they will recover," Evie said.

"If they are in prison, visit them," Joan added.

"You see, we are the ones responsible for that alien being running loose on our planet." Vicki poured herself another cup of tea. "Well, Adam and Eve were actually the ones responsible, but we inherited him. So, we are the ones that need to take care of him."

Ruth picked up her Bible. "In Romans 5:12 . . ." She flipped through the pages. "Therefore, just as through one man sin entered the world, and death through sin, and thus death spread to all men, because all sinned . . . even over those who had not sinned according to the likeness of the transgression of Adam."

"Do you know the scripture that says 'all have sinned and come short of the glory of God'?" Vicki asked Sheila.

"No."

"That scripture is found in Romans. Paul is telling us that we inherited the devil's nature of sin leading to death, because of Adam," Vicki explained.

"That deceiver tricked Eve, but Adam fell willingly," Ruth said.

Now all the women nodded in agreement and started talking in little groups.

"Ladies, I know we have hit on a sensitive subject, but let's not bombard Sheila with too much information," Vicki said.

"Oh, no don't stop because of me. I may have never heard anything like this before, but I love hearing it now," Sheila told them.

"Personally, I think we need to take it easy on Adam. He probably thought he was going to lose Eve," RubyMae said. "You know, she must have been a knock out!"

"Jesus said that satan was the god of this world's system, but he illegally entered this earth. He caused man to lose God's covering as a Father and satan became our stepfather. Jesus gave us back to the Father, but only those who choose to accept the Blood Covenant. He was the first-born son and we were adopted by the Father through the Blood of Jesus into the family of God. We are now kings and lords and should be ruling and reigning on earth through the authority of Jesus," Vicki taught.

"You make it sound so simple to understand," Sheila smiled.

"Paul said by one man sin entered the world and by one man death was conquered once and for all," Ruth sensed the anointing of the Holy Spirit. "God's plan is simple."

"I heard a preacher on TV say that AIDS is God's judgment on homosexuals."

"Sheila, God doesn't use sickness, disease and natural disasters to judge us. Evil spirits of sin and death entered earth when Adam bowed his knee to the master of rebellion and pride. AIDS is a direct result of sin, and satan is trying to kill men and women as fast as possible," Vicki told her. "God is trying to hold back judgment as long as possible, but soon He is just going to run out of time."

"Then, why do most Christians believe that God sends judgment on people?"

"They believe the lies of the kingdom of darkness and they don't know the heart of the Father." Vicki told her.

"They don't know Father God period!" Kathy said as she got up to pour herself another cup of tea. "Some of those same people think God cursed the black people by turning their skin black."

"I've heard that one several times!" RubyMae said with an angry tone. "Forgive me, Lord, but that snake convinced many white folks that God was white and hated all other races but the white race."

"There is an evil alien loose on this planet and he has come to steal, kill and destroy," Vicki repeated. "His kingdom is the one that has taught men to hate each other, especially pointing out our differences."

Ruth stood to get a glass of water. "People don't know how to interpret scriptures in the Bible. Jesus came to destroy the works of the devil, not races."

"The Bible tells us that God has placed Jesus far above all principalities, powers and rulers of darkness of this age through His victory over satan. Jesus is the High Priest over His body, not satan," Vicki added.

"Contrary to a popular doctrine, satan is not running around earth as an agent of the Lord!" RubyMae exclaimed. "How ignorant can some Christians be?"

"I've heard that preached by some very famous preachers," Sheila told them. "I got saved watching Christian television."

"Praise the Lord for Christian television, but honey, you've got to test every word you hear!" RubyMae warned her.

"Some have even said that hurricanes and tornadoes are the result of God's judging an evil world," Vicki told her.

"God sure has gotten a bum rap," Ruth said.

"Yes, and who do you think is responsible for that?" Joan asked sarcastically.

"I know," Sheila smiled. She was getting the picture. "The devil!"

They all laughed with Sheila.

"Our judgment for Adam's sin came upon us immediately. Adam and Eve had to leave the garden of eden and then they had to contend with the curse that came upon their spirit, soul and body and the whole earth," Vicki said.

Kathy spoke up. "I never thought of it like that."

Ruth agreed with Vicki. "We inherited satan's carnal nature. We got severed from the goodness of God and were joined to the evil nature of satan."

"When Jesus defeated death, God ruled that Jesus has paid the price for sin that was or ever will be necessary for the entire race of man from Adam to the last human ever born." An anointing, a spirit of teaching, entered Vicki. "Sin has no more power over those of us who walk in the spirit of life in Christ Jesus and not in the flesh. The only catch is that the human has to make the choice for God from his heart and out of his mouth."

"How do you walk in your spirit and not the flesh?" Sheila asked.

RubyMae picked up her Bible and pointed it at Sheila. "This is how we walk in the spirit and defeat the devil . . . the Word of God."

The early morning sun sent rays peering through the tree house of metraloas. He was angry and tired. He was ordered back to earth and told that if he ever came back to hell uninvited, then he would be terminated as an android. He tried to explain that this assignment was wrong from the beginning. He was tired of being abused and neglected and especially tired of daylight on earth. He hated light and God.

Forcing himself to open his lookout window and begin surveying the Knights' house, the only thing that made him get up was thinking of his plan for his demotion and a reassignment in hell. But before he could begin his morning ritual and get everything in place, he heard several car doors slam. Quickly, he transported himself outside his bunker to a better position and focused his radar eyes.

It looked like several large angels were following some humans into the house. He spied more activity of angels taking place around the perimeter of the property; the wall of angels standing shoulder to shoulder was reinforced. He tried to zero in with the special zoom lenses in his eyes, but it was no avail, everything was blurry again. Nothing was wrong with his ears because he could clearly hear the cackling laughter from a group of female humans. He might have dismissed it as being one of those female parties, but the reinforcements of the angels made him know better than that.

It was a prayer meeting.

Deciding that there was nothing he could do about it, metraloas closed his eyes to rest.

BAM! SPLAT!

Someone knocked him out of the tree. Looking up, he thought he saw two chemah's.

"Are you stupid? Look what's going on over there! You fool!" chemah finished screaming at him using terrible cuss words. "You were asleep on the job! I ought to terminate you right now!"

Metraloas tried to look at his assignment as his eyes focused. Huge crystal ladders with angels climbing up and down were forming a connection between heaven and the inside of the house. A glory cloud descended and the radiance was blinding all the evil spirits outside the radius of the circle of light in the neighborhood. Many little demons were running for cover.

"Go up there and tell me what in the——is going on!" Chemah yelled at him.

"I'm not getting close to that light!" Metraloas disappeared and reappeared on a big limb higher up in the tree.

Chemah cursed as he watched the next display of fireworks. Crystals were forming as beacons of towers over the house.

"I just closed my eyes for a second!"

"You didn't see anything suspicious? Like people who belong to all those cars parked out in the driveway!"

"It could have been one of those scrap booking things."

Chemah raised his arm and shot a fireball at him, singeing the hair of metraloas. The stream of fire knocked him out of the tree.

Metraloas stood and looked over at the house again. He was angry over his singed smelly hair, but he felt worse over this new development with the Knights. He flew back into the tree to gather his things.

"What do you think you're doing?" chemah followed him.

"I'm leaving. I've tried to tell you for two years that my assignment is a strange Christian family. They read the Bible and quote the written words of Jesus continually."

"You have seen this type of spiritual fortress and you're just now letting me know?"

"No, it has never been like this. But the glory covers that house day in and day out, week in and week out, month by month and that has never changed in two years. I've told you about that fact thousands of times! It's all in the reports that you haven't read."

Metraloas was losing it as he threw his things into a container to transport back to hell. He picked up a black book and shook it in chemah's face. "This is a copy of all the reports I sent you!"

Chemah pointed his weapon at it and burned it with fire.

Metraloas laughed at him. "I suspected you might do that, so I have two other copies hidden." *Never trust another evil spirit, especially a fallen angel,* he thought. "I'm sure the master will enjoy reading some of my comments and suggestions that were ignored by you!" He refused to back down to chemah this time.

SWOOSH!

A sound of a mighty rushing wind from another dimension pierced their ears. They stopped screaming at each other and ran to the observation window. What they saw caused both of their hearts to miss a couple of beats. Tongues of fire were dancing above the rooftop of the house and floating down through the Holy Spirit's covering. The anointing entered the house and sat on top of each woman praising and worshiping the Lord. The glory cloud shrouded the house and waves of cool refreshing breezes were showering all the ladies meeting inside.

Enormous warring angels circled the house guarding the human's time with the Lord. Worshiping angels appeared as waves of clear-blue water proclaiming the glory of the Lord. Flying around and in and out of the glory cloud, they said, "Holy, Holy, Lord God Almighty, which Who was, and is, and is to come."

"You are hearing true worship!" chemah pointed to the atmosphere distortions outlining the angelic beings flying in and out of the glory cloud. "You are seeing worshipping angels from another dimension appearing in ours. They sing about Jesus' victory and His coming!" chemah screamed out loud. "I hate true worshippers!"

Metraloas fell to his face and tried to find something to hide under. He heard about the angelic display the day that Jesus was born, but he was in hell working and never experienced the power of worship like he was now witnessing. The light became so intense that all the spirits within several blocks had to leave their posts.

Chemah cursed metraloas, kicking him all the way to hell.

CHAPTER 12

"You don't believe in a judgment?" Sheila was shocked. She thought all Christians believed in judgment. Mentally, she pictured weird looking people who stand around street corners carrying signs that say "Judgment is coming" or "The world is coming to an end."

"I didn't say that I don't believe in judgment," Ruth countered.

"Judgment has already come," Vicki told her. "We are living in judgment. When Adam and Eve had to leave the garden, the world they encountered was cold, dark, cruel and harsh. Even the animals changed."

"They could no longer see or hear angels singing and worshipping God," Joan added. "They couldn't walk and talk with the Lord like they did before sin entered the world."

"Then why do people talk about the end of the world and judgment?"

"Judgment is coming to satan and his kingdom. They have not received punishment for deceiving Adam and Eve and bring sin, sickness, disease and death to our world," Vickie said.

Ruth added. "God is going to restore this earth from all the evil created by the kingdom of darkness. That day is called the judgment day of God."

"Or the day of wrath, but whatever you want to call it, it's the day that all evil will be wiped off this earth and the kingdom of darkness with its curse will be totally gone!" Vicki added. "Praise the Lord!"

"So, you believe that judgment day is only for the devil and his kingdom?" Sheila confirmed.

"Judgment is for all, because the Bible says that whatever you sow you are going to reap. Judgment for the evil ones is curses and punishment in the lake of fire. Judgment for the righteous ones is blessings and inheriting the earth. You can choose your judgment. And the only way of escape from the curse is through Jesus His Son," Vicki told her.

"If you choose to serve sin over Jesus, then you will experience the judgment that has been reserved for satan and his kingdom of darkness," Ruth said.

"And that might start sooner than death," RubyMae added.

"But the sad thing is the unbelievers will finally see who the devil is and how he has deceived them, but it will be too late for them," Vicki explained.

"Jesus will expose the devil and the entire world will see what a small being he really is," Ruth told her.

RubyMae shouted happily. "No more devil to harass us and tempt us!"

"No more curse upon the earth!" shouted Joan.

Vicki nodded her head. "Even though there is a day that all eyes shall see and know that Jesus is our Lord and King of the earth, we need to be crushing the devil's kingdom under our feet until the kingdom of darkness is removed from this earth!"

"God is going to do it through His body now. We've got to know that He is waiting for us to preach the gospel to every nation on this earth before He comes back!" Ruth said.

"Satan is going to be defeated totally in several nations before He comes back!" Vicki proclaimed. "Maybe all nations, if we would just believe God's Word and receive it."

"Wait!" Sheila put her hands up as she lowered her head. "Everyone's talking at the same time!"

"Girls," Vicki said. "I think we are overwhelming Sheila."

"God revealed to us in Genesis 3:14–15 that satan was responsible for the curse that came over earth. God then prophesied that the seed of a woman would defeat satan," Ruth said as she opened her Bible. "Jesus crushed satan. Just as God said He would in the garden of eden; the Seed of a woman defeated him."

"The earth and all that is in it belongs to the righteous, the children of God." Vicki added with a more subdued tone. "That is us."

Ruth looked directly at Sheila. "Satan has an intense hatred for us. Mankind received the special covering from God called the anointing. Satan was after our anointing because he lost it after he was severed from God."

"Boy, did he ever get a surprise!" RubyMae laughed.

Ruth explained. "Flesh is nothing but dirt without the anointing."

Vicki added. "After the fall, men became the illegitimate children of satan and man's nature and flesh changed. The life force in our blood was changed. Satan is limited to our dead fleshly bodies and puny power without God's anointing."

Quiet Kathy was excited. "You know, that does explain why satan hates us so passionately."

"Most Christians believe that God pronounced curses on us after Adam sinned. But what God really did was reveal that satan is the curse and that Adam allowed the curse on earth," Ruth said. "Then God revealed what the curse would do to man and the earth."

"He pronounced judgment over the curse, satan, and prophesied that the Seed of the woman, who is Jesus, would restore the earth to its rightful owner. God and man who will once again be One together," Vicki said. "We will be ruling and reigning with Him from earth."

The girls shouted, "Praise the Lord!"

"Satan was judged and given a sentence. In the context of Hebrew if you interpret the word bruise as crush or annihilate, then you would understand that God was prophesying the total destruction of satan and his kingdom would come through a man," Vicki said. "Then, God our Creator would be restored as our legal Father again. Which is exactly what Jesus did!"

Ruth added, "A bruise sometimes indicates a light wound, but this says that the Seed of a woman would totally crush satan's head, which means that the kingdom of darkness will be completely removed from any interference of God's plans for the nation of Israel and us, the body of the Anointed One, Jesus."

"From the book of Galatians, in the New Testament, we know that the Seed of the woman is Jesus the Anointed One of God," Vicki said.

"Praise the Lord!" RubyMae could feel her spirit rise within her." We are going to rule over all the worlds to come!"

"The worlds to come?" Sheila was amazed at the things she was learning.

"I heard a well known scientist say that currently there are about 60 billion galaxies out in space," Ruth told her. "And knowing that our God has a purpose for everything He created, He must have plans for them."

"The Book of Ephesians tells us that the same power that worked in Jesus when God raised Him from the dead and seated Him at God's right hand far above all powers and every name that is named is in us. And further more that same power in us comes with the authority to exercise it over all the power of the enemy," Ruth pointed out.

"When Jesus conquered spiritual death, the Father said all authority belongs to His Son. Then Jesus in turn gave that authority to His disciples before He ascended into heaven. When we take authority over the kingdom of darkness on earth, we give honor and glory back to God. That is a completed circle," Vicki continued teaching.

"Honey!" RubyMae sang out. "The Father loves circles!"

Sheila held up her hand. "This is what I think I've learned today. Jesus died on the cross. He defeated death and recovered our position with God. But to receive blessings and life, you have to accept Jesus in your heart and with your mouth."

They all clapped.

"Don't forget judgment is coming for the kingdom of darkness and anybody that didn't ask Jesus to be their spiritual head," Vicki added.

"Who made hell?" Sheila asked.

"The devil did." Vicki explained. "It is a prison for the souls of man who are separated from the life of God. Death takes every soul that dies in the spirit force of fear straight to hell when the spirit separates from the body. Jesus is the only man that conquered death and fear of the grave."

"When we choose Jesus, we are actually given a personal chance to once again choose not to eat from the tree of good and evil," Joan revealed.

"No wonder Jesus said that we had to 'eat of His flesh and drink of His Blood!'" Evie stated.

"He is the Bread of Life; the Fruit from the tree!" RubyMae said.

"Bread and Fruit?" Sheila repeated what she was hearing.

"God revealed that to not eat of that tree, Adam would be obeying Him and choosing to be in right standing with God and righteous. When Adam ate of the fruit from that tree, he committed an act that resulted in separation from God. Sin will take us from spiritual death to physical death. The result of disobedience was immediate spiritual death," Vicki explained.

"Obedience to God is fellowship with Him and life. The sentence or reward of obedience is spiritual life. The sentence or judgment of disobedience is spiritual death." Ruth was trying to be as basic as she could with Sheila so she could begin to understand the teachings of Jesus.

"I think I understand." Sheila's face changed. "Man was judged immediately for his disobedience, but satan and his kingdom haven't been punished yet."

"And we will be God's agents of judgment and wrath in the ages to come, because we have been purified by fire through the Lamb of God, Jesus," Ruth told her.

"What will happen when Jesus comes back to earth?" Sheila asked.

"Jesus is coming back to save Israel because of His Covenant with Abraham and for the earth because He made it," Ruth told her. "He will rule and reign over earth with His body, us, for one thousand years. Earth will not end until that is fulfilled."

"God wants His earth back into the hands of His Son and God wants us back!" Vicki proclaimed throwing her hands up to the Lord. "So God is going to restore the garden of eden, not destroy the world!"

"The earth was made for humans, not for satan and the fallen angels. Satan is the alien!" Ruth told her. "Some people on earth have many homes. Heaven is one of our many homes that we are going to have when satan's kingdom is destroyed."

"That is good! That is so good!" RubyMae proclaimed. "My generation has been told that they were the aliens on this earth, but we've been *lied* to!

This earth belongs to us!"

Vicki explained, "Most born again people do not know that God has an agenda to recover all that satan has stolen from Him. Earth will belong to those who claim it and believe that the coming of the Lord is to reclaim earth and not destroy it."

"Jesus said that the meek will inherit the earth," Ruth reminded them.

"And, baby, that sure ain't the devil and his gang!" RubyMae sang again

Tell them about the transfer of My throne from heaven to earth, the Lord told Vicki.

"Yes, Lord, I will tell them. The Lord just reminded me that His throne is going to be transferred from heaven to earth. That's the New Jerusalem in Revelation. We are going to rule and reign over God's creation from earth," Vicki prophesied.

"Girls don't forget that there is coming a new heaven and a new earth," Ruth remembered. "I believe that the Lord once told me that after the earth is restored and the devil is thrown into the lake of fire, He is going to give us a new place to live. A place that was never touched by the evil one and that will be far greater than His original creation. He believes that we deserve the best of everything."

Everyone sat in total silence. The Spirit of the Lord's presence was awesome. "This is what the Lord must have meant when He wrote, 'eye has not seen or ear has not heard what God has prepared for those who love Him,'" Vicki whispered.

Evie said quietly, "Just think about it; a new heaven that is better than the old?"

"And a new earth," Ruth whispered.

"My, my, my," RubyMae exclaimed quietly.

The Holy Spirit moved over Vicki to speak. "The Lord is speaking in these last days through the believers in His Word. Those who are bold enough to proclaim the truth in righteousness will rule and reign with Me on earth. Earth is mine. Is it not written in My Book that the gold and the silver belong to Me? Didn't I say that I own the cattle on a thousand hills? I put man in charge of the works of My hands and I did not change My mind. A man disconnected from Me and a born-again Man, My Son, reattached My children to Me and recovered it all. I have reclaimed what was lost to Me in the garden. Once again My glory will cover the earth and will be funneled through My body. I am not a loser! I do not intend to destroy the works of My hands. I will recover all."

"Thank You, Jesus! We receive Your words," Ruth worshipped the Lord.

All the ladies praised and worshipped the Lord. After a time of worship and being quiet before the presence of the Lord, Vicki looked at everyone sitting quietly in her family room. "The Word reveals to us that there is the judgment seat of Christ where His body will judge the evil angels and those who followed them. For those who refuse to judge themselves while they were on earth, they will be judged by their own words."

RubyMae held up her Bible. "This is our judge. This book will judge every word or deed we did while here on earth. Every word you ever said that wasn't wiped out by the Blood of Jesus, you will be held accountable for their release into the spiritual and natural realm. Think about it; every last word you ever said! You can't be a child of God and live like the devil, act like the devil and talk like the devil and not be held accountable for your words."

Vicki glanced at her watch when she heard the grandfather clock in her foyer. "Oh my goodness! I don't think we're going to have any trouble praying together everyday. I am going to dismiss us in prayer and tomorrow we can start. I hope we haven't overloaded you Sheila."

"You've given me a lot to think about, but most of all you've given me hope."

‡ ‡ ‡

"What do you think they are talking about?" Marilyn asked Ann as she noticed that Jeff had been in Pastor Ben's office for the last two hours.

Ann got up from her desk and put her ear to the door again. "I still can't hear a thing. They must be whispering!"

"Sit down Ann!" Marilyn looked up and down the hallway. "What would you do if someone saw you?"

She turned around and acted unconcerned if she was caught. "I can get myself out of any situation." Walking back to her desk, she leaned forward and lowered her voice. "You and I both know what they are talking about."

Marilyn went back to her typing. She hated to admit it, but Ann was probably right. After she got the financial book back from Pastor Ben, she added the monthly contributions from the Knights. It was absolutely unbelievable the amount of money the church was receiving from them.

"I heard that Pastor Ben went over to the Knight's house last night and got kicked out."

Marilyn stopped typing. "Ann," she sighed, "that is an outright lie! You better be careful what you are spreading!"

"I got that straight from the horse's mouth!"

Marilyn knew she was talking about Pastor Ben's wife, Linda. "If you tell anybody that, I'm going to call Linda and ask her what she told you."

Actually, Ann overheard Linda asking Pastor Ben if he was going to set up a board meeting since he visited with the Knights last night. "Don't bother. I don't want to be guilty of gossip. I only mentioned it to you because you know everything about Pastor Ben anyway."

Marilyn turned back to her computer thinking what she said probably didn't help the situation. She suspected that Ann embellished conversations and no matter how she admonished her, Ann would still gossip the first opportunity that presented itself.

Jeff sat across from Pastor's Ben desk observing his six foot frame slouched in his chair. The Senior Pastor's black hair was receding faster than he could grow the few strands out that he used to cover the pink skin of his scalp. His eyes were bloodshot, his face looked a little flush and his whole demeanor was that of stress.

"Maybe you should take the day off and go home."

Pastor Ben looked at him. "I'll get more stress at home. Linda's upset with me for going over to Dan's house. You know the temperament of red-heads. She feels I should call a board meeting and get this all out in the open."

"What do you think?" Jeff asked wondering what he was going to do.

"I don't know. I've tried to pray, but I'm hearing nothing."

"You think maybe the Lord is telling Joshua to go to public school?"

"No! Why would the Lord tell us to build the school and then tell our best financial contributor to go to another school?"

"Then you think the Knights are listening to the . . ."

"Devil? Yes I do. I don't believe that God is talking to Joshua. Dan is letting a fourteen year old lead him."

"Well, we've sort of expected something like this since they go to all those conventions."

Although Pastor Ben has learned not to mention any names in his sermon, he tried to be as specific as he could about some of the wrong doctrines that he believed were being taught on Christian TV. "I feared something like this was going to happen sooner or later." He leaned back in his chair and slumped down with his head looking up at the ceiling.

"They really asked you to leave last night?"

"Dan didn't even walk me out to the front door."

"Hmm, what does that mean?"

He sat up and stared at his young assistant pastor. "Probably that he was upset with me! I don't know." Sometimes the younger generation frustrated him. Even though he was only 45, he was glad he wasn't 25 again.

"I just wondered what you read into Dan's motives."

"I think that someone has convinced him to leave our church and that someone has a lot to gain at our loss."

Jeff shook his head. All day yesterday he wondered how much money the church would lose, but he didn't think it would look right if he asked Marilyn to let him see the financial records like Pastor Ben.

"I just can't believe that God would move Dan and Vicki from the church they have been attending for over 20 years."

"Yeah, and take all their thousands of dollars with them."

Pastor Ben replied very sharply. "It's not about money! It's about the will of God!"

Jeff couldn't believe what he just heard. Who was Pastor Ben kidding? It was all about money! He even heard the pastor say so yesterday.

Pastor Ben saw the look on his face and explained. "In reality it is a lot about money, but now I'm concerned about the Knights being deceived and traveling the wrong path. Sometimes the wrong path can lead to hell."

Did I just hear you right? A look of unbelief registered on Jeff's face.

"I don't mean a literal hell. Don't forget that Jonah stayed three days and nights in the belly of the whale. You can't tell me that wasn't hell! That's what happens to a lot of Christians who miss God; they end up in their own personal made hell."

That was about the second or third time he had mention something about hell in connection with the Knights. "Well . . ." Jeff started to get up when the phone rang.

"Hello?"

"This is Pastor Ben. Just a minute . . ." He put his hand over the mouth piece of the phone. "We will continue this later."

That was Jeff's cue that his boss wanted him to leave. Closing the door behind him, he wondered who was on the phone.

Ask Marilyn.

He walked past her desk and went to his office. Now was not the time to be nosey. Pastor Ben would figure out something he could do.

He always did.

CHAPTER 13

Joshua spent the next week writing down ideas for the ministry. His dad called the telephone company to get a couple of new lines into their house with 800 numbers. They were starting with four phones. Almost immediately things came together like a plan that someone had been working on for months instead of days.

Vicki came up with the idea of using the least-liked family room in their house as the location for the Devil Chasers. The location was perfect since they seldom used that room even though there was an outside entrance into the pool area and the inside entrance had big French doors that could be closed for privacy.

Dan hired an architect and a carpenter with a crew that could completely gut the room. He asked the architect to design an office type area for ten to twelve people that had cubbyhole like partitions on top of the desks to give phone warriors privacy. Even though they were starting with only four teenagers, he figured that the ministry would grow and expand with time.

Vicki painted the room a light green and decorated with hunter green and navy blue to give it an atmosphere of authority. On the wall she paid an artist to paint a vine with leaves and fruit as a border in the center of the walls. She added scriptures entwined above and below the wine. She placed a large plaid, hunter and navy, couch in the back of the room by the fireplace. A couple of giant overstuffed hunter-green leather chairs surrounded the couch. She thought it would be a great place for prayer or Bible reading. Two leather navy wing chairs were moved to the front of Joshua's large cherry wood desk.

Joshua opened the front door of his house and started to the intercom when a crew of painters almost ran into him carrying their supplies out the door.

"Oh! Be careful!" Vicki followed behind them and out the door.

He stood aside watching the whole scene wondering what his mom had been up too. He knew that she was probably going to want to show him everything, even though he wasn't that interested in house decorating and design.

"Joshua, come look." She closed the front door. "They just finished the room." She hadn't told the men in her life what she was going to do with the Devil Chasers room. Dan always let her make all the decisions concerning the decorating of their home.

She opened the French doors and Joshua walked through. "Well, what do you think?"

He walked over to the walls and began reading the scriptures on the walls. "'I am the vine, you are the branches. I am the way, the truth, and the life. In My Father's house are many mansions' . . . Mom, this is awesome! I like the way the vine is painted with fruit and the scriptures." He was impressed. The minute he walked into the room, he felt the presence of the Lord. For the first time he really appreciated his mother's concern for details.

"I've always wanted to put God's Words on the walls of our house. I think this has inspired me to redecorate the house."

"Dad's gonna love that idea."

"I've got another surprise. Come with me down the hall."

Vicki opened the door to one of their spare rooms that had been used as a guest room. She removed the bed and put in its place a couple of chairs, a desk, and a couch. At the end of the room, she had the carpenter make one whole wall of shelves.

"What's this?"

"This is the Devil Chasers special room for study of the Word or prayer. I guess you could say it is kind of a break room. I've got a refrigerator, a microwave and a table and chairs on order."

Joshua went over to the shelves where a brand new stereo unit sat. She already bought a bunch of tapes for worship and study. *Leave it to my mom to think of a break room.*

"Maybe later we can build on to the family room and put this room closer to the phones. But for now . . ."

"Mom, I think this is more than enough. Did you talk to a printer?"

"Yes. I got some ideas to go over with you. Mr. Gottman had hundreds of different designs to choose from. I told him that we would come over tomorrow after you looked as these." She took him to her study which was located close to them, by no coincidence, where she had left the catalogues on her couch.

Joshua picked up one of the catalogues and flipped through it. "How much is all this costing?"

"Don't worry about the cost. Dad's paying for everything. I thought about 2,000 cards would get you started."

"Lincoln High has over 2,000 students."

"We can order more. That was just the initial order." She sat down on the couch. "Are you excited about next Monday?"

"It seems to be happening so fast."

"When the Lord moves, you've got to be ready to move with Him."

"I still can't get over the church's reaction. Does it bother you that so many people think we are missing the will of God?" Joshua sat next to his mother.

"It only bothers me that no one from our church has joined our morning prayer group." She felt like Pastor Ben and Linda had influenced every one to stay away from them as a form of punishment.

"Mom, I don't think they liked our name."

"It's more than the name, Joshua. When your Dad and I first married, we didn't believe that committed Christians should have money." She closed the book. "I know we've told you all this before. I've prayed for so many bull-headed . . . uh . . . traditionally thinking Christians that their spiritual eyes would open. I pray constantly that they would see how bound they are thinking about money through old traditional ways. Riches are a by-product of a commitment to the Word of God. It is still hard to believe that 25 years later some Christians won't receive the prosperity message, but they sure want our money!"

He told her that it seemed to him that money was a hidden agenda in all the objections for them leaving both the church and the school.

"It's not just money, Joshua. The Lord revealed to me a few months ago that a spirit of Christianity controls many of our organized churches. The doctrines of demons fill the pews of our churches in the minds of Christians and most of them don't have a clue! Your Dad has decided to resign tonight at the church board meeting."

She sounded a like one of the girls on his team. "I wondered when he was going to tell them." He made a mental note to pray for his mom.

"When did he tell you?"

"Last night, he said that the Lord told him to cut his fleshly ties with the church."

"It's almost too hard to leave our church."

"Mom, how can you and Dad not realize how traditional thinking could destroy this ministry before we even have a chance to get it going?"

"We know that Joshua. We have prayed and interceded for the pastors and people in our church for many years. It's not easy to break ties."

"You're acting like Samuel did when God told him to stop mourning over Saul. I don't understand why he couldn't just stop thinking about Saul especially since he disobeyed God and he kept trying to kill David?"

"That's because you didn't have a personal interest in Saul like Samuel did and that goes with your connection with our church. You don't have the same emotional connection that we do."

"I know that you were strong supporters of starting the school and that you convinced many members of our congregation to lend their physical and financial support." His Mom was very dedicated in volunteer work at the school. He wondered if she would stop helping them now since they were going to quit.

"We might have stayed at our church if, oh well . . . I don't want to think about that right now."

It was hard for him not to be upset with the people at that church. He'd been hearing her cry a lot in their prayer room. Personally, he was excited about leaving especially because he didn't have very many close friends in his youth group.

"I was thinking today about designing some note pads of different colors that designate different prayer requests." She deliberately changed the subject. "You know like white for salvation, red for applying the Blood, green for healing, and blue for miscellaneous."

"Good, idea." He stood to leave her office. "When can we get started?"

"You can start the count down after today."

Now that was something he could get excited about.

‡ ‡ ‡

After dinner that night, Joshua and his parents continued with their recently formed habit of praying and confessing scriptures over the new ministry. They applied the Blood of Jesus to anything remotely connected to the ministry building the foundation for the Devil Chasers in the spiritual realm. As they prayed, angels were busy constructing the communication tower linking their house between heaven and earth, and the Holy Spirit's headquarters on earth. Joshua heard the Lord telling him during prayer that it was very important to establish a prayer link that the devil and his evil kingdom could not destroy.

Dan led the way as the head of the family. "Lord God, we pray for the special warriors of the end times and the ones called for The Devil Chasers phone ministry. Give them the spirit of wisdom and revelation in the knowledge of Jesus and Your Word. Let their eyes and ears be opened to the understanding of the spiritual war taking place. Let them know what the hope of their calling is, and what the riches of the glory in His inheritance are toward them. In all the phone calls, let young warriors speak forth in boldness and Your power and with the anointing of the Holy Spirit to break the yoke of bondage."

"Let us understand that Jesus has put all things under our feet and that we are the head of all principalities, powers, mights and dominions on this earth as we exercise our authority over the devil," Joshua prayed.

They exercised the law of binding and losing as Dan prayed, "Kingdom of darkness, we take authority over you and bind you from interfering with the formation of this ministry. We bind any evil spirit you assign to the Devil Chasers phone warriors. Cease and desist from all maneuvers against us. Jesus said what we bind on earth is bound in heaven. What we loose on earth is loosed in heaven. We bind the forces of evil around this ministry and loose the angels of God to interfere in the operations of the devil. We apply the Blood of Jesus over the phone warriors."

"Jesus is Lord over the Devil Chasers," Vicki declared.

"Demons cease and desist from your maneuvers against our son and his partners."

"The Blood of Jesus comes against you demons."

Dan, Vicki, and Joshua walked all around the family room laying hands on the furniture, walls and phones. They anointed everything with oil. They prayed over the smallest details like the printing of the cards and the colored note pad paper.

"We apply the Blood of Jesus over the cards being printed. We bind you demons from touching anything to hinder the printing or the date to receive them."

"We bind demons from touching the phone lines. We call them free from your hindrances kingdom of darkness. The Devil Chasers dwell in the secret place, the Blood Covenant, and the shadow or defense protects our children!" Vicki declared.

"We command you in the Name of Jesus to loose the eyes and ears of the young people that will be calling on these phone lines. You are a liar devil and you can't have the teens of Lincoln High School," Dan declared.

"We call all teens to salvation from the north, the south, the east, and the west of this city and schools," Joshua added. "Be saved! Be healed! Be delivered!"

"Jesus is Lord over Lincoln High School and all the public schools in our city!" Joshua declared.

"Greater is he in us, than he that is in the world."

"No weapon that is formed against the Devil Chasers shall prosper. Every tongue that shall rise against us, we shall condemn."

"Thank you Lord, that we are delivered from the power of darkness, and are translated into the kingdom of the Your dear Son."

"We proclaim the Lord's will over the Devil Chasers."

"We are victorious! We are more than conquerors through Jesus Christ our Lord," Joshua declared over and over.

"Jesus, our elder brother, made an open show of you devil! He spoiled your goals and intentions with the human race. We intend to do the same thing.

We spoil your plans with the teenagers who are going to call the prayer line!" Dan declared as they finished their nightly ritual.

In between declaring in English and speaking in their heavenly language, Vicki heard herself speaking in a forceful manner. Sometimes she would hear the English interpretation in her mind and other times she didn't have a clue what she was saying. As she prayed, she believed by faith that they were praying perfect prayers according to the will of the Holy Spirit.

Every day, the intercessory prayer group prayed in the family room and special prayer room in the Knights' house. Vicki was excited that God's plans were being guaranteed by the law of agreement. Day and night prayer was ascending into the throne room of God.

The angels were busy collecting all the prayers and delivering them as sweet odors in vials to the throne room. A special bowl held them until the day the angels could release them against the works of the devil.

Later that night as he was studying the Bible, Joshua saw an open vision of satan's kingdom built out of straw and stubble. He saw a great field of ripe wheat standing tall and strong when a powerful wind of the Holy Spirit swirled around the stalks and blew down houses and walls all over the field.

He heard the Lord say, *when My anointing mixes with the prayers of the saints, a great spiritual force is released and it overcomes any work of the devil and his kingdom. Anyone who builds his house upon the rock of My Word, builds a Kingdom that the evil forces cannot pull down or destroy.*

Then, he saw the communication link being established between heaven and earth over his house. After knocking and entering his parents' room just before they were to go to sleep, he told them of the vision.

"Where did you see it?" Dan asked.

"Come here, Dad," he excitedly walked over to the French doors and opened them to go outside.

Dan got out of bed and put on his robe by the chair. Vicki followed him.

As Joshua looked up and through the arbor that protected the balcony he saw a beautiful clear sky with twinkling stars. Through the open end of one side of the balcony, he could see the huge roof over the main part of the house. He pointed to it and said to them, "There, it is over that part of the house."

His parents looked and all they could see was the clear sky and roof shingles. Normal things they would expect to see with natural eyes.

"Can you see it now?" Dan asked.

"Yes."

"Describe it," Vicki said.

He tried to think of English words that could possibly describe what he was seeing. "I see hundreds of angels." He looked around the house. "The angels that guard and protect are standing shoulder to shoulder all around the perimeter of our property right now."

"What do they look like?" Vicki smiled.

"They are dressed in white, with swords hanging from their sides. They are different sizes and shapes, but mostly tall. There are hundreds of smaller angels working on this crystal tower structure that is reaching far into the sky."

Joshua leaned over the balcony to see if he could see an end of it.

Vicki gasped and grabbed for him. "Be careful Joshua!"

"Don't worry!" Joshua grabbed onto a vine and leaned as far as he could. "I don't see the end to this tower that they are building."

"What did they call it?"

"I heard several angels talk about a communication link that they were establishing between heaven and earth."

That gave Vicki an idea. She went back into her room to get her Bible.

"Where is Mom going?" Joshua looked back just in time to see her leave.

Dan shook his head. "I don't know."

She came out reading a passage in Genesis 28. She looked up at Joshua still watching from the balcony. "Why don't you go outside to see and hear what they are doing?"

"Okay."

"Come back here when you can no longer see what's going on." She called after him as she sat in her lounge chair in her room and searched the Word.

Dan could tell that the Lord was leading her to read a certain passage in the Bible. He went over and got his Bible and sat at a chair close to hers.

"You found what Joshua is seeing?"

"Yes. This is fascinating."

"Where?"

"Genesis 28."

Dan turned to the passage in the book written by Moses long ago. He did not have a clue about what she found.

"Look at verse 12."

Dan read it out loud. "Then he dreamed, and behold, a ladder was set up on the earth, and its top reached to heaven; and there the angels of God were ascending and descending on it." He looked at her. "You think that this is what Joshua is seeing now?"

"I think it's possible! What else could Moses call the thing that Jacob saw in his dream but a ladder? Doesn't the description seem to indicate something like a modern day tower for electrical lines or telephone lines?"

Dan reread the passage trying to imagine the ladder that Jacob saw.

Joshua came back into their bedroom. "The vision stopped, but before it did I heard two angels talking and one of them said that our prayers have almost finished this link from the house of God through the heavenlies to the gateway of heaven."

"They said those exact words?" Vicki could hardly believe what she heard Joshua say.

"Yes. They said that this gateway was going to provide a direct link as a highway between the Devil Chasers ministry and the throne room of God. They definitely called it a gateway. I looked up and at one point I could see a porthole open. It looked like clouds were swirling around this opening. As I strained to see what was happening, I saw a multi-colored stone archway at the top of the structure and a scene straight from heaven stared back at me."

"What kind of scene?" Dan asked.

"You know a sparkling, beautiful kind of blue-green sky with green meadows and multi-colored flowers and people in white waving at me."

"People or angels?" Vicki asked.

"They could have been either."

Dan and Vicki continued reading the story from Genesis.

Joshua read verse 17 out loud. "And he was afraid and said, 'How awesome is this place! This is none other that the house of God, and this is the gate of heaven!'"

"Did what you see sound like maybe what Jacob saw?" Vicki asked.

"Maybe. The communication tower that I saw could have been described like the ladder that Jacob saw." He couldn't wait to meditate on the passage.

"Why do you suppose that the Lord wants Joshua to have this spiritual insight?" Dan asked.

"Dan, read what the Lord told Jacob."

"And behold, the Lord stood above it and said: "I am the Lord God of Abraham your father and the God of Isaac; the land on which you lie I will give to you and your descendants. Also your descendants shall be as the dust of the earth; you shall spread abroad to the west and the east, to the north and the south; and in you and in your seed all the families of the earth shall be blessed. Behold I am with you and will keep you wherever you go, and will bring you back to this land; for I will not leave you until I have done what I have spoken to you."

"I have this sense that Joshua's calling has something to do with fulfilling the Lord's promise to Abraham and his descendants," Vicki told him quietly.

A peace came over the three of them as a breeze softly flowed around them. The presence of the Lord caused them to sit in quiet awe meditating as they praised the Lord quietly in silence.

CHAPTER 14

Joshua and his team were eating lunch at the Hut. More than two weeks had passed since their first meeting at his house. The Hut was always full of young people, because it was located a couple of blocks from the school. As soon as the lunch bell sounded everyone ran as fast as they could to save a booth.

"If you think this is full now, you should see it on Friday and Saturday evening," Mose noticed Joshua looking all around him like he was feeling crowded.

The four of them could hardly hear each other talk.

"When did you say the cards are going to be ready?" Kellie was putting ketchup on her fries and looking at Joshua from across the booth.

Joshua raised his eyebrows indicating he couldn't hear Kellie's question. Raising her voice and shouting, she repeated her question.

"My mom is picking me up after school today and we're going to check on them. They should be ready next week some time."

"I can't wait to see them!" Hannah squealed with delight.

"Hey! I want to go with you!" Mose decided.

"Yeah! We wanna go too!" Kellie and Hannah nodded their head in agreement.

"Uh, my mom is checking me out early from school."

"How are we going to hand these cards out?" asked Hannah drumming her fingernails on her can of diet Coke and watching them stuff their faces with fries and hamburgers oozing with ketchup and pickles and onions! She breathed out loud and looked at her diet drink. She was trying to lose some extra pounds.

"I've got some ideas," Mose put his hamburger down. "How about sticking them in lockers?"

"I thought about that," answered Joshua as he cut the lettuce in his chef salad. "But I don't want to have to clear it with my new principal after my first day of school, so I think we better hand them out one-by-one."

"How about our youth group?" Hannah tried to think of something else besides eating. She had started going with Kellie to the youth meetings a couple of months ago.

"I think that is a great idea!" Kellie agreed.

The smell of the salty French fries was getting to Hannah. "Can I have a couple?"

"Sure Hannah, I'm not that hungry," Kellie said as she passed her the plate of fries.

"We all should keep extra cards with us and hand them out as the Holy Spirit leads us," Joshua instructed.

"How about putting them on bulletin boards around school?" Mose had put some serious time into thinking about how they were going to get their phone ministry started.

"That will work, because all the other clubs in school get to announce their clubs." Being a member of the Student Council, she reminded him that all clubs, religious or secular, got the same treatment at the high school as long as they were operated and run by students.

"So what else are we going to do?" Mose' words were muffled as he stuffed fries in his mouth.

Joshua told them about his idea for the weekend.

"Cool," said Hannah

Mose choked on the fries in his mouth and sputtered for a few seconds coughing and gagging.

"If you can clear it with your parents let's make it an all night thing starting on a Friday night and ending Saturday. My mom will stay with you girls upstairs during the night and my dad will stay downstairs with us guys," suggested Joshua after Mose told everyone he was okay.

"How about inviting our parents to come?" asked Kellie.

"Hey, that's a good idea. But, let me clear it with my mom before we make any more plans." Joshua thought he better get permission first.

"When are we officially going to open the phone lines?" Hannah asked as she wiped the ketchup off her chin. She finished the whole plate of fries by herself.

"Hopefully within a week or two. I'm going to work on a schedule of manning the phone lines for you this weekend," Joshua replied.

"Hey Joshua, I was thinking about a scripture motto."

"Like the three musketeers . . . 'all for one and one for all' kind of thing?" asked Hannah.

Mose glared at Hannah. "I'm serious. We should have a scripture theme that we say over the phone with every caller."

Joshua thought of a scripture. "Do you have one in mind?"

Mose reached for his notebook on the floor and pulled out a piece of paper. "It just so happens that I have an idea for the Devil Chasers creed written down." He looked up to see if he had their attention.

"We're listening," Joshua said.

Mose sang the rap he wrote.

We are, the Devil Chasers,
Working on this earth
as evil erasers.
In His name we cast out the devil.
No fooling around! We're on the level.
In a new language we speak
fighting evil spirits making'em weak.
when they try to lie and steal
we take away their power to kill.
Laying hands on the sick
Knowing they recover quick.
We trust in Jesus Christ God's son
The Lord of glory, the only One.

"Hey, that sounds great!" Hannah hit him on the arm playfully.

"I like it to," Kellie laughed.

"Can I take that with me and get Mr. Gottman to print our creed on the back of the cards?" Joshua was impressed with Moses' creation.

"Is it too late?" Mose replied with enthusiasm hardly believing that Joshua liked his rap.

"Well, if it is then we can get them on the next bunch."

"We've got a name, we have a scriptural creed in rap form and after this weekend we will have cards and the phones hooked up. Praise the Lord! I can hardly . . ." Kellie stopped as she looked at her watch and stood. "Hey! Guys! We gotta go. I don't want to be late and I have a longer way to go than you guys."

They all stood but Hannah. "Hey, Mose, you didn't finish your hamburger and Joshua, you left some of your salad!" She grabbed a napkin and started stuffing fries into it.

Kellie rolled her eyes. "It's beyond me how someone as skinny as she is can eat so much."

"That's why she is always on a diet!" Mose said with a laughing smile.

"Hey watch it! I know you guys are talking about me," she hurried to catch up with them.

‡ ‡ ‡

Chemah and metraloas sat in the big oak tree down the street again looking at the Knights' house. Satan ordered chemah to stay with metraloas to give eye witness accounts concerning the changes occurring at the Knights' house. The build up of warring angels was not a temporary tactic as chemah had hoped it was.

"I told you what it's like trying to torment and harass the Knights." For a long time he had wanted to get rid of this cursed assignment. "This family is too weird! I cannot come against them since they are always praying and quoting scriptures. They only turn on their TV to watch Christian stations and Christian movies!" He spit out the sentence with disgust. "Have you ever heard of a family like them? He looked over at chemah who was deliberately not talking to him. "How about reassigning me to the pits?"

"Where's that bat that has been your shadow?" He ignored his question.

Metraloas shrugged. He hadn't seen him in a week or two. *It looks like the warring angels are building a major offensive headquarters with a communication tower reaching into heaven.* He couldn't understand why chemah hadn't perceived what was going on in the invisible realm of the Kingdom of God.

"Shut up! I heard that thought!"

He glared at chemah with hate in his eyes. He had given up a year ago, because he knew that the Knight family had established firm habits that he could never break. Some stupid demons and lower class androids were idiots when it came to knowing when to give up, but this was the first time he ever saw a higher spirit act so ignorant.

Chemah refused to let metraloas know the reason that he couldn't reassign him. Lately, his divisions of demons have been failing their assignments. The *agony of defeat* was a phrase the demons made up after having to face satan with news of failure.

"What do we do?" asked metraloas. He had his own plan that called for him to act ignorant and stupid around chemah.

"I don't know, yet!" Chemah slapped metraloas out of the tree again. "Don't ask me any questions!"

Metraloas got up from the ground and gave chemah the evil eye. Lightning had begun to spray from the firework display over the house as they turned around suddenly and stared at the display.

"If they continue building this prayer communication network, big spiritual eruptions are going to take place over the heavenlies surrounding the

Knights' home."

Then you won't be able to hide your defeat any longer. "How many days can they keep praying for four or five hours?"

"They can pray indefinitely without the spirit of division at work among them! There have been a few humans that have committed themselves to the fight faithfully, but when there is a group, we can always find someone that will start thinking out of their flesh and provide openings for us to cause them to fall!"

"These Christians are not ignorant to our methods of deception. Before I got this assignment, I thought humans were too stupid and blinded to know about the true battle that is going on around them."

"Most of them are stupid! They cannot see into our spiritual domain nor do they understand. You have the misfortune to be assigned to the minuscule few humans who really live by God's Word."

"How can we fight the Knights?"

Chemah angrily knocked him in the head with his hand. "You know what to do, fool! Watch them until they make a mistake and then you report it to us." *This android is as stupid as they get.* "Maybe you need an adjustment in your brain because you're so old."

I need to be reassigned.

"I heard that!"

"Why don't we just walk away from them and never look back?"

"Because! We can't walk away from this assignment."

Metraloas wouldn't let it go. "I don't understand. If the Knights are operating under the true force of faith, why can't I be reassigned?"

"You never know when humans can be forced through trials and tribulations to give up their faith."

Read my reports then you would know if this was the real faith or not. "This assignment is lost."

"Shut up, fool! Don't ever let me hear you blaspheme like that again!" chemah turned red and fire spewed from his weapon hand.

Metraloas barely missed getting burned. He was tired of taking physical abuse from the kingdom of darkness and the Kingdom of Light. Swords cutting and butting him from the angels of the Lord causing him pain. Evil beings from the kingdom of darkness slapping, hitting, buffeting and burning him had increased his pain adding torture from both sides. He hated being an android that was created by satan.

"We've got to formulate some kind of plan before we inform lord satan of these developments."

"How about I follow a female coming to the meetings and see if there is a link to any evil spirit from a generation curse in her family?"

Chemah eyed him suspiciously. "Report to me when you find something . . . and metraloas, this is your last chance. Fail at this and it is all over." He disappeared into one of the gateways putting down the irresistible urge to wipe him out forever.

Metraloas turned his eyes toward the Knights' house after watching chemah disappear. He settled down to wait. The next time the ladies came to the prayer meeting, he would be ready to follow his prey. Hopefully the path would lead back to hell.

‡ ‡ ‡

Joshua and Vicki exited the printer's office after school satisfied that everything was going as scheduled. The cards would be ready to distribute sometime next week. By the following Friday they would have a live phone number and a new room ready for action.

Getting into his mom's white Cadillac, Joshua asked her if they had any plans for the weekend before they officially opened.

"I don't think so. I was hoping that we could relax and get ready for the first week that you start answering phones."

"Well, I was thinking about a weekend sleep-over with the gang. We could pray and fast together before that big day."

"I'm not sure about having both boys and girls over," Vicki hesitated. "We don't want any gossip starting about . . ."

"I was wondering about that when Kellie had an idea that maybe we could invite the parents over, too. You know, the girls could have the upstairs and we could have the pool house."

"That's an idea. It is short notice though." Vicki looked over at Joshua sitting in the passenger seat. "It would be a great way to kick off the Devil Chasers," Vicki thought it sounded like a teenage idea, but it sounded good.

"It would be a good way to get the parents involved and for you and dad to get to know them."

"Okay. Go ahead, call and invite them."

Vicki looked at her son with love and admiration. The Lord was so good to give them a special child, especially since they were told they couldn't have any children. The reports didn't agree with the Word of God, so she chose to believe God and ignore the negative report. As she sought the Lord several years for a child, one day she learned about Hannah's prayer in the Bible. She told the Lord if He would give her a son, she would give him back to Him for His service. God blessed them with a son, Joshua.

They had brought Joshua up in strict care with the Word of God and prayer living a life totally dedicated to the things of the Lord. In all that they had done, God had richly blessed them. Dan's law practice was very successful and that made it possible for Vicki to quit working after Joshua was born. She made it her mission in life to raise Joshua as a man of God.

Thank you Lord, she thought, *we are living proof that there is a place in the Lord where the kingdom of darkness can't touch your children and that the blessing of the Lord follows His Word.* She heard an evangelist one time call that place of living in the Lord in victory above the snakeline.

"Lord, we abide in the secret place, the Blood Covenant, and under the shadow of the Almighty," Vicki said out loud as she drove down the road thanking Him for their Covenant protection.

Joshua looked over at her and began quoting the protection Psalms 91 with her, "He that dwells in the secret place of the most High shall abide under the shadow of the Almighty."

"I will say of the Lord, He is my refuge and my fortress: my God; in Him will I trust." Vicki quoted the next verse after him. It was a habit she had started with Joshua when he was just five years old.

"Surely, He shall deliver me from the snare of the fowler, and from the noisome pestilence."

"He shall cover me with His feathers and under His wings I shall trust: His truth shall be my shield and armor."

"I will not be afraid for the terror by night; nor for the arrow that flies by day." Joshua shouted.

"Nor for the epidemic that walks in darkness; nor for the destruction that destroys at noonday."

"A thousand shall fall at my side, and ten thousand at my right hand; but destruction shall not come near me," Joshua continued quoting.

"Only with my eyes shall I behold and see the reward of the wicked."

"Because you have made the Lord, my refuge, the most High, your habitation . . ."

Vicki spoke with authority, "There shall no evil befall you, neither shall any plague come near your house."

"For He shall give His angels charge over you, to keep you in all your ways."

"They shall bear you up in their hands, to keep you from hurting your foot against a stone."

"You shall tread upon the lion and the snake: the young lion and the dragon shall you trample under your feet."

She thought about the time as a little toddler that he used to pretend that he was stomping the devil's head. "Because you have set your love upon Me, therefore will I deliver you: I will set you on high because you have known My name."

"You shall call upon Me, and I will answer you: I will be with you in trouble; I will deliver you, and honor you."

"With long life will I satisfy you, and show you my salvation," Vicki concluded.

Stopping at a red light, she looked at Joshua, "How many times have we quoted Psalm 91 together?"

"To many to count . . . Mom, the light turned green."

That was a quick light, thought Vicki.

Instantly a sequence of events flashed like a picture in Joshua's mind as an open vision. He saw a blue truck speeding down a street, running through a red light and crashing into the driver's side of a white car. He turned to tell his mother what he saw with his spiritual eyes when his natural eyes connected with a truck coming toward them. His spirit communicated to his mind quickly even though it seemed like slow motion. *The car looks like Mom's,* he thought as he realized that the truck wasn't going to stop. *Oh no!*

"MOM!" yelled Joshua as he pointed to her side window . . .

. . . Kientay and Kara were sitting in the back seat enjoying Psalm 91 being quoted out loud when suddenly they received communication from the Holy Spirit.

The driver of a blue truck directed by a demon a block away is going to run a red light and hit the Knights' car with the intent to kill them. In a few seconds Joshua and Vicki could be standing at the entrance to paradise without intervention. Go!

Immediately, they flew into action. The Holy Spirit demanded total evasive action against this plot by the ruler of darkness, chemah and no injury or property loss was to occur because of the Knight's consistent daily confession of supernatural protection that activated their Covenant.

Chemah followed the Cadillac and saw an opportunity to strike. He summoned one of the demons that possessed the driver of a truck about to stop at an intersection opposite the Knight vehicle to take control away from the human. He wanted Joshua dead.

Spirit of drunkenness, take over the driver of the truck and smash the Knight car to——! chemah demanded through the evil spirit communications network, the graveline.

Kientay flew outside of the car to position himself between the truck and Vicki's side of the car. Kara was to make sure Vicki was safe. Natsar appeared faster than a speeding bullet and joined Kientay. They both held up their shields. Milchamah joined Kara as she positioned herself above Kientay and Natsar to guide the truck to a stop without killing the driver. Other angels were given orders to position themselves to protect any innocent bystanders.

Warring angels fought in the heavenlies to keep demonic spirits from interfering with the orders the Holy Spirit had decreed. Everyone was in place and prepared for this split second plot of evil. Kientay held his sword up and faced the truck gaining speed toward the Knight car. His sword glowed with the anointed fire of the Holy Spirit.

"Get out of the way you —— —— angel!" The maniac crazed devil screamed and glared at Kientay with a determined look to kill.

"The Knight family dies!" shouted chemah. His evil hormones flooded his veins as anticipation excited him about the crash.

"No evil shall befall the Knight family in the name of the Lord!" shouted Kientay as he moved the shield of faith in front of Vicki and Joshua.

"The Knights live by the sword of the Word!" Kara shouted as a light-piercing sword appeared in her hand and she took a warrior stance.

"Oh!——!" Cursed chemah as his eyes filled with the reflection of many warring angels. He knew that the Spirit of Faith had intervened and His plan would fail, but he couldn't stop the course of action he had started . . .

. . . Vicki turned her head to see what Joshua was pointing at. She saw a blur that looked like a blue truck fly over the top of their car. "Jesus!" Vicki screamed and instinctively hit her brakes as she ducked her head.

The driver of the car behind Vicki saw the truck and took her eyes off Vicki's car and didn't see that she hit her breaks. Not able to stop in time, she ran into Vicki's bumper. The impact pushed the white Cadillac in the opposite direction of the truck as it seemed to smash into a light pole. The actual time it took for all this to take place was seconds. When the car stopped, Joshua got out of the car and ran over to the driver of the truck.

"Did you see that!" someone screamed.

"Oh, Jesus!" someone else said.

Several people ran to the truck that was turned on its side. The driver's side of the truck was smashed and glass shattered everywhere.

"He's dead!" screamed a lady as she watched the truck land on its side, skidding to a stop.

Joshua made it to the truck first and tried to see into the cab. The front windshield was completely gone and his door was crushed against the curb. The man still had his seat belt on. The only way out was through the windshield. “Are you okay?” he asked scanning the inside of the cab to see if the steering wheel or anything had pinned him in.

“I think so.” The injured man tried to undo his seat belt. “Oh ——! My arm is broke,” he cursed through clenched teeth.

Joshua looked at his arm and saw that it was in a weird angle. “In Jesus name, bone in this arm be healed!” He grabbed the man’s arm and popped the bone in place.

“What the ——?” The man shouted out with pain and cussed when he realized the pain was gone. He looked at Joshua with shock in his eyes.

“Here, take my hand and I’ll help you out.” Joshua stuck out his hand.

As he emerged from the truck everyone started clapping. A siren blared through the noise of the people standing around them and a police car pulled up close to the accident . . .

. . . Natsar and Kientay deflected the truck with the shield of faith. Milchamah with his great warrior strength grabbed on to the truck as it flew into the air. He glowed with infused power by the earlier prayers of Dan and easily stopped the force of the sliding truck to keep the driver from being smashed to death by the impact and sudden stop.

Kara held the seat belt of the driver to keep it from snapping and throwing the driver out the windshield. Chroni positioned himself behind Vicki’s car to keep the car behind her from smashing her fender on impact when hitting Vicki’s car and causing a three car pile up.

Immediately, demons came out of the truck driver with fierce anger and started fighting Kara. Milchamah flew over to help her with his sword.

“Give it up! You are defeated by the Word of the Lord!” shouted Milchamah as he stabbed the demon and green bloody gunk spewed out. Leaking his power source, the android disintegrated and vanished.

“Thanks for the help!” shouted Kara as she fought with another demon that came out of the truck driver. Swords were swinging and clanging everywhere. The anointed swords overcame all opposing weapons.

THWART! Milchamah cut off a demon’s head. It rolled down the street. “You have more strength than you realize!” shouted Milchamah at Kara to encourage her.

Kara stabbed the evil spirit in the side and started slicing him in pieces. “You are so right!” She was amazed at her strength and accuracy, since she rarely practiced using the warrior weapons. “They’re falling like flies!” She proclaimed as power surged through her angel veins. She looked at her sword. “It’s like demolishing a machine.”

“You are!” Milchamah informed her.

The other angels fought demons that gathered from all quarters of the city at chemah's command. Not realizing the strength of the Knights' confession of the Word daily, the battle was futile. Chemah let his anger overcome a wise decision to retreat. Because he tried to reinforce the battle scene with more evil spirits, more of satan's android army was destroyed causing greater harm to the kingdom of darkness.

The warring angels continued quoting Psalm 91. "He has given us charge over them and we have lifted the Knight family above this evil with the power of the voice of the Lord!" shouted Natsar.

"All glory to the Lord of Glory!" yelled Chroni.

"This is fun!" laughed Kara as an android disintegrated before her eyes.

It was an overwhelming victory for the Knight family. The angels bowed and raised their swords to the Lord of Host and gave Him a shout of glory!

Chemah turned his head in disgust and started to dematerialize. He didn't want to see any more defeat. Satan would be furious when he learned of his defeat.

Milchamah looked up just in time to see him try to leave. "Should we?"

"Yes! We should!" shouted Natsar.

They chased him in the spirit realm all the way to one of the gateways to hell, releasing several arrows into his backside.

"Remember this defeat the next time you decide to attack the Knight family."

They both shouted praises to the Lord God.

CHAPTER 15

"Please clear the way folks." The police officer expected to see some dead bodies or at least some critically hurt people from the look of the cars involved. After he checked everyone involved in the accident, he only found a few scratches.

"Can someone tell me what happened?" He took out his note pad to record what was said. Everyone talked at the same time. "Please, please, one at a time. I only have two ears."

"My son and I were driving east on Main Street, when a truck driving south ran a stoplight and hit, excuse me, looked like he was going to hit us," explained Vicki.

"What is your name Ms . . . ?"

"I am Vicki Knight and this is Joshua, my son."

"Okay and which car is yours?" asked the officer.

Vicki pointed to the white Cadillac over at the other corner.

"Now, who owns this truck?"

"I do," said the man as he rubbed his arm and stared at Joshua. He was stunned from the events that had just taken place.

"Your name is?"

"Jerry Lake. I . . ." the man started getting dizzy.

The officer looked up as he heard the ambulance sirens about a block away. He put his hand on Jerry's arm that should have been broken. "Take it easy. Sit in the ambulance when it gets here and let the medics check you over. Looks like I have plenty of people to talk to."

"Officer, officer!"

"Who are you?"

"I'm the red Mazda behind the white Cadillac. My name is Mrs. Kim Moore."

"Okay, what did you see?"

"You're not going to believe it!"

"Try me lady, I've heard it all." He had taken plenty of accident reports before. They all said the same thing.

"We were going east like she said on a green light, when this truck ran a red light from the driver's side."

"Okay, your light was green." He noted that down. *Driver of white Cadillac had right of way with green light.* "Go ahead," he looked up, "What happened next?"

"When he should have plowed into her car," Mrs. Moore pointed at Vicki. "He flew over the top of or her car!"

Truck flew over top of. . . "What did you say?" The officer stopped writing and stared at the lady talking to him. He thought he heard her say that the truck went airborne.

"You heard her right, officer," said a bystander. "My whole family walked out of the bank standing at the corner waiting for a green light, when we all saw this truck flying in the air."

Now I've heard everything! He had heard of the flying nun, but never a flying truck! *These people must need medical attention.*

The officer casually walked over to Vicki's car. Circling it slowly he looked for damage that showed she had been hit from behind. He got down on his knees to look under the car and saw a perfect showroom underside. He walked around to the front of the car and looked for a dent from the light pole that she hit. He couldn't find a scratch, but he found a huge dent on the light pole. On the red Mazda the front bumper was caved in and both lights knocked out.

He made himself look one more time. How was it going to look on his report that the white car was totally void of even a scratch, and the truck that supposedly hit the car was totaled? The officer scratched his head. *Something's not right here.*

"Let me get this straight. That blue truck ran a red light while the white Cadillac was crossing the intersection, but instead of hitting your car, which is the normal action when one car inters into another one's path," he stared intently into her eyes. "That truck flew into the air over the car and landed across the street on its side, with no major damage to anybody?"

"That's correct sir," Vicki said.

The policeman shook his head and walked over to the ambulance to talk to the man from the truck. "Does he have any injuries?" He asked the medic.

"He checks out okay. A few bruises and a couple of minor scratches. I don't think he needs to go to the hospital, unless he wants to."

The medic pulled the policeman's arm and walked a few paces away from everyone to whisper in his ear confidentially, eyeing Joshua while he spoke. "This is a strange one. The man claims his arm was broken and that the kid (he nodded over at Joshua) prayed for him. Says the pain went away instantly and then he could move his arm to get out of the truck."

Oh great! I get all the fruitcakes! “A head injury?”

“I can’t tell for sure.”

The officer walked over to the man sitting in the ambulance still in shock about what had just happened to get his side of the story. “Uh . . . sir, your name is?”

“Jerry Lake.”

“Mr. Lake, can you tell me what happened?”

“I was driving south, about twenty-five miles an hour, when I saw the light turn yellow. I went to put on my brakes, like I normally would, you know nothing fancy just move your foot from the accelerator to the brake pedal. I’ve done it thousands of times before.”

“Okay, so you didn’t brake.” He let out a sigh. This accident was strange and the explanations were taking too long. “What happened next?”

“I’m trying to tell you when I tried to raise my foot, it wouldn’t move!”

His foot wouldn’t move? “You couldn’t move your foot?” *Give me a break! Does everyone connected with his accident have a brain injury?*

“Believe me officer, I tried. When I broke loose of whatever was holding my foot down, I couldn’t push the break. It was like the brake froze or something. Then the next thing I felt was the truck being gunned full force. I looked at the accelerator and it was being punched, only not by me.”

“Say that again?” He couldn’t believe what he was hearing.

“I said I was driving south . . .”

He angrily interrupted him. “Not the whole story, just the part about the accelerator.” *This guy definitely has a head injury!*

“The accelerator was pushed all the way to the floor, but my foot was on the brake!”

“Sir, I think you’re a little dazed by a head injury. It’s not uncommon for people to hit the accelerator instead of the break when they loose control.”

“I did not lose control of my truck! I am a trained professional truck driver! I know when to hit the breaks or when to hit the accelerator! Instead of plowing into her, I flew over her and missed her completely!”

“What do you think caused that?” The policeman asked sarcastically. *This guy is crazy!* He decided to tell the ambulance driver to take him to the hospital and get his head examined.

“I have no idea!”

“Officer . . . uh . . . I’m sorry, you never told us your name,” Vicki inquired.

“Officer Daniels, Ms. Knight.”

“There is a simple explanation. We are devout believers in Jesus Christ as a miracle working God. Everyday I cover my vehicle with the Blood of

Jesus. That is why our car does not have a scratch on it."

Oh No! Not one of those Jesus freaks. She covers the car in the Blood of Jesus? Who does she think she is?

The Lord opened her spirit ears and she heard what he was thinking. "I'm not a Jesus freak, officer, but I do live my life totally in His Word. Jesus clearly says that if I abide under the shadow of the Almighty, His deliverance and safety net, then He will deliver me from all evil. If you cannot believe me, then believe your own eyes and ears."

This woman must be one of those 'psychic' people I've seen on one of those commercials.

"No, I am not a psychic. I am a woman of God."

"Lady, how are you reading my mind?" An angry spirit rose up inside him coming against Vicki.

"The Holy Spirit is telling me what you are thinking."

"Well, what in the —— is *HE* telling you now?" he spat out sarcastically. His favorite people in the world to hate were Christian people. His mother-in-law topped his list as one of the biggest all time hypocrites in the world!

"Sir, you wouldn't want me to tell the whole world what I just heard and saw in my spirit."

Suddenly, Officer Daniels shook from the inside out. Something strange was happening to him. His pen fell to the ground.

"You are having an affair with a woman named Linda."

"How in the —— did you know about Linda?"

"Officer Daniels I don't get my understanding from hell; I get it from heaven. You better stop listening to the voices you hear, because they are from hell and they are going to take you to hell when you die if you don't accept Jesus. You will not be able to escape from that prison like your last prisoner did."

He shut his mouth and listened to her. *How did she know . . . ?*

"Your wife is a faithful Christian and has been praying for you for 10 years. She suspects you are cheating on her, but she has decided to stay with you so that you won't die and go to hell. She has forgiven you because the Lord Jesus Christ is giving her the strength and power. Repent and accept Jesus Christ as your Savior. If you don't, I see you spending an eternity in hell with burning flames."

Officer Daniels was stunned. His heart was pierced and he fell to his knees crying.

"Repeat after me; Jesus, forgive me of my sins and my committing adultery with Linda."

"Jesus, forgive me of my sins and my committing adultery with Linda."

"Come into my life. I give myself totally to you."

"Come into my life. I give myself totally to you."

"Jesus be the Lord of my life. I renounce satan and his influence over me."

"Jesus be the Lord of my life. I renounce satan and his influence over me."

"Now look at me."

Officer Daniels looked up at Vicki.

"Spirit of adultery, spirit of lying and spirit of rebellion come out of him and do not ever reenter again!"

The spirits resisted. Natsar stood behind the officer and stabbed the head demonic spirit with a sword and demanded that he leave. "I said GO!" Vicki hit the top of the officer's head and he fell over and looked like he was dead.

The Christian people who watched and heard what Vicki did shouted out loud and praised God. Unbelievers gasped in shock not believing what they were hearing and seeing.

"Come out of him, devils!" She commanded them over and over relentlessly to obey her. With each command, Natsar stabbed and cut out each demon.

Another officer walked up behind Vicki. When she turned around, she had the fire of the Holy Spirit in her eyes.

The officer held up his hand and said, "Whoa! Wait a minute," he explained as she looked like she was going to lay hands on him. "I'm a born again Christian. I understand what's happening." He looked down at Officer Daniels who was shaking like a person with a spastic attack. "At least I think I know what is happening."

Grabbing a hold of his arms, he helped Mr. Daniels get up and put him into his police car. He took Daniels' note pad and started reading the notations he had just jotted down. Then he walked back to Vicki. "It looks like his notes cover everything. I'll make sure he gets home to his wife." He looked at Vicki with a misty sparkle in his eyes. "Thank you for obeying the Lord. We've been praying for his salvation."

"God is good. He answers the prayer of faith. Can we leave?" Vicki was charged with supernatural energy.

"Sure, we have your address if there is anything else."

The driver of the wrecker, after hooking up the blue truck, was examining Vicki's car. She heard him say, "I've never seen anything like this in my life!"

Vicki went over to witness to him. Joshua finished talking with Mr. Lake as Mrs. Moore came over to talk to Vicki. Before this wreck, she thought she was a Christian. She wanted to question Vicki to make sure they were both serving the same God. The God she just witnessed acted more like the God of the Bible than the God her pastor talked about every Sunday. She wanted to personally know the God of this woman.

A tall evil spirit, cloaked in a black, hooded robe watched chemah orchestrate the largest defeat of the kingdom of darkness in that area that he could remember. The demonic yellow-red eyes closed as he struggled to keep his composure. The scene before him sickened him.

The black bat landed on the ground in front of the sinister being and transformed himself into a large, ugly black gargoyle with grotesque broken wings. "I am sorry master," the evil spirit begged forgiveness as he lowered his head to grovel in the dirt.

A low rumble greeted him. "Why?"

The gargoyle swallowed as he thought of an explanation.

"Don't think of an answer. Tell me NOW!" He roared like a lion.

A hurricane force of wind swept over the gargoyle and plastered him to the ground. "Chemah was trying to destroy a human family that is erecting a communication tower between earth and heaven." He struggled to speak.

The dark figure fumed as fire and smoke consumed him. "Which family?"

"Dan and Vicki Knight."

"Finish your assignment!" A gust of wind twisted the being out of sight.

The gargoyle stood and shape-shifted back into a bat and flew away.

Dan walked into an empty house. He was in the kitchen getting a glass of tea when his family came home.

"Dad!" Joshua couldn't wait to tell his dad what happened. "Dad!" he yelled as he walked down the hall.

"I'm in the kitchen." Dan put down the pitcher of tea.

Joshua came running in with a smile on his face. "We were just in an accident!"

He saw the smile on his face. "What did you say?"

"We were stopped at an intersection . . ."

"Joshua, slow down," Vicki interrupted as she laid her purse and jacket down on the table and went over to hug and kiss Dan.

Dan looked over Vicki and Joshua. "No one was hurt . . . right?"

"No! Dad, listen!" Joshua was so excited he could hardly contain himself.

"Anyone else hurt?" Dan inquired.

"No." Vicki told him.

"Dad, you gotta hear this!"

"I think the truck driver broke his arm," Vicki interrupted.

"Okay, tell me the whole story." Dan sat at the kitchen table.

Joshua told him all the details of the accident while Vicki started dinner for them. "Then Mom led the police officer to the Lord!"

"Well, that explains why I was led to pray in the Spirit this morning. Court was delayed until this afternoon and I rescheduled a meeting."

"What time was it?" Vicki asked as she removed a casserole from the refrigerator and vegetables for a salad.

"I shut the door to my office around 10:00 a.m. and prayed in the spirit for at least thirty minutes."

Vicki stopped chopping lettuce to hug Dan. "Praise the Lord you listen to Him!" They gathered in a circle in the middle of the kitchen to thank the Lord for their deliverance.

Dan kissed her. "I thank the Lord that you guys are okay."

Vicki went over to check the lasagna in the oven. "We all felt this intense desire to pray in tongues with authority this morning."

"I didn't think I could eat with everything that has happened but," Joshua said smelling the lasagna when she opened the oven door, "I've changed my mind. I'm starved!"

"Spiritual warfare makes me hungry," Vicki told him. She shut the oven door and turned around to give Dan another big hug. "It happened so fast, but you should have seen the look on the policeman's face when I told him he was having an affair!"

"Mom even told the officer the woman's name!"

Dan quoted a memorized scripture from I Corinthians 14: 24–25, "But if all prophesy, and an unbeliever or an uninformed person comes in, he is convinced by all, he is convicted by all. And thus the secrets of his heart are revealed; and so, falling down on his face, he will worship God and report God is truly among you."

Vicki grinned. "I've been asking the Lord to use me in that way."

"The officer sure fell on his face."

"Praise the Lord!" Dan was excited with them, "That's the Word of God in action!"

The lasagna permeated the kitchen with a delicious aroma.

"Be doers of the Word, and not hearers only, deceiving yourselves. The Knights' are doers of the Word of God," Vicki confessed.

"Were you confessing scripture?" asked Dan.

"Our favorite. Psalms 91," she told him.

"Thank the Lord that His Word is sovereign on this planet." Dan was truly grateful that they had learned about speaking scriptures out loud and calling forth protection. There was no doubt in his mind that he would either be at the hospital or morgue right now if it wasn't for the Word of God coming out of their mouth daily.

Vicki told them it would be about thirty more minutes for the lasagna to cook so they could spend some time giving thanks to the Lord for His supernatural help.

The guardian angels joined them in worship with excitement and praise.

‡ ‡ ‡

They just started eating when the front gate buzzed.

Dan looked at Vicki while Joshua went to the intercom system on the wall and answered the caller. "Were you expecting anybody?"

"No." Vicki replied as she stood to follow Joshua.

"I hope Pastor Ben hasn't decided to talk with us again!" Dan put his fork down.

Joshua released the gate to open. "Mom, it's the driver of the truck."

"What truck?"

"You know . . . the guy from the accident."

"What does he want?" Dan stood concerned.

"He wants to talk to Mom," Joshua told him. He waited at the door until the man parked his car and walked up the steps with his family. He opened the door just before they rang the bell.

"I hope we're not disturbing you, but my family and I would like to talk to your mother," stated Jerry Lake.

"Come in," Joshua said leading them into the living room.

Dan and Vicki walked up behind Joshua to greet the visitors.

"Mrs. Knight! I got your address from a policeman at the police station. Excuse me, but this is my wife, Cindy."

"Pleased to meet you," Vicki shook hands with her.

"These are my children, Mindy, Tom, and Heather."

"This is my husband, Dan and of course you met Joshua already. Please, come into the living room." She led them down the hall to their less formal living area.

The Lake family sat on a large floral couch and matching love seat. The living room was elegantly decorated in white, off white, mauve and pink.

A baby grand piano stood in the corner of the room near a grand, stone fireplace.

Even though the room would have normally intimidated the Lake family, Jerry didn't notice. He opened a large manila envelope and handed the contents to Vicki with excitement. "This is an x-ray of my arm that was just taken at the hospital."

Vicki looked at the x-ray that looked like a normal arm bone.

He pointed to the color differences on the picture. "This is where the emergency doctor told me I once had my arm broken in three places. He says that they healed very nicely considering the extent of the damage."

His wife Cindy spoke. "The doctor said it looked like some new bone had grown where it had been previously crushed."

Vicki gave the x-ray to Dan. She waited for them to explain.

Jerry's smile covered his face. "Because of your son, I believe that there is a God. I mean before today I didn't believe in a God!"

"Please sit down." Vicki said.

"I've never ever broken my arm before. When I told that to the doctor, he said that was impossible. We have the proof in black and white. He pointed at the x-ray again and went over the calcification of the bone. He circled those areas saying the bone was enlarged at the breaks."

"When Jerry told him that he had just been in an accident and a boy had prayed over his arm and grabbed it to help get him out of the truck, the doctor didn't believe my husband!" added Cindy.

"Your son prayed. Uh . . . I think what he said was a prayer. But even if I had doubts about my arm, I saw your car."

"Jerry said that your car didn't have one scratch on it," Cindy stated.

"God protects our car with His warring angels," Vicki confirmed.

"I want to know the God you know," he looked Joshua straight into his eyes. Grabbing his wife's hand he added, "And I want my family to know your God."

Inside, Vicki could hardly contain herself. "Do you know anything about Jesus?"

"No. We don't go to church," answered Cindy.

"My dad was an alcoholic and I . . . I am too," Jerry confessed.

Cindy turned her head to look at Jerry. She had never heard him admit he had a problem with alcohol before. Her eyes filled with tears. "We party and go dancing, but lately we've felt such emptiness. I started reading a Bible my sister gave me a year ago."

Jerry shuddered. "Someone upstairs was looking over me."

"We never took time to think about God or anything like that. Nothing has ever happened to us before, until today." Her misty eyes looked at Jerry's as she put her hand on top of his. "I don't know what I would have done if he would have gotten killed today."

"I want my children to know about God. Mindy has a problem with telling the truth, and Tom is drinking and our little one doesn't obey us." Jerry looked at his children and burst out crying, "Can Jesus help us?"

"He wants to very much," answered Vicki. "For God so loved the world that He gave His only Son, Jesus, that whosoever believes in Him should not perish, but have everlasting life."

"That sounds like my sister, she is always talking about Jesus like she knows him personally," Cindy said crying as she opened her purse and took out a couple of tissues to wipe away their tears.

"Jesus died on the cross to pay the price for our sins and our separation from God. God raised him from the dead, defeating the devil like you experienced today, Jerry, even though you couldn't see him with your eyes," Vicki explained to him. "Jesus can give you victory over every thing that is evil in your life."

"I believe in Him now. After what I saw today, I can't deny that Jesus is real. I still don't understand what happened, but I believe that God delivered me and healed me."

Dan reached over to get the Bible off the coffee table and handed it to Vicki. She turned to Romans 6:23 and read, "For the wages of sin is death, but the gift of God is eternal life in Christ Jesus our Lord."

"I have to tell you . . ."

Vicki stopped to listen to him. "Go ahead."

"I've mocked God and laughed at preachers."

"God knows everything you have ever done, but He doesn't condemn you." Then she turned to the tenth chapter of Romans and continued reading, "If you confess with your mouth the Lord Jesus and believe in your heart that God has raised Him from the dead, you will be saved. For with the heart one believes unto righteousness, and with the mouth confession is made unto salvation. For the scripture says, 'whoever believes on Him will not be put to shame.'"

"For," Dan continued, "whoever calls on the name of the Lord shall be saved."

Jerry fell to his knees and cried out to the Lord, "I want to confess Him as my God and get delivered from alcohol!"

Cindy and his children got on their knees with him. They were all crying.

"Father," Vicki stood to place her hands on his head. "We are grateful that You revealed Yourself to the Lake family and revealed their need of a Savior. Satan tried to kill Jerry today, but YOU delivered him," Vicki couldn't stop the emotions that enveloped her and tears came to her eyes. The Spirit's presence was very strong around them. She looked at Dan and with her eyes asked him to lead the family in a prayer of salvation.

"If you will repeat after me, I will help you pray," Dan said.

They nodded yes.

"Jesus forgive me of my sins."

"Jesus forgive me of my sins." They all repeated what Dan told them.

"I recognize I need a savior to set me free from the bondage of sin."

"I recognize I need a savior to set me free from the bondage of sin."

"I accept Jesus Christ as my personal savior."

"I accept Jesus Christ as my personal savior."

"I renounce satan and all his works in my life."

"I renounce satan and all his works in my life."

"Cleanse me with Your Blood."

"Cleanse me with Your Blood."

"You are now set free!"

Joshua moved over to Jerry and said, "I would like to pray to set you free from the generation curse of alcoholism that was passed down to you from your father.""

"Yes! Please! I want to be free from this compulsion that drives me to drink. Streams of tears were falling down Jerry's face, a man known for the hardness of his heart. "I've tried to stop, but . . ."

"Satan, I bind you from all generation curses on the Lake family. Jesus has delivered them from the curse of the law. No longer can the iniquities of the fathers follow this generation. It stops now, satan!" demanded Joshua speaking to the evil spirits that had been assigned to the Lake family. "Spirit of addiction be gone. Spirit of lying be gone. Spirit of rebellion be gone. Spirits of partying, drunkenness and alcohol be gone. I apply the Blood of Jesus to the mind and body of each member of the Lake family."

Joshua and his dad were laying hands on each member as they were falling out under the Holy Spirit's power.

"Holy Spirit, after cleansing them, baptize in Jesus' baptism with the evidence of speaking in tongues," Vicki asked.

Dan, Vicki and Joshua listened to each member of the Lake family speaking in a heavenly language

As the Word of God was being spoken, an army of angels were released to fight with the demonic implants in the Lake family. A menacing looking warring angel with a glowing sword greeted each demonic implant. They were

eager to do serious damage to the kingdom of darkness. The demons started screaming and shape-shifting into vultures flying like lightening to the nearest doorway to hell or somewhere to hide. Some saw the previous fight and hid deep into the flesh of Jerry Lake hoping that they would not be discovered and forced out of their house.

The power of the prayers collected in heaven for this battle was released on the warring angels anointing them with great strength to annihilate all the evil androids associated with the Lake family. The angels were excited about being able to administer the Covenant in the life of a new family through the Knights' bold witness. They quickly found out how true it was that there was never a dull moment with the Knight family.

Sounds of swords slicing through air with demonic body parts flying through the spirit realm occurred as the power source of the demons, a green blood-like substance, was squirting everywhere. Demons of hate and lying came out and screamed. "Don't terminate us! Send us somewhere else! We will obey you! We beg you! Send us back to another dwelling place!"

"No longer do we have to put up with your foolishness, now is the day of salvation and now the long awaited time of the body of Jesus Christ is here." Natsar cut off three heads with one swipe. "No mercy for you evil creations of the devil!"

"No mercy!" Other warring angels were shouting.

Kientay fought along side the warring angels. Again, he felt the joy of executing the demons with the Word of God coming from Joshua's mouth. He flew through the air consumed with the battle. "Jesus is coming to defeat you in the heavenlies and then off the face of the earth! This is just the beginning!"

"We hate the works of evil that you perpetrate against the humans on earth!" Chroni shouted.

"Did you have mercy when you drove the father and son to drink?" One of the guardian angels from the Lake family stabbed a demon of alcohol in the throat against the wall.

He choked out, "It . . . was . . . my job . . . Ugh!" The angel whacked off his head and green blood spewed from his body.

Kientay gave him a high five. "Way to go!"

"I've wanted to do that for a long time!"

"It feels good doesn't it?" Natsar slapped one of the Lake guardian angels on the back.

"Yes. It does, even though . . ."

Kientay warned the angel as a demon spirit raised a sword to stab into the angel's body. He ducked and Kientay cut off his head.

They stood in the middle of the living room as the fight continued outside the walls of the Knights' house.

"You are torturing us before the time!" One of the demonic androids screamed as a sword pierced his body. Green blood, mixed with liquid fear flowed from him.

"Before the time! Before the time!" Natsar mimicked them with each stab. "You demon spirits need to learn that this is the time! This is the day that you are cut off from the land of the living!"

"Time has run out and they don't even know it!" Kientay laughed with the other angels.

"Now is the day of salvation for the Lake family and now is the time of your torment!" declared Milchamah.

"Tell all the evil children of darkness, no mercy to the kingdom of darkness." Kientay laughed with the other angels as some escaped the room in terror for their lives. This was the age that the angels had been long waiting for.

The demons fleeing couldn't believe the strength and power of the warring angels surrounding the Knight family. Putting their hands over their ears they screamed with pain. Every word was like a knife thrust through their heart.

"Kientay," Chroni appeared. "You were right. No angel will say that they were bored with this assignment!"

CHAPTER 16

Joshua watched his dad and mother praying for the Lake family. He moved to the back of the living room and sat at the piano. As he started playing a tune of worship softly in the background, his heart was overflowing with praise and worship to the Lord.

Suddenly before his eyes, an angel appeared sitting on the end of the piano. She had on a white gown and robe with a gold belt and halo with long beautiful curly blond hair that seemed to sparkle and glitter like diamonds and gold. She was singing and giving praise to the Lord with the music he was playing.

Another angel appeared next to him and pointed behind Joshua. He stood as the angel took over playing the piano for him. The Lord opened Joshua's eyes to see the battle going on in the spirit realm in their living room and in the heavenlies above their house. The thought entered his mind that the angels fighting in their living room were fierce looking. He had seen them guarding his house, but they didn't look anything like they do now.

He estimated the warring angels to be about eight to twelve feet tall. Most of them had huge wings spanning at least six to ten feet. They had broad shoulders with swords and armor that seemed to be as big as their body. Their swords looked like the weapons he had seen on *Star Wars*. Long shafts of light from a metal base, seemed to look like light and then solid metal. The armor glowed with light covering different colored tunics and army type pants. Others were dressed in all white tunics and pants. Joshua could see them flying and moving fast in his living room. Some of them seemed to be moving so fast that all he could see was a trail of light behind them like a falling star.

The guardian angels were also fighting. Joshua estimated their size to be similar to the human size, but their swords were as big and powerful as the warring angels. He noticed a couple of extremely tall warring angels clothed in white holding massive glowing swords powerfully wiping out several demonic spirits. The demon spirits showed faces filled with terror. Their insides didn't look like human or animal. He heard a lot of crunching like metal hitting metal.

The angels' swords had a yellow-white iridescent glow around them. He wondered if the flaming swords represented the anointing of the Holy Spirit. It surprised him to see the green fluid come out of the demons when they were stabbed. He wrinkled his nose at the sulfuric smell that was released whenever a demon spirit was stabbed and disintegrated. Everywhere it spewed the green liquid left a glittery trail of green fire. When the head was severed from the demon's body, it seemed to vaporize into nothing and disappear. Eventually, their spilled power source did the same thing.

Actually, it was a lot like some of the science fiction movies that Hollywood had made. Joshua was thrilled at the scene that was open to his eyes. He had an intense desire to grab a sword and join in the battle. The Lord's angels were making mincemeat out of the demons and it seemed to Joshua that they were enjoying it. It was exciting to see the angels doing some serious damage to the kingdom of darkness.

Just as fast as it appeared, the scene closed around him and he found himself sitting back at the piano playing and praising the Lord with his parents and the Lake family. A family of long lost sons and daughters had come home to the Father. He continued worshipping the Lord with his parents in the natural realm and in the spiritual realm with the angels.

Metraloas watched from a distance at his regular spot in the oak tree when he saw a mini van drive up in front of the house and a family of five walk up to the Knight house. He recognized some of the demons nesting in the humans.

Raising his head and sitting up, he yelled at them from the tree. "Don't go in there!"

A few poked their heads out of their human host's body to see who it was that was yelling at them. When they recognized it was metraloas the moron, they just wagged their heads and shouted obscenities at him.

He raised his arms up in disgust and slapped his forehead. *Of course! Who would listen to a failure like me?* "You stupid demons are going to be sorry!" He relaxed into a horizontal position and floated about half way between the top of the tree and the ground. Humming to himself, he wondered how long it would be before the fireworks would begin.

He didn't have to wait long.

It was like lightning with sounds of sonic booms. Suddenly inside and outside of the house, blinding lights appeared. He could see the glory spikes falling from heaven like grenades causing sparks and fire everywhere. Dark smoke with a putrid sulfuric smell began spewing from the walls and rooftop.

The android demons materialized every where. Metraloas counted two gigantic warring angels for every demonic android fleeing for his life. He had never seen so many warring angels in his life at such a small insignificant event.

The demons were different shapes and sizes. Some looked like monkeys with extra arms and long, pointed snouts with dead, shallow yellow eyes. Others were like weird proportioned spiders and snakes. Many of them shapeshifted into vultures so they could escape by flying, but it didn't matter what spiritual powers they possessed; the Lord's angelic army was wiping them out.

Metraloas enjoyed the sight. He floated above the tree to watch everything going on. Lying horizontally, a white bag appeared in his hand and he started tossing popcorn into his mouth. *This is better than the movies,* he thought. He watched demons streaming from the house with warring angels hot on their tails.

Several hundred demons were screaming and running around like chickens with their heads cut off. The warring angels even started attacking demons assigned to other families in the neighborhood. He started laughing so hard he fell to the ground as the bag of popcorn flipped into the air and spilled the contents all around him. The battle lit up the neighborhood like a fireworks celebration.

A demon in the form of a bird with a pitch fork tail flew passed him. Metraloas was instantly beside him, "Hey you coward! Go back and fight to the death you yellow-belly night crawler!" Grabbing him around the throat, he caused the bird to do a one-eighty, throwing him back into the center of the fight. The demonic bird hit an angel who turned around and whacked him to pieces with his sword. He fell like ashes to the ground.

Metraloas looked at his hand. He didn't know he had that much strength, but all the years of abuse he had suffered from the name calling of sniveling idiots like him was being released from him with power. A diabolical laugh came out of his mouth.

"What are you doing?" The bat appeared.

Metraloas acted like he was unimpressed by his entrance. He picked up the bag of popcorn, flew back to the balcony of his headquarters, sat down in a lounging chair and popped a couple more kernels into his mouth. "Revenge is so sweet!" He spoke to the bat as he perched on a railing.

"You are enjoying the fight."

"Why not? I tried to warn them and they wagged their tongues at me."

The bat glared at him.

"Where have you been?"

The bat cloaked his real thoughts. "I've been looking for another place to go since you are so sure that you are getting reassigned."

Metraloas looked over and cussed. "You're — right. I will be reassigned and some other sucker will be stuck here." He was too pleased with himself to notice something was different with the bat. "It won't be long now."

Recording angels entered a golden horse chariot and flew directly to heaven. They were the witnesses to the conversion of the Lake family. Their mission was to appear before the angel in charge over one of the rooms of records in heaven and personally give testimony to what they witnessed. They handed a scroll to him with writing on it describing the Lake family and all the details of their conversion.

High praises of God were ringing with the bells of heaven all around the angels in the room. Every time a person on earth accepted Jesus as his or her personal Savior and was delivered from the chains of bondage to the kingdom of darkness, a bell sounded.

In the room where the salvation of Jerry, Cindy and their children were to be recorded, the angels were busy writing into each individual record book of each person the exact day, hour, minute and second the salvation occurred. It was then written down at the word of two witnessing angels and signed by them. The recording angel also witnessed the country, state, county, city and place of salvation. No one in the eons of time would ever question the validity of any person's birth into the kingdom of God. It was used as a legal document to prove to the kingdom of darkness if a soul's place of eternity was ever questioned.

"Were you witnesses that the man Jerry Lake, the woman Cindy Lake and their children, Mindy, Tom and Heather were born again at the house of Dan and Vicki Knight at 8:00 p.m.?" asked the recording angel.

"Yes, we witnessed that Dan Knight led them to repeat a prayer that proclaimed Jesus Christ as Lord and Savior. We saw it and heard them say it with their mouth."

The recording angel handed them each person's record book and took the scroll to officially enter it into the room of records. The messenger angels then took that person's record book to a table with angels sitting behind it and in front of them golden buckets. Each page of the record book was washed with a bloodstained cloth. The power of the Blood of Jesus glowed from the bucket like radiation.

The recording angel declared, "All sins and all evil deeds no longer exist. They are undisputedly removed by the Blood of the Lamb." She called out each individual name and declared that they were perfectly righteous in the eyes of the Lord God Almighty.

Another angel announced that they were forever forgiven and all transgressions no longer stood in the hall of unforgiveness. "It is written in His Blood and now delivered to the Almighty to be signed, sealed and totally adopted into the family of God."

Michael materialized in the hallway leading from the rooms of records. He was waiting for the angel who was carrying a golden tray with five record books. "Are these the records of the Lake family?"

"Yes, sir."

He had heard from Chroni that a first-fruit of the ministry of the Devil Chasers, a family of five, had entered the archive's record system. "I will personally take these to the throne room."

The messenger angel bowed recognizing his authority as he handed the tray to Michael.

Michael entered an enormous room. Horns and trumpets blared through the vast immeasurable room as he walked to the front. "This is the first-fruit works of the Devil Chasers." He bowed before the Lord Jesus giving Him glory and praise and then handed him the tray.

Jesus turned and looked into the cloud of glory surrounding the Father sitting on His special seat of authority. He could see the total image of the Father while those surrounding the Him could only see an outline of a man sitting on an indescribable golden throne of glory. A rainbow of colors surrounded the center of worship. The light radiating from it seemed to be brighter that white. Precious gems of amethyst filled the floor beneath the throne casting a beautiful glow of purple under the Father's feet.

"Father, a family has been saved at the house of Joshua Knight, son of Dan and Vicki Knight; the first-fruit of the Devil Chasers ministry and of many yet to come." Jesus laid the books on the altar in front of the feet of the Almighty Father.

A voice that sounded like thunder and lightning spoke from the cloud. "A family has been redeemed by the Blood of My Son! Together they have been saved and have received eternal life!" Each family was recognized personally by the Father and their names were announced one by one.

A shout of praise sounded throughout heaven.

God's hand came out of the cloud and opened each personal record book of the Lake family and initialed it with His name: He officially adopted them into the family of His Son. They were now His children. He then personally wrote their names in the Lamb's Book Life. Their former lives were forever forgotten. Being officially adopted, they now belonged to the family of God.

The Father proclaimed with a loud booming voice, "The Lake family and all of their children belong to My Son and our family!"

Joshua sat in bed reading his Bible when he heard footsteps coming down the hall. His door opened and Jesus walked in.

"Hi Joshua." Jesus walked over and again pulled out his desk chair and moved it along side of his bed to talk to him.

He was not surprised that Jesus was visiting him again. He figured He might come after seeing into the spiritual realm tonight.

"What did you think of the battle?"

"It was too cool!"

Joshua thought he sounded like a teenager, but he couldn't think of another word to describe what he saw. He suspected there wasn't a word that could express human feelings after an open vision of the spiritual realm. "If only the kids of my generation could see what I saw! Can I tell the team about it?"

"Yes, I want them to know."

If only they could see the truth, they would never serve satan again!

"A spirit of murder and suicide has been released over teenagers in your nation's schools. You need to know your enemy so you can teach your generation how to fight against the kingdom of darkness."

Joshua's desire to teach young people about satan had grown stronger in the last few weeks since Jesus' first visit.

"You will be released soon. I have come to teach you about our enemy's kingdom on earth. In Ephesians the sixth chapter the four classes of evil spirits are explained. The lowest two classes are principalities and powers."

"They seem like robots or androids," Joshua commented. He figured they were the ones he saw fighting with the warring angels.

"They are children of the devil and androids are as good of a name as any other. Any Christian speaking the Word of God can easily combat and defeat principalities and powers."

"What is that green gunk coming out of them?"

"It is their power source, like gas in one of your cars or blood in your veins," Jesus explained in terms he could understand. "They have been programmed to harass and torture mankind. You can resist them easily."

The door to Joshua's bedroom opened and a pint size monkey-like creature scampered into the room. He paused and looked around seemingly shocked that it was so easy to get inside the Knight house. He checked every room in the house and found that everyone was asleep but the young boy.

Not seeing Jesus, he observed Joshua sitting in bed with his Bible on his lap. Running over to him quickly, he hopped onto the bed and sat on the open

Bible and proceeded to put his hands over his ears.

Reacting faster than he could think, Joshua pulled his hands off his ears and threw him off his bed. "Get out of my room you little demon!"

The monkey rolled a couple of times and stood up with a shocked expression on his face. He couldn't believe that Joshua could see him. That had never happened to him before. He initiated telepathic communication. *I don't have to get out of here! I was minding my own business walking down the sidewalk in front of your house, when I noticed a hole in the hedge of protection surrounding your house. Someone in your house has used a word of fear.* He waved a pointed finger in the air as to say naughty-naughty!

Joshua shouted at him using his voice. "I don't care what hole you found, this house belongs to the Knight family, this bedroom belongs to me and I belong to Jesus. Get out of here now!" Jumping out of his bed, he chased the annoying demon out of his room, down the stairway, and out the front door.

An angel of the Lord greeted the demon with a sword and hacked him to pieces. Joshua ran back upstairs realizing he left Jesus. Opening the door, he saw that Jesus was still in his bedroom. "I'm sorry, Jesus! I didn't mean to leave you like that." His face was blushed as he sat down on his bed. It was embarrassing that he left the room without even thinking about Jesus.

"Don't apologize. You did exactly what you should have done. If you didn't do it, then I couldn't have."

"Did you say that you couldn't have taken care of that demon?"

"Yes. My people ask me daily to take care of the devil for them, but *they* have to take authority over satan's kingdom on earth."

"We have to do it? I must have heard you wrong. I think you said we have to take care of the demons who attack us."

"That's what I said. I did My part when I defeated the devil in hell, now it's your turn. Take what I did to him in hell and do it to him on earth."

Joshua walked over to his desk and got a yellow note pad and pen to write down everything that Jesus was saying. The scripture came to his mind about Jesus expecting his enemies to be put under his feet.

"You are thinking correctly. I am in heaven waiting and expecting My body on earth to put every evil being under My feet. You have to enforce My victory!"

"But many expect You to take care of the devil for them."

"I know. But that is unscriptural. Where in the New Testament did I tell anybody to ask Me to take care of the devil for them after I rose from the grave?" Jesus asked.

He couldn't think of one scripture.

"There isn't one. But there is a scripture that says 'Resist the devil and he will flee from you'; and another, 'neither give place to the devil.' 'You' is understood in those sentences and they are scripture commands, not suggestions."

"But why aren't we taught how to fight the devil?" Joshua asked.

"The doctrine of demons." It was a simple answer. "A teaching that could have some truth and lies mixed in it, but it is mostly a doctrine of total lies. Do you remember what Paul told Timothy?"

"He said that the Holy Spirit has declared that 'in latter times some will depart from the faith, giving heed to deceiving spirits and doctrines of demons.'"

"These are the latter times. Demons have disguised themselves among my congregations in false beliefs, but I am coming to flush them out." Jesus knew that the Holy Spirit deposited into Joshua's spirit the understanding of His coming.

"You're coming in Your glory before the rapture of the church?" He was waiting for the Lord to confirm the thoughts in His mind.

"It's in My Book. I am coming in glory and in physical manifestations. Just like now. I am coming to gather the strength of My body in prayers and use that authority to war with the fallen angels that still have control of the heavenlies."

"Isaiah the prophet told of this great event in chapter sixty. And James, he wrote about it in his letter." Many more names and passages came into his mind. "Lord, how did we miss it?"

"Because many of My people are asleep and have become dull of hearing. They refuse to study My Word for themselves. They want to take the easy way out and live in this world without conflict. Didn't I say that offenses would come? Doesn't My Word record that I said if they hated me, they will hate you? But those few who walk the straight and narrow way and endure persecution and preach the truth will lead the way for My glory to cover the earth!"

"Lord, some ministries have formed to attack the Word of faith movement. Why are Christians attacking Christians and wounding each other?"

"My grace is sufficient for all ministries. The Word of Faith movement is inspired by Me. The Father has willed the end-time ministries so that prophecy will be fulfilled. Those coming against My ministers will be held accountable, but they also are accomplishing their calling in this world through their own ministries."

"Your Word says that the world will know that we are Christians by our love. How can you be so merciful to Christians who are fighting with other Christians?"

"They are doing it in ignorance, but the fighting among brethren has to stop now. When My glory is released on earth in these last days those with unforgiveness in their hearts will not be able to stand. Keep your eyes on Me when you start receiving the same attacks," Jesus warned him. "Don't let yourself be caught in the sin of idolatry."

"Idolatry?"

"Yes. Do not let your mind think or meditate on anything but Me and My Words."

"Yes, Sir! Can I ask you a question?"

"Yes."

"I read about a ministry that is strong in deliverance, but they also are fighting against the faith movement. Is it wrong for me to read what Christians are saying about other ministries?"

"It is none of your business what others are doing in their ministry unless I give you a message to deliver from Me to them. If you read what is said about you, your flesh will get involved and pride could come in."

"So you don't want me to read what they are going to say about me?" He repeated what Jesus said to confirm it in his mind.

"I don't want you to read what they write about you," Jesus reconfirmed his command.

Joshua never thought about them writing about him. "It makes me wonder how they can continue casting out demons when they walk in discord? They even write books and name men and women that are Your prophets and call them heretics!" It was still amazing to him that the attacking ministry could continue to minister in Jesus' name.

"Do you remember Mark 16?" Jesus asked him.

"Yes. 'Go into the world and preach the gospel to every creature. He who believes and is baptized will be saved, but he who does not believe will be condemned. And these signs will follow those who believe. In My name they will cast out demons, they will speak with new tongues. They will take up serpents and if they drink anything deadly, it will by no means hurt them. They will lay hands on the sick, and they will recover'."

"What did I say is the first thing that a believer can do after he preaches the gospel?"

"Cast out demons in Your name," Joshua replied.

"What is the second thing?"

"Speak in tongues."

"Who can cast out devils?"

"Those who believe and preach the gospel."

"Did I say only Spirit-filled believers can cast out demons?"

"No. Oh, I see. That explains a lot about some ministries that cast out demons without believing in spiritual gifts."

"I know that you have been wondering about that. Any born-again believer in My Word can cast out low-level demons. Any human can say no to their suggestions and temptations."

"Any one?"

"Authority on earth has been given to humans. All you have to have to cast out demons is a body. They have no right to exist in a body when they have been cast out by a human."

"Ah . . . now that makes sense. No wonder You said that people can cast out demons in your Word and You might say to them to depart from You because You never knew them. That really shows it doesn't take much power to cast out demons."

"Low-level demons and evil spirits can easily be cast out by even the youngest baby in the body of Christ if they know My Word. There are some evil spirits that only come out with greater power from the Holy Spirit."

"One time Your disciples couldn't cast out a demon spirit from a boy. Is that an example?"

"Yes. I said that he could only be cast out by prayer and fasting. But what did I say before that?"

Joshua couldn't remember. "I need to look in my Bible." Instantly the exact location came into his mind. Matthew 17:20. He picked up his Bible beside him and turned to the chapter and verse. He looked up at Jesus. "You said that it was because of their unbelief that they could not cast out that demon."

"I called them a faithless and perverse or unbelieving generation. If they were filled with unbelief, where were all the words I had been speaking to them?"

"They let the devil steal Your words from their heart."

"Your faith has to hook up with God's faith for manifestation to come into the natural realm," Jesus explained. "Now do you know what I was saying to them?"

"It would take fasting and prayer for them to receive Your words into the good ground of their heart for them to grow into the harvest of great faith."

"The seed of My Word has to be planted in a prepared heart."

"So people who are fasting and praying and asking You to give them the power to cast out demons are going about it the wrong way."

"Fasting and praying prepares your heart. Reading and mediating on My Word causes the seed of faith in your spirit to grow and become stronger. My Word cleanses you of wrong thinking and speaking wrong words. What example did I give them to cure their unbelief?"

Joshua again looked down at his Bible. "You said, 'If you have faith as a mustard seed, you will say to this mountain, "Move from here to there" and it will move, and nothing will be impossible for you.'"

"I gave you the process for cultivating the faith to cast out unbelief. Plant My Words in you like a seed and speak them over and over out of your mouth while the roots are growing inside the good ground of your heart. Then out of the abundance of your heart My Word will burst forth as a tree out of your mouth with power to take care of any serpent on earth."

"That is the third thing you said in Mark 16. Taking up serpents."

"What did I say after that?"

"You said that if we drink anything deadly it will not hurt us."

"Notice the word drink. When you drink you take something from the outside and put it inside. A Christian who is strong in spiritual gifts and speaks in tongues will not be harmed. No poison can kill the seed of My Word growing in the heart of a believer. No devil on earth or in the heavenlies no matter how powerful he is can kill or stop a believing born again Christian who speaks in tongues and walks in the power and listens to the wisdom of the Holy Spirit."

"So a believer who walks in the Spirit and anointed in the power can lay hands on the sick and they will recover," Joshua concluded.

"Believers filled with the power of the Holy Spirit will walk in demonstration and power of signs and wonders. These are the ones that will take dominion over the earth and the works of My Father's hands."

"Most of Your body wants to leave earth instead of reclaiming it. My mother was raised on songs about the *Sweet by and by* or *The mansion over the hilltop* in heaven. Most people look to the rapture as the great escape from planet earth."

"Dinner in heaven will only be for those who are not looking for a way of escape. It is a reward for those who have been in the heat of the battle and on the front lines fighting."

"Some people are going to be disappointed when they are left behind."

"They will be forced to live by faith in the time of Jacobs's trouble. But for those who choose My ways over tradition or doctrine of demons, the Father has planned a special awards celebration. Remember what I told you? It will be a victory celebration over all the works of the enemy from Adam to the last believer who hears and does My Word."

"What is our part of the rapture?"

"Departure by faith."

"Which only comes from knowledge of Your Word."

"Your response to that low- level principality was exactly what I expect from My body. Train others to do what you just did. The younger generation will overcome all the attacks of the devil. They will know how to unite no matter what their background is and they will destroy all the works of the devil!"

Jesus was pleased with Joshua's quick response revealing that his mind stepped aside and let his spirit lead him. "Many in My body let reasoning take over and then question why it happened or have doubt about it happening. They get bogged down with questions that lead to serious doubts and form habits that weaken their power source of faith."

Joshua was writing as fast as he could so that he could remember everything Jesus was telling him.

"Your commission on earth includes teaching young people how to fight the devil. The first and second class of principalities and powers are easy to fight . . ."

"Like that monkey looking imp?" Joshua asked.

"Yes. They are easy to resist by just saying no, but they will come back over and over to put suggestions in the mind of the human they are assigned to. You have to aggressively attack them like you did. No retreating!"

"Hmm, that means that they don't give up very easy."

"They have been instructed to watch and wait until the human flesh opens a door for them to reenter into the life of their victim. Resisting them by saying 'no' will cause them to leave for a season, but their ultimate destruction is only caused by My Word coming out of your mouth as you chase them!"

"You said that Your Word is spirit and it is life." He looked up and smiled at Jesus. "I get it. That's why You are calling this ministry the Devil Chasers."

"My Words coming out of your mouth are the only words that will take care of the spiritual roots of problems that exist in any human's life. The third class of evil spirits is the rulers of darkness. My angels, empowered with My Word coming out of your mouth, take care of the rulers of darkness. Intercessory prayer with fasting, depending on the situation, will destroy their works and words coming against you. Fervent, righteous prayer, prayers prayed according to My Father's ways will destroy their ability to regroup and rebuild what My angels tear down in the spirit realm."

"That's why you had my Mom form a prayer group to pray for us, right?"

"I have called several young people to join you. With parent prayers, you will experience the anointing of the Holy Spirit. He will provide you with the power you will need as you glorify Me to destroy the works of the enemy and intercede for others. Speaking in your heavenly language will give you the advantage you need over the rulers of darkness."

"What about the last category?"

"The last category is the spiritual hosts of wickedness in the heavenlies. Fallen angels are part of the spiritual hosts that reside in the heavenlies above earth. I will take care of them. Praying in the Spirit breaks their power. The Holy Spirit who knows the Father's will prays perfect prayers through you."

"Is that 'taking up serpents'?"

"Yes. Only those who speak and walk in the Spirit can take on the wicked spirits in the heavenlies. Only the Holy Spirit can speak the words that will cause their destruction. Only those who walk close to me can take up the torch of My presence and the sword of My Word and fight with Me in the heavenlies."

Joshua was busy writing down all that Jesus was teaching him. "Wow! This is awesome stuff!"

Jesus smiled. He loved the enthusiasm and first love of youth. "You are the leader of the Joshua Generation."

"Me?"

"The Joshua Generation will look, act and talk like Me. The kingdom of darkness will not know if they are looking at Me or you."

"Wow." He needed time to let that sink down into his spirit.

"The Father's will has been ordained to be accomplished perfectly on earth when you pray in tongues." Jesus stood to leave. "I want you to teach the members of the Devil Chasers how to cast out demons, pray in the spirit and fight with Me in the heavenlies. Tell them I am coming."

He watched Jesus open his door.

"Joshua, this is the generation that shall live and not die. Again I say, teach them to live for me and not die. I am calling this generation to live in total victory. I am calling you to train many young people to openly combat the forces of evil and defeat them for all to see. And remember tell them I am coming."

Jesus smiled at him, walked through the open door and shut the door behind Him. Joshua heard footsteps going down the hall this time.

CHAPTER 17

Pastor Ben rolled over and looked at the clock on his night stand. The red numbers blared out at him, 4:00a.m. He sat up and rubbed his neck. Two hours of sleep wasn't enough for him to function properly at the church in just five hours, but he didn't know what else he could do to make himself sleep. Today was Joshua Knight's last day of school.

He tried every thing he could think of to change Dan and Vicki's mind, but nothing worked. Finally, Dan resigned from the church board the other night and then told him that his family would be leaving the church for good. He couldn't believe his ears. *How could this be happening to me*, he thought one more time as he rubbed his hand over his eyes and face.

"Ben, what are you doing?" Linda asked groggily.

"Nothing . . . go back to sleep."

She raised herself half-way to look at the clock on his side. "How can anybody sleep with you tossing and turning all night?"

Looking back from the bathroom door he reassured her, "I'm going to my study so that I won't bother you anymore."

"Ben . . ."

"What?" He hesitated knowing what she was going to say next.

"Let it go," she pleaded with him.

"I'm trying to." *Oh God! How I am trying.*

"God will take care of things."

How many times have I told someone else those very words? He turned back to the bathroom refusing to think about what she just said.

Linda fluffed her pillow wondering if she could go back to sleep or not. Having lived with Ben for the last twenty years, she knew that he might never let it go. Even though Vicki Knight and she had never been close friends, she thought that they were people that would be loyal to them. Being a pastor and having close friends wasn't easy. Often their so-called best friends had an ulterior motive. The Knights were very wealthy, but she didn't think that they were the kind of people that used their money to control people. She always considered them as good, down-to-earth committed Christians.

She closed her eyes and sighed. Now she was doing the very thing she was trying to get Ben to stop doing; wondering and analyzing and wondering and asking God why.

‡ ‡ ‡

Ben sat at his leather desk chair in his dimly lit home office and noticed how quiet it was this early in the morning. A shower relaxed him, but it did not make him want to go back to sleep. He looked over at his cold, dark and empty leather couch. A worn out spot where he usually met God in prayer stared at him. For the last two weeks he had spent hours pouring his heart out to God and begging him not to let the Knights leave, but it seemed to be a waste of time. God had been and was still silent on the matter.

He looked up and quietly asked out loud, "Why God? Why don't you say something to me?" The frustration of the situation started to rise up inside him and overwhelm him. *Answer my question!* "Why did you let Dan Knight leave my church?" . . .

. . . In the dark corner of Pastor Ben's office a coiled snake with fire-red eyes quietly watched the pathetic looking man crying out to God. A black vulture flew into the room and landed next to the snake.

"Is he doing what it looks and sounds like he is doing?" The vulture inquired.

The snake hissed back. "Yessssss."

The vulture's eyes grew intense. "What are you waiting for?'

"I am waiting for the right timing."

"One of God's preachers is shouting at him and you are waiting?" The vulture couldn't believe his ears. "I heard him all the way into the second heaven."

The snake slowly uncoiled. "This day is the day of breaking." He answered nonchalantly.

The vulture shook his head.

"How many men of God have you taken down?" The snake hissed at him.

"Well, uh, none."

"How long have you been a watcher?" Slowly the snake wound himself around the vulture.

"I'm a courier."

"Then mind your own business!" The snake flexed his muscles and tightly choked the vulture.

The vulture let out a shriek and pulled himself free cursing the snake. As soon as he could, he disappeared. Finding the nearest entrance to hell, he decided someone in hell might be interested in a watcher who is not doing his job . . .

. . . Hearing a noise, Ben's eyes darted over to the dark corner of the room. Standing, he went over to the light switch and flipped it on. Looking intently all around the room, he saw that he was alone. Turning off the light, he went over to the couch and fell to his knees.

"Oh, God . . . where are You? Why can't I hear anything from You?" He covered his face with his hands and began seeking God by pleading Him to talk to him.

The snake slowly slithered over to the kneeling pastor. He thought that his latest victim might continue his pathetic prayers to his God, so he decided to plant a few evil thoughts in his mind before he reported what he discovered. Slowly, he wound himself around the Pastor's body while he made his way to his head and ears. It was easy to get close and move around or upon the body of a human who was self absorbed and filled with worry, doubt and fears.

Laughing and mocking the Pastor gave him such a high. He loved his work and assignments. This was his food. This was his reason for existing. Watching the fall of God's servants was so exhilarating, it was beyond understanding.

He whispered in his ear as his tongue licked the flesh. *Surely God has not forsaken me. I am a man of God. I know His Word . . . I preach His Word . . . I am the right one in this situation. The Knights are wrong. The Knights are going against the will of God. Time will reveal who is right and who is wrong. They will come back to me and beg for my forgiveness.*

As he released his hold over the pastor and fell to the floor, he watched the pastor's lips freeze and the black dots representing the words he had just spoken from the spiritual realm sink into this skull. The snake's diabolical laughter pierced the dawning light as he slithered out of the room. He couldn't help but think that this pastor was yet another notch that he would add to his list of fallen pastors.

"I don't think that I really know how to pray," Sheila announced to the women of the prayer group sitting around her. Being an observer for several days now, she finally got the courage to speak out for more instruction.

Vicki started their meeting with the usual singing and praising the Lord about 20 minutes before they individually prayed. Earlier she gave another word from the Lord like the first time the women met to pray. She wondered if

Sheila understood what prophesying and speaking in tongues were all about. "I hope you understand that I spoke forth a word from the Lord. It is one of the manifestations of the Holy Spirit."

"Oh yes." Sheila replied. "I believe that you were speaking words that the Lord put in your heart. That's not what's bothering me. I really don't know how to pray."

"Why don't we go over some scriptures and techniques for prayer," suggested Joan. "For years I wanted to pray, but no one ever taught me how."

"Good idea." Ruth and the other women agreed.

"First Sheila, you need to know that prayer does not change God. It changes people and situations," taught Vicki.

"Satan, leader of the kingdom of darkness, has blinded the minds of people. So we have to stand in the gap for them," Joan said.

"I once heard a preacher say that no man in his right mind would drive his car a hundred miles an hour into a concrete wall. But a drunken man or a doped up man might, not realizing what he was doing. That is what happens to sinners. They are blinded by the deceiver of this world," added Ruth.

"How do we pray to get them delivered?" asked Sheila.

"We take authority over demons and tell them to let the person we're praying for go," Vicki said. "We ask the Lord to send workers to get into their faces in every path they walk."

"I'm sorry that I'm asking so many questions."

"Please don't apologize," Vicki was quick to tell her that was why they were meeting. "We are learning from each other and praying for God's intervention in the affairs of our children."

"When you first become a Christian it is like being a baby. You have to learn how to walk and talk," Ruth said.

"We owe the Lord thanks for sending us the written Word and the gifts of preachers and teachers, because from them we know a lot about prayer. We know that each and every Christian is called to pray! Especially to pray for intercession for our country, our family and sinners," explained Vicki.

"And don't forget we are to pray for Israel," Kathy reminded her.

"Yes. The Bible promises a blessing on those that pray for Israel," Vicki said.

"This is how I pray for the lost; 'In the Name of the Lord Jesus Christ, I break the power of the devil over . . . Insert that person's name . . . I claim his or her deliverance from the bondage of blindness. I claim his or her full salvation in the Name of the Lord Jesus Christ.' Satan has to release his hold," instructed Ruth.

"What if he doesn't let that person go?" asked Sheila.

"That's why the Lord has sent a host of warring angels to live with us down here on earth," Vicki told her. "Every knee has to bow at the name of Jesus. The angels make them bow. This is where intercession comes in. We need to pray until the sinner or situation is loosed from the blindness of evil spirits, so that the light of Jesus Christ can shine into their heart."

"There is power in numbers and agreement," Ruth added.

"Fasting, prayer, and intercession, using the Blood of Jesus and His Word, are the weapons of our warfare that pull down strongholds of the enemy," Vicki said.

"We will be giving them a prayer covering from the kingdom of darkness." Ruth and Vicki continued to flow together in teaching the word to Sheila.

"How can we do that?" Sheila asked.

"We are going to apply the Blood of Jesus for protection daily over every phone warrior and person involved with this ministry. We don't kill any animals like Moses instructed the children of Israel to do so the death angel would pass over them, but we apply the Blood by speaking with our mouth," Vicki told her.

"Why do you have to apply the Blood daily?" asked Sheila.

"The Blood of Jesus purchased our salvation from satan. Jesus' Blood destroyed our sins, birthed us into His kingdom, bought us back from the power of sin and death, put us back in right standing with God, gave us overcoming power, and released us from the powers of darkness and set us free," Vicki said.

"Say that again?"

Vicki repeated it slowly as Sheila wrote it down. "Satan did not know that God would accept a blood sacrifice for sin."

"We apply the Blood daily because every day and night, a 24 hour period, is a new beginning on earth," Ruth explained. "God's mercy is renewed every day."

"Jesus prayed in the garden that God would count every man, woman or child that believes in Him with His own righteousness. That is mercy and the Word says His mercy is renewed every day," Vicki told her. "Jesus didn't demand that every person be saved like satan demanded that every person be in bondage to death."

"God wanted us to have the choice to accept His Son or reject Him," Ruth continued.

RubyMae spoke out. "Jesus will even defend your right to go to hell!"

Sheila shuddered as she thought about her husband.

"We remind demons of their master's defeat when we talk about the Blood of Jesus! Glory!" shouted RubyMae. "This is praying in the Spirit and shouting territory! The old timers knew this. They use to pray using the Blood of Jesus until demons released their hold over what ever they were praying about. They didn't quit until the victory was manifested in the natural realm!"

"Wait a minute! What did you say? Praying in the what?"

"Praying in the Spirit. We pray in the Spirit by speaking in a new language. Paul called it tongues. It's in Acts chapter two," explained Vicki. "I call it the language of the angels."

"Vicki, I've got the scripture in my Bible." Evie held up her Bible, since she knew where this discussion was headed. "Chapter one, verse four 'but wait for the promise of the Father, which, you have heard of me. For John truly baptized with water, but you shall be baptized with the Holy Ghost not many days from now. And when the day of Pentecost was fully come, they were all in one accord in one place. And suddenly, there came a sound from heaven as of a rushing mighty wind, and it filled all the house where they were sitting. And there appeared unto them cloven tongues like as of fire, and it sat upon each of them. And they were all filled with the Holy Ghost, and began to speak with other tongues, as the Spirit gave them utterance.'"

"How do I speak in tongues?" asked Sheila.

"Ask Jesus to baptize you with fire and power and receive the gift of the Holy Spirit with the evidence of speaking in tongues," replied Vicki. "Raise your hands as we pray for you. When you are ready to receive, I will lay my hands on you and you will receive Jesus' gift and speak in other tongues. Ladies, gather around Sheila."

The ladies prayed in English and then some started praying in their heavenly language. Faith began to rise as Vicki spoke the word over Sheila.

"Father, Jesus prayed and asked You to give us another Comforter. Jesus said He would not leave us comfortless, but the Spirit of truth, whom the world cannot receive, He would dwell with us and in us. Jesus also said the Holy Ghost, our Comforter, shall teach us all things, and bring all things to our memory, whatsoever His Word says to us. When we were saved, The Holy Spirit put us into the body of Christ. We know Your Spirit is inside us. Now we ask You to give this gift that Jesus taught us about to Sheila. Let her allow Your Spirit to come out of her like rivers of waters."

"Amen!" agreed RubyMae.

"Holy Spirit teach Sheila to pray. Teach her to pray in her heavenly language. We thank you for answering our prayer." Vicki stopped praying and spoke to Sheila. "Ask the Lord to fill you with His baptism."

"Jesus, I want to be baptized like the disciples in the upper room on the day of Pentecost. Fill me with your Spirit."

"Sheila, when I lay my hands on your head, believe you will receive and speak in tongues." Vicki touched Sheila on her forehead and she lifted up her hands praising the Lord in another language. They all raised their hands and started praising the Lord in the language of tongues.

"Praise the Name of the Lord!"

"The Lord is a mighty Warrior!"

"Oh, give thanks to the Lord, for He is good! For His mercy endures forever."

"Bless the Lord, O my soul; And all that is within me, bless His Holy Name!"

"Let everything that has breath praise the Lord."

"From the rising of the sun to its going down, the Lord's name is to be praised!"

The gray, clouded sky made special surveillance almost impossible. Metraloas cursed. Chemah was right in suspecting that he needed an overhaul, especially since his special eyesight was blitzing off and on again. All of a sudden, his night vision started working and he was able to pierce through the dim morning light to keep a close watch on the Knight house. He was diligently looking for a woman that was the weakest link in the newly formed prayer group of Vicki Knight.

The bat materialized. "What are you doing?"

Metraloas didn't trust the bat. Something was up with him. "I'm watching. That's what I do in the kingdom of darkness. What do you do?" He eyed him suspiciously.

"I told you."

He had made up his mind not to tell the bat anymore of his secrets.

The bat impatiently waited with him for over five hours. It seemed like a waste of time until the prayer meeting was over. The first woman that came out of the Knight house by herself was Sheila Coyle. The other women left in pairs. Metraloas decided to follow Sheila home.

The bat didn't comment, waiting to see if the stupid android really did know what he was doing. Following Sheila into her house, they encountered many demons.

"What are you doing here?" asked a demon of fear.

"I'm metraloas, watcher over the Knights."

Several demons started laughing, "We've heard of you before. You're the one that sits in an oak tree a couple of houses away from your assignment!" one demon shrieked laughing.

"I wouldn't be laughing if I were you. Do you know where this human female has been?" he pompously asked.

The head spirit of fear spoke. "Where has she been?" He had been angry ever since Sheila received Jesus as her Savior and he was cast out of her body.

"I don't think I'll tell you." metraloas turned around and acted like he was leaving.

The spirit grabbed his arm and forced him to turn around. "Tell us, you arrogant fool!" he hissed.

Metraloas looked with fire in his eyes. "Apologize!" he shouted as he hit the spirit of fear's arm to release his.

The spirit growled and squared off for a fight . . .

. . . The front door opened and Wade Coyle walked in.

"Sheila!" he shouted as he slammed the door.

Sheila ran into the foyer from the kitchen. "What are you doing home?"

Wade stared at her with the evil eye of the gatekeeper demon that possessed him. "Where have you been? I've been calling you all morning!"

"I've been at a friend's house."

"Who?"

She turned away from him as Wade grabbed her arm and the demon inside him slapped her face. "What's her name, stupid!"

Sheila put her hand to her cheek. Tears brushed her eyes from the stinging blow. She turned around to go to the kitchen.

"Don't turn your back on me! Come here!"

Sheila tried to ignore him, but lately that was impossible. He had only recently started hitting her. The first time was after she got saved and she told him she wouldn't go to the bars with him anymore.

"Lord," Sheila whispered, "I need your help." . . .

. . . The spirit of drunkenness in Wade looked into the living room after hearing a commotion. He saw metraloas and the spirit of fear fighting each other. Leaving Wade, he instantly flew between the two spirits. "What in the——is going on in MY house?" he screamed at them.

"This low-life android has some information about the female Sheila and he won't reveal it!" explained the spirit of fear.

"Who are you?" The strongman of the Coyle family yelled at him.

"I am metraloas, murders of mothers and a spirit from the division of powers!"

"I've heard of you. You're failing in your assignment. How can you help us?" The spirit of fear demanded an explanation.

"I am on a special assignment from chemah!"

"I am shathah, spirit of drunkenness! I demand you tell me all you know about the human, Sheila Coyle."

"I will reveal that information only if you are in agreement with a plan of mine and he gives me an apology for calling me a fool!"

Shathah turned toward the spirit of fear. "Apologize!"

"I am also from the division of powers. He is not over me!" He turned around to disappear, but shathah stretched his hand and pulled him out of the dimension he was going to hide in.

Shathah had the greater power being from the rulers of darkness and was the strongman over the Coyle family. "He isn't over you, but I am! Tell him that you are sorry for calling him a fool!"

Fumes started coming out of the spirit of fear's head. "Ohh! I apologize!" he said spitting the words out with rage.

He released the spirit and kicked him out of the house with his foot. "What do you know?" demanded shathah.

"I know that chemah ordered me to follow the human Sheila as she was leaving the Knights' house."

All the little demons in the house shrieked and started trembling. Every demon in the city had heard of the Knight family. They had been warned to stay away from them.

"Did you hear what happened to the demons involved with the truck accident the other day?" asked metraloas.

"We heard several are missing and probably will never return to their assignments on earth again," answered shathah. "Several privates in my special division of drunkenness were cast out of the driver of the accident. I have vowed to get revenge on the angel that was responsible for my workers displacement. We were told that the whole family are . . ." he spit with disgust, " . . . are believers in JC now!"

The demons shuddered when they heard the name JC.

"You mean our human, Sheila, is going to their house?" asked the spirit of fear.

"It's worse than that," reported metraloas. "She's been going Monday through Friday every morning for four or five hours. And they are not making a quilt!" He knew what the women were doing.

The bat shook his head. He was almost positive that he added the last sentence about the quilt to make them think he was stupid.

"Wh . . . What are they doing?" stuttered a monkey-like demon.

"Chemah believes they are praying." He liked being able to throw chemah's name around like they were buddies.

The trembling demons gasped out loud!

"No" The spirit of fear moaned and cursed.

"Are they reading the . . . the . . . the . . ."

"Spit it out stupid!" Another demon shouted.

"The WORD!" They all trembled with fear.

"Shut up you stupid demons. I can't think with you whining and sniveling!" shathah yelled at them.

"The glory cloud is getting bigger and stronger everyday around and over the Knight house," answered metraloas. "They must be in the . . . the . . . the . . . WORD!" He mocked the demons making fun of them.

Shathah cursed. "I knew something was up, but I've been too busy recruiting and training my spirits of drunkenness to pay attention to her absences."

Metraloas was thrilled to see that shathah was worried.

Shathah started pacing back and forth in the living room. Muttering to himself he said, "What terrible timing! His dad is about to wash his hands of his son. I can't lose Wade now. I have two serious potential alcoholics on the line." As he paced, he shape-shifted into several different human and animal forms, from an old man, to a young woman and then a cat and last a dog.

"I have a plan," metraloas told him as he grabbed a hold of his arm and stopped him from shape-shifting. It was obvious that he had trouble handling stress.

Shathah changed into his original form of a grotesque snake. "Terrible timing! I've got several new converts starting to drink."

"Uh . . . ump!" metraloas cleared his throat. "I said I have a plan!"

"What?" He turned his shape into a man dressed in a black hooded robe.

"If you come with me, I can introduce you to chemah and he could introduce you to satan as our secret weapon into the Knight home."

He turned himself into an old wrinkled woman. "How can I be a secret weapon?"

"Stop that infernal shape-shifting and listen to me!" metraloas screamed at him. "Through Wade, we could get to Sheila. From Sheila we might cause a door to open enough to cause a breach in the Knight operation." The android was exhibiting unstable personality tendencies.

"That might work." He stopped pacing. "How would we do that?" shathah was interested. If he succeeded, he thought, maybe he could get a higher commission and rank in satan's army.

Metraloas looked into shathah's eyes. *All right! He took the bait!* His plan was working, even though shathah was a jerk. The demon spirit in charge of a legion of demonic alcohol androids who could hardly control his own image isn't exactly a sure thing, but it was the only thing he had at the moment.

"Let's go then."

The bat couldn't believe that metraloas was going through with his plan. It seemed to him that shathah was very unbalanced.

Shathah looked over at Wade talking to Sheila too nicely.

"Before we go, I've got some unfinished business to take care of." Shathah flew over to Wade and entered him.

The bat materialized next to metraloas. "What are you doing?"

"Where have you been?"

The bat sighed. "Listen, don't you think this shathah spirit is a little unbalanced?"

"I think he is very unbalanced."

"Then what's the deal?"

"The unstable ones are the easiest to lead around. The nature of his assignment lends itself to distressed personality traits. Exactly the spirit I need in case this plan takes a wrong turn."

"Okay, if you know what you're doing," the bat shrugged and disappeared again . . .

. . . Wade ran over to Sheila. He was going to slap her around a little, but the desire left him.

Instead, he said, "Sheila, sit down at the table. I want to talk to you."

Sheila heard and felt a change in him. *The demon is gone! I can talk to him.*

"I don't know why I act this way. Sometimes the rage and anger builds up in me so strong that I feel like I'm going to bust. I just have to hit something or someone." Wade sat down at the table and lowered his head into his shaking hands.

Sheila wasn't surprised. She knew when the rage started growing in him. The spirit of rage and anger were lower demonic implants under shathah in him, but Sheila didn't know the exact number of demons inside Wade's body or their names. She just knew that he was demon possessed. "Wade, you need to get some peace into your life."

"I know you're going to tell me I need Jesus." Wade looked up at her as his voice quivered. "What I need is a drink."

"Jesus can deliver you from your drinking problem."

He stood and yelled at her. "I told you! I don't have a drinking problem!"

"Yes you do, Wade. You were drinking before we got married."

"Okay! Okay!" He got up and started looking through the cabinets for some booze.

"I've been going to Joshua Knight's house."

"Where did you put it?" He was slamming doors looking for the bottle he had hidden. He couldn't remember where he put it.

"Wade, are you listening to me?"

"Why do you always throw away my bottles?" He grabbed her arms and shook her.

"Are you going to slap me again?"

He let her go and put his hands behind his head closing his eyes. He breathed deeply a couple of times and then opened his eyes as he immediately began to think about a bottle of booze. Forcing that thought out of his mind, he sat back down at the kitchen table. "Where did you say you went?"

"Joshua Knight's house. Joshua is a school friend of Hannah's."

Suddenly, Wade's eyes turned evil looking. His whole countenance changed and his voice became harsh because Shathah entered him.

"Look at me Sheila!" Shathah demanded that she submit to him. He wanted total control over her. "I am warning you Sheila, you are never to go to that house again!"

Sheila stood indignantly. She knew she wouldn't obey him because the Holy Spirit inside her let her know that she wasn't dealing with Wade anymore. She stared at him. With no fear, she turned away keeping her mouth shut.

Shathah lunged to grab her and then froze. Sheila's guardian angel was blocking him with a sword drawn ready to hit him. "You can't stop me!" shouted shathah sensing that she was way too confident, he left Wade and flew with metraloas into one of the gateways leading to hell.

He would take care of Sheila another day.

CHAPTER 18

Joshua and Mose planned to meet after school at the Hut. He couldn't wait to tell him about the Lord's latest visit. "Hey!" Joshua spotted him walking through the door.

"Word! What's up?" Mose stuck out his hand for the special handshake that he invented just for them as he sat with him in their favorite booth.

Joshua told him about his second meeting with the Lord last night. "I don't know why Jesus is personally visiting me."

"I can't believe you talked to Jesus again in person!"

"You CAN'T believe?" Joshua emphasized his negative response.

Mose rolled his eyes. "Okay, I said the wrong thing. I can believe," he said as he took the menu from their waitress. Seriously, he looked Joshua straight in the eye. "I've never known anyone like you. It's like the supernatural is natural to you."

"God is the God of the supernatural. Miracles, signs and wonders are His middle name," Joshua opened the menu. "That's why I wouldn't stop doing what I'm doing for anything in the whole world. Serving the Lord is exciting!"

"Go figure, since you get personal visits from the Lord."

"A lot of people have seen Jesus."

"You've got to admit, it's not a normal . . ."

"What can I get you?" The waitress asked.

"Man, I could eat a horse. I want a burger with fries and a Coke," Mose handed her his menu.

"What's in your house salad?" Joshua asked. He wasn't hungry enough for a chef salad.

"Lettuce, tomatoes, and cheese."

"Do you have any cucumbers?"

"Yeah, I think I can find you some . . . dressing?"

"Fat free ranch."

"Anything else?"

Joshua handed her the menu. "Bottled water."

"Do you ever eat junk food?" Mose asked as the waitress left their table.

"No."

"I thought only rabbits eat the food you eat."

Joshua laughed.

"Like I said before, I don't think there is anything about you that is 'normal.'"

"You mean normal by the world's standards, or normal by spiritual standards?"

"Are you sure you will be able to handle public school?"

Joshua thought about his question. "I'm only sure that Jesus wants me to go to public school and He is with me every wherever I go."

"Word answer. That's why I think I'll call you Wordman."

"That's about all you'll get from Joshua," Kellie added as she sat down in their booth. "I've known Joshua for three years now and the Word is his specialty."

Hannah sat next to Joshua, "You know that you are going to be, like, a rare species at our school, don't you?"

"Jesus said that all things are possible to them that believe and I believe that He wants back into the public schools more than we do," Joshua explained. "Besides, didn't Peter say that we are peculiar people?"

Kellie looked at Joshua with sad eyes. "I'm gonna miss you a lot."

"Next year as a senior you will forget all about me."

"No way!" Kellie raised her voice.

Mose interrupted her. "By the way, update, Joshua has now had two official visits from Jesus."

The waitress interrupted their conversation by delivering their food. "Can I get you girls anything?"

Hannah drooled over Mose's food, but ordered a salad.

Kellie passed on food. "Now," she quizzed Mose when the waitress left, "what did you say?"

"Jesus appeared to Joshua again last night," Mose said as he stuffed a big bite of hamburger in his mouth.

"Sh!" Joshua didn't want anyone to hear what they were saying.

"Like, what did he tell you?" Hannah asked.

"He gave me instructions about evil spirits and what I saw last night. He wants you to know because you are a part of this ministry."

"You saw something again?" Mose asked.

"I saw a spiritual fight between angels and demons."

Metraloas was summoned to the center of hell.

The bat followed metraloas. “Do you know what he wants?”

“Does anyone ever know what the master wants? I don’t have a clue.”

The bat asked a thousand questions. Metraloas cursed him. “How in —— should I know? I only know he wants me to go to the fun center. And if you’ve never been there, that’s the place that he gets immense pleasure torturing former witches, warlocks and fallen preachers from earth. He likes to show off his power by sitting on his throne in the center of hell and threatening those who fail at their assignments by taking away rewards, disembodiment or, if you survive the fun-center, termination. “

The old android is losing his memory, the bat thought. He was with him when they went to the fun center to find chemah earlier. “Have you ever been tortured?”

“No. Chemah is the only one that has ever hit me. I’ve kept my nose clean and stayed away from hell politics. Satan likes to rule us with threats of evil action. The more fear embedded in our heart, the more he can take control of our mind and body.”

“How come you hate chemah so much?’

“Because he is lazy and treats all androids like slaves. Since we are all members of the kingdom of darkness, we should share responsibilities but he receives all the credit and rewards.”

“Isn’t that the way of humans on earth?” the bat asked.

He didn’t answer. Descending down the long tunnel he again endured the comments of the spirits chained in the sides of the walls.

“This is it, metraloas the moron. You are history!”

“Yeah, the graveline told us that lord satan is livid!” Evil laughter bounced off the wall and the voices magnified in his hearing.

He ignored them as long as he could. “At least I am free. I’m not chained up until the appointed time!”

“Yes, but when we are released we will not have to worry about those Christians who have the power!” They cackled with sinister laughter. “They will be raptured!” They screamed obscenities at him as he landed at the bottom of the tunnel.

“Shut up you tribulation spirits! When you get released, the Christian God has already determined your failure; you will only last a few years on earth’s surface!”

“They really are scary looking,” the bat commented.

“They don’t scare me. The only thing they can do is curse and torment people after they die and are taken to hell."

"Are you sure that they are absolutely bound and embedded in the walls of the tunnel?" The bat asked.

"Yes. After all these years, they have never come after me. As humans are free falling to the bottom of hell, all they can do is mentally abuse them. But I've learned how to use my front and back long sharp talons by clawing them as I travel to the bottom floor."

Now the bat understood why the chained spirits hated him so passionately.

Chemah was waiting at the bottom of the tunnel. He put his hand out and grabbed metraloas around the neck. "What are you going to tell him?"

"What do you think?!" He sputtered out.

"What do you want?" Fear was building inside of chemah.

Groveling might do okay for starters. "I want you to take all the blame for the Knight family!"

The bat couldn't believe what he was hearing. Metraloas must have a termination wish.

Chemah's blood boiled red-hot. It was all he could do to keep from blasting him with his fire. "I can take the heat from satan! After all, I survived the war of rebellion in heaven." Chemah used his power to lift metraloas off the ground with an invisible chokehold determined to terminate the android.

Anger kept chemah from reading metraloas' mind. The bat decided to highlight that fact in his memory card and discipline the emotion of anger. In the future maybe he could use that knowledge as leverage over the higher ranking fallen angels.

"But you on the other hand can be taken out: silenced for eternity by one blast from me!" He slammed him into the ground. "I am an angel! Never forget it!" chemah kicked him hard in his side a couple of times.

"Go ahead, terminate me!"

Chemah stopped kicking him. Satan wanted to talk to metraloas and he still needed him to be a watcher over the Knights until he found their weak spot. It was so frustrating to have to depend on androids to keep humans in line. He let out a string of cursing.

"I'm sure that satan, the master deceiver, the dragon of the Old Testament, the snake in the garden of eden and as the first arch-angel of light, the most beautiful creation in all of our universe would be very interested in your extra-curricular activities." metraloas stood and dusted hell's dirt off his dry-leather skin.

Oh, shut up you stupid, stupid android! The bat wanted to throw-up. Listening to another tirade of metraloas' trivial words sickened him. *He's like one of the nerdy humans who say wrong words at wrong times,* he thought as he rolled his eyes and sighed.

"I've known satan since before the beginning of time. I was one of the first to follow him when he was Lucifer, son of the morning. I know exactly what he believed when he talked to us about the plans of God. I know of his plans now and I am a member of his inner circle. Who do you think he is going to believe . . . me or you?"

"He can't be everywhere at the same time. So he invented me, the spiritual robot, so to speak. I am a member of the billions of armies of androids that were created to deceive, torture and harass humans. Who do you think he needs most?"

The bat was thoroughly engrossed in the conversation. He couldn't believe that metraloas had developed to the degree that he was challenging a spirit from the heavenlies. *Amazing,* he thought. *Who would have ever thought that an android as old as he was could evolve? The master will be very interested in my next report.*

Chemah was shocked. "You are unbelievable. You think I care if you stand before the master or not?" He raised his hand to blast him to pieces.

Metraloas used his ace card. "I have found a weak link in the Knights' prayer warriors."

Chemah lowered his weapon hand.

"Destroy me and I promise you . . . you will never find out."

"I don't care if I find out or not. You are an android that has run amuck." He stared him down.

Metraloas kept his mouth shut.

"What can you do as an android that I can't do as a created angel of God?!" He grabbed metraloas by the throat.

"Give me a chance to show you my plan and if I fail, you can terminate me."

"You help me and I might let you exist. If you try to deceive me, I will make you painfully pay before I terminate you." chemah released metraloas and dematerialized to transport himself into the heart of hell.

The bat materialized again next to metraloas who was struggling to breathe sitting on hell's dirt floor. "I hate to ask, but what did you think you were doing?"

He swatted the bat away from him.

"Oooo! Green blood?" Hannah squealed. She sat down her fork that was full of dark green leafy lettuce. "Anyone want my salad?"

Joshua continued, "Just like the movies. Only these demons are uglier and smell terrible."

The four were still sitting in their favorite booth in the back of the restaurant with their eyes and ears totally focused on Joshua.

"They just vanished after they were stabbed?" asked Kellie.

"They left a residue of ashes that kind of disintegrated."

Hannah quickly unzipped her backpack and pulled out her Bible.

"How can Hollywood know so much about the spiritual world?" Kellie wondered out loud.

"Some of the writers must have a personal view of what's going on," Mose told her.

Joshua stopped talking to see what Hannah was up to. She turned to the books of the prophets near the end of the Old Testament. She was flipping through the pages. "I have it marked here somewhere . . . yeah . . . Listen to this scripture guys. It's in Malachi 4:3. I underline all the passages with red ink that talk about defeating the devil. 'You shall trample the wicked, for they shall be ashes under the soles of your feet.'"

"Cool!" Mose slapped the table with his hand.

"Why do you think you are getting so many visits from Jesus?" Hannah interrupted.

"I've only had two, Hannah."

"Man, that's two more than I've had," Mose exclaimed.

"Jesus told me that I would receive the gifts necessary for the operation of this ministry. You need to ask Him. You know He is the one running this ministry, not me."

"I'm glad it's you and not me." Some of the things that Joshua has experienced scared Mose, but he sure wouldn't let Joshua know that.

"Joshua, I'm really grateful to be a part of this ministry. I can't wait to get started. Just think of the miracles we're going to see," Kellie said.

"My parents told me that God has a special work for me to do since before I can even remember. I seek to prophecy like Paul wrote."

"Wordman, whatever the Lord gives you blesses us. So I hope that He gives you more."

"One thing's for sure," Hannah interrupted.

"What?" Kellie asked.

"Without a vision the people perish," quoted Hannah.

"So can we pray for visions?" Kellie asked Joshua.

"It's how you word your prayers," Joshua cautioned them.

"How?" asked Mose.

"If you use the Words from prophecies in the Bible, then you will never pray a wrong prayer. I know that the manifestations of the spirit are given out by the will of the Holy Spirit according to Paul's teaching in Corinthians.

I want a vision from the Holy Spirit and only the Holy Spirit," Joshua told them.

Hannah started flipping pages again back to I Corinthians looking for the scripture to which Joshua was referring. "Is that in chapter 130r 12?"

"Chapter 12 around verse 10 or 11," Mose answered.

"Yeah, here it is in verse 11. 'But one and the same Spirit works all these things, distributing to each one individually as He wills,'" Hannah read.

"We do have to covet the best manifestations and especially to prophesy. The manifestation of prophecy was the one my mother was anointed with at the accident. It was so cool to see that police officer fall flat on his face," Joshua said.

"Isn't that the same as seeking gifts?" asked Kellie.

"No. We are not to seek the manifestation, but the Giver. The Holy Spirit distributes manifestations of Himself among the body of Christ as He needs. So we should seek and desire the Holy Spirit to manifest Himself through us for other people." Joshua felt the teaching anointing coming upon him. "Paul told us to pursue love and desire spiritual things. Manifestations of the Holy Spirit are anointings, not gifts. The highest anointing is prophesying. A prophet reveals the plans of the devil and gives us warning so we can pray against the evil purposed on earth."

"Doesn't a prophet also reveal plans of God?" Mose asked.

"Sure. The Lord doesn't do anything on earth that He doesn't first reveal it to His people."

"Yeah, but the question is, is anybody listening?" Hannah asked half sarcastically.

"I think more of the Lord's body is listening now than ever before," Joshua answered her. Everyone was listening intently to Joshua while oblivious to the time.

"But is there such a thing as good prophesying?" Hannah was a little confused.

"That's what Jesus was doing when he told me to start this ministry. If I would have done nothing after he talked to me, then His coming to me would have been for nothing."

"I don't get it," Hannah told him.

"Hey! I get it. Jesus gave you direction about what to do and we are praying over it until it comes to pass," Mose said.

"Are you saying when a man speaks the will of God that we have to intercede for that to come to pass?" Kellie wanted to make sure she was hearing what Joshua was saying.

"If the prophecy warns of coming judgment, or works of satan, then we need to stop his plans against us. If the prophecy is a ministry revealed, then prayer is needed to bring it to pass." Joshua said.

"What if someone tells you that the Lord wants you to become a missionary or something like that?" Mose asked.

"You should never let a prophecy from someone else change the course of your life unless it is a confirmation acknowledging what the Lord has already shown you. They should only confirm what the Lord has already told you."

"If prophecy is judgment, then why should we be interceding to stop it from coming to pass? I thought that all judgment in the Bible was final?" Kellie asked.

"Kellie, look at Nineveh. Jonah was a prophet and what he said didn't come to pass," reminded Hannah.

"The law of mercy is greater than the law of judgment. That is how satan is defeated. He operates his kingdom out of judgment and wrath. God operates His Kingdom out of mercy and grace," Joshua explained.

"So, if prophecy is judgment, how can we pray and change what is going to happen?" Kellie asked again.

"Prophecy or visions of judgment concerning men are warning of coming works of satan to inform the believers how to pray and intercede that destruction doesn't come to pass."

"You don't believe that it is judgment from God?" asked Hannah.

"Think of judgment as harvest. There are two harvests blessing and cursing. I believe that we are under the law of seed time and harvest. And since people are doing the sowing, they are the ones responsible for the harvest that they receive."

"Hm . . ." Mose pondered what he just said. "You know, I like that. It makes us responsible for the things that happen to us."

"Yeah, like, I like knowing that God isn't condemning people to hell on earth and then to hell after death," Hannah said.

The waitress came over to the table looking at her watch, "Can I get you anything else?" She had long ago cleared the table and she was wondering how much money in tips this group of kids was costing her.

"Can I have another bottle of water, please?" asked Joshua.

"Sure, anyone else?" She tried to be polite.

They all shook their heads no.

"God wants to prosper, protect and perfect His children and remember He loves everyone, not just those who have already have accepted Him, but . . ."

Hannah interrupted, "For God so loved the world that He gave . . ."

"Yeah, it just doesn't fit that God would love only a select few," Mose agreed. "Jesus died for us when we were yet sinners."

"What about judging a prophet in the Old Testament by his words?"

"That's something different all together. The Bible is a book of God's Words about three different groups of people."

"Like who?" asked Hannah.

"The Jews, the Gentiles and the body of Christ," explained Joshua. "God deals with each group differently."

"Okay, how did that answer my question?"

"Think about a prophecy that was spoken over someone you know that did not come to pass. Do you consider the person that gave the prophecy a false prophet because he missed it?"

"Or," Mose interjected, "because the person he prophesied to missed it!"

"My mom was told that she would have a music ministry, but it never came to pass," Kellie told them.

"Did that agree with her spirit?" Joshua asked. "Did she pray about it and then practice music everyday?"

"She loved playing the piano and at first she practiced until she met my dad."

"When someone speaks a word of prophecy to you and it agrees with your own spirit, then you have to work and pray for it to come to pass. Demons hear prophetic utterances and listen to them. They can gain insight on where to attack people and their ministries."

"Maybe, the person that spoke to her missed it," Hannah said.

Kellie nodded, "That explains a lot of things to me, Joshua."

"Whether a prophecy is a warning to stop a work of the devil or a vision to start a work of God; both need prayers to come to pass on this earth," Joshua taught them. "satan and his kingdom are here on earth to wreak havoc with God's creation."

"Wreak havoc?" Mose snickered. They all laughed.

Joshua laughed with them. He took the bottle of water from the waitress. "Thank you." He made a mental note to leave her a big tip.

"God does have a plan and will for every human being on earth. He gives us the ability to choose His plan or reject it. He gave us His Word to warn us of satan's plans and actions that cause judgment. From the beginning He prophesied that a man would crush his kingdom and recover and restore all that satan stole from God."

"So the day of wrath is judgment against the kingdom of darkness?" Hannah asked.

"Yes. Satan and his evil system are the only beings from that fateful day of temptation that haven't received judgment for the evil that they caused to come into this earth and upon man," Joshua explained.

"Yeah, like in the words of Hannah, like why didn't anyone ever teach us that before . . . I mean like why are we so clueless?" Mose mimicked Hannah's voice and face. He loved to tease her.

"Cut it out Mose! I'm serious about this!" Hannah hit him back on the arm.

"Think about it. God's plans never change. His way of thinking and doing things are forever set in stone, but satan's plans can and should be changed."

"That makes sense to me," Mose said.

Glancing at her watch, Kellie stood up. "Hey! It's almost time for dinner and I've got to run."

"Why don't we meet at my house tonight."

Kellie grabbed Joshua's arm. "That's a great idea, but if I don't get home now, I'll be grounded."

Mose stood at attention. "Onward Christian soldiers!"

Hannah pushed Mose out the door. "Not another song!"

CHAPTER 19

A black throne materialized in the center of the fun arena located next to the cells in hell. Metraloas and the bat traveled down the dusty crowded trail filled with vile and disgusting creatures. Suddenly, the evil spirits paused sensing the arrival of the prince of death.

As the ground shook, Metraloas grabbed the wall to steady himself. "The master loves transporting his throne from earth and ruling the underworld."

"He was a genius in designing this place of detention for the souls of men and women who die in their sins. Have you ever seen his true form?" the bat asked.

"Yes. Once, when his hood fell down and exposed his wrinkled, gross decaying skin. It was totally awesome, but he immediately transformed his face into a youthful looking man. Several of us saw him before he could recover. On the surface he always looks like an extraordinarily handsome man," metraloas said. "Did you know that he has many homes around the earth?"

"He does?" The bat had been in a couple of them.

"Yes." They turned a corner to descend down into the heart of hell. "He even takes many humans as wives."

"How do you know this?"

"There are a lot of things that I know since I do a lot of listening and little talking."

They arrived just as satan stood, demanding all spirits in hell bow to him and proclaim that he is the god of earth, of hell and of the heavenlies above earth. Standing on the last step before entering the fun center, an invisible force swept around them making them bow whether they wanted to or not. The dark, ominous atmosphere was highlighted with fire dancing and swirling around them. With their night vision they could see all the stands surrounding the fun center filled with hordes of demons of all sizes and shapes. They were bowing and chanting that "satan is lord over earth above and below!" The evil beings in the kingdom of darkness worship him out of fear.

Metraloas leaned over and whispered to the bat. "I have seen him torture humans and androids with the most ruthless, perverted evil acts that a being could possibly imagine." He laughed. "Jesus said that satan is the father of lies and the one that allowed the curse to plague earth."

The bat looked around quickly to see if anyone heard them. "Shhhh . . . you mentioned the name of JC!"

"Metraloas looked around them. "Most of these beings around us are like zombies. They can't think for themselves. The human's God put the blame of Adam and Eve's fall on satan. God said that he was cursed more than all the beast of the field."

"Humans are our enemies."

"The humans think that their God created satan. They think our master is jealous of them."

"What do you think?" the bat asked above the noisy crowd surrounding the throne.

"I hate light. I hate the Word and I can't stand humans." They watched satan torturing a former witch from earth. "Did you know that one of the devil's future punishments is because he didn't open the house of his prisoners and offer forgiveness to them?"

"What?" the bat was shocked. "Where did you get that?"

"It's in the Bible."

"Do you know where we are?"

"Sure," metraloas boasted. "This is Sheol, known as hell, the great underground prison designed as a body in the middle of the bowels of the earth. Satan demanded the incarceration of every soul of every human who died on earth."

"You didn't answer my question."

"I don't know who to believe. It is the master's system that control humans on earth. He has successfully brain-washed them with a language of death. He has trained the body and the mind to think death after the first few seconds of life."

An ear-shattering scream interrupted their conversation as a horde of demons began piercing the soul of a human with pitch forks.

He bent over and whispered by the bat's ear. "Why do you think the master wants to totally control all humans?"

"Their power?"

"Their authority over the earth through their mouth."

"I think I am beginning to understand. The master has successfully found a way to channel the power of humans into his kingdom."

Another earth-shattering scream stopped their discussion as a new human was thrown into the fun center. The crying sounded like a female. She was wrapped in chains and pulled around by a miniature demon in a black robe.

Satan waved his hand and an evil grotesque spirit with a monkey body, the face of a bat and long arms with claws at the end appeared with a large black book. She crumpled at his feet begging for mercy.

Hideous laughter came from the black-hooded being. "You want mercy? You weak, sniveling peace of trash! Have you confused me with another god? The Christian God gives mercy and is weak and lacks power. The strong inherit the earth and my kingdom! My kingdom is the strength of this planet!"

The evil spirits around the arena in grand stands jeered at the human and cheered for satan. They repeated over and over that "satan is lord! He is master and ruler of all!"

He opened his black book. "At last I have destroyed you from the earth." He ran his finger down each page looking for the name of the human.

"Here you are . . . oh my, my! You worked hard for me. I see that you won many people to the New Age movement. As a teacher you influenced many to believe in the doctrine of devils! HA! HA! HA!"

His laugh sent fear trembling through the human bones crumpled at his feet. He came off the throne and pointed his finger at the human. The dead flesh was ripped off her bones.

The bat laughed. "I had no idea that dead flesh looked like that!"

"Their pain is more real down here than on earth, since the soul is more sensitive to pain without the body. Don't you just love the smell of dead, rotten, stinking flesh?" metraloas turned his face upward and inhaled a long, long breath and froze enjoying every scent.

"Why is their body a blue-gray color?" the bat asked.

"The life of the body is in their blood and they have to breathe to be alive. Since they are dead, they have no more need for oxygen and no more red color. Look! Watch how the flesh falls off the bones as it is burned with fire and then reappears as the fire recedes."

"How often does that happen?"

"This cycle is repeated over and over in every prison cell and pit covering every part of hell. When the dead flesh disappears, inside the skeleton a gray mist resides that is their soul. If you noticed, it is only when the soul talks that you can tell the sex of the human."

A look of horror washed over the face of the human as patches of dead flesh started reappearing over her skeleton. "I believed in your kingdom of darkness." She pointed her bony finger at satan. "I brought many to this place. You promised me a part of your kingdom!" As she talked she dragged her bones over to the feet of satan and begged him to honor his word.

"Me, honor my word?" He looked at the evil spirits laughing in the stands. "ME . . . honor my word? I am the father of lies. I was the first to lie and I have made many children of lies!" His laughter was hideous. "I am proud of my lies." He directed his yellow-red eyes into the woman's eyes. "After all, they brought you here didn't they?" Again, he threw back his head and laughed. His hood fell off his head and everyone who saw his face gasped.

Immediately a handsome young face replaced the wrinkled decrepit face that was exposed when his hood fell off. Satan pulled the black hood back over his head immediately. He kicked the soul groveling at his feet so hard that her bones detached and fell on the ground like dice. What little flesh had formed on her was scattered. Little black-hooded gremlins ran over to gather the bones to scatter them all over hell. They loved to play the game of hide and seek.

Satan laughed at them and nodded his head. He gave them permission to play the game they loved.

"Did you see him?" metraloas grabbed the bat in his hand.

"Hey! Watch it!" he struggled to fly away from metraloas. His hand was big enough to crush him while he was shaped like a bat. "I saw his face for a second."

"Didn't I tell you his true form is hideous?"

"Shhh . . ."

One of the gremlins passed them carrying a leg bone of the human. The gray mist followed the demon screaming in excruciating pain trying to find her bones.

"Notice that each bone that is torn from her dead body gives that soul intense pain. Pain is more acute to them after death. The flesh is a buffer between the spirit and soul on earth."

"You know a lot about these things."

"I've been around for a long time."

"How long does this game last?" the bat asked.

"The human will be tormented for days during the game and then put back together, chained and put in her prison cell until another time of torturing. It's a non-ending cycle of torture for eternity."

Another human was brought before satan.

Chemah communicated with the master on their special communication line separate from the graveline. Satan waved his hand and indicated the human soul was to wait until he heard from chemah.

"Come forward."

He signaled to metraloas to come forward with him. "Lord satan, we have disturbing news. The family that metraloas was watching is trying to connect with a host of warring angels from the army of JC." Chemah bowed.

"Connect?" Satan stood as he motioned for metraloas to come forward. Satan put his arm around metraloas. "Connect? What exactly does chemah mean by trying to connect?" He stared into chemah's eyes. His spy had already told him about the communication tower.

"An army of warring angels is guarding the house and it looks like angels are building a communication tower between heaven and earth," metraloas explained.

Chemah was horrified. *Of all the stupid ignorant things!*

"Now, now chemah. It was smart of him to tell me all the facts! Don't call this intelligent android stupid and ignorant!"

Chemah bowed, "But my lord satan, he is lying! We have no proof of a communication line!"

Satan let out a blood-curdling scream and a power force hit chemah and flattened him on one of the walls in hell. "I know about the communication tower! Do you really think that you can con me?"

Immediately, long roots of slimy, black tentacles attached themselves to him and pinned chemah against the wall.

Metraloas fell to floor and spoke to satan. "Oh great one. Let me tell you that I had no part in keeping this from you. I have record of all my reports that I gave to chemah recommending he tell you about their heavy church involvement and prayer groups that Vicki Knight started."

Chemah let out a blood-curdling scream. "metraloas, you throat-cutting———! When I get loose, I will kill you!"

Quickly, satan was next to chemah putting his long filthy, crooked nails on the sides of his face. "What were you thinking? You know the prime directive. I am always to be informed of any human that can plug into God's communication system, BEFORE the system is in place!"

Satan was furious that chemah had kept the operation from him. He started scratching his cheeks until the sharp nails pierced the fallen angel's red skin and blue blood began dripping on his hand. "Why did you not make me aware of the warring angels' positions around that property?" Following the flow of blood, satan looked down and saw the fire blaster fitted at the end of his arm. Slowly his anger subsided as he remembered how chemah lost his hand in the war of rebellion while saving him from serious disfiguration.

Patting his face and then licking the blood off his own hand, satan spoke quietly into chemah's ear. "You are one of my favorites! Why do you have to disappoint me, son?" He walked back to his throne. "Release him!"

Fear reigned in the hearts of those that follow the prince of death. This was exactly the picture he wanted his subjects to register in their mind. Immediately, the slimy tentacles let go of him. He fell to the floor trying to recover his breath. The tentacles were slowly squeezing the breath of death out of him.

When chemah could stand, he walked slowly back to the throne and fell to his face. "Master, forgive me. I thought that I could take care of this situation without adding extra burdens to your many campaigns on earth," he choked out holding his hands to his throat, his stringy, red hair drenched in blue blood.

"So you don't think I can handle more campaigns?"

"No, I know that you are superior in every way to a mere mortal and to those you have created. I didn't think that they were that dangerous. Christians that live such pious lives are seldom so dangerous."

Satan laughed. "How true! Religious, traditional Christians are a favorite of mine."

Chemah was an excellent orator and deceiver. He knew exactly which words to use to give his master pleasure. "It is true that metraloas tried to tell me about the Knights, but I thought he was just a sniveling idiot and a coward. I didn't know if I could trust him. Several times I came to his base and checked on the things he was reporting, but I never could see anything that matched his findings." Chemah was lying. He turned his head and growled at metraloas with disgust. "He set his base in an oak tree two houses from the house he is suppose to be watching."

Laughter roared from the demonic stands.

Slowly, satan pointed his finger at metraloas and an invisible spirit put his hands around his throat and started squeezing the green liquid power source flowing inside of him.

Metraloas felt the pressure on his throat causing his veins to bulge. "Master, I was wrong for not making sure that chemah understood the situation, but I want a chance to correct it."

Satan waved his hand for the invisible spirit to stop. "Why should I give you another chance?"

"I have observed the Knights for two years. If you would assign chemah to help me, I am positive that together we could discover a weak place to get into their home or flesh. It might take years for someone else to gain my understanding of that family! No one knows them like me." He was talking fast. Time was running out on him.

Again satan waved his hand for the invisible spirit to let him go. "What do you think about his idea, chemah?"

"It has merit." He tried to answer calmly even though anger was building inside him. Chemah knew that he could crack the Knights. It wouldn't take him long to prove what a failure metraloas was.

"Ah, I love your thinking chemah. You are an angel after my own heart! I will grant your request."

The evil angels and demons stomped their feet on the floor of hell in recognition of satan's evil authority over all his kingdom.

He pointed his finger at both of them. "I'm warning you! If you fail, chemah, you will be chained in tartarus and you, metraloas, will be recycled spare parts for my latest model android! Leave me now so I continue with my favorite sport."

Immediately an invisible force removed them from satan's presence.

On the surface of earth metraloas spoke to the bat as he rubbed his neck. "The master wasn't like this at first. Evil desires with time have turned the prince of death into a bloodthirsty sadist. If this was Noah's day, the offending androids would have been given a second chance. His own inventions are driving him toward an insatiable diet of evil continually that is causing his mind to go insane."

The bat absolutely could not believe his ears. "Are you insane or do you just have a death wish?" He looked all around them to see if any evil spirit heard what the crazy android just said. "I know you have been around for a long time, but don't you know how dangerous it is to say such things?"

Metraloas didn't reply as he flew back to his headquarters. He knew that he was treading on dangerous ground, but he figured his days were numbered anyway. He couldn't think of any android his age that still existed. Most of them were considered defective and then destroyed.

Chemah looked behind him and saw metraloas and the bat talking with each other. A desire boiled within him to terminate metraloas, but his position with satan disturbed him more. It was obvious that their leader was changing. Satan was either forgetting the past or changing the facts to fit his purposes. But either way, he wasn't the same being that was created by God with wisdom and understanding of the secret places on the mountain of God in heaven.

Thoughts of doubt were continually invading his mind.

He was convinced that the suspicious thoughts were direct attacks of a cloaked spy from the Kingdom of God. Several times he had a feeling that one of God's angels was in his private quarters, but he could not see anything. It had to be one of God's angels that was sending him thoughts with the power to torture him.

Chemah couldn't understand how the thoughts could dominate him, since evil spirits were the ones that were supposed to put wrong thoughts in the minds of humans. It made him fuming mad that his mind could still be subjected to the goodness of God. The thoughts harassed him and he had no power to stop the agony. He wondered how that was possible that good could penetrate the force field of evil surrounding hell and earth. Could it be possible that . . .

NO! He shouted in his mind. *I refuse to think about it!* He was so consumed with the thought, that he didn't follow metraloas. Instead he transported himself to his ship in the heavenlies. Even as every spiritual cell in his body was being beamed between earth and the heavenlies, the question survived the transport of his scattered brain cells.

How can satan win?! HE CAN NOT DEFEAT HIS CREATOR!

As he appeared in his personal quarters the thought was like a swarm of good spirits chanting over and over and over in an invisible dimension that he could not see.

"Get away from me!" Chemah put his hand to his head and screamed out loud.

Earth is governed by the law of sowing and reaping and satan's kingdom has no power to change that law, the good spirits said over and over. *Satan won't win,* they chanted.

Chemah fell down on his bunk and tried to use the power of mental control to stop the thoughts assailing his mind. It was true that satan had become so satiated with evil desires, that an unquenchable thirst for wickedness was causing him to become unstable and out of control. Many of the fallen angels could see that even though satan was convinced that evil was triumphing over good, the reality was that good was winning on earth.

He refused to recognize his obvious defeats and that concerned chemah. The prophecies from God's prophets were coming to pass despite all the plans and schemes of satan's to stop them. It seemed to him that they had never been able to stop the appointed times of God. Especially the prophetic Word from God in the garden. Even though satan killed several different generations of baby boys, the deliverer always survived. Jesus himself being the biggest example of a Word from God that satan couldn't stop. Chemah closed his eyes and banged his head on the wall next to his bunk.

I will not think of this . . . I will not think of this . . . I will not think of this!

He stopped to listen and heard silence.

Satan can not change the predetermined plan of God that he and his kingdom will be brought to the lowest depths of the pit and cast into the lake of fire!

Chemah jumped off his bunk and grabbed his head and let out an ear-piercing scream. "NOOOO!"

CHAPTER 20

Mose called his mom and asked her if he could go home with Joshua. She wanted him to come home, but she liked that he was becoming close friends with Joshua.

"Wordman, hey, does it bother you that I call you Wordman?"

"No. I've spent all my life making the Word a part of me."

"I should have been with you yesterday!" Mose tried to ignore Kellie honking the car horn as they drove around the circle drive way with Hannah hanging out of the window yelling that they would call if they couldn't come over.

They were talking about the accident that occurred yesterday after the visit to the print shop. Suddenly Joshua stopped. "You should have seen my mom . . ." Mose ran into the back of Joshua as he stepped up to the front porch " . . . when she told the policeman he was having an affair."

"Man, I wished I could have seen his face!"

"It was like my Mom pulled a gun on him and shot him dead! He fell to the ground. Nothing can be hid from the Holy Spirit." Joshua pushed in the number code on the key pad and opened the front door.

"The truck flew over your car?"

"I didn't see it. That's what the eye witnesses said."

"Word! That is unbelievable!"

"No it isn't. Angels caused the truck to fly!"

"Oh yeah, just a common occurrence people see trucks flying every-day!"

"Attitude?"

"My attitude's just fine." Mose rolled his eyes. "You know ever since I've met you, I have to watch every word I say around you."

They walked into the foyer. "Hey, you are the one that used the word 'unbelievable,' not me. You want me to agree that what happened is unbelievable?" Joshua stopped and looked him straight into his eyes.

He had him cold. "No, I want to see it myself."

"You do every week."

"What are you talking about?"

"People get saved at your church every Sunday."

Mose stopped at the steps to the winding stairway. Joshua's house still amazed him every time he walked into it. He couldn't help think it was something out of the program *Lifestyles of the Rich and Famous*. "I know, 'Salvation is the greatest miracle of all.'" He quoted his dad. "But, you can't see salvation."

Joshua started up the stairs.

"I want to see something that will make my eyes pop out."

"If that's your confession I believe every word of it."

"You know, Knight, one of these days I'm gonna . . ." . . .

. . . Kientay and Malcolm followed closely behind the boys.

Suddenly a couple of evil vultures flew over their heads, diving close to the top of the boy's heads.

"I don't like the way this conversation is going," Malcolm materialized his sword.

"They can hear words filled with fear, doubt, or anger from miles away!" Kientay moved closer to Joshua as he looked around the sky above the house; the most common entry that most demons used to enter a human's physical house.

One of the evil vultures spoke to the other. "Isn't this the house that metraloas is assigned to watch?"

"Yeah! Call him and tell him to get here fast. It looks like we're going to get in."

Malcolm heard that they were contacting reinforcements. The angels surrounding the house of Knight strengthened their ranks. "It won't be easy for the vultures to break through . . ."

Kientay finished his sentence for him. "But there is a remote chance that it could happen if Joshua started thinking and talking through his flesh."

The warring angels at the entrance gate appeared before the guardian angels. "We are prepared for battle, if necessary."

The sky over the house across the street started to fill up with dark clouds. Evil spirits were gathering a force.

"I don't believe that we will have to fight," Kientay said.

Metraloas appeared before Kientay. "Let me in!" He demanded. His evil heart was pumping fast. He hadn't been this close to the inside of the house of Knight in years.

"Not so fast, metraloas. A door to this house hasn't opened yet. Words of offense have not come out of Joshua's lips."

Metraloas looked around. It had been over two years since he had gotten this close to walking into the physical house of Knight. "You can't deny that his friend is offended."

"He may be, but Joshua isn't." Kientay materialized his sword and raised it. "You cannot come through us unless Joshua speaks the words."

Metraloas honed his eyes and ears on every word that Joshua was saying . . .

. . . Mose stopped climbing up the stairs staring at Joshua. "As a comedian, it's kind of hard to watch every word that comes out of my mouth."

"I'm not your judge." Joshua turned around at the top of the stairs.

"Yeah you are. Why do I feel I have to watch every word I say around you?" Mose was letting his flesh get a little riled.

"What you're really saying is that as a comedian you can't make people laugh unless you cut someone down or use negative words," Joshua faced Mose as he moved to the top of the stairs.

"Did I say that?" Now Mose was getting irritated.

"Then, what are you saying?"

Mose stopped to think about the question he just asked. What was he saying? He decided to keep his mouth shut. It was obvious he already said too much and besides, he could feel the temperature in his body rising . . .

. . . Metraloas was posed to pounce on the boys as soon as Joshua said anything remotely opposite of what Jesus would say or think. He pushed forward as he listened to the words coming out of the boys' mouths. A devious grin appeared on his face.

Kientay knew that it wasn't going to happen. "You might as well leave. You are wasting your time." He held his position.

"You know you guardian angels are all alike; so full of optimism and crap like that."

"It isn't crap, metraloas. It's what the world was created with, faith, but then you know nothing of the things of God." Kientay knew it was a waste of time to talk to the evil android. Soon his time would run out and all creations of satan would be totally destroyed by fire.

"I know that your God is weak, and we will win this war on earth and the struggle for the souls of man," metraloas sneered.

Chroni materialized with the glory of the Lord reflecting from his armor. He blinded the evil spirits that surrounded the hedge of protection. "You know nothing but the lies programmed to you from your father, satan. Your time is almost up and the kingdom of darkness will see defeat and all human beings will see with their natural eyes your defeat by the glory of God, the Son of the living God!"

"Be gone, metraloas! Joshua is resisting you with the Word of God!"

" . . . Are we getting ready to slug it out?" Joshua asked.

"No!" Mose shouted at him.

"Mose, I don't want to be the one that judges the words that come out of your mouth."

Suddenly it dawned on him what Joshua just asked him. "Wait a minute . . . did you just ask me if we were going to fight?"

"Yes."

"REALLY fight, like physical?"

Joshua shook his head yes.

Mose continued to stare at him and burst out laughing. "Me . . . and you . . . fight?"

When the picture of them physically fighting entered Joshua's mind, he started laughing with Mose.

When they stopped laughing, Joshua took him to his bedroom. It was as they entered his room that he realized that they may have come dangerously close to allowing their emotions to overcome their spirit. Anything in the flesh could open the door to demonic presence.

"Hey, we need to pray." Joshua dropped his stuff on his desk.

"Why?"

"I think we might have been close to opening a door for demons."

Mose dropped his stuff by Joshua's desk. "You think so?" He looked around the room as if he could see something.

"Yes. Satan assigns watchers that report on every move that we make and every word that we say."

"Word! Is that why you are so careful about every word you say?" Mose sat on one of the chairs in Joshua's large bedroom.

"Yes. Believe me Mose, I don't listen to every word you say just so that I can nail you and make you think I'm better than you."

"The second I say something negative, I know it's wrong."

"If I caused you any offense, please forgive me," Joshua asked him from a sincere heart.

"Hey, you didn't offend me. I was just allowing my flesh to raise its ugly head a little," Mose replied. "I sure don't want a demon coming into your bedroom because of me. So forgive me for getting a little ticked off."

"Let's pray." Joshua raised his hands up to the Lord in Heaven. "Forgive us Lord for saying any words that were idle and powerless. I forgive Mose and he forgives me . . ."

"Amen!" Mose said in agreement.

"We bind any spirit that may have thought he could gain entrance into this house, or bedroom or our lives."

"Yeah!" Mose interrupted looking around the bedroom again.

"We submit ourselves to God, to one another and we resist satan and his kingdom in the name of Jesus!" . . .

. . . Several warring angels left the wall of protection to fight with the evil spirits who had gathered to enter the property of the house of Knight.

Metraloas knew the moment Joshua asked Mose to forgive him and prayed he lost the opportunity to gain entrance into the house of Knight. He took off, hoping the angels wouldn't chase him.

Kientay followed at his heels. It was too tempting to whack him a couple of times with his anointed sword. It was so sweet to hear the Word of God coming out of the boy's mouths. It was a close call. The other warring angels were diligently holding back the forces of evil and defeating them soundly. The demons had no chance to defeat the division of warring angels guarding the house of Knight. Swords and other weapons were clanging and scattering the evil demons, many of them were being destroyed.

"Look!" Kientay pointed out after he returned from harassing metraloas. "Look how far the warring angels are chasing the demons from the neighborhood!"

"Every Word of faith coming out of their mouth pushes the devil and his forces away from them and gives us more power!" Malcolm announced.

All the angels returned from chasing the demons shouting victory.

"Nothing can stop the force of faith that is released when a believer speaks God's Words from his heart with faith," Kientay declared.

Chroni appeared and told them what was going on in the throne room of heaven. "The recording angels told me that the force of prayer is great enough to overcome the power of the weapons formed against them. The prayer group started in Vicki Knight's house is releasing prayers filled with the Word of God. They are in agreement and are one with the Father, Son and the Anointed One. Because a link between heaven and earth has been established, the Knight house is to be known officially as the house of Knight!"

"Praise the Lord!" the warring angels lifted up their hands and fell on their faces praising the Father for His infinite wisdom and grace.

"Great mercy has the Lord for His children!" shouted Malcolm.

"Great love has the Lord for His children!" shouted Kientay.

"Great rewards has the Lord for His children!" shouted Chroni.

While on their faces before the Lord, the Anointed One spoke out of His throne room in His headquarters on earth:

This is the time of great judgment on earth. Did I not say in My Word that I will never again allow the curse to destroy every living thing on earth? Did I not say that even though the imagination of man's heart is evil from his youth because of the curse, that I would not allow the curse to destroy all humans? While the earth remains seedtime and harvest, cold and heat, winter and summer, day and night shall not cease.

There is coming a great harvest of increase to My body. First, this world's wealth will transfer from the wicked hands into the hands of My children. Then, the second harvest is a harvest of miracles. Signs and wonders follow the Word coming out of the mouth of My children. Miracles are going to happen that this world has never seen before. Great manifestations of My Word are coming to this generation on earth. And before that great and wonderful second coming of My Son, I will bring a harvest of souls that has never occurred on planet earth before. I will fill My body to overflowing. Just as Jesus overflowed Peter's boat so that it started to sink, I will overflow My body with a great number of souls that no man can number!

The first harvest is to provide the money needed to preach the gospel to every person on the face of the earth. Nothing will stop this predestined plan of God. The second harvest is a calling to all people to believe in a supernatural God that can heal their body and provide for their needs like no other god on earth. With great signs and wonders and supernatural miracles the last harvest is the great harvest of souls.

Souls . . . souls . . . souls! The Father loves His creation and is not willing that any should perish but that all should have eternal life. This is the time of salvation. Signs shall abound. Lift up your head the King of Glory is coming!

The warring angels rejoiced and gave great praise to the Lord of Glory.

After a time of worship, the angels went back to their assignments. Kientay, Malcolm and Chroni walked through the walls of Joshua's house and went upstairs.

"This message that we heard from the Anointed One is going to be received by several of the Lord's prophets around earth," Chroni told them. "This is the beginning of the Joshua Generation. They will sweep America like locusts covering every inch of the land!"

"Will Joshua be one of the prophets?" Kientay asked.

"Yes."

Praise the Lord! Kientay thought to himself. He knew that Joshua's faith was being developed for the level necessary for the last and greatest battle of this earth before the Tribulation. "Will he be one on the front line?"

"Yes"

All the angels shouted. It was like a dream to be involved with one of the called out ones to fight the great battle that will prepare the way of the Lord.

"This battle is the battle that we've all been waiting for!" Kientay thanked the Lord that Joshua would be personally involved with the fight that will make a way for the coming of Jesus to end earth's wars for one thousand years. "Thank you Jesus!"

‡ ‡ ‡

Pastor Ben entered the small entry way of his home. He placed his briefcase on the little side table in the short hallway leading to his undersized kitchen. He wondered how long the church would be able to meet his salary. A picture flashed into his mind of the large and elegant foyer that he had been in the other night. For a second, he felt jealousy arise in his heart over the Knights' home. Different thoughts like that had been plaguing him all day.

Linda heard him from the kitchen and called to him.

"Yes," he replied, "it's me."

He walked into the cramped family room and sat on his favorite chair. Linda noticed that he didn't have the daily newspaper with his shoes off like usual. She was afraid to ask him how things went today. She wiped her hands on her apron and went over to take his shoes off. "Dinner will be ready in about thirty minutes."

His eyes were closed. He looked drained and very tired.

"I made your favorite meatloaf with mashed potatoes, gravy and . . ."

He turned his head toward her and said without emotion, "I'm not hungry. I want to take a nap." He closed his eyes and turned his head back toward the wall letting her know that he didn't want to talk.

Linda walked back into the kitchen and turned off the stove burners. It didn't look like dinner would be when she planned. Taking off her apron, she walked into Ben's office and shut the door. Dialing Marilyn's phone number she sat in his desk chair.

"Hello?"

"Marilyn?"

"Yes?"

"I need to ask you some questions about Pastor Ben's day."

"Linda?"

"Yes, I'm sorry, I thought you would recognize my voice."

"Well, you sound a little different."

"I'm concerned about Ben. How did things go?"

"Not so good. The calls started today about Joshua's decision to leave school."

"From who?"

"Well, several teachers and a few from the school board." She was hesitant about telling her the specific names of those who called.

"You can tell me, I know just about everyone that counts anyway."

Marilyn told her.

"I was afraid those families would be the first to say something."

"Well, the worse thing was Mr. Smith."

"What did that stiff-neck accountant say?"

"He said that he knew that one of these days Pastor Ben would run off the church's meal ticket."

Marilyn sucked in her breath. "No!"

"Yes and he indicated to me that maybe the board should contact the Knights and see if a new pastor would change their mind about leaving the church."

She couldn't believe what she was hearing. "Marilyn, did you tell Ben what Mr. Smith said?"

"No, but I think he found out."

"How?"

"Well, you know how Ann likes to talk."

"Oh brother! Don't tell me she told him."

"No, not Pastor directly . . ."

"She told Jeff."

"Oh! I could just strangle that woman!"

"I know what you mean. I get so tired of having to listen to her mouth! I pleaded with her not to tell, but she takes every opportunity she can to get into Pastor Jeff's office."

"That little busybody! She doesn't care who she hurts!" Linda was seeing red.

"I told her that if she tells Pastor Jeff anything else that is said about this situation that I was going to tell Pastor about all the gossip she leaks out of his office."

"If it's the last thing I do, that woman is going to lose her job over this!" Linda was furious.

"How is Pastor?" Marilyn asked.

"He's taking a nap, but I don't want him thinking about this matter anymore. That is why I called you. From now on, call me and let me know what is going on in the office. I don't want Ben to have to tell me what is going on when he comes home. I want this home to be a sanctuary for him."

"Oh, I agree with you totally. I will tell you everything that is going on. I know that Pastor Ben needs a knowledgeable, praying wife."

"He's depressed enough as it is. When he comes home, I want him to leave all this stuff back at the church office."

"Oh, most definitely! Don't worry, Linda, I won't let you down."

"Uh . . . Marilyn lets keep this between you and me, okay?"

"Sure. You can count on me not to tell anyone else. I am not like Ann."

"Good. Talk to you later."

"Uh . . . Linda, I just wanted to say that I don't think the church board will lower your salary. They might not give you a raise this year, but I don't think they will reduce Pastor's income."

Linda held her breath. "Who said they were thinking about that?"

"Well, I think one of the board members suggested that Pastor think of all the ways that they could cut the budget. I looked at last year's budget and Pastor received a pretty big pay increase and bonus. You know how people think when looking at shortfalls; big salaries are the first to go."

Linda felt a little offended. "How about your salary? When was your last raise?"

"My salary? Oh, secretaries make nothing compared to the pastors of this church." *Surely*, she thought, *they wouldn't look at cutting my salary!*

"Are you sure? Maybe they might cut one or two of the secretary positions."

Oh God no! Her husband was thinking about retiring. There was no way that they could make it if she lost her job. *Don't panic*, she thought, *you have seniority over all the other secretaries.*

It was almost like Linda could read her mind. "It's a good thing that you have been a secretary at the church for so long."

A sigh of relief could be heard over the phone.

"But then again, you would be the perfect cut, because you make more than all the other secretaries."

Fear took hold of her heart. "Well, one thing is for sure . . ."

"What?" asked Linda.

"If I leave, then the church will be in a pretty bad way."

"How?"

"I'm the one that knows everything about anything that concerns this church . . ."

Linda hung up the phone a little harder than usual.

Marilyn looked at the phone not believing that Linda hung up on her. *Not even Pastor Ben knows as much about the church as I do and every member of my church knows that's the truth! If you want anything from anybody in the church I can direct you. It isn't the board that orientated the new pastors.* "I do!" She held the phone away from her ear and spoke out loud into it. "In fact I have been the church secretary for the last five pastors. Just because Pastor Ben had been the longest running pastor of this church in a long time doesn't mean squat! I've seen better ones than him run out of our church!" She slammed the phone down on the receiver.

What started out as a good idea finished with a bad feeling in the pit of Linda's stomach. Even though Marilyn claimed that Ann was responsible for all the gossip that leaked out of the church office, Linda wasn't entirely convinced.

It was almost like she had just made a pact with the devil.

Slithering down a porthole into hell, the android snake reported to his supervisor. His division of watchers belonged to a special division; one that was assigned to the five-fold ministry workers. His last four assignments were pastors. So far all of them had fallen to adultery, except the one he was assigned to currently; Pastor Ben Baker.

After several years of faithful watching, he finally discovered a door of temptation; worry over money. Laughing out loud, he could hardly believe his luck. Sometimes the life of a watcher can get pretty boring, especially if the Christian he is assigned to does any amount of praying or reading of the Bible. Pastors were tough, but they usually cracked. He hadn't found one yet that was impervious to his flesh.

They all fall . . . sooner or later . . . they all fall.

Winding around the corridors of hell, the snake searched for his supervisor. It was time he reported all that he knew about Pastor Ben. He spotted him over in the pits.

"Snake 666–782, where have you been?"

"I've been watching my assignment, sir, very closely I might add."

The mammoth brown grizzly bear with a long snout and numerous whiskers in his nose started flipping through his binder. "Yes, here it is." He transported them both as fast as a twinkling of an eye into his office. He looked down at the snake coiled on the ground by his desk. "What do you have to report?"

"My assignment, Pastor Ben, is very depressed and worried over . . ."

"Yes, it says here," he wrinkled his nose to get a clearer look at the notes he had written, "ah, yes, he is worried over the Knights."

"He is worried over . . . how did you know?"

"I have it written down here in my notes under your name."

"I haven't reported this before now!" the snake hissed.

He closed the book and slammed it down on his desk. "I am well aware of that fact you idiot!"

The snake remembered the vulture and said, "You know about this because of a stupid vulture, right?"

"He was a little concerned about your timing."

"How could a courier vulture know anything about the art of watching?"

"I took that into consideration before I gave him your job."

"What?!" The snake hissed.

"He thinks that you have bungled this assignment."

"That vulture has no idea how to overcome my pastor, especially this particular one!"

"If he doesn't deliver like he said, then he will get terminated and you will return." The bear returned to his business.

"I know this pastor better than any being in the kingdom of darkness. I know his favorite food, his favorite sport. I know which side of the bed he sleeps on. I know his favorite . . ."

"I will not change my mind!"

"Then, I have no choice than to report to your supervisor."

He stood ready to attack the snake. "I will tear your head from your body!"

"Did the vulture tell you that this pastor has a congregation of over 2,000 humans?"

The bear looked surprised. "Uh . . . no."

"Did he tell you why he is worried about the Knights?"

"No."

"He is worried because Dan and Vicki Knight are two of the most important members of his church."

"Spit it out!" the bear was tired of waiting for the answers.

Clenching his teeth the snake hissed, "He is worried because the Knights are the wealthiest members of his church."

His supervisor had a puzzled look on his face.

He sighed. It was obvious that his supervisor knew nothing about human living on the surface of earth. "He is worried over finances! I finally discovered the pastor's weakness and you sent an idiot to take my place? He doesn't have a clue about my assignment!"

"Don't panic . . . stay calm."

The snake uncoiled quickly and with a sudden leap, he wrapped himself around the dumb—bear. One squeeze and his powerful muscles could take him out. He rattled his tail as he slowly wound himself around his neck with his tongue going in and out as he was face to face with his supervisor.

Hissing slowly and directly with every word he spoke, "I have invested several years in this pastor. He has resisted women and teaching false doctrines. Finally, the pressure of finances is pushing him into the temptation of worry and you want me to calm down?" Slowly the tone of the snake was rising as his words were stirring his emotions. "I don't think so!" he hissed.

The bear cursed. "Release me you idiot! I promise, you will get he credit for the fall of this human."

The snake looked into his eyes. Slowly he uncoiled.

The bear breathed deeply and brushed off his rigid, rough brown coat with his hands. He hated the thought of the snake coiled around him. He went over and called for his computer notebook. "Show me the file on Dan and Vicki Knight." After his voice was scanned for security level and confirmed for clearance, the file materialized in front of him. "Hm . . . here it is. Just what I remembered hearing, the master has assigned a very important angel to the Knights."

"Who?" the snake leaned over to look at the file.

The bear snapped the notebook shut. "What is in this for me?"

"I have the information and you have . . ."

" . . . the security clearance to arrange a meeting with this angel."

When he put it like that, it looked like the snake was going to have to strike up some kind of deal with the bear. "What do you want?"

"Equal recognition with you."

"You want half?"

"Half or no deal."

The snake thought about his demands and wasn't sure he could trust him or not. "How do I know that you will keep your end of our deal?"

"You don't. But I'm the only one that can call off the vulture that has been officially assigned to your Pastor Ben Baker."

"I agree, but hurry, we have to stop that stupid imbecile."

"Let's go!" The desk and computer disappeared.

"Wait. The name first!" The snake uncoiled to stop him.

"No! The name after I see if the vulture has succeeded or not."

Instantly, they disappeared from hell.

CHAPTER 21

When Kellie and Hannah arrived at Joshua's house, Mose immediately told them what happened to them earlier.

"Oh man!" Hannah exclaimed. "I miss all the fun."

"Don't worry. I have a feeling that this is just the beginning of the fun we're going to have," Mose told Hannah as they followed Joshua to one of the family rooms. It was a mystery to him how Joshua could find anything in a house so big. "Is this our space?"

"No, it's not finished, yet." Joshua didn't want to reveal their newly remodeled family room until the special weekend he was planning.

"This is their plain family room," Kellie explained. "It doesn't have a fireplace and it's a lot smaller than the others."

This is smaller? One whole wall of shelves was dedicated to books and a collection of figurines. There were two desks with computers. Mose visualized his living room and family room in this room with space left over.

"What just happened is a great example of what Jesus told me." Joshua went over to one of the desks in the room and took out his notes and Bible from his backpack.

"What?" Mose sat down on the couch and put his things on the coffee table in front of him.

"He taught me about the devil's kingdom and the classes of demons in it," Joshua said as he joined him on the couch.

"Pastor Pearson taught on the devil once and he said that the Old Testament doesn't say much at all about the devil accept in Isaiah 14 and Ezekiel 28," Kellie said as she opened her Bible sitting next to Joshua.

"The people in the Old Testament didn't have a revelation of the devil. Hannah, why don't you read Isaiah 14:12?" Joshua asked.

She sat down on one of the wing chairs at the side of the couch and opened her Bible to the passage. "How you are fallen from heaven, O Lucifer, son of the morning! How you are cut down to the ground, you who weakened the nations! For you have said in your heart: I will ascend into heaven, I will exalt my throne above the stars of God; I will also sit on the mount of the congregation on the farthest sides of the north. I will ascend above the heights of the clouds. I will be like the Most High."

Joshua interrupted her. "We know that satan, known as Lucifer before his fall from heaven, had a place of high honor among God's creation. Pride entered his heart and I believe he wanted to become the first son of God."

"Whoa, wait a minute, you don't think he wanted to be higher than God?" asked Mose.

"I don't think anyone in their right mind would ever think they could ever be greater than God, especially since he was created by God," Joshua explained.

"Who thinks that satan is in his right mind?" asked Hannah.

"Didn't we just read he wanted to exalt his throne above the stars of God?" asked Kellie as she opened her notebook to take some notes.

"If you look up the Hebrew word for stars, you will find it also figuratively means a prince or star gazer. Satan wanted to be the Son of God who would be equal to God because they are family."

"You think he wanted to be us?" Hannah asked as she took her notebook out of her backpack.

"I think he wanted to be the one chosen to father the children of God," Joshua added. "Remember, it's just my opinion."

"Why do you think that?" Mose asked. "Can I have a piece of paper Hannah?"

"From the first chapter of Hebrews, I meditated on the phrase 'to which of the angels has He ever said.' The Holy Spirit told me that if God could have called an angel to be His son, then they have the capabilities of fulfilling that position."

"Wordman, that makes sense," Mose said as he wrote down what he said.

"Read that first chapter." Joshua told them.

Hannah closed her notebook and juggled it around with her Bible. "What book?" she asked opening her Bible.

"Hebrews," Kellie said impatiently.

Hannah stared at Kellie thinking how rude she was getting.

Joshua read the verse. "For to which of the angels did He ever say: You are my Son?"

"So, you think satan wanted to be Jesus?" asked Hannah getting her notebook out again and writing frantically.

"Let's go to the dining room and sit around the table." Joshua saw that they were having trouble taking notes from what was turning out to be a teaching session.

"How about the kitchen? Then we can get a drink," Kellie asked.

"And something to eat!" Hannah added.

"Sure." They walked through a hallway that led to another main intersection and back around to a big kitchen with a great big room attached to it that was used as an informal dining room. On the other side of the kitchen, a big formal dining room could be seen through closed French doors.

"How many rooms does this house have?" Mose asked.

"There are six bedrooms and seven bathrooms; does that give you a clue?" Kellie answered his question.

"I think my mom told me that she was going shopping, so we should have the house to ourselves." He said as he sat down all his stuff on the kitchen table.

"How can you know for sure?" Mose said with a little attitude.

Kellie glared at him.

Even though his house was super big, Hannah thought it was cool. "Joshua, do you have some pop?"

"Actually, I do. Kellie knows where the fridge is."

"Hannah, you need to drink water," Kellie put her things down on the table.

"Whatever, mother!" Hannah quipped.

"For every can of pop you drink, your body needs four to six glasses of water to flush it out of your system," Kellie informed her.

"Kellie, can you get me a glass of water?" Joshua asked.

"Sure. How could satan even think about being the father of our race?" She asked as she took glasses from a kitchen cabinet and filled them with ice cubes. Opening the refrigerator she was surprised to find a couple of cans of coke inside. No one in the Knight family drank pop.

"Think of it like this, before Lucifer sinned, he discovered God wanted a family. And maybe he figured that since he was filled with all wisdom and beauty he should be our father." Joshua reminded them that these were thoughts from mediating the Word.

"Man, I have absolutely no neuron networks in my brain that have ever thought like that!" Mose exclaimed taking a can of pop from the tray Kellie carried in.

"I know this may sound strange but . . ."

"Strange? That doesn't even come close. Like, how could satan ever be like Jesus?" Hannah gave Joshua a puzzling look.

"Not like Jesus. He wanted to be the first Adam," Joshua explained.

"Hmm," Mose closed his eyes trying to get his brain to get into a deeper thinking mode. "If he wanted to be a son of God like Adam, then he could have gotten angry at God when he created Adam."

"Okay! Like maybe that's why he hates us so much?" Hannah thought out loud.

Mose turned his Bible to Ezekiel 28 and read out loud. "You were the seal of perfection, full of wisdom and perfect in beauty. You were in eden, the garden of God; every precious stone was your covering . . . The workmanship of your timbrels and pipes was prepared for you on the day you were created. You the anointed cherub who covers . . ."

"What does that mean, 'the anointed cherub who covers'?" asked Kellie as she turned to that passage.

"Cherub doesn't mean angels, it means cherub."

"How do you know?" Mose asked.

"I looked it up in the concordance. Cherubs could be spirit beings in a different class than angels."

"Hey, like we are human beings and they could be cherub beings and angels are angelic beings. Cool." Hannah nodded her head.

"Covers is a word that indicates protection and defense. It would appear that Lucifer had authority over the cherubs. He had a throne . . ."

"Wordman!" Mose interrupted Joshua. "If you have a throne, you have a kingdom."

"If you have a kingdom, then you have subjects." Hannah continued reading, "Listen to this, 'You were on the holy mountain of God; you walked back and forth in the midst of fiery stones. You were perfect in your ways from the day you were created, until iniquity was found in you. By the abundance of your trading, you became filled with violence within, and you sinned' . . ."

Joshua interrupted her. "Satan was the first created being to sin. His heart was lifted up because of his beauty and his wisdom."

"Okay, let me get this straight. Satan was created by God, but somehow he discovered God desired a family. How do you think he knew?" asked Mose.

"The word of God indicates that timbrels and pipes were prepared for him on the day he was created," Joshua finished his drink of water.

"My mother thinks he probably directed all of heaven's music," Kellie told them.

"Many Bible scholars believe that he was in charge of praise and worship in heaven. That could explain how he might have known about the Father's desire for a family." Joshua stood.

"You lost me, Joshua," remarked Kellie as she laid her Bible on the table and took the empty glass from Joshua. She waited on him without even thinking about what she had done.

"God sometimes reveals a portion of His character to those who are worshiping Him in Spirit and in truth. I sometimes get a revelation from the Lord when I move into worship from my whole heart." He took the full glass from her. "Thanks."

"I get it! He thought he should get the honor of being the one chosen to become the son of God," Mose said.

"Like, how can satan have children?" Just thinking about that made Hannah disgusted.

"The Bible indicates that satan does have children."

"What?" Kellie and Hannah said together.

"Where?" asked Mose.

"Turn to Genesis 3:14. 'So the Lord God said to the serpent . . . I will put enmity between you and the woman . . . between your seed and her Seed.'" Joshua quoted.

"I thought satan's seed was the seed of evil?" Mose questioned.

Kellie crossed her legs in the chair with her Bible opened on the table in front of her and leaned forward. She was looking at the scripture intently. "I've never heard this before."

"There are other scriptures," Joshua pointed out.

"Well you might as well show us all of them," Hannah said.

"Turn to Revelation 2:20–23," Joshua read the passage out loud. "I became suspicious of the passage in verse 23. Now you and I both know that Jesus would never kill human children."

"Yeah, that passage has always bothered me," Hannah admitted.

"So, you think that the children in this verse are talking about satan's children?" Kellie asked.

"Satan's system on earth is called Babylon the great, the mother of harlots. Her children are the seed of satan's."

"This is awesome!" Mose said. He had never been at a Bible study that was so exciting.

"How do you do it?" Again Kellie was dumbfounded at his thinking.

"When you meditate on the character of God, then you know that it just doesn't sound like Jesus to kill human children. I started thinking that the seed of satan could be demon spirits. Now this is my opinion, but I don't think God created demons."

"Wait a minute. What about the disembodied theory?" Mose asked.

"Huh?" Hannah asked as she stood to stretch. She had no idea what they were talking about.

"He's talking about Christians who think that demons once had a body during the time on earth between verse one and two in the first chapter of Genesis," Kellie explained.

"Remember, this is just a theory, it's not written in stone. I don't think that demons are fallen angels."

"I've always heard that satan can't create anything," Kellie said.

"It depends on your definition of creation."

"Yeah," Hannah enthusiastically sat down, "after all men have created robots."

"How about cloning?" Mose added. "That's really weird."

"We do know that after satan was kicked out of heaven, he was stripped of his authority on God's planet," Joshua continued teaching. "So whatever he has done on earth, he's done it through our authority. He came to our atmosphere . . ."

"Like on a spaceship?" Hannah asked excitedly. "There was a sci-fi movie once that showed alien ships establishing their headquarters in the bowels of the earth. Is that hell?"

"Hell is a prison for humans who have died physically, not satan's headquarters. I believe satan has homes on earth, but he doesn't live in hell permanently." Joshua had their full attention. "I believe that he started the rebellion in heaven because of his intense jealousy and hurt over what he thought was disloyalty from God."

"If he wanted our position then he hates God and us!" Hannah opened her can of pop.

"Man! That makes sense!" Mose said. "But it also sounds too weird."

"Yeah, like what traditional Christian is going to believe this."

"As long as what we believe doesn't violate scripture, I don't think it will hurt us. In fact, I think meditating on these things helps us to make spiritual connections in our mind, since we can't see into the spiritual world."

"Wordman, it does make sense that he could have become extremely offended because of the pride in his heart over his wisdom and beauty." Mose was getting excited.

"I think that satan lives in a space station located above earth and that explains UFO sightings."

"What about the issue of satan exchanging places with Adam?" Kellie didn't want to get off the subject. Especially since UFO's was a favorite topic of Hannah's

"In the garden of eden on earth, when Adam sinned and disobeyed God, the devil didn't take Adams place, he took God's place," Joshua told them.

"What?" Mose, Hannah and Kellie said together.

Hannah slapped her forehead. "Not another new thing."

"Is it too much?" He looked at the clock. "Do you want to stop?"

"No, you can't keep us hanging," Kellie protested.

"Scripture reveals that God made us in His image, according to His likeness. In Genesis 1:26 He said, 'let them have dominion over all the earth.' God gave us earth and told us to rule over it."

Mose suddenly realized that the devil doesn't have a body.

"Yeah," Hannah agreed with him. "Neither do demons."

"Then why is he still in control?" Kellie asked.

"Because we have let his kingdom of darkness take over our world."

"Hey man, we didn't do it, Adam did!" Mose protested.

"We inherited what Adam did and Jesus paid the price for it. But we haven't finished what Jesus started after the resurrection."

"Oh," Kellie realized. "That's why Jesus is in heaven now waiting for us to put His enemies under His feet."

"Adam disconnected us from our true Father and Jesus reconnected us. Now we should be obeying Genesis 1:28. Subduing the kingdom of darkness until God says it's time for dinner in heaven."

"You forgot to tell us about man's relationship to satan."

"Adam lost his relationship with God. So he was cut off from God. Satan became the stepfather of mankind. Jesus said in Matthew 11 verse 27 that 'all things have been delivered to Me by My Father and no one knows the Son except the Father. Nor does anyone know the Father except the Son, and to whom the Son wills to reveal.'"

Kellie realized that satan continued to lie to humans. "That's what you found through the names of Adams descendants."

"Jesus began teaching the people about their real Father. The One in heaven; the One that they didn't know or couldn't know until the Anointed One sent from God showed the truth," Joshua taught.

"Jesus said that satan came to steal, kill and destroy," Mose said.

"That rat!" Hannah exclaimed. "Even after causing our race to get kicked out of the garden and lose our real supernatural life, his kingdom of darkness began to destroy our earth!"

"I see it. He took over God's position as father."

"Yeah, but he is the evil wicked stepfather like Cinderella's wicked stepmother!" Hannah growled.

"Jesus told the disciples not to call anyone on earth their father for only One is our Father and He is in heaven," Joshua pointed out.

"I never could understand what Jesus meant about that. I mean I call my dad, Dad, but . . ." Kellie said.

"Jesus wasn't talking about your biological father; He was talking about your heavenly spiritual Father, God. Every human has to have a spiritual head," Joshua told them. "Now we can choose. Jesus or satan; good or evil; light or darkness; life or death. Jesus asked the Father to allow us the choice. He didn't demand that all men be saved like satan demanded that all men die because of their sin."

"Man, if only everyone could understand how great God the Father really is," Mose shook his head.

"He won't force you to love Him or choose to live with Him for all eternity. In fact, He will fight for your right to go to hell if that's where you want to go," Joshua looked at them intently. "That's why we have to share the good news about Jesus.

"Joshua," Kellie picked up her Bible, "where in the scriptures does it say that satan became the stepfather of mankind?"

"The Jews were very upset with Jesus' teaching about the Father. In John 5:18 it says 'they sought all the more to kill Him, because He not only broke the Sabbath, but also said that God was His Father, making Himself equal with God. They were never taught that God was their Father. If you remember, God said that He was the Husband of Israel."

"Like, I'm really confused," Hannah threw up her hands. "Is God the Father or is God the Husband?"

"Think of it like this. After Adam was cut off from the Father and satan became the illegitimate stepfather of mankind, God had to find a way to reintroduce himself into the earth since sin separated Him from His creation. He cut a covenant with Abraham and started a love relationship with the nation of Israel and until Jesus came, He couldn't be their Father, since he was rejected as a father, so He became their husband. As their husband, He had the authority to protect them from the curse."

"Oh, that is so beautiful!" Hannah felt like crying as her spirit was moved.

Kellie turned her Bible to Isaiah 54:5 and read, "' . . . for your Maker is your husband, the Lord of hosts is His name; and your Redeemer is the Holy One of Israel; He is called the God of the whole earth. For the Lord has called you like a woman forsaken and grieved in spirit. Like a youthful wife when you were refused,' says your God. 'For a mere moment I have forsaken you, but with great mercies I will gather you. With a little wrath I hid My face from you for a moment; but with ever lasting kindness I will have mercy on you, says the Lord, your Redeemer.'"

Joshua said, "In the Old Testament, God took the position of husband over the descendants of Abraham so that He could protect them and legally pour out His blessings over them even though the earth is covered with the curse. Moses taught them the terms of that covenant so that when they exchanged blood, God accepted the curse from them as they accepted the blessings from Him. He showed them how to walk in the blessings, but He also showed them what would happen if they didn't walk in His law or covenants through obedience."

"The curses of Deuteronomy are not from God, but they are actually from the nature of men inherited from satan." Kellie reasoned.

"Exactly. You see when God gave them blessings, He received their curses. That was okay with Him, because He is the only One that can handle the curse. But when Israel refused to obey His covenants, laws and statutes, God had to give back what He received from them; the curse," Joshua explained. "The terms of their contract with God as husband was written in the Torah."

"You make it sound so simple," Hannah said.

"It is simple. God taught them about curses and blessings. Blessings are from Him and curses are from satan. Kellie, here is the scripture that reveals satan's office or position of father on earth. Look at John 8:37. Jesus said, 'I know that you are Abraham's descendants, but you seek to kill Me, because My word has no place in you. I speak what I have seen with My Father, and you do what you have seen with your father.'"

"Whoa . . ." Mose started to say something.

"Hold that thought Mose. Verse 39 says 'they answered and said to Him, Abraham is our father. Jesus said to them, "If you were Abraham's children you would do the works of Abraham. But now you seek to kill Me, a Man who has told you the truth which I heard from God. Abraham did not do this. You do the deeds of your father." Then they said to Him, "We were not born of fornication; we have one Father-God." Notice that they finally received from Jesus the teaching about God in heaven being their father. The verse before that, they said Abraham was their father. Now they just said that God is their Father. But look what Jesus says in verse 42, "If God were your Father, you would love Me, for I proceeded forth and came from God; nor have I come of Myself, but He sent Me. Why do you not understand My speech? Because you are not able to listen to My word. You are of your father the devil and the desires of your father you want to do."

"I guess that settles that," Hannah declared.

"It's right here in scripture," Kellie reread what Joshua read.

"So then, satan is the illegitimate father of mankind!" Mose declared.

"Jesus said that those who don't believe in Him, then their spiritual father is satan. That is the position that satan received after the fall of man. Every man, woman and child on earth has a spiritual head. It is either God the Father in heaven or satan, a fallen being from heaven who lives in the heavenlies. Those are the only two choices. God's kingdom is operated by faith and produces blessings. Satan's kingdom is operated by fear and produces curses."

Mose exclaimed. "It is all making sense."

"The Lord God knew all this would happen. That is why he predestined Jesus to die on the cross for us. I John 3:8 says that 'He who sins is of the devil, for the devil has sinned from the beginning. For this purpose the Son of God was manifested, that He might destroy the works of the devil'!"

"Praise the Lord for Jesus," Kellie raised her hand.

"In Isaiah 14:24 'The Lord of hosts has sworn, saying, surely as I have thought, so it shall come to pass, and as I have purposed, so it shall stand: I will break the Assyrian, *or satan*, in My land, and on My mountains tread him underfoot. Then his yoke shall be removed from them, and his burden removed from their shoulders. This is the purpose that is purposed against the whole earth." Joshua closed his Bible. God's purpose is to destroy the kingdom of darkness from the face of earth. That is what the day of wrath is all about."

"Joshua, my Bible doesn't say *or satan*," Hannah pointed out as she leaned over her Bible scanning the verse again to make sure she didn't miss something."

"I added that so that you could see that the 'Assyrian' can spiritually apply to satan. We are to continue the works of Jesus and do like he did. It all started with Jesus' death on the cross. He gave Himself as the sacrificial lamb. Satan messed up and condemned a just man and sent him to hell. Jesus died on the cross not just to cover our sins, but to annihilate them. Death spread to all men, because all came from the blood of Adam. Even if you are a good person, death still reigned over you, but Jesus destroyed death and utterly took away his power!"

"You know," Kellie added, "Jesus' Blood is different from ours.

"You can trace the father of a child through the blood. Jesus' Blood has direct DNA from His Father, God, which could destroy sin before He was ever born. Therefore Jesus was like Adam before he sinned. Adam and Jesus' Blood came from the Father."

"So are you saying that Jesus' Blood was perfect?" Hannah asked.

"Yes. There was no sin in his Blood. I believe that, because Jesus said with his own lips that satan came again to tempt Him, but he could find nothing in Him. The 'nothing in him' was no sin or death seed in His Blood or thoughts in His mind contrary to the Word of God."

"Wow! This is cool," Mose exclaimed. "I never thought about Jesus' Blood having supernatural DNA."

"Is that why some Christians sing so much about the Blood?" Hannah asked.

"Yes. Satan didn't know what the blood covenant was until after Adam and Eve sinned. So even though the blood of bulls, goats, and the ashes of a heifer sanctified and purified the flesh, satan had no idea that the Blood of the Anointed One would cleanse our conscience from dead works so that we could serve the living God."

"Didn't the writer of Hebrews say something like that?" Kellie asked.

Hannah opened her Bible. "It's in Hebrews 9:22, 'And according to the law almost all things are purified with blood, and without shedding of the blood there is no remission.' Isn't that remission of sin?"

"Yes." Joshua said. "The Blood Covenant is the secret place and it was kept a mystery from the kingdom of darkness. Satan didn't realize that Jesus' Blood was Blood that more than covered sin, but it obliterated it totally."

"What does obliterate mean?" asked Hannah.

"It means to destroy or wipe out without any trace," Kellie said.

"Like the sin never existed before," Mose added.

"Jesus Blood is precious Blood. He was like the first man before sin entered mankind. His Blood was perfect. And satan never did find a way to pollute Jesus' Blood. Jesus never sinned in thought, word, or deed," Joshua said.

Mose laughed. "The dude was stupid! He didn't know that he was crucifying the Lord of Glory!"

"But a lot of people deny that Jesus was perfect," Kellie reminded him.

"Of course they would deny it, because satan doesn't want anyone to know that Jesus' Blood defeated sin totally," Joshua said.

Mose was getting a clear picture in his mind about the power of the Blood and sacrifice of Jesus. "He wasn't just any lamb, because He had to be one without blemish or natural disfigurement."

"Men also deny that Jesus was physically raised from the dead," Kellie added.

"That's because the foundation for Christianity is the belief that Jesus body was raised from the dead after three days. But Christians have missed it!" Joshua told her.

"Like how?" asked Hannah.

"The power isn't that His body was raised up after three days. Remember Jesus raised Lazarus' body after four days! His body was a perfect sacrifice, but it was the uniting of his spirit and soul that was born again in the depths of hell that defeated the devil! Don't you see? Without understanding what Jesus totally did to the devil, how can you understand the power that is available to you through the name and Blood of Jesus?"

"I get it, I think," Kellie said slowly.

"Christians, who understand the new Blood Covenant made in heaven with Jesus' Blood, can walk all over the devil and his army. They can pulverize and sterilize the devil and never think twice about it."

"I think I'm going to like stomping the devil's head," remarked Kellie.

"Yeah! The Devil Chasers make a real statement!" Hannah grinned. "We've been giving too much credit to the devil,"

"Satan came to earth after the anointing. That's what he lost when he fell, his connection to the Creator. And after man sinned and the anointing departed, all he got was flesh. I don't think the devil knew what was under the covering of the anointing of the human," Joshua told them.

"Didn't he get a surprise when all he got was rotten, ugly, old flesh," Kellie said.

Mose laughed. "My dad calls flesh, the devil's food."

"Speaking of food . . ."

Kellie interrupted Hannah. "Who is speaking of food?"

Hannah wrinkled her nose at Kellie. "Is anybody hungry besides me?"

"Are you kidding?" Kellie asked incredulously. "We are eating the bread of life which is feeding our spirit. How can you be hungry?"

Joshua went over to the kitchen pantry and pulled out a couple of bags of chips and brought them back to the table.

"Hey, what's up? This is junk food!" Mose picked up one of the bags and looked at the label.

Joshua stammered. "I, uh . . . I thought maybe we might meet this weekend and I wanted to be prepared."

Hannah took the bag from Mose and opened it. "Are you sure the crunching won't bother you guys?"

"Go ahead, Hannah. Forgive me for not offering you guys something before now."

"I knew it was too good to be true," Mose thought he caught Joshua cheating.

"What?" asked Hannah as she crunched a chip.

Mose and Kellie looked annoyed with Hannah.

"What?" She asked Kellie. "I'll stop if it is annoying you!"

"I thought Joshua was one of those health food nuts," Mose answered her question.

"Go ahead, Joshua, don't mind these rude people," Kellie ignored them.

His concentration was interrupted. "I'm not sure what I was going to say."

Mose reminded him. "You were talking about flesh."

"The Bible says that if you are fleshly minded then you have set your life on the course of hell," Joshua remembered what he wanted to say.

"I would like to remind you, Kellie, that the body has to have physical food to live," Hannah spoke in her defense.

Joshua interrupted their conversation. "Kellie, don't get offended just because Hannah is eating."

"It's not that she is eating, it's the crunching that is bothering me!"

"I'll stop."

"How can you separate eating and crunching chips?" Mose was confused.

Kellie apologized. "No, I'll eat a couple with you and then maybe the crunching won't bother me."

"I think our flesh is trying to move us into the soulish realm. When something is irritating you like that, you can trace it back to a thought or a feeling from your flesh. And once you get into the natural realm then a demon can get involved. Remember that Jesus taught that when the seed of God's Word is being planted in your heart, demons immediately come to steal it from you."

"Hey, man! I felt irritated too. Forgive me Hannah, I don't want no demon around me!" Mose's eyes widened as he looked all around the room.

"Sure, you want a chip?" She stuck out the bag of chips so they could all crunch together.

Realizing that Hannah needed someone to eat with her, Mose and Kellie stuck their hands into the chip bag at once and then laughed at each other. Hannah held out the bag to Joshua.

He shook his head no. Joshua decided to tell them the mental picture that he got one day when he was meditating on the second chapter of Acts. "Immediately when Jesus gave up His body, His soul was captured by demon spirits and taken to the pit of hell. The evil spirits put ankle and wrist chains on Jesus and dragged him throughout hell while the devil was celebrating his victory."

"Wordman . . . where is that in the word?"

"Acts 2:31 'his soul was not left in hell, nor did his flesh see corruption' . . ."

CHAPTER 22

In the lower regions, the dark secret caves and caverns of the underground world, shouts of victory were shaking all the parts of hell to its core. Wild abandoned dancing and rejoicing could be seen through the fires of hell. The one man that the forces of evil could not destroy on earth had finally arrived as a prisoner.

"This is the Messiah! King of the Jews!" Several short demons in black robes surrounded Him and wrapped Him in chains.

"Bow, you evil spirits!" A spirit from the division of death mocked Jesus and laughed in His face as His soul was released from His body on the cross. "This is Jesus, the one who cast many of you out of your human hosts on earth!"

They bowed and began to mock Him unmercifully.

"If You really are the Son of God escape from us now!" The demons mocked Him as He shouted out that His God had forsaken Him on the cross.

Jesus allowed them to take Him to the depths of hell through a gateway. The living evil forms embedded in the walls taunted and jeered at Him as He free-fell down the tunnel to the floor of hell. They lusted to get their hands on His dead flesh, but could not because they were chained.

The foundations of hell shook as the darkness descended on Jesus and an evil force snared Him. The stench of the place took His breath away and the heat burned His lungs making the pain and difficulty He felt on the cross of breathing intensify and continue after death. The smell of decaying flesh greeting His nostrils and the sounds of piercing cries assaulted His ears. Red and yellow colors from the fire of hell greeted Jesus' eyes. Blue phosphorous creatures slithered around His dead soul.

"Escape from us, Jesus of Nazareth!" mocked a gross looking green snake slithering through the powdery dust of hell who wrapped his body around Jesus' feet tripping Him as He fell to the ground.

"If You really are the Son of God, then You could escape from this prison like You escaped the mobs on earth!" Another demon in the form of a bear with a long snout and protruding teeth jerked one of the chains around

Jesus and jeered at Him as He slowly got back to His feet.

Satan waited in the center of hell feeling the rise in power at his latest conquest over the human race. He snickered with evil joy and a smile revealed his pleasure. Hell was receiving a great reward!

The devil classified Jesus' death as the greatest event that ever happened to him since the fall of man. In his wildest fantasies, he could never have imagined how great he felt at the moment when Jesus passed from life into death. Jesus by far had been his greatest adversary. No man ever born of a woman had defeated him as much as Jesus did when He walked the face of earth.

I'm bad. I'm so bad!

As satan's heart rejoiced, his mind laughed at the irony of the meaning of the word bad. This was his world and he wanted the definition of words in all the languages on earth to reflect his kingdom of darkness. He desired his language of lies to replace the language of truth. The Bible said that good was God and satan was bad, so he wanted to be very bad. The intensity of his desire to destroy God's words from the face of the earth knew no boundaries.

He laughed and raised his fist in victory as he thought about how the words that described God's kingdom were being twisted and mangled beyond recognition. All humans would soon be brainwashed to believe that day is night and night is day; good is bad because truth would no longer be accepted in any form on his planet

I captured Jesus! Satan stood and raised his fist at God. *I won! I beat you again!* "This is my place. This is my territory. My prison for Your dead creation! I designed this place to capture the souls of fallen men and women for eternity. You will never, NEVER gain entrance into my prison!"

The man Jesus was being dragged through out hell as He was spit on, tripped, hit and buffeted just like He was only hours earlier. On earth after His capture, the Roman soldiers beat Jesus, plucked His beard out and put a crown of thorns on His head. His back was stripped of all flesh from the whipping He received and then the soldiers covered His body in spit. He did not try to hide His face from the shame. Every prophecy about the suffering Messiah in the Hebrew Torah and the Prophets came to pass on that day of crucifixion.

On the cross, His bones were all out of joint. Pain was a constant companion for Jesus since His capture in the garden of Gethsemane. Even though His disciples felt comfort that Jesus was finally out of His misery because He was physically dead, they didn't know what He was experiencing right now in His soul.

"It didn't end because You died Jesus." A demon taunted Him. "Your torture before You died was only the beginning of sorrows."

Another demon lifted His face off the ground shouting, "No matter what you suffered on earth, it cannot be compared to the suffering in the bowels of earth!"

All hell was rejoicing and throwing a party. Creatures that were gross beyond description filled the prison of hell. Demons mixed in their form with man and beast flew around the top of Jesus, rejoicing in His capture. Beings of gross proportions and perverted human form spit on Jesus as He was led to the center of hell. The evil kingdom of darkness celebrated that their master was victorious in another battle with Almighty God. Satan kept his word and defeated another would-be Messiah. The evil spirits believed their master caused another spiritual abortion of the plan to redeem man by the Christian's God.

Satan stood and applauded his evil workers as they dragged Jesus to the fun arena and presented Him before their master. The cries of laughter and celebration drowned out the screams of the tortured damned. He was shocked when Jesus was captured so easily on earth, and then even more surprised at the trial of Jesus. Who would have guessed that Jesus wouldn't open His mouth in defense of the false accusers that the he had produced for the Miracle Worker's conviction.

Satan was fairly sure that his false witnesses would be successful, but he had no idea that Jesus would submit Himself to death like He did. Humans are double-minded, he reasoned. One day they were positive that Jesus was going to deliver them from Roman bondage and proclaim Himself their King, and the next day they were yelling "Crucify Him! Crucify Him! We have no king but Caesar!" Forgetting about all the good Jesus had done for them, they were quick to believe all the lies that were told to Pilate about their Precious Savior.

I did it! I captured Jesus! And he is guilty of the same sin that God accused me . . . ME! God said that pride filled my heart. "What do you think about this man now?" satan proclaimed to the prince of hell. "He is the one that delivered those that I made blind and lame. He cast out several demons by His word and those who I brought to you, He took them away by force!"

"If He was such a powerful man, how did you capture him?" The prince of hell wondered.

"He said that His soul was sorrowful even to death!" satan lifted up his head and laughed. "He proclaimed on the cross that God had forsaken Him."

"I don't understand . . . is this the Man that by His word only took away the dead from me without prayer to God?"

"This is the very one, Jesus of Nazareth!"

"How can it be that one so powerful in His human nature could not resist fear?"

"Because I am the one that moved the soldiers to beat Him without human compassion or restraint before they hammered the nails into His hands and feet. I am the one that mixed the gall and vinegar and commanded the soldiers to give Him the drink. I am the one that subjected Jesus to death and now hell!" he bragged.

"This must be a trick of His to ensnare you," the prince of hell warned satan. He had a nagging feeling that something was terribly wrong.

"Why do you doubt me?" satan yelled at the prince of hell. "He is our enemy! He did major damage to you and to my kingdom! When He couldn't escape the cross, fear invaded His mind and slew Him! That led Him to sin, which led to defeat, which led to death!"

"I could not keep this Man from taking Lazarus from me and neither could any in my division of fear prevent his reappearance on earth. Do not bring this Man down here. He will release all my prisoners that I hold in unbelief and have bound with their own sins. He has devised a plot to conduct them into everlasting life!"

Satan scorned hell's suggestion and ignored his warning. "You will see. This Man will not escape your prison. No man on earth will ever see Him again!"

Boasting before the prince of hell, satan strutted around Jesus like a proud peacock. "Here He is . . . the great destroyer of my works on earth." Satan blasted out curses for all hell to hear, especially the souls in paradise. A shout of triumphant laughter burst forth from satan's mouth as the demons pushed Jesus down in front of his throne. Several short demon spirits in black robes surrounded Jesus and pierced Him with their spears.

Satan stood and stretched his arms up in the air. "Look and behold! I told you that I would defeat the self-proclaimed God, Jesus of Nazareth!" He circled around Jesus in the center of the ring again raising his arms and pointing at Him as He stood. "You thought You were God!" He looked at all the ugly deformed half human and half animal looking demon spirits in the stands surrounding the arena. "I told you that I would defeat every man and woman born on earth! No seed of a woman will ever be able to defeat me!"

He walked over to Jesus and kissed Him. "How did you like that kiss of betrayal Jesus? One of Your own disciples turned You over to me for profit!"

Jesus wiped His mouth.

They laughed at the mocking kiss that satan gave the King of the Jews.

"What are you going to do now God?" Satan lifted his fist again shaking it at God. "Who are you going to send next, since Jesus failed?"

The demons cheered in triumph. The entire world of darkness had been waiting for this day to take place for the last three and half years.

The chains tightened around Jesus' wrist and neck, sending excruciating pain to his bones. The torture of the cross seem to pale in significance to the torture He was now experiencing.

"What are you going to do now, God?" Satan repeated triumphantly in his victory. "I've got Your Son! Your only little Boy!" An evil vicious laugh roared throughout hell. "I got Your first son, Adam. Now I have Your self-proclaimed God-man, Jesus! Ha! Ha!"

The mocking laughter that filled the room surpassed the laughter directed toward Him on earth. Tens of thousands and thousands of evil spirits and demons filled the center of hell drooling at the prospect of torturing Jesus.

Looking at Jesus with eyes filled with evil intent, satan cursed Him, "See how deluded You became to think that You were equal to God? What happened Jesus? Did all that power go to Your head? Did you believe that maybe You were God? Don't You think it might be a little impossible for me to lock God up in a cage in hell?" With a sick sneering scream, he spit on Him. "You are not GOD!" He screamed. "You're just a man like Adam. It doesn't matter what You did or what You thought! I have You now and You will never escape this place."

Jesus looked directly into the dark hooded face of the devil and proclaimed, "I and My Father are One and you will never change that truth."

Satan laughed at him hysterically. "Listen to the deceived fool! He still thinks that He is God!" He went back to his throne to enjoy watching the torment of Jesus.

His body was so deformed from the brutal beatings that the Romans gave Him that He didn't even appear human. He was feeling the pain in the five areas of the soul acutely. It was far greater than the senses and feeling when alive back on the surface of earth.

"What do you think, Jesus, should I let them play hide and seek with Your bones first?" Satan lifted his hand to his chin and stroked it a couple of times. "Should I let You experience Your dead flesh ripped from Your dead bones. Hmmm . . . decisions, decisions."

The evil spirits sitting in the stands around the fun center shouted the different types of torture they wanted Jesus to experience.

"Did you know that on earth Your flesh is like a veil that protects Your spirit and soul? But down here Your dead flesh is just for added pain. Oh, did I forget that You are One with God? Then forgive me, but You know all about the flesh body that Your God created." He took great pleasure in mocking Jesus.

The prince of hell reserved his comments as he observed satan.

Suddenly, an intense flood of fire roared through hell like a tidal wave. It engulfed Jesus' dead blue-gray bloated flesh and patches of it began to burn and started falling off his dark gray skeleton.

"This . . . this is the Anointed One of God?" A tall glowering spirit in a black robe made his presence known. "Surely this can't be Him, the Son of God!" the spirit of fear roared out as he jabbed Jesus with a long black spear.

"My God! My God! For this You have forsaken Me!" Jesus screamed out in pain.

Demonic rats ran up and bit His legs. Jesus kicked them away from Him. Worms appeared inside His skeleton and a few seconds later dead skin began to reappear over His skeleton. All forms of creepy insects surrounded Him. Roaches and spiders laughed, continually grating on the mind of Jesus. When the flesh was totally gone from His skeleton, His soul looked like a gray misty cloud caught in His bones.

The spiders laughed that Jesus saved other people on earth, but He couldn't save Himself. "We can torment You night and day and day and night," spiders chanted.

"We can torment You whenever we want!" The roaches declared.

"Didn't You say on earth, Jesus, that the worm doesn't die even though fire burns everywhere in hell?" A demon laughed. "Save Yourself from the worms!"

Jesus looked at the patches of skin falling off His skeleton and groaned within Himself. The fierce, pitch-black darkness surrounded Him with suffocating hot air. He could not feel the soft refreshing cooling breezes of the Holy Spirit that He lived for on earth. His soul panted after His maker like a deer that pants after water. His thirst was so devastating that it was all He could do to keep His thoughts centered on His Lord and Father.

"You saved others Jesus! Save yourself!" The laughter sounded like a hammer coming against His skull.

Long lines of demons were waiting for their turn to pass by Jesus to mock and torture Him. They were reveling in the fact that they didn't have to fear Him or His words. He was in their territory now. He was in their prison forever and ever. The rejoicing was out of control. A spirit of frenzy permeated every evil demon and fallen angel throughout the regions of the damned.

Jesus took authority over the pain and torture. He began to quote the written word of God from Psalm 22. "My God, My God, for this purpose I have been born."

"What purpose?" A demon spit on Him. "I have waited a long time to repay you for forcing me to leave my human house!" He stabbed Jesus with a long pitchfork.

"He believes He was destined for hell?" An evil spirit in the perverted form of a dinosaur laughed. "No wonder it was so easy to bring Him down here!"

The demon faced the stands of evil spirits to tell them about bringing Jesus to hell. "Usually humans fight us as soon as their spirit and soul leaves their body and they realize the truth of hell and eternal damnation. But we all know they struggle and fight to no avail." He walked around the arena shouting. "No lost human soul can escape from our clutches after physical death if his spirit is dead and his soul is lost and without God. He is void of faith in God or they would have never entered this prison of the damned. But this Jesus, Savior of the world, did not struggle or fight. He accepted defeat because He was forsaken by His God. He even said so out of His own mouth on the cross!"

Jesus ignored the pain and the evil spirit's cursing and set his mind once more on scriptures. He could remember every scripture He ever memorized back on earth when He was living in His flesh body. "You are but a few days from helping Me, and from the words of My groaning. Oh My God I cry in the daytime. You will hear Me. I cry out in nighttime! You will hear My cry."

Jesus moaned as He felt the pain of several spears piercing through His skeleton and hitting His gray misty soul. The demons hated hearing the Word of God quoted from a soul in hell.

"Shut up!" They cursed Him.

"Cry out all you want to! Satan is your god now!"

"Worship satan, Jesus!"

Jesus spoke through clinched teeth and vowed, "I will never worship satan!" He spoke loud enough for all to hear Him. "I worship my Father with all my might and strength. Him only do I serve!"

"Get a grip Jesus! You have no spiritual strength in hell to resist our master and his desires!" A demon smote His skeleton face. "You are in hell! Everyone in hell worships master satan."

"My Father and I are one. I will rise in three days with His Spirit," Jesus declared despite the pain.

Laughter broke out spontaneously throughout hell.

"No one has ever raised from this place of the unrighteous damned!"

"I am the Resurrection and the Life!" Jesus repeated the words He spoke on earth's surface.

"Tell us Jesus, how are You going to escape me?"

Jesus did not answer him.

Satan exclaimed for all in hell to hear his declaration. "This demented soul is ours for eternity! He will not answer me because He knows that I am the one telling the truth now." Satan laughed at his own words. "The truth is . . . I won! I won! I won!" He couldn't contain himself as he jumped up and down with excitement.

Jesus didn't wait for the roar to settle down. He began to repeat the words He had memorized as a boy in Israel. "But You are Holy, enthroned in the praises of Israel. Our fathers trusted in You; they trusted, and You delivered them. They cried to You, and were delivered." Jesus ignored the facts that faced Him. "I raise My voice in praise to You. I will be delivered!"

Suddenly, the devil screamed and ran off his throne pushing all the demons out of his way. Getting in Jesus' face he yelled at him, "There is no deliverance from this place of torture, Jesus! No one has ever escaped hell! You are no different than any other poor miserable soul in this place!"

Undaunted, lifting His face and His voice, Jesus continued to quote Psalm 22. "They trusted in the Lord God, and were not ashamed. But I am a worm, and no man; a reproach of men, and despised by the people. All those who see Me ridicule Me."

"He called himself a worm," laughed a demon.

"No! He said He looks like a worm!" An evil spirit disagreed with him.

The demon cursed and shoved him in the back. "I heard what He said! He said He is a worm!"

"What does it matter what He is saying?" yelled another demon. "His words mean nothing in hell!"

"Look at Him!" satan spit out with scorn. "He said He was the Truth, and the Way. Does He look like Truth now?"

"NO!" they shouted.

"Look around you, Jesus. This is Your world now. Be these wretched human's God if you can. Free yourself if You are that One that was coming to crush my head!" The devil slowly bent his head down giving Jesus time to respond to his challenge.

"IF you are the Son of God, leave hell now. Tear down these bars and walk out of here." satan yelled into His face. He had a fierce desire to make Jesus admit that He failed at God's plan and purpose. "Do You understand that You are in hell for eternity? You failed!" He screamed into the rotten ears that were once again falling off His dead bones. "Admit that you failed God and You are not the Messiah, Redeemer of mankind!"

Jesus refused to admit failure. "My Father and I are One and no one can defeat Us."

Satan stared at him incredulously. Not one man or woman has ever resisted him this long in hell. "I won!" He yelled looking up toward heaven, shouting and shaking his fist again. "This Man is insane! He can't even admit defeat in hell!"

Jesus directed His words toward heaven proclaiming, "God is the one who put Me in the womb. He made Me trust while on My mother's breast.

I was cast upon Him from birth. From My mother's womb He has been My Father. He is not far from Me, even though it seems like trouble is near. For He will help me."

"Shut up! The Word of God has no authority down here!" a demon screamed.

"Amazing! He still believes that God is going to help Him!" Satan rolled his eyes and waved his hand as if saying His Words were useless and meaningless.

All the demons laughed out loud as they circled Him and taunted Him again and again for His sin of being a man and believing that He was equal with God and letting fear enter his mind.

Jesus quoted the Ten Commandments. "I worship the Lord God that delivered Israel out of the land of Egypt and out of the house of bondage. I do not have any other gods before the Lord God of Abraham, Isaac and Jacob."

Satan grew weary of hearing Jesus speak scripture from his mouth. "So, You think that You are the Messiah and that You can still worship God even in hell? This is my territory Jesus! God is not in this place! Do you understand? I am Your god now! Worship me!"

"The Lamb of God has been sacrificed for the sins of all mankind," Jesus said as He slowly raised his body from the ground.

"Shut up!" Satan slapped Jesus. "Look at You! You are no Messiah!" satan waved his hands wildly and shouted at the demon spirits crowding in to see what he was going to do with Jesus. "Would you bow to this Man as Lord?"

"No!" they shouted.

"Begin the torture!" another evil angel yelled.

"He tortured us on earth before the time! Now we will do the same to Him!" yelled a dirty, foul stinking demon.

"Let me get revenge on Him." A spirit that was cast out of Mary Magdalene was drooling over his chance to torture Jesus.

Jesus looked directly into the eyes of His accusers. "Many bulls have surrounded Me; Strong bulls of Bashan have encircled Me. They gape at Me with their mouths, like a raging and roaring lion."

"Listen to him! The fool is still speaking scripture!" Another evil spirit said with disgust.

"Are you sure that is scripture?' Another asked.

"I am poured out like water. All My bones are out of joint."

As Jesus spoke, His flesh once again fell off His bones and the demons took their spears and stabbed His skeleton. Hot searing pain flashed through His soul. He felt every stab as unbearable anguish on his soul.

"My heart is like wax; It has melted within Me. My strength is dried up like a potsherd, and My tongue clings to My jaws; you have brought Me to the dust of death."

"Finally!" Satan rolled his eyes again, "We finally agree on something! God delivered You to me. You are mine now!"

Jesus knew the scriptures. Men thought He was stricken, smitten and afflicted by God. But He knew better. He had the power to lay down His life for all men and women and He had the power to take it up again. In the fullness of time, He would take up His life again through the power of the Holy Spirit. He willingly chose to pay this price for the sins of all human people. Not some sins, but all sins, all sicknesses, and all diseases. Jesus thought of the book of Isaiah chapter 53.

He kept thinking about the Word of God and all the faces of His family and friends on earth that would be so happy when these next three days and nights are finished and they would see that God's Word is true. Each smiling face helped Him to withstand every torturing blow to His soul body. "Greater love has no man than to give his life for his friends." Jesus said through gritted teeth filled with pain.

In the pitch-blackness of hell, He was cut off from God and totally engulfed in hopelessness and despair. His soul was oppressed beyond measure in the pit. Quoting the Word of God He memorized and confessed daily as a Jewish boy in the land of Israel, He concentrated every cell of His dead soul on the righteousness of God.

Satan directed his voice toward the saints in paradise. "Jesus is not the One you were waiting for. He failed. Too bad!" satan laughed. "Maybe someone else will come your way in another couple of hundred years! For all you souls in paradise, I declare that Jesus will not be delivering you from this place of torment!" He release a diabolic outburst of laughter and cursing.

Jesus continued quoting the Word. "For dogs have surrounded Me; The congregation of the wicked has enclosed Me. They pierced My hands and My feet; I can count all My bones. They look and stare at Me. They divided My garment among them. And for My clothing they cast lots."

Satan smiled and sneered, "I thought that was an appropriate ending for the Son of God! The great Anointed One of God hanging on the cross, stripped and beaten: naked for all men to gaze upon. All your disciples ran and hid. All of them were easily frightened wimps!"

Jesus ignored satan. "But You, O Lord, do not be far from Me; O My strength, hasten to help Me."

Satan stood and hit Jesus with a bolt of lightning and knocked him to the ground. He cursed Him. "Shut up fool! Where is Your legion of angels, Jesus? You said you could pray to Your Father and He would provide You with more than twelve legions of angels."

"My Father will send His angels according to the Scriptures."

"It is illegal for God to help a human once they give up their body and I receive their soul in this place!" satan told the crowd. "He can't! Jesus, You are in my control now! I rule over death and the grave! Fear delivered You to me and there is not one little mustard seed of faith left in that soul of Yours. If there were, You would not be in the bowels of earth with me now!"

"Deliver Me from the sword, My precious life from the power of the dog. Save Me from the lion's mouth and from the horns of the wild oxen." Jesus trusted completely in the Word of God to deliver Him from spiritual death.

"Did you hear that! He called satan a dog!"

All the evil spirits let out a roar and started jumping up and down! They were incensed that Jesus had the gall to speak to their master that way.

"Satan is god!"

"Satan is master and lord of all!"

"Hail satan! king of kings and lord of lords!"

Jesus raised His hands toward heaven. "You have answered Me!" He declared unto the Lord God Almighty.

"Hey! Look at that! He is raising His hands in worship to satan!"

Jesus looked into the eyes of satan. "I will never lift up My soul to an idol!"

"Hey, what is He saying?"

"Oh,——!" A demon cursed. "I think He is quoting scripture again!"

"He thinks God is going to answer His prayers down here?"

"They all think that! You know how crazy in the head they get down here!"

Satan pointed his finger at Jesus and forced Him to the ground. "I would have been the better savior of the world! My system works. His," he pointed is finger up to the throne of God, "His system has failed. No man will ever defeat me in my domain on earth!"

Even on hell's dirty floor, face down, Jesus refused to submit to satan and give him worship. The pressure to bow was great, but He withstood the evil onslaught. When the pressure stopped, Jesus stood again before satan. Turning from side to side, Jesus looked in the eyes of His tormentors and proclaimed that He would never worship satan.

"I worship the God of Abraham, Isaac and Jacob. Him only will I serve."

Standing before the evil congregation in filthy, stinky garments soaked with the sins of mankind, He determined in His soul that He would not worship a false god. He remembered that the scriptures said that He was made sin for all of mankind, but He himself was sinless.

"I came to hell of My own free will by submitting My Spirit to the prince of death. No one took My life from Me. I willingly gave My life as predestined by the Lord God Jehovah in heaven."

"You really think that we are going to believe that You willingly came to hell?" the devil asked looking incredulously at the dead soul before him. "How stupid do you think I am?" he roared into Jesus' face.

"Have you never read the scriptures from the prophet Isaiah? 'Who has believed our report? And to whom has the arm of the Lord been revealed? For He shall grow up before Him as a tender plant. And as a root out of dry ground." Jesus bent over and picked up a fist full of dirt letting it slip through his fingers as He continued quoting from the 53 chapter.

"He has no form or comeliness. And when you see Him, there is no beauty that you should desire Him. He is despised and rejected by men. A Man of sorrows and acquainted with grief. He was despised and you did not esteem Him. Surely He has borne their sicknesses and carried their sorrows. Yet you esteem Him stricken and smitten by God, and afflicted. But He was wounded for their transgressions, and He was bruised for their iniquities. The chastisement of their peace is upon Him and by His stripes they are healed!" Jesus paused and then said, "I am the One the scriptures reveal. I am He that was dead and is alive forever more!"

His words incensed the congregation of evil spirits. "Kill Him! Kill Him!"

The prince of hell roared at the evil spirits. "He is already dead, you stupid fools!"

How can it be that Jesus still refuses to accept where He is? Satan was baffled. "The Word of God didn't keep Him from MY hands! His words are worthless! Don't be deceived by His claim of rising from hell in three days."

A nagging thought arose in satan's dead spirit. He put it down immediately. "NO!" He shouted going back to his throne, he sat down.

[illegible]

"Bow to ME Jesus!" he stood and shouted. "Admit that I am the god of this world! Worship me and I will stop Your torture."

"I worship the Lord God Almighty and Him alone," Jesus said looking straight into the eyes of satan. "You are a liar and the Father of lies!"

Satan sat back down on his throne. He broke contact with Jesus. Even in hell, he couldn't stand to look at His eyes.

[illegible] have set My face like a flint, and I know that I will not be ashamed!"

The prince of hell whispered into satan's ear. *Release this man, he will make a fool out of you!*

Satan raised his hands to cover his ears. Lightning and fire started falling all around his throne room. "Enough!"

"Who among you fears the Lord? Who obeys the voice of His Servant? Who walks in darkness and has no light? Let him trust in the name of the Lord and rely upon his God!" The flesh came back on His skeleton. He continued to speak the Word of God through a clenched jaw.

"Look! All you who kindle a fire, who encircle yourselves with sparks: Walk in the light of your fire and in the sparks you have kindled. This you shall have from My hand: You shall lie down in torment. I speak praises to the Name of My God the Creator of heaven and earth!"

"OH, SHUT HIM UP! cried the evil spirits as they covered their ears from the words He was speaking. They screamed over and over as the whole arena erupted into chaos. "We HATE the WORD OF GOD. Shut up! Shut up! SHUT UP!"

Satan's eyes grew hot with rage. Every Word cut into his heart like knives. He couldn't believe this Man still believed in God's Word. As he stood, he screamed as loud as he could. "I SAID ENOUGH!" His eyes were blazing with fire. He lost control.

Lifting up his arm to release all his power against Jesus, the prince of hell constrained satan and spoke privately to him. *Wait until three days and three nights have passed then release all your power upon Him. Prove that Jesus is a false Prophet. Prove to your entire kingdom in front of their own eyes that Jesus' words are powerless against you.*

Satan sat down very agitated. After gaining control he calmly said, "We have all of eternity to torture Him for speaking God's Word in hell." He could wait. "NO man has ever escaped from me. NO man has EVER escaped hell. This man is NO different!"

Taking Jesus to a cell, the evil spirits laughed and jeered at Him, believing the words of their master. He was captured by the prince of death, satan, and in the captivity of the prince of hell. As far as they were concerned, Jesus was defeated and dead.

End of story.

CHAPTER 23

In the upper regions of hell, some of the saints who were kept in captivity because of sin in their souls, but died in the hope of the promise of the Savior bowed their heads in disappointment. The rumor had been circulated throughout the region of paradise that a man had suffered the martyr's death on earth and had entered through the gates of hell. He had been killed like the prophets of old had prophesied that the Messiah from God would suffer at the hands of the Gentiles on earth and in sheol.

Many were watching the events taking place in the lower regions of hell. Those in paradise could not get to those in the torment of hell because they were separated from each other by a gulf. They had been waiting thousands of years for the Prophet from God that would deliver the saints from the jurisdiction of hell. They died having never received the promise of the Messiah. Even though they obtained a good testimony, they could not be made perfect until Jesus defeated death. Because Adam sinned, death had a hold over all men.

They were not sure if the man being tortured was the One they were looking for and waiting with hope or not. But they were hoping He was the One. The greatest test that He might be that prophet was the words that He was speaking. His words pierced every place of residence in the souls of paradise and all believed that He was the One.

One of those who felt the pain of disappointment looked up when Abraham put his hand on his shoulder. He was on his knees praying to God. "Father Abraham, we thought that Jesus was the One."

Abraham, the father of faith, and the one in charge of all that entered paradise comforted the captives. "Don't despair my children. The Man that you are looking at now said on earth before He died that the only sign He would give this present evil generation, was the sign of Jonah."

"But what did he mean, father?"

"Son, just as the man Jonah was caught between the lower regions and upper regions of hell, so is the Son of Man to be in the 'belly' of hell for three days and three nights," Abraham answered.

"Father!" A woman came and bowed before him. "I was there when

Jesus walked on earth. He always did good. I never heard one unkind word come out of His mouth!" She was crying. "He has to be the One! I know that He is the One that will set us free!"

"The coming prophet has to yield Himself to God, fulfilling scriptures from the prophet Isaiah who said, 'Surely He has borne our sicknesses and carried our sorrows. Yet we esteemed Him stricken, smitten by God, and wounded for our transgressions, and bruised for our iniquities,'" Abraham quoted.

"Just like this Man, Jesus?" asked another. "He was cruelly beaten on earth, but look what they are doing to Him now!" She cried for Him.

"Yes," answered Abraham. "The beating He endured was for our sins. 'And by His stripes we are healed. All we like sheep have gone astray; we have turned every one, to his own way; And the Lord has laid on Him the iniquity of us all.'"

"But we don't understand father? Why must He suffer so?"

Isaiah walked through the crowd and stood by Abraham. He quoted his own prophecy. "He was oppressed and He was afflicted, yet He opened not His mouth. He was led as a lamb to the slaughter, and as a sheep before it shearers is silent. So He opened not His mouth."

"But this man is still quoting scripture, even in the torment of the lower region!" A man pointed out.

"Yet, He has not opened his mouth to bow before satan!" Abraham proclaimed. "And finally in this region He is with us because we can hear His Words clearly!"

"And," Isaiah pointed out, "Jesus did not open His mouth in defense because He would have stopped the plan of redemption. He is the sinless Lamb of God. One word of defense would have cancelled the plan of God to pay for our sins and buy us back."

"Father Abraham," a woman stood, "I was there. I came to Jerusalem to seek the One who people said would lay His hands on you and heal all manners of sicknesses and diseases. I had a form of cancer. But I was too late. I saw Him stand before the judgment seat of Pilot and His accusers speaking words of lies and blasphemy against Him. He did not open his mouth on earth to bow to any man or any of the gods. He did not defend Himself."

Another spoke, "Isaiah, didn't you say through the Spirit of God that the Messiah would be taken from prison and from judgment?"

"Yes and I also said, and I quote, 'Who will declare His generation? For He was cut off from the land of the living, for the transgressions of My people He was stricken. And they made His grave with the wicked . . . but with the rich at His death, because He had done no violence. Nor was any deceit in His mouth.'"

"I believe that man down there in the center of hell is the Messiah," she told everyone around her.

"I believe He is the One, father." Many were voicing their faith.

"Me too!"

"Even if they take Him to the lowest bowels of the region of hell, He will arise!" Isaiah proclaimed boldly.

Another disciple of Jesus came forth. He died of a heart attack from the stress of the imprisonment of Jesus. "Jesus, told us on earth that He was the sacrificial lamb making intercession for the transgressors." He turned to another eyewitness. "How many times did He say that He would spend three days and three nights in the middle of the region of hell?"

The other witness said, "Several times!"

They both turned and looked at Abraham. "We missed it. We didn't understand what He was trying to tell us!"

Everyone was listening to these eyewitness reports.

"He told us that He came into the world to do God's will and destroy the works of the devil. Several times He said that the Son of Man would be delivered to the Gentiles and would be mocked, insulted, spit upon and scourged. And on the third day, He would rise again. But we refused to listen to Him. We were so stubborn about establishing Jesus' physical Kingdom on earth at that time. We had no idea that it wasn't God's timing!"

Abraham stood and raised his hand toward heaven and pointed his other one to the Man standing in the middle of the fun arena, being savagely tortured for the sins of all men. "Jesus fits every description of the suffering Messiah and the prophetic prophecies."

"But why isn't He here with us, since the Messiah never sinned?" A former priest asked.

"He is here with us, only He has to make atonement for our sins, not just physical atonement, which He did on the cross. But the Messiah has to pay the price for our sins with spiritual suffering," Isaiah explained. "If he doesn't suffer the pains of hell and escape it, then none of us will ever be able to escape this place of torment."

Although the saints in the upper regions were not in torment like those souls in the lower regions, they could still hear, see and smell the torment of souls. It was a terrible place to be.

Isaiah continued, "Because He made His spirit and soul an offering for sin, all of us here and those who accept him on earth will be made righteous once again in the eyes of the Lord."

"When will we know if it is Him, father Abraham?"

"After three days my son."

In His cell, Jesus completed speaking Psalm 22; "I will declare Your Name to My brethren; In the midst of the assembly I will praise You. All you descendants of Jacob, glorify Him, and fear Him, all you offspring of Israel."

He lifted his eyes and looked into the upper regions of hell. He knew that they would despair of Him being the One sent by God for their release. He continued to speak with authority, shouting to the saints in paradise. "For He has not despised nor abhorred the affliction of the afflicted; nor has He hidden His face from us; but when I cry to Him, He heard. My praise shall be of our Father in the great assembly!"

With every word that He spoke, a demon stabbed him with a spear. "Shut up! Or we will triple your torment!" They cursed him unmercifully.

His words tormented the tormenters.

"I will pay My vows before those who fear Him. The meek shall eat and be satisfied; those who seek Him will praise the Lord. Let your heart live forever! I am He that was to come into the bowels of earth. I am He that will rise again!"

No amount of torture could stop Jesus from quoting scriptures from His cell in hell. Even though they did not cease from inflicting pain, Jesus would not bow to satan. In their frustration and anger after three days of quoting scripture day and night, and their continual determination to break Jesus and make Him bow to satan, they forgot what He spoke on earth.

On earth, the chief priests and the Pharisees remembered that Jesus said, "After three days I will rise." They asked Pilate to secure the tomb with guards and seal it so that His disciples couldn't steal Jesus' body away.

One day passed

Two days passed.

Three days were almost passed.

On the third day His words were far from their heart and mind.

Satan thought about it once or twice, but completely dismissed the possibility. It was too ludicrous to believe that with only His words, Jesus could escape hell. Who would believe anything that Jesus said while on earth now that He was in hell? The prince of death was certain that Jesus belonged to him for eternity.

He comforted himself with the fact that Jesus was in chains and caged. No one convinced satan that Jesus could escape. Jesus would stay in his unregenerate dead soul for eternity. Forever and forever . . . dead life without end! He was to be with him forever.

"He is just a man!"

The prince of hell watched and waited.

Time was ticking click by click.

They couldn't wait to announce that Jesus belonged to satan and forever his dream was going to come true. The Man Jesus, who refused to bow to him on earth, would soon bow to him in hell; the three days and nights were almost up. On the fourth day, satan would proclaim to all that Jesus was a liar and failed at escaping from hell.

Satan made plans to ascend to the earth's surface and proclaim to all that Jesus was his prisoner in hell forever by wiping all memory of Him off the planet in every heart and mind of every believer that he could find. Jesus wasn't the first failed deluded human Messiah to show up on earth and probably wouldn't be the last.

Not one evil demonic spirit or fallen angel was able to break Jesus. They were not able to make Jesus bow to satan or worship him with His mouth in hell.

Late into the third day on earth, the evil spirits began to celebrate early. "Satan did it!" The evil spirits rejoiced. "Our master is greater! He has defeated God!"

Three earth days and nights were enough for the devil! He stood in front of his throne throwing up his arms ranting and raving like a lunatic, "His resistance to me has continued long enough. Go to the lowest region of hell and bring him to me! I am going to end it now!"

Jesus was again brought out to the fun circle.

"I am the ruler of this world." Satan stood and raised his hands in front of all the assembly. "I rule the earth and everything above it, on it and under it! Resistance to me is futile. I caused the first man Adam, who was sinless, to fall. Now I have You, Jesus, the self-proclaimed Son of God. You belong to me!"

The evil angels and demons added their mocking, they surrounded Jesus and started to spear Him again with knives, spears and pitch forks when a rumbling began to shake hell.

It started out like a small earthquake tremor.

Then the trembling began to intensify.

Not knowing what was going on, all the demons stopped dead in their tracks and looked to satan for the answer. Immediately, they could see he was not the one causing this shaking.

Satan ran back to his throne in the center of hell and grabbed the arms of the chair. A look of horror came upon his face. He held onto his throne as if he was holding on for his life. A feeling of dread and doom descended over hell.

Even the spirit of fear was taken over by fear.

Demon spirits tried to steady themselves as the floor was rocking and rolling. They all knew something was very wrong. As the floors and walls began to shake violently, large boulders started falling around the entire evil congregation surrounding Jesus; they could not stop hell from moving.

Then a voice like thunder reverberated throughout hell. The Father spoke, "Let all the angels of God worship Him."

A host of angels invaded hell and made every being bow to Jesus.

"Arise, My Son! Arise, My Love! Hell no longer has a hold over You!" No one could move when the force of the Spirit of God entered that place.

The Spirit of God fell upon Jesus in bodily form. A blinding light burst onto the scene and caused the demons to writhe in agony and pain. Instantly, Jesus became born again! His countenance was like the sun shining in its strength.

The angels lifted up their voices and proclaimed, "Jesus is the firstborn from the dead!"

He received a new spirit from the Holy Spirit and became a new creation. The chains of darkness were loosed from His body and soul. The neck, leg and wrist chains fell to the ground. Angels of light surrounded him and threw his chains away from Him.

Angels and humans from paradise shouted praises to the King of kings and the Lord of lords. An explosion of light burst through the portholes of hell!

The blue-dead flesh disintegrated as fresh new flesh formed over his bones and spirit. His new flesh was clean, pure, lily-white and fresh as a newborn baby. A robe of pure light surrounded his flesh. Legions and legions of God's angels proclaimed Jesus as Lord and celebrated the victory of Jesus' new birth in the center of hell.

"No!" he screamed. "No! God can't do this! You can't walk out of hell! You died in Your sins! You belong to ME!"

"I am the Resurrection and the Life," proclaimed Jesus as He took the keys of hell from him. "I am the Light of Life. Darkness has to flee!"

Demons started scampering and fleeing like roaches, when the light from the manifested presence of the Holy Spirit entered Him. That light continued to radiate from Jesus and pierce the darkness of hell. All the evil angels were screaming and running from Him, the light of glory. The decrepit and degenerative state of hell was exposed by the fierce brightness of His glory.

The light had a deafening sound like the roar of a tornado. It was cracking like thunder and lightning as Jesus was born again and given a new spirit in hell.

Adam, first created of all mankind, shouted and rejoiced. "The light that you see is the author of everlasting light! This is the One that God told me would rescue me and Eve and return us to paradise!"

"This is the light that comes from the Father and the One that I prophesied on earth would come!" Isaiah the prophet shouted out for all in the locked prison to hear.

"Jesus!" the saints in paradise were shouting His name over and over again with victory. "Jesus, the Messiah!"

Jesus was the first man to be born again by the Holy Spirit. His Spirit came to life as a new creation! Fire and lights like a fireworks celebration on earth revealed that all of hell was bowing before Jesus.

"Ugh! You are blinding us!" they screamed looking for a place to hide. They couldn't run fast enough or far enough!

"Fall on us!" Evil spirits cried to the rocks in hell. They couldn't stand to be exposed to the light. "Fall on us, you worthless piece of real estate!" The rocks refused to obey them.

The holy angel Michael walked over to the gates guarding paradise and proclaimed with a loud voice. "Lift up your gates, O you princes! Open up you everlasting gates and the King of Glory will come in!"

The prince of hell fell to the side of satan and shouted at him, "If you are a powerful warrior, fight with the King of Glory!"

Satan turned himself into a powerful fire-breathing dragon and tried to destroy the new body of Jesus. Immediately Jesus grabbed the neck of the dragon and slammed his body to the ground. He stomped the dragon's head with His foot and crushed the life out him.

All the saints watching cried out in anger to the prince of hell, "Open your gates so that the King of Glory may come in!"

Jesus walked away from satan's throne with the keys in his hand. He was headed to the prison across the gulf. This was the hour that was promised to them who believed the Messiah was coming. He preached to all who died in faith, not having received the promises, but believed in them and confessed them during their life on earth. He crossed the gulf that separated them preaching to the spirits in hell.

He was the first Man to ever cross the gulf.

"I am the resurrection and the Life. He who believes in Me, though he may die, he shall live. And whoever lives and believes in Me shall never die. Do you believe this?"

The prophet David cried out saying, "I prophesied on earth through You that men would praise the Lord for Your goodness and Your wonderful works to the children of men! For you have broken the gates of brass and cut the bars of iron away from us!"

"Didn't I rightly prophesy of You when I was alive on earth?" The prophet Isaiah said, "The dead men shall live and we should rise again who are in our graves. For the Almighty God has sent us a deliverer!"

"Yes! Yes, Lord, we believe that You are the Christ, the Son of God, who is to come into the world." Many raised their hands to praise and worship Him.

They held out their hands to Jesus. "Praise be to the Lord! The Anointed One of God has come for us!"

"The prophets said you would come!" A woman dropped to her knees and worshipped Him.

Jesus unlocked the gates of paradise.

The Father spoke again to all in the regions of the dam as hell stood still paralyzed with fear. "Your throne, O God, is forever and ever; A scepter of righteousness is the scepter of Your Kingdom. You have loved righteousness and hated lawlessness; therefore God, Your God has anointed You with the oil of gladness more than Your companions."

Jesus held out the keys and gave them to father Abraham. "I am the One you prophesied and saw many years ago. You have been waiting for Me."

Abraham bowed before Him and worshiped Him. "The Father has called you God and I call you My God!"

Across the gulf, those humans in the pits and cells of hell were listening and saw what was going on. They didn't believe in Jesus. They died in their sins without faith or hope in the promise of a savior. The sinful lusts and desires of their flesh blinded them to the truth of Jesus being the Messiah.

"He is lying to you!" they shouted.

"Don't believe Him, it's a trap!"

"Lord satan will torture you for believing in Him!"

"Life? Ha! There is no life in this god-forsaken place!"

One man screamed, "No one can break out of hell! He's crazy!"

"He is a lunatic." A dead human cursed Him.

"Curse God and accept Your death!"

The souls of evil men joined with the evil spirits, cursing and reviling Jesus even with their faces in the dust of hell. But their worthless, idle, evil words went unheeded in the hearts of the faithful ones.

As the souls in paradise received the words of Jesus, the words of the evil souls became silent. They were drowned in the sea of nothingness by the voices of praise!

When Jesus said He was the Resurrection and Life, one of the men in paradise dropped to his knees and bowed before him and cried out, "I believe Lord, that you are the Messiah! I will follow you anywhere!"

"Truly, we believe you are that Prophet!"

"I am the Bread of Life. He who comes to Me shall never hunger, and he who believes in Me shall never thirst. I am the Living Bread that comes down from heaven that you may eat of it and not die. If anyone eats of this Bread, My Words, he will live forever; and the Bread that I gave is My flesh, which I gave for the life of the world."

Some who had recently departed from earth and lived in the holy city, Jerusalem, recognized Him. "He was the one who fed the thousands from the few minnows and crackers."

"He is the one! He is the Messiah, the Anointed One of God!"

A woman, who sat at Jesus' feet on earth said, "I saw this Man heal a blind person and cast a demon out of my sister."

"This is the hour that I spoke about! The dead hear My voice and those who believe will live. All power and authority has been given to Me in heaven, on earth and in hell. As the Father has life in Himself, so He has granted the Son to have life in Himself."

Jesus began to breathe on those in paradise and said, "Receive the Holy Spirit."

A light exploded throughout the upper region with a sound of a rushing mighty wind. It filled all paradise. Tens of thousands and thousands of humans were becoming born again. The spectacular light show was beyond human words and comprehension. Because of the Blood of Jesus and the power of the Holy Spirit, the souls waiting for the promise of God were being made perfect.

The Holy Spirit replaced their old spirit with a new spirit to those who believed in Jesus, as He preached the Word, the power to get born again in the very pit of hell. Warring angels filled the entire gulf between the upper and lower regions of hell. They helped the Lord as he unlocked the gates of paradise with the keys He took from the devil.

The spectacular show of lights, which exposed all the evil spirits, caused hell to shrink in disbelief and they could do nothing but bow and wait for them to leave.

Hell would never be the same again.

"I have come to declare unto you that our Father has made a way for you. You are a new creation in Me. The power of sin and death cannot stop My resurrection or yours. You are now born again into My Kingdom. But you must wait until I have been reunited with My body in the grave and present My Blood before the Father at His altar. I will cleanse everything between hell and heaven. Even the very tools of worship in heaven have to be cleansed first."

Abraham spoke. "We praise Your Name, Jesus. We submit to You and anything You tell us to do."

"You are LORD!" All of the recreated men and women bowed to Him.

"My angels will help you build a new paradise outside the gates of the Father's city. There father, Abraham, you will greet all the saints that are cleansed by My Blood."

"Oh! Praise be the Lord!" Abraham bowed before Him again. "You are Lord!"

As the saints of old were released, many hugged and kissed the Lord. Some cried and fell at His feet, worshiping Him as the Messiah. They kissed His nail scared hands and touched the wound in His side. Jesus as the sacrificial lamb paid the price sin demanded and now they would live forever in a world without end.

The congregation of saints and angels cheered Jesus as He reappeared before satan. The demon spirits watched in horror as satan, who reappeared in his true form, slinked like a snake off his throne. On his hands and knees, he bowed before the Lord of glory.

Jesus stripped him of his robe and put a chain around his neck. He paraded satan naked and stripped of all authority all over the body of hell on his hands and knees. Disarming principalities and powers, He made a public show of them. He was triumphant over the devil and his entire kingdom of darkness in every way and everything.

The saints of old were praising and worshiping the Lord God. The angels were shouting their praises and flying around demanding all evil spirits to continue bowing to the Son of God. The kingdom of darkness looked small in comparison to the Lord's army of angels.

"Bow to Jesus! King of kings! Lord of lords!" proclaimed Michael.

"Jesus' Name is higher than all living beings in heaven, in earth and under the earth." Gabriel declared. "He has been declared God!"

"Glory to God in the highest! Jesus has delivered the Lord's people from the power of this present evil age!" proclaimed all the other angels.

"I am the manifested will of God. The first man Adam became a living being made of dust from the earth. I am the last Man. I have received the power from My Father to give life unto all who seek Me."

Jesus pulled on satan's chain, and lifted up his hands toward heaven. "O death, where is your sting? O hell, where is your victory?" Jesus overcame the spiritual and physical power of the devil and all the evil kingdom of his was horrified.

The power radiating from Jesus was electrifying to every being that came in contact with Him. Not one demon or evil angel could stand in his presence. A look of shock and terror filled satan's face. He was stripped of everything he thought he owned. He was not prepared for this hour.

"I am the firstborn from the dead!" proclaimed Jesus like a boxing champion on earth that had just been declared victor of the fight. "I have the victory over death and hell!"

Satan gritted his teeth with his face licking the dust. "I have been tricked! You are God!"

"I am the Lord of glory. I gave My life for the sins of mankind, so your works would be destroyed. Now the manifold wisdom of God is made known to all principalities and powers and to all rulers of darkness, even throughout all the heavenlies. I will give my authority and power to My body, the called out ones!"

All of the evil spirits gasped! "The called out ones? Who are they?" Questions erupted all over the regions of hell. "What did He say? Who is He talking about?"

"My new body!" Jesus proclaimed for all to know. "Believers in Me who will be joined with My Father and I as one new Man!"

Satan tried to lift up his face and stand. "Foul, I cry foul! You could only do this . . . this thing because You are God."

"No, Satan! I beat you as a Man of God. The wisdom of God was hidden in a mystery. I was ordained and predestined for this time. I now enforce the authority and power that God, the Creator put into the hands of the men and women of earth as a Man of God. I have all power over death, hell and the grave. I have all power and authority over you!"

The saints in paradise and all spirits in heaven shouted with a voice of praise.

"No, no, NO! No fair! You had to beat me as God! No other man has ever defeated me!" He raised his body to his knees. "It's not possible for a mere man to defeat me!"

Jesus put his foot on the devil's back and pushed his face back into the dirt. "I live and breathe by every Word that proceeds from the mouth of God. I am a born again Man. No longer can sin or death dominate Me. You are defeated satan, by the Word of God who was made flesh and walked and talked on earth. You deceived yourself because you refused the truth. You are the father of lies. You rejected truth to reign over you."

He pounded his fists on the ground. "No! If I had of known you were God, I would have NEVER crucified You . . . The Lord of Glory? Oh——!" he cursed himself as he was beginning to understand what he had done.

Satan stayed prostrate on the dust of hell's floor and started pounding the ground with his fist and his head. Jesus put more pressure on his head to stop his thrashing around. "I am the Light that gives light to every man who will accept Me. I am the Anointed of God. I came into this world through the womb of a woman. I have a legal right to this earth. You, satan, entered this world through deception and lies. You are an illegal alien."

Satan's mouth was in the dirt of hell. He was being strangled by it. The dirt of hell was dead flesh. Literally Jesus fulfilled Genesis 3:14 . . ."On your belly you shall go, and you shall eat dust all the days of your life."

Directing His speech to all in hell, Jesus proclaimed in a loud booming voice. "I am the Son of God and the Son of Man. As a man, I legally take all power and authority in the heavenlies, on earth and under earth back from the kingdom of darkness! I am He that was spoken of in the book of Genesis. For a moment satan bruised My heel, but for all eternity I have crushed your head!"

A shout of praise from heaven and hell rang out among the sons of God. All of heaven rejoiced.

"Jesus is alive! The prince of death and hell cannot keep Him in the grave!" Michael announced.

Hell was immobilized and stunned. Not one evil demon or evil angel could believe this was happening. How deceived could they have been to believe satan? He didn't know the plan of God! Nor did he recognize that Jesus was the Anointed One from God. Many of the fallen angels that followed him began to feel sick as their life force drained from their spirit bodies.

Jesus released satan and immediately rose through all levels of hell, through the gulf and the region of paradise and back to the sepulcher to retrieve His physical body. He arose to heaven to present His Blood before the Father and cleanse all the holy vessels in the throne room of heaven.

He arose triumphantly!

Jesus was the One! *Stupid, stupid, STUPID*! Satan was pounding his fist into the ground and repeating over and over.

"JESUS WAS THE ONE!"

CHAPTER 24

"Cool!" Mose shouted.

"Cool?" Hannah looked at Mose in amazement, "Like, that is all you can say about the story Joshua just told us. That was too awesome for words!" She wiped her eyes as the tears rolled down her cheeks. "I wish I could have seen what *you* did!" In the middle of his story, Hannah had folded up the chip bags and put them back into the pantry. Joshua had their undivided attention as he told his vision of Jesus in hell to them.

"After totally humiliating satan in front of all his evil spirits and rebellious angels and retrieving His body back in the tomb, Jesus ascended to heaven with all His angels and the saints from paradise." Joshua continued the story that was revealed to him by the Holy Spirit through his years of meditating the Bible.

"So, that's what Jesus meant when He told the thief on the cross that He would be with him in paradise!" Kellie said.

"I always wondered about that," Mose added. "Especially since the Word in Acts states that Jesus' soul was not left in hades."

"Yeah, like, how could the Lord be in heaven and hell at the same time?" asked Hannah.

"He wasn't. Paradise was in an outer region of hell, but set apart by a gulf. Remember the story about the rich man in hell and the beggar in the bosom of Abraham? They both could see and hear one another. They just couldn't cross over from one part of hell to the other," Joshua told them.

"How do you know that Jesus continued to suffer in hell?" asked Kellie.

"Let me ask you a question. After Adam and Eve ate of the fruit from the tree, did they die spiritually or physically?"

"Spiritually," they all said.

"How do you know?" Joshua asked them.

"If he didn't die spiritually then God lied," Kellie answered.

"That's right. God said they would die. Adam died spiritually."

"Then how could Adam still hear God when He came to walk and talk with him after he sinned?" Hannah asked Joshua.

"Adam was first a spirit and God created him a body. The planet earth was a nursery and the body was the house for His baby, Adam. Now Eve's body was a cell taken from Adam when he was asleep and God breathed into this body a female Adam."

"See what I mean guys?" Kellie commented. "Have you ever heard anyone tell a story like Joshua?"

"Wordman! God was the first to clone?"

"It wasn't a total cloning," Joshua blushed. "I mean, obviously, we have differences."

Hannah laughed. "Like totally. We have different parts."

"God calls it a male body or a male body with a womb. Remember after God created Adam and Eve's bodies, we all got one the same way," Joshua said.

Mose smiled real big. "Yeah, I get it. When two cells called the sperm and the ovum get together then . . ."

"We get it, Mose," Kellie looked annoyed.

"Spiritual death is separation from the Father. Remember, he wasn't seeking the Father, the Father was seeking him," Joshua pointed out.

"Isn't that the same as us?" Kellie asked. "We say that we found Jesus, but isn't it really that He found us?"

"Yes and the Holy Trinity has been chasing us ever since Adam fell in the garden. We just couldn't see or hear them."

"If you study the rest of Genesis, you will find that by the third generation, Adam's grandchildren didn't know how to walk and talk with God." "We don't really know exactly what Adam saw or knew about God, but we do know that gradually the generations after Adam started losing knowledge about God."

"How do you know?" Kellie was always curious how Joshua knew these things.

"In Genesis chapter four, we see in verse three that time is referred to as 'and in the process of time.' Here God is speaking to Adam's sons Cain and Able, the second generation of people. But at the end of the chapter in verse 26, it was in Seth's son, Enosh's generation that man began to call on the name of the Lord. This is significant. The second generation still talked to God openly, but the third generation began to 'call on the name of the Lord.' That suggests that they were praying to God, but not openly talking to Him."

"Word!" Mose looked at the scriptures. Joshua was amazing. He looked over at Hannah. "Can I have another piece of paper?"

"Sure," she tore a sheet out of her notebook.

"That understanding came from the Holy Spirit through meditation. If you look up the Hebrew meaning of the name Enosh, it means mortal. It was in the third generation that man began to live out of his soul instead of his spirit. If you continue reading in Genesis by chapter five you will learn that the generation before Noah believed lies about God and His true nature and character. Look at the meaning of the name Noah in verse 29."

Hannah read it out loud. "And he called his name Noah, saying, 'This one will comfort us concerning the work and the toil of our hands, because of the ground which the Lord has cursed.'"

"Explain please," Kellie didn't get it.

"God did not curse the ground of earth. Man allowed the earth to become cursed by allowing the devil who is the curse access to the garden. He said in chapter three and verse 17 of Genesis that earth and the ground became cursed because of Adam's disobedience."

"I always heard that God cursed the earth," Hannah was tapping her pencil on the edge of the table.

Mose stared at her.

"What?"

"You're tapping your pencil."

"Sorry. Joshua, everybody believes that God cursed the earth. Why?"

"God doesn't curse. In Genesis, God saw that His works were good and called them blessed. Satan is the curse and Adam received the curse through his own actions. Hannah, you heard a lie from the devil that began in Lamech's generation. By Noah's generation, God looked from heaven and 'saw that the wickedness of man was great in the earth and that the thoughts of his mind and spirit were evil continually.'"

They were trying to follow Joshua in his Bible, but he was going too fast.

"After the fall, satan continued to deceive Adam and his descendants."

"Wordman, so that is why men blame everything on God," Mose realized.

"Yeah, like tornadoes, floods, hurricanes and fires and call them acts of God instead of acts of satan!" declared Hannah. "That makes me mad."

"How did death take Jesus to hell?" Kellie wondered.

"Jesus was the Word made flesh, He submitted Himself to death by declaring, 'My God, My God, why have You forsaken Me?'" Joshua told them. "Jesus said that God is life, when He declared that life had forsaken Him, death took over."

"WORD!"

"I always wondered why Jesus said what He did on the cross," Kellie mused. "I mean if He didn't know what God was doing, then what chance do I have of knowing His plans?"

"Jesus was perfectly aware of God's plan. God hadn't forsaken Him like we think that means. Jesus had to speak separation from God, or death could have never claimed Him."

"Word!" Mose said. "Are you saying that Jesus could not die?"

"Yes."

"Is that why Jesus didn't say a word at His trial?" Hannah asked.

"If He would have said anything in His defense, then Pilot couldn't have killed him."

"Why?" Kellie asked.

"Because there is not death in life." Joshua knew that he was talking about things hard to understand. "Jesus said that He and His Father were One. He didn't mean that God had a flesh body or that Jesus only had a spirit body. He meant that they are One like God explained when a man and woman marry; the two become one. Jesus was perfect in thought, word, and action. Death did not have legal right to take Him because He had no fear and His thinking and speaking was perfect. His soul was conformed to the image of His Father."

"In Proverbs . . . uh . . . chapter 18, I think, the Word says that 'the power of life and death is in the power of the tongue," Kellie remembered.

"The big issue here is that fact that most Christians don't believe that Jesus went to hell," Mose interrupted.

"To really understand what happened to Jesus for those three days and nights, you need to seek the Holy Spirit for revelation. You need to go over and over it and meditate the scriptures and God will show you. Satan doesn't want us to know how completely he was defeated. And he certainly doesn't want us to know the whole truth about anything that pertains to our status as newly created beings. That is what born again means. We are a new creation in Christ."

"That part about satan not wanting us to know what really happened makes sense," Kellie said.

"This is a great teaching, Joshua," Hannah commented.

"Why did He have to suffer for three days and nights?" Mose asked.

"I'm not sure. But do like Jesus would do," Joshua told her.

"What?"

"Forget the past! He's not suffering now! He is the triumphant Lord. He has a name higher than all names. No other name but the name of Jesus is worthy of praise and honor and glory." Joshua shouted.

Hannah and Kellie raised their hands and began to worship and praise the Lord. Mose and Joshua joined in for a few minutes.

"I wonder what his new name is?" Asked Mose.

"His new name is recorded in Hebrews," Joshua told them.

"Where?" They all asked at the same time.

"In the first chapter. God called Him God and told all the angels to bow down to Him." Joshua explained.

"Well, Jesus is God! That's not a new name," Kellie told him.

"Yes, it is. No man has ever been called God before. Man has been called the Son of God. Like Adam and all his descendants have been called sons of God, but they have never been worshiped as God!"

Hannah stopped praising the Lord. "What are you saying Joshua?"

"I'm saying that Jesus as a new man has been called God by God and He will be the only Man that will have that distinction. Yes, we are in the family of God and yes, we are sons of God, but Jesus is the only man that is the firstborn." He wanted to emphasize this understanding over and over. "We are sons of God born again after Jesus."

"I'm not a boy . . . I'm a girl," Hannah protested.

"Same thing," Joshua explained. "You are in the body of Christ and there is no male or female."

"Doesn't Paul also say that there is no Jew or Gentile?" Mose asked.

"He said in Galatians that there is neither Jew nor Greek, slave nor free, male nor females, because we are all one in the Anointed One, Jesus," Joshua answered him.

Kellie turned her Bible to Hebrews the first chapter and read out loud. "Therefore God, Your God, has anointed You with the oil of gladness more than Your companions."

"But," Hannah protested. "I still don't understand. Wasn't Jesus God because His Father is God?"

"Yeah, but His mother is flesh and blood, human." Mose reminded her.

"Think about it. What part of Jesus was God?" Joshua asked them.

"Part! You mean body parts?" squealed Hannah.

"I mean what part of Him was human and what part of Him was divine?" asked Joshua.

"Well," Hannah reasoned. "When He left hell, He stopped at His grave to pick up His body. His body had not seen corruption."

"That is right according to scripture in Psalm and Acts. Remember it was three days later and David testified saying that Jesus' body would not see corruption," Joshua said. "The disfigured body was immediately healed except for the holes in His wrist, the wound in His side and scars on his back; physical proof throughout eternity that He paid the price of sin. He is no longer the crucified Christ . . . He is the Resurrected Christ! The only thing that reminds us of the crucifixion is the cuts made in His physical body. These are the markings of the New Covenant between Him and His Father," Joshua taught them.

"So, what part is divine?" asked Kellie

"His Blood," Joshua told them

"But didn't He tell Mary not to touch Him when she saw Him in the garden around the tomb?" asked Kellie. "Wouldn't that make His flesh special?"

"He hadn't yet presented His Blood sacrifice before the Father in heaven," replied Joshua. "He cleansed all of heaven and earth of the sin that had invaded the Father's creation with His Blood. He made intercession for the transgressors."

"That must have been a long vision." Mose commented.

"I saw a movie screen in my head over just about everything I told you," Joshua explained. "The details of hell I got from a woman who made over 40 visits to hell with Jesus."

"For real?" Hannah asked.

"How do you know she really went to hell?" Kellie asked.

"I believed her testimony and I got a witness from the Holy Spirit in my spirit."

Mose thought of a passage and turned his Bible to Matthew 27. "Here is another scripture that confirms your vision."

"What verse, Mose?" asked Hannah flipping through her Bible.

"Verse 52 . . . Look, I've always wondered about this scripture; it is so way out there! Listen." He began to quote, "and the graves were opened; and many bodies of the saints who had fallen asleep were raised; and coming out of the graves after His resurrection, they went into the holy city and appeared to many!"

"How do Christians who don't believe that humans can come back to earth after they die explain this story?" Hannah asked.

"They probably explain it away like they do speaking in tongues. You know that it only happened in that day because of Jesus first resurrection or something like that," Kellie answered.

"Or they think that they could only walk on earth because they hadn't gone to heaven yet," Mose added.

"Those are the people from paradise?" Hannah asked.

"Who else could they be?" Joshua added. "The men and women of that verse who followed Jesus after His resurrection, are the ones who died believing in the promise, but never saw Him."

"Then Jesus preached in hell." Mose said.

"Where do you find that in the Bible?" asked Kellie.

"Well, actually that last part was revealed to me through meditation on the events that took place when Jesus was in hell and rose from the dead. The rest is from another saint's account of his visit to heaven. He wrote in the book that before you pass through the gates of heaven, father Abraham accepts you into the city of paradise."

Mose added. "The Bible does say Jesus preached to the souls in hell."

"No way!" exclaimed Hannah.

"Yes . . . way!" mimicked Mose with his hands on his hips.

"Where?" asked Kellie.

"1 Peter 3:19," answered Joshua.

Kellie turned to the scripture to read it. "By whom also he went and preached to the spirits in prison, who formerly were disobedient, when once the Divine longsuffering waited in the days of Noah. While the ark was being prepared, in which a few, that is, eight souls, were saved through water."

Kellie looked up at Joshua, "I don't understand . . . I thought the spirits in prison were Noah and his family?"

"Some people think that the spirits in prison are the fallen angels. Look at verse 18 . . . 'For Christ also suffered once for sins, the just for the unjust, that He might bring us to God, being put to death in the flesh but made alive by the Spirit, by whom' . . ." Joshua looked up and asked them, "who is the whom?"

"What?" asked Hannah.

"The 'whom' in this verse. Who is it?"

"Where?" asked Mose.

"Verse 18," Kellie pointed out.

"The whom in that verse is the Holy Spirit. Jesus preached to the spirits in prison by the Holy Spirit. Noah was a figure or a type of what was going to happen. While Noah built the ark he spoke what God said to him over and over and over. Eight people believed and got into the ark. The resurrection of Jesus is the ark that saved us through the Holy Spirit, the power of God. And the Word of God cleanses us from all unrighteousness," Joshua answered. "Some of the people who died before Noah were in that holding cell called paradise because they were once disobedient, but they were waiting for the promise of the Anointed One who would crush the head of the serpent who caused sin and death."

Mose's brain was beginning to register overload.

"Jesus said that whoever believed in Him, out of his belly would flow rivers of water," Hannah remembered.

"We are washed with the water of His Word," Kellie affirmed.

"A lot of them had waited a long time for the Messiah to come. It must have been a great time of rejoicing in the victory over death and hell and they stopped to celebrate in Jerusalem before going on to heaven," Joshua said.

"I don't think I've ever heard a sermon on this subject," Mose rubbed his head. "I've got to go to the bathroom."

"I sure don't remember reading these scriptures!" Hannah put her hands in the air, "And I've read the whole Bible!" She stood and stretched.

Kellie shook her head at Hannah. "Get real. No one can remember everything they read in the Bible!"

Joshua looked at his watch. It was getting late so he decided to stop teaching at this point. "After teaching his disciples 40 days and night, he ascended up to heaven in front of 500 witnesses."

"Word! That's a type of what's going to happen in the future isn't it?" Mose said as he paused before going into the bathroom.

"This is awesome, Joshua," Hannah loved reading the Bible with Joshua.

A question came into Kellie's mind. "What was God saying when He spoke to Jesus and said, 'Sit at My right hand, until I make Your enemies Your footstool'?"

Joshua turned to Hebrews 10:12. "Listen to this . . ."

Mose shouted at him. "Wait until I . . ."

"Okay."

"What time is it?" Kellie asked Hannah.

Hannah pointed to the Coo-coo clock on the wall.

"Oh my! No wonder my b— uh, tailbone hurts!" exclaimed Kellie.

Mose ran back from the bathroom.

"This is the last scripture, 'but this Man, after He had offered one sacrifice for sins forever, sat down at the right hand of God, from that time waiting till His enemies are made His footstool.'"

"I thought God was going to do that, you know make His enemies His footstool," Hannah stated.

"That's what most Christians think," replied Joshua. "No where in the New Testament does it say that God is going to take care of demons for you. He has done all He is going to do with satan. God is waiting for us to put the kingdom of darkness under Jesus' feet."

"God is waiting for us?" Hannah asked.

"We are responsible for the kingdom of darkness still running loose on planet earth!" answered Joshua.

"Word! That's right! When Jesus left he was under His feet!" Mose was finally getting it.

"He sent His Son to destroy the devils works and defeat death. He did that. All authority is in the hands of Jesus and He commissioned His body to enforce His defeat of the devil," Joshua said.

"I don't get it? Why is the devil still here on earth?" asked Kellie.

"Because we, the body of Christ, have not put him and his kingdom under our feet, which would be Jesus' feet," explained Joshua. "God will allow anything we allow, but personally I think it's so we can have some fun enforcing the defeat of satan and his kingdom."

"Fun?" Kellie was shocked that he used that word.

"You haven't met 'fun' yet!" Mose was thinking about the public school he hadn't experienced yet.

"Most Christians may not think it is fun," Joshua smiled, "but it should be."

Mose looked at Hannah, "I don't think he knows how different he really is."

She shook her head agreeing with him.

"God is waiting for us to put the devil and his kingdom of darkness under Jesus' feet. He's not waiting for Jesus to do anything . . . Jesus has done everything that needs to be done."

"Wordman you are right on. The only thing that is left is for the body of Christ to enforce Jesus' victory and totally crush satan's kingdom!" Mose thought out loud.

Vicki stood at the door listening to their conversation for a few seconds. She walked in wondering if they realized what time it was, but couldn't resist joining them. "There is another reason why Jesus might have left the devil on earth for awhile."

"Mom . . ."

"Why, Mrs. Knight?" Hannah asked.

"Do you know the place where Jesus asked a question about when the Son of Man returns to earth will He find any faith?"

"Isn't that in Luke chapter 18?" Mose asked flipping through his Bible.

"Yes." Vicki walked over to the table they were sitting.

"Here it is," Hannah found it first.

"Read it Hannah," Vicki said.

"I tell you that He will avenge them speedily. Never the less, when the Son of Man comes will He really find faith on the earth?"

"I thought that when Jesus comes back the second time that He won't find faith on the earth," Mose stated.

"What is faith?"

"Faith is a substance or a spiritual force," Joshua answered.

"How much spiritual force of faith was on earth when Jesus rose from the dead?"

"Since they all ran, I guess not much," Mose thought about it.

"Yeah and Peter denied Jesus, I think he was afraid of what would happen to him," Hannah said.

"Try none. Not one of Jesus' disciples was looking for Him. On the third day after His death, they should have been camped around His tomb. A couple of disciples even talked with Jesus and didn't know it was Him. After His death, His disciples were drowning in the spiritual force of fear. Jesus had faith for Himself, but He could not have faith for His disciples," Vicki taught them.

"Faith has to be developed in us," Joshua said.

"Faith like a seed is deposited inside our spirit man when we get saved and it takes a process for it to grow into a powerful force in our life. It has taken the church almost two thousand years to get a revelation of faith and other powerful truth's from God's Word. But faith is the force that will deliver this creation from the curse of satan. Great faith in the body of Christ will be required for God's purposes to be completed on earth in these last days."

"So, you believe He will find faith on earth?"

"Yes. Those that go up in the rapture have developed their faith to the point that people on earth will think that they are seeing God in the flesh. I believe that those left behind will be forced to develop their faith. Remember faith is a seed that is deposited in all born-again people."

"I thought the earth will be totally controlled by the anti-Christ?" Mose asked.

Vicki thought about it for a few seconds. "Let's shelve that topic until another time, it is getting late."

"That's fine with me," Hannah let out a breath of relief. "I don't think my brain can take anymore."

"So, do you think that satan is part of God's plan?" Kellie asked.

"Well, that's another topic that we better leave to another time, but God is a great planner and since he gave us all the right to choose, He has back up plans for His back up plans for His plans."

"Joshua did say that God is not the author of trials and tribulations, right?" Hannah asked.

"Trials and tribulations come to take the Word of God out of your heart. If you understand that truth, then you will have to develop your faith through the force of patience by hearing and hearing the Word, because the Bible says that we overcame him, satan, by the Blood of the lamb and the Word of our testimony. The Word of our testimony is the Word of God coming out of our mouth creating and releasing the power force of faith," Vicki explained.

All of them were writing down what Vicki was saying.

Kellie closed her notebook. "That's the most writing I've ever done at a Bible study!"

"That was great, Mom," Joshua stood and stretched.

They all stood up with him and stretched.

"Man, my brain feels like mush," Mose rubbed his head.

Hannah walked outside with Kellie as she opened the French doors. "This is so great. My brain is so full, I feel like its going to explode."

Mose was going to say something, but decided not too. Hannah was too easy to attack. She was always opening herself up for teasing.

"You do know how late it is, right?" Vicki asked again.

"We lost track of time, Mrs. Knight," Hannah said as she looked up at the stars. "But I'm with Kellie. Whatever she does, I do with her."

Kellie picked up her purse to turn her phone on. "Oh my goodness! I have ten messages and I bet half of them are from my mom!" She went outside the French doors to use her phone.

"Are you hungry?" Vicki asked.

Mose rubbed his stomach, "I am starved!"

"Your mother called hours ago, Mose, and I told her that you guys were having a Bible study. So, she came over and brought you some clothes so you can stay the night," Vicki told him.

"My mom is the greatest." It was hard to believe he was going to stay the night at this house.

"Joshua, I was wondering . . ."

He held up his hand to stop Hannah. "Let's call it quits for the tonight."

"Yeah," Mose pleaded. "My flesh is overwhelming my spirit at the moment."

At that exact moment, Mose's stomach made a loud growling sound and everybody cracked up laughing.

Vicki stood, "Come to the kitchen and I'll fix you something to eat."

"Then, we can go to the media room and watch a movie or something," Joshua added

"Media room?" Mose shook his head. "Now, why am I not surprised?"

Kellie came into the room just as she heard them talk about the media room. She grabbed his arm. "Joshua has the most awesome movie screen, you're not going to believe . . ."

"Don't tell me. I already feel like I've died and gone to heaven."

CHAPTER 25

Joshua woke up and looked at his clock. It was 3:00 a.m. He froze, because someone put his hand on his shoulder. Through the haze of sleep, he remembered that Mose spent the night with him, so he relaxed. He turned his head to look at Mose and saw that he was fast asleep. He felt a hand on his opposite shoulder shaking him.

He jumped.

"Don't be afraid! I have come to deliver a message to you from the Lord."

Joshua sat up and put his hand on his heart. "Isn't there another way for angels to deliver messages?"

At first Kientay was confused. Then he understood. "I didn't mean to scare you."

"It's a natural reflex." Joshua turned on the light and looked at his visitor. "Who are you?" He was looking into the eyes of a medium built young man around six feet tall. He had brown eyes and brown hair cut a lot like his, short. He was dressed in regular people clothes.

"I'm Kientay, your guardian angel."

"I thought angels had wings and wore robes. Your shirt looks like one of mine," replied Joshua.

The plaid shirt had wild bold primary colors in it. He wore jeans all the time while on earth just like Joshua's. "I like to dress like you."

"It never occurred to me that you dress like us."

"If we wore our angel clothes and had wings, then you would know you were entertaining angels."

"That makes sense. I guess I always had you pictured with white robes and wings," Joshua whispered. "The warring angels I saw the other night had tunics that looked like combat fatigues, well almost."

Getting out of bed, he checked his back he asked, "Where are your wings?"

"Guardian angels don't have wings, usually. Only certain angels have wings. Warring angels can have wings, but they can also disappear. Angels around the throne of God have wings. The living creature around the throne has six wings and . . ."

Interrupting Kientay, Joshua asked, "What is the message you have for me?"

"The Lord asked me to show you the spiritual battle that was taking place when the demons tried to kill you and your mother in the car."

"Were you there?"

"Of course, I am your guardian angel and I rarely leave your side. I was in the back seat listening to you quote the protection Psalm with your mom's guardian angel," informed Kientay. "I have been assigned to stay with you until you finish your course here on earth."

"That's cool."

"I am going to take you back into the past on the timeline."

"The timeline?" Joshua ran over to his chest of drawers to get his jeans and a shirt. He didn't want to go with Kientay dressed in plaid bottom pajamas.

"Look at yourself."

Joshua realized that he was dressed in his regular clothes. "I'm ready."

"Time is one of the dimensions of your existence," explained Kientay.

"I've wondered about time relating to the past and present and future. I've seen several movies that have dealt with traveling back in time. I always thought that was make-believe, you know, you never know what is possible and what is impossible because of the special effects and computers and what they can make you believe from Hollywood."

"It is possible to travel back into the past and into the future, but only by faith. That is why satan hasn't been able to access time travel."

"If he could time travel, I bet the first thing he would do is change what he did to Jesus on the cross!"

"God Almighty would never let that happen!" Kientay commented as they walked outside of the wall together. "That's what happened to John on the island of Patmos."

"Wait!" Joshua stopped in mid-air and looked at his feet. "What am I standing on?" Then it occurred to him that he could fall out of the air like Peter did when he walked on water. But falling on the ground was a whole lot different than falling into water!

"You are standing on the timeline like John. He traveled on the timeline into the future in the book of Revelation."

"Cool!" Joshua turned back and walked through the wall into his bedroom looking at his hands and body as he walked through. He felt a tingling sensation as he passed through.

Kientay followed him.

"This is too cool. Can you change what will happen if you go into the future?"

"Some things have the ability to change. Specific events have been predestined from before the beginning of time."

"Like Jesus dying on the cross?"

Kientay followed him back through the bedroom wall. "Yes. The end of the age of grace has been predestined to take place. No human being evil or good or any other spirit can stop that from happening. A new heaven and a new earth have been predestined. It will come to pass."

Joshua couldn't tell the difference between the floor of his bedroom and the air outside that he was standing on. "Then the people of Nineveh didn't have an appointment of judgment?"

"All people have an appointment of judgment. Judgment is harvest time. Some choose the judgment of mercy and blessing or some choose the judgment of wrath or curses. God prefers that people receive the judgment of mercy and choose the blessing over the curse. Those who do not receive the Redeemer, Jesus Christ of Nazareth, have an appointment at the end of time, we just hope they will see the light before their time runs out."

"So, it wasn't Nineveh's time."

"They were about to reap what they had sowed, Jonah received a prophetic vision of a plan of satan to destroy them. God was warning them. Satan demanded that they die according to the law of sowing and reaping. Remember Jesus called satan the god of this world. The Great One that created them was giving them an opportunity to live and receive His divine intervention of mercy."

"Mercy triumphs over judgment."

"Yes. You know the scriptures. Mercy to receive blessings is greater than the judgment of the curse until the times of the Gentiles have been fulfilled," Kientay explained.

Joshua turned to stand on the roof of his house. He sat down to look at his neighborhood. "So you are telling me that Jonah was sent to warn them of a plan of satan to destroy them?" This was exactly what he tried to teach the team the other day.

"The fullness of time was coming to pass over their wickedness. God sent his prophet to warn them that they would be destroyed if they didn't repent. Their fasting and praying stopped satan cold. God's Word has made allowance in time and judgment for a true repentant heart. The law of mercy is greater than the law of judgment. Repentance always reverses judgment of the curse."

Mercy is greater than the law of sin and death even in the Old Covenant, because it is based on the prophetic Word of the Messiah. But we can't discuss that now. I have been instructed to let you see into the spiritual realm so that you can learn more about the forces of evil you will be fighting.

"Let me ask one more question. What did you mean by saying, 'allowance in time'?"

"I know you think of your existence in a measurement of time. Time is a particular characteristic of earth, a dimension. But when you accepted the Son of God as your Savior, you received redemption through His Blood, the forgiveness of sins and were immediately placed into eternity. Time does not rule in the spiritual realm. Remember when Paul wrote that you have been 'raised up together in the heavenlies in Christ Jesus'?"

"Christians are already in eternity." Joshua knew that was true from the scriptures.

"You are one of the members of His body on earth and other members are in heaven, but you are members one of another. You are already in the heavenlies with Christ, therefore not subject to time," explained Kientay.

"Is that what Paul is saying 'that in the dispensation of the fullness of the times He might gather together in one all things in Christ, which are in heaven and which are on earth in Him'?"

"That is correct. Therefore because the Lord of the dispensation of times is Lord, we can travel on the timeline; although the Lord can choose to reveal future or past events in a dream, a vision, a trance or on a screen with a panoramic view. Very similar to your movie screens of today, but far more advanced than your technology."

"Cool!"

"We can travel off the timeline." Kientay moved off a line that revealed itself to Joshua, and he floated safely down to the ground outside of the house.

Joshua followed him.

"Or we could move backward." He moved backwards and ran in place like he was running on a treadmill. Suddenly, the landscape changed from fall to winter and to spring and summer all before Joshua's eyes.

Joshua put his hand on Kientay shoulder. "When you did that, could I have stopped you on lets say winter and it would have been winter last year?"

"Yes."

"Do it again!"

"I need to obey the Lord and take you to the scene of the accident the other day. I choose to take you traveling in another dimension of eternity, off the timeline, and back to the accident that occurred on earth's past timeline." Kientay and Joshua floated again in the air and above the rooftop of his house.

"Whoa!" Joshua felt his heart sink to his knees. The sensation of lifting was tingling through his body. They started moving faster and faster through the sky. House tops and trees looked like little toys. Then it seemed like everything was moving fast. He couldn't tell where they were going. He was amazed that the dizzy feeling left. A peace surrounded him like a shield. The space outside of the shield became a hazy rose color growing darker the faster they flew. It seemed as if he was flying like Peter Pan.

Slowing down, Joshua saw they were back in familiar space. They were following his mom's white Cadillac. It came to a stop at the red light. Kientay took Joshua to the top of one of the buildings overlooking the accident that had taken place earlier.

"What the Lord wants you to see is the spiritual battle that was taking place in the heavenlies and on earth at the same time the accident occurred."

Kientay pointed up to the sky that was open to Joshua. He could see all the angels surrounding the intersection. A great battle was taking place in the heavenlies with Michael leading a legion of angels against several of satan's generals.

Joshua looked around. "Where is satan?"

"He seldom comes to battles that are so insignificant. He focuses on the heads of state and the leaders of nations. He has appointed most of the fallen angels referred to as the 'spiritual host of wickedness in the heavenlies' in Ephesians, over the nations of the world."

"He probably is most concerned with Israel and the United States."

Pointing to the scene of the accident, Kientay wanted Joshua to see all the angels getting in the position for the crash. As soon as the truck went airborne, the angels started fighting the evil spirits. Joshua saw the evil spirits come out of the truck driver. Immediately, two warring angels withdrew their swords and started chasing the evil spirits. He also saw Kientay fighting.

"How can you be there and here at the same time?" asked Joshua.

"Remember, we left the present timeline when we left your bedroom and went back into the past timeline. But now, we are actually not in any past, present or future timeline observing this. We are in eternity. Think of it this way. We are in the now of the Lord God. His time is always now, not later, not yesterday, not tomorrow, but now. Or think of watching a movie that you acted in. You could watch yourself acting in the movie."

"True." His analogy helped him to understand.

"The most important thing is to understand the spiritual battles that were taking place during the would-be fatal accident. This is what the prophets of time past understood," explained Kientay. "A servant of satan tried to kill you."

"This is like Elisha, who asked the Lord to open the eyes of his servant to see that the mountain was full of horses and chariots of fire all around them."

"The Lord wants you to be aware of your enemy. He wants you to know that because of the Word of the Lord that is in you, that seed is enabling you to see spiritually and physically into the spirit realm. Even though you did not see, you believed. You have prayed and asked for wisdom and understanding of walking and talking in the Spirit. This is part of the answer to your prayer of revelation knowledge," Kientay explained to Joshua.

Demons were fighting to keep the observers from seeing the miracles God was working. Little monkey-looking imps were sitting on human shoulders. Octopus-type beings with many arms were covering the people's eyes and ears so they couldn't see or hear.

"God's Word says that the gospel is veiled to those who perish 'whose minds the god of this age has blinded. Who do not believe, lest the light of the gospel of the glory of Christ, which is the image of God, should shine on them.' But you never really think of the reality of the Word of God when you can't see the spiritual realm all the time."

"Joshua, the Word of God says that you wrestle not . . ."

" . . . against flesh and blood, but against principalities, against powers, against the rulers of the darkness of this age, against spiritual hosts of wickedness in the heavenlies,'" he interrupted Kientay.

"Yes and the word *wrestle* is the Greek kind of wrestling. It was nothing like the wrestling you have seen on TV. They wrestled cheek to cheek, hand to hand, stomach to stomach, leg to leg. They bit each other's ears and noses off. That is how close demons can get with believers, if they don't use their authority over them."

"This is hard for my mind to accept." He cringed as he saw the work of demons coming against humans.

"Most Christians refuse to meditate in the Word and let God reveal the truth of the spirit realm. You are a very different human, because you walk, talk, act and breathe the Word of God. God is opening your eyes because He knows that you will teach others what you see and hear through His Word. He can trust you with revelation knowledge. Just remember the young people that you will be teaching need baby food first. They will choke and gag on the things that you know."

He made a mental note and felt a tinge of guilt over his first meeting with the team. "They are choked already."

"Don't allow your feelings to interrupt the purpose of God."

He immediately went back to the scene before him. Some of the demons had long evil sword like darts piercing the human host's brain in and out and wrapped around their head. They looked like octopuses with tentacles going in and out of their brain sitting on top of their heads. It looked like those humans would have unbelievable migraine headaches.

"They do. The source of most migraines is spiritual," Kientay read his mind.

Some were wound around the necks and backs of the humans. Snakes were also wrapped around some of the arms, legs and middle sections of the people who came to see the wreck. He had seen demons before and they still were disgusting and shockingly hideous. They urinated and vomited green gunk all over the people. "This is hard to take."

"How do you think the Lord God feels about it?"

"Do any of them know Jesus?"

"Some have accepted Jesus and have a new spirit. Their spirit belongs to Jesus, but their soul belongs to satan. They haven't accepted all the terms of the Covenant because they don't renew their mind to the Word of God. Humans need to realize that they are always in a battle with the forces of evil," reminded Kientay. "Believers have to claim their rights in Jesus and demand that satan cease and desist from attacking them. That is how born-again humans activate the Blood Covenant between God and Jesus. They declare what God's Word says about them."

"That's how my mom and dad taught me, but its one thing teaching it to the team and another thing actually seeing it."

"You have been commissioned to teach others how they are being attacked by demons." Kientay was glad the Holy Spirit was opening his eyes.

"What about the Christians that don't believe that demons can influence them like this?"

"Your only hope is to pray for them, that the 'eyes of their understanding will be enlightened.'"

A vulture-like demon started urinating on one of the human hosts. Yellow-green urine bathed her starting from the top of her head running down her body. At one point it almost looked like the she was enjoying the feeling. It was grossing Joshua out. Turning away, he looked at Kientay with a sick expression, like he was going to puke.

"Many humans enjoy the pleasure of sin for a moment," Kientay sadly said.

"If they could see what I am seeing, they would resist demons, sin, sickness and disease." *And they would puke!*

"It makes us want to puke, too!" He read Joshua's mind again.

Joshua noticed how the angels protected the car. They seemed to absorb all contact from the car. "Hey, that's awesome! No wonder the car didn't get one scratch!"

Fierce fighting began after the demon spirits failed in their plan to kill Joshua and Vicki.

"What won the battle for us? When we were quoting scripture in the car?" asked Joshua.

"It gave extra strength to Kara, your mother's guardian angel, and me. But the intercessor was your father, who prayed as the Holy Spirit led him in his office earlier. Usually, God deals with his people days before the intercession is needed. He knew He could trust your earthly father to pray even when he did not understand what he was praying."

"Thank the Lord!" Joshua understood the importance of obeying the urge to pray immediately.

"The Lord also wants you to understand about the connection between Spirit-filled prayers and spiritual warfare. You might not know who or what you are praying for, but whenever or wherever you sense the Lord calling you, you better pray!"

"If my dad wouldn't have answered the call, would my mom and I be in heaven right now?"

"No. There are other factors involved. Another weapon for protection on earth is applying the Blood of Jesus every day. Your mother and dad apply the Blood of Jesus night and day continuously," explained Kientay. "She also dispatches angels of protection over you everyday."

"What about the people who were involved in the accident?" Joshua watched himself ministering to the man in the truck. It was really weird seeing himself.

"God used your dad as an intercessor to stand in the gap for them."

"What if Dad hadn't prayed when the Holy Spirit called him?" He wondered about the Lake family.

"Mr. Lake would have been killed and gone to hell without accepting the Lord."

"Oh, my!" Joshua was quiet as he pondered the significance of Kientay's revelation.

"Your dad's prayers were very critical to the over all outcome of this scene." Kientay was glad that Joshua was beginning to understand. "God looks for a son or daughter that is willing to pray and cover every person on earth. Sometimes, His children refuse to answer the call to pray. Many humans have perished because of it. He is longsuffering and patient, not willing that any should perish, but many believers refuse to use their authority over demons and give their time to the Lord."

"What happens to the Christian who refuses to pray or doesn't understand his role in intercession?"

"That person will be held accountable for intercession of the souls that were appointed to him."

It was a mind-boggling thought.

"God has a plan for everybody, but if they refuse His plan, He always has a backup."

"You mean the perfect will of God and the permissive will of God," Joshua heard that doctrine in the church ever since he was little.

"I mean plan A or plan B or whatever it takes."

Kientay and Joshua started flying again. Joshua tried to remember everything he was hearing.

"Don't struggle with remembering. The Holy Spirit will bring these things back to you when you need them."

They were traveling faster and faster and faster. The sky changed colors and looked like a blue-gray haze to Joshua. They stopped on the roof of his house.

"What are you thinking?" asked Kientay. He could only read his mind when the Holy Spirit gave him the ability. It was closed to him now.

"I'm thinking of all the people who suffer needlessly because Christians won't take time to pray. Some have been taught that God teaches them humility and humbleness from suffering. They think that sickness, disease and bad things come from the Lord to keep them humble."

"Humility and humbleness come from casting all your cares on the Lord, and submitting yourself to God. Angels are aware of the doctrines of demons that permeate the mind of some of God's children. It is up to you to cleanse yourself of all filthiness of the flesh and mind."

"I call it stinking thinking." Joshua looked at his house. He wondered what they were going to do next.

"We are now in the future of earth's timeline. It is the weekend that you are planning."

Slowly, they descended into his house through the roof. Joshua was surprised to see himself with the team talking and reading the Bible in the library. They were preparing themselves for the first day of answering phones. Joshua had many scriptures prepared and compiled them into the computers at each phone station. He watched as he turned on the computer that was in the formal library to demonstrate the files he had installed. It was so weird looking at himself. "Why are we here?"

"The Lord wants you to see a very important spiritual battle that is going to take place. Watch closely" . . .

. . ."What kind of calls do you think we are going to get, Joshua?" asked Kellie.

"I'm not sure, but I hope I have enough of the right scriptures to get us started."

"You mean like salvation scriptures?" asked Mose.

"Yes. I have put many different categories or subjects we might get calls about in these files." He opened the windows program and clicked onto the yellow file folder. "For example, we could get a caller that tells us he or she is depressed. Then you could click onto the folder labeled depression and find a list of scriptures dealing with that subject. The subjects are arranged alphabetically."

"We don't have to read those scriptures if the Lord gives us something else do we?" asked Hannah.

"You are to do whatever the Lord leads you to do. The first thing we want to do is always pray for the Holy Spirit to lead us and guide us on the right path. Since we are talking on the phone, our primary concern is to be the voice of the Lord. The most important thing is to pray with all callers and be led by the Holy Spirit at all times. And if you don't know what to pray . . . pray in the Spirit until you hear from Him," Joshua instructed them.

Suddenly, the doorbell rang like someone was using it as a punching bag.

Vicki was in the formal living room with the mothers of the team. Dan was in the family room with the fathers. Vicki went to answer the door.

"Where is my —— wife!" A drunken man stood stooped over at the door.

Vicki stood speechless.

"Are you deaf?" screamed the man. "I said, where is my—- wife?"

"I heard you the first time," Vicki replied trying to steady the shaking she felt inside the pit of her stomach.

Joshua came into the foyer with Hannah. Sheila walked up from behind them.

"What are you doing here you ——!" Sheila's husband Wade was screaming obscenities at her. "I told you, you couldn't come!"

"I'll get my coat," Sheila said quietly trying not to agitate him anymore.

"No!" Hannah grabbed her mother's arm. "Please, don't go!"

"Hannah, it will be all right. Don't worry." Her mother patted her hand. Sheila was trying to leave as fast as she could so Wade wouldn't embarrass Hannah.

Hannah turned to Joshua and begged him not to let her dad take her mom. "Don't let her leave! He gets really crazy when he's drunk."

It was happening so fast. Joshua turned around to find his dad. They were back in the family room and hadn't heard the doorbell. Sheila was gone before Joshua could get help.

"Mom!" Hannah cried as she turned to leave.

"Don't worry, honey," Sheila kissed her goodbye. "Everything is going to be fine!"

"Sheila! Get your ——— out here!" yelled Wade as he grabbed her hand and pulled her out the front door.

Hannah screamed one more time, "No!"

"Girl! Get your —— —— self back in the house if you know what in the —— is good for you. Do you want some of me?" Wade put his finger in her face.

Hannah wouldn't back down. Sheila moved between them, and Wade Coyle slapped his wife instead of his daughter. He grabbed Sheila's arm and pulled her to the car forcing her to get in.

Kientay motioned for Joshua to follow them. Joshua saw the gun in the front seat. A sick feeling registered danger in his spirit. When he looked into Wade's face, he saw a demon laughing at Sheila. Joshua watched the demon pick up the gun and put it to Sheila's head as they were driving away . . .

. . ."No!" he yelled. "Don't let her drive away!" He forgot he was observing the future and they couldn't hear him.

The scene faded as he turned to Kientay. "What's going to happen?"

"That was the spirit of murder in Wade. He has many spirits inside him from the generation curse of alcohol. He's been addicted since he was a teenager."

"How does it end?"

"That's up to you. The ending hasn't been written yet."

"What do I do?" asked Joshua.

"Joshua, do like you have done in the past," reminded Kientay.

"Okay, I know. I always ask myself what would Jesus do if He was in this situation."

As fast as a blink of an eye, Joshua and Kientay were back in his bedroom.

"Wait, you are going too fast. I would like to see the future one more time."

"Joshua, trust the Word of God in your spirit. You will know what you should do through the Almighty's Word and the leading of the Holy Spirit."

Joshua caught a glimpse of his clock. It was 3:05 a.m. Only five minutes had passed since he left his bedroom.

"Yes, we are back in the present timeline."

He was fighting a feeling of anxiety. He didn't feel like he was given enough time to survey the situation.

Kientay sensed a feeling of anxiousness trying to invade his mind. "Joshua you know what to do. Pray and ask for wisdom from the Lord. Seeing the future is no different from getting visions or reading the book of Revelation. You still have to depend on the Holy Spirit for everything you receive."

"What about what I said? Will I say the same things again?"

"Were the words you spoke written in stone?" asked Kientay.

Joshua laughed half-heartedly.

"Relax. Be anxious for nothing. God knows you can handle it."

"Can I tell my mom and dad?"

"Your mom knows about Wade. Sheila has confided in her a few things, but she doesn't realize how severe the situation is."

"Should I tell her?"

"The Holy Spirit will tell you what you should do. I want to give you a word of caution. You have a strong fortress around your house and your life. Because your parents heed the Word of God, a hedge of protection surrounds you. But there will be times you will be tempted. Remember, Jesus was tempted. No man is above temptations on earth; use those times as stepping stones, not stumbling blocks."

"Will I see you again?"

"The Holy Spirit directs our paths. Until you are absent from your body, I will always be your own personal guardian angel."

Joshua watched Kientay gradually disappear. He turned around and got back in bed. Suddenly, he was very tired.

CHAPTER 26

Chemah sat at his computer table looking over all the data he had on metraloas. He was disturbed over his last encounter with him. He buzzed his assistant to come into the private quarters of his spaceship. It was hovering over the city of the Devil Chasers.

"You rang?" A vulture appeared in his quarters and changed into a tall black robed skeleton.

Chemah looked at him with disgust. "Put some flesh on your skeleton." He didn't like talking to skeletons.

His assistant laughed. He called himself 'nitro' after the chemical compound on earth known for blowing up things. Chemah wanted him to change his name to nero after the Roman emperor who burned Rome. Of course fire was chemah's specialty.

He changed himself into a gorgeous male hunk with bulging muscles. He took the stance of a body builder showing off his muscles in competition.

Chemah looked up from his computer. "nitro! You are disgusting! Ever since you received the ability to shape-shift you've gone stupid!"

"Stupid is as stupid does."

Chemah cursed him. "You've got to get over your infatuation with Hollywood movies. Did you finish your report?"

"Yes, master." He bowed as it appeared in his hand and he handed it to him.

Chemah quickly scanned its contents. "Just like I figured."

"He has a plan. I'm just not sure what it is yet."

"That ———!" He released a string of cuss words. "No wonder we are losing so many battles recently. We have to use too much of our time and energy policing these —— —— androids!"

Nitro wasn't offended at his comment. Androids were the ones that were keeping satan's kingdom operating. He was designed especially for chemah and was an expert on chemah's feelings and thoughts. "My . . . my . . . my aren't we grouchy today."

"If it wasn't for those — humans reproducing themselves like rabbits, we wouldn't have to rely so heavily on androids!" Chemah hated the creation of satan. He was always trying to create a super race of beings like God. They were a nuisance to him and to most of the fallen angels. If it they weren't so necessary, he would torch every android he saw.

"What are you going to do?"

"I can't trust metraloas." chemah stood and walked over to the window that revealed the star-studded black space that surrounded his spaceship.

"Since when could you ever trust an android but me?" Nitro put his hand on his chest and acted like a gay male. "What do you think he is going to do?"

"I think that he is going to try and trap me into taking his position over the Knight family."

"You? He couldn't be that crazy. You are a member of the spirits in heavenly places and were once a member of the holy angels of God in heaven." He was proud of his master's former status. "How in——could he be such a stupid fool to think that you would be assigned to a mere Christian family?"

"They are not a mere family. I've been looking over metraloas' reports for the past two years and he is right, this family is dangerous." chemah walked back to his desk and handed nitro a black folder.

Nitro opened the folder and scanned some of the contents. His eyes bugged out when he read how many people the Knight family had led to Jesus and discipled. He let out a string of cuss words.

Chemah raised his hand and sent a fireball to disintegrate the folder.

"Ouch!" He released the burning folder as it fell to the ground. "Why did you do that?"

"The prince of death would be furious if he read that report!"

"Metraloas probably has a hidden copy of his reports."

"He has two copies. The little —— will probably try to blackmail me." Chemah got up and walked the floor again. "I hate androids!"

"It would be very hard to control the souls and the bodies of humans without us," nitro pointed out.

"I know it! But androids seem to be evolving into machines who can think for themselves."

"Of course! Without free-will-created beings, satan will never be able to touch God's creative ability."

"Have you prepared the report of the incident that happened the other day?" chemah changed the subject with a growl.

"Uh . . . I am working on it. There were far too many demonic androids to bribe all of them. I am trying to think of some way to take the blame off you."

"Have you found a way?"

"Uh . . . no."

Chemah cursed. "What is the biggest obstacle?"

"The number of androids that were destroyed by angels and the many homeless demons cast out of the humans."

Chemah cursed again. "I did not know that Vicki and Joshua Knight would turn a near disaster into a healing and deliverance campaign." He pushed some of his files off his desk onto the ground. "Most Christians are destroyed spiritually, mentally and physically with car accidents."

Nitro laughed. "They get hung up on asking God questions. Why God . . . How God? . . . where, when, why, how . . . It is so cool when they get angry at God because they think He allowed their family to get killed or hurt."

"I have never seen a Christian respond like the Knights. How could I have known how they would react?"

"Oh, you are so right! Most of them fall apart when they receive bad reports. Well, I personally went down to earth to see the car they were driving in . . ." nitro shook his head. "I could not believeeee what I saw. Not one scratch . . . not one dent!"

Chemah sat down. "Another breed of Christians has appeared in this generation."

"What kind?"

"Humans that closely resemble the 120 Christians on the day of Pentecost."

Nitro trembled. "You mean the first humans that received the infilling of the Holy Spirit?"

"Yes. The ones that received the secret language of the Kingdom of God and speak it even though they themselves don't understand what they are saying!"

"That is terrible news!" nitro almost fainted as he sat down on the couch and fanned himself.

Chemah bent over and picked up a few of the papers on the floor. "It is worse than that." He didn't bother using his thoughts to pick them up.

Nitro noticed his action and realized how shook up he really was. "What could be worse?"

Chemah stood. "The ones walking the earth now have the benefit of two thousand years of experience. Secret manuscripts from eye-witness accounts during Jesus days on earth are showing up everywhere. They have revelation knowledge and understanding of the force of faith from past generational seeds that have not been harvested."

Nitro shook his head again. "I am at a loss for words. I have no idea how you are going to get out of this one."

They were both silent for a few minutes.

"What is the master going to say about this turn of events?"

"I don't know. It will depend on his mood. You never know what satan is going to do next, but his unbelievable ego and pride could take us all to the lake of fire!" chemah cursed again.

Nitro stood up "According to the book of Revelations that is where we are all going."

"Shut up you stupid fool! You have been reading that foul Book again!" Usually nitro was good for a laugh, but today he was irritating him. "Only those who believe God's Word quote it!"

"Don't kid yourself. Look at all the fallen preachers that are constantly quoting the Book down there." He pointed to the place below earth's surface. "Look at what good it does them," he tossed back his long dark wavy hair and flipped his chin.

Chemah sat back down. "Leave me!" He needed to think of a plan. "This used to be easy."

"It's not your fault that this last generation of Christians has received lots of revelation."

"There is still one *big* stumbling block on our side."

Nitro smiled. He knew the answer. Turning himself into a blonde sexy negligee-clad female, he walked over to Chemah and sat down on his lap. "What would that be?" purred his female voice.

Chemah laughed lustfully and decided to indulge in nitro's fantasy. It was a welcome release from the stress of thinking about his report to satan. He grabbed at him, now her, and whispered like a snake into her ear.

"Flessssssh!"

‡ ‡ ‡

Dan poured a cup of coffee and opened the blinds of the French doors overlooking his back yard property. It was pitch black outside, since it was an hour earlier than his usual five o'clock in the morning. Watching the sunrise and praising the Lord for the day was a great way to start his workday and today he wanted to give the Lord extra praise as an offering for the protection of his family from a disastrous accident.

He lived by the scripture, "seek you first the kingdom of God and His righteousness." Righteousness was being in right standing with God and that meant doing things God's way. A preacher once said that God's kingdom was God's reign inside us. That struck a chord in Dan's heart, so every morning at least an hour every day before going to work, he prayed for God's way of doing things.

Being in business for himself, Dan learned early that he needed help.

Not being raised in a Christian home like Vicki, he felt that his way of doing things were far from the way God did things. But it was his thinking that was so trained in the world's system, especially since he received his law degree from a godless university that bothered him the most. After finding Jesus, a great desire to know God and His way of thinking took over his life. He found himself spending every free minute of his day or night studying the Bible and then he met Vicki at a Bible study.

Their life together started in the Word of God and has continued that way. Starting the day with prayer over all his cases and clients has resulted in God's wisdom making him a very successful lawyer. Together, Vicki and he had grown from baby Christians who started their marriage in a one bedroom apartment and now owned several homes and lived in one that would be considered a mansion. They were very careful to give all the glory and credit of his success to their Lord, Jesus Christ.

Vicki woke up sensing that Dan was missing from their bed. Smelling the coffee aroma that floated upstairs, she knew exactly where he was. With so much happening lately, she decided to get up and spend some time with him before he left for work.

Hugging him from behind, he turned around and she gave him a big kiss on the lips. Sometimes she would turn her face and he had to kiss her cheek. Dan laughed. "I can always tell when you've brushed your teeth."

Vicki made a playful face at him. They had just celebrated their twenty fourth wedding anniversary. They were more in love today than they ever were. Dan told her she just got better and better.

"When does your case go to the jury?" She opened the refrigerator door and took out a carton of eggs.

"I should do my summation Monday or Tuesday. We are meeting early to go over the type of questions Mr. Gottman will probably face one last time." He watched her break the eggs into a bowl and begin to scramble them. "He really needs to settle down before he is put on the stand Monday."

"I wondered why you were going to your office today." He usually worked on things at his home office on Saturday. She placed the eggs in an omelet pan and put strips of bacon in another.

"Are you hungry?"

She stopped and turned around laughing at herself. "No, I'm not hungry." She looked at the clock. "Why are you up so early?"

"I need to spend some extra time meditating the Word." He felt a stirring inside his spirit, but he had no idea what it was all about. "How's Joshua?"

"It was after midnight before they got into bed." She put away the eggs and food until later that morning.

"They?"

"I forgot to mention that Moses Pearson stayed the night with Joshua."

"Hmm . . ."

"Joshua's life is changing fast."

He got up to pour himself another cup of coffee. "You know with the divine revelation that Paul received, he received severe attacks from a demon. I know Joshua can handle the knowledge and revelation of scripture, but will we be ready for the mental and emotional, maybe even physical attacks?"

"You mean when he starts attending public school?"

"Yes."

"I could get up with you and we could pray together," Vicki suggested.

"Early morning is the only time I ever get with the Lord . . . alone." He didn't want to offend his wife, but he needed his own time with the Lord.

"You're right . . ."

He interrupted her. "No, you are the one that is right. I can give ten or fifteen extra minutes with you. After all prayer is the only thing that keeps us several steps ahead of the devil."

"Satan doesn't have a clue to what is going to hit him," Vicki said. "Joshua and the team . . ."

"Is he actually calling them the team?" Dan looked up.

She shook her head yes. "He doesn't even realize that the words he speaks makes him sound a lot older than fourteen years old."

"He will learn." He put his hand on Vicki's and asked, "Did you crash their time together?"

"Dan, it was almost ten o'clock and they hadn't even taken a break for dinner. You know when Joshua's talking about the Word of God, he sometimes gets carried away."

"You don't have to defend yourself."

She had been waiting a long time for Joshua's ministry to begin. "I can't wait to pick up their ministry cards from Mr. Gottman."

The dark sky started to lighten a little. "Let's go outside and watch the sun come up."

She went over to a closet and got a light sweater coat to put over her thin gown and robe.

"Who?" He asked as they sat down on the deck lounge chairs.

"Dan, it's still real dark out here." She couldn't even see the trees on their property.

"Don't be impatient, now who were you talking about?"

"Mr. Gottman, you know, your client? They one that's getting sued from that guy who looks like that singer guy from the sixties . . . uh . . . what's his name? Oh, yeah, Tiny Tim." Vicki laughed thinking there wasn't anything tiny about that super, tall, big man with long, black, stringy hair playing an ukulele with a squeaky voice. "When we showed Mr. Gottman what we wanted printed, he laughed and told Joshua he needed us to take care of some business for him."

"I didn't know that you were having him print the cards."

"I told you, Dan."

"I'm sorry but something is bugging me this morning," Dan explained as he was having a hard time listening to her.

"Didn't you spend extra time with the Lord?"

"I was going to, but now I'm spending time with you."

"Why don't we pray together?"

Dan stood. "Okay and you know I'm glad you didn't fix breakfast. I think I'll fast today. I have a feeling we need to be on our guard again."

"I can call my prayer chain. I have the best one in the whole world. All this week we asked the Lord to help us remember to pray and cover every thing demons could possibly get their hands on." Vicki stood with him and put her hand out to hold his.

"He hit on you and Joshua. Maybe the Lord is warning me that he will try something on me."

"Well, like Paul would say, 'Don't think it strange when a fiery trial comes your way.' We know demons are trying to kill us."

Suddenly, a gorgeous, purplish-pink color invaded the sky above their trees.

"Let's go sit on the bench by the shore and pray." Dan loved praying outside.

Their backyard looked like a garden showcased in the magazine, *Better Homes and Garden.* A variety of flowers surrounded beautiful trees and a pond with a waterfall was a perfect place to meet with the Lord in prayer. They walked down to the waters edge holding hands taking in the harmonious sounds of the birds making music and the colors of nature provided by the Creator.

"Father, we come to you in Jesus Name and claim Psalm 91 as our protection and covering over us today. We abide in the secret place, the Blood Covenant. We say that You are our refuge and fortress. We put all our trust in You. We will hide under Your covering and take refuge under Your wings. No evil shall befall Vicki, Joshua or me in Jesus Name," claimed Dan with authority in the knowledge of God's Word. "You are the Most High God over us!"

"Father, as Moses commanded the children of Israel to apply the blood around the door posts of their home, in like manner I apply the Blood of Jesus to our home, our cars, our minds, and our bodies by faith in the Blood Covenant," prayed Vicki.

"Kingdom of darkness, in the natural realm, I am the priest of my family, and I command you to cease and desist from your maneuvers against my family and the Devil Chasers. The Blood of Jesus and the Holy Spirit comes against you because Jesus is Lord over the Knight family and the Most High God is our spiritual Father," ordered Dan. He looked at Vicki and gave her a big hug. There wasn't a day that he didn't thank God for her.

"God bless your business today. The favor of the Lord is over you, Dan, and your business, your clients, judges, jury and prosecutors. God bless your mind and give you His understanding words. Amen." Vicki always gave Dan a blessing before he left the house.

He gave her a long kiss. One she wouldn't forget for a long time.

‡ ‡ ‡

Joshua's eyes opened. He sucked in his breath trying to get his bearings.

What time is it? He wondered. *What day is it?* He was quiet waiting to see if someone was next to him trying to wake him up. He heard someone breathing.

Who is with me? He closed his eyes. *Think Knight . . . think.*

An arm hit him in the stomach; he jumped slightly. He opened his eyes. It was a black arm.

Calmly, he remembered. *The arm belongs to Mose.* He turned his head and saw Mose's face and that his eyes were firmly shut.

It was slowly coming back to him. *Today is Saturday*. He gently removed Mose's arm and turned to the opposite side. *I should be sleeping!* He groaned. His clock revealed that it was 7:00 a.m.

Allowing the semi-warm water of his shower to slowly wake him, he thought about his experience earlier in the morning. After dressing and looking over the notes he had written down, he knew that his experience was real and not a dream. He found his mom in the kitchen reading her Bible and told her about his encounter with his guardian angel.

"Your Dad and I talked about all the spiritual encounters you're experiencing lately."

"It's like a dream. I think I could easily wonder if it really happened like I think it happened."

"Paul indicates that very same idea when he talks about a man that he knew whether in the body or out of the body who went to heaven."

"I think it was my spirit that went with Kientay and saw all those things." It was amazing to him to think about his body back in his bed, while his spirit journeyed on the timeline.

"Are you writing everything down?"

"Yes. I am very careful to immediately write down what I've seen and heard before I go back to sleep."

"Joshua . . ." Vicki just realized what time it was. "I'm concerned about the sleep you're missing."

"Don't worry, Mom. I looked at my clock and I was only gone about five minutes, even though it seemed like a couple of hours."

"Hmm . . . that's interesting. Are you hungry?"

"No, I'm going back upstairs to do some studying before Mose wakes up."

"Oh, I forgot about Mose!"

"I'll wait to eat breakfast with him."

She got up to clean off the table and to assemble the ingredients for their meal.

Joshua stopped at the doorway and looked back at her, "Oh Mom, don't get in a hurry. It might be noon before Mose gets out of bed."

Linda rolled over and noticed with her hand that Ben's spot was empty. She groaned and sat up in bed as she remembered. All during the night Ben tossed and turned. One time she awoke to see him pacing up and down at the end of their bed. She put both her hands over her face and thought that the worse thing about yesterday was that he went to bed without eating or talking to her.

Yanking the covers, she hopped out of bed grabbing her robe on the chair and angrily tied the belt around her. She was determined to have it out with him face to face. It was time for him to face facts and move on. Dan and Vicki Knight were gone and he can do nothing to change the situation.

In his office Ben was pacing back and forth thinking about the past events and how he might be able to change them. Looking at his watch he wondered how early he could call Dan. He was worried about disturbing them too early since it was Saturday. *If I could just talk to him one more time.*

Linda opened the door. "Ben, what are you doing?"

"Not now Linda." He didn't even make eye contact with her.

"Yes . . . NOW!" She walked over to him with her hands on her hips unwavering from backing down.

He looked up and saw the resolute look on her face. Walking over to his desk chair, he sat down. "Okay."

She stood looking at him.

"Will you please sit down?" He didn't want to look up at her. "I'm waiting."

Sitting down she told him, "I'm waiting for you to come to your senses."

She always knew what to say that hacked him off. "Don't make me mad at you Linda," he said calmly, trying to control a desire to speak ugly to her.

"You're already mad at everyone else; Dan and Vicki Knight, God . . . why not add me?"

"What do you want from me?"

"I want you to talk to me about your feelings."

He stared at her blankly.

"Ben it is not the end of the world just because the Knights quit our church."

That's what you think! He continued staring at her.

"Look at you! You look terrible!"

"Thanks, I can always count on you to encourage me," he snapped at her sarcastically.

"I'm not trying to criticize you; I'm trying to help you face reality." . . .

. . . The vulture flew into the room and sat on a table to the side of the desk. It sounded to him like they were getting ready to fight. He decided to join in. This assignment was going to be easy . . .

. . ."How much sleep did you get last night?"

He rubbed his head and sat back in his chair. "None to be exact."

"Ben, look in the mirror. Your eyes are bloodshot and the bags underneath your eyes look like they are growing bags. You have not gotten over four or five hours sleep a night in weeks!"

"You really don't understand the consequence of the Knights leaving our church, do you?"

"What's to understand? They believe God is calling them some where else. They have free will from God just like we do."

It's not free-will when you are being influenced by an evil spirit! The vulture suggested.

"It's not free will when you are being influenced by an evil spirit!" Ben raised the tone in his voice.

"Ben, lower your voice, please."

What, you let your wife tell you what to do?! The vulture laughing at him, mocked him.

Ben felt irritation rising from his flesh. "Don't you understand what the ramifications of their so-called free will is going to cost us!"

"Ben, you're getting upset, please settle down."

The vulture flew over and sat on Ben's shoulder. *Linda is trying to control you.*

"Quit telling me what to do!" he said through clenched teeth.

"I am not telling you what to do!"

He thinks you are stupid! The vulture whispered in Linda's ear.

"I know you think I'm stupid . . ."

"I never called you stupid!" Ben half-yelled at her.

"You're yelling at me!"

"Linda, you don't understand."

He doesn't want you to understand.

"Oh right, and you think you know everything!"

Ben stopped responding realizing that their conversation was dangerously getting out of control.

The vulture hopped back on his shoulder and whispered again, *you do know more than she does. You are the chosen of God, the one called to know His will. She is not the minister of your church . . . you are!*

"I'm the one who is called of God to preach."

Those words cut her heart. "So, what are you saying?"

You are saying that she cannot tell the man of God what to think or say. She has no part of your life in the ministry . . .

. . . The bear and the snake materialized in the office just as they heard the last words the vulture said.

"No!" shouted the snake. "Don't say that!"

They startled the vulture and he fell off the shoulder of the pastor. Stumbling from around the desk he flew over to them. "What are you doing?"

"You stupid idiot! Listen!" . . .

. . . A former memory instantly flashed in his mind. He remembered his words to Linda when he asked her to marry him. He told her to pray about their union, because he was called to the ministry and if she married him, she would be joined to his calling. He said it would be the same as her being called into the ministry because they would be one new being.

He came around the desk and fell to his knees in front of her. "Linda, please forgive me. Satan is influencing me. I heard him say that you have no part in my life or ministry. I know that thought is not mine! Can you forgive me?" He laid his head on her lap and started crying.

Compassion filled her soul and she immediately forgave him for the words he had spoken. She stood holding his hands and led him over to the couch as they both cried and prayed together. "I love you, Ben, of course I forgive you!" . . .

. . . The bear and snake cursed.

"I told you that this stupid ignorant vulture didn't know what he was doing. I was there when the pastor proposed to his wife. STUPID! STUPID! STUPID!" the snake ranted.

The bear couldn't believe what he just heard. "Get out of my sight before I wipe you out!"

The vulture disappeared immediately.

"Look at them kissing and making up!" The snake cried out angrily. "Do you know how long it will take me to undo what this moron has done?"

The bear turned around and walked outside through the wall. He couldn't stand to be in the same room with married humans displaying true passion and love for one another.

"I know something that might make you feel better."

"What?" asked the snake.

"The name of the high-ranking angel is chemah."

CHAPTER 27

Sitting at his desk at the opposite end of his room, Joshua read Jeremiah 18. Reading the Bible was more than just gathering information, it was about receiving revelation from the Lord which was one of the greatest experiences in his life. Nothing could compare to the high that he felt when the Holy Spirit opened his eyes and he could understand a deep spiritual truth from God's Word.

One thing that Joshua learned early in his search of the scriptures was the fact that apparently the translators of the Old Testament did not have an understanding of the nature of God. He talked to the Lord about it. "Why didn't they know You as their Father?"

I wasn't their Father at that time.

"I can't find where they were ever taught to have faith in You. I mean look, Lord. If the harvest was good and plentiful, they gave You the credit, but if the harvest was destroyed, You were responsible."

Remember, the Anointed One was only given to a few prophets and kings in the Old Testament.

His parents taught him how to meditate. They said it was like digging for gold. The work was tedious and sometimes a great deal of time passed before he discovered the nuggets of truth. But he found when the revelation came, the work paled in comparison to the awesome reward from God. Many times it would seem as if a word would jump out at him in bold big letters. After he looked up the Greek or Hebrew meaning of the word in the concordance, he found a connection to understand the meaning as the Holy Spirit inspired the writer. His mom told him that scripture always interprets scripture. The Word says line upon line, precept upon precept.

His mother also taught him that God dealt with two groups of people in the Old Testament; the Jews and the Nations. In the New Testament Jesus dealt with one group, the Jews, and the Pauline letters dealt with the body of Christ. She said that the only way to keep end time doctrine straight was to know which group the scriptures were talking about; the Nations, the Jews or the body of Christ.

Joshua thought about how many Christians got confused when they tried to apply passages of the Old Testament to the body of Christ when God had clearly addressed them to the Jewish people. The Holy Spirit later confirmed what his mom taught him.

Jesus first called His body of believers the called out ones. Jews and Gentiles, men and women, rich or poor, have become One together in His body. In the New Testament Paul said the body of the Anointed One, Jesus, was a mystery. Satan had no idea what I was planning. The body of Jesus was hidden in the Old Testament.

Ever since that time, Joshua made sure that he knew which group of people the scripture applied to that he was reading. He realized how important it was to keep his end time thinking straight. It concerned him that many Christians were replacing prophecies that applied only to Israel to the body of Christ.

The more he researched the topic of judgment and mercy the more he realized that from the beginning God made it clear to His creation that they are responsible for the judgment they would receive. Chapter 18 of Jeremiah clearly revealed that the nations of the world are judged according to their works, but Israel was judged according to their Covenant with God.

The story of Jonah came into his mind. He turned to the pages of the Bible to the story about a prophet of the Lord that was told to warn Nineveh of judgment that was coming upon the nation. It was an awesome story. The whole town repented, even though Jonah didn't want to warn the people.

He read out loud to himself. "Now the Word of the Lord came to Jonah, 'Arise go to Nineveh. Cry out against it: for their wickedness has come up before me.' Hmm." *I wonder what 'their wickedness has come up before me' means?*

He turned his computer on to look up the words in the Hebrew. He found out many things about wickedness, but one thing caught his attention; God's mercy has to depart from a nation or person before judgment can come upon them. A judgment of wickedness was the result of the curse that came from satan. Over and over he meditated on the phrase '*their wickedness has come up before me.*' Nineveh was a very wicked city and they did terrible things to the Jewish people. It wasn't a wonder to him why Jonah didn't want them to find the place of repentance.

Joshua read in Proverbs 11:5, *'the wicked fall by his own wickedness'* and Proverbs 13:6 *'wickedness overthrows the sinner.' Wickedness is the opposite of righteousness, and righteousness is right standing with God or doing things God's way. Therefore wickedness is the way of the devil because he was the first to take the path opposite of God,* he wrote down in his study journal.

The Lord spoke to Joshua. *They had no knowledge of My ways. Nineveh repented at Jonah's words, but Jonah should have stayed and taught them about Me. He knew that the law of mercy is greater than the law of wrath. He knew about My compassion and that I would rather see obedience than sacrifice.*

"He knew that they would repent before he went?"

Yes. I tried to tell Jonah that it was good for Me to have pity on humans who did not know the difference between good and evil, blessing or cursing.

Joshua read that they turned away from their evil ways and idols with fasting and prayer. "Lord, satan was prevented from destroying a whole nation. He lost them to You. Is that how the wickedness of the people of Nineveh came up before You, because satan is the accuser and tester of the human race?"

As the stepfather of the human race, he took it upon himself to test humans because he can't be every where at the same time and he can't read your mind. But there is another purpose for testing and trials.

Joshua waited for the Lord to tell him, but he knew from previous experience that the Lord wanted him to search for the answer.

Joshua leaned forward. "Lord, You know that most Christians think that You are testing them so they can learn something, but You know that I don't believe that way. I know that You don't have to test us to know what is in our heart, because You already know."

Who doesn't know? The Lord asked.

"I don't know!" A light bulb switched on in his mind.

I know what is in the deepest parts of your heart. I know every thought and neuron pathway in your mind. I know how many individual hairs on your head. I know what is in the secret places of your spirit, soul and body. But you don't know. Tests, trials and tribulation reveal what lies in secret inside you.

It was after he read the whole book several times that he saw another great truth in God's Word.

Read it again, the Holy Spirit encouraged him.

Joshua meditated on each verse again walking the floor. He knew the Lord wanted to reveal something to him, so he continued reading the scriptures to his spirit out loud so that the Holy Spirit could anoint the words and give him understanding. Then it happened; he saw something he had never seen before.

Do you see?

He sat down again at his desk and looked at the verse in his Bible.

"Lord, I never saw that word before!" In verse six of the first chapter of the book of Jonah, the word "sleeper" jumped out at him. "Jonah was sleeping while the men on the boat were about to perish."

When My people disobey Me, many suffer.

"Sleeper!" *Lord he was asleep!*

Mose woke up hearing Joshua yelling at him. "Hey, are you talking to me?" Mose rubbed his eyes.

Joshua didn't hear Mose.

The wicked are wicked because of the wicked one. They are under the curse. When my people are sleeping, they can not rescue the lost.

"That's what You meant when You said they didn't know how to discern between their right hand and their left."

I have no pleasure in the death of the wicked. Jonah wasn't in a whale.

"Not in the whale?"

Mose watched Joshua talking to himself and then realized he was talking to the Lord. He got out of bed, picked up his bag and went into the bathroom.

"I must have heard you wrong."

I said Jonah wasn't in a whale.

"Oh, I get it he was in a great fish, right?"

No.

"If he wasn't in a whale or a big fish, then what was it? Can You give me a hint? I know its right in front of me, but I need You to open my eyes to what I am missing."

He was in disobedience.

"I know he was disobeying You, but where was he physically?"

Joshua, it matters where you are spiritually! I am concerned about every area of your life. This story is about My compassion, My love, My mercy and My willingness to forgive.

Mose entered the room. "Am I interrupting you?"

"Mose, you're up?"

"Yeah, someone yelling 'sleeper' woke me."

"Uh, I'm sorry; I've been studying the Word."

"I heard something about a fish?" Mose picked up a pillow and threw it at Joshua.

Joshua put the pillow on the bed.

"So, what's up?" Mose asked as they finished making the bed together.

"Let's go eat breakfast, then I'll tell you everything."

‡ ‡ ‡

"After talking to your guardian angel, that's why you were reading about Jonah?" Mose asked Joshua as they were walking up the stairs back to his bedroom.

"Yes." Joshua pointed to the underline passage as he sat down.

Mose read out loud, "So the captain came to him, 'What do you mean, SLEEPER? Arise, call on your God; perhaps your God will consider us, so that we may not perish . . ." he stopped. "Why did you circle the word sleeper?"

"Jonah was asleep in the middle of the storm. If God's people are sleeping during their life on this earth, then they cannot help the people that are in bondage to death."

When you sleep, you are unaware of the physical and spiritual conditions of the people around you.

"Word!" Mose started to read when Joshua signaled him to wait.

"The Lord just said that when we sleep, we are unaware of the physical and spiritual conditions of the people around us."

"When I am in deep sleep, my mom says not even a bomb could wake me. Hey, that's what the men in the boat said to Jonah!"

"I think that Jonah could have interceded and calmed the storm for the sailors, if he had wanted to."

It was Jonah's disobedience that caused the storm.

"Wait a minute; the Lord just said that it was Jonah's disobedience that caused the storm."

The hair on Mose's arm stood up and goose bumps traveled up and down his spine. He slowly looked around the room thinking that maybe the Lord was standing behind him or something.

Joshua laughed at him. "The Lord's not physically here."

"But you said He is talking to you."

"I hear His voice talking through my spirit. It's not an audible voice. Don't you talk to the Lord?"

"I've heard a word or two, but not whole sentences, like you're doing right now."

Joshua didn't comment. Mose was in the baby stage of fellowshipping with the Lord. He pointed to another passage in the Bible and quoted the rest of the verses. "I know that it is because of me that this great tempest has come upon you." He closed his eyes and leaned back in his chair. "Lord, the fourth verse in chapter one says You sent out a great wind upon the . . . wait a minute!" Joshua sat up and opened the concordance sitting on his desk. He looked up the Hebrew word wind.

Mose wondered what he was doing.

"The word wind in Hebrew is *ruach*. It also can be interpreted as to blow, to breathe or spirit that is of a rational being; including expression and function."

"Why is that important?" Mose asked.

"Sometimes I have find that translators will choose a meaning of the word according to their understanding of the circumstances."

"Are you saying that our Bible was translated wrong?"

"No, I'm saying that sometimes I choose to meditate over certain words and let the Holy Spirit tell me what the word means and the passage is saying. The Holy Spirit inspired the scriptures through men. The original text is perfect, but sometimes the translation can use a little help."

"You don't think the translations are inspired by God?"

Joshua hesitated replying. He didn't want to say the wrong thing and give Mose the wrong impression. "I'm not saying that exactly, but I am saying that you have to meditate and let God tell you what He wants you to know about the Word. Mose, if you read the Word without revelation then all you are getting is information. Revelation takes you into a higher level. To one that the demons can't mess with you."

"Cool!" Mose accepted his answer.

"You need to know the word you are studying and how many times the translators chose to use it and in what way." Joshua picked up another concordance. "See," he pointed to the word in the concordance, *ruach* was translated as 'wind' 92 times and 232 times as 'spirit' out of the 370 times that it appeared in the Old Testament."

"So?"

"In this case, it's easy to interpret *ruach* as wind, because the people in this passage were in a boat floating over water."

"Okay, I see what you're saying."

"But what if the wind in this passage was more than just wind?" Joshua challenged his thinking.

"You mean like the Holy Spirit?"

Grabbing another concordance from the shelf over his desk, Joshua looked up all the scriptures which used the word *ruach*. He pointed out the first scripture in the Bible using the Hebrew word *ruach* was in Genesis 1:2. "Read that passage."

Mose went to his bag and got his Bible. "I like to read from my Bible."

"The Spirit, *ruach*, was hovering over the face of the waters." He looked up at Joshua's face. "What are you thinking?"

"I think the Lord sent the Holy Spirit to save Jonah and the men in the boat!"

The Holy Spirit convicts the world of sin to save them and He convinces

My children to obey Me so that they won't perish. I do not send the Holy Spirit to destroy.

Joshua repeated what he heard. "The Lord sent the Holy Spirit to bring Jonah back to Him, not to cause a storm that would punish him or kill innocent men. He convicts the world of sin to save them and convinces His children to obey Him so that they won't perish and cause others to perish."

"The Lord just told you that." Mose was catching on. "Man, that totally changes the meaning."

"I know. Most people read the Bible and see a God that kills, destroys and takes away."

"Word! I see a God that loves us so much that He chases after us!"

Joshua closed his eyes as he felt an overwhelming feeling of compassion inside him. The realization that men were making God's Word of no effect because of traditional thinking and teaching was heartbreaking to him. "Many people could be delivered from suffering and pain if only they knew about God's love for them. That's why we're starting the Devil Chasers."

I came to save those who are lost . . . not destroy them. If your son ran away from you, would you send a hurricane or tornado to punish him?

"No."

"No what?" Mose was feeling love surround him, but he still wasn't hearing the voice of the Lord.

"No, I wouldn't send a hurricane or tornado to punish my son if he disobeyed me or ran away from me." The Holy Spirit was letting him experience the heart of the Father and Son. In his mind, he saw Jonah rejecting the Word of the Lord and fleeing on a boat to Tarshish. When the boat was in danger from perishing, Jonah was fast asleep. "Mose, the storm didn't wake Jonah up, the men of the boat did. Trials and tribulation don't teach us anything. God sends His Spirit, uses His Word and other people to teach us. Trials and tribulations come to destroy us and get us off the Word."

"That means that God sent His Spirit to chase Jonah down and bring him back."

"He loved Jonah, but He also loved the men and women of Nineveh. He is the lover of souls. He is not the one that is killing, stealing or destroying His people or the people of the world. The kingdom of darkness is the one."

"Word! I can see it now, but . . ." Mose rubbed his arm.

"But what?"

"I'm feeling it! I always thought that feelings were of the flesh."

"You have spiritual feelings too. If your feelings are based on the Word of God, then they are okay. You just have to know which one is which."

"There is still something . . . never mind."

"What."

"It's nothing."

"Please tell me."

"Why did the storm get worse when the men decided to take Jonah back to shore? I mean, look, the wind didn't stop until the men threw Jonah overboard."

Read it again

"The Lord says read it again."

Mose immediately obeyed, "Nevertheless the men rowed hard to return to land, but they could not, for the sea continued to grow MORE tempestuous against them." He noticed the word more.

"It looks like they were trying to return Jonah to land," Joshua said.

"That's what I don't understand, why wouldn't the wind stop if the wind was the Holy Spirit?"

"I'm not sure. Let's pray." Joshua bowed his head and asked the Lord to reveal to them the rest of the story.

When the wind of My Spirit blows to move things . . . all things get moved.

Mose thought he faintly heard something about the wind, but he didn't want to say anything. He knew the Lord would talk to Joshua.

Joshua looked up. "The Lord is giving you the answer."

"ME?"

"Did you hear anything?"

"No, but I think I saw something."

"Was it like a picture?"

"Yeah, I saw the wind picking up and moving things."

How do you know it's the wind?

Mose sat up.

"You heard something right?" Joshua asked.

He repeated what he heard. "How do you know it's the wind? I heard it just like you said! Inside me!"

"That's the Lord speaking to you." Joshua heard the Lord in his spirit too, but he kept quiet wanting Mose to experience the Lord. "Meditate on the question."

Mose sat back down and closed his eyes. He pictured tree tops moving, flags blowing and waves on the oceans; all were indications of the wind moving.

Joshua knew the answer. Satan saw the wind moving. He knew something was going on.

"Okay, I got pictures in my mind of the wind. Now, what do I do."

"Now you can go back to the scriptures and read again, or you can ask the Lord to direct your thinking and start looking for clues."

Mose opened his eyes. "My mind went blank."

"That's when you reread the passage you were meditating."

Mose picked up his Bible and reread it out loud.

"Now meditate again."

Mose closed his eyes.

Joshua silently prayed for him. *Lord help him to see this without me telling him.*

Satan looks for the wind, the clouds and the fire moving over the earth.

"Wait!" Mose sat up again. "If I can see the wind, then satan can see it too!"

"The wind and the fire are two manifestations on earth that indicate where the Holy Spirit is working. The devil is always looking for physical manifestations of the Holy Spirit."

"Do you think that's what happened to Jonah?" Mose was very excited now.

"Yes, I think demons moved the natural wind to stop the wind of the Holy Spirit."

"Oh, man! The devil saw it too!"

"I've studied past moves of God and the one thing that always happens to them is that the devil gets involved. It never fails!" Joshua said. "Like the move of the Holy Spirit during the early 1900's. Did you know that several different Pentecostal denominations were formed after two of the leaders started fighting over doctrine?"

"I heard about the revival, but I don't know anything about it."

"The devil found a way into their flesh and the move of God was stopped."

"My dad says that the devil works the hardest to confuse the experience of speaking in tongues more than any other spiritual manifestation in the church."

"That's not hard to believe. It's our secret coded language that the devil can't understand or break. Look at all the confusion and wrong teaching over the experience," Joshua agreed with him.

"Getting back to Jonah," Joshua wanted to stay on their task until Mose received what the Lord wanted him to know. "I think satan was now causing the sea to grow violent to kill a prophet of God and probably kill all the men in the ship as a bonus."

"Well, since Jonah disobeyed God, satan probably thought he had a right to kill him."

"Probably," Joshua agreed with Mose again.

Where did Jonah say he was when he cried out to Me?

"Where was Jonah when he cried out to the Lord?" Joshua asked.

Mose read in Chapter two verse two, "Out of the belly of Sheol, I cried . . . where's Sheol?"

"That is the Hebrew word for the underground world of the dead. You know, below the earth. It's been translated equal times between the English words hell and grave and a few times referring to the pit."

Joshua thought about the story that Jesus told about the rich man in hell and the beggar Lazarus with Abraham. "Look up a story for me in Matthew chapter 16."

Mose read it out loud.

"I remember looking up the word gulf. If you investigate the Hebrew word for fish, you will find a cross reference that leads to the word gulf."

Mose wasn't seeing it. "So?"

"From this parable, we know that both Lazarus and the rich man went to hell, but they were actually in different parts."

He had Mose's attention now. "Okay . . . ?"

"So, what if there is a name for that gulf?"

Now Joshua lost him again. "I don't get it?"

"Well, Jesus said that Jonah was in the 'whale's belly' for three days and three nights' . . ."

"That's what the word says," Mose agreed.

"But Jonah's prayer doesn't say that he was in a fish's belly. His narrative indicates that he drowned in the sea and then went to hell. I'm not saying that his body wasn't in the fish's belly, but what if at the same time his soul was in the great gulf that separated parts of hell? And what if that gulf was nicknamed the Whale's Belly?" Joshua smiled at the connection. "I love the way the Lord thinks!"

It was just like God to have a dual meaning with a play on words with this story. He loved how awesome it was to dig deep into His Word. This was the very reason why he spent so much time searching out the Word.

"I think that Jonah's body was in special fish prepared by the Lord to protect it from being eaten by the fish in the sea. He drowned, and while his soul was in the gulf in hell, he repented. And then, God caused great fish to vomit him on dry land, and God put his soul and spirit back into his body."

"Wordman! I always thought that Jonah was in a whale for those three days and three nights." Mose shuddered. "I can't imagine all that slimy stuff inside the fish surrounding him."

Children should be taught that Jonah was in disobedience. It wasn't a great fish and it wasn't a whale. Jonah was in disobedience.

"This is a story of God's mercy and satan's failure at killing humans. He failed because the sailors survived and probably accepted Jehovah, Jonah was saved and the people of Nineveh were saved."

"You know, children should be taught about Jonah's disobedience, not about Jonah and the whale," Mose added.

Joshua knew in his spirit that what Mose just said was straight from the Lord, but he didn't think that Mose had that revelation yet.

My children open the door for judgment when they disobey me.

"Word, again! When we disobey the Lord, it opens the door for the devil to kill and destroy!"

Joshua smiled.

"What?" Mose froze. "That was from the Lord wasn't it?"

"He's talking to your spirit and you're repeating Him."

"He's talking to me?"

"See how easy it is to hear from the Lord?"

Mose was really excited now.

Satan was fighting hard to kill Jonah. He figured out he was in disobedience and could kill him. He hates My preachers and prophets with a passion.

"Satan hates God's preachers, prophets and teachers," Joshua said.

"With a passion!" Mose added.

How long was Jonah in the belly of hell?

"Three days and three nights," they both answered at the same time.

"You heard too?"

"Yes."

"All the time?"

"Pretty much," Joshua admitted.

"Cool."

How long was My Son in the belly of hell?

"Three days and three nights," they answered together again.

Jonah in the belly of hell for three days and three nights was a sign for My people that Jesus was that prophet that was to come. Jonah died in the storm like Jesus was to die.

"Did you hear that?" Mose asked.

"Yes, Jonah was like the Lord Jesus, except Jesus obeyed God."

Why did Jonah disobey Me?

"Why do you think Jonah disobeyed the Lord?" asked Mose.

"Jonah somehow knew that God was going to give them mercy that would block judgment."

"Look at chapter four verse two!" Mose exclaimed. "He angrily accused God of being gracious and merciful, slow to anger and abundant in loving kindness . . ."

"A God that doesn't like to do harm," Joshua added.

"Wordman, this story is really about God's love for all people."

"The amazing thing is that it is a book that is devoted to the Gentile nation. We know that God loves Israel, because He said that they were the apple of His eye. But in this story, we now know that He cares about the Gentiles too."

"God is really a good God."

"This is the beginning of your understanding that most people, even Christians, don't know the heart of God and how good He really is."

I want and need the souls of men and women. That is what I want My children to learn about Jonah. I have compassion and a deep desire for men and women to come to Me.

Mose looked up at Joshua with a lump in his throat. "It's about souls, isn't it?"

Joshua felt like he had swallowed a fish. He couldn't talk, so he shook his head yes. It was then that the Lord allowed them to experience a portion of His overwhelming love and compassion for all the people in the world. It welled up inside them like a dam of water and suddenly burst.

Both of them got on their faces and started crying from their spirit before the Lord.

"Oh, Jesus," Joshua cried out.

Moses didn't even care that he was crying in front of Joshua. His heart felt like it was going to break.

Suddenly, the Holy Spirit used Joshua's voice to release His desire.

"My children . . . My children . . . My children . . . oh My children! My children need to be in obedience to Me. My children . . . My children . . . oh my children. Love the lost . . . love the lost . . . My heart . . . My children. Show them My love . . . My grace . . . My mercy . . . My mercy . . . My mercy and My love.

My children . . . My love. Tell all . . . My children My love. My mercy . . . my grace . . . tell all . . . tell everyone of My love . . . oh My love . . . tell them . . . tell them I love them. No matter what they have done . . . I love them. I love . . . oh My heart My love. I love them."

Mose heard every word in his spirit that Joshua was speaking. Never had he experienced anything like this before in his life. Out of his belly came a deep wailing of tears for God's children who will not tell the world that He loves them with an everlasting love.

Joshua also cried out for the teens his age that were wasting their time with the things of world. "Oh, Lord God, so many of the things we do are so worldly and useless! Please forgive us for wasting time!"

Mose heard what he said and agreed with him. "Please help us Lord to make good use of our time!"

"Oh, Lord! Your heart is mercy and grace. Your heart is forgiveness. Your heart is crying for lost souls."

Mose spoke out in tongues. It was a message from the Lord.

Joshua heard the Lord speak the interpretation and said, "I am dreading the day when My Father declares that the time is come for the harvest. The end of harvest is the day of judgment. It's the time when I will command My angels to separate the sheep from the goats. It will be the end of the age of the nations. The nations will be judged according to their compassion on the My people, the nation of Israel. It is the day that our Father is going to wipe the tears from My eyes and I will not be able to cry for the lost nations ever again."

Mose immediately got off the floor to write down what Jesus was saying through Joshua . . .

. . . the door to Joshua's room opened for a few minutes and then closed quietly.

Vicki looked at Ruth, "Do you want to disturb them?"

"No way. I've prayed too long and too hard for Mose to have an experience with the Lord like that. As far as I'm concerned, you can adopt him!"

As a mother, Vicki understood what she was saying.

CHAPTER 28

Mose looked over at Kellie sitting in the chair next to him at his father's church. He handed her a long note that he wrote to her after he got home yesterday from Joshua's. He half-listened to his dad's preaching and half-watched her face as she read the note.

After reading the note, she turned it over and scribbled, *why didn't you call me last night?*

He read it and scribbled back, *because I had to spend sum family time after being with Joshua 4 almost 2 days!*

Kellie had to fight off jealous flesh. Up until a week ago, she was the one that got to study and pray with Joshua all the time. She wrote, *didn't I tell you?* She told him that Joshua and he would hit it off.

You were right. He wrote back.

She leaned over and whispered, "What did you talk about?"

Mose scribbled down his answer while shaking his head, *too much!*

"When will you tell me?" She forgot to whisper.

A lady sitting behind them bent over and said "Shh!"

Mose pointed to the note paper.

Kellie shook her head no and put it away in her purse. She was feeling a little left out. Just a couple of weeks ago, she was Joshua's best friend.

Mose sensed her feelings. He motioned for her to give him the note paper. He wrote, *after lunch, come with me to J's house.*

"Okay," she whispered . . .

. . . Joshua sat at the back of the church with his mom and dad. They were visiting the Pearson's church and waiting for the Lord's confirmation that it was going to be their permanent place to worship. He enjoyed Pastor Pearson's sermon so far, but truthfully he was looking for Mose and Kellie. He forgot to mention to Mose yesterday that they would be visiting. In his heart he felt that this was the church that they should attend, but his head was wondering about the youth group. It would take an unusual Christian youth leader to understand his anointing and his history with youth pastors was not as successful as he would have liked. He believed that they were intimidated by his knowledge of the Word.

It wasn't their personalities that bothered him the most; it was the lack of knowledge of the Word through their teaching and preaching that he had to endure. He wanted to quit going to Wednesday night church services so many times in the past that he couldn't count all of them. Even though his parents understood how he felt, they told him that under no circumstances would they allow him to quit church.

When Pastor Pearson dismissed the congregation, Dan and Vicki waited in the huge lobby to meet with the Pearson's to go out to eat.

"Joshua!" Kellie squealed and waved at him, motioning him to come over to her.

He forged through the crowded lobby.

"I didn't know you were coming today!" She hugged him.

"I forgot to tell Mose, where is he?"

"He is looking for Hannah to see if she wanted to come over to your house later this afternoon. He said that you guys have a lot to tell us."

"Joshua!" Hannah squealed like Hannah. "It's been so long since I saw you last!"

Mose rolled his eyes. *The only down thing about this ministry is the girls,* he thought.

"Well?" Kellie asked.

"Well what?" Joshua replied.

"Are you gonna make our church your home church?" Hannah asked.

"I don't know yet. My dad wants to talk to Pastor Pearson first."

Mose asked. "When?"

"Today, during lunch."

"Lunch?"

"Your mom invited my mom out to lunch yesterday."

Mose turned around and looked at his mom talking to a group of ladies. "That's just great! I'm always the last to know!"

"Why don't we all go out to eat?" asked Joshua.

"Like, I'm free. My dad doesn't care about what I do," Hannah announced.

"That must be nice," Mose liked to pick on her.

"No. It's the pits. My dad drinks and I stay with Kellie until I have to go home." Kellie was the only one that really knew about the situation at Hannah's home.

"Just kidding," Mose sounded genuinely concerned.

"No, you're not. You really like to pick on me," Hannah acted offended.

"I really am sorry." *Man, she is really gonna make me pay.*

Kellie laughed with Hannah who smiled back and pointed at Mose. "Got ya!"

Ruth came over and told them that they were all going out to eat, except Hannah's mother who said that she couldn't go with them.

"Everybody ready?" Dan asked the group once Pastor Pearson was free to go. "Great let's go."

Metraloas watched the Knights enter church that Sunday morning knowing that they would be busy worshipping God for the next three to four hours. He also noticed that they were visiting a new church. Standing a far off, he saw Sheila and her mother enter the same church. He decided now was a good time to introduce shathah to chemah since they hadn't made a connection with each other yet.

Hesitating, shathah was keeping a close watch over Sheila to make sure that she wouldn't hatch another scheme with the angels to save her husband, Wade. Together they flew into one of the tunnels leading to the gate of hell.

"Are you sure he is here?" asked shathah.

"Does a dog return to his vomit? Besides, he told me he needed a break. The left leg of hell is where he works out his frustrations."

Shathah laughed. "Why couldn't we connect the first time?"

"He was in his ship in the heavenlies," metraloas answered.

"Ah, the fallen angels are so bad and lucky!"

"Yeah, and they get all the breaks."

They enjoyed going to the place of the damned as they flew down the gateway to hell. Metraloas lead them through a narrow corridor that was crowded with slithering snakes and other grotesque beastly evil beings. The horrible smell of decaying flesh was filling their nostrils.

"Ah! The smell of dead flesh is so sweet!" metraloas sniffed absorbing every thing he could. Once again he thought about how he missed his home and wanted to come back.

"There is nothing like the smell of rotting, dead flesh!" exclaimed shathah.

"Even better than the drunken stupor you lead many of your victims on earth?" asked metraloas.

Shathah thought about the smell after a drunk vomited. Laughing with delight he said, "Vomit from drunks on earth is what helps me stay on earth. But there is nothing like the vomit from a dead human!"

They were both laughing as they descended lower and lower through winding tunnels and stairs that would take them into the pits of fire.

"Is it true of what I've heard about him?"

"All the things you have heard about him are probably true. Besides what is truth in the kingdom of lies?"

Shathah laughed heartily and slapped metraloas on the back. "I really like the way you think! I've heard about his infamous fire-blaster at the end of his arm. I would love to have one like his!"

"It's not so great if you are one of his targets!" metraloas spoke out loud what he was thinking.

"That's why you hate him so much!"

"I loathe him. He has kept me from doing what I love the most."

"What is that?" A snake hissed as shathah accidentally stepped on him.

"I want to be down here torturing souls," metraloas explained.

"You want to be down here in hell?" shathah thought that was weird since most demons desire assignments on the surface of earth.

"I know that I am considered a freak of satan's design, but I have never had a successful assignment on earth."

"That is really strange. I've never met a human I couldn't deceive."

"If you ever meet a true Spirit-filled Christian who knows the Word, run like hell." A smug laugh rolled from his lips. Telling the truth was a rare thing for an evil android. They are programmed by satan to lie whenever possible and he could care less how much they lie to one another.

Arriving at the entrance to the left leg, once again metraloas surveyed the pits looking for chemah. "How old are you?" He wondered if he knew how much hell had changed from its original design.

"About a thousand earth years," shathah replied.

"Then, you don't even know that satan remodeled hell after JC escaped."

"Why?"

"He changed it to look like a body. He is always copying God and since the day of pentecost when Jesus started building His body, satan announced that hell was going to look like a body lying down in the depths of earth. That's his copy of the body of Christ."

"So, that is why we have a left and right leg . . ."

He interrupted. "A right and left arm, a center with a brain and a heart pulsating through out it. . . ."

"Don't forget the best place, the fun center in the middle of hell."

"My favorite place is the left leg of hell. Millions of pits of fire are in the acres and acres of hot-burning land. I love the darkened land of death, fire and torment. I love the screams and especially the smells."

Shathah looked shocked. “How old are you?”

“I am one of the first created by the master,” he told him.

“That is why you love hell so much. What’s in the head?”

“I don’t know for sure. The head of hell is a secret place for satan and the fallen angels. No demon spirit has ever been there and only one man has ever gone in the farthest reach of hell and plunged to its deepest depths.”

“Satan took JC there?”

“All the way,” metraloas told him.

Shathah’s shocked look betrayed what he was thinking. “You know that one of the prime directives is to never talk about the three days and nights that JC stayed here!” He looked around the corridor to see if any demon was spying on them. He saw a procession of dead mules with humans chained and thrown over them like a sack of potatoes. “Where are they going?” shathah asked.

“To the pits. Look at their faces! Imagine what those dead humans are thinking right now! They land on the floor of hell with a ‘thud’ that takes their breath away. Little diabolical demonic androids greet them with chains for their feet and hands. After they are bound, these scary little creatures have the power to throw them on the back of a dead mule and once again they feel the breath of death knocked out of them. They pass through tunnels seeing, hearing and feeling such atrocities that a permanent expression of fear is ingrained upon their ugly faces for eternity! And the last stop is the pits. Welcome to hell home for eternity!”

Metraloas belted out his little scenario while shathah was laughing so hard, he could barely stand.

“That was great! You should be a writer or something. Now, even I wouldn’t mind if I could work on one of those welcoming committees of demons.”

“I didn’t even tell you the best part. When they arrive in the pit area, demons are allowed to bite, claw, scratch and torture the humans while they remind them that they are in hell for not receiving JC as their Savior,” metraloas sighed. “I almost forgot. The hot atmosphere hurts their lungs to breathe. It hurts so much that they think they are going to die, but wait . . . they’re already dead!”

Metraloas and shathah cracked up laughing.

“See I told you this is a fun place to work.” metraloas slapped him on the back hard as he led shathah out of the tunnel and into a land that looked like it had just been destroyed by an atomic bomb. “Look and behold!”

The ground was scorched and burned black and red with fire. Orange, yellow and red colors dotted the landscape as fire flashed and lighted up the scene before them. Hundreds and thousands of pits could be seen as far as the spiritual eye could see and fire was flowing like hot lava from a volcano. It would sweep like a tidal wave over the pits. Many cried out for water as the fire covered them in their pit. Metraloas and Shathah looked over the pits with their night eyes. The scene before them appeared like a special night scope on a rifle; only it appeared to them in light and dark gray color with heat magnifying itself in various degrees of red hues.

They spotted chemah. He was flying over one of the pits laughing with great pleasure and power as he shot more fire into the center of the pit where a lost soul in the form of a skeleton stood.

"There he is!"

Shathah looked over and saw this weird looking human-like being flying through the air. He got close to metraloas and whispered, "What's with the red hair?"

"It's a long story, but he got burned in the war of rebellion and lost one of his hands, so he decided to make himself look like a total freak."

"Wow! I've never seen a fallen angel look so weird."

"Shh! He hates androids with a passion! And he will probably hate you especially when he realizes that you have been promoted to the division of ruler."

"It's easy to win promotions and favors when you work with humans and alcohol!" shathah roared with laughter just as a wave of red-hot lava rolled over the pits and human beings began screaming everywhere. "I bet many humans in this land of pits think that hell was going to be one big drinking and dancing party!" He laughed at the thought that the pits were in the shape of the top of a martini glass. "If there could be a party in hell," shathah laughed, "this would be the place!"

"Believe me when I say that there is no party in this desolate land filled with humans." Metraloas thought for a second. "In fact, I don't think there is a party any where in all of hell for humans. Just screams of excruciating pain."

Shathah pointed out. "Look at chemah! He sure looks like he is having a party! Man that fire-blaster at the end of his hand is hot!" He looked over at metraloas as they both snickered. "Uh, pardon the pun!"

When metraloas stopped laughing he realized that this was the first time he ever had fun with another android.

"How did that feel?" chemah laughed hysterically with growing power. "Just think! You could have escaped this punishment if you would have accepted that name we curse down here."

"Jesus have mercy!" The person from the pit cried out just before the roar of another wave of fire drenched her trembling body and one more time ripped off the dead flesh.

"Shut up! You stupid woman!" chemah flew over her and gave her another burst of fire. "Jesus can't save you now." He cursed her with every known word used for cursing on the face of the earth.

She screamed louder. "Jesus! Please release me from this constant torment!"

Chemah turned to one of the guards and asked mockingly. "Do you see Jesus down here?"

The guard shouted a wicked "NO!"

"You should have cried out to Jesus while you lived on earth. Not now you stupid ——! You listened to the lying spirits who told you God was too good to send you to hell," chemah laughed scornfully.

Groans of despair were continually being spoken from the gray mist inside the skeleton bones. She stopped calling out for Jesus to help her and instead began cursing His Name. When she lived on earth, she cursed the name of Jesus. She told many that she would rather party in hell, than give up her fun on earth. She believed the lie that hell was one big party with satan as the leader. Satan promised her that he would put on the biggest and best party in hell.

When she was alive, she would say, "I can party with the best of them! I will be the biggest and best party person hell as ever seen!" She boasted as she downed a shot of vodka. "Give me another! I bet I can drink more than you can before we pass out." She would challenge anyone to drink with her.

Chemah was told of her boasting by the party spirits that had to leave her body when she had passed out on the couch. Rolling over she fell on the floor and landed face down in her own vomit and suffocated to death. No one was around to roll her out of her puke and take her to the hospital to keep her from dying. The party spirits loved to torture her with the memories of people the Lord sent her way.

"You could have accepted Jesus, but you spit in the face of the people He sent you. Many tried to get you saved to keep you from this damnation. Curse Him now! You did while you lived on earth!" They laughed at her continually for 24 hours. She would never leave the torment of hell.

Chemah laughed and turned to another miserable soul. He waited for the dead flesh to come back on his next victim so he could burn it off again.

"See what I mean about their flesh?" metraloas pointed out to shathah. "The flesh of dead humans looks like gray dead matter. See now how it forms on the bones and then gets burned off and then reforms again. It is an endless cycle. The bones never burn to powder. They burn black. Look how the soul of the human looks like a gray mist. Now, look at the worms forming in her skeleton." He looked up smiling. "She can feel every one of those worms; they are boring into her flesh."

"Where does the flesh come from?" shathah asked.

"I don't know. It's just part of the package. The Christian book warns them about this place, but hardly anyone believes it," metraloas told him.

"So a dead human can feel the torment of worms, spiders, roaches, rats and snakes?"

Metraloas couldn't believe what he was hearing. "Where have you been for the last one thousand years?"

"My assignment was to develop the division of alcoholism. I don't get to visit hell very much. I have more humans now addicted to alcohol than ever in the history of mankind."

"Yeah, they feel everything. The soul can feel cuts, stabs, bites, and blows given by us. We make sure that they receive endless torture, horrendous screams, hideous moans and despair and not to mention constant cursing and death rock and roll music. There is no rest here for the soul."

"What about their memory?"

"They remember everything, especially all the times that they could have received JC and escaped from the constant burning and torment with fire. And best of all, souls suffer by themselves. There is no fun in hell for a dead human soul. They are isolated in these individual pits or cells." Metraloas scanned the horizon. "Watch that guard over there."

"The snake?" shathah asked.

"Yes. Every time a soul in the pit cries out for Jesus, a demon guard comes and pierces the center of the gray mist in each skeleton until that soul stops crying out Jesus' name. Their pain becomes so unbearable that they stop saying His name after awhile."

The soul they watched started cursing God for sending them to hell and the guard stopped stabbing them with the spear and cursed JC with him.

Shathah was very amused when he heard the man cursing God with every curse word he knew. "They think God sent them here?"

"Yeah! Isn't it great? I love it when they curse God!" laughed metraloas.

"Death sends them to hell because they didn't accept the one way of escape," shathah said. "JC wrote it in His book that He is the way, the truth, and the life. He's the only door to escape the wrath of hell."

Chemah flew over the two androids and cursed them. "Shut up you stupid demons! I can't believe you would quote His words!" chemah landed next to metraloas and punched him in his stomach. Chemah screamed at him and called him many terrible names.

Shathah backed away from metraloas. It was self-preservation in the kingdom of darkness. There were no self-help courses to learn how to get along in satan's kingdom. He watched chemah beating metraloas until he fell to the floor of hell weakened and barely able to move. Fallen angels had the right to treat an android any way they wanted too. He didn't defend metraloas, he was just glad it wasn't him.

"You're lucky I don't destroy you right now!" He pointed his fire-shooting arm at metraloas' green-bloodied face.

"Even if a soul in these pits had heard me, they wouldn't have believed me!" metraloas barely said as he lay on the ground. It was the most harm he had ever experienced at the hands of chemah.

Shathah was stunned. He didn't know if he wanted to meet chemah or not.

Metraloas slowly raised himself off the ground. "You know that they are in this place because of fear and unbelief that led to imprisonment!" He wiped the blood off his face with his arm thinking how he wished he could return just a portion of chemah's cruelty back on him. His tough leather skin can take more punishment than chemah's. "They have no faith to take them out of this place!" He growled at chemah.

"What in —— do I care!" chemah screamed obscenities at him. "Never quote JC again! Do you understand me?" He released a shot of fire at him scorching his leather-like skin.

Chemah turned his attention back to the pathetic souls in the pits. *Metraloas is history!* He thought as he released more fire to burn the dead humans. "God wants us to punish you like this for all eternity!" He yelled at them.

Shathah listened to the words he was saying. He slowly moved over to metraloas. "Do they really believe him?"

"Why not?" he said as he bent over and rubbed his stomach. "The souls in the pits lived years on earth believing that God was too good to send them to hell. So, now that they are here, they blame Him." He breathed slowly in and out while he was talking.

"They have a little help with chemah telling them that God sent them here," shathah noted.

"It's not any different from all the brainwashing they got on earth. We were made to hate God and humans made in His image. We blame God for all the evil works that we commit. The master has successfully convinced the world that God is responsible for everything bad that happens to them."

Shathah thought it was ironic. "Those bad things that satan orchestrates drive humans to drink. It makes my job easier. I teach androids how to increase the addiction of alcohol into the lives of children, teenagers and adult humans. Since the invention of television, my division has exploded with humans becoming addicted by the hundreds of thousands. I really don't have time to be here now."

Chemah flew over to the two after he watched them for a couple of minutes. "Who is this?"

"I found an android living in the house of a friend of . . ."

"Another moron?"

Metraloas ignored the insult. "This is shathah, spirit of drunkenness, the director over a division that controls one of the prayer intercessor's husband that meets in the house of Knight. He is from the class of rulers of darkness."

Chemah didn't recognize him. "Which division?"

"I am in the division of drunkenness and alcoholism."

He especially hated those androids that were successfully promoted to the class of ruler of darkness. "Who is your target?"

"Her name is Sheila Coyle. Her husband is Wade. Shathah has controlled Wade since he was a teenager with alcohol."

"What are your accomplishments in that family?"

Shathah boasted of all his accomplishments. "I have led many to the life of drinking through working at the Coyle family business. Many of the executives are becoming alcoholics."

"What about the Coyle family? I'm more interested in them," demanded chemah.

"Wade Coyle is an alcoholic in denial. His youngest child, a boy is just now starting to experiment with drinking and teen sex."

Shathah conveniently left out Hannah and Sheila. Since becoming Christians, the grandmother had commanded all evil spirits to leave them alone, but he didn't think it was necessary to let chemah know the whole truth. *After all*, he thought, *it only takes one thought to change a human's life for all eternity.* All demons were encouraged to keep on using different thoughts until one worked. He still had an opportunity to re-infect her and then possess her.

Chemah grabbed shathah's throat and started squeezing him with his death grip. "I'm interested in more than his addiction to alcohol! What other spirits are operating in his flesh?"

"The spirit of anger, depression, lying and violence abide in his fleshly house," choked out shathah gasping for air. He could hardly believe that angels were so strong that just one could handle him so easily with one hand.

Chemah released him. "Would you invite a spirit of murder to come in with you and then we could use him in a greater plan for destruction of the Knight family?"

"I would be agreeable." *Who would say no after that display of power?* "Of course I would need another house to live in."

"What do you want?" In satan's kingdom, everyone has a price.

"What's in it for me?" shathah decided he might as well ask.

Chemah's eye's glared at shathah. "What do you want?"

"I want an introduction to satan. I want him to know that I am a part of this maneuver to bring the Knight family down."

"You are either totally stupid or . . ."

"Or he has a full proof plan to bring down the Knight family. Why don't you introduce him to satan now?" interrupted metraloas. "It would look great for you, chemah, especially now that you know about a door opened into the Knight family."

The moron might have a point. Chemah started thinking about how he could brag that he was the one who brought down the Knight family. Satan was developing an intense, personal hatred for Dan, Vicki and Joshua Knight.

"Follow me, satan just happens to be in the center of hell at this very moment."

CHAPTER 29

Sitting at the country club restaurant, Kellie felt uncomfortable. She knew that Dan Knight would pay for everybody's lunch, but she had never eaten at a place where she needed instructions to know how to use the silverware. She looked at her mousy blue dress and wished she would have chosen something a little more chic this morning.

Looking across the table at Hannah, Kellie thought that she looked like she belonged in a place like this. The Todd family didn't come close to having the money that Joshua's family had, but neither were they close to Hannah's family. Everything matched Hannah's clothes, her shoes, her purse and even her nails. She reminded Kellie of one of those plastic girls from a teen flick, only she knew that inside Hannah was nothing like that.

Hannah looked at Kellie and thought she looked great sitting next to Joshua. Even though her family was considered well off, she didn't remember ever experiencing a table setting like the one in front of her. She tried to brush out a few wrinkles in her off-white linen dress and forget about what anybody thought about how she looked.

They were sitting in a table next to their parents with a view that was fabulous. Overlooking the lake was a well-known golf course that featured a golf tournament televised around the world. Mose felt like he was getting a glimpse of the *Lifestyles of the Rich and Famous* again. He picked up one of the forks and exclaimed. "Word! Why are there so many forks?"

Joshua told him which fork to use and when. He wondered if his parents would be able to talk with Pastor Pearson about their personal beliefs. He needed a church home for the ministry; a congregation that he felt comfortable being around. He needed a pastor that could mentor him and one that he could recommend to future converts. His family was only a few days from stepping into the biggest move they had ever made and he still had no idea what his parents were thinking about the church they would be attending.

While everyone else was thinking about themselves and their surroundings, Joshua was thinking about the Lord and the ministry, again.

An evil, eerie atmosphere permeated every inch of hell. A foreboding feeling took the breath away of all human souls that entered through hell's gates. Demons were created to withstand the heat of hell and to love the smell of burning, rotting flesh that reminded humans of rotten eggs. Passing through the tunnel, flashes of a strobe light revealed metraloas, chemah and shathah rushing hurriedly.

The guard standing at the entrance of the tunnel leading to the center of hell gave them a great report. "Satan is sitting on his throne in the center of the fun arena. He is in an ecstatically 'happy' mood. Something from earth has given him great pleasure."

That information gave metraloas the courage he needed to go on with his plan. Walking toward the crowd of demon spirits surrounding satan, they could hear much revelry and commotion carrying on.

Chemah grabbed a tall skinny bear and spun him around. "What is going on?"

"Lord satan just received a copy of an editorial from one of earth's newspaper. It says hell is a many-splintered place. Splintered, not splendid! Get it?" The evil spirit laughed and hit chemah in his arm with his elbow.

A blood-curdling laugh echoed throughout the entrances to the fun center as satan read more from the earth newspaper. "Listen to this! Imagine me enjoying a human this much," satan cackled. "Everyone listen to what this human has written, 'In hell, all the warm-blooded animals you ever barbecued are lined up to have a chat with you!' HA! HA! HA!" He was overcome with fits of hysteria. "Here's another, 'In hell nothing is open on Sunday. When you take a number to get waited on it's always more than a million.'"

All the demons roared at that one.

"This article is the bomb!" satan looked at one of his gargoyle guards and hissed with pleasure. "Oh, I just love that latest expression from the hip generation on earth. Don't you just love them saying 'it's the bomb' when something is good?" The demons in the center of hell gave satan their total attention and nodded their heads enthusiastically.

"Where in the hell do you tell your friends and relatives to go when they are already in hell?" Satan almost fell out of his throne in another fit of laughter. "Isn't it great how ignorant these humans are about hell! Here's another good one, 'In hell an electronic dialer will instruct you saying: Hell-O. Please hold for Mister Lucifer.' I love it! I love it!" pausing he said, "You know, that's a good idea."

It was a scene not many inhabitants of hell had ever seen or heard before; evil spirits and demons listening and laughing with satan while he read a human newspaper from earth.

"Imagine," satan spoke seriously, "we send each soul here in hell to our store of various torments and tell them they can purchase any torment for the right price." Every being paused, not knowing exactly how to respond. Satan's held his stoneface look for a few seconds and then he-hawed with laughter. "Just kidding! This human writer said that, not me!"

Chemah was stupefied, "Can you imagine a human writing something so ignorant?"

Metraloas wasn't surprised. "Human's don't have a clue about hell. Imagine that writer dying, entering the underworld and remembering every word that he wrote in that article while one of us is torturing him?"

"Why is the master laughing so much?" shathah asked.

"The master loves to make fun of humans and he especially loves the liberal left-wing news writers," chemah told him. "They are responsible for more lies perpetrated against the Kingdom of God and Christians than any other scheme that he has ever devised in America."

When he was no longer amused, satan called for the demon spirit who brought him the newspaper. "The human who wrote this, uh . . ." satan was looking over the article for a name. "Ah, yes. Is she one of ours?"

"Yes, sir," one of his assistants answered him. "There's not many in the news reporting field that don't belong to us."

"Yes, I know. The church handed over the media to me in the fifties. I like controlling the media. Their little pea brains are too small for a mind of my ability. I tell them what to think and how to believe. I am the one that master-minded their liberal system." satan stopped to catch his breath. He put his hand on his chest. "I am so bad . . . so bad . . . I'm one of a kind bad! One of these days, I'll introduce myself to them."

Chemah looked at metraloas. They both knew one of his favorite things to do was to subvert the meaning of words because he could not tolerate any words that belonged to the Kingdom of Light. He hated saying or hearing good, great, awesome, blessed or happy words. He felt all these words were too optimistic and hopeful. It was his plan to rid earth of any words that would point to Jesus as the Messiah.

Satan stood from his throne and boasted about his accomplishments, heaping glory upon himself. "They would never be able to correctly report the facts without my spiritual insights." He strutted in front of his throne like a peacock.

"What does he say about the Christian network that is gaining ground on the big networks and growing daily?" shathah asked.

"He doesn't say anything," chemah scolded him. "Listen."

Satan stood from his throne and pointed his finger up above his head. "All the angels carried on so pathetically sick when He created man. They made a big deal of His new creation! I wanted to puke! I knew His new creation would fall! I knew they would sin when tempted! Didn't I say to God, 'what are you gonna do now, God?'" Satan's eyes were hot with hatred for the disgusting human creatures. He held out the paper and hit it with his hand. "Look at them now. How pathetic they are! How ignorant they are! They can only make such idiotic jokes about hell because they don't think we exist!"

He sat back down on his throne. Satan waved his hand and lightning started cracking everywhere with sparks of fire hitting the ground and burning the paper he had crumpled up and tossed. "Humans are the most stupid creatures that God ever made!"

He stood and screamed at the top of his lungs, "I told you so GOD! I hate You, and I hate Your creation! I will win! I WILL WIN!" Satan flung his head up and shook his hand at God. At that moment, the black hood that covered most of his face came off. A gasp could be heard all through the crowd of evil spirits. More spirits witnessed the truth of his real face this time than the last time. Many closed their eyes and put their hands over their mouths.

Satan's face was fear inspiring with its grotesque rolls and rolls of wrinkled skin. Sin scared and marred the once most beautiful perfect creation God created. Once again a handsome young man's face appeared over the ugly one. Every evil spirit who had seen the real satan acted like they never saw what they really did see.

"Spirit of evil reports!" satan sat down pulling his hood over his head.

The evil spirit walked up and bowed, "Yes, my lord satan?"

"I want to give this reporter a special reward."

"Yes, sir!" replied dusphemia, the spirit of evil reports.

"Make sure she gets money and fame from this well-written article about hell and make sure she knows she got this reward especially because of her writing about hell! I want more of this kind of powerless, fruitless talking and illusion written about hell on earth."

Dusphemia started to disappear when satan called him back. "Don't forget to make a note that I personally want to thank her when she arrives at our 'holiday hilton' permanently." He chuckled at his own humor. "The less they know about us on earth, the more we can surprise them when they arrive!" He jumped to his feet. "The less humans know of our true identity, the more power we hold over them. You know what they say on earth, the more the merrier!" He shouted viciously.

"Your wish, is my command!" dusphemia left immediately.

He sat back down on his throne. "Now, back to business. Who else has a great report for me?" satan glared at the many demons in the crowd around his throne.

Chemah decided this was a good time to tell satan about his plan. He walked up to the front of his throne and bowed before him. "lord satan. I have a report from a special family on earth that you have targeted for destruction."

"They are not special. I target everyone on earth for destruction. Are you talking about the Knight family? Is it true that they are officially the house of Knight?"

He bowed again. "Yes, my lord, I am and I haven't heard they are official."

"My special spirit of fury, what are you planning?" satan snapped his fingers for his servants to bring him his special liquid potion to drink. Not one evil being knew for sure what he was drinking. Some think it has to do with the energy he needs to survive.

"I have put off reporting to you until I had some exceptional news!" chemah was trying to find the right words.

"Take your time. You know that your future rests on your next few words. I wouldn't like to terminate your service on earth." satan raised his eyes, to raise the temperature around chemah.

Chemah was sweating and wiping his brow. "I have found a way to stop the Knight family."

"Is that the family that you tried to kill in the car wreck the other day?" satan seethed as he remembered how many evil spirits that little episode cost him. He snapped his fingers for his book of records to appear.

"I can explain that, lord satan!"

"Go on." satan thumbed through the book's pages sitting on a black steel table in front of his throne trying to find the recording of the accident. He wanted to see what the exact cost was to his kingdom from that failure.

"I saw too late that the Knight family had protection from the Blood of JC and His armor. So few know how to apply His Blood for a covering, well, I just thought it was worth a try just in case we could do some damage."

"It says here that I lost a total of seven souls and hundreds of demons. That 'little' incident did do some damage! TO MY kingdom!" satan stood.

Chemah motioned for shathah to come up next to him.

"Who do we have here?" satan inquired.

"This is shathah, spirit of drunkenness. He possesses the house of Wade Coyle on earth."

Shathah bowed.

"What does that have to do with the accident we were discussing?" satan roared.

"Lord satan, it is common knowledge that after a victory of the enemy, they can be made to fall through over confidence or pride."

"No human is immune to pride on earth," satan sat down.

"Shathah has control of the husband of one of the women that attends a prayer meeting at the uh . . . house of Knight," informed chemah.

"And?"

"We have formulated a plot with the help of another indwelling spirit to cause a murder to take place."

"You think the Knights may not be expecting another attack so soon?"

"Yes, and with a couple of more small attacks, even if they fail, I think we could pull them off guard." chemah was talking fast, trying to sell his plan to satan.

"How did you find shathah?" asked satan.

"I followed each female human attending the prayer meetings of Vicki Knight," lied chemah.

Suddenly satan's eyes darted over to metraloas.

This was what he was waiting for. He cried out and threw himself prostrate before satan. "Lord satan, I have failed miserably at my assignment on earth with the Knight family. I beg you for my old assignment and ask that you assign chemah in my place. He is deserving of this commission more than I. He is a worthy opponent for the humans, Dan and Vicki Knight! They are a highly developed praying family and they need a powerful worthy opponent to take them out. I am not worthy or powerful enough."

"So, chemah, you have devised a plot against shathah's assignment that includes bringing down the house of Knight?"

"Well, I . . ." stammered chemah. He was shocked at what he was hearing, because he didn't have a clue about a plot. What he told satan earlier was a lie.

"He has worked and worked with me lord satan. He had all the ideas. I am not worthy to continue with this assignment." metraloas was giving it all he had.

"Very well, chemah, you are now assigned to the house of Knight. Bring them to me or cause them to be ineffective in the kingdom of JC." satan then turned his attention to metraloas.

"Now, what should be done with you?"

Metraloas slithered over to satan and kissed his feet. "I am only worthy for the lowest position in hell!"

Satan looked at metraloas. He put his hand on his shoulder and spoke so all could hear. "I will not punish you. I do not want to disturb the inspired mood of the newspaper article I just read to all of you. Very well, metraloas, report to the left leg of hell. You will help dig the pits of fire as hell is enlarging itself every day."

Metraloas grabbed satan's hand and kissed it over and over. "Thank you, lord satan! You are merciful and kind!"

A scowl came to his face. "Shut up you stupid fool!" He slapped him away. "I hate mercy and I hate kindness!" He zapped him with an electrical charge before he waved his hand and metraloas disappeared.

Satan looked at chemah and shathah, "Now, back to earth! See to it that your plan does not fail!" With a wave of his hand, he disappeared and only a puff of smoke remained.

Chemah screamed with rage flying as fast as he could to the left leg of hell. Looking everywhere he was trying to find that deceiver. He went to the end of the deepest part of the pits and searched for him. Spotting metraloas he flew with full fury and hit him with all the force of hatred he could build up.

"You set me up!" shouted chemah with vengeance in his heart.

Metraloas rolled when he was hit. He was laughing so hard that it didn't even hurt when chemah hit him. "Of course, I set you up! You're were so full of thoughts of self-pride and glory, it was easy. Now, see how you like it when you come against the prayers of the Knight family."

"Never! Don't try to curse me you miserable————android! You are counting on my failure. I will not fail," chemah was trying to convince every evil spirit around him with his boasting. But a terrible dread, an invisible evil spirit became a seed of torment in his spirit mind. Chemah faded slowly out of his sight. *I will destroy you metraloas!*

"Oh, I didn't even tell you the best part! This is just a rumor, but then again you know how rumors are. I heard that a new ministry is forming, and Joshua Knight is the one called to form it and that he received a personal visit from JC Himself. And can you believe it? The Knight house is the headquarters. Oh yeah . . . one last thing. The communication tower between heaven and earth has been built and established on their property. They are now the official house of Knight! And I heard from the graveline that satan knew about the communication tower before you told him through an informant. So, if you continue lying to the master, he knows that you are lying."

Chemah rematerialized. He was seething hot with boiling rage.

"One more thing. That cloud covering that you saw and the glory of God that kept our eyes from seeing what they were doing? It was constructed without interference from *any* ruler of darkness or the high spirits in the heavenlies. And that pathetic attack of yours? It resulted in first fruits from Joshua Knight's new ministry called the Devil Chasers."

Chemah was about to explode.

"I knew all along what was going on. Guess I fooled you, but don't worry since you are smarter than I am. I'm sure it won't take you as long as it took me to ditch them."

Words could not explain the emotional dam that was building inside chemah. *You are about to be barbequed!* He raised his fist to blast him out of hell and incinerate him to cinders. "I am going to love destroying you. You know that I can never die, but you, one blast and poof you are gone! Satan gave you life and I'm going to snuff it out! The master won't even miss you!"

"Remember me, when the master receives my reports and names all the people and demons you were responsible for losing for the past two years."

Chemah stopped his blaster just in time. If he terminated metraloas and the reports were delivered to satan, then he would be furious with him. He turned his blowtorch off. "I will get revenge if it's the last thing I ever do!" chemah screamed curses at him as he flew out of the left leg of hell and into the tunnel. Venting his anger, he left a fireball trail over all of the pits until he disappeared. The screams were pitiful.

Metraloas watched him leave. Evil laughter rocked his soul. He grabbed the shovel and started digging. He smiled. *Home at last! Home at last! Thank satan, I am home at last!*

He was finally free of the Knight family.

‡ ‡ ‡

Joshua waved goodbye to his friends and got into his parent's car as they left the Country Club. He couldn't wait to find out if his parents talked to Pastor Pearson.

"We invited them to come over Monday night," Dan answered him. "Sunday is a very busy day for a pastor."

"But we did find out a few things about them," Vicki added.

"What?"

"They follow the faith movement like we do," she said.

"And they watch TBN." Dan knew that Vicki was relieved to know that they watched her favorite Christian network.

"Praise the Lord!" Joshua was relieved to hear that they listened to the Christian television network. He especially loved to watch the new JCTV network and couldn't wait to watch it with his new friends, especially Mose. It was the first time that he could really talk to a male besides his dad.

Turning into the long winding driveway of their home, Joshua told them that he invited the team over.

"That's okay," Vicki replied. "Your Dad and I have some things to talk about, so we will be in our room."

‡ ‡ ‡

Kellie, Mose and Hannah walked up to the Knights' front door. It was open.

"Hello?" Kellie peaked around the door.

Mose grabbed her arm. "You're not going in are you?"

"Sure."

"Maybe we should ring the doorbell?" Hannah reached for the bell.

Kellie blocked her hand. "There's a reason the door was opened. Come on."

They quietly walked into the foyer.

"Mrs. Knight?" Kellie whispered.

Walking down the hall and around a corridor into the kitchen, they saw coffee cups on the kitchen table. "This is weird." Hannah grabbed Kellie's arm. "You don't think that the rapture took place, do you?"

"Don't be ridiculous!" Kellie left the kitchen.

"Where are you going?" Mose followed her.

"I'm going up to Joshua's room."

"Maybe we should leave?" Mose said.

"I think the rapture happened!" Hannah commented again as they walked up the stairs at the back of the house.

Mose whispered, "What if the rapture took place and we were left behind?"

"Not a chance. I've been studying the Bible with Joshua for over a year," Kellie said out loud. "My faith is so much greater since I've been studying with him. When Jesus blows the horn, I will be ready!"

Slowly, they walked down the hall towards Joshua's room. "Wait!" Hannah whispered.

"What?" Mose jumped.

"What's that noise?" Hannah asked.

"Come on," Kellie said. "Let's find out."

"You find out!" Mose said shaking his head.

Kellie counted to 10 slowly. "Fine!"

She continued down the hall and stopped at Joshua's door. Slowly opening the door, she went inside his room.

Mose and Hannah waited for her to come back out.

Hannah tapped Mose on the shoulder. He jumped. "Don't do that!"

"Shh!" She whispered. "I hear voices down the hall."

Kellie came out of his room. "He's been here. His church clothes are on the bed."

"Are they folded all nice and neat?" Mose asked. Kellie didn't answer him so he stuck his head in Joshua's bedroom and took a look himself. "Oh no!" he whispered softly.

"What?" Kellie asked.

"That's what people do when they get raptured!" Mose said excitedly. "They fold their clothes in little neat piles; it was in that book . . ."

"Shh! Do you hear it?" Hannah asked.

Kellie looked down the hall. "Yeah, it's coming from Vicki's bedroom." She moved toward the noise. She looked behind her and no one was there. She motioned for them to follow her.

"No way!" He yelled at a whisper shaking his head no.

"I'll stay with Mose," Hannah spoke a little louder.

"SHH!" he said in her ear, happy to return to her what she did to him all the time. A few seconds later they were still waiting.

"This is stupid," Hannah said. "I'm going to see what's going on."

"Go ahead, I'm right behind you," Mose put his hand on her shoulder.

Hannah slowly opened the door at the end of the hall and saw Joshua, his mother and father and Kellie on the floor praying in the spirit. She looked around for Mose and saw that he was on his knees in the hall praying. She fell to the ground and joined them.

They were all transported by the Holy Spirit into the realm of interceding for the lost.

CHAPTER 30

Michael opened the door to the Lord's office. He had been summoned to his office to discuss the progress of Joshua's ministry.

Jesus was sitting at his desk looking over some of the reports His generals sent Him from earth. Since His resurrection and ascension into heaven, He worked intensely and tirelessly for His body. His undivided attention was vigilantly applied to every detail of the care of each one of His people. He was constantly at work, bringing as many people as He could into the Kingdom of God.

"Michael!" Jesus arose from behind his desk and hugged him with kisses on each cheek as the people in the Middle East practice. "It is good to see you." He motioned for Michael to sit down. "Do you feel the level of anticipation that the time of the end of the age of grace is just a breath away?"

"Oh yes, Lord. Even the inhabitants of earth are sensing a change. Heaven is as busy as usual, but there is a special atmosphere that seems to be permeating all around us that is a different."

Jesus looked at the files on his enormous desk. "My body is working hard, but I sense we may run out of time before the end of the age. Many evil people have been planting wicked seeds in these last days and the harvest of judgment is pressing upon the earth demanding retribution."

"This harvest of judgment from the wicked evil spirits and their followers will destroy earth if it wasn't for Your intervention, Lord."

"The Father intervened during the first harvest of judgment and He has made provision to spare earth a second time."

"If it had not been for Your presence, Lord, in the Ark, the world-wide flood of waters would have destroyed earth," Michael remembered the greatest event on earth since the beginning of its existence, Noah's flood.

"But this next time you, with all the warring angels and My body from heaven and earth will be with Me to rescue the earth from being destroyed by fire in the last judgment." Jesus smiled.

"Your heavenly host of angels is waiting for that day with great anticipation of wiping earth clean of all evil influences!" Michael bowed and praised the Father with Jesus.

"I have dispatched the warring angels for protection and healing from the spiritual war raging on earth even though some of My own are working against me. But now is the time that all members unite as one new body of believers for the war in the heavenlies. I have been reading the reports from the recording angels." He picked up a golden folder filled with special reports about salvation, healing and prayer requests from the saints. "I see that recruitment is increasing by leaps and bounds in all areas of earth."

"I read the report about the Africa, and it has been projected that by the year 2020 the nation will be 95% members of your body."

"I talked to My Father about Africa and He said that they will actually reach that number earlier than reported on earth."

"Oh, blessed be Your Name, Lord. That nation has suffered so much cruelty in the history of earth."

"The Father also told Me that over one billion Muslims will be turned to Me before the great and mighty day of My second coming. He has not forgotten His promise to Hagar regarding Ishmael, Abraham's son. He said He would make a great nation from his descendants and He did not intend for that great nation to be separated from Him for eternity. I have a great desire to bring them into the Covenant between My Father and I. The enemy will not succeed in destroying the seed of Ishmael!"

"Oh, blessed be the Father's Holy Name and Word!" Michael declared. "Lord, if only your children could see that their spiritual growth is constantly on Your mind. If they could only know Your heart, that You want all humans saved and rescued before that terrible day of wrath. If they would only know Your Word that You have a commandment from the Father to be the finisher of their faith."

"Many know and believe, Michael. I have several reports of victory. My Word is growing and developing many members of My body into My image as I have commanded. I dread that day when My Father wipes all tears from My eyes and I can no longer sow them as seeds for the people of earth."

"Lord, Your work is being richly rewarded. Several new ministries have started on earth."

Jesus realized that they were still standing and moved behind his desk to hear Michael's report. "Please sit down. I am ready to receive your report."

As Michael walked to the golden chair in front of Jesus' desk, he once again let the beauty of the Master's office thrill all his senses. Jesus' office was absolutely gorgeous and there were no adequate words in any language to describe it. The walls glistened with transparent gold revealing the splendor of the city of God. Next to the Father's office, Jesus had the best view of the entire city. The furniture was handcrafted by some of the best carpenters in heaven. Michael admired the profession in which Jesus was trained on earth during His early years before the ministry. The ornate pattern and design of his desk and chairs were out of the universe. He noted that Jesus had designed his office to make any visitor comfortable and completely satisfied. All of His furniture conformed to the body when anyone sat on the chairs and sofas in His office.

A beautiful rainbow of colors danced from the ceiling and swayed to the music that was perfect to his ears. Before any visitor could think of a need, angels would appear instantly to take care of it, but Jesus was the one that made His office so special, Michael thought as he sat down in the cushy arm chair. Just being in His presence was all the joy Michael wanted in heaven or earth. Jesus was so stunning that one flash of His smile lit up the whole universe with warmth and love. Michael coveted the times he could be in His presence. Just one Word from Jesus changed people or circumstances forever.

"I bring great news of a special heavenly visit between Dan, Vicki and Joshua Knight and the Holy Spirit." Michael handed him a folder.

Jesus opened it. "This is good news." He barely glanced at the contents and knew everything that the folder contained. "The Father will be pleased that the Knights have adequately supplied all the angels with the power they will need for the next attack of the evil one. Does satan have knowledge of the Devil Chasers yet?"

"Yes and no. He has assigned a fallen angel over the house of Knight, because he blames him for the communication tower, but he is still unaware of the Devil Chasers calling and potential danger."

"Which fallen angel?"

"Chemah, my Lord."

A small tweak of pain disturbed his heart. "He was such a big loss to the Father."

Michael thought about the angels that followed Lucifer in the rebellion and how it broke the Father's heart that they chose to believe the lies that Lucifer circulated in heaven. "It isn't like satan to assign a fallen angel to a family of humans."

"I see that Satan has received a report of the many souls that the house of Knight has won for My Kingdom, and their extensive knowledge of My Word. He is probably furious that he wasn't informed earlier. I believe the angels in charge of the house of Knight need a special commendation for being so diligent in listening to My Words spoken out of the Knights' mouths. I see in your report that the communication tower was constructed without any interference from the kingdom of darkness. The spirits in the heavenlies were not alerted in time and we have a stronghold established in My name. This is an excellent report!"

Michael made a note to carry out the Lord's command of a reward for the many angels guarding the house of Knight. "This generation is going to become a thorn in satan's side."

A look of regret registered on Jesus' face for the fallen angel. "It is time for chemah to reap the harvest of thorns that he has put in members of My body. No more thorns in My side!" He has been waiting for this generation for over 2,000 years. "The Father told me that this generation would see the former and latter rain that will bring great harvests. All the prophecies recorded in the Old Testament will surface. Chemah is going to suffer from being assigned to the Knight family."

"It is fascinating to watch the prophecies of Daniel taking place in this age."

"Yes and the world will see the great deceiver, satan, in his true form," Jesus said.

"What a shock it is going to be for them," Michael commented.

"The transgressor's life is a hard one. Satan chose his path."

"It is ironic that the very thing that caused him to lift up himself against You, is the one thing that alludes him now." Michael was talking about the devil's beauty and wisdom that was sealed with the anointing from God.

"He was the seal of perfection until sin was found in him. To cover the ugliness that has overtaken his spirit body, satan has to use human power constantly to maintain his human appearance. It was the anointing which he desired from mankind more than anything else."

"It must have been a shock when he realized that the anointing departed from Adam and all he was going to get was naked flesh." Michael remembered how shocked all the angels were when they saw Adam and Eve without the special covering from God. "Satan mistakenly allowed his true from to be revealed before his kingdom in hell. Several angels were on assignment in the fun center when they reported the emotional tirade that overcame him and his black hood fell off. He recovered within a couple of seconds, but not before several saw the ravage of sin on his true form."

"He still believes that he will defeat My Father," Jesus said as He shook His head realizing the futility of his plans.

Michael was aware of the fact that God didn't like to lose. "It's almost impossible to believe that Lucifer thinks he can change the Word of God!"

"The pride of his heart corrupted his thinking. He was given many chances to change his mind and repent of his evil thoughts."

Everyone in the Kingdom of God knew that God gave Lucifer several chances to repent and change his way of thinking. "The Lord God Jehovah is a God that loves to forgive and extend mercy and restoration, but He refuses to force any created being to repent. Satan will torture chemah unmercifully when he fails."

Jesus had personal knowledge of the fury of his enemy. "He sowed seeds for his own judgment when I was in hell."

"He did torture you more than any other fallen angel." Michael could hardly watch. "It was chemah's choice, my Lord."

"They think they chose the more powerful force; the force of fear and hatred." Jesus knew satan believed that God was weak because He was merciful. "His wisdom perverted his thinking and caused his downfall. Pride goes before destruction."

"Soon they will be made to know the truth." Michael with all angels was waiting for the trumpet that was about to blow, signaling the last battle when truth would prevail.

"In satan's failure, he will take many with him," Jesus said with sadness. He cried oceans of tears for His Father's creation that had been destroyed by pride that led to sin and death.

Michael felt Jesus' pain. "He will fall short in his efforts to cause the Devil Chasers to fail. The force of faith coming from the house of Knight is powerful. We have secured all doors, all possible pathways; there is no stone left that is uncovered. His attempts will not only fail miserably, but they will bring more souls into Your Kingdom."

"I trust you completely, Michael. I am excited about the rewards the Father and I will hand out at My dinner to the members of the Devil Chasers and the many others involved in this campaign."

"How are the preparations coming for the coronation, Lord?" Michael hadn't gone to the banqueting hall in a long time. The last time he looked into the room the tables were being decorated.

"The invitations are still going out." Jesus stood receiving a call from the Father. "Michael, take these reports to the tactical room. Make sure they are logged in and that the appropriate screens are programmed for these events. Tell all My angels that this report is exceptional. They are doing a great job with the Devil Chasers!"

Michael bowed and left the room.

Joshua sat up on the floor and turned to look at the clock by his parents' bed. Out the corner of his eye, he saw an arm he didn't recognize on the floor. Looking around the room and standing, he saw Kellie. Following Kellie's form he then saw Hannah in the doorway and behind her he saw a couple of legs out in the hallway that probably were Mose's. He didn't even know that they had come into his parents' room. His mom sat up with his dad and saw that they had guests. Behind her Kellie and Hannah sat up.

"Mom? Kellie?"

"Wow," Hannah pushed her hair back from her face. "What a trip."

They all stared at one another for a second trying to remember where they were. "That trip was a spiritual experience." Vicki tried to stand.

"What are you guys doing here?" Joshua asked.

"You invited us, remember?" Mose reminded him.

"I remember, but I don't remember letting you in." Joshua replied.

"The front door was open," Kellie said.

"It was?" Vicki stood. She looked over at Dan who was still down on the floor. "I'm sure your dad locked the front door."

The house was so big that they had made it a habit to lock the doors. There was a security system around all the doors and windows. A keypad outside and inside made it impossible to enter without a code.

Dan sat up. "I did."

"I promise," Kellie told them. "It was wide open!"

"Hm . . . I guess one of our angels let you in," Vicki smiled.

"The last thing I remember was changing clothes at home," Kellie looked at her watch. "Whoa . . . over two hours ago!"

"Hey, where's Mose?" Hannah asked.

"He's out in the hallway," Joshua told them.

Hannah went to the doorway and saw him sitting up with his head on his knees.

"What's up?" Mose looked half-asleep.

"Come on Dan. Help me get something to drink for everybody."

Dan was still sitting on the floor. "I don't know if I can move." He looked up and saw what looked like a thin cloud covering in the room.

"It's the presence of the Lord," Vicki said.

"I kind of feel like I'm drunk or something," Hannah announced. "And I'm probably the only one in here that has been drunk before."

Dan laughed. "Uh, I don't think so."

"Oh," she embarrassingly said.

"You're drunk in the Spirit," Vicki told her.

"Whatever, I've never felt like this before," Hannah replied.

Dan stood. "Get your Bibles and let's go to the kitchen."

Pastor Jeff walked into Pastor Ben's office after knocking and waiting for an official okay to enter. He wanted to talk to Pastor all weekend, but he was told that the Pastor was unavailable. Since it was a couple of hours before

Sunday evening service, Jeff didn't want to bother him if he was still preparing his sermon.

"Are you busy . . . I mean are you . . ."

Pastor Ben interrupted him. "Go ahead and sit down,"

"I don't want to interrupt your time with the . . ."

"I'm not praying at the moment."

It was hard to talk about all that had transpired in the last couple of weeks, but Jeff was concerned about him. "I noticed the Knights were not in attendance this morning."

He started to reply that he hadn't noticed, but that would be a lie. He did notice. He caught himself looking throughout his church all during his sermon trying to find Dan and Vicki's faces. "Yes."

Oh boy! Jeff thought. "You're not making this easy on me."

"There is nothing more to say about the situation. Dan and Vicki have made their choice and we will have to accept it."

"Several others didn't show up this morning either. What about the offering?"

"I don't know what the offering was." Ben answered honestly. He didn't know how much money they received, because he deliberately didn't ask to see the receipts. As far as he was concerned, it was going to stay that way for a long time. He and Linda decided to make some changes in the church operation and their own personal life. His ulcer and stomach condition was worsening and the stress on his heart was beginning to concern him. "Dan did officially resign from the board, so it is probably safe to assume that some of his friends will go with him."

"Yes, but how many?"

"Jeff, look . . . I don't know what is going to happen, but I am determined to put all of this behind me and look forward to the future that God has planned for my family, this church and myself." . . .

. . . in the corner of his church office, the snake and his new counterpart, the bear heard every word.

"Did you hear what he said?" the bear asked.

"I'm not deaf, you stupid idiot!"

Fury came over the face of the bear.

The snake realized his mistake and apologized immediately. "I was really thinking about that——vulture."

The bear understood. He never should have listened to that deceiving android. "Well, I see what you were trying to tell me."

The snake hissed releasing a string of cuss words. He was in a very foul mood.

"How much damage has he done?" The bear asked.

"I won't know until I listen and watch him."

"Oh."

The snake coiled his body and rattled his tail acting like the reptile that he was designed to look like. "But, that's what I've been trained to do. I'll just slither around and lisssten to every word he sayssss. Ssssooner or later he's going to get back into his flessssh. It might happen at church, it might happen at home, or somewhere else, but ssssooner or later every human opens a door for us through their flesssssh."

The bear decided it was time to terminate his association with the snake. He really didn't like the subtle nature of the crafty species anyway.

The snake snickered at his obvious exit.

‡ ‡ ‡

After getting something to drink and eat, Vicki took the group to their favorite family room and Joshua told everyone about his experience with his guardian angel. "It started the other morning on my trip with Kientay. He told me about the law of repentance. He directed me to read the book of Jeremiah and from there I went to Jonah."

"Kientay?" Kellie, Mose and Hannah said together.

"I met my guardian angel the other morning."

"Before we talk about Joshua's visit, do you want to discuss what just happened?" asked Vicki.

"Word! What just happened?" Mose asked.

"What do you remember?" asked Joshua.

"I remember hearing myself speak in tongues, but that's the last thing I remember," Mose said.

"Me, too," Kellie and Hannah spoke at the same time.

"I know we've been speaking in tongues, but I can't believe we've been praying for over two hours." Kellie had never prayed that long before.

"I think we entered the anointing of the Holy Spirit upon Joshua," Vicki told them.

"Like a time warp?" Hannah asked.

"You watch too many *Star Trek* movies!" Mose kindly reprimanded her.

"She might be closer to the truth than you realize," Vicki said. "I believe that there is a dimension of prayer that can remove us from our present time dimension."

"In my past experiences, I always thought a lot of time had passed, especially when Kientay took me on the timeline of times past. But when I get back to my room, the clock only shows that a few minutes have passed."

"Well, the Holy Spirit forgot to stop the clock," Kellie looked at her watch again.

"I've never heard of praying in the Spirit over two hours and not knowing or realizing it." Mose was concerned. "I mean . . ."

"I have to stop praying and walk around to try and keep my mind from wondering," Kellie admitted.

"I have never prayed over five minutes in my heavenly language ever!" Mose said.

"We have just entered the *Twilight Zone*," Hannah laughed.

"No, not the *Twilight Zone*, the Holy Spirit's zone," Vicki told them.

"Actually," Dan interrupted, "I have had a couple of experiences like this in the Lord before."

"I don't know about this . . ." Mose was wondering what his dad would say about this experience. "Uh, I'm sorry Mr. Knight for interrupting you."

"That's okay. It's good for us to test our spiritual experiences."

"Like, we don't want to get deceived or anything like that," Hannah said.

"I don't think this experience would stand the test of current theology," Kellie was starting to agree with Mose.

"The Lord told me long ago that His truth is not theology," Vicki explained.

"The Lord blows my theological thinking away all the time," Joshua added.

"Is this like being 'slain in the spirit'?" asked Hannah, preoccupied with this experience. "I've seen something like this on Christian television, but I've never experienced it before."

"For lack of a better term, you could call it that," Vicki answered her.

"Cool," Mose replied.

"But what is the purpose?" Kellie asked.

Vicki laid her pencil down. She had been writing notes for their first meeting. She moved over to the chair facing the couch. "I know that the three of you are aware that you are a spirit and that you have a soul that lives in a body."

They nodded at her confirming what she said.

"Have you ever gone to sleep praying in the Spirit and woke up praying in the Spirit?"

They all shook their head no.

"Okay, let me try another approach. Your spirit mind knows things that your head doesn't. God is a Spirit and the Bible says that they that worship the

Lord worship Him in Spirit and in truth," Vicki said. "Do you understand your prayer language?"

Again their response was no.

"Then wouldn't it be safe to say that there may be a level of prayer that your head and body wouldn't understand?"

"Uh, Mrs. Knight, then being slain in the spirit is worshipping the Lord with our spirit with a loss of consciousness?" Hannah asked.

"Some people have reported a loss of time and awareness; others say that they remember everything that was said and all that was going on around them. I really don't think that we can classify any spiritual experience with specific phenomenon that happens every time," Vicki explained.

Dan added, "As long as you are seeking God and His way of doing things, He will not let you experience anything bad."

"I believe that," Hannah said. "Mr. Knight, what was your experience?"

"I was praying in the Spirit and lost all track of time. My secretary came in and told me I was going to miss court. I would have sworn it had only been about five minutes instead of the hour that had passed."

"I'm still wondering what is the purpose?" asked Kellie. "I mean not knowing what we are saying and the loss of time?"

"We won't always know the purpose," Vicki told her. "The Holy Spirit directs us to pray when someone else needs help. We don't have to know all the particulars about the situations."

"And we don't always need to know other people's business," Joshua added.

"Yeah, like, my grandmother says that the Lord has her praying for missionaries around the world at all times, day or night," Hannah said. "You never know if one might have a head hunter chasing them or something."

Mose shook his head and rolled his eyes.

"Remember what John tells us to do in I John 4:1." Vicki turned the pages of her Bible. "Beloved, do not believe every spirit, but test the spirits, whether they are of God; because many false prophets have gone out into the world."

"How do we test the spirits?" Kellie asked.

"It depends on how they manifest," Vicki replied.

"If an angel appears to you and says that he serves the Lord of Hosts, both demons and angels can say that, so you would need to question them," Dan said.

"Is that what you did?" Kellie asked Joshua.

"I knew it was Jesus and the same with Kientay."

Hannah asked. "Haven't a lot of denominations started because an angel appeared to them?"

Vicki explained, "If they deny that Jesus is the second person of the Trinity and came in the flesh, then we call them cults."

"And if they deny the Holy Spirit, too," Joshua added.

Dan explained, "but remember not all people know exactly how their religion was started."

"Yeah, my dad told me that most religions change their message and their mode of operation to fit the times," Mose commented.

"But how do you know the good angels from the bad?" Hannah asked.

"They will usually deny some part of the Bible," Vicki explained.

"Or they will add or take away from the written Word," Dan added.

"The best way is to know the Word and judge everything from the law of love," Vicki said. "Most cults have some rule that violates the law of love."

"Mom, don't forget the law of life in the Anointed Jesus."

"Can demons look like angels?" Mose asked.

"The Bible tells us that satan and his workers can appear as angels of light and beautiful humans," Dan replied.

"Then not every angel is of God?" Hannah asked.

"That's right," Dan said. "Many have been deceived into thinking they are talking to angels sent by God and they are really demons or fallen angels sent by satan."

"Man, it makes you wonder . . ." Mose talked out loud.

"Wonder what?" Joshua asked.

"Excuse me. I was talking to myself," Mose told him. "But are we really ready to chase demons?"

Chemah and shathah sat in the tree headquarters that use to belong to metraloas. It was almost impossible to look into the cloud of glory that surrounded the house.

"Are you sure that we are at the right house?" shathah asked.

With an evil eye, chemah stared down the android. "Don't even go there." He was in no mood to put up with stupid questions. Being assigned to a low-level android position was like a demotion and a royal put-down in the kingdom of satan, even though he knew that the house of Knight has turned out to be a very dangerous human assignment.

"What do you think they are doing?" shathah asked.

"Are you totally ignorant at the meaning of that cloud?"

"I've never seen one like that before! I usually only see the inside of a smoke, filled bar, but I can see everything that is going on in that place . . ."

"Shut up!"

Shathah clamped his mouth once he saw the red in chemah's eyes. It was a lot darker than his skin and even though he had the look and the body of a superman, his deformed hand kept every being from wanting to ignite his anger.

"If you are like that perverse android metraloas then I'm going to terminate you now," he pointed his arm weapon at his face.

Shathah guarded his face with his arm and shouted, "I am nothing like him!"

"Then shut your mouth while I think!" It was imperative for him to come up with a plan. "As long as that glory cloud stays around the house we are wasting our time here. That cloud tells us that one of the three, either God the Father, God the Son, or God the Holy Spirit is manifesting Himself."

"How are we going to overcome them with that covering?"

"I don't know, but by satan I will find a way!"

‡ ‡ ‡

"We are more than ready to chase demons!" Joshua answered passionately, "We overcome demons, evil spirits, fallen angels and anything else in the kingdom of darkness by the Blood of the Lamb and His Word coming out of our mouth!"

"Yeah!" Hannah and Kellie jumped up with arm and fist lifted in the air like they were going to knock out the devil.

Mose was embarrassed when he realized what he just said. "Word! I can't believe I let that come out of my mouth."

"Do like Job did and place your hand over your mouth!" Kellie told him. She picked up his hand and put it over his mouth.

Mose acted like he just slapped his face and fell over on the couch.

"We all need to realize that we have the answer for anything the devil tries to do to us," Vicki picked up her Bible. "It's all in here. Everything we need. And God knowing what we would face sent the Holy Spirit to reveal to us everything He said and exactly what He meant."

They were quiet for a few minutest when Vicki asked if she could make sandwiches for everyone before church time. Hannah and Kellie got up to help her.

"Moses, you had a legitimate question. We need to know that you are ready to tackle the sometimes dangerous situations you may encounter when you are talking to teenagers over the phone," Dan told him.

"If demons can look like humans, can they talk like them?" Mose asked.

"Good question," Hannah turned around to hear the answer.

"Girls, I can handle the food. Go on back into the room and listen." Vicki thought that learning the Word was more important than preparing food.

Kellie and Hannah sat back down on the couch to hear Dan's answer.

"The answer is yes. They can talk and sound like humans."

"Whoa!" Hannah cried out. "How am I going to know which one is which?"

"I don't know if there is a sure way to know except through the Holy Spirit," Dan didn't know if he should mention at this point or not that demon spirits could imitate the voice of the Holy Spirit too.

"Demons can imitate the Holy Spirit's voice," Joshua added.

"Oh no, I don't think I will know the difference," Hannah moaned.

"Don't confess that!" Joshua said sharply.

"What Joshua meant to say is give yourself and God some time. This is why we are talking together now," Dan said trying to put down a feeling of irritation. He had decided not to tell them about demon's ability to mimic the Holy Spirit.

"Excuse me, I didn't mean for that to sound like I was getting on to you, but when you say things like that, evil spirits are watching and waiting for open doors into your life," Joshua explained.

"They are watching me?" Hannah looked all around the room. "Like, right now?"

"Satan assigns evil spirits to watch people," Dan told her.

"Yeah, like preachers. My dad has to watch everything he says or does. He told me he couldn't make one mistake without the devil hearing about it," Mose told them.

"Are they watching when I take a shower?" The thought of them in her bedroom and bathroom bothered her.

"Hannah!" Kellie was embarrassed that she asked a question like that in mixed company.

"Like, I'm only telling you what I'm thinking! Come on! You can't tell me that you've never thought about taking off your clothes and angels watching you? Come on Kellie, it's never crossed your mind?" Hannah pushed her in the side.

"Okay, I may have thought about it once or twice, but I would have never brought it up in mixed company!" Kellie slapped her hand away from her.

Vicki brought out a tray of food and sat it down on the large coffee table between the two couches and chairs. "Can someone help me bring in the rest of the food and drinks?"

"Sure," Dan stood to help.

Now was a good time to take a break. Knowing Joshua's love for the Word of God, he wondered if Joshua was giving the team too much knowledge all in one or two meetings. It seemed to Dan, that the young people facing him were taking in a lot of revelation in a short time. At least he observed they all looked like they had an open mind to learn from the Lord. He was very happy with the teenagers that Joshua chose to make up his first ministry team.

Dan's part of the ministry was to make sure that he kept a discerning spirit for any weak areas in the flesh of the team that the kingdom of darkness could exploit. With the prayer group meeting during the week, he believed that the team would be adequately covered by the Lord. Application of their Covenant rights regarding protection and deliverance was a major role for him as a parent. All parents and adults should understand the spiritual war taking place on planet earth, he thought. He was thankful that the Lord had given them special insights for protection and security.

The more he was around the young people that formed the Devil Chasers, the more he was convinced that they were walking into God's destiny and call on their lives.

CHAPTER 31

Joshua slowly turned the combination lock after missing his last number the first time. Mose stood behind him waiting for him. One more time he tried as the lock opened and he took off his backpack and unzipped it. He looked around, taking in all the sounds of his new school. The hallway was crowded filled with noisy, obnoxious and barely clad teenagers.

"Hey!"

"What?" Joshua couldn't hear a word he said. Someone was screaming at the top of their lungs.

"I just said 'hey'!"

Joshua shook his head as he looked up to see what the commotion and noise was all about. Another person screamed "fight" and everyone ran down the hall to see what was going on.

"Welcome to public school," Mose proclaimed when he could finally talk to him.

"Where did everyone go?" he looked around to see the hallway almost empty.

"A fight in the cafeteria, probably."

"Is it always like this?"

"Uh, yeah, but not usually on Monday or this early." Mose shook his head. "Man, someone's gonna get kicked out for a full week!"

"Out of school?"

"Mr. Williams is tough about the rules."

"Tough?" Joshua put away his last book and closed his locker door.

"Yeah, I've never had a principal as strict as he is. He won't give any slack."

The school bell rang.

"Remember where your first hour is located?" Mose ask.

"Sure, my brain still works," Joshua hit his arm playfully.

"Se ya second hour."

Joshua turned around and walked into the chest of Justin Walker.

"Hey watch it you . . . Knight? What in —— are you doing here?"

He grabbed Joshua's shirt and pushed him as a group of upper classmen surrounded them.

Mose turned back just in time and saw Joshua pushed into his locker. He yelled at Justin.

"You know this loser?" One of the older boys with him asked.

"Yeah, he's my freakin' neighbor." He looked him over and then saw the folder in his hand. "Don't tell me you're going to my school, what happened? Did you get kick out of that ——— Christian school?"

"Let him be, Walker!" Mose ran back to help Joshua.

Justin started laughing. "Do you guys hear something?"

"Yeah, it's a shrimp!" Another laughed with him.

"A skinny black one!" Justin shoved Mose into his buddy who then shoved him back.

Another shove around and Mose stumbled over the foot of one of Justin's friends who deliberately tripped him. Laughter erupted from the crowd of kids gathering around the locker.

"Pick on me Justin!" Joshua moved between them.

"You are a little bigger, but I think you stink more." He made a couple of sniffing motions. "What do you think guys?"

"I think we need to show him who rules at our school!"

Justin grabbed Joshua's shirt and pulled him toward him. "I've wanted to do this for a long time now!"

"Hit him! Hit him!" The crowd started chanting.

"Don't do it, Walker!" Mose stood up and grabbed his arm.

"Let go!" Justin jerked his arm and his elbow caught Mose's nose.

"Hey, it's Williams!"

"Let's go, Walker!" A friend grabbed Justin's arm.

Justin put his finger in his face. "Next time Knight!" He pushed his book and folder out of his hand as he brushed by him. They all took off running down the hall.

"Break it up!" Mr. Williams sternly said to the crowd as they were scattering every where. "Everyone here is late to class and will receive a tardy!"

Joshua went over to Mose who was bent over. "Are you okay?"

"Is there any blood?"

He bent over to look. "Move your hand."

Mose stood up.

"No, there is no blood. Does it hurt?" Joshua put his fingers on the bridge of his nose and wiggled it.

"Ow!" Mose lightly hit his hand away. "That hurts!" Mose bent over and picked up his things. "What did you do to him?"

"Are you boys okay?"

"We're okay, Mr. Williams," Joshua answered.

"Joshua, how did you get a locker in the senior section?" Mr. Williams asked.

"The freshman and sophomore sections are full. I already asked the office," Mose told him. He noted that Mr. Williams already knew Joshua by his first name.

"I'll check it out, but for now you better try to stay clear of some of those seniors," the principal said as he turned around to clear the halls of students.

"I'll try, Mr. Williams."

"So, what's the deal?" asked Mose.

"Tell me and we'll both know." Joshua brushed off his books as they walked to the office to get their tardy slips.

"I bet you've been praying for Justin."

"Yes."

"You think he'll ever get saved?"

"The trouble is he already thinks he is saved."

"No kidding?"

"I never kid about salvation," Joshua said as they entered the office. "Justin probably did accept Jesus when he was a kid, but he didn't transform his mind to the Word."

He rolled his eyes. He keeps forgetting how Joshua takes every word he says seriously. "It's just a phrase," he said talking about the word kidding. Leaving the office, he apologized to Joshua.

"Hey, don't concern yourself. Justin has tried to make my life miserable ever since I first met him."

"I don't want you to get a bad impression of the way things are around here."

"I'm not totally ignorant, Mose, I knew this wouldn't be a walk in the park."

A walk in the park? Man, he sounds like someone from an older generation, Mose thought as he lightly rubbed his nose. He was trying to decide if it was broken or not. "Later, Joshua," He walked the opposite way from Joshua. *What a bad beginning for a guy who had never been to a public school before today.* Mose shook his head; *I hope he doesn't talk too much in his classes.* He hated to see kids make fun of Joshua. But then again, ever since he began spending so much time with Joshua, there had never been a dull moment.

It didn't look like that was going to change any time soon.

‡ ‡ ‡

"Vicki, I have to tell you how blessed I've been since we've started these morning prayer meetings." Evie stood just outside of Vicki's front door and hugged her. "I am so glad the Lord prompted you to call me. I don't feel the loneliness I felt when my Tom went to be with the Lord."

"For years, I have prayed by myself," Joan added. "There is such a joy in fellowship with Jesus when you give yourself to intercessory prayer, but the joy in fellowshipping with other Christians is a great blessing to me that I never knew existed." She leaned over and kissed Vicki's cheek. "God bless you."

"God is so good!" shouted Vicki. "God bless and keep you. The Lord make His face shine upon you, and be gracious unto you. The Lord lift up his countenance upon you, and give you peace. See you tomorrow morning."

She waved goodbye. "Remember, in just a few days our kids start handing out their calling cards with the phone numbers."

Sheila waited until they all left to talk to Vicki. "Do you have a few minutes?"

"Sure. Let's go into the kitchen." Vicki went to the cabinet to get glasses for drinks. "What would you like to drink? Would you like a sandwich or something?"

"Water is fine, but no thank you on the food. I have something very important to ask you."

Grabbing a fresh cup of tea and handing her a glass of water, Vicki sat down at the table waiting for Sheila to begin talking.

"You know I told you that Wade is not saved. Well, I was wondering. Is it possible he might be demon possessed?"

"Very possible. Didn't you tell me he drank heavily?"

Sheila nodded her head yes. "He refuses to accept he has a problem."

"I believe that drinking definitely opens the door to demonic possession. When you are drunk, the normal safeguards against devils entering your body are not in operation. In fact, a drunk might as well stand up and shout, 'Come on in devil, the door is not locked.'"

"I think I can tell when a devil leaves Wade and when it comes back."

"How?"

"One way I know for sure is that his eye color changes and he gets this strange look. Then his voice becomes rougher and his facial countenance is different. I just know it's not Wade."

"I would say from what you just described, there would be no doubt he has demons. That's not all is it?"

"No. Since I got saved, well, things went from tolerable to intolerable. You know, getting by, to not getting by."

"Sheila, is he hitting you?"

Tears came to her eyes. "How did you know?"

"It's not hard to know." *I really didn't even need the gift of discernment for that deduction.* "Demons are not original. They use the same tactics generation after generation. When did he start hitting you?"

"After I got saved. The other day he found out that I'm coming here every morning. He told me not to come and he threatened me with violence."

"The next thing he will do is demand that you not go to church and not watch Christian programs on television."

"The Bible teaches wives to submit to their husbands. Was I wrong not to obey him by coming here?" Sheila asked.

"No, you are not wrong by coming here or by going to church, because demons are trying to block you from the things of God. Let me get my Bible and show you what I am talking about."

Sheila opened her Bible and waited for Vicki.

"Turn to Ephesians chapter 5 verse 22, 'Wives, submit to your own husbands, as to the Lord.'"

"That is the verse I heard this preacher use for submission. Is he right?"

"Paul is teaching about submission, but there is a key phrase here that many people don't see with their understanding eyes. Look at verse 25, 'Husbands, love your wives, even as Christ also loved the church, and gave Himself for it.' Now look at the last verse because it is summed up in right order here. 'Nevertheless let each one of you in particular so love his own wife as himself, and let the wife see that she respects her husband.' Now go back to the first phrase."

Sheila looked down at her Bible. "What phrase?"

"Verse 22, 'as to the Lord.'"

"What does that mean?"

"It means that you submit to a husband that is submitted under the headship of Jesus Christ. Your husband must love you with the love like Jesus. God qualifies that love. It's not sexual love, selfish love or controlling love. It's the kind of love that a man would give up his life for you, like Jesus did when he died on the cross for us."

"Wade isn't under the headship of Christ."

"Demons rule any person who isn't submitted to God. We have to be careful in understanding your situation. Satan is the spiritual stepfather of sinners. Jesus never submitted to anyone who was coming against a divine plan of God for His life or a violation of scripture."

"Didn't Jesus obey the law?"

"Yes. He submitted to the Law of God. He only submitted to the laws of man that did not violate God's Word or will. Several times He was in conflict with Jewish tradition. He never submitted himself to Jewish tradition if that practice kept him from obeying God. The Bible says 'that to obey God is better than sacrifice.' Several people in the Old Testament would not submit to a law that commanded them to break God's law."

"How did Jesus know the will of God?"

"He was in constant fellowship with Him. He sought the Lord with all His will, strength, soul, body and spirit. He had a tradition of getting alone and praying, or going into the synagogue and reading the Word and praying. He memorized God's Word."

"So we submit to God by praying and reading His Word?"

"Yes. You will never find a scripture where Jesus submitted His authority to demons until He handed His life over to the prince of death according to the plan of our Father to redeem mankind."

"I think I understand. Demons are using my husband to destroy my growth in the Lord and keeping me from developing a relationship with the Lord."

"If he is trying to stop you from establishing a habit of praying or reading the Bible and getting around people who are in the body of Christ, then those motives are evil. Praying and reading the Bible caused Jesus to grow and mature in wisdom, knowledge and understanding."

"But, I love my husband. I don't want to divorce him."

"There are always exceptions."

"How do you know those exceptions?"

"They are in the Word. If you have a husband who is not a Christian and he treats you with love, you should not have a rebellious spirit toward him. You can love him and submit to him and believe the Lord for his salvation."

"If your husband really loves you, he wouldn't stand in the way of your going to Bible studies and church, right?" asked Sheila.

"If it wasn't for the wicked evil spirits controlling him, he would probably let you go. In your husband's case, I think his alcohol addiction interferes with his love for you. Satan holds those who don't know Jesus in bondage and controls them with evil spirits."

"So it's the devil in my husband that is trying to make me submit and give me confusion about submission?'

"Without a doubt. He loves to confuse Christian women over the doctrine of submission. Don't get me wrong, there are some women that should be submitting to a loving husband and they don't."

"I think I would submit to my husband if he was a Christian."

"The devil wants you to disobey God and submit to evil. Jesus submitted to the law of God with love. God is love. God will never force you to submit to Him. That's the way your husband should treat you. He should never force you to submit to him. Women submit willingly to their husbands because of the love that is showered on them."

Sheila smiled. "I agree with that. Women will submit to true love."

"As long as satan is the spiritual head over your husband, he will never let your husband truly love you. But what is worse is that the kingdom of darkness is gradually replacing Wade's love for you with alcohol. The Bible says that strong drink is a mocker. That is why the situation is getting worse for you."

"I keep having the thoughts that if I don't obey my husband, then I don't love him."

"Those thoughts are from a demonic spirit. He his trying to keep you confused so you won't take authority over the demons in your husband. When it is a demon using your husband, and in control, Wade has no ability to stop what he is saying and doing."

"So, you don't think that he really wants to hit me."

"If he didn't before, then I think that a demon is angry with you because you gave your life to Jesus," Vicki explained. "And if it isn't his nature to lose his temper, then I don't think it is really him hitting you."

"I thought so."

"You know you don't have to be afraid of him."

"I never was afraid of him, but if this keeps up . . ."

"You have authority over fear through Jesus. Hate the demons in him, but love your husband. Love covers a multitude of sins and it is the way to defeat the demons in your husband."

"Then I should get mad at the demons."

"Get mad at satan's kingdom and love your husband. The key is to realize that you have to deal with the demons in charge of your husband. Don't think of Wade being Wade, think of Wade being used by demons."

"It makes me mad to think about how demons are destroying Wade."

"That's good. You need to get a holy anger against demons. Then you can stop them from blinding Wade at their will."

"So, what do I do?"

"First of all, submit yourself to God. Second, lean not to your own understanding, but pray and the Lord will direct your path. Remember, submit yourself to God and resist demons. And don't bother talking to Wade when an evil spirit is controlling him."

"Don't speak to Wade?"

"Speak to the demons in Wade and make them bow to the Spirit of God inside you. Remember, every knee shall bow and every tongue confess that Jesus is Lord."

"How do you make the demons bow?" Sheila asked.

"Use the power of God's Words and speak to them. Angels make them bow when they hear the Word of God coming out of your mouth. Jesus defeated the devil in the desert by saying, 'it is written.' Memorize the scriptures that apply to your situation and think about them over and over until they permeate every fiber of your mind, will and emotions. When you need the Lord to move for you, He will be there because 'greater is He in you than he that is in the world.'"

"When the demon leaves Wade he is a different man; he's the man I married."

"According to I Corinthians 7:13–17, if you stay with your husband, then you will sanctify him even though he is an unbeliever."

"What does that mean?"

"That means that your authority given to you through Jesus can be used to cover your husband with God's authority."

"Me?" Sheila asked as her eyes filled with hope.

"You. Whatever you allow, God will allow. Whatever you bind on earth, God will bind in the heavenlies."

"You said heavenlies not heaven?"

"The atmosphere above earth, or heavenlies, is where satan and his fallen angels live. Warring angels will bind those who operate out of the heavenlies when you take authority over them."

"Why doesn't God do it?"

"Jesus already did all He is going to do for you. He did it when He died, suffered in hell, then defeated satan, restored the Father's rightful place of authority over us and then gave us a choice to decide which father you want to submit yourself to."

"I remember you told us that satan is the stepfather of mankind."

"Since Jesus defeated him in hell, satan is only a spiritual father to those who reject Jesus or know nothing about Him. That is why He told us to preach the gospel to every creature in every nation. They don't know that the good news is that Jesus died for them, defeated satan in hell, and was resurrected from the dead so that we could have eternal life with our real Father in heaven if we choose Him over the devil."

"I'll choose Jesus any day over satan, but it sounds too easy." It was hard for Sheila's mind to comprehend what Vicki was saying.

"It really is that easy, but we have an enemy alien that has made it hard if you don't know your Covenant rights. God told us that His people perish because of a lack of knowledge. Take authority over demons and tell them to leave! The only way we can determine if your husband wants to continue to live with you is if he is able to make up his own mind without being influenced by the forces of evil."

"What if Wade doesn't accept Jesus?"

"Don't let him have a choice."

"What?" Sheila was really confused now.

"Demand that the demons leave your husband and then claim his salvation as part of your family! I always told Joshua as a little boy that he didn't have a choice but to love Jesus and then I told demons everyday to keep their hands off him because he belonged to Jesus."

"I wish I knew about this before my children were born."

"You know it now. It's never too late to start confessing the scriptures over them and to command demons to get their hands off your children and out of their flesh. Be diligent and consistent and you will start seeing a harvest soon."

"Will you pray with me?" Sheila asked.

"Do you want to ask the Lord if you are to stay with Wade?"

"No. I know I love him. I know that the real Wade Coyle loves me too. I see it in him when the demon comes out of him." Sheila started crying. "He told me he has such rage and anger! Sometimes he doesn't know what to do! I know it's the demon in him that is making him hit me. Before I got saved, he was a weak, crying drunk. When the demon takes over him, he is a mean, angry and very strong drunk."

Vicki took Sheila's hands. She was moved with compassion for her. "I'll pray and be in agreement with you. Remember that you have to be in total agreement with everything that I say. If you have any doubts then let me know. The prayer of agreement works only if both people agree exactly on the same things and believe with no doubts."

"I want to stay married to Wade. I want all demons out of him! I want him delivered from alcohol and saved and Spirit-filled!"

"Father, Sheila and I are joining together with the Holy Spirit in the prayer of agreement. We are claiming Wade Coyle's salvation, deliverance and baptism in the Holy Ghost with fire and power. Your word says that if we agree on earth as touching anything, You will give it to us. We are doing that now. We are in total agreement together that Wade Coyle is delivered, healed, saved and Spirit-filled, Amen."

Sheila opened her eyes.

"Stand with me. In the Name of the Lord Jesus Christ, we break your demonic power over Wade Coyle, demons. We claim his deliverance from the bondage of blindness. We claim Wade's full salvation in the Name of the Lord Jesus. Demons, release your hold on him now!"

"Amen!" Sheila said wiping her eyes. "I agree with Vicki."

Vicki took hold of Sheila's hands and squeezed them. "If thoughts come to your mind and give you any doubts, tell that demon that he is a liar and to get behind you. Command those thoughts to be gone. Then, reaffirm your faith in the prayer we just prayed by giving Jesus thanks for saving your husband and setting him free."

Sheila hugged Vicki, "Thank you. How can I ever repay you?"

"By loving Jesus and growing in His Word daily and don't forget to pray for our children every day. Develop a close walk with Him. That's all the thanks I will ever need!"

‡ ‡ ‡

Hannah, Mose and Joshua walked the half a mile from the high school to the Hut to eat lunch. Hannah wanted them to confirm the juicy gossip that she heard from various friends at school.

"Like, I missed it!" Hannah exclaimed as they sat at their usual booth.

"Next time, you can take my place," Mose rubbed his nose lightly.

"You didn't miss anything, Hannah, it wasn't very exciting," Joshua told her.

"I miss Kellie," she sighed as she ordered her usual salad.

The waitress took the other orders and left their table.

"I miss the rides she gives us," Mose added.

"Serves you right for all the complaining you do every time you get into her car!" Hannah said with a huff.

"I don't complain! It's Joshua that's . . ."

Hannah interrupted Mose, "Don't blame this on . . ."

Mose closed his eyes and put up his hands over his ears. He didn't want to hear or see her.

Hannah leaned across the table and grabbed his hands. "You're acting like a baby!"

"Listen guys you have to stop talking about negative things and be positive," Joshua said.

"Yeah!" Hannah agreed. "We still have some decisions to make before this week is over."

"This is our last week to plan and study before we officially open," Joshua reminded them.

Hannah let out another sigh, "I can't believe that we are going to make decisions without Kellie here!"

"You're the only one talking about making decisions and will you quit complaining about Kellie?" Mose raised his voice in frustration.

"No!" Hannah defied him.

"Trust me, Hannah," Joshua explained. "We are not going to do anything without first talking to Kellie."

"Good, especially since she came up with the idea in the first place," Hannah voiced what she heard.

"What idea?" Joshua asked. He wondered what Kellie might have told Hannah.

"Naughty girl," Mose pointed at her. "Pride goes before destruction!"

"I don't have the kind of pride that destroys a person. Get off my back!"

A little teasing was starting to turn into a full-blown squabble.

Joshua couldn't believe his ears. He bowed his head and started praying quietly. "Lord, I'm not sure what is happening, but You know. Please let me know what is going on and give them eyes to see what they are doing. I give You the glory and honor. All power belongs to You. I thank You that Your Word says that You are with us always. You said that You would never leave us nor forsake us. I am so thankful for Your Word."

Hannah and Mose stopped squabbling when they noticed that Joshua's head was down with his hands on his forehead.

"Are you okay?" Hannah asked.

Joshua didn't hear them.

"Joshua!" Mose said a little louder.

He looked up just as the waitress delivered their food.

"Anything wrong?" Mose asked.

"I'm fine. Mose, pray and let's eat."

They were quiet as they began eating.

Mose put down his hamburger. "Okay, what's up?"

"Are you upset with us?" Hannah asked.

"Do you really want to know?"

"Yes." They said together.

He placed his fork to the side of his plate and took a deep breath. "Your little squabbles and put-downs are opening doors for attacks from the kingdom of darkness. You have violated so many scriptures in the last fifteen minutes that it would be impossible to go over all of them with you in the amount of time we have left in our lunch break. The consequence of this habit that you are forming between each other is going to eventually harden your heart and it will definitely quench the Holy Spirit. If it keeps up, then I will not be able to eat lunch with you."

Hannah's mouth dropped open and Mose's eyes widened. For the first time that Mose could remember, he was totally speechless.

"Wow! That was straight up," Hannah looked at Mose. "I think that

Joshua is right, and I want to apologize to you, Mose. I definitely don't want to open any doors to demons. She looked at Joshua. "I want to eat with you because I learn so much from you."

"That's cool. You said what I was going to say and I am sorry for arguing with you Hannah. And Joshua will you forgive us?"

"Yes. It's already forgiven and forgotten." Joshua picked up his fork and returned to his salad.

Mose and Hannah's appetites left them.

"Mose, I don't want to give you a canned apology, so please forgive me. We can't keep nipping at one another."

Nipping? Mose started to say something about her choice of words, but he decided to be quiet instead.

"I don't want to seem harsh, but what we're getting ready to do is very serious. It may even be the difference between life and death." Joshua sounded very grown up when he talked serious. He knew how he was sounding, but at the moment he didn't care. There was a lot more at stake than his reputation.

"Death?" Mose asked.

"Yes."

"Uh . . ." Hannah thought for a second. "Natural death or spiritual death?"

"You better pray to God you NEVER experience spiritual death." Joshua stopped eating. "If you experience spiritual death, then that means you have gone to hell."

"Can we go to hell after being born again?" Hannah asked.

Joshua stood after looking at his watch. "We don't have time to talk about this now."

Mose and Hannah ran after him after grabbing as much of their food as they could.

"Come on Joshua give us a clue," Mose asked him as they walked back to school.

"Read Hebrews Chapter 6:1–6." . . .

. . . Kientay, Malcolm, and Chloe, the guardian angels, followed the somber students as they walked back to school. They were all dressed in human clothes, jeans and shirts or blouses; they looked like high school students.

"Your charge," Malcolm stated, "surely put mine in his place."

"It was about time," Chloe added.

"I wondered how long Joshua would take all that idle chatter," Kientay commented.

"Did you see the watchers straining their heads to hear?" Chloe asked.

"I saw them," Malcolm told her.

"I saw that chemah has assigned two more watchers to Joshua," Kientay added.

"Well," Malcolm added, "from what I've heard out of Joshua's mouth so far, I think he could assign 300 watchers and it won't do him any good."

"I agree," Chloe said. "Do you think Joshua will answer her question?"

"The one about going to hell after the spirit has been born again?" Kientay asked as they walked into the hall of Lincoln High School with their charges.

"Yes."

"As soon as he gets an opportunity, he will address her question."

Malcolm followed Moses. "Later guys."

Chloe stood by Hannah who was still talking to Joshua. She looked over at Kientay. *Why do we guardian angels assigned to teenagers like talking and looking like our charges?* She was thinking about Malcolm's choice of words and how they have changed since he was assigned to Moses Pearson.

Because we've learned to add a little interest to our life on earth.

She looked over at Kientay and stared at him. *I thought it was because we can sometimes fool a low-level demon.*

He wondered why she was using her mind to communicate with him instead of her voice. "Well, that too." . . .

. . ."Hannah, I don't think this is the right place to talk now." He didn't want to be rude, He looked around to see if he could see Justin. He wasn't afraid of him, but he decided to heed Mr. Williams's advice. He was going to try and avoid him.

She followed him. "I just feel so bad right now."

He shut his locker door and turned to go to his fifth hour class. "Your feelings are hooked up with your flesh. Do you have a flesh scripture memorized?"

"Yes." She was following him as she quoted it. "Those who are in the flesh cannot please God."

"Good. Now quote it out loud several times until your flesh lines up with the Word of God."

"Those who are in the flesh cannot please God."

"Again."

"Those who are in the flesh cannot please God."

"Hannah."

"Those who are in the flesh cannot please God."

"Hannah!" Joshua stopped in front of his class.

"Those are in the flesh . . ."

Joshua shook her slightly. "Hannah, the bell just rung, you have to go to class."

"This is my class."

"You have this hour with me?"

"Do you have Biology?"

He looked at his schedule. "Yes."

"Are you sure? I don't think we have any freshmen in this class."

Justin walked up behind him and flipped Joshua's hat off his head. "She is right, nerd! Only seniors and juniors are in this class."

He grabbed his hat and quickly put it in his backpack. He was sure.

Joshua entered the class and gave his schedule to the teacher. He added his name to the roster and told him to take the only seat available in the room.

Right next to Justin Walker.

CHAPTER 32

Vicki searched the students exiting the high school. She had to cast her cares on Jesus three times after her morning prayer session. Every time she thought that she was worry free about Joshua attending a public school, she found herself entertaining several thoughts about him. She saw him coming through the doors talking to a girl.

Joshua opened the car door, "Mom, do you mind if Hannah comes home with us?"

"Of course not."

"Thank you, Mrs. Knight." Hannah got in the back seat.

Vicki waited a few minutes before she asked the big question. "How was your big first day?"

Joshua thought about the exact word he wanted to use. "It was . . . interesting."

"What does that mean?" She pulled away from the circular drive.

Hannah decided to keep quiet and listen to Joshua's answer. She knew that his fifth hour wasn't very fun. Throughout the whole hour Justin gave him an evil eye at every opportunity. Joshua seemed to be unaffected, but how he ignored Justin, she had no idea.

He knew that his mom wanted a minute-by-minute run down of everything that happened to him, but he really didn't want to talk about school. "Mom, everything was great. When anything happens that is worth talking about, I'll let you know."

Vicki read between the lines. She pulled up to the gate of their home and put in the security code. From experience she knew that it was impossible to talk to him when he didn't want to. If she would endure with patience, he would eventually come to her and talk.

He always did.

Walking past Joshua's old locker, Kellie stopped. She pictured in her mind the many times that they met at that locker after school and she gave him a ride home. Several times she would stay over his house and they would study the Bible or do homework. They weren't girlfriend and boyfriend, just good friends. They both started school together when it first opened. He entered school after being home schooled all of his life and was a couple of grades ahead of everyone else. Since she was two years older than him, they had a lot of classes together. His parents wanted him to develop his social skills, so they had a special reason to help build the new church school, especially since he didn't have any siblings.

It was so hard to believe that after a few years he was gone. She turned to walk out the front door when she heard her name called.

"Kellie," Pastor Jeff called out to her.

"Hi, Pastor Jeff. I was leaving school."

"I saw you standing by Joshua's locker."

"Yeah, it's kinda hard to believe he's not here."

"I need to talk to you. Do you have time to talk to me in my office?"

"Uh . . ." Kellie looked at her watch. She wanted to go by Joshua's house and see how his first day went before she was suppose to pick up her sister from basketball practice. "I guess I have a few minutes."

He closed the door to his office because he didn't want Ann to eavesdrop. Kellie sat on the chair across from his desk grabbing her long hair and putting it behind her shoulder. She could almost sit on the ends of her hair and by the end of the day she was tired of it getting into her face.

"I heard about a club that Joshua is starting. Uh, what is the name?" He didn't forget the name. He just wanted to see if Kellie knew anything about it.

"The Devil Chasers."

"That's what I heard. What's it all about?"

Kellie didn't think it would hurt to tell Pastor Jeff, since they were going to officially open the phone lines next week any way. "It's a phone line for teenagers."

"Why the name Devil Chasers?"

"Joshua believes that is the name that the Lord gave him."

"The Lord?"

"Pastor Jeff, don't you think you should talk to Joshua about this and not me?"

"Why, is it a secret organization?"

"Of course not!"

"I was just wondering if there was anything to be concerned about. I mean, I'm hearing so many strange things lately. I wanted to get some facts together before I talk to him."

"What strange things?"

"You know like a lot of talk about satan, demons, and witches . . . things that the Bible expressly forbid us to get involved in or have anything to do with; things from satan's kingdom."

"It's a prayer ministry."

"Then why are you chasing devils?"

"We're going to be praying with kids over the phone. Our prayers are going to chase demons away from the callers. We should be recovering people from his kingdom."

"What you are really doing is playing with fire and someone is going to get burned. You know satan won't take it sitting down if you start disturbing his kingdom."

Kellie couldn't believe what Pastor Jeff was saying. *What are you thinking?* She asked herself as she began to feel uncomfortable about being in his office. "You know what it's like at the public schools."

"Of course, I know what it's like! That's why we voted to start a church school. If everyone was as involved with the youth of this city as I am, then the public schools might be operating under a Christian influence instead of the atheistic humanism level that it's operating under now," he stood because she stood.

"Then you know that demons are not sitting down and that everyday they take hundreds maybe even thousands of teens to hell to be with them forever."

"I don't know what Joshua is going to teach you and that is a very big concern to me!"

"The Devil Chasers' only mission is to get the gospel of Jesus to teenagers outside of the physical church. You know, help them to read the red print in the New Testament. And if 'they' and anybody else thinks differently, then 'they' don't know what 'they' are talking about." Kellie replied with attitude. She turned to leave because if she stayed any longer she might get mad.

"Wait a minute, Kellie, I didn't mean to offend you. I'm not saying those things. I just hear them and report then to Pastor Ben if necessary."

"Don't you go to church on Sunday and youth group on Wednesday?" Kellie asked dispassionately.

"You know I do. That's what I was hired to do!" Pastor Jeff took offense.

"There are about 1,000 kids at this school, pre-k through the 12th grade and there are over 2,000 students at Lincoln High School with just four grades and most of them are unbelievers!"

"Your point is?"

"My point is that most of our youth meetings are for believers and

Joshua has a vision to take church to the kids on the outside. And that is all there is to it."

"Are you sure?" He moved closer and put his hand on her arm gently.

She looked down at his hand. "I think I better go now."

He put pressure on her arm and turned her toward him. "Wait, one more question. I noticed that Joshua wasn't at our church Sunday."

Kellie was surprised that his hand was still holding her arm.

"Did he attend your church?"

No use not telling him, she thought, *he's gonna find out sooner or later*. "Yes."

"Did he tell you if they are changing churches?"

"No." She pulled her arm lose.

"But he did talk to you about going to public school, right?"

"Why don't you ask him?" Kellie was beginning to feel very uncomfortable. She put her hand on the door knob.

He put his hand on the door and leaned up against it. "I know that you are good friends with Joshua, and I am very concerned about Joshua making a big mistake." He really couldn't stand how much time she spent with Joshua.

"Pastor Jeff, you need to talk to Joshua." She opened the door hoping he wouldn't try and stop her. Feeling relief when the door opened, she walked out making sure that he heard the door shut behind her.

Ann looked up and was shocked to see Kellie walk out of Pastor Jeff's office. She walked straight through the middle of the two desks and out the side front doors without saying a word.

"Was that Kellie Todd?" Ann asked Marilyn.

"Yes."

"Did you know that she was in the office with Pastor Jeff?"

"Yes."

"Alone?"

Marilyn stopped typing. "Now don't make a big deal out of this Ann!"

Ann stood and walked closer to her desk so that she wouldn't have to talk so loud. "Not make a big deal?! He . . . they were in his office with the door closed!"

"So?"

"Marilyn, in case you didn't notice, Kellie is a 17 year old girl and Pastor Jeff just broke Pastor Ben's rules about single girls in single men's offices with the door closed!" Her tone was getting louder and louder.

"I'm sure that there is a perfectly logical explanation."

"Well, I'm not so sure!"

‡ ‡ ‡

Jeff watched Kellie shut his door with attitude and smiled at her. The feeling to pull her into his arms almost got the best of him. He went back to his desk chair and sat down. He had broken out into a sweat and his heart was beating fast. That was the longest physical contact that he had ever experienced with her. No female had ever affected him like Kellie Todd.

In the hallway earlier, he couldn't help but notice her cute little behind in her pretty tight jean skirt and her sexy, long hair. Even though there was eight years difference in their ages, he had his eye on her for two years. He couldn't wait until she turned eighteen. The first thing he was going to do was ask her out on a date.

He didn't just invite her in his office to talk about Joshua.

Hannah waited for Joshua in the kitchen. His mom was fixing them some raw vegetables and low-fat ranch dressing. She put her stuff down on their kitchen table and walked over to Vicki. "Can I help you do anything?"

"No, thank you. I figured someone might come over after school today with Joshua."

"I think the others are coming. Joshua said we ought to take this next week to study and get to know one another better."

Vicki set the tray down on the table. "Go ahead and eat something. You don't have to wait for Joshua." She looked at the short flowery chemise and her sandals. The weather would change soon and she wouldn't be able to dress so skimpy. "Do you have anything to change into?"

Hannah picked up her back pack and pulled out a pair of jeans and a t-shirt. "Where can I change?"

Vicki led her to the guest bathroom.

Hannah shut the door and turned around and looked at the most elegant red, white and black bathroom that she had ever seen. A red glass bowl sat on a black marble shelf with a long pewter faucet coming out of a black marble wall above the sink. Black and white large marble stone covered the floor. Shiny glass and modern art with red towels lined the walls. At the end of the bathroom a large glass shower with several shower heads with very shinny chrome looked at her. A large vase of red roses perched on a glass shelf in front of a glass window was on the opposite wall. She couldn't find the toilet until she opened a door and saw that it was completely out of sight in a closet.

Changing her clothes, her thinking switched from her surroundings to the lunch fiasco. She really couldn't wait to talk to Joshua and get everything out in the open.

‡ ‡ ‡

Kellie got into her car quickly. She couldn't wait to tell Joshua what just happened until she got a call from Mose asking her if she would pick him up. She had to turn around and go back to his school where he was stranded.

"Is that all that happened?" Kellie was a little put out with Mose that he missed getting a ride with Joshua. Mose had just finished telling her about lunch and she wanted to make sure that she got everything straight.

"That's everything. I've been going over it and over it. I really have this bad feeling."

"Bad because of what you and Hannah are doing to each other or bad because of what you think Joshua is thinking?" She stopped at a red light and looked over at him.

"I don't know. It's like my stomach is turning over and over."

The light turned green, but Kellie was looking at Mose when she heard someone behind her lay on the horn.

"The light is green," Mose pointed out.

Kellie took her foot off the clutch and the car died. "Sorry!" She looked in the mirror to see the person behind her giving her the finger and screaming at her. "Look at that jerk, uh, guy behind us."

As she tried to start the car an older car sped by right in front of them. It couldn't have missed them more than a few inches.

"Did you see that?!" Kellie screamed. "That old man just ran a red light!"

Mose couldn't speak, he just nodded his head.

The car behind them honked again and then, sped around them. Kellie sat there for a second as reality just set in at what happened. "We would have been hit."

"Yeah," the color drained from Mose' face, "maybe even killed."

Kellie turned the key again and the car started right up as the light turned yellow . . .

. . . Natsar flew over the top of Kellie's car protecting the occupants. Two warring angels stood in front of the Mustang and refused to let it move into the intersection. Other warring angels were fighting with demon spirits in the air above the intersection.

Malcolm and Marisa exited the backseat and joined in the fighting.

"They never give up do they?" Marisa said as a sword materialized in her hand and she swatted a bat out of the air that was flying toward Kellie and Mose.

Malcolm cut down two of the demonic bats. "No, they don't."

Green blood squirted all over the car. A couple of angels appeared with golden buckets and cleaned off the car in the spiritual realm.

Natsar landed next to the guardian angels.

"That was quick," Marisa said as her sword disappeared.

"It wasn't very much of an offensive."

"Did it come from their conversation during lunch?" Malcolm asked.

"Yes." Natsar confirmed what they were thinking. "Mose and Hannah are opening doors for these little pests!"

Malcolm and Marisa watched the car moving through the intersection. They transported themselves back into the back seat.

Natsar flew over the car and got close and stuck his head through the roof. "Be of good courage, the Holy Spirit has a plan." He encouraged the two guardian angels.

Their attention was directed back to their charges who were praising and worshipping all the way to Joshua's house. Malcolm and Marisa were grateful that at least their charges understood the gravity of the situation that almost occurred, and were giving thanks to their Heavenly Father.

‡ ‡ ‡

Joshua sat at the front of the kitchen table listening to Mose and Kellie telling them how they were almost involved in an accident. Earlier, he thought about what they were going to study tonight when he realized what a great opportunity it was to talk about their lunch experience.

"After we left the scene of the near wreck, my stomach settled down. Do you think that was the Lord trying to warn us?" Mose asked.

Everyone looked at Joshua when Vicki asked. "What do you think?"

Mose thought about it. "I think he was trying to warn us."

"Yeah," Kellie said. "I think so too."

"I've felt bad all afternoon since lunch," then Hannah remembered, "until Joshua told me to say a scripture over and over."

"I think this would be a good time to look at scripture," Joshua said.

Getting out their Bibles, Joshua told them to open them to James 3:16. "For where envy and self-seeking exist, confusion and every evil thing are there."

Mose looked up, "But I don't think what we were doing at lunch was strife."

"Why?" Vicki asked.

"It wasn't like we were arguing or fighting. We were just kidding, you know playing around," Mose answered.

"What do you think Hannah?" Vicki asked.

Joshua decided to back off and let his mother run this. That way they could get upset with his Mom and not him.

"I know that Mose likes to cut me down and make fun of me sometimes, but I see it as his need to make people laugh so that he will be accepted. So, I don't hold it against him. Like, if I really thought he didn't like me, then I would have it out with him."

Mose couldn't believe his ears. "You really see my teasing you like that?"

"Yes, I do. I come from a dysfunctional family, Mose, I know what it means to want acceptance." Tears filled her eyes and she quickly brushed them away.

Mose looked back at the scripture. "Then you are right, Joshua. I am in violation of the scripture because of the words 'self-seeking.'"

Kellie just didn't get it. "Are you sure that what they were doing was strife?"

"Let's look at the meaning of strife." Joshua got up to get a dictionary from his mother's office.

"I think in my heart I really know that I am seeking to lift myself up at the expense of her feelings. Hannah's just an easy target," Mose said.

"What do you mean easy?" Kellie asked.

"You know, like, the blonde jokes. She just acts like a dumb blonde sometimes," Mose replied.

"Mose, Hannah is not a dumb blonde. She is very smart."

"Hellooo? Hannah sang. "Did I leave the table or something?"

Kellie couldn't help herself and she broke out laughing with Mose.

"What?" Hannah asked.

"See what I mean, I don't mean to make fun of her, but she opens the door so wide, it's hard not to walk through."

"Did you ever think that I know what I'm doing and that maybe I am giving us all a chance to laugh?" a different Hannah answered.

Mose and Kellie were a little surprised at her response.

"You see, it's like this. It's not fun to live in my family. Living with a father that's a drunk; well, you never know what to expect. I've kinda built this image to cover up my true feelings. I like people thinking I'm a dumb blonde and Kellie is right, I'm not one."

Joshua sat back down and set the dictionary on the table quietly.

"But lately, I've noticed that I am getting . . . well . . . forgetful. And my mind sometimes wonders, and I'm getting a little scared that maybe I can't control it. You know this image that I created. I mean, sometimes I wonder maybe I am that dumb, forgetful blonde."

"You're not a dumb blonde, Hannah. I think it's exactly like you said," Vicki said compassionately. "You have a demon assigned to you that is putting those thoughts into your mind. Don't give that pesky little demon the time of day. Ignore those thoughts."

"Since this is confession time, then I should confess. I have this problem with my size. Ever since I can remember I've been the littlest and the shortest kid out of every kid in my class," Mose spoke out. "I learned real fast that if I could get the bullies to laugh, then they would lay off me."

"This is good," Vicki told them. "You need to share your feelings and thoughts with one another.

"I agree," Joshua said. "We need to know one another and why we do the things we do. You guys know me, I don't think like other kids my age. So I don't worry about what anybody thinks about me. I just figure if they don't like Jesus, then they won't like me."

"That's not news to us, Joshua," Kellie smiled.

Everyone turned to look at Kellie.

"What . . . oh, you want me to confess or something?" She put her hand up to her face and leaned over tapping a finger on her cheek. "My parents are Christians, I fight with my sisters once in awhile . . . I can't think of anything else."

"Okay . . ."

"Wait, I just remembered something. I am embarrassed to say anything about this, but I felt some feelings of jealousy toward Mose."

"Me?!"

"For three years now, I've been Joshua's best friend and yesterday I felt left out when I found out all that Joshua and Mose did together."

"I still love you, Kellie. You're like a sister to me," Joshua told her.

"Ahhh . . ." Hannah sang again. "That is so sweet."

"This is very good. Being open and honest with each other will help keep the demons away," Vicki said.

"Confess your trespasses or faults to one another and pray for one another, that you may be healed. The effective, fervent prayer of a righteous man avails much," quoted Joshua. "That's in James."

"I still don't understand why some kidding and joking around is bad," Mose spoke up. "I mean, there's gonna be a lot of changing in the way I talk and the words I use if teasing is wrong."

Joshua turned to the word *kid* in the dictionary. "Let me read the definition of the word *kid.* To try to make a person believe what is not true; deceive; fool; delude; hoax. To tease or ridicule playfully with jokes, banter, misleading talk, etcetera."

"What?" Mose put his hand on the dictionary. "Can I look?"

"Sure." Joshua handed the book to him.

"Word! I didn't have a clue!"

"You would be surprised, Mose, if you really did a word study about the subject."

"Lay it on me . . . uh, I mean, tell me."

"Ephesians five talks about 'walking in love, as Christ also has loved us and gave Himself for us'; verse four talks about foolish talking, nor coarse jesting, which is not fitting. Verse six tells us let no one deceive you with empty words and do not be partakers with them, for you were once darkness, but now you are light in the Lord. Paul says we are to walk as children of light. Notice that he didn't say that once they were in the dark, but he wrote they were once darkness."

"It only makes sense that if our power truly comes from the Word of God, then the words we speak and the meaning of those words would be very important," Kellie thought out loud.

"I think the more we search the scriptures, the more we might be surprised what we find out," Vicki said.

"In Titus, Paul talks about insubordinate, idle talkers and deceivers whose mouths must be stopped. He also says in chapter two verse seven 'in all things showing yourself to be a pattern of good works; in doctrine showing integrity, reverence, incorruptibility, sound speech that cannot be condemned.' In chapter three he begins again by reminding them to be ready for every good work, to speak evil of no one, to be peaceable, gentle, showing all humility to all men."

It was so quiet, you could hear the grandfather clock ticking in the foyer.

"Do you want me to continue? The Bible has so much more to say about words involving the tongue and the mouth." Joshua repeated everything he said from memory. He didn't have any notes in front of him.

"Joshua and I did a study of the mouth once. There were a lot of scriptures in Proverbs," Kellie added. "It was very interesting."

Joshua quoted several memorized scriptures. "Proverbs 4:24, 'Put away from you a deceitful mouth, and put perverse lips far from you.' Proverbs 6:2, 'You are snared by the words of your mouth; you are taken by the words of your mouth.' Proverbs 6:12, 'A worthless person, a wicked man, walks with a perverse mouth."

"Can I say something?" Kellie asked.

"Yes."

"Look in chapters seven and eight of Proverbs at what wisdom says; 7:24 'pay attention to the words of my mouth'; 8:7 'for my mouth will speak truth; wickedness is an abomination to my lips. All the words of mouth are with righteousness; nothing crooked or perverse is in them.'"

"What is perverse?" asked Hannah.

"It means to be wicked or deviating from that which is considered right or acceptable," Joshua told her. "Substituting the word bad for good is perverse in God's sight."

"Man, I hope you're kidding."

Joshua stared at Mose not believing that he just said what he said.

"Uh . . . I know. I know. You never kid." Mose lowered his head shaking it.

"Mose, we just looked up that word!" Hannah pointed out.

"Major slip. Man, I need time to change my thinking."

"Don't worry, Mose, I understand," Joshua told him.

"I think if the Spirit of Wisdom says that we should pay attention to wisdom's words, speak truth and speak nothing wicked, crooked or perverse; then it must be something that we need to do," Vicki said.

"Joshua," Kellie asked. "Do you remember when we found out that one of the definitions for wicked is naughty in a playful way?"

"I remember."

"Couldn't jesting, kidding or joking be considered naughty in a playful way?"

"I think so," Joshua answered Kellie. "Wicked can also be bad moral character which describes satan's behavior."

"In all of these scriptures that Joshua is teaching, you need to know who God is talking to and not do what most Christians have done," Vicki taught them.

"What is that Mrs. Knight?" Kellie asked.

"Most Christians look at these words, perverse and wicked, and think that the Bible is talking about the sinner. Don't look at it like that or you will never apply God's Word to your own actions and words."

"Who is the Holy Spirit talking to then?" Hannah asked.

"Is the Word written for sinners or Christians?" Vicki asked her.

"Mostly Christians I think," Hannah said after thinking about it.

"Are you saying Christians can be perverse and wicked?" asked Kellie.

"Yes. You can love the Lord and even be filled with the Spirit and say words that are considered by the Lord to be wicked, unkind, selfish, etcetera." Vicki explained.

"Man!" Mose realized that he had really never thought much about some of the words he spoke. "Now, I'm going to have to study and check out every word that I'm saying."

"Well, Mose," Hannah said seriously, "it's either that or be guilty of using wrong words."

"Besides, Mose, what about what Jesus said about words?" Kellie asked.

"Uh . . . give me a clue . . ." He was still a little put out over Joshua's attitude.

"I'm sorry. Matthew chapter 12:36 'I say to you that for every idle word men may speak; they will give account of it in the day of judgment.'"

"The Lord once told me that *idle* words are powerless words. We are to speak words that will release the power of faith," Joshua told him.

"So, we really do have to watch every word we speak." Hannah repeated.

Vicki answered her. "I think we really need to know if the words we are saying are something that can give glory to God and can edify and lift up the one that we are talking to or about."

"I agree," Joshua said. "In our ministry words are going to be real important. We will be the voice of God."

"How do you feel about this?" Vicki asked the group.

"Since we confessed to one another, now we need to pray for each other," Hannah said.

Mose sat there deciding if he was going to swallow his pride or wrestle with it. They were all staring at him. "I have to admit, I felt pretty annoyed with Joshua. Oh, shoot! I'm ticked off with him. I think that he is picking on me and being too hard. I can feel anger rise inside of me whenever Joshua challenges the words that I'm using. I think he is extreme and says and does some things that make me mad. But when I really take time to pray and think about what he is saying, I know in my heart that he is right and that I'm wrong."

Joshua started to say something and then decided to keep his mouth shut until Mose was finished.

"If God wants me to watch every word I use, then I will seriously work on changing my vocab, but I'm going to need some time."

"I want to add to what you just said, Mose. I'm really not trying to prove that I am right and that you are wrong. My purpose is to establish our ministry and fellowship with each other on the Word of God. I want to do things God's way. His way is the right way. His way is the only way."

"That's good enough for me, Joshua. Let's pray," Hannah said.

"Yeah, I think I will feel better once I pray for Hannah," Mose added.

"Since the half-brother of Jesus said that if we pray for one another, we would be healed; then we better pray." Kellie looked at Hannah. "I want to ask you to forgive me for getting upset with you for acting like a dumb blonde. There were a lot of times that it felt good laughing with you. And Mose, I really am glad that you and Joshua are becoming great friends."

"I want to ask Hannah to forgive me for cutting you down and lifting me up," Mose confessed.

"Let's pray." Joshua stood and went over to the middle of the room where they could hold hands in a circle. He waited until they were in place. "Lord, we want to praise You and lift You up. We ask you to forgive us for moving in the realm of our flesh toward each other. We love You, and we want to be like You. You want us to love each other as You love us and gave Your life for us. Holy Spirit guide us in Your Word because You, said that love covers a multitude of sins and the Word will cleanse us of all unrighteousness."

Hannah prayed next. "Lord, You said that those who are in the flesh cannot please God. I want to please You and love You. Forgive me for being in the flesh and getting angry at Mose. Please help me Holy Spirit to look at Jesus in times that I feel offended, so that I can remember that He paid the price for me and I owe everything to Him."

Kellie lifted up her voice to the Lord. "Please forgive me, Lord, for thinking thoughts against my friends. I really do love Hannah, Mose and Joshua and I want Your love to flow through me to them and those who call us. Help us to minister Your grace and mercy."

"Lord, I think You know what is in our hearts right now. Please forgive me for walking in the flesh joking and using words that cut people down. Give us wisdom to understand the words that we are speaking and reveal the attitudes and the real power behind them."

"Group hug!" Hannah put out her hands to everyone.

"Remember what Jesus said, 'This is My commandment, that you love one another as I have loved you. Greater love has no one that this, than to lay down one's life for his friends.'" Vicki told them.

Forming a circle, they put their hands in the middle and shouted; JESUS IS LORD!

CHAPTER 33

Wade Coyle entered his home full of whiskey, anger and demon spirits. He had gone to his usual bar after work and stayed until the bartender refused to serve him any more drinks. He hated it when they forced him to leave before he was ready. Normally, he wouldn't have even considered fighting the bartender, but before he thought about it, he swung at him. It was a good thing he was drunker than he thought because the bartender backed up and he fell to the ground. The bartender could have kicked the snot out of him with one hand tied behind his back.

He cursed as a couple of big men picked him up and threw him out the door. He stood up and fell down. Finally, standing on his own, he told them that he would be back and finish the fight. "You can't throw me out! You don't know who I am!"

"Yeah we do! You're a . . ." the bouncer spit a wad of tobacco at him, waved his hand at him and turned around cursing him. "They're all alike. Those —— —— drunks, not worth the time of day!"

"You guys were just lucky I had one two many . . . the next time I could teach you a thing or two." His speech was slurred and his vision was blurry. He lost his balance falling backwards and stepping on the side of the curb, he fell into the gutter.

Shathah materialized outside the bar and spotted him as he rolled over in the street to get up. Wade felt revived when the evil spirit entered his body and thought about going back into the bar and fighting the bartender now.

Go home, Wade. Shathah ordered him as he examined Wade's internal organs and functions. At least his bladder was empty, he couldn't control himself when he tripped over the curb and landed on the street. Just like a dog he relieved himself; his pants and his shoes were soaked with urine.

Shathah directed him home. He was anxious to start a fight with Sheila and rough her up. It was evident that Wade would have never made it home if he hadn't taken over driving. It was a little harder than usual because Wade's body was growing weaker day by day. Forcing Wade's eyes to focus, shathah was able to keep his car on the highway. The last thing he wanted to happen was a highway patrol pulling him over because the car was weaving back and forth.

In his drunken condition, Wade could have a fatal accident, go straight to hell and then Shathah would receive immense pleasure torturing him. *No, that won't work.* His smile faded thinking about receiving a new assignment. He would have to start at ground zero with another human and miss the opportunity for advancement in the kingdom of darkness that he has a shot at now.

He violently shook Wade's head as he was slowly falling asleep. *Wade!* He yelled at his unconscious mind. *You can't sleep now!*

Wade's eyes popped open.

Who would have ever thought that that this human piece of trash was going to be my way into a greater realm of power. This was the one that was going to make him important in the master's eyes. *I'm going to have a shot at the house of Knight!*

Erasing his mind of future thoughts, he decided to think about how great it was going to be when he could slap Sheila around. A smile came to his unattractive face. He loved the feel of flesh exploding against flesh and the smell of blood, but nothing compared to a female's eyes filled with fear. His plan was for Wade to eventually kill his wife. Then he and the other demons could make fun of the judicial system during Wade's arrest and trial. He wouldn't remember a thing and swear that he was innocent all the way to the electric chair.

Evil laughter erupted from Wade's mouth in a different voice than his. He was working hard to change Wade's personality to suit his goal. The nonviolent sniveling human was turning into a real man consumed with anger and violence. He was pleased with himself. Wade was becoming a wife-beater and soon murderer. Everything was going great except one minor detail; how was he going to get Wade involved with the house of Knight?

Shathah parked Wade's car in the driveway of his two-story house. He forced Wade to get out of the car and walk without falling over to the front porch. Opening the door, he let everyone inside know Wade was home. "Sheila!"

The living room was dark.

"Where in the——is everybody?"

The light on the stairs turned on and Sheila looked down from the banister. "You're drunk, Wade."

Shathah laughed inside him. *What did you expect?*

Unexpectedly, Wade's stomach growled. That was a sign to shathah that Wade's body needed energy.

Shathah spoke through Wade's voice. "What's for dinner? I'm starved!"

"Jared and I have already eaten." She walked down the stairs. "I'll warm up what was left." She was surprised that he hadn't passed out.

He followed her into the kitchen and sat down at the table. Shathah decided to wait until she finished fixing his body something to eat before he started a good fight. He had to stay physically strong to have a decent fight.

Sheila stirred the homemade chili in a pan on the stove. She got a bowl out of the cabinet and put some left over salad in it and placed it in front of Wade. She was glad to see Wade wanted to eat, because most of the time the bottle was all he ever wanted at night after work.

"Hmm . . . that smells good. Chili is my favorite." The smell of the food triggered Wade and aroused him from his drunken stupor.

Sheila quickly turned her face to look into Wade's eyes. She recognized it was Wade talking and thought that maybe he was free of the demonic influence. As soon as she sat down she realized her mistake.

"What in the——do you want?" Shathah stared through his eyes as his personality took over Wade.

She quickly stood. "Nothing from you!" She recognized an evil spirit was talking to her.

"What do you mean 'from me'?"

"You know what I mean?"

"You think you're so smart." He stabbed the fork into the bowl full of salad and then into Wade's mouth. Shathah cursed the limitations of the human body.

"I can do all things through Jesus Christ who strengthens me!" Sheila went back to the stove to stir the chili.

"Shut the——up!" Shathah cursed.

So, the scriptures bother the evil entity in Wade. She smiled as she placed a bowl of chili in front of Wade. It was important that Wade's body get the food it so desperately needed. The alcohol he consumed was destroying his cells and eternal organs. She was praying for the protection of his body until his spirit was born again. Sitting down across from Wade, she stared into his face. *This is going to be fun.*

Shathah didn't like the look on her face. He never saw a smile on the face of a female who was afraid of her husband. He felt like she had the advantage over him and he didn't like the feeling. Something was different about her. She radiated self-confidence. He cursed. *Of course it was that — prayer meeting!* He sensed her confidence in the Word of God. She must have learned something from the scripture that was planted in her heart and he hadn't been around to destroy the seed. "You went to that —— prayer meeting again."

"Yes." Her smile pierced his heart. "Don't you want to know what I learned?"

"No."

"Of course you do. I learned that because I am a child of God I can demand that the spirit of alcohol leave my husband's body NOW!" . . .

. . . POW! The instant the word left her mouth a powerful blow from a warring angel's sword came crashing down on shathah's skull like lightening.

He felt a strong force start to pull him out of Wade's body.

HELP! He cried out to other demons. Panicking, he allowed the other spirits inside Wade to join their power to his to overcome the power in the words she released against him. Other spirits outside of Wade's body came to their rescue to combine forces and hold off the spiritual attack . . .

. . . Resisting her command, shathah successfully survived being cast out of Wade's body. Changing his eyes to a glaring yellow he spoke to her using his own voice. "You're not as strong as you thought" He laughed demonically. "You can't do that Sheila. He doesn't want to quit drinking."

"He would if he knew that you were driving him to drink!"

"Ask him."

"Wade." Sheila pleaded. "Wade, talk to me."

His eyes went back to normal.

"Wade." She kneeled in front of him. "Wade, listen to me. Please say with your mouth that you don't want to drink."

It took a couple of seconds for his eyes to focus. He realized that he was sitting in the kitchen and Sheila was talking to him. "What?"

"Wade, think with your heart. You know that you love me."

"Love?" His heart started racing and it felt like the blood vessels in his brain were going to burst. All he could think about was a drink. He needed a drink. He put his hand up to his hair and brushed it over his head. He couldn't think. *What is Sheila saying?*

A drink. You need a drink. Shathah whispered as he stood facing his ear. That was all Wade could hear. *You need a drink.* It was so compelling that he thought he was going to die right then if he didn't get a drink now.

"Sheila!" He desperately grabbed her hands. "I've got to have a drink."

"No, Wade. You don't know what you're saying."

"What do you mean I don't know what I'm saying?" He cussed. "Don't you understand I have to have a drink and I have to have it now!" He stood and pushed her aside as he ran to the living room bar.

Sheila followed after him shouting "No!" She wanted to fight for him. "Wade, I got rid of the last bottle you brought home." She grabbed his arm and turned him around. "Please listen to me."

The voices in his head were still screaming at him that he needed a drink. They were pushing him to the breaking point. "Sheila, if I don't get a drink, I'm going to die!" He pried her hand off his arm.

"Wade, fight the feeling!"

"Fight? Are you crazy!" The pain in his head increased. His breathing became labored. He put his hand to his chest thinking he was having a heart attack. "Sheila! I can't breathe!"

"Okay." Sheila was talking to shathah.

He took over Wade and glared at her. "I told you."

"I am a child of God. Don't talk to me."

Shathah laughed at her.

"I want to talk to Wade."

Wade sat down on the couch clutching his heart and breathing heavily. "What is going on?"

"Your body has been taken over by a spirit of alcohol."

Shathah wouldn't let Sheila talk to Wade so he disguised himself as the belligerent Wade that she thought was the real him. "Not again." Shathah took a few seconds to calm Wade's fast-pumping heart and rising blood pressure under his demonic attack. "Sheila, you sound like a broken record. Why don't you give it up?"

He stood and turned away from her. He didn't want Sheila touching Wade. There was a soul connection between them because they were husband and wife, so he was always careful not to let her connect with the love part of Wade.

She stood and started to say something.

Wade held up his hand. "Please don't give me any of the religious crap now." He cursed again. "I'm going to puke if you say anything more about that God of yours!" The more cursing words he could get out of Wade's mouth, the more power he could enforce against her words of faith.

When he started swearing and cussing, Sheila decided to leave.

Shathah remembered something. "Where is Hannah?"

Sheila ignored him wondering why he would even bother asking. She left him to go upstairs to her bedroom.

"Sheila, I'm talking to you! Come back here!" He ran after her.

"I'm going to bed."

"I'll ask Jared."

Sheila stopped him. "She's at a friend's house." She continued up the stairs.

"What friend?"

Sheila ignored him again. She knew that the demon didn't want them associating with the Knight family. She walked into her bedroom and shut the door wondering if she should lock it.

Shathah ran up the stairs. For some reason it occurred to him that Hannah could be visiting the Knight family. *What a perfect opportunity!* He forcibly opened the door as it banged the wall. *She is my connection to the house of Knight!!*

"I will not fight you." For a fleeting moment fear tried to enter her heart.

"I don't want to argue with you now. I would like to spend some time with Hannah. I've been ignoring her lately." That was a true statement from both Wade and shathah, even though he had another purpose in mind now. "Doesn't Hannah need a ride home?"

"We've made other arrangements." Sheila moved to the closet.

"What?"

"Why are you so interested in Hannah? You haven't showed interest in the children in a long time."

"What are you doing?"

"Changing."

"You're going to go get her."

Sheila ignored him and sat on the bed putting on her socks and tennis shoes. "I'm going jogging."

Shathah got mad. "You're lying."

Sheila stood.

He released an intense desire for Wade to slap Sheila, when he noticed the red button flashing on the answer machine near the bed. When Wade moved close to her, Sheila flinched like he was going to hit her. Instead, he pushed the playback button on the machine.

"No!" She tried to stop him.

He pushed her back on the bed.

"Mom, this is Hannah. Umm . . . you're probably out jogging before dinner like you always do. I'm at Joshua's house. It's a long story, so I'll tell you when I get home. Mrs. Knight asked me to stay for dinner. Umm . . . I'll call you to come get me when we're finished. Bye."

Shathah glared at Sheila. "Stay here. I'll get Hannah." Wade walked out of the room, down the stairs and out of the house.

She finished dressing and ran into her son's room. "Jared, I'm going to pick up Hannah! I'll be right back!"

He was playing a computer game. "Sure, Mom."

She ran down the stairs, picked up her purse and ran out the kitchen door to her car. "Please, Lord, cause your angels to delay Wade from getting to Hannah before me."

Backing out of the garage she fumbled with her purse trying to find her cell phone. "Come on!" She dialed Hannah's cell phone as it directed her to the message center immediately. Her phone was either dead or turned off. "Lord, Jesus!" Sheila cried out. Anxiously throwing on the brakes and putting the car into drive, she clutched the phone drawing a blank in her mind for Joshua's phone number.

"Oh, Lord! Help me remember the number!" Seven digits came to her mind and she quickly dialed.

‡ ‡ ‡

Joshua stared at his parents who were laughing with Hannah. "I don't see what so funny about that joke."

"That makes it even funnier." Dan put his hand over his mouth and coughed.

"Just because my humor is different from other people doesn't mean I don't have any." Joshua laid down his fork. "Besides, you know what Solomon said about joking and jesting."

"What?" Hannah asked.

"'Like a madman who throws firebrands, arrows and death, is the man who deceives his neighbor and says, 'I was only joking!''"

"I'm surprised at you Joshua!" His dad acted offended. "Solomon wasn't talking about a harmless joke. He was talking about cutting down someone and then saying 'I was only joking.'"

The phone interrupted their laughter.

"I'll get it." He was glad to get away from the table. Understanding jokes was a weak side of his personality. They just didn't seem as funny to him as they did to most people. Some of the jokes he had heard were down right discriminatory against people. He knew that God truly did look on the heart of man and not on his physical appearances. He couldn't think of one joke that didn't make fun of some race or human differences.

Kellie was always telling him he was too serious about life. And now Hannah was getting to see a side of him that he wasn't so sure he wanted her to see. Why that might bother him, he had no idea.

"Knights' residence."

"May I speak to Hannah."

"Just one moment please." Joshua brought the phone to Hannah.

"Hello?"

"Hannah, your dad is on his way to get you. I've asked the Lord to send some of his angels to detain him. But just in case, why don't you be outside waiting? And don't get into the car with your dad. I'm on my way."

"What's going on?"

"I'll explain when I get there." Sheila looked up and saw the light turning red at the intersection she was crossing. She gunned the engine and ran a red light. "Oh, Jesus!"

"Mom, are you alright?"

"I just ran a red light. Baby, go ahead and tell Vicki that your dad got worse today. She knows what's going on with him."

"Okay."

"I'll be right there, honey. Forget about standing outside. I know that the Lord has sent his angels already, so don't worry!" . . .

. . . Shathah was speeding as fast as he could. He sent a spirit of fear to make chemah aware of the situation. He couldn't believe why he didn't think of it before. Hannah was the open door into the house of Knight. She was the key to an entrance inside their house and it was right in front of his face all the time. No angel can stop Wade from entering the physical house of Knight to pick up his own daughter, he thought anxiously.

Seeing bright flashing red lights in the car mirror, Shathah knew that a police car caught him speeding. Cursing angrily, he connected with a spirit of fear on the graveline. *Is he one of ours?*

An evil spirit responded. *No. He has no demons in his flesh nor do we have any androids masquerading as a policeman in the vicinity.*

Is he an angel or not? Shathah asked desperately.

He hated that angels could look and assume any role of a human just like demons could. But using their cloaking devise, they had the ability to hide the fact that they were angels from them.

The officer waited for the driver to come back to his car.

Come on . . . is this a human or not? Shathah hit the steering wheel impatiently.

The officer slowly opened his car door. He edged close to the car and stood behind the passenger door with his hand near his gun ready to use just in case. "Come out of the car, slowly."

No reading is possible. Treat subject like a human with the possibility of being an angel.

Shathah sighed. The officer was acting like a real human, not like an angel with authority over him. He had to act sober. With Wade's alcohol content level it was going to be difficult. He slowly got out of the car. "I'm sorry officer, how fast was I going?"

"Would you stand away from the car."

"Sure." Shathah shut the door and kept his hands and arms away from the sides of his body. He slowly raised his hands over his head so the officer could see that he wasn't going for a gun. It would be rotten timing to lose Wade's body now.

"I need to see your driver's license." The officer shined his flashlight in his eyes.

Wade's eyes looked clear. He slowly reached into his pocket and pulled out his wallet.

"Would you remove your license?"

He handed it to the officer.

"Sit in my car. I have to do a vehicle check."

"Sure thing officer."

Shathah was proud of himself. He was going to pull it off. He opened the door and sat in the police car.

The policeman typed in Wade's license number. He looked over at Wade. "The computer went down and we are going to have to wait until it comes back on line."

"Yes sir Officer . . ." He couldn't see his name tag.

"You know the radar gun locked you at 10 miles over the speed limit."

"Yes sir . . . Officer . . . ?" He waited for the policeman to tell him his name.

He looked straight into Wade's eyes. "Officer Natsar." . . .

. . ."You really don't have to stand out here with me, Joshua." Hannah looked at him as they walked through the gates to the sidewalk.

"You don't think that my mom and dad would let you stand out here alone do you?"

"I hope you know how blessed you are."

"You mean because my mom and dad know Jesus?"

"Yeah." Hannah looked down at the ground. She was trying to keep from crying.

Joshua could feel her hurt. "I do."

"I spend a lot of time with Kellie's Christian family . . . but your family shows me that Kellie's family isn't the only one out there." She turned away. "My dad drinks alot. The only time we have any peace is when he is passed out."

"Through Jesus, we will overcome the demon of alcohol in your dad," Joshua tried to encourage her.

"I know. It's just . . . I wish I could have a dad like yours."

"Don't waste your time wishing and thinking about something that will never happen."

"What do you mean?"

"I mean whenever you think about your dad, speak out loud that satan can't have his soul and spirit. Take authority over him every time a thought comes into your mind about your dad being a Christian. Speak out loud that he belongs to Jesus. You have to be very careful because you could waste a lot of time thinking about what your life could have been or what it would be like to have parents like mine. Demons are trained to keep thoughts like that in your mind so the Word of God gets choked out of your heart. That is their main work against us, using thoughts to become idols against God."

"Thoughts as idols?"

"Yes. Anything that keeps your mind occupied and away from God can become an idol." He looked up and down the street to see if any cars were coming. "When I first started attending Christian school, a demon sent a boy into my class with a sole purpose to make my life miserable. Soon, all I could think of was how much I didn't want to go to school. I thought so much about what he did to me at school . . . I couldn't eat dinner at night. I started getting sick to my stomach even after mom and dad prayed for me. It didn't take mom long to seek the Lord and find out what was going on. She showed me in the Word of God how I allowed that circumstance to become an idol by thinking about it all the time. I actually transgressed a commandment of God. 'You shall have no other gods before Me.'"

"How can thoughts be gods or idols?"

"If you spend all your time thinking about your circumstances instead of the Lord and what He has done for you, that is idol worship."

"Oh."

"Paul said through the Holy Spirit that no covetous man, who is an idolater, has any inheritance in the Kingdom of the Anointed One and God. Covetousness is to desire ardently or crave or long for something someone else has or something you don't have. That is how thoughts can become idols. I thought about what this boy was doing to me every waking minute. He became an idol to me."

"I never thought of it like that." His words were penetrating her heart.

"I didn't know until my mom showed me and then my dad taught me how to bring every thought under captivity of my spirit and the authority of Jesus."

"It's hard not to covet when I think about being robbed of a decent family life."

"Hannah, thank God for changing your dad and keeping your mind on Jesus. He is the only One that can meet your every need. No matter what your dad does, God can be the Father that you need if you let Him."

"How?"

"Covet after the Words of your Heavenly Father. Desire understanding and discretion from the Holy Spirit and on top of that, desire to be conformed to the image of Jesus. You won't have time to think about your situation at home. Soon you will be walking in that anointing that will keep Jesus first place in your life."

"Thanks, Joshua."

It was really hard for him to imagine what it would be like to have a parent not saved, but he knew that he couldn't speak to her out of his soul. He had to speak to her from his spirit.

"I . . . I don't know what to say." A couple of tears fell down Hannah's cheek.

"Hannah, there is hope for your dad. God doesn't base what He does for us through any other person, or emotion, or even need. He bases what He does for us on faith in His Word. 'Without faith, it is impossible to please God.' Begin speaking the Word over your dad and a task force of angels will be assigned to your family. It is only a matter of time before the power of those prayers will penetrate through the evil in your dad."

Sheila pulled up in front of the house. Hannah turned to get in the car. "Tell your parents thank you, again." She got in the car and rolled down the window. "I'll see you tomorrow at school. Bye." . . .

. . . . Kientay and Chloe stood in the driveway watching over Hannah and Joshua. It always filled him with strength when Joshua was a vessel for God to use.

"That was great," Chloe said. "I hope that Hannah was really listening."

"I've been a guardian angel over a couple of children in abused situations," Kientay remarked. "It's really tough."

"Once, I had a female charge that was being physically abused by her father."

"That must have been tough."

"It was awful. The Holy Spirit cried with her the whole time. The Lord God gave me many breaks by allowing me to work with children that were being taken care of in heaven."

"What happen to the child?"

"She made it through the difficult situations and God gave her a great ministry. He healed her emotions, memories and pain. He didn't give me more than I could handle." Chloe felt tears come to her eyes. "I don't know why most humans think we don't have emotions."

"Because if they have an experience with angels it's usually with warring angels instead of us," Kientay replied. "Warring angels are trained like the human military on earth,"

"I don't think so. Look at all that screaming and cursing they do at boot camp training!"

"I'm talking about disciplining their emotions," Kientay explained. "They are trained to mask their emotions."

They listened to Joshua sharing his personal story with Hannah.

"The other angels don't know what we go through here on earth," Kientay said as Joshua was teaching Hannah about idols.

"The Father's heart is hurt more over abused children than any other thing on earth. It's very difficult for me to hear humans blaming God for the evil that is perpetrated on children."

"I agree. But every abused child needs to grow up, get over it and forgive."

"Do you think that you could do that Kientay? Forgive? I mean if you were human and being abused, would you forgive?" Chloe asked.

"I hope that I could make the decision to forgive."

"Lucifer couldn't. He thought God abused him by not favoring him."

"Even if he felt God had done him wrong, he could have forgiven the Lord. But he chose not to forgive God because of his wrong thinking. He had long ago given up thinking righteously. God was never responsible for the corruption of his mind." Kientay didn't like to think about Lucifer.

"But he took an offense against God," Chloe reminded him.

"Satan was already too far gone in his mind to ever consider forgiving the Lord. Look at what he has done to this planet and God's children! He created rebellion and sin. He is responsible for the curse that covers this earth!" Kientay didn't like to think about God's forgiveness toward satan.

Chloe turned and looked at Kientay as Sheila's car drove up. "The Lord God would have forgiven Lucifer if he would have repented."

Kientay watched Chloe fly to the top of the car and sit down. Her long golden hair blew behind her in the wind and her beautiful white robe glistened as she drove away with her charge, Hannah.

She was right about what she said. Even though it was a hard truth to think about, it was true. He looked up and saw an endless black sky filled with twinkling stars repeating what Chloe said. God is love and He would have forgiven Lucifer if he had asked for forgiveness.

But Lucifer, day star and son of the morning, never sought God's mercy for forgiveness.

CHAPTER 34

Dan took his watch off and set it on his dresser. Vicki was in their bathroom washing her face and changing into her nightgown. Yawning, he took off his shirt. He had been on his guard all day. Several times during the day he took time to pray in the Spirit in his office. Vicki came out of the bathroom and sat down at her vanity. She started brushing her hair thinking about Hannah.

"Don't worry," he threw his waded shirt by the laundry basket through the doorway. "We prayed and they are going to be alright."

She told Dan about Sheila's marriage and home situation just before she took her shower. "Earlier this morning, you felt that an evil spirit was going to try to attack you. What do you think now?"

Dan walked up behind her and began massaging her shoulders. "Nothing happened to me that I know about."

"Good." He was right. They had given the care of Hannah and Sheila to the Lord and she should not touch it with her thought life. "What about your court case?"

"It went great." He went into the bathroom.

She followed him and stopped at the entrance of the door. "Nothing happened at all?"

"Nothing." He bent over to brush his teeth. His day had been routine.

"What about Mr. Gottman?"

He gargled with mouthwash and spit it out. "He was very good on the stand. He had proof from two witnesses that he recommended several other prints shops. Uh . . ." he wiped his face with a towel. "I think the jury will see it our way."

"Open and shut?"

Dan moved to his side of their bed. "Almost."

Vicki sat on the other side. "Almost?"

Dan smiled remembering the testimony of Mr. Gottman. "You know, I think his family living in Germany at the beginning of World War II helped his case a lot. The judge and several of the jury members were at least his age or older." He was very pleased at the jury selection. "The Lord helped me pick a great jury."

She removed the throw pillows from her side of the bed. "I know, you always say that the jury makes or breaks a case."

He removed the throw pillows from his side of the bed. "Court adjourned a couple of hours early today. "I didn't want to start my summation until I pray."

"I know, you always allow extra time to give your summation just in case the Lord changes anything you are going to say." She removed the bedspread from their bed.

Dan jumped into his side of the bed. "Why do I tell you how my day went if you already know all about me?"

She tugged at the sheet he was laying on. "I like to hear you say it, but you can correct me if I'm wrong."

Dan lifted his body as she pulled the sheet and blanket down. He opened the notebook of scriptures that they confessed every night before turning off the light. It was their habit to pray with one another until one or the other went to sleep.

Vicki got into bed next to him. "Wait a minute Dan, you said almost."

"I still have a small, tiny feeling in the pit of my stomach." He really felt that something was still going to happen. But he didn't know what.

"Do you think it has anything to do with Hannah?"

He thought for a moment. "No."

"Do you think we need to do some warfare praying?" Vicki started to get out of bed ready to hit the floor running.

Dan grabbed her arm. "Wait, I said it was a small feeling. I have a bigger feeling of peace. Let's say our scriptures together and then enjoy the peace of the Lord."

"That reminds me of something."

"What?"

"I invited everyone for a dedication service of the Devil Chasers ministry Thursday night. And the parents and kids are going to have a sleepover with us this weekend."

"Is that why you cancelled tonight?"

"Yes, I thought since we will be spending all this weekend together that we would have time to talk to the Pearsons alone."

"What if we don't get a chance to talk to them alone?"

"Then we'll visit their church one more Sunday and make up our minds after that."

Dan fluffed his pillow. "How are we going to fit all this in?"

"It won't be a big deal. I want Pastor Pearson to pray and to pronounce blessings over the team. Then, afterwards we can eat a small assortment of finger foods and have something to drink."

"Why can't we do this over the weekend?"

"Because . . . I am inviting other family members. I promise I won't go overboard. Besides . . ."

"Vicki, can we stop talking and say our confessions?"

"Just one more question. Are the phones and computers ready to go?"

"The computer programmer is coming over tomorrow to make sure everything is okay."

"So, we will be ready after this weekend?"

"Vicki, everything is fine. Are you worrying?"

"ME? Worry? You know better than that Dan Knight! I'm just making sure everything has been taken care of and that's all."

"Then let's confess and pray."

"That's what I love about you." Vicki set back and fluffed her pillow.

"What?"

"You always know when to quit talking." She moved in close to him and snuggled against him. He was her best friend and he always knew just the right thing to say.

Dan started their nightly ritual of quoting scripture. "I am a believer."

Vicki repeated each sentence after him.

"I go into all the world and preach the gospel to every creature. These signs follow me because I believe. In Jesus' name I cast out demons. I speak with new tongues. I take up demons and if I drink anything deadly it will not hurt me. I lay hands on the sick, and they recover." He turned to the section in their notebook labeled the authority of the believer. "We need to confess our authority over the kingdom of darkness. Let's start with Luke 10:19."

This time Vicki quoted the scripture first. "Behold I give unto you authority to tread on demons and evil angels, and over all the power of the enemy. Nothing shall by any means hurt you."

"Lord, we declare that we have the authority from Jesus to stomp demons." Dan declared. "Jesus delegated to me, as a member of His body, the right and the authority to speak in His name on earth."

Vicki loved the next part. "Listen to me, demons, I submit myself to God and I resist you and the Word of God says that you have to flee! No weapon that you form against me will prosper. Get away from Joshua. We deny you access. Dan, Vicki and Joshua Knight belong to Jesus." Vicki breathed in a strength that seemed to permeate her body whenever they confessed God's Word over them. "Jesus is Lord over the Knight family!"

"Lord, we submit ourselves to You and to the Covenant of peace, nothing broken and nothing missing. Thank you, Lord for sending angels of protection surrounding our property. Amen."

‡ ‡ ‡

Joshua was in his bedroom sitting at his desk writing in his journal. He was trying to remember everything he heard from the Holy Spirit earlier that day. Once again, he felt the exhilarating feeling every time he received revelation knowledge from the Holy Spirit. "Lord," he asked, "Do you like the name the Devil Chasers?"

I was the first Devil Chaser.

Joshua thought of the pictures in his mind that the Lord gave him about His victory over satan in hell. He saw the Lord put a yolk around satan's neck with a chain attached after the Lord became born-again. He took that chain and dragged him all over hell. Jesus openly showed satan's entire kingdom that He had conquered death, and that He is the Lord of every thing above, on and under earth.

I dragged the devil all the way around hell, but I had to chase him down first. He thought I was there because I could not overcome the power of death.

Joshua laughed. "I can't wait to see that day." He believed that he would be able to see Jesus stomp the devil from the pit of hell. He imagined it like a special family movie that all believers will be able to watch with the Father one day in heaven when everyone was together. "The day you beat the devil in his territory has to be the greatest day in the history of earth! It sure was a day that satan will never forget."

My body has the same commission from the Father that I did when I lived on earth in My flesh body.

"You came to destroy the works of the devil." He visualized a strong defeat over the enemy, through believers on earth. He saw the enemy like a blob of darkness run from believers and disappear into a teeny, tiny dot that was eliminated.

Joshua got into bed and turned off his light. "Holy Spirit, lead many kids to call the Devil Chasers phone line."

Joshua, you are going to have fun kicking the devil's butt.

Joshua smiled as he fell asleep. It didn't surprise him to hear the Lord say "butt." After all He was the Creator of them.

Outside the safe rooms of the sleeping family in the house of Knight, a cloud of darkness surrounded their property. The once clear, cool star-twinkling night became murky, and hidden as a swirling black mist blocked out their light. An eerie feeling permeated the air with the stench of sulfur like the familiar smell of rotten eggs.

Michael stood with the wall of angels surrounding the property of the house of Knight. The Holy Spirit sent him to warn the warring angels of an attack that chemah was organizing with the local coven from the brotherhood of satan.

Chemah told the demon that controlled the high priest of the coven to organize an attack against the house of Knight. Satan had ordered the termination of the family because they were causing many of his plans to fail with the newly organized intercessory prayer group. Humans were coming by astral projection in their spirits to try to destroy them.

Chroni appeared beside Michael and walked the ranks of the angels. The tall warring angels dressed in white robes stood shoulder to shoulder holding hands. Being forewarned of the attack, they were in position and ready for anything the enemy would try to do to them. They had faced similar attacks countless times. The occult members would try to break through the hedge of protection. The angels could hear Dan and Vicki Knight quoting scriptures before they went to sleep. They smiled knowing that this attack was futile. It was doomed for failure before it was ever planned.

All of a sudden, the skies above the house filled with human spirits. A clear dome of protection like plexiglas stretched from the bottom of the edge of one side of the property to the other side. The high priest screamed obscenities at the warring angels wanting to distract them, while others chanted and tried to center their power at the angelic hedge of protection causing a breach.

Chroni laughed. "Come on, give it your best shot!"

They could not concentrate and pool their power. It seemed to defuse when they tried to aim it at the angel wall. Confusion and disorder came against their minds.

The leader of the occult group called all the humans back into a huddle trying to rally their strength together. "Try harder, maybe we're not concentrating enough!"

Angels laughed at them. They dared them to try to break through their wall of protection.

One of the coven members screamed out and threw a spear with all his might. It stopped before it even touched the garment of the angel and fell to the ground.

The angels continued taunting them. "Come on! You can do better than that! Your grandmother can throw better than you."

The angels' words angered the occult members. They threw all manners of weapons, knives, arrows and spears against them. Some even tried to shoot bullets at them. But to their horror, no weapon could do them any harm. They tried to call demonic spirits to join and fight with them. To their dismay no spirit would answer their call.

"Try calling your god and see if he will come and help you overcome us," Chroni told them.

"Maybe he is going to the bathroom," another angel mocked.

"Maybe he is sleeping."

"Maybe your master doesn't really care about you at all."

Several cult members stormed the angel wall with the spirit of fury guiding them. As they touched the angels their hands burned like they were on fire. They screamed out in pain.

A woman, who was a high witch with great power in the coven, fell down on the ground and stared at the angels. She couldn't believe what she was seeing. She was told that satan was more powerful than the Christian God. Her mind could not handle this situation. Never had it ever occurred to her that the angels of God had more power than the power of satan. Her belief in satan being all-powerful was a lie.

Other human spirits continued trying to break through the angels to get to the house of Knight. With each frustrated wave of attack fury was building up inside them with more rage and hate. None of the occult members had ever been unsuccessful at attacking another human. They kept on trying not accepting what was taking place before their eyes.

An angel looked directly in the woman's eyes on the ground and said, "Please, accept Jesus as your Lord. If you stay on the path that you are pursuing, then you will be destroyed." Lovingly the angel told her the truth. "Satan really hates you. But Jesus loves you so much that He died for you. His power is greater than satan's. Jesus has all power in heaven, in earth and under earth."

The woman sat on the ground not believing the beautiful loving voice of the angel that was speaking to her. It spoke peace into her heart. Unknowing to her the angel deposited seeds of doubt toward satan's kingdom in her heart. She gave up trying to fight the angels and backed away. Satan told her that he loved her, but she never heard his voice sound as beautiful as the angel who just talked to her.

Michael gave the command to end the attack.

Suddenly, the countenance of all the angels turned fierce and the look from their eyes made all the occult members fall backwards onto the ground. They were powerless to move until the Holy Spirit released them. Without using one weapon or moving an inch, the angels of God defeated the human spirits like they were toothpicks. Standing up the occult members flew away as fast as they could. They could do absolutely nothing to penetrate the wall of warring angels.

The angels shouted as the occult group retreated from the property of the house of Knight in defeat. They praised God and rejoiced that the Knights prayed and confessed the Word out of their mouth daily.

"Nothing is more powerful than the Word of God coming out of the mouth of a believer!" a warring angel shouted.

"What a wonderful manifestation of power," another shouted. "If only the children of God on earth could understand what the children of God in heaven know!"

"They will, my son," Michael said. "The Lord is coming soon and He will manifest His presence to every human on earth. They will see the power of His dominion and might through the power of His body of believers!"

Chroni looked into the house and saw that Dan, Vicki and Joshua were sleeping peacefully. They never knew that satan had organized an attack against them. They were sleeping in the bosom of the Lord and trusted totally in His Word.

Maybe sometime in eternity they might learn of the Covenant protection that was bestowed on them this night, but if they don't, he thought, *it really won't matter. God's love is all that matters in this life and the life that is to come.*

Looking upward, the warring angels could see and hear the stars rejoicing in the love of God that has been bestowed on every human on earth. They heard the stars excitedly saying, "The Lord is coming! The Lord is coming! The Lord is coming soon!"

‡ ‡ ‡

Hannah was in her bed sleeping when she awakened by a loud noise.

"Sheeeeeila!"

Her dad screamed from downstairs. Immediately, she knew what woke her up. She looked at the clock it was 2:30 in the morning. Her dad was announcing his arrival home from the bars that closed at 2:00 every morning. She heard her mom go to the top of the stairs.

Trying to keep her voice down she whispered loudly. "Wade! Shhhh! You'll wake the children." She wondered if he would remember about Hannah.

He yelled at her. "Com her . . . I need to . . . *hic-up* . . . talk wif you." He was staggering drunk. Seeing everything double, he looked like he was going to pass out as his eyes crossed and his lids closed.

After the police officer detained Wade and shathah missed picking up Hannah, he took Wade to another bar to drink so that he could think of his plan of action. Chemah would be on his back soon if he didn't come up with something.

Shathah left his body and tried to get him to stand straight. "Stand up you weak-kneed————!" He cussed at him.

A spirit of fear came out of him to help him. "This is getting us nowhere! I couldn't see a thing to help him drive! He almost killed himself driving on the wrong side of the road."

"I know . . . I know! He's supposed to be my ticket to the next level of power. I don't want to lose him now!" shathah was huffing and puffing. Drunks were like lead weights.

"I wouldn't want to be negative or anything like that, but I don't think your luck is going to hang with you," fear told him as he let go of Wade's body.

Wade opened his eyes and saw the two demon spirits trying to help him stand up. "Thanks guyz . . . whar hav ya gin . . . I meen bin? Huh?" He was still staggering back and forth. "Ya know . . . we haft t'be quiet . . . we haf to beee . . . you know . . . shh! The kidsz . . ." His eyes rolled back and he passed out.

"This is no fun," the spirit of fear complained as he let him fall to the ground.

"Yeah, he is a no-good bum going no where!" cussed shathah. "That's why I want out of here. We should have let him hit that car head on!"

"You can't do that until you find a door into the house of Knight!" fear yelled.

"I know, I thought I could tough it out, but I want a new assignment."

They heard Sheila come down the stairs.

She bent over to help him get up. He was passed out cold. "Come on Wade. Get up and I'll help you shower." She tried to move him but he was too heavy for her.

Standing up she felt a cold breeze around her. Rubbing her arms, she discerned that evil spirits were around her husband. She shivered with goose bumps. "I know that you are here. I know that you think you have my husband. You listen to me, you devils from hell. Wade belongs to Jesus. I have interceded for him. Satan can't have him any longer. Get out of my house now and keep your filthy hands off my husband!"

Can she see us? Fear shrank along side of the foyer wall.

No, look at her eyes. She's just guessing! shathah observed.

"I told you to get!" Sheila demanded again.

She knows that we didn't leave!

Great guess! shathah said sarcastically. His green blood started to boil. "Who do you think you are?" He roared at her.

Two warring angels appeared before them. They towered over the demonic spirits by twice their size. "She knows who she is and so do we."

"She is a child of God, a royal priest, a joint-heir with Jesus!" One of the warring angels announced.

They drew their swords and pointed them at their throats. "Who are you?" the other angel roared at him.

"Nobody! We know that we are nobody." Fear could barely speak with the sword pointed at his throat. They both inched backwards. Then, fear backed out through the wall and took off running for his life.

"This human belongs to satan," shathah half-heartedly declared. "Can't you see that he is a drunk and an alcoholic?"

"We only see what the Lord sees." The angel looked up to heaven. "The Lord says that Wade Coyle belongs to Him."

Shathah didn't know what to say.

"Flee!" they both yelled at him.

Shathah took off running, fully expecting them to chase him and cut him to pieces.

The two angel's put their swords back into there sheathes and chuckled.

Sheila sensed the evil spirits were gone. She went back upstairs and got a blanket to cover Wade. This time at the foot of the stairs, she felt warmth surrounding her and smelled a wonderful smell like roses. As she bent over Wade, a sense of strength invaded her being. In her spirit, she knew that two towering warring angels were guarding him.

Hannah watched her mother lovingly put a blanket over him. She also sensed that angels were present. In her heart, she knew it wouldn't be long.

"Mom?'

"Oh! Hannah, what are you doing up?" She put her hand on her chest.

"Do you sense the presence of angels?"

"Yes." Sheila put her arm around Hannah and walked her back upstairs and into her bedroom.

"Joshua told me how to pray for Daddy."

"What did he tell you to do?'

"He told me to tell the demons that Daddy belonged to Jesus and that I should thank the Lord for His salvation every time I think about Daddy."

"Are you doing it?"

"Yes. I heard you do it downstairs."

"Mrs. Knight is teaching me how to stand for my rights as a believer."

"That means that we are both agreeing together for the same thing in Jesus' name."

"I know." She led her daughter over to her bed.

"I don't think it is going to take very long now." Hannah got into bed.

"Neither do I." Sheila tucked her in and sat down on the side of the bed. "No matter how long it takes, I will not get discouraged."

"I won't either. Do you like going to the prayer group?"

"I love it. I am learning so much about Jesus. When we all lift up our voices in praise and worship, it is the most wonderful thing I have ever experienced. I have this intense desire for your father to experience Jesus with me."

Hannah looked over at her walk-in closet filled with the latest fashionable clothes. One wall of her closet was ceiling to floor shelves with shoes. Her vanity was over-flowing with makeup, perfume and jewelry. She had two dressers crowded with clothes. Any thing she ever wanted was given to her, but it was nothing to her since she discovered Jesus. "Mom, I would give all this up for Jesus."

"I know. I've seen the change in you Hannah. I'm glad that you have decided to be a committed Christian."

She laughed. "Joshua would never let a shallow Christian become a member of his team."

"What's a shallow Christian?"

"He says that a shallow Christian is a carnal Christian, one that lives out of his soul."

"He is teaching you a lot of things."

"He makes the Bible open up. I love it when the Holy Spirit anoints him to teach."

"Be careful that you don't make Joshua an idol," Sheila warned.

"That's interesting."

"What?"

"Joshua was talking to me about the very same thing tonight."

"What did he think was your idol?"

"Envy over his family life."

"Is it?"

"Not now. I prayed before I went to sleep earlier and asked the Lord to forgive me for thinking that way. I don't want to live out of thoughts from the past or regrets that might carry over into my future. And I sure don't want to have any idols before the Lord."

"I'm glad to hear you say that. Whenever I talk to you, I realize that the Lord has protected us from many things that could have gone wrong because your dad drinks. We have a lot to be thankful for. Do you want to pray?"

"Yes. I would like to pray together every night for Daddy."

Sheila took a hold of Hannah's hand. "Father, thank You that You love us so much that You sent Your Son to die for us. Help us, Lord, to put You first in everything that we say and do. Help us, Lord, to keep a watch over our mouth so that we would not grieve the precious Holy Spirit. Thank You, Lord, that Your angels watch over us and keep us safe day and night. In the name of Jesus, we declare that the Coyle family belongs to Jesus. No weapon formed against us will prosper. We walk in health and in the supernatural protection and deliverance in Jesus the Anointed One."

"Demons, we again give you notice that Wade Coyle, my daddy, belongs to Jesus. He is saved and filled with the Holy Ghost in Jesus Name! No weapon formed against him will prosper in Jesus' Name. Get your hands off him, demons. Listen to us. You are under our feet and we trample any right you think you have to my daddy's spirit and soul," Hannah commanded.

"You have no right to Wade. You are a liar. Jesus paid the price for his sins and I accept what Jesus did for my husband. Amen."

"Wow! Mom! You really have learned how to pray. You don't even sound like the same mother."

"I received the baptism of the Holy Spirit."

"I did too!"

"That is so great Hannah. I'm so excited for both of us. Pray in your prayer language until you go to sleep and I will too," Sheila stood to leave.

"Wait until Grandma hears about us."

"I already told her. Good night." Sheila turned off the light and shut her door.

Hannah turned over and went to sleep feeling great about her family for the first time in her life.

CHAPTER 35

Dan sat back in his comfortable desk chair and looked out at the beautiful view of the two full-length windows in the corner of his office. He loved to look at God's creation. Whether it was the sun rising or the sun setting it was always spectacular. Framed scriptures decorated with pictures from various nature scenes covered the other two walls. Anyone who entered his office knew that Dan was intimately connected to the words of God. A large black Bible sat on his desk, permanently. He didn't care who came into his office the Bible was never removed. Dan was not ashamed of the gospel of Jesus Christ.

Laying his pen down, he put his head in his hands on his desk and began speaking in his heavenly language. Coming into his office earlier than usual, he felt that the Holy Spirit wanted him to make some changes and add some things to his summation. He learned to never question the prompting of the Holy Spirit in any area of his life. The Lord taught him how to test the spirits to make sure that he was listening to Him alone.

His secretary buzzed him.

"Yes?"

"Dan, the court recorder just called, court has been postponed again. Something strange happened to their computer system. He said they couldn't get a programmer in for at least two or three more hours." His secretary informed him.

"Call Mr. Gottman and inform him of the court delay."

"Yes, sir."

"Thank you. Uh . . . Gloria, please hold all calls or visitors for an hour or so."

"Yes, sir."

Gloria hung up her phone and resumed her typing. She was used to Mr. Knight calling her and asking her to *freeze* everything while he prayed. It was because of his close relationship to the Lord that she accepted Jesus as her own personal Savior. Before she started working for him, she considered herself a Christian, since she was raised in a Protestant Church. But the more she knew about him and his walk with the Lord, she felt like she didn't know the God that he worshipped. He never condemned her. He just kept showing her the love of God. The more she observed him the more she desired a personal relationship with his Jesus.

After he got to know her, he came to her and asked her if he could pray with her before she started work everyday and speak a blessing over her before she left to go home at the end of the day. Of course she had no objections about anyone praying, especially over her and her family. Every time Dan prayed she couldn't keep from crying. She cried for a week before she asked Jesus to be real to her and come into her life.

It had been 10 years since she came to work for Mr. Knight. Everyone in her immediate family was now saved and filled with the Holy Spirit. Whenever she thought about her husband, Bob, she realized what a blessing the Lord had provided for her when she started working for Mr. Knight. It only took one week of fasting and praying instigated by Dan for Bob to beg to get saved. Just thinking about Dan praying for Bob brought tears to her eyes. Every morning, she thanked the Lord that she worked for Dan Knight.

Several times before he got saved she had begged her husband to go to church with her. Dan told her to stop begging God to save Bob. He showed her in the Bible that she should ask the Lord to send other Christians to cross his path. He told her how to command demons to loose his blinded eyes and then thank the Lord that Bob was saved. Then, Dan told her to keep her mouth shut around her husband. Well, he didn't say it quite like that, she thought, but she got the picture.

The Lord appeared to her husband one night and she woke up to find him on his knees by the side of the bed begging for forgiveness from his sins. She never dreamed that the Lord would come himself. In the months after she had been saved, she had sowed a lot of seeds of begging Bob to go to church with her and now he was begging to be saved.

You couldn't convince Gloria that the Lord doesn't have a sense of humor . . .

. . . Matthan was in the office with Dan. He got down on his face and worshiped the Lord while Dan laid his head on his desk and prayed. Matthan hadn't heard from the Holy Spirit yet, but he was looking and watching. He knew in his spirit what Dan sensed; an evil spirit was going to strike.

Suddenly Chroni stepped through the outside wall and stood behind Dan. Floating several inches over him, he spoke to Matthan. "chemah has sent an evil spirit in the form of a beautiful woman to compromise Dan."

"What is the Holy Spirit's plan?" He asked as he floated up to Chroni.

"When she comes through the door, shut the door on her. Chemah is trying to set up several temptations to hit the house of Knight hard and often. This spirit is going to act like Dan attacked her."

"The old sexual harassment trick?"

"Yes."

"But Dan always has his secretary in the office with him or he leaves his door open," Matthan said.

"The evil spirit is going to make a quick entry and try to take him by surprise." Chroni floated down to the floor just behind Dan. "The Lord has ordained that Joshua receive a lesson in spiritual judgment. We will plant a seed of suggestion into the evil spirit to relay to chemah, who desired entry into the house of Knight the other night."

"How exciting!" proclaimed Matthan. "Joshua loves to fight the enemy. He knows the benefits he receives from spiritual warfare will add to his growth in the Kingdom of God." Chuckling to himself, he thought about Kientay and the prospect of seeing chemah groveling.

Chroni paused as he received a communication from the Holy Spirit. "The demon is coming!" . . .

. . . Gloria was typing a letter at her computer when she looked up to see a beautiful blonde standing at her desk.

"I didn't hear anyone walking down the hall." *Or the elevator doors open,* she thought. "Can I help you?"

"I need to see Mr. Knight immediately!" Reaching into her purse, she pulled out a compact to see how she looked. Her hair was pulled into a French twist with bangs and long tendrils of blonde hair curled around her hairline.

"Mr. Knight will be busy for another thirty minutes. Can I help you?"

The female in front of Gloria's desk leaned over and exposed cleavage. She had on a tight jacket and a short bright pink skirt.

Gloria pulled her head back and gasped. *This woman is dangerous*!

"Girl, tell him it's an emergency!"

"If you will sit down, I will announce you in exactly thirty minutes." *And not a minute before,* she thought stubbornly.

The woman let out a long sigh. She turned around and acted like she was going to sit down. Instead she ran around her desk and opened the door to Mr. Knight's office . . .

. . . Opening the door the evil spirit froze. She saw Chroni standing in front of Dan protecting him with the shield of faith.

"Come in!" Chroni smiled.

Analyzing the size and strength of the warring angel, the evil spirit decided to proceed. All she had to do was come into the room and shut the door. Then she was going to tear open her front jacket and expose herself claiming Dan attacked her. It was a tactic she had used before and it always worked. "I think you're bluffing. You don't look fast enough to fight me. I don't think you have the stuff!" She started to advance when Matthan shut the door in her face . . .

. . . Dan heard his door open. He lifted his head to see a sexy young woman standing in his doorway. He was surprised that Gloria let someone come into his office without his knowledge. "May I help you?"

She started to come through the doorway, when all of a sudden the door shut in her face. Dan ran around his desk to open the door and see what happened. He heard a smacking sound like a THUD when the door connected with her nose. He was prepared to pray for her healing immediately.

Gloria jumped up to stop her from going into Mr. Knight's office. She knew something was wrong when she saw the door close. Sirens were going off in the inside of her.

Dan opened the door. "Are you alright?"

The woman had her hand over her nose. She looked like she was trying to keep blood from going everywhere. "YOU broke my nose!"

Dan bent over trying to look and see the extent of her injury. But the woman had her body bent over and turned away from him. He moved around her to try and help. "Let me look at it."

She was resisting him, using one of her hands to keep him away from her.

"If you don't mind, let me pray for your healing. I know God can heal your nose," Dan was still trying to look at her nose.

When Dan said *pray* the demon panicked and ran down the hall to the woman's bathroom.

"Gloria, do you think you could go after her and see if she is okay?" Dan was puzzled by the woman running down the hall.

"Sure," Gloria started walking down the hall. She stopped and walked back. "Uh . . . did she say that you broke her nose?"

"I couldn't have possibly broken her nose. I wasn't anywhere near that door!"

"So, what happened?"

"You were behind her; I thought you could tell me."

"If you didn't close the door, who did?"

"I don't know," answered Dan.

Gloria turned around to find the woman.

He stood there stunned. Something was going on, but what? He still wanted to talk to the woman, to find out what had happened.

Gloria came back with a shocked expression on her face.

"Is she okay?"

"I don't know. Did you see her?"

"No."

"She is not in the bathroom."

"No one has passed your desk," Dan reported.

"Did you see anyone go out the exit to the stairs?"

"You would have heard the door alarm if someone would have gone out the emergency exit. Are you sure she's not in the bathroom?" asked Dan.

"I checked everywhere! She's not in the bathroom! Go see for yourself."

Dan walked down to the hall. "Coming in!" he yelled as he walked through the bathroom door. Checking each stall and the powder room, he came to the same conclusion that Gloria did. "It's not that I didn't believe you, I just wanted to be a witness and confirm what you saw."

"I told you!" Gloria's face was white. "What do you think?"

"I think we may have encountered an evil spirit." Dan could think of no other explanation. "Did you have a funny feeling being around her?"

"I sure did." She rubbed her arms unconsciously feeling cold. "Even if you weren't busy, I probably would not have let her in your office. Something didn't smell right. She had this look on her face, but her eyes . . ." she shivered.

"What look?"

"Her eyes looked cold and demonic; you know . . . no life!"

"Well, what or whoever it was, I've got a release in my spirit that the attack from a demon was thwarted. We are more than conquerors through Jesus Christ our Lord!"

"Praise the Lord!" shouted Gloria has she went to sit back down at her desk. *Thwarted?* She giggled at the word he used.

Dan went inside his office and started to shut the door. He looked back at Gloria. "What's so funny?"

"Thwarted?"

Dan chuckled with her. She was right. Thwarted was one of those barely used words in everyday conversation. It was funny in view of what just happened. Using that word seemed to release a supernatural laugh from within her spirit. He sat down on the chair besides her desk to enjoy the comic release from the preposterous situation they just encountered . . .

. . . Chroni drew his sword and brought it down in front of the demon pointing it at her throat.

She screamed. "You broke my nose!" Then she ran down the hallway after she heard the word *pray*.

Chroni and Matthan followed her.

She released her image from the natural dimension and began cursing them appearing in the spiritual realm only as she ran into the bathroom. "You broke the nose of my beautiful human body!"

"That's not all that will get broke if you don't leave," declared Chroni.

Matthan and Chroni chased her as she went back into the hallway trying to escape through the emergency exit. Cut off, she flew back into the bathroom. They followed her flying through the wall of the bathroom and surrounded her stopping her from exiting through the wall to the outside.

She stood frozen, "What are you going to do to me?"

"Go tell chemah that the Blood of Jesus comes against him. He might as well know that protection is all over the house of Knight. We won't let him cross over the circle of blood that surrounds them. Their hedge of protection is in tact. No holes! Do you understand?"

Matthan looked at Chroni, "I thought you said Joshua has a hole in his protection and that he could be attacked tonight?"

"Hold your peace angel!" demanded Chroni.

The evil spirit disappeared from the bathroom when they broke eye contact with her.

Chroni and Matthan laughed together as they walked down the hall back to the office. "Do you think the demon took the bait?" asked Matthan.

"Without a doubt she took the bait, hook, line and sinker. What an actor! You should go to Hollywood and try out for an angel part in one of their ridiculous movies about angels. You could teach them a thing or two." Chroni put his arm around Matthan.

"No way. They might give me a part like that one movie about angels who drink, swear and mate with humans."

"Did you watch that movie?" He was surprised.

"Joshua wanted to see it only to know how Hollywood was misrepresenting us, but he waited until he could view it at home."

"What did you think?"

"I think the world is going to be shocked when they finally meet one of the Lord's angels," Matthan answered him. "Why do you think that so many Hollywood writers believe that angels can be turned into humans?"

"That is a direct desire from satan himself. He thinks that if he could become human then he could defeat Jesus."

"That thinking comes either from the mind of a totally psychotic being or a totally deceived human!" Matthan laughed.

"He has convinced his kingdom of darkness that they will defeat the body of Jesus. Like the teens of today say, 'go figure.'"

"Demon spirits are so gullible and ignorant," Matthan smiled as he watched Dan and Gloria releasing the spirit of laughter.

The Holy Spirit thought the whole incident was humorous, and he chuckled with them, but Jesus thought it was hilarious and couldn't wait to see the ending through His little brother, Joshua.

‡ ‡ ‡

The evil spirit appeared before chemah. "Speak!" He commanded her like a dog.

The infuriated android had her hand over her nose. "Don't call me! I'll call you!" she said with disgust.

"What happen to you?" he demanded.

"I got ambushed!" The deceiving spirit was holding her nose.

"How close did you get?"

"I opened the door to his office. Look what happened to my nose! I'll have to go to the dark planet to get it fixed!" The evil spirit pointed to her nose that was bruised and clearly broken.

"Did you find out anything?"

She took out the compact in her purse, looked at her nose and screamed. "I hope I can get this fixed before I go out on the streets tonight!"

"Did you learn anything?" yelled chemah.

"This is going to cost you big time, chemah!"

Chemah raised his hand to release a ball of raging fire.

The evil spirit looked up just in time to stop chemah. "Okay, okay, take it easy! I think the smaller angel goofed and gave me some scoop on the boy, Joshua."

"What is it? Come on!" He couldn't wait to hear.

"I didn't get everything. The larger angel stopped him before he revealed any details."

Rage was building up on the inside of chemah. "You have two seconds to tell me."

"Okay already. Shish! You're as bad as the human males I have to deal with! He said something about Joshua doing something he shouldn't do and a door or a hole or something would be open for someone to tempt him tonight."

"I knew it! I knew it! I told that miserable quitter metraloas that I would not fail." chemah disappeared to make some plans for confrontation with Joshua.

The evil spirit looked at chemah with disgust. "That ungrateful . . . !" she cursed. "See if I put myself out for you again!" She disappeared to find an outpost station with a departing ship to take her to the dark planet where androids were produced and repaired.

Dan picked up his phone and buzzed Gloria.

"Yes?"

"Can you come into my office please, Gloria?"

"Sure." She giggled again before she could hang up.

Gloria sat at one of the chairs in front of his desk with a smile on her face trying to contain herself.

"I was just thinking." Dan tried not to look directly into her eyes. "I know that we just had a brush with a demonic plan to ruin my reputation, with the door shut." He saw her put both hands over her mouth out of the corner of his eye. "There is no telling what she would have done or claimed that I did. So I want us to pray together and ask the Lord for wisdom for the coming days."

Gloria took down one hand from her mouth. "I didn't know demons could look like a human." She released a slight snicker.

"You know the Bible says that satan can appear as an angel of light. It also says that we can 'entertain angels unaware.' So then they must look like humans. After this experience, we also know that we can entertain evil spirits unaware."

"That gives me goose bumps!" She shivered.

"You didn't let fear get you, did you?"

"Are you kidding?" Her words were muffled, because she kept one hand over her mouth as she was trying to control the occasional outbursts of joy. "You can't be afraid and laugh at the same time," she answered him.

"I think it's because of the power of God that was released to defeat the demon. Spiritual power is responsible for this light feeling of joy."

"Light feeling?" She hee-hawed again.

"Don't you feel good?" he asked her.

"Yes. But this isn't light . . . trust me." She sensed the feeling was building inside her again. "I thought that demons looked like monsters in science fiction movies."

He nodded his head trying not to look at her again. "I think their real form is ugly and evil looking. Remember the magician's rods turned into snakes in Moses' day."

"You mean that woman could have had snakes inside her?"

"Who knows what she really looks like?" replied Dan.

"Oh! That is so repulsive!" She bent over laughing.

Dan couldn't block the urge to let it rip from down inside him any longer. He laid his head on the desk releasing a deep rolling chuckle. They laughed so hard that tears were rolling down both cheeks. When they could finally contain themselves, Dan suggested that they pray. Gloria noticed that the door to his office was closed and wondered about another plot to ruin Dan's reputation.

"I've got an idea." He went over and opened the door to his office half way. "You don't mind people listening to our prayer, do you?"

"If they can hear us laughing, then they can hear us praying."

"Father, thank You that the Holy Spirit and the Blood of Jesus was here to protect us from an evil plot of satan. We know there were angels here to protect us. You are an awesome God. We hide under the shelter of Your wings of protection and salvation. No weapon formed against us will prosper. Every tongue that rises against us will be pulled down by the power of the spoken Word. No evil shall befall us here at the office of my business. All my clients are blessed with Your protection. The Blood of Jesus protects all my cases. Lord, thank You for leading us with the Spirit of wisdom."

Gloria agreed thanking Jesus quietly, when she felt the Holy Spirit lead her to pray. "Father, thank You for all the blessings on this family and business. God bless Dan, Vicki, and Joshua. God bless this new ministry the Devil Chasers. God bless them with Your angels surrounding them. God bless Dan and his family with clear direction, courage, creativity, and favor in this endeavor You are leading them. God bless them with hands to bless others with protection, provision, safety and strength. Amen."

"Thank you, Gloria, for speaking blessings over my family."

"Dan, you have been pronouncing a blessing on me and my family for years now. It's about time I blessed you and your family."

"We love you, Gloria. We are so grateful to the Lord that your family is saved."

"Please tell Vicki, that I will give thirty minutes a day to pray specifically for Joshua and the Devil Chasers."

"Thank you, Gloria. God bless you and your family."

Gloria stopped and looked at Dan. She couldn't help herself. "It's a good thing that you thwarted the plan of satan."

Another burst of hilarious feelings hit Dan as he leaned over his chair laughing so hard his sides were hurting. "I think . . . ha ha . . . that we . . . ha ha ha . . . are caught in the spirit of laughter!"

Gloria put her hand over her mouth giggling like a little school girl "I've never . . . ha ha . . . experienced . . . ha ha . . . laughing . . . ha ha . . . in the . . . ha ha . . . spirit before. I know that this must look strange," she tried to breathe a couple of times, "but it feels too good to stop."

"So we can get back to work, I will be careful not to use the word . . ." He couldn't even finish his sentence before the chuckles were spilling out of his mouth.

Gloria left the office thinking how much God has blessed her family since she started working for Dan Knight and how exciting it was to know Jesus, like Dan, knew Him. She couldn't wait to tell her husband about the demon in the form of a blonde that Dan, through the Holy Spirit, thwarted!

CHAPTER 36

Three very hot and impatient teenagers stood outside Lincoln High School. It was an unusually hot fall day. Even though it was late in the afternoon, the sun was emitting heat that caused an overdressed person to sweat and be very uncomfortable. Life happens fast when the last bell at the end of a school day sounds. A spirit of anxiety was working on them.

Mose looked around, wiping the sweat off his forehead. "Man, it is not a good thing to be in the way of kids leaving school, especially ones with temperatures rising."

Joshua looked at the front doors of the school. "Where is she?"

Today was the day they were going to the print shop together. Kellie was taking her car with Hannah. Joshua and Mose were riding with Vicki to pick up the Devil Chaser cards they ordered. Everyone was at the bottom of the steps, except Hannah.

Mose looked at his watch and wiped the sweat running down his brow again with the long sleeves of his shirt. He made no effort to resist his feeling of irritation. With a harsh tone in his voice, he interrogated everyone, "Are you sure you guys mentioned to Hannah that we were ALL going to meet together after school?"

"Mose, remember Monday?" Kellie reminded him.

He shook his head. How could he forget so soon? "Lord, have mercy, it is hot!" He was irritated that they had to wait for Hannah.

"Hannah has never been on time in her life! Trust me, I know," explained Kellie. "Phew! The weatherman's prediction took a hike today." Her long sleeve sweater was tied around her waist. She could feel the puddle of sweat around her middle section.

Joshua was the only one that was dressed in knee-high denim shorts and a bright yellow short-sleeved cotton shirt. "You guys need to change weathermen."

"Who do you listen too?"

"The Lord."

"Now, I wonder why that doesn't surprise me?" Mose smirked.

"Are you all waiting for me?" Hannah ran down the steps breathing hard.

Kellie stared at her and felt like saying "duh!" But that was the old Kellie, the new Kellie would forget that they had been standing there waiting in the sweltering sun for at least fifteen minutes.

Stopping to get her breath and put her books in her backpack, she explained, "I'm sorry I'm late. I had to stay after school. Mrs . . ."

"Let's go," Kellie interrupted. They turned around and left Hannah talking to herself. Without realizing it, she picked up the spirit of irritation from Mose and Joshua.

"Hey! Wait up!" Hannah yelled after she realized everyone was leaving her behind. She ran after Kellie. "Is everybody mad at me?"

Kellie opened the door to her car, not speaking to her.

Hannah opened the door and sat down. "Give me a break. It's not my fault that I'm late!"

Kellie refused say anything else. As far as she was concerned, Hannah was always blaming someone else.

Joshua and Mose got in Vicki's car.

"Are you excited about getting started tomorrow?" Vicki asked the boys as they were putting on their seat belts.

"Yes." Mose sat in the back seat of the car. "Mrs. Knight, could you turn up the air conditioner?"

"Sure. How about you Johsua?"

"What?"

"Are you ready to hand out cards?"

"Yes." Joshua was thinking about the weekend. His thoughts were becoming dangerously close to anxiety and concern.

Mose noticed the tone of Joshua's voice had changed and he didn't sound irritated. Now he seemed distracted. As his body cooled down, Mose realized he was thinking better.

Joshua looked at Mose. He thought about telling him about what he saw in the future, but decided not to. It was hard enough controlling his thoughts let alone trying to control the thoughts of the team. It had been on his mind constantly today and he had to work hard not to let the thoughts carry him into a state of worry.

Vicki looked at her son tenderly. "Are you okay?"

Joshua heard the motherly love oozing from her and felt a little irritation toward her. "I'm just thinking about the big day."

"I hope you guys have time to pray over the cards before you hand them out," Vicki voiced her concern about them being ready.

"Mom, we've been praying over them for a month now."

She ignored the tone of his voice. "Joshua, some works of God take months, even years of prayer and preparation."

"If we hand the cards out tomorrow what if we start getting calls this weekend?" Mose asked. "Joshua, are you feeling okay?"

"Yes."

"Answer Mose's question."

"What did you say?" asked Joshua.

"If we hand out the cards before this weekend, what if we start getting calls?"

"If we get calls, then we start answering them."

"What if we get a caller that we can't handle?"

"You pray," Joshua said.

"Do you guys feel something a little strange?" Vicki sensed a spirit of irritation around her.

Joshua quietly spoke in his heavenly language. "Let's pray and take authority over the spirits attacking us."

"Yeah! It started with me then it went to Joshua and now it is on you Mrs. Knight."

"I think I opened the door," Joshua told them. "I was totally irritated with Hannah for making us wait for her."

"As soon as we park, you can talk to them," Vicki told them.

"Here I go again," Mose groaned.

"What?" Joshua asked.

"Here I go sucking up . . . oh sorry, Mrs. Knight!" Mose turned red. "I've got to say I'm sorry to Hannah again."

Vicki turned into the parking lot of Mr. Gottman's print shop. "You can be self-controlled in the things concerning Hannah, Mose, if you want to be. Do you know the Words of Jesus . . ." She was putting her keys into her purse when she realized she was by herself.

Mose and Joshua waited for the girls to park.

Hannah saw the look on their faces. "What did I do this time?"

"What are you talking about," Kellie asked as she opened her car door.

Joshua was first to speak. "We need to say something to you."

"Me?" Hannah and Kellie asked at the same time.

"Both of you, we want to . . ."

"I interrupted you," Mose confessed. "I just did it again didn't I?"

"Go ahead," Joshua said.

"I interrupted you, Hannah, back on the steps."

"That's okay."

"Mrs. Devlin kept her after school," Kellie explained.

"She thought I was talking in the back of the class. It wasn't me, but I didn't want to tell her who it was, so I accepted her punishment. I figured you guys would understand."

"Please forgive me for interrupting you Hannah," Mose asked her with real repentance.

"I'm the one that interrupted Hannah," Kellie confessed. "I should be the one asking forgiveness."

"Forgive me too," Joshua told them. "I realized a spirit of irritation was working on me and I asked the Lord to forgive me."

"I think demons have been working on all of you," Vicki said as she approached the group in the parking lot. "And no wonder with this abnormal heat wave."

"Let's pray now!" Hannah looked around them. "I don't like demons!"

"Demon be gone in the name of Jesus!" Joshua spoke with authority . . .

. . . the demonic spider had to remove his web of thin black thread-like tentacles which he had started weaving and attaching to the physical heads of the teenagers and Mrs. Knight, as Kientay and other guardian angels blasted him with light from their swords.

The spider let out a scream as the light burned him. Sulfuric smoke appeared with a sizzle and pop as each tentacle was scorched. The smell was horrible. He was a flying deformed spider with a human head and long leg tentacles. He vomited out worry and anxiety with thoughts that moved along the black tentacles as they wove themselves around the minds of the humans. His job was easy when the natural physical temperatures were high and discomfort caused tempers to flare.

He cursed them as he fled from the scene. When the Word was spoken out of the mouth of believers, he had no choice but to flee or be destroyed.

Kientay wrinkled his nose. "I can't stand their smell!"

Malcolm agreed. "It will be a great pleasure when we can finally rid earth of these black spider-like demons!"

"It would be so easy to keep those terrible spiders away from them if they would only watch their attitudes, especially when unseasonable temperatures occur," Chloe said.

"It is not like God didn't worn them by creating natural spiders in their world," Marisa said. "Demonic spiders weave webs to catch humans just like natural spiders weave webs to catch other insects."

"We know, Marisa, they eat them!" Malcolm raised his voice.

"But so many humans haven't made the connection between animal characteristics and human behavior," Chloe lamented.

"Praise the Lord that their spiritual senses are becoming sharper!" Kientay didn't want Chloe's statement to bring down the festive mood of the adventure with their charges.

The warring angels surrounding the car lifted up their swords in praise and worship to the Lord. Taking authority over the demonic spiders gave God much glory and revealed that the team was learning spiritual things.

"Thank God that they spoke His Word out of their mouth so that we could defend them and defeat the enemy!" A warring angel declared.

"Our day is coming!" Kientay exclaimed as each guardian angel stood next to their charges as they prayed outside the print shop. "When they can all see in the natural what a spectacular scene in the spiritual dimension surrounds them, they will never allow a tiny demonic android to control their feelings and emotions ever again" . . .

. . ."It's gone!" Hannah declared.

Mose breathed deeply. Even the air smelled better. "You would think we would know by now when to recognize an attack."

"I'm sorry, Josh I think I let my feelings of being so hot and uncomfortable open the door for this attack," Kellie said softly.

"You're forgiven. Every time we do recognize what is happening in the spirit realm and do something about it, we grow in spirit perception and sharpen our spiritual senses. I don't think the kingdom of darkness has any idea about what we are going to do, because the attacks would be more serious," Joshua told them.

"Oh, Joshua, don't say that!" Kellie said.

"Don't let fear get you, Kellie. We will be able to overcome anything the devil tries to bring against us!" Joshua pointed out.

"We are more than conquerors!" Hannah said with intensity.

"Yeah, a demon was probably just taking advantage of the situation. After all, it is easy to get frustrated with Hannah," Mose commented.

"You better break that habit of your flesh wanting to attack Hannah. That will be a weak spot that satan can take advantage over you at his will if you don't," Vicki warned them.

"Even if it wasn't the devil, like it was a natural situation, we still have to be on guard not to get into the flesh," Joshua said.

"Joshua!" Kellie shouted. "Did you say the word *like*?"

Joshua laughed at himself. "I did."

Mr. Gottman saw them out in the parking lot and thought his eyes deceived him. It looked like they were praying. He took off his glasses to clean them and then put them on to see them talking and crossing the street. The older white haired gentleman with a matching mustache, a jovial laugh and sparkling eyes, figured his glasses were dirty. Even though the Knights were believers in Jesus, he knew that they were here to pick up their order. But then again, Dan told him that his family was praying for him to accept Jesus as the true Jewish Messiah, so maybe they really were praying for him out in the parking lot. He chuckled out loud. He told Dan he would really like to believe in Jesus, but something was holding him back. He was a young Jewish boy in Germany during the war . . .

. . . Dan liked Mr. Gottman the moment he met him and an instant friendship developed between them. After a few weeks of working together, they felt comfortable enough with one another to start talking about religious beliefs.

"During my early years in school, we Jewish children were ridiculed when we did not celebrate Christmas with the other children. And after Hitler's rise to power in Germany, we were told Hitler was a Christian," explained Mr. Gottman.

"You should know that Hitler was the cause of an estimated 13.5 million Christian deaths."

"No, I guess I am only aware of the six million Jews that were exterminated," Mr. Gottman answered.

"Hitler may have thought he was a Christian, but in truth he was listening to a familiar spirit, if not satan himself. Can I show you a passage in the New Testament?"

He put his hands up and chuckled lightly, "You know, I may not be an Orthodox Jew, but I do not believe in your New Testament."

"Did you know that our New Testament was written mostly by Jews?"

"Well, no. I am ashamed to say I did not know this." Mr. Gottman was a little surprised.

"My favorite writer of the New Testament is a Jewish man named Paul." Dan picked up the Bible off his desk and turned to Philippians 3:5. "Please listen to this, 'Circumcised the eighth day, of the stock of Israel, of the tribe of Benjamin, a Hebrew of the Hebrews; as touching the law, a Pharisee. Concerning zeal, persecuting the believer's in Jesus; touching the righteousness which is in the law, blameless."

Mr. Gottman got his glasses out of his pocket; "Please, let me read. I am from the tribe of Benjamin. I would like to read of a Jewish man who can say he is blameless in the law."

Dan handed him the Bible. "You will like Paul very much."

Mr. Gottman became so curious about the man Paul, that he accepted a New Testament from Dan and started reading it. From time to time, he would ask Dan questions about what he was reading. He also studied the prophecies of the Old Testament and compared them to the scriptures Paul was teaching. Dan and Vicki prayed everyday for the blinders to be removed from his eyes . . .

. . ."Hello, Mrs. Knight. How are you doing today?"

"I am doing very good Mr. Gottman, how about you." Vicki was praying for him silently in her spirit.

"The world is looking better everyday. I testified yesterday and I feel very good about this case. We even finished early today and that is why I am here to help you."

"We prayed, and we believe you will be victorious in your trial," Vicki said.

"I thank you for your prayers. We have not had time to discuss the letters of Paul that I am reading. You tell that husband of yours I am reading Paul's letters over a second time. I am convinced the Christian religion should really be another Jewish sect." They both laughed at his remark.

One of Mr. Gottman's workers brought their order out from the back.

"Ah, yes! Here it is." He opened one of the boxes and showed them to Joshua.

"Mr. Gottman they are beautiful!" Kellie exclaimed when Joshua handed her a card. She looked like she was going to cry.

The lettering on the cards was embossed over an opened Bible. A shield with a cross and a dove was to the side. A sword was on the other side. The embossed letters were royal blue on a white Bible with blood red edges. On the back of the card, I John 4:4 was printed: *'Greater is Jesus Christ in us, than satan that is in the world.* Their Christian motto was under the scripture.

"I understand that John was a Jew that was very close to Jesus," Mr. Gottman's eyes were gleaming. "We Jews do not have a great understanding of our enemy the devil, but I thought you would like the quote from John's letter."

"Word of God!" Mose exclaimed. "These cards are cool!"

"They're awesome!" Hannah said.

Kellie thought she was going to cry. She handed the card to Vicki.

"Mr. Gottman, you did a beautiful job." Vicki thought the cards were perfect.

"I am happy for a family that will take such a stand against the evil in this world."

Vicki got out her checkbook to pay for the cards.

Mr. Gottman put out his hand to stop her. "I am paying for this first order. You are not to give me a penny."

"We can't let you do that," Vicki protested.

"I insist. It is the least I can do for the blessing of your family in my life."

"Well, we insist that you let us pray for you."

"I accept."

"Gather around, everyone. Mr. Gottman would you get in the center of our prayer circle?"

Mr. Gottman looked pleased at the way they were going to pray for him.

"Jehovah, Father, we thank You for Mr. Gottman's creative design with the cards we ordered. They were more than we could ever think or ask. Now, with the seed that he has planted into Joshua's ministry, we ask You for a one hundred fold return. We ask You for a not guilty verdict in his case. We also ask that You reveal to Him that Jesus Christ of Nazareth is the Messiah that the Jewish people were promised was coming. Give Mr. Gottman a Saul on the road to Damascus experience, so without a doubt, he will be able to say, 'Jesus is my Lord.'"

"Mr. Gottman, God bless you with abundance, creativity, good health, faith, clear direction and spiritual perception of God's truth. God bless you with goodness and mercy following you all the days of your life. May you dwell in the house of the Lord forever. Amen."

Mr. Gottman hugged Vicki. He was crying. She sounded more like a Jew to him than he did.

‡ ‡ ‡

It was a beautiful star shining and twinkling night. Joshua could picture the hedge of angels that surrounded their property. When he got home from the print shop, his mom and the team laid hands over the boxes of cards and prayed in the spirit over them. Then, they prayed over the atmosphere around their house and in their house. Tonight was a special night.

It was a time of prayer and dedication.

The doorbell rang. When Joshua opened the door, he spotted a falling star above the head of Mose. "Hey, Mose!"

"Hey, Joshua. How's it going bro?" They exchanged the special handshake that they had created with each other.

Joshua remembered the first time he met Mose and smiled. "Great!"

"No demons?" Mose asked referring to their earlier encounter.

"None!" Joshua looked up into the sky and saw three more falling stars.

Vicki walked up to the door. "Come on in, Pastor Pearson. Ruth, you look great. Where's RubyMae?"

"She's coming." Ruth looked back at the car parked in the horseshoe driveway. "Mother?"

"I'm coming . . . hold your horses . . . I'm coming!"

They went into the living room to join the others. Everyone was excited about the gathering to pray over the cards and dedicate the newly formed Devil Chasers to the Lord. Vicki introduced all the parents to one another. Several family members and other prayer warriors had been invited for the dedication ceremony. Pastor David Pearson had been asked to dedicate the ministry to the Lord.

"I thought we would wait a few more minutes for Dan. He got held up at the office."

It almost seemed too quiet in the room. Especially since Vicki had gotten used to the two girls talking non-stop. The four of them were sitting on the smaller sofa together. "Is everything okay?" Vicki asked the team.

Mose spoke. "Sure, I guess we're realizing what an awesome responsibility this is going to be."

"Yeah," agreed Hannah, "people are going to be calling us up for answers to their problems."

"Now, I think it is important to realize that you are not going to give them answers, but you are going to pray with them and give them God's Word." Pastor Pearson commented like a pastor and a parent.

Joshua spoke up for the team like always. "We want to seek the Lord for His presence and anointing over the phones."

Looking at one another, they all silently nodded their heads in agreement with Joshua. "We need to be quiet sometimes so we can hear from the Lord," Kellie commented.

"I'm impressed," Vicki said enthusiastically as she sat down. "This is the first time that I've witnessed this group being so quiet." She smiled. "It's good to have quiet meditation before the Lord, especially since we've been talking so much for the last month." She winked at them. Not very many people knew about all the things that they had been through just in a few short weeks.

"Pastor, we would like you to dedicate us and this phone ministry to the Lord, as a prayer ministry," Joshua didn't have a chance to talk to the Pastor Pearson before tonight.

"As I was seeking the Lord on what to say, He told me the same thing."

"Joshua, I would really like to wait before we start at least a few minutes to see if your dad will make it."

Dan walked through the doorway almost out of breath, "I'm here! Sorry I'm late."

"Dan, our kids have put together a pretty impressive work for the Lord." Pastor Pearson stood to shake his hand.

"Praise the Lord! I agree with you."

"If everyone will follow Joshua, he will take you into the newly decorated family room that will now be called the headquarters of the Devil Chasers," Vicki told them.

Walking down a hallway to the back of the house, they entered a large area that had dark cherry desks with individual cubby like partitions with a phone, a computer and space to write. A grouping of cotton plaid and leather sofas and chairs surrounded the back of the room facing a huge wall of windows and a centered fireplace overlooking the lake behind the house. On the other end was a miniature kitchen with bar stools and an island. Joshua watched the faces of his phone team.

The guests greeted the room with "oos" and "ahhs." Dan set up folding chairs so that everyone could sit around the fireplace. He moved a small clear plexiglas podium in front of the fireplace for Pastor Pearson.

"Before we dedicate our children to the Lord, why don't we give Him an offering of praise for this wonderful room and equipment that He has provided for us," Vicki said.

Dan joined hands with Vicki. "Father God, we are so thankful to You for giving us this opportunity to join hands with our children and engage in a ministry that will glorify the name of Jesus. I ask You to go before us with Your Holy Spirit and guide us in Your ways of truth with mercy and grace. In Jesus Name, Amen."

They all lifted up their hands and began praising the Lord.

"Lord, we bless Your Holy Name."

"We give you praise."

"We are the seed of Abraham. We thank You for the blessings of Abraham that are on us and our seed."

"We love You, oh Lord, our Strength and Redeemer."

"All glory and honor and power to the Name of the Lord."

"The Lord is a mighty warrior, strong in battle."

"The Name of the Lord is an awesome Name."

"Praises to His Name."

"Holy, Holy, Holy, Lord God Almighty."

Dan gave everyone time to praise the Lord and then leaned over to the pastor and said, "Whenever you are ready, Pastor Pearson, please feel free to begin."

He picked up his Bible and turned to I Kings Chapter 8 and 9. "I had no idea I would have a podium. A preacher always feels welcome with a podium. My name is Bishop David Pearson, but you can call me Pastor David. I recognize some of you and some I don't. So, I want to introduce you to my son, Mose Pearson. I am proud that he is a part of this outstanding team of young people that the Lord has called into a phone ministry. Thank you, Dan and Vicki for this wonderful room and equipment that God has given to you. We stand in awe of the Master's thoughtfulness." He opened his Bible.

"I have chosen parts of Solomon's prayer for the dedication of this ministry tonight. When I finish praying and blessing this ministry, the workers, and the cards," he looked at the four sitting on the sofa, "I want everyone in this room to take some of that anointed oil and anoint the whole room." He pointed to a basket at the side of him sitting on a table with card and Bibles. Vicki bought a special Bible for each of them with the name of the ministry and their names inscribed on them.

"God has given Joshua a marvelous vision to reach his generation for Jesus. Since this ministry will involve much prayer, I have chosen to ordain the Devil Chasers, a ministry of prayer and intercession. I have changed some of the words and inserted the correct names."

"Joshua, Kellie, Mose and Hannah, stand up in a line in front of me. Parents and grandparents, stand behind each child and lay hands on them while I am praying."

All the adults stood and did as Pastor Pearson instructed. Joshua's grandparents on his father's side were around him. Mark and Kathy Todd and one set of grandparents were around Kellie. Ruth and her mother, RubyMae with Pastor Pearson's parents gathered around Mose. Sheila and her mother stood by Hannah. Other family members were also invited to attend. Several aunts, uncles and cousins of the various families had shown up. Vicki felt that it was important that as many family members as possible be present. She wanted many prayers offered as protection against the forces of evil for each teenage member of the Devil Chasers.

Pastor Pearson spoke. "As Solomon dedicated the Temple in Israel, he was fulfilling a dream and a vision his father, King David gave to him. As we dedicate the Devil Chasers to the Lord, we realize a vision and dream of Dan and Vicki Knight was to have a child and raise that child like Samuel was raised in the house of the Lord. When I first entered Dan and Vicki Knight's home, I recognized this house was indeed a house of prayer in my spirit."

He spread forth his hands toward heaven and said, "Lord God of heaven and earth, there is not a God like You, in heaven above, or on earth beneath, who keeps the New Covenant and mercy with Your servants. These members of the Devil Chasers, members of the body of Christ walk before You with all their heart."

He motioned for the parents and grandparents to come forward. "Now lay your hands on your children." The parents and grandparents laid hands on their children. Other family members laid hands on the parents and grandparents.

"I am asking you to anoint these children with the command that Jesus spoke before He was taken back to heaven when He said, 'You go into all the world, and preach the gospel to every creature. He that believes and is baptized shall be saved; but he that believes not shall be damned.'"

"Father, Your Son then said, 'These signs shall follow them that believe; In My name shall they cast out devils'; we are asking that all demon possessed teens who call these lines will be delivered and set free from the chains of darkness!"

All of the adults added amen and prayed words of agreement with Pastor Pearson's prayer. Vicki's heart was jumping with joy.

"Jesus continued by saying, 'In my name they shall speak with new tongues.' Father, we are asking many children be filled with the Holy Spirit and speak with tongues over the phones!"

"Amen!"

"You said 'They shall take up serpents.' Father, we believe that all the evil works that are reported over these phones will be broken by the power of the Blood of Jesus and the written Word spoken!"

"Amen!"

"You continued by saying 'and if they drink any deadly thing, it shall not hurt them.' Father we believe that anything demons devise against our children and those involved in this ministry will fail. I render all maneuvers against the Devil Chasers null and void. Harmless in every way! No evil shall befall them according to Psalms 91."

"Yes, Father, we are in agreement," Dan said.

"'They shall lay hands on the sick, and they shall recover.' Father, we claim that all shall be healed over the phones. We call spiritual hands from your angels and from the words spoken over the callers. We ask that You will touch the callers with Your anointed power and loose them from the spirits of infirmity in Jesus Name!"

"Glory!" Vicki and Ruth shouted together. His prayer was moving their spirit with great emotion of joy.

"We claim this passage of scripture from Mark chapter 16 as the working Word of God over this ministry. These messengers and the phones are contacts to the world Jesus called us to go into. Surely these children are obeying Your Word!"

A quiet hush fell upon all in the room as the presence of the Lord appeared like a cloud over their heads.

Kathy Todd started a song of praise as the Holy Spirit moved over them. They all joined in the singing, worshiping and praising the Lord. It was beautiful how she was singing in the spirit. At one point, they stopped to listen to the Holy Spirit sing to them through Kathy

She interpreted her song from tongues into English. "O Lord, our God, listen to the cry and prayers which Your servants are praying this night before You; that Your eyes may be open toward this house night and day. Listen to the prayers over these phones in this room and cause their prayers to return unto them answered in one hundred fold with all glory, power and honor going to Your Son, Jesus Christ. Hear these prayers that the stranger that calls may know Your Name, to believe on the Lord Jesus Christ. We claim many, many salvation's to occur through this phone ministry."

"Blessed be the Lord, that has given this vision to Joshua and his friends. Blessed be the Lord God that will perform His Word. It will NOT return unto this ministry void, but a harvest of 100 fold will come unto this ministry. Let all of the teenagers of Lincoln High School and this city know that there is a God. Amen," Dan prophesied.

Pastor David spoke to the family members. "Stretch forth your hands as I speak blessings over your children and mine."

Many were crying. The anointing of the Lord was strong in the room.

"In the Name of Jesus Christ, I bless you with the promises of God which are 'yea and amen.' The Holy Spirit make you healthy and strong in body, mind, and spirit to move in faith and expectancy in your lives and over these phones. May God's blessed angels be with you to protect and keep you."

Pastor David walked down the line of young people touching each one lightly on their forehead with oil.

"Be blessed with supernatural strength to turn your eyes from foolish, worthless and evil things. Be blessed with the Words of the Lord to speak wise counsel from His Word for the callers. Be blessed with beholding the beautiful things of God as you speak His Word into ugly, evil situations."

"I bless your ears to hear the lovely, the uplifting, and the encouraging and to not remember or meditate on the demeaning, negative, ugly things you will hear. May your feet walk in holiness and your steps be ordered of the Lord. May your hands be tender, helping hands to those in need, hands and mouths that bless."

"May your heart be humble and receptive to serve one another and the phone callers. Be blessed with the things of God, and not the world. May your mind be strong, disciplined, balanced and faith-filled. May everything you hear go to the Lord only and not to others for gossip."

"God's grace be upon this home, that it may be a sanctuary of prayer, rest and renewal. May many spiritual battles be manifested in this room. May love reign at all times and unconditional acceptance of one another and the callers be consistent."

"God give you success and prosperity in this ministry. May your needs be met according to His riches in glory. God give you spiritual strength to overcome the evil one and avoid temptation. God's grace be upon you to fulfill your dreams and visions. May goodness and mercy follow you all the days of your long life."

"The Lord bless you and keep you. The Lord make His face shine upon you, and be gracious unto you. The Lord lift up His countenance upon you and give you peace. I bless you in Jesus' Name!"

The power of the Lord's Spirit descended on all, manifesting in waves upon waves of cool, billowing breezes of pure air sweeping over the faces of everyone in the room. Many were slain in the Spirit and some became drunk in His presence. The Holy Spirit revealed Himself with waves of joy and love permeating the heart and soul of everyone standing, sitting, or laying on the floor. The sweet Spirit from the Lord anointed the Word of God that came out of the pastor's mouth and inspired them to sing and worship the Lord for a couple of hours before going home.

Joshua barely made it upstairs to his bedroom. He was drunk in the Holy Spirit, the new wine of the New Testament. He always wondered from a natural inquiry what it would be like to truly experience a supernatural occurrence. In the space of one month, he personally witnessed several of the stories he had only read in the Bible and other books of great men and women of God: laughing from deep within, unable to control the five senses like someone drunk, falling under the power of God, a miracle rescue and flying through the skies with his guardian angel. In his spirit, he heard the Lord say that many would experience His power in the last days, and this was only the beginning.

He did know one thing about being drunk in the Spirit, tomorrow when he woke up, he wouldn't have a hangover.

CHAPTER 37

Joshua laid his head on his pillow in his bed and fell fast asleep.

Someone or something woke him up again. He turned his head and saw a blurry 3:00 a.m. in bright red letters on his clock. The inside of his body still tingled with a super charged presence of the Lord. Trying to clear his head, he heard his spirit man speaking in the heavenly tongues inside him, but his flesh was cool and felt creepy. It was hard to separate his spirit from his soul and understand why he woke up. Shaking his head, he had a strange almost indescribable, weird feeling come over his skin. Then, an eerie feeling crawled up his back and made him believe that a supernatural guest was in his bedroom.

"Okay, who is it this time?" He wasn't scared even though goose bumps were traveling up and down his arms. He swung his feet out from the bed to sit up. His body felt like lead. He tried to open his eyes but couldn't as he lowered his head into his hands. He expected Kientay or another angel to put their hand on his shoulder and wake him up.

Suddenly, he felt a blast of icy cold air swoosh across his face. Instantly, he was awake and realized that a bad dream seemed to be interrupting his heavenly experience.

"Joshua!" a voice thundered from the corner of his bedroom.

Turning on the light, he saw an evil spirit with a black hooded cape and scythe in his hand. Joshua was so filled with the Holy Spirit from all the praising and singing that his first response was to laugh at the evil spirit. It came out of him spontaneously without fear.

That made chemah mad.

"Is this a joke, Kientay?"

"Don't you know who I am?" roared chemah with the scariest voice he could imitate as he released another cold blast of air against Joshua thinking that maybe he wasn't quite awake.

"Let's see," Joshua realized that he was looking at a demon spirit. The blast of air didn't faze him. He decided to play with him. "I think you have a Halloween costume on masquerading like the grim reaper."

"I am the spirit of death! I have come to take you to hell!" lied chemah.

Joshua couldn't keep a straight face. He cracked up laughing. "That's a lie, chemah. You'll have to do better than that." c*hemah? did I say chemah? Who is chemah?* The knowledge of his name didn't come out of his mind, but it came from his spirit.

Chemah cursed. *He knows my name!*

The Holy Spirit spoke through Joshua "Yes, I know your name, and I know your thoughts!"

"How do you know?" chemah heard Joshua's voice, but he had this funny feeling that he wasn't talking to the boy.

"Your evil thoughts are so loud that a baby Christian could read them. The thoughts of the wicked are an abomination to the Lord!" The Words from the Word of God that Joshua spoke roared through chemah's spirit. "For the Word of God is quick, and powerful, and sharper than any two-edged sword, piercing even to the dividing asunder of the soul and spirit, and of the joints and marrow, and is a discerner of the thoughts and intents of the heart."

Joshua heard those words come out of his mouth. He was completely aware of the Holy Spirit talking through him. "Your thoughts, chemah are continually evil. You gave up the peace of light for the chaos of darkness. You are an easy angel to understand. Nothing but evil is your way. You walk, talk, act and think evil. You chose darkness over the light of your Creator. Your end is the lake of fire!"

Chemah started trembling. Few of the beings in the kingdom of darkness knew he was a fallen angel. Because of his mutilated body, many thought he was a special creation of satan. His disguise was removed, and the real chemah stood before Joshua—exposed. Sweat poured out of his leather, burned-red skin.

"In eternity past, you experienced the love of the Creator. Why did you believe the lies of Lucifer when he told you that you were no longer useful for the Lord? While you were His, did He not bestow on you special honor and give you love and attention? You were once the special . . ."

Chemah screamed at the top of his lungs! "Enough!" He refused to listen to the truth and put his hands over his ears. "I won't listen to your words! You are trying to take away my peace and happiness in the kingdom of darkness!"

The anger of the Holy Spirit flared through Joshua's mouth. "There is no peace and happiness in your realm of darkness! You were created perfect; nothing missing and nothing broken, but you chose to be separated from the Father and accepted a life that included brokenness of spirit, soul and body. You chose to walk opposite of Your Creator."

Father God opened chemah's eyes, and he saw the Lord God talking through Joshua and started shaking. The power source within his body drained from his face and he grew weak "Of a truth, Lord."

"You have taken away your peace by your own wickedness. Destruction will come to you because you are a worker of iniquity. You will never inherit the earth and your power and riches will profit you nothing in the day of My wrath."

Slowly he regained his evil thinking. *I . . . will . . . fight the goodness of God!*. Fury was boiling out of his pores as he sweated angel blood. He was so angry at the truth, that he could not control his natural inclination to use his weapon.

Michael and Gabriel appeared and grabbed each hand as he started to blast Joshua away. Michael spoke. *You will never be allowed to hurt Joshua. He is under the protection of the Blood of Jesus Christ the Lord of Glory! He lives in the secret place, the Blood Covenant of the Almighty.*

Joshua pronounced judgment on chemah. "But the day of the Lord will come as a thief in the night; in which the heavens shall pass away with a great noise, and the elements shall melt with fervent heat, the earth also and the works that are therein shall be burned up. You shall perish in that day. You will burn in the lake of fire for eternity."

The words caused chemah unbearable pain. He wanted to leave so bad that he started having thoughts of killing himself. Even in the war of rebellion in heaven he never felt like this.

You are going to listen to Joshua! This is a taste of what the white throne judgment is going to be for you fallen angels, Michael told him. *Born-again humans will be your judge.*

Chemah shouted out, "No! You are tormenting me before the time." Chemah wanted God to judge him. He would be more merciful than humans would.

God has already revealed sin and rebellion through the man, Jesus Christ, Michael declared to chemah. *Jesus with the members of His body will judge you.*

"No . . . NO!" chemah could only guess what the body of Jesus the Anointed One would do after the trial and punishment that satan caused Jesus to endure. "I will plead for mercy from the Creator!"

"He will not hear you. What you say has to go through the body of Christ. That is the only way that God will listen to you," Gabriel said sternly.

Joshua was in great faith and the power of the Almighty Holy Spirit. He heard the conversation going on in his spirit. He sensed that warring angels were restraining chemah even though he couldn't see them.

"But the fearful, and unbelieving, and the abominable, and murderers, and whoremongers, and sorcerers, and idolaters, and all liars, shall have their part in the lake, which burns with fire and brimstone: which is the second death. That is your part, chemah. You are headed to the lake of fire and you chose that path with your eyes wide open!"

Chemah screamed in torment. "You can't do this! You cannot do this to me before the time!"

"Who said, chemah?" asked Joshua. "This is the time of the Almighty. This is a sliver in time that He hid from satan and his kingdom."

"The lease is not up yet! Satan is still god of this world!" He was grasping at anything he could think of. He was desperate to get out of Joshua's room.

The lease is up! Spoke the Father from heaven. His voice sounded like a lion roaring through chemah's spirit being. *This is My time. You will listen to My son!*

Chemah screamed to be hidden from the voice of the Almighty as a gust of wind burst through his body.

Joshua spoke. "satan was defeated by my elder brother Jesus the Anointed One! He gave me the keys to hell. I can do all things through Jesus Christ my Lord! Your time is up. Be gone." Michael and Gabriel were going to personally escort him to one of the entrances to hell, when Joshua called him back. "chemah!"

Chemah hated it, but he had to obey Joshua just like satan had to obey Jesus in hell. Jesus proved to all the evil demons and spirits that He was the One with all authority.

Joshua looked at chemah with authority through the Blood of Jesus. "Bow before the Holy name of my elder brother, Jesus, the Anointed of God from Nazareth."

He gritted his teeth. As his rage was being restrained, the noise of his grinding teeth was as irritating as fingernails scraping a chalkboard.

"The Father has said, 'Let all the angels bow to Jesus, who is God. Confess that Jesus is Lord over you!'" Joshua commanded. "You are an angel, even though you are a fallen one."

"I, already bowed!" he proclaimed from gritted teeth. "When . . . Jesus was . . . in hell."

"Do it again."

Michael held up his sword to chemah's neck.

Chemah choked out an objection. "I can't confess Jesus. Don't you know that demons and evil spirits can never be saved?"

"I only know scripture," Joshua replied. "The Word says every knee shall bow and every tongue confess that Jesus is Lord. You have knees, even if they are ugly. I'll tell you one more time, and then I'll let the angels that are beside you stab your heart."

Confess that Jesus is Lord! Michael was about to physically make him obey.

"I will not," chemah defied Joshua.

"My elder brother, Jesus, defeated you 2,000 years ago and gave me His power to make you bow! All authority and all power belongs to me because I am joint-heir with Jesus and with the new name that God the Father gave Jesus, you *will* bow! Jesus is Lord to the Glory of the Father!" quoted Joshua.

An unseen force made chemah obey Joshua's command. "Jesus . . . is . . . Lord . . . to . . . the . . . Glory . . . of . . . the . . . Father!" chemah finally choked out as the rebellious spirit deflated inside him. The goodness of God prevailed again.

"You desired to get inside the house of Knight," Chroni told him. "It was your choice chemah to follow the deceiver. The Word of God defeated you and you will never overcome the body of Christ."

"A believer in the Blood Covenant of Jesus just defeated you," Michael announced.

He could not disappear until all the angels finished speaking.

"A believer and confessor in the name of the greatest Devil Chaser in the entire world, the first Devil Chaser, Jesus Christ, the Son of God," Kientay added.

"Joshua is an overcomer through Jesus, and he just overcame you, chemah," Michael said. "You will be forced to give up your plans and pursuits against the body of Christ in these last days."

"Count on it!" The Holy Spirit spoke through Joshua as He opened Joshua's eyes to see into the spirit realm so he could watch chemah disappear.

Escorted outside, the angel zone that protected the property of the house of Knight, chemah realized he had been set up. There never was a hole in the wall of protection. The angels let him in. He glared at Michael. "You miserable . . ." Again, curses spewed from his mouth like a pipe full of sewage filling up a cesspool.

He dematerialize with his head down into the cold, dark, ugly night that was his world; a realm that had just been violated by the greatest power of all; a believer and a Devil Chaser, Joshua Knight.

Early the next morning, after Dan finished his quiet time with the Lord, he woke Vicki. "I know it's early, but I need to talk to you." He usually let her sleep in especially if she got up to pray through the morning hours.

"Oh, Dan! I overslept! I was going to fix your breakfast."

"No, I don't need breakfast, but I wanted to go into the office a little early this morning. The jury will be going into deliberation today, after my summation, if there isn't another delay." His latest trial was inundated with endless interruptions of various problems.

Vicki sat up. "Mr. Gottman's case? I thought you were going to do that yesterday afternoon?"

"It was postponed again, another surprise interruption. Anyway, we do it today."

Vicki got up and put on her robe. "So much is going on."

"I know and I have a feeling that we've only just begun." Dan hugged Vicki as she was going to the bathroom.

"Dan!" She put her hand up to block his kiss.

"I know, I know. You have to brush your teeth first." Dan stood at the doorway to the bathroom looking at his lovely wife.

"Dan, don't look so close this early in the morning, I don't even have my makeup on."

"You are beautiful with or without it."

After Vicki finished brushing her teeth and washing her face, she put her arms around his neck to give him a good morning kiss. They went downstairs to the kitchen to get some coffee together. Sitting at the table, Vicki asked him what he wanted to tell her. Dan told her about the incident yesterday at his office.

"Why didn't you tell me last night?"

"We went to bed too late. It wasn't a big deal. The Holy Spirit manifesting Himself with signs and wonders was the big deal!"

Vicki smiled. "Wasn't that great that Mose's grandmother was healed of diabetes last night?"

"Praise the Lord! How about the cancer in Kellie's grandmother?"

"That was great. The Lord is so good." They took a few minutes and worshipped the Lord.

"I admit last night was good, but I don't think seeing a demon spirit in the body of a human was a small thing!"

"I agree with you, but I didn't want a demon to overshadow what the Holy Spirit did last night. If that's the best thing the kingdom of darkness can use against us, then without a doubt they will fail."

"But a blonde with . . ." The coffee was done and she poured them both a cup.

"Now, Vicki," he interrupted her, "you can't get upset about a little thing like that. You know the Lord protected me."

"You didn't know that she wasn't a real human until after she disappeared."

"I can't believe that we are having this conversation over a demon spirit! You can't tempt me with . . ." Dan put his hands on his chest.

"Ohhhhh . . . Dan!" Vicki got up to hit him, playfully of course.

He caught her and stood to pull her close to him for a big kiss.

"Hey, Mom and Dad, aren't you a little old to be carrying on like that?" Joshua walked into the kitchen: his eyes still half-closed. "Mind if I get a cup?"

"I guess one won't hurt you," Vicki said. "And how old is old? Remember, I'm the one that fixes your breakfast, lunch and dinner!"

"One of these days you'll find out you're never too old for . . ." He swooped Vicki in his arms and gave her another big kiss.

Joshua tried to ignore them. "Dad, it's too early . . . spare me!" It wasn't cool to see your mom and dad kissing.

"How about some toast?" She asked gently pushing Dan away.

"Okay, but don't start preaching to me this early in the morning."

"Why in the world would I do that?"

"I didn't get much sleep last night. I had a visitor."

"Again?" Vicki asked. "Do you want some toast, Joshua?"

"Where did you go this time?" Dan asked.

"Two slices. I didn't go anywhere. I got a visit from a fallen angel named chemah."

"What?" She came over to the table to sit down.

"I woke up knowing someone was in my room and turning on the light I saw what looked like the spirit of death. His timing was terrible and I couldn't help but laugh."

A thought came to Vicki's mind. "Maybe your guardian angel set him up."

"The Word of God flowed out of my mouth before I could even think and the anointing was still so strong from our meeting last night. I could feel the glory surging in my blood. It was really cool."

"What else happened?" asked Vicki.

"I told him to leave, but then before he left, the idea came to me to quote the verses from Philippians 2:10 that you taught me."

Vicki smiled. "The scripture that says everything has to bow at the name of Jesus."

"I know that many Christians believe that the event of bowing to Jesus will take place in the future. But I found out from chemah that all the angels bowed when Jesus was born again in hell."

"Did you find scripture to support what the fallen angel told you?" Dan asked.

"Yes. In Hebrews 1:6 'But when He again brings the firstborn into the world, He says: "Let all the angels of God worship Him."' That happened in hell before Jesus went to the grave to get His body."

His dad warned him. "Uh, you might not find very many Christians that would understand your experience last night."

"I think a couple of huge warring angels were in my room to make him obey what I told him to do."

"Did he try to do anything to you?" Vicki asked as she stood to get the toast that had just popped up.

"Well, he tried to curse me with death. I heard myself quoting scriptures in a very calm voice. I woke up still speaking in tongues."

"Wasn't that your first time to ever get drunk in the Spirit?" Vicki asked.

"Yes."

"It was an awesome time with the Lord," Vicki said buttering the toast and pouring some orange juice for both of them. "I woke up speaking in tongues." Vicki noticed he stopped talking. She put down her toast. "Is there anything else?"

"Yes. The Holy Spirit talked directly through me. I heard Him speaking."

"How did you know?" Dan asked.

"I heard the Holy Spirit tell him things about the past that I didn't know about."

"What things?" Vicki asked.

"Chemah's past in heaven before he fell." Joshua told them what the Holy Spirit said. "When the Holy Spirit finished, I started to forbid him to ever come back again, but I decided it was too much fun to take authority over him in Jesus name."

"Fun?" Dan didn't know if he liked his son using the word *fun* when talking about demons and fallen angels.

"It's okay, Dad. I know the scriptures and besides, Jesus told me that I would have fun chasing devils."

"If the Lord told you it was fun, then who are we to say otherwise." Vicki looked over at Dan intently.

"I'm aware what other Christians think, but Jesus commissioned me to teach kids how to fight the devil. And one thing I know about fighting, if you don't like it, you won't last long in the heat of the battle."

"He has a point, Dan."

"I know what you are saying Joshua, but a lot of Christians won't understand you."

"They didn't understand Jesus either."

"Does it bother you that he found a way into your bedroom?" She placed a plate of toast in front of Joshua.

"No, why should it?"

"Some Christians would ask the Lord why he allowed a demon spirit to get to you," Vicki told him.

"It was awesome when I heard the Holy Spirit speaking through me and pronouncing chemah's punishment for his war crimes."

"What?" Vicki almost choked on a sip of orange juice.

"When I was doing that study on judgment, I took a side tour and looked up all the scriptures in the Bible on wickedness. I discovered that Proverbs said a lot about the result of wickedness. The Holy Spirit used those scriptures against chemah."

"How did that make you feel?" Vicki asked.

Joshua paused to think about his mom's question. "It was hard to separate me from the Holy Spirit, but I actually heard the Lord speaking through me. I had this feeling that at one point chemah saw the Lord, not me."

"That's pretty heavy, Joshua." Vicki wondered if he really knew what he was saying.

"I think that's the way is suppose to be," Dan answered.

"But judging angels?" Vicki asked.

"That is what the Lord is grooming us to do. We are going to rule and reign with Him throughout eternity." Joshua took a bite of the toast.

Dan said. "It is in the Bible. Paul said that we are going to judge angels. I can guarantee you that it will not be the ones in heaven that we judge."

"I know that scripture, Dan. But Joshua did that last night, not in the millennial reign of Jesus that is going to occur in the future."

"Mom, I didn't do it. The Holy Spirit did."

She stood to get Dan some more coffee. "I'm going to have to pray about this. Joshua's revelations are going to seriously affect the kingdom of darkness."

"No more coffee, Vicki."

"We can't be afraid of what demons might do to us. You know Jesus said that He gave us authority over *all* the power of the enemy and that nothing would hurt us!" Joshua said. "I'm not afraid of demons!"

"Joshua, be careful," his mom admonished him. "Knowledge puffs up."

He couldn't believe his ears. "Mom, Paul said first, 'now concerning things offered to idols; we know that we all have knowledge. Knowledge puffs up, but love edifies.' My knowledge came from the Spirit of God through the love of God. This experience has nothing to do with idols."

"You're right. I misused that scripture. We now have three major things that the kingdom of darkness has done to us since you started this ministry."

"Three? What's the other one?" Joshua asked.

"I'll let your mom tell you all about it. I've got to go, family."

They prayed together, and then Dan opened the door to the garage. "I'll see you tonight."

"Dan, don't forget about our sleepover," Vicki called after him. "Bye!"

Vicki told Joshua what had happened while she cleaned up the kitchen.

"That was more of a big deal than mine!"

"What makes you say that?" she said wiping off the kitchen table.

"He saw a demon spirit in the form of a beautiful woman?"

"Wait a minute did I say beautiful woman?"

"Let's get back to what Gloria and Dad saw . . . okay?"

"The Bible tells us that satan can appear as an angel of light. If he can do that then it shouldn't be a problem for a demon to appear as a female or male human. Besides, I believe your dad."

"Hey, I believe Dad and Gloria too." Joshua shook his head. "What will demons think of next?"

"What ever they try, the Holy Spirit will always warn us," his Mom reminded him.

"Cool!"

Vicki looked at Joshua. Every time he used the word *cool*, it reminded her that he was still her little boy.

He recognized the look. "Mom, don't look at me like that. I'm not your little boy, okay?"

"Whatever." She finished putting the dishes in the dishwasher.

He shook his head because she sounded like a kid. "I can't wait to tell the team about what happened."

"That reminds me, you never did tell me about your meeting with your guardian angel." She sat back down at the table.

Joshua told her about what he witnessed in the spirit realm of the near accident they almost had. Then he told her about seeing the future.

"Can you tell me about it?"

"I almost forgot about it. I was dangerously close to worrying over it. Kientay told me to just ask the Holy Spirit what to do. I think last night was His answer."

"What are you supposed to do?"

"I know I don't have to be concerned about what I'm going to say, because like last night, the Holy Spirit is going to speak through me," Joshua stood to go upstairs.

"Isn't the Lord wonderful?! He gave you help with the experience you gained last night."

"Yes. Hopefully that's enough training not to react like I saw us doing."

"Us? You mean you saw me in the future?" Now Vicki was curious.

"Yes."

"Did I panic?" Vicki could hardly believe what Joshua was saying.

"No, we both just hesitated too long."

Running up the stairs, he had to hurry and rush through his morning routine. He couldn't wait to get to school and tell Mose and Hannah about his visit. He wasn't worried about tonight either. He decided not to tell Hannah about what he saw was going to happen, because he didn't want her to worry.

She thought about the thing Joshua revealed to her as she finished wiping down the counters and got dressed to take him to school. *Above everything, Vicki Knight,* she told herself, *you cannot worry. Worry is your greatest enemy. Worry is the enemy of casting all your cares on Jesus.*

As she watched him get out of the car and enter his new school, she prayed. "I cast all my cares on You, Lord, for You care for me. No weapon formed against this family will prosper. We are more than conquerors through the Anointed One and His Anointing. Greater are You in us, than He that is in the world. And above all things," she continued. "We dwell in the secret place, the Blood Covenant, of the Most High God!"

The angels shouted and rejoiced with her as she praised the Lord with all her heart, mind and soul.

CHAPTER 38

The first light frost of the fall season occurred the night before the official opening of the Devil Chasers ministry. The day before was almost unbearably hot, but the next day hats, light coats and umbrellas were taken out of storage by most of the kids going to school. It had to happen sooner or later, but to the four members of the Devil Chasers standing at the top of the steps by the flagpole of Lincoln High School, they would have preferred it happened later. A cold front moved in with a storm overnight causing a clash of weather fronts producing severe lightning and thunder. Joshua thought it was symbolic of the two spiritual fronts that would soon meet head on. It was an early *thank God it's Friday* morning. They joined hands and prayed over the day and the cards they were going to hand out.

Several guardian angels joined them in prayer as the warring angels stood guard watching for any attacks from the enemy. Although the enemy was still unaware of the total scope of this new ministry, all of the angels were aware it wouldn't take long for the kingdom of darkness to figure out what was going on. Healing angels appeared behind the team with golden buckets filled with golden flakes of healing dust. They were prepared to touch the minds of those reading the cards to prepare their hearts to receive the seed of the Word on the cards.

All kinds of evil and unclean spirits watched the proceeding from a far. The lower demons were wondering who forgot to inform them of another prayer gathering around the flagpole.

"Hey, who changed the date of our prayer around the flagpole?" someone came up to the group while they were praying.

"No one did Kyle," answered Kellie after they finished praying. Taking the morning off from her school to hand out cards with them, she justified her absence because she was part of the team. Kyle attended Hannah and Kellie's youth group. "Here," she told him. "Let me give you one of our cards. We're starting a Christian phone line to pray with teens needing help."

An angle threw some gold dust on Kyle's head and hands as he read the card, "The Devil Chasers . . . Have Bible will Travel . . . Hey, this sounds cool.

Can I have some to pass out?"

"Sure!" Kellie handed him about a dozen. "We have enough to pass one out to every kid in this school."

Joshua looked around at the kids starting to congregate around them. *Thank you, Lord. This is exactly what we prayed for.*

Many came up to see what was going on because they were attracted to the crowd gathering around them. Joshua asked the Lord to not let one card be wasted. "If you know of anyone that needs any help, please pass them around." Joshua told a group of Christian kids.

A couple of kids spotted the glittering gold dust on their hands and head. "Hey look!" One of them pointed.

"Hey! Look at the gold sparkles on that group," a girl said.

"What is it?"

Joshua looked at Hannah wondering what they were talking about.

"Do you see anything?" Hannah asked.

"No, do you?"

"No."

Another boy pointed at them. "It's all over your hands."

"I see an angel throwing golden dust all over you guys. Man! It's all over you!"

"Hey! I see angels, too!"

"Look! Angels are every where!"

Kids began running to the four teenagers passing out cards with gold dust sprinkled all over them. Rumors of seeing white glowing angels with golden buckets of gold dust started spreading like wild fire all over the school. The first bell rang.

"Okay, everyone, divide and conquer! We'll meet here at lunch time," Joshua said.

Mose walked with Joshua to his locker. "What do you think is going on?"

"I think that the Lord thought of a supernatural way to get our cards passed around."

"Cool, but how do they know they are angels?" Mose asked.

"Man, I saw one." A kid said as he was walking by. "They are dressed in white holding shinny golden buckets tossing out this glittery gold like dust."

"Did you hear what that kid just said?" Hannah asked Kellie as she walked her to her car in the parking lot.

"Yeah! What a supernatural God we serve!" Kellie got into her car.

"He is awesome! See you at lunch." Hannah waved goodbye as she turned around and went inside the school to go to her locker. She saw Shannon, a friend of hers since elementary school, at the locker next to hers.

"Hey," Shannon opened her locker and looked at her straight auburn hair to see if it needed combing before going to her first class. "I hear you're handing out some kind of card. What's going on? Something about angels?"

"God sent His angels to help us pass out our cards. Remember, the club that I told you I joined?" Hannah removed the books she didn't need from her backpack and threw them into her locker with a thump.

"What?" she asked as she reapplied her lipstick.

Hannah unzipped the front pocket of her purse and handed her a card.

She scanned it quickly. "What's it all about?"

"It's about helping kids and their problems with prayer and scriptures."

"You think anyone's gonna take you guys serious?" She put the card into her locker and closed her door.

"Are you kidding? How many angels have you ever seen?"

"I just heard about the angels, I didn't see them," Shannon replied.

"Ask someone who saw them." They started walking down the hall.

"What's happenin' tonight?" Shannon changed the subject. It was Friday. She didn't have a date and thought about going to a movie with Hannah. "Hey! We haven't gone to a movie together in a long time!"

"I'm spending the night with Joshua."

Shannon spun her around before they entered their classroom. "Joshua who?"

"Joshua Knight."

"Who?"

"Oh yeah, I forgot that you don't know him. He's a new kid at our school . . . he's the one I told you about. You know . . . the one that started the phone club I joined with Mose Pearson and my friend Kellie."

"You're spending the night with him?"

"Me, and the rest of our team with our parents. We're spending the night at Joshua's tonight to pray and read the Bible."

"You better be careful how you tell kids around here what you are doing. They gonna think you're doing the nasty."

"Shannon!" Hannah put her hand over her mouth.

"And what's this thing you're gonna do? A Bible study? On Friday night? Are you insane?"

"No, it's a special deal like a kick-off party."

"Oh, why didn't you just say it's a party? Who's invited?"

"It's not open to everyone." Hannah thought about what she said and how it sounded to Shannon. "You're right, I'm not gonna tell anyone else about what we are doing." She reached into her front pocket and pulled out a handful of cards. "Here, why don't you hand these cards out to some of the youth at your church?"

Shannon took about a dozen cards, "How are you going to stop kids from calling you and playing pranks on you?"

"We'll let the Holy Spirit take care of the pranksters. We're not worried about that. Anyway, this ministry was started by the Lord, not us."

"The Holy Spirit? Man, Hannah what's gotten into you?"

The Holy Spirit, she thought. "I'll tell you later when we have more time." She forgot that Shannon wasn't a committed Christian. She mainly went to church because her parents made her.

"You think the angels will help me pass out your cards?"

"I wouldn't be surprised. This ministry is a blessed ministry."

Hannah and Shannon stopped talking as their teacher started the class. Hannah pulled out one of the Devil Chasers cards and held it in the palm of her hand. Quietly under her breath, she prayed in tongues. The team had been dreaming and waiting patiently for this day, but they never once thought that Jesus would send His angels to help them get this ministry started.

God you are so good!

Joshua and Mose were waiting for the girls to show up for lunch in the parking lot.

"Hey, Joshua. Why don't we let the girls go to the cafeteria and we go to the Hut to pass out cards?"

"How are we getting to the Hut?"

"Oh yeah! We don't have any wheels."

"How about getting the driver's license first."

"I'm 15 years old. How old are you?" Mose realized he didn't even know Joshua's birthday.

"I turned 14 last July."

"Wordman! You won't be able to drive until you're a junior!"

"I know."

"Hey guys! Where are we going?" asked Hannah calling out to them from the car window.

"To the Hut . . . to the Hut, to the Hut, Hut, Hut," Mose sang as they got in Kellie's car.

"Has anyone given out any more cards?" asked Joshua.

"I've given out a lot of cards to guys that are Christians," Mose told them. "Word! That angel thing really helped!"

"I gave away a few to Shannon, a girl next to my locker," Hannah replied. "She's going to hand them out to her church group and she's hoping to see an angel."

"Have you ever heard of gold dust appearing like that?" Kellie asked.

"I've heard about it, but I've never seen it," Joshua told them.

"Did any of us see it?" Hannah asked.

They all looked at one another shaking their head no.

"Do you think it was real?" Kellie asked.

Joshua thought about it for a second or two. "Yes, I think it was a manifestation of the Lord. We prayed over each card."

"Word! Angels were announcing the beginning of this ministry!"

"That's like the stars twinkling and glowing when Jesus was born," Hannah proclaimed.

"We should have known that Jesus had a plan to help us get the word out. We've got a lot more to pass out," Joshua said.

"Give one to every teen you see," Mose said. "If we don't, it will take us a long time to get this ministry rolling." That reminded him of an old, very old, TV series. "Rollin, rollin, rollin . . . keep them doggies rollin . . . RAW HIDE!"

This time Hannah cracked up laughing. She loved the way Mose could keep them laughing all the time.

"Where did that come from?" Kellie looked back at him as she changed lanes.

"Don't any of you guys watch *Nick at Night*?"

Kellie exclaimed. "Who has time for TV?"

"I've watched it," Hannah told him.

Mose couldn't believe the look on Joshua's face. "You have no idea what I'm talking about do you?"

"I don't watch TV."

"How about movies?"

"Rarely," Joshua replied.

Kellie pulled into the driveway of the Hut.

Mose couldn't believe that Joshua knew nothing about TV. It almost seemed un-American.

Hannah hit Mose in his back lightly. "At least we know how dedicated Joshua is."

They all laughed again as they sat down at their regular booth and told the waitress all they wanted was water. None of them were eating because they were fasting. It was easy for Hannah to fast, but Mose looked at the glass of water on the table and made a face like a dying man's last request who had been marooned in a desert.

His stomach growled loudly.

Hannah and Kellie laughed.

Mose swallowed. "Uh, Joshua . . . how long are we fasting?" He rubbed his aching stomach.

Kellie grabbed his hands across the booth and looked into his eyes. "The . . . whole . . . weekend!"

Mose laid his head on the table. "Jesus, help me!"

"Hey!" Hannah stood and called after a table of friends she recognized.

"What'sup?" one of the girls asked.

"Yeah, like, what's with this angel thing?" another girl asked.

"Like, I've got these cards to pass out to everyone and the angels are helping us," Hannah explained.

"What's the 411?"

"A phone ministry," Hannah answered. "Call us and you will get help with prayer and scriptures from the Word of God."

Joshua looked at Kellie and Mose. "Let's get started like Hannah."

"Yeah, we can't let Hannah show us up," Mose said as his stomach growled loudly again. "I need to keep my mind off this growling stomach."

"Let me see!" One of the girls took a card from Hannah and started reading it out loud.

"The Devil Chasers . . . whoa . . . hey girl you gonna chase spirits like they did in the movie *Ghostbusters*?"

"Let me see!" One of the girls took another card from Hannah. "You go, girl!"

"Like, give me a break!" Hannah stared at the girl that said 'you go, girl.' She handed her the card. "Like, here! Read it and get a clue."

"Have Bible will travel?" The girl had a puzzled look on her face.

Hannah put her hand on her hip. "It's one of those sixties or fifties show . . . you know the western series about a guy with a gun?"

"All the movies back then were about a cowboy with a gun. Big deal!" commented another girl.

"No, never heard of it." The girl started to hand her back the card.

"Keep it. You never know when you might need a friend to pray for you."

She put it in her purse.

"Here, you can all have one. We don't chase ghosts. But we do kick butt!" Hannah announced.

"Man! They don't talk like that at my church."

"Have Bible will travel . . . I've heard that phrase before," one of the girls named Allison commented.

"Hey, listen to this, We deal with fear, unbelief, doubt and sickness."

Another girl said. "What's the deal?"

"The deal is that demons have been ragging on us and it's time to expose them." Hannah pointed to the number on the card. "You can call our digits starting Monday."

"Joshua did you hear Hannah?" Kellie asked.

"No, I've been busy handing out cards"

"She's telling the girls that we kick butt."

"We will be kicking the devil's butt. Don't let it bother you, Kellie. She's just trying to relate to the group of girls she was talking to. It's like Paul saying that he knew how to be all things to all people."

Kellie just wanted to know who the real Hannah was.

"Is this a religious thing with a church or something?" asked Allison.

"No, but we will pray for every caller," answered Hannah.

"Okay, cool." Allison put the card in her jean pocket.

Another girl looked at Allison's pants. "Hey! You've got gold dust all over your jeans!"

She turned her head to look and then looked at her hands. "Like, gold dust is all over my hands!"

Kids all over the restaurant flocked to see Allison's hands.

"I didn't think you could do religious stuff at school," commented one of the boys eavesdropping. He couldn't see the gold dust everyone was going crazy over.

Hannah handed him one of the cards. "We answer phone calls off campus. Members of the Devil Chasers ministry are teens talking and praying with teens."

Another boy came up and asked for a card. Looking Hannah over he said, "I'll call if you'll answer."

"In your dreams," Hannah gave him the brush-off and turned to talk to others gathered to see what was going on. "Listen, if you're having a problem with anything, I mean anything, just call us. I promise you we can help you with prayer."

"Is it 24/7?" asked Allison with a dazed look on her face, as people were feeling of her hands trying to get the golden flakes onto their hands.

"Not yet. Monday through Friday after school hours until 10 or 11," Hannah said handing out the rest of her cards to everyone around her.

"Hey! I want some gold dust!"

"How's it going?" asked Joshua seeing the big crowd around Hannah.

"I gave a lot of cards away. That girl, Allison has gold dust on her hands. I think this is going to be a happening thing."

"Praise the Lord!" Joshua could hardly wait for Monday to come. But first, he had to take care of Friday night.

‡ ‡ ‡

Chemah was camped at the old headquarters down from the house of Knight. Even with his far superior powers, he couldn't get any closer than metraloas did. He was fuming mad.

Every time he thought of metraloas, he would get so furious that his skin seemed to get redder and tougher. He vowed to pay him back for his deception. The demonic androids were a necessary evil, but one that was sometimes intolerable. He had plenty of time to think of ways for metraloas' demise, but he reigned in his thoughts disciplining himself to concentrate on the brat Joshua and his family.

The bat appeared beside him. "Where is metraloas?"

"Who are you?"

"I'm the bat that has been talking with him."

"He is in the pits in hell."

"I will take care of him for you."

"Why?"

"Because I would like to join your division."

"You see where I am?" chemah laughed at him.

"You are an angel, and we both know that this is only temporary. I am one of the latest androids that satan has invented. I have more capabilities, but I would like to be in a division of the highest authority of angels," the bat told him.

"What is your real form?"

He shape-shifted into a large, black gargoyle.

"What else can you do for me?"

"I will help you take down the house of Knight."

"How?"

"The master promised to give me the reward from the division of powers with the ability to cause murder. I think the anointing of murder would help your work against them."

A cloud moved over the house of Knight's neighborhood and it started pouring down rain. Chemah used his shield of protection from earth's weather to keep himself from getting wet. The weather fit his mood perfectly. It was foul, and he was foul. A bolt of lightening sounded and shook the tree. It hit the invisible dome of protection surrounding the house of Knight. The electrical current was diffused into what looked like thousands of tributaries surrounding the half circle and then went into the ground with a sizzle. It would have been a spectacular show for humans if they could see into the supernatural world, but for chemah it was another reminder that he couldn't break through the hedge of protection.

"A spirit of murder would be useful."

"I just have one thing to finish before I can work for you."

"Finish your assignment with the master and report back to me. I will allow you to join my division."

The bat disappeared.

Chemah looked down and realized that several demon spirits had gathered around his base. "What are you fools starring at?" He screamed at them.

"We are looking for metraloas."

"The moron is in the pit."

They were scared of chemah. He was a higher spirit in power and authority than metraloas and all of them put together. "We came to inform him that Joshua Knight has formed a phone ministry."

Chemah moved at the speed of light and stood among them on the ground.

Metraloas said something about it, but he didn't listen to him. "What is he doing?"

They handed him a card.

Chemah quickly scanned it. "Where did you get this?"

"We stole it out of a pocket of a teenager. Knight's gang is passing them out all over the school."

Chemah cursed and threw it on the ground. He turned his fire blaster on it and tried to burn it. It refused to burn. "What in——is going on?" He bent over to look at the card to see what it was made of.

A warring angel materialized and took the card out of chemah's fingers. "I'll take that card and return it to its rightful owner." He disappeared faster than a blink of an eye.

"——!" chemah hated it that some warring angels could translate themselves right in the midst of them and leave unharmed. "The house of Knight must have prayed over the stupid cards!"

"You've haven't heard the worst yet," another sneered.

"What?! Tell me you stupid idiot!" chemah grabbed the demonic vulture and began strangling him.

"Angels are throwing the golden healing dust all over the hands and heads of the kids that are receiving their cards." He choked out.

Chemah turned white.

"You should see the kids that have already seen the golden flakes and the angels!"

Chemah cursed. "How many?"

The two snake watchers looked at each other. "Um, maybe a hundred or so?"

He cursed again. "Do you know that one witness will tell a minimum of seven others? Go to hell and get reinforcements. Take them to the high school and see if you can contain the outbreak that the Devil Chasers have started!"

Watching the house of Knight gave chemah a better understanding of what metraloas was up against. He quickly fastened his eyes on the sound of many car doors closing. He couldn't believe it! Even in pouring down rain the women were meeting for intercessory prayer. He looked up to the sky. It wouldn't be long before the communication beams from the house would be sent to heaven and the answers would come back just as fast as they were sent. There was nothing that the kingdom of darkness could do to interfere with God's response since the communication link between heaven and earth was completed.

He cursed again as he watched the glory cloud surround the house. It was so thick that even with his special angelic eyes, he couldn't see what was going on. He was sure that either Jesus or the Holy Spirit was manifesting His physical presence. He hated it!

This assignment was disgusting and made him sick. *No wonder metraloas wanted to go back to hell.* He cursed again. He was really losing it thinking about metraloas. That's it. *I'm visiting shathah.*

Before leaving he tried to curse the house of Knight, but he felt like the evil prophet Balaam who could not curse the nation of Israel. It was like every curse word he spoke fell on dead ground.

A black cloud moved over his tree and a bolt of lightening appeared and struck the tree causing it to split down the middle destroying the former headquarters. Chemah moved and screamed out loud.

A voice bellowed out from the cloud. *I will bless those who bless My people and curse those who curse My people.*

Chemah disappeared trembling.

"I told you! You are not going over to their house tonight!" Wade shouted at Sheila as she fixed his breakfast. He hit the table and stood screaming and yelling at her.

Sheila turned around and walked away.

"Come here, Sheila! Don't walk away from me." Wade grabbed her arm and turned her around.

Sheila pulled away. She knew she would have bruise marks where he grabbed her. Staring at him and seeing the demonic eyes, she decided to speak out. "I am going, and you can't stop me. I am speaking to the devil inside of Wade!"

"Did someone tell you that I am demon-possessed?"

"No one had to tell me that, Wade or whatever your name is. I've know since the first day I got saved that you have a demon and probably many more."

SLAP! The spirit of rage and fury hit Sheila through Wade.

She put her hand to her face. "That is the last time you will ever hit me in the Name of Jesus! I apply the Blood of Jesus to my body. I bind you evil spirits in my husband in the Name of Jesus! You try to hit me again and angels will cut you to pieces!"

Sheila stood and faced the devil in her husband . . .

. . . Shathah's fury raged against Sheila. He wanted to crush the spirit inside her! As he started to move Wade to hit Sheila again, two big warring angels appeared with huge swords drawn against shathah.

"Sheila is a child of the most High God. She has used the Name of the Lord and the Blood of the Almighty Son of God. She now has us to defend her. Before you can strike her again, you will be hacked to pieces by the order of the Holy Spirit."

Shathah's rage was so out of control, he could barely contain himself.

Chemah appeared and tried to calm him down. "I wouldn't do it if I were you."

"What are you doing here?" asked shathah.

"I've come to see how you are doing with your assignment." chemah was really running out of patience and time.

He looked over at the warring angels now guarding Sheila. "The female———is growing in spiritual strength and learning how to use the Word of JC against me." He grabbed chemah in desperation. "She has learned about the power that JESUS . . ."

Chemah slapped him hard. "Don't say HIS name!" chemah slapped him again. "Get ahold of yourself!"

Shathah fell to his knees after the last slap. "Did you hear what she said?! She applied *HIS* Blood against me! That gives me the creeps! I've heard that the good angels appear and smear His Blood all over your body!" He rubbed his arms frantically trying to remove the invisible Blood that he could feel. "LOOK!" He yelled at chemah, "I can't shape-shift now!"

Chemah looked over at the warring angels surrounding Sheila; they were smiling. He whispered, "shathah control your tongue! The Blood will wear off after twenty-four hours. Christians rarely consistently apply the Blood of Jesus. They can't see you in the spiritual realm. Most of the time they forget the revelation knowledge that they receive about us, so remember that the next time you start to lose it."

He whimpered, “I don’t think I will be able to knock her around like I use to.” He was still rubbing his arms.

“Those are very powerful warring angels surrounding her now. Since she has learned how to apply the Blood and the Word against you, you won’t be able to touch her again, unless she gives you access.”

“Get it off me!” He screamed bloody murder. “Get it off me!!!”

Chemah released fire from his weapon and showered him. It burned his upper body and shathah’s skin turned black like charcoal.

“Thanks, I needed that!” His skin stopped tingling and irritating him. Shathah looked over at Wade crying and asking Sheila to forgive him. “He grovels like a dog when I’m not in him. He isn’t a man at all unless I make him act like one. When she leaves to go to her meeting at the house of Knight, I’ll get him good and drunk. Then maybe I can think of something else evil to do to this family.”

“Listen, shathah, the master thinks you’re helping me to get into the house of Knight.”

“How can I help you if I lose Wade?”

“She didn’t cast you out did she?” asked chemah.

“No! But she tried! It took all of our combined power to keep from being cast out. Who knows how long it will be before her power is greater than ours? She prays everyday with many believers!”

“You’re right. We need to do something quick.” chemah paced back and forth. “It’s been my experience that we need to strike fast and hard before they grow in faith.”

“I’m not sure about that. Maybe I should back off Wade and use the ‘I’ll change and go to church if you don’t leave me’ con.”

The thought came to chemah that maybe they should drop the adults altogether and work on the teenagers. *The Devil Chasers . . . I wonder, do they really know how to fight demons?* There’s no time for that.” chemah wanted to get the house of Knight as soon as possible. It was embarrassing to be assigned to humans with little authority on earth and with lower class androids. “I have to get rid of this assignment.”

“You want to get to the house of Knight because of your ego and for revenge. That means that this assignment is already compromised.”

“Shut up, you fool! The house of Knight is going down with or with out you!” chemah glared at him with his bulging, inflamed eyes. He was determined to get out of the mess he was in now. “I don’t need you!”

“Your pride will get in your way. You’re not thinking right!” shathah realized he better not listen to him.

Chemah was furious with anger. “Who is in charge of this operation?”

“It is not a matter of who is in charge! It’s only a matter of results.

Which plan will work and which plan is stupid."

BAM! Chemah flew into shathah and hit him full force with a blast of fire and then his other fist. Shathah's jaw reeled backwards and cracked. He retaliated and gave chemah an upper cut with his fist. Shathah then turned himself into a demonized snake so he could squeeze all the fire out of him. They were screaming and yelling so loud that the demonic world heard them all around the earth.

"Fight! It's a fight!" demons gathered all around them from the heavenlies and the near by neighborhood by the thousands. They were cheering and taking bets.

As chemah flew by, shathah grabbed him and began to squeeze him with all his might. Then chemah opened his mouth and latched onto one of shathah's arms. He spit out a huge chunk of his arm as green blood squirted all over them. Shathah screamed out in pain and hit chemah on the top of his head revealing the power he had even though he wasn't an angel.

The noise and revelry of the fight entered the portals of hell. The fighting evil spirits tumbled out of the house and entered the skies above the Coyle house. Rage so filled chemah's heart, that he completely forgot his assignment and lost his focus.

As they continued fighting ruthlessly, four mammoth, winged flying dinosaurs flew out of the pit of hell and latched on to each arm of the perpetrator with their sharp and long talon claws. They separated both of them and carried them down to the pit to report to satan.

‡ ‡ ‡

Sheila went into the bedroom and shut the door. She decided to pack her suitcase and leave Wade until the situation changed.

Wade ran after her and pounded on the door.

"Sheila let me in!" He hit the door three more times. "Sheila, pleeeease, please, please . . . PLEASE! I beg you . . . Please let me in! I am sorry! I don't know why I do what I'm doing to you. We can work this out if you'll just talk to me!"

She refused to let him in the bedroom. The pounding quit, and she heard Wade go downstairs. The front door slammed. He started his car and drove away. She figured he was going to his favorite bar to get drunk, because that was his solution for everything. There was nothing else to say to him. She decided not to talk to Wade again until the demon was cast out of him.

Never again would she let the evil spirit in Wade hit her.

CHAPTER 39

Joshua went to his front door for the third time that night. Everyone he invited showed up with their parents even though the cold and stormy weather persisted all day. By the time everyone started coming to the Knights' home, the rain had stopped, although a cloud cover returned and hid the night stars. A hint of precipitation was still present in the air and a sensation of anticipation hung over Joshua like a cloud as he shut the door behind Hannah and her mother. He couldn't decide if knowing the future was a positive or a negative, especially since the stakes were so high.

Tonight, a literal life or death situation was going to take place in his home. Joshua could only hope he would do the right thing. Since he was not aware when the events would occur, he wasn't sure how much time he had. He looked at his watch realizing that in the last five minutes he checked the time three times. He told himself that he had to get it together and stay calm, because everything was going to be cool.

Sheila walked through the front door and followed her daughter into the living room. She hadn't told Hannah about their clothes in the back of the trunk of the car, because she didn't have any plans yet. She only knew that after they stayed the weekend at the Knights' house, they were going over to her mother's house. Her mother already picked up Jared and wasn't surprised at the suitcases she loaded in the car. More than once she had encouraged her daughter to leave her husband. Sheila intended to keep on fasting until something changed; in her heart she didn't think that would be very long. Actually, she had a persistent feeling that something was going to happen soon. Trying not to think about her personal situation, she sat down on the beautiful white couch. This was a home that maybe she and Wade could have had if he hadn't spent most of their married life drinking.

Vicki pushed a serving cart into the living room containing an ice-cold pitcher of water and an ice bucket with glasses. It was hard for her to serve only water and not provide finger foods for her guests. "I hope everyone is in agreement about fasting for the Devil Chasers ministry."

"I think it's a great idea." Ruth picked up the glass water pitcher and poured herself a glass of water.

"There is nothing like being able to hear from the Lord so much clearer after a couple of days of fasting," commented Pastor David. "It is very good to let the flesh know who is boss once in awhile."

"Word on!" Mose raised his fist half-heartily. He was getting weak and didn't know if he could last the whole weekend.

Dan called everyone to attention. "Vicki, Joshua and I have been praying and asking the Lord how to conduct this weekend. I have divided rooms for prayer into three areas: The family room for prayer over the tools of the ministry, like the phone, the cards, and the room. The living room can be for corporate prayer. The library and dining room can be used for instruction. And there are three bedrooms upstairs designated for private prayer anytime anyone wants to get alone with the Lord."

"We believe this is a long-term ministry commitment for as long as the Lord wills, so we feel we need to keep the communication lines open between us and the Lord. We want to be ready for anything with the help and guidance of the Holy Spirit." Vicki handed Dan a glass of water. He continued talking after he took a couple of sips. "I know that our children started fasting today. Let me know if any of you want any meals tomorrow. If you haven't fasted before, twenty-four hours is a good start."

"One meal was a good start for me," Mose said under his breath.

"Let's begin with us all praying together and then we can split up. I'm sure our kids want to be alone with each other for awhile." Dan took a drink and started the prayer.

Not too alone, thought Joshua.

Shathah flew out of a gateway from hell, thinking how much he wished he had never gotten involved with chemah. He doubted he would get any recognition of any value now that satan had to discipline both of them for fighting. *How embarrassing!* He had to wrestle with chemah without any of his powers, but neither could the fallen angel use any of his evil powers. He rubbed the spot where his ear was supposed to be. Chemah had gotten so furious with him that he bit off his ear and a chunk out of his arm.

Satan thought that was so wickedly funny and amusing that he refused to allow chemah to terminate him. Ordering shathah to get his arm fixed, but not replace his ear, irritated shathah. Satan told him that his ear would remind him of the fight that caused him to forget about his assignment. It was shathah's unfortunate luck that satan was visiting hell at the same time that chemah and he started fighting.

"Wouldn't boxing on earth be more entertaining if men who wrestled and boxed would once again start biting chunks of their flesh from one another?" Satan sat back down on his thrown and started reminiscing about the 'good' old Roman days. "Now those were the days of real men fighting real fights," he thought out loud.

He stopped the fight because he got bored. He issued them both one more warning and sent them back to earth. He gave chemah a personal threat. "If you fail at this assignment, I will strip you of all your powers and banish you to the dark planet." Even though he couldn't destroy chemah, he could chain him up if he wanted to. "Besides, I'm surprised at you chemah," he said to him after shathah left the arena, "one blow should have destroyed that android."

"Your androids are becoming more and more powerful," chemah said with a warning tone in his voice.

"I know what you are thinking . . . I have all power over them. Not one of my creations would dare confront me!"

Chemah dared to speak. "Might I remind my lord, that you dared to confront God our Creator."

"Ah, but you see that was different chemah. I know the heart of God. He is like a cream puff compared to me."

"But my lord, God has handed over the authority of His kingdom to Jesus. The born-again newly created human is the one that you are going to confront."

"ENOUGH! Don't remind me, chemah. One of these days you will push me too far." He glared with fire-red eyes into the cold eyes of the fallen angel. "I will overcome Jesus at the final hour when He descends on earth with His army. I will be ready with a stronger army. Remember, when Jesus comes He won't find any faith here on earth. I will have successfully destroyed all seeds of faith. Only the force of fear will remain. The question is . . . will you be at my side or on the front line?"

"I will be just behind death and hell, like always."

Satan disappeared in a whirlwind of fire.

Chemah sensed an overwhelming feeling of dread. It occurred to him that satan wasn't as ready as he thought he was and that just maybe he wouldn't be at his side either.

"Chemah!" The bat flew behind him out of one of the trap doors from the center of hell and screamed after him.

He barely heard the bat. Chemah stopped as the bat materialized in mid-air.

"I've been looking everywhere for you."

"Why?"

The bat could barely talk. He took a couple of deep breaths and spit out great information for the angel. “I found *the* copies of the report metraloas hid from you.”

Chemah’s eyes sparkled with evil joy. “Where?”

“I figured out they had to be close to him. He made a fake hollow stone by his home base. I could only search when he was gone, but I knew if I watched him long enough that I would find them.” The bat shape-shifted as the documents appeared in the gargoyle’s hand.

Throwing them on the ground, chemah used his fire blaster and burned them to ashes. “I’m going to discharge enough heat into that android to explode him to smithereens!” Immediately, he flew to the nearest gateway back into hell. “Are you coming with me?”

“I wouldn’t miss this for anything in this world!” the bat laughed. “I hate that old android. He’s long outlived his usefulness in the kingdom of darkness. He should have been destroyed years ago!”

“I believe that we are going to get along fabulously!” Chemah patted him on the back as they materialized on a dusty trail in the pits.

“Metraloas told me that this was your favorite place to be when you visited hell. I’ve only lived in hell and the surface of earth. I was immediately shipped to earth from the dark planet.”

“There are billions of planets out in space.”

“Then why are we stuck on this planet?”

Chemah stopped, turned around and stared at him. “Long story . . . maybe one of these days I will tell you about it. Let’s find metraloas.”

“I know exactly where he is.” He hurriedly flew to the back of the left leg of hell where metraloas was digging new pits. “There he is.”

Chemah took off flying and hit metraloas full force knocking him off his feet and landing on top of him.

Metraloas was shocked. “I thought I was finished with you chemah!” he yelled.

Chemah stood and pointed his fire blaster at him. “Soon, I will be finished with you.” He screamed obscenities at the android. “I told you that I was going to terminate you!”

“What about the copies of my report?”

“Burned to ashes and scattered to the four corners of the earth!”

“How . . . ?”

“Meet my new assistant!”

The gargoyle materialized and sneered at him. “I found your copies,” he mockingly told him where he found them.

Metraloas recognized the bat that befriended him. “Why? He pleaded with his old friend. “We are both androids.”

"You are a pathetic excuse for one." The gargoyle cursed him. "I was sent by the master to destroy all androids who are evolving beyond what they were created to be. You have developed several abilities that the master didn't originally design you to have."

Chemah released a sadistic chuckle. "The master doesn't want his inventions to develop on their own. He doesn't care about education or freedom. He wants his androids to be puppets and humans to be zombies. Whatever gave you the idea that the master values you at all?"

Metraloas could barely think. Fear took over all his abilities and his mind went blank. The last thought he had was that this must be what it felt like just before the end.

"I would like to make your end slow, painful and filled with suffering like we torture humans. But too much of my time on earth has been wasted because of you as it is and you are not worth it."

Chemah released a fireball that engulfed metraloas and before he had time to run, the fire hit his skin. He screamed and fell down to the ground to roll. Chemah ran over and kept the fire stream going. Metraloas could not believe that the fire from chemah was so much more intense than the fire of hell as it penetrated the defenses of his skin. The inside of him started to melt as he looked up and saw the gloating smiling eyes of his enemy. The last thing he heard was chemah saying what a fool he was to believe that he could escape a mighty angel and then . . . nothing.

‡ ‡ ‡

Shathah entered the Coyle's house. No one was home. He checked every room. Passing the master bedroom, he did a double take and backed up and went into the bedroom. Drawers were left open. He checked the closet and clothes were gone. It was just as he suspected. Sheila left Wade.

He flew out of the bedroom in the direction of Joe's bar. He knew the stupid fool would be at his favorite place drowning his sorrows in liquor. An evil spirit intersected him and directed him to the roof top of the Coyle's house.

"Who are you?" demanded shathah as he folded his wings and they disappeared.

"I am phonos, spirit of murder. I've been sent by chemah to help you with the downfall of the house of Knight."

Phonos presented himself in his human form. He looked like a model from the pages of *GQ* magazine. He could appear either in black or white flesh. He chose white this time, because it was a white male he was to enter and influence to commit murder.

Shathah cursed. He didn't like the idea of so many new spirits getting involved with Wade. Looking at phonos, he wondered what his real form looked like. So many demon androids were receiving their human body and choosing to keep it permanently.

"My original form is a gargoyle." He shifted back into his original form and hissed like a snake at him. "Does that ssssatisfy your curiosity?"

"How long has it been since you reached attainment?"

Phonos smiled. He had only recently reached attainment. He liked being able to shape-shift into a human form. "What does it matter if the master believes I can do the job?"

"That doesn't tell me if you know what you're doing."

"Believe me, I earned this good-looking body and it was worth anything I had to do to attain it," he ran his hands over his body as he shifted back to his male form. "Let's get down to business."

Shathah waved his arm and they left the roof appearing in Wade's bedroom. "The female, Sheila, just packed up and left."

"Is she necessary? Couldn't we have Wade show up and just start shooting everyone at the house of Knight?"

"It's not that easy to get into the house of Knight. They apply the Blood of JC everyday and over anything that can move or anything that can't move. Huge warring angels are standing shoulder to shoulder around the borders of their property. Wade could get in, maybe. I might have to leave him for a time, but then he would never kill anyone without me inside him."

"How about the female?"

"She is getting stronger everyday with the teaching of Vicki Knight!"

"Teaching?" Phonos scoffed at his concern over Christian teaching. "So, what's the problem?"

"No, you don't understand. She's not a normal Christian and it's not normal Christian teaching. There are no doctrines of devils mixed with her teaching. She teaches in the Holy Spirit with power and truth!" shathah warned him.

Phonos yelled at him. "Why do you say His name? He is the God that gives the humans all their power and knowledge about us!"

Shathah ignored his response. "This Knight woman has already taught Sheila to understand the secret place, the Blood Covenant and how to activate her blessings."

"Yes, I've heard what God has blessed we can't curse. So what?"

"You've only heard? What's the deal?" shathah raised his voice cursing. "You are a novice!" He cursed again. "What the——is chemah doing. This assignment is too complicated for an inexperienced android!"

Phonos wasn't concerned about his doubt. "I am very capable of pulling off this operation. I am one of the first prototypes of a new line of hybrid androids. I am the latest success of our master."

Shathah knew that satan was always working at creating a being like the human. So far, all his experiments had failed. But each new generation of androids improve and become more complex. "So you are the culmination of his latest experiments."

"I am the best."

"Then, why is it that you don't understand about committed Christians who have revelation knowledge about the kingdom of darkness?"

"I have just accumulated and analyzed my first assignment. You will see that I learn everything quickly and I will process the information I learn faster than any android on the face of his earth."

"Just in case you don't know, humans can hear our words from the spiritual realm, but most of them do not realize it."

Phonos was insulted. "I understand all that!"

"I don't know what you know and I don't have the time or the desire to be in a situation that is dangerous for me because of you!"

"Don't we need to find Sheila?"

"I know where she is. *Where* was I?"

"Humans don't know that they can hear our voices. But actually, they can only hear the words that we don't block. If they don't accept our words as thoughts in their own mind, then we have no way that we can influence their decisions."

"Okay, so you know," shathah said. "But you don't know about how they activate their Covenant of Blood . . ."

"With my analytical processes I believe I can answer that question. The humans probably activate their Covenant with their mouths."

Lucky guess, shathah thought. "They don't understand how important their own words are either. But we are more concerned about the thoughts that they receive from us. So, you better get it straight. Their thoughts influence their words. Humans have the ability to cause their words to come to pass. But they do not understand their own human authority on this earth. If they understood about the power of thoughts, then they would not accept our suggestions as their own!"

"It was not a lucky guess. I told you that I have a superior central processing unit than you earlier models."

Shathah fumed. "You don't know that Sheila has activated her authority over us and bound me with faith-filled words and now I have been forbidden by two warring angels to inflict any physical attacks on her body."

"Do you think she knows how to activate her Covenant every day?" Phonos heard that all Christians have some kind of wrong thinking causing a stronghold of doubt and unbelief in them. "What about any former doctrine of demons? Isn't there anything in her neuron pathways that can interfere with her understanding?"

"Sheila wasn't raised a Christian. She doesn't have any strong networks of wrong thinking or doctrine of demons in her brain. I might have prevented her from leaving Wade if I had not been fighting with chemah."

"You were going to steal the seed of His Word from her heart through Wade?"

"That was the plan." Shathah again surveyed their bedroom groaning within himself. A perfectly good opportunity was gone. "Chemah thinks we should attack now before the situation gets any worse. I want to wait for a better opportunity. Maybe even come from a different direction."

"So, that's why you fought."

"There is a lot at stake here. If we are successful, a big promotion is in my future."

What's in it for me? Phonos cloaked his thought from shathah testing the android's power level. "Why don't you find Wade and I'll go and talk to chemah. Maybe we can come up with a plan that he will like?"

"I think I better cancel my original agreement with him." His instincts were telling him to cut his losses and run from chemah.

"Listen, I might have a new perspective for this situation," phonos almost pleaded with him. This was his chance for a big promotion.

"I'm going to find my house. You go talk to chemah. If you come up with a plan, I'll listen."

Flying out of the Coyle house and in different directions, phonos was determined to finish this assignment with honors and recognition from satan and shathah was determined to beat chemah out of a reward and watch satan torture him.

Once again the kingdom of darkness was divided.

CHAPTER 40

Michael and Chroni were summoned before the Lord of hosts in the tactical room that was located on the planet heaven. Taking one of the pathways that led directly between heaven and earth, the journey seemed like it was instantaneous. All of the offices of the Trinity were housed in a triune set of buildings in front of the throne of God on the mountain of God. The auditorium surrounding the throne room was immense. No created being knew the exact number of worshippers it contained. Acres of fountains and gardens surrounded the building complex. The outside of the buildings were framed in gold and studded in diamonds that formed a crown, representing the crowning glory of Jesus at the top of the buildings.

They entered the headquarters of the Lord Jesus situated on the right of the Father's building. It was one of the most magnificent gold buildings constructed in the city of God and housed the offices of the 24 elders. On the left of the Father's building was the Holy Spirit's building. All three were connected with gold spun corridors that looked like a type of glass never before seen on earth. It glistened and twinkled like the stars in heaven. The whole compound rested on a foundation floor built with the Word of God. The very top of the building housed the office of God the Father.

The duo walked into the lobby on a marble floor greater than the marble of earth. It had strands of gold entwined through it reflecting the light of God. A specially designed framework of gold covered the walls reflecting images of humans and angels working together. Gigantean doors made out of mother-of-pearl that seemed transparent, opened to the expansive information desk where many angels directed all visitors. Michael was recognized immediately, as all angels dressed in bright white angel attire stood at attention. Turning to the left and walking down the elongated connecting hall, called the hall of faith, Michael and Chroni stopped a busy angel to ask him how things were going with the coronation celebration.

"We are so excited! The Master told us the time is very soon, very soon. All the gold place settings have been arranged on the tables. The gold cups are getting the names engraved as we speak. It is so exciting! Come and see!"

"Thank you for stopping to inform us, but we are on a mission for the Master," Chroni said restraining his joy from the angel's obvious enthusiasm.

The angel smiled at them. "Thank the Lord that the invitations are still being handed out on earth. We workers in heaven want God's celebration to be full to overflowing. It was very pleasurable to answer your question. May I be of further service?"

"No. Thank you very much, but we must be about the Lord's business," Chroni replied. "I don't understand how anyone can reject the King's gracious and merciful invitation." They continued on their journey.

"Those who don't accept the Father's invitation are going to regret their decision," Michael said as he stopped to look at a portrait of David when he defeated Goliath. "I remember what it was like before iniquity was found in Lucifer. When I first started training the angels for combat, Lucifer would laugh at my assignment from the Lord God. Before he sinned, there were no enemies of the Lord,"

"Now, we are involved in the greatest conflict of the universe- the battle over the souls of men from earth because of his iniquity." Chroni asked, "Why couldn't Lucifer live on his own planet and leave man alone?"

"Because of his intense hatred of God and all that He made. You know that satan was very jealous of God's children, and now he wills to destroy as many of them as he can. He wants all of God's creation to go to hell and worship him while he tortures them. He really is deluded into thinking that he can still defeat God," Michael said.

"Does he not believe that God has prepared the lake of fire for him and his kingdom?" Chroni asked.

"I don't think he knows that evil men and women will torture him and his kingdom at that place for eternity."

"Evil torturing evil for all eternity," Chroni shook his head. "The kingdom of darkness is going to be shocked. Every human he has deceived and tortured will become their tormentors."

"The more humans satan deceives the greater punishment he will receive for all eternity," Michael told him as they continued walking.

"He doesn't even know that he is adding to his own misery."

They entered the tactical room still talking about God's enemy. "He couldn't defeat Jesus, the Son so how can he think he will defeat God the Father?" Chroni asked.

Jesus appeared before them. "That is the way of a mind separated from the Creator. We cannot comprehend the ultimate horror of facing eternity without God's light and life. But satan's own lies have deceived him and he is deceiving many." Jesus put His arm around Michael to give him a big hug. "What do you think, Michael? Is My body on earth growing in revelations and getting stronger every day?"

Michael bowed to Jesus and said, "Yes, Lord. All glory goes to You, Lord!"

Jesus hugged Chroni. "Many believe that you are coming soon, before the rapture," Chroni added as he bowed before the King of kings.

"A sleeping giant is about to awake on planet earth. Every thing will soon be restored to My Father." He heartily put His arms around both angels. "Is everything in place with the Devil Chasers Ministry?" Jesus placed His hands on Chroni's shoulders.

"Yes, Lord. I am here to report that all the assigned angels are waiting in their places at the headquarters of the Devil Chasers. The prayer covering is the best and I am privileged to be a part of this campaign." Chroni bowed and gave glory to Jesus.

Jesus transported them to a screen that was focused on the house of Knight. Every movement and every word was clear to them just as if they were there in person.

"What do you think Joshua will do, Chroni?"

The Lord knew because the Father had already revealed it to Him. But sometimes He liked to give the angels opportunities to learn about humans. Jesus knew that in the next age they would be co-workers together judging the many worlds the Father has and will create.

"He will cast out the devil in Wade Coyle."

"What makes you think that?" asked Jesus.

"Because, he did not tell his dad about his trip to the future," replied Chroni. "And he is relying on the Holy Spirit to lead him."

Jesus looked at Michael, waiting for his comment.

"I don't believe he is afraid of demons. I observed that the child, Joshua, is filled with Your Word and he relies totally on You leading his life. That was obvious after what he did when he faced chemah. He will stop this evil work purposed against Wade and Sheila Coyle," added Michael.

Jesus laughed. "Wasn't his confrontation with chemah great?"

"Joshua is a most unusual teenager. He invests all his time in Your plans, pursuits and purposes. It is most pleasurable to be guarding him on earth," Chroni said.

"I am glad you are enjoying your assignment, Chroni. The Father has ordained that Joshua will walk on earth as a prophet," Jesus revealed. "Joshua will pass this first phase of the prophet's test."

Michael and Chroni understood that the Lord's prophets were His voice on earth. It was imperative that His prophets understood how the kingdom of darkness operated evil on earth through the law of sin and death. Jesus operated His Kingdom through the law of the Spirit of life through the Anointing.

"We understand the test of a prophet, but the believers on earth sometimes do not know why testing is so important for them," Michael commented.

"You are doing a great job, Michael and Chroni, revealing the voice of the enemy to My body. They cannot be confused about good and evil. Wisdom is the principal thing and knowledge is pleasant to the soul, but discretion with preserve them and understanding will keep them to deliver them from the paths of evil. They must know mercy and truth and bind them around their neck and write them on the tablet of their hearts." Jesus looked at Joshua on the screen. "Just as My Father wrote every man, women and child on the tablet of His heart for all eternity."

Jesus looked at other screens around the room. "Look at all of my children working the Father's will on earth!" As far as the eye could scan, millions of screens manned by an immeasurable number of attending angels and humans living in heaven were watching, observing and recording all deeds. No detail escaped their attention because the Lord was concerned by the smallest detail in every human spirit on earth. "I am excited about the Joshua Generation."

Jesus started chuckling. The more He thought about Joshua's response to chemah, the more joy rolled from His belly. When Jesus laughed, waves of refreshing breezes were released in heaven and both angels knew what was coming next; the people and angels around Him stopped what they are doing and received a heavenly lift in their souls.

"You must learn to release more joy, Michael," Jesus put his arm around his shoulder and patted him on the back. "Laughter has a chain reaction. When several of God's angels and children release waves of joy from their soul in heaven, it is released through the Holy Spirit on earth in the form of laugher."

Michael smiled. The Lord had told him this before and he tried to understand, but Jesus, an immortal being, had experienced a mortal body and soul.

Jesus looked at the two angels in front of Him and recognized their inability to truly understand what it was like to be human. "One of these days, Michael, Father God will release the good human emotions that will benefit all beings, but not before evil has been completely destroyed and locked away for all eternity."

"We remember, Lord, that it is written, 'the joy of the Lord is their strength,'" Michael quoted the written Word from the Bible on earth.

"Laughter infuriates the enemy!" Chroni thought of the many times he had noticed the Knight family indulging in the practice in the last few weeks.

"Earth needs the splitting-the-side kind of rolling joy liberation to remove the spirit of heaviness from it. Many miracles, signs and wonders have been planned for this last age before My coming with the spirit of laughing."

"The kingdom of darkness will be shocked when they see what Your Father has planned," Michael chuckled a couple of times.

"But the greater power comes against the kingdom of darkness when My people discern demonic presence," Jesus reminded his head angels. "My sisters and brothers have to know and understand that they are My mouth on earth. My body has authority over the forces of evil! I told them when I was living in My old human flesh that they had power over *ALL* the enemy then, not just when they came to heaven! *All* is *all*. I can not stand it when My body gives satan authority and power through their mouths, like the kingdom of darkness *really* has power. They need to understand that when I said *ALL*, I meant *ALL*. I have *ALL* power over the enemy and I transferred that power through My Word before I was translated back into heaven!" Jesus was becoming extremely emotional. "The coming army of prophets will blow the kingdom of evil clear off the earth with the weapon of My Word coming out of their mouths!"

"Praise Your Name and Your Word." Michael and Chroni bowed themselves on the floor in front of the Lord. When He got excited and started preaching with passion, the presence of God moved over Jesus and it was almost always impossible for them to stand.

Chroni praised God for appointing Jesus as Highest Apostle and High Priest over the saints' confession. The thought entered his mind that the challenge for their ministry on earth was getting the Lord's people to recognize and understand that all of heaven was waiting to hear what they were saying. Every being that God ever created was waiting for His voice to come out of their mouths and then the warring angels would make sure that the demons complied.

Jesus continued preaching, "The devil, living on planet earth, commands and trains his forces of evil spirits to block faith words. He is getting his people prepared to fill their mouths with words of doubt and unbelief. Few people realize that it is the devil that is stealing, killing and destroying them because he lives outside of the dimensions that humans can detect with their natural abilities. But soon, that will all end and satan will not be able to find faithless words that he can fill and use for his glory! He thinks that I won't find faith on earth." Jesus paused as the Father laughed from His Throne. "I will find great faith before the great translation that will remove My body from earth to heaven!"

The humans and angels in heaven paused as they heard Jesus preaching. When He finished, they all worshipped God and gave thanks for His marvelous plans for the future of heaven and earth.

"I believe Joshua will take authority over the evil in this situation," Michael once again affirmed after a time of worshipping the Lord of Glory.

"Go, and take care of My brothers and sisters," commanded Jesus as He hugged His angels again and blessed them.

"We will carry out Your every command!"

Leaving the tactical room, they disappeared and conveyed themselves to the transport system on the outer edge of the City of God. Instantly, they were traveling on the highway back to earth. Chroni looked out of one of the space ship's windows seeing the stars pass as lightening streaks surrounding them and wondered how many times he had traveled back and forth between earth and heaven.

Michael heard his thought and answered him thinking, *thousands and thousands of moments in eternity and time on earth.* "With countless moments yet to come," he declared out loud.

He smiled. "I hope I did not disturb you."

Michael opened his eyes and shook his head.

"It is going to be different when we can travel back and forth openly and can be seen in the natural dimension," Chroni said. "I will enjoy working with humans after the kingdom of darkness is chained for a thousand years."

"It will be great to see earth restored to its original creation," Michael agreed with him. "Once again, we will all hear the stars of God singing out His glories. Earth will have peace for a season. Then, we will be visible in the human dimension and they will see into the spiritual dimension. The veil of darkness will be stripped from covering the earth." It was good thinking about the coming day of wrath and destruction of satan's kingdom from the face of earth. "We have waited a long enough for this time."

"Wiping out poverty, sickness, disease, famine and wars with all inhumane treatment will be great to our senses." Chroni thought about all the things God's angels on earth for the last six thousand years have had to endure.

"I agree." Michael looked out his window enjoying the slow way of traveling between heaven and earth.

"We need a rest before the Lord God settles the issue of evil, sin and death forever. Has the Father given you a hint of the worlds to come?"

"Yes. He has thought about the human creation and those things that have given Him and all creation the greatest pleasure . . ."

"Let me guess," Chroni interrupted excitedly. "Because we were created in celestial regions and learned our lessons in eternities past in the presence of God, and because the first man before the fall was created like us, but the rest of mankind was born . . ."

"Created like us, but the first to be created in the image of God," Michael corrected him.

"I know that the Father has received great pleasure in babies and children. I think He will create beings that can form families and procreate."

"The Lord has told me that marriage between a man and a woman was such a successful union of passion and love with mankind on earth, that He intends to perpetuate it in eternity, only changed," Michael revealed.

"Oh glory to God. What a great and perfect planner the Lord is! Even though we do not have descendants and creations of our own, I agree with the Lord; children in heaven and earth are the greatest humans to be around. Having to endure the gross ravages of the curse on earth is eased greatly when I look at human babies with their faces reflecting the love of God. It just seems to make all of this worthwhile."

Michael thought Chroni summed up the whole story of mankind perfectly. The joy of the angels on earth, through all of the depravity of sin, was human children. Babies made in the image of God. Nothing gave them or God more pleasure than children.

Looking around the formal living room during prayer, Joshua started feeling warm. He wasn't sure how long it was before Wade Coyle would show up because when Kientay showed him the events, they were off the timeline. He had to flood his mind with scriptures to keep anxiety under his feet. Under his breath, he started quoting the Word over and over.

Greater is Jesus in me than satan that is in the world! No weapon formed against me will prosper . . . I have all power and authority over the devil through Jesus Christ my redeemer . . . No evil shall hurt me or anyone in my house in the Name of Jesus! Behold! I give you all authority over serpents. No evil shall come near my house! I speak to the mountain of fear to be gone! God has not given me the spirit of fear but power, love and a sound mind! I have a sound mind. The power of God in His Word through love resides inside me.

When they finished praying together, Dan suggested that the men go into the family room. He wanted to show them the carpenter's work on the cubbyholes that he had made for their desks and the phones.

"No!" Joshua shot up from his chair. "I mean, Dad, I've got some things to show the guys in the family room. Why don't you stay here, while Mom and the other mothers go out and look at the pool house?"

"Why would we want to go out to the pool house, Joshua?" asked Vicki.

"You know, Mom. I thought the mothers might want to look at where the guys are going to stay the night."

"We'll be fine, Joshua, *in* the formal living room." His mom was adamant in the tone of her voice and gave him a look to match.

"Okay, we want the family room then," Joshua said.

I wonder what's wrong with him tonight. "Joshua, I want to show the dads the set up with the phones. We're not going to stay for a long time."

Joshua didn't know what to do. "Dad, all the computers are in the family room."

"We will only be a couple of minutes, then you can have the room for the rest of the night." Dan couldn't understand why Joshua was acting the way he was.

"Joshua, you can look at the computers after your dad." Vicki thought that he sounded like he was panicking.

If I was in the family room and didn't hear the doorbell, then Dad might react the same way I did. Then Mrs. Coyle could be killed. "Okay, I'll get one of the binders and start going over the procedures with everyone in the formal living room."

"Joshua," Dan stopped him. "I already put a computer in the library room for you to demonstrate."

"Okay, Dad." Joshua looked after his dad wondering why he didn't tell his dad about his visit to the future. He shared a special relationship with his dad and now it seemed to him like he might have made a mistake about not confiding with him about what soon to take place.

He took the team into the library.

‡ ‡ ‡

Shathah stepped inside the darkened bar and switched to his night vision. It gave his eyes the ability to see like the room like a night scope as he began scanning faces looking for Wade. He spotted Wade, in a corner with a drinking buddy from work, slumped over the table almost passed out.

"Hey! Wade . . . hey . . . good buddy? I thought we were going to have another round of drinks?"

Wade looked up with eyes that looked into a hazy and blurry scene before him. He thought he saw this misty gray-black ugly thing coming at him. "Leaveee . . . meeee . . . alonne! I don't need aneeee . . . buddy . . . to tell me whattttt . . . ta'do! YAH hir me?"

"Yeah! Good buddy. And so can everyone else in the joint!"

Shathah entered Wade. As usual it was a simple process. He briefly checked the condition of his alcohol, soaked and overworked organs. He spoke to the lower principalities living in his body. *How much alcohol has he consumed?*

We lost count after he ran out of money and his friend started paying for them. It looks like we're going to lose this body sooner than expected, a demon complained.

Why are you complaining? shathah cussed him out. *Alcohol deadens the natural safeguards their God has given them to fight our invasion of their flesh and it gives you demons quick control over the five senses.*

A spirit of fear agreed with shathah. *It is a wonderful tool to use for possession, even if it is hard on the body and quick to destroy it.*

But you two can easily find a new human to possess after this one kick's the bucket! Another demon complained. *It is hard for us lower level demons to find new houses.*

SHUT UP! shathah cursed again. *I get so sick and tired of listening to you whining crying babies! Will one of you morons tell me how much alcohol Wade consumed!*

The recording demon told him and shathah cursed again. He was three times over the legal limit for driving.

Wade sat up and opened his eyes wide. His strange, yellow-gray blank eyes frightened the guy facing him. Shathah possessed Wade's soul immediately so that he could make him do anything that he wanted. Putting all of his power into Wade's eyes, he realized that he was close to totally possessing his spirit. *See what I mean*, Shathah spoke to the many demons living inside Wade's body. *A controlled will totally dedicated to evil is the ultimate goal of all demonic possession and I am in total control of his body and soul,* shathah boasted to them. *The next possession, I will control is his spirit!*

"What are you looking at?" shathah's demonic voice blasted out of Wade's mouth. He looked daggers evil looks to Wade's drinking buddy hot enough to burn the hair off his head.

His drinking buddy felt the force of the demon hitting him in the face as he fell over backwards. Shathah rushed Wade's body out of the bar and got into his car. His destination was the house of Knight, but first he had to stop at Wade's house.

CHAPTER 41

"What kind of calls do you think we are going to get, Joshua?" asked Kellie.

It was starting. Joshua remembered seeing and hearing Kellie say that before. "I'm not sure, but I hope I have enough of the right scriptures to get us started." *I think that is exactly what I said. This is so strange*, he thought. *It is more than a feeling of having said the same thing before, but it is knowing what I'm going to say before I say it!*

"You mean like salvation scriptures?" asked Mose.

"Everything in this binder is loaded in the computers on your desk. I'll show you when we go into our room." They followed him. *Hmm . . . I don't remember this, but Kientay said the events weren't set in stone. So, maybe things won't happen exactly the way that I saw it.*

They sat around the desk in the library and looked at the computer Joshua turned on. "I arranged this binder into different categories or subjects. For example, we could get a caller that tells us he or she is depressed, and then you could pull up a folder in Word and click to the folder labeled depression." He showed them on the computer. "Each station will have a binder like this with the same information that your computer does in case the electricity is off and you can't use your computer. You will find a list of scriptures dealing with that subject. The subjects are arranged alphabetically."

Joshua's heart leaped. The future timeline was getting closer.

"We don't have to read those scriptures if the Lord gives us something else, do we?" asked Hannah.

Joshua hesitated. *Oh boy, that's the exact question that Hannah asked.* He slowly answered her. "The first thing we want to do is always pray for the Holy Spirit to lead us and guide us on the right path . . ." Inside his spirit, Joshua started praying. *Holy Spirit . . . lead me now to say and do the correct things to save Mr. and Mrs. Coyle.* "Since we are talking on the phone, our primary concern is to be the voice of the Lord and not the voice of our nature which is the voice of reason . . ." Joshua jumped.

"Wait . . . !" Kellie interrupted. "What is the voice of reason?" She didn't remember ever hearing Joshua talking about that before.

"The voice of reason is the voice that you hear inside you that thinks and talks from the natural realm."

"Is that from satan?" asked Hannah.

"Our natural reasoning was thinking formed after the relationship between Adam and God was severed by disobedience. That thinking was inspired by satan and prevails on earth today."

"We know," Mose interrupted. "That was when satan became our step-dad."

"Yes, satan has designed this world's system through the natural five senses of your body and soul . . ."

"The mind, the will and the emotions!" Mose, Kellie and Hannah said together.

"Uh . . ." Mose thought out loud. "Is that what Jesus meant when He said that He was a Man that told the truth which He heard from God?"

"I believe that Jesus personally talked with God. But I also believe that during His ministry years on earth He heard from His Father through His Spirit, and that He saw the Father with His Spiritual eyes. He is our example, and I think He operated then exactly how we are supposed to operate through our spirit, which is right at this moment, *now* in touch with God's Spirit."

Trust Me. The Lord spoke to Joshua's spirit.

"Remember the most important thing is to be led by the Holy Spirit, Who is the eyes and ears of God, to and through your spirit."

"We know," Kellie repeated for what seemed to her like the hundredth time. "We are a spirit, who has a soul, mind, will and emotions and live in a body."

‡ ‡ ‡

Shathah drove Wade's car fast, skidding the tires as he pulled up into his driveway and stopped the car by supernaturally killing the motor. He was anxious to get the gun into Wade's possession. When he entered the bedroom, shathah woke Wade so he could see the open drawers, Sheila's empty closet and missing suitcases. The sudden jolt of realizing that his wife had left him caused pain, depression and anger to fill Wade's spirit man.

Shathah laughed. *Those emotions will give him added strength to cause him to kill Joshua or his parents or maybe all of them.*

Chemah entered Wade's body as his power overwhelmed Wade's body and caused him to fall to the floor shaking. "We are going after Joshua Knight," he declared.

"What are you doing in here?" shathah shouted at chemah as he spoke to Wade's mind to calm down and get up off the floor.

"You will need my rage to get Wade mad enough to kill several people," answered chemah as he looked around. "There's room. There's plenty of room."

"I have plenty of rage against you to do this without you!"

"Channel your rage toward the Knight family and away from me. Did it ever occur to you that I allowed that fight so that we both could be full of the spirit of rage?"

Shathah paused.

"Don't think about it now, you might disperse the rage inside you. We need a concentrated effort to kill the Knight family!"

"You're right!"

"Excellent. Anger, hatred and rage is fuel for murder!"

Phonos entered after chemah. "Hey, great place! This is a nice house you are staying in shathah."

"Look again."

"He has a very hard heart," remarked chemah.

"Look at his liver," shathah said with disgust.

Phonos shook his head. "If he dies prematurely, where are you going to stay?" His liver was almost gone.

The other demons in his body groaned.

Shathah lowered his voice. "Could you cool it about the condition of this body? We need the other demons to cooperate with us and they are a little sensitive about having to move at the moment! I am grooming his son, Jared, for the position. He has already yielded to me and has been to his first wild party and gotten stone drunk. I forgot how nice organs look that haven't been polluted by alcohol."

"Wine is a mocker, strong drink is raging: and whosoever is deceived thereby is not wise," quoted phonos from Proverbs 20:1.

"I HATE SCRIPTURE!" chemah screamed obscenities.

"Don't get so upset," shathah told chemah. "The latest androids are taught more Word before they are assigned to earth nowadays."

"We have been told that more humans know the Word today than ever before in the history of earth," phonos told them. "They teach us the latest doctrines of demons that we are to introduce to the young minds in school. So that means we have to know the Word to be able to distort it by adding and subtracting words."

Chemah laughed at the thought of using scripture to deceive Christians. "The only *good* word is a twisted word!"

Phonos continued boasting, "I've been taught how to drive many of the humans to murder. Satan wants them quoting scripture while they are killing.

The feeling we get is unbelievable! Spilling human blood while quoting scripture is beyond satisfaction. I experience a feeling of total power. The psycho ones, you know . . . the serial killers are the best. They always say that voices were telling them to kill. We are. Several of us spirits in the division of murder drive them crazy." He fabricated his experience because he only read about the division of murder. This was his first actual case.

Shathah asked him if he ever lost a victim by quoting scriptures.

"No. Reading scriptures or quoting them has to be mixed with faith that works by love. We mix ours with fear and say them with hate. Have you never read that 'faith works by love'?"

"Yes," shathah replied.

Chemah sighed. If they continued talking they might water down the rage that had built up inside Wade.

"Then, there is no way for the scriptures to work when I quote them. I hate humans! I hate the Word of their God! I can't get rid of His Word since I've memorized it. The scriptures actually torment me!" phonos revealed.

"When you all are finished visiting, can we continue our mission?" chemah was frustrated working with these android imbeciles.

Wade got into the car and drove away as the spirits were talking inside him.

"What about us spirits of division," another spirit who resided in Wade's body piped up. "If it wasn't for us, many humans would never allow you to get into their bodies!"

"Hey, it's the doctrine of demons that has taught the majority of the church goers that Christians cannot be possessed with us!" another evil spirit spoke out. "We can possess their body because of their ignorance."

"Yeah. They don't know that they are a spirit that is having a natural experience!" phonos enjoyed giving information to evil spirits.

POW! chemah blasted the spirit of fear with fire.

Fear immediately caused pain in Wade's body and he bent over while he was driving, causing the car to veer to the left. Crossing over into the wrong side of the road, the car was traveling straight for a head-on collision.

The demons inside his body all screamed at once.

Shathah grabbed the wheel turning them to take them back to the right side of the road. "You fool!" shathah shouted objecting strenuously to the use of weapons inside the human body. "Besides injuring his internal organs, you almost gave him a heart attack! If you kill Wade, we will be without an entrance into the house of Knight and we could become homeless!"

"No one calls me a fool and lives!" chemah shouted.

Phonos stepped between them. "We are about to complete our mission. Who wants to take the blame if we fail?"

"Hey! Look what you did to his pancreas! That blast could have knocked down many of the strongholds that I have built and killed this body!" The spirit of fear yelled at him.

"He is turning into the driveway now. Where are you going to be?" chemah asked phonos ignoring the spirit of fear.

"I have to be in the brain center," answered phonos. "Where are you going?"

"I am going to be in his spirit, so the rage and fury can come out of this heart. That's why I always notice the heart."

"I have to enlarge myself to cover his face, voice and brain. He was really drunk before I took over, and to keep him from staggering and falling over!" remarked shathah, still filled with anger at chemah.

Chemah looked at shathah sternly. "Keep that anger and rage so that you can release it at the correct time!"

Wade parked the car. He got out of the car so fast, that no one reminded him of the gun.

"Phonos! What were you thinking?" screamed shathah.

"I didn't have time to position myself. My order to put the gun in his pocket was not received." Since this was his first mission, he didn't remember to get it for Wade.

"Why in the——didn't you make him keep it in his pocket in the first place?" chemah yelled.

Wade's face began to jerk and twist with muscle spasms. Chemah gave him a couple of pains near his heart. Wade's hand went up to his chest.

"Stop it, chemah! How can we complete this mission if you give him a heart attack?" shathah yelled at him.

"If I do, you can be sure you will receive all the blame!" Chemah screamed.

"If I didn't have to break up a fight between you two, I would have been in position!" phonos screamed at them. "You can be sure that I will tell the master who was the blame for failure of this mission!"

"Don't blame it on me!" shouted shathah.

Chemah groaned. It was like an omen to him that the mission was doomed to failure. He released a string of expletives.

Wade cursed as he rang the doorbell. He couldn't control himself. The words came from his spirit which was one with chemah at the moment.

"Don't worry," shathah ignored chemah's cursing. "I'm great at improvising!" . . .

. . . Suddenly, the doorbell started ringing over and over. Joshua jumped again. Vicki jumped up to open the front door.

"Where is my — wife?" The drunken Wade stooped in the doorway tripping over his feet.

"Come in." *said the spider to the fly*, Vicki was thinking.

"Are you deaf?" screamed Wade as he cussed her out again with slurred speech. "I said . . . where is my — wife?" *Look at her face! There is no fear!* shathah yelled at the demons. *ABORT! She's been warned by the Holy Spirit. We need to abort immediately!*

No! yelled chemah. *Everyone freeze! Let's see what we can salvage and let's combine our powers. We can do some damage!*

"I heard you the first time," Vicki said calmly.

Hannah and Sheila walked up behind Joshua wondering what all the commotion was and who was at the door.

"What are you doing here, you ——?" shathah screamed obscenities at her through Wade. He was very angry that he could no longer intimidate her with fear. "I told you, you couldn't come here!"

"I'll get my coat," Sheila said quietly trying not to agitate him anymore.

"No!" Hannah grabbed her mother's arm. "Please don't go!"

"Hannah, it will be all right. Don't worry." Sheila put her hand on her daughter's shoulder. She was trying to leave fast so that Wade wouldn't embarrass Hannah in front of her friends.

Hannah turned to Joshua, "Don't let her leave! He gets real crazy when he's drunk!"

Suddenly, the next few seconds went into a time warp of slow motion in Joshua's mind. The people and the words sounded like they were falling down a long tunnel . . .

. . . All of the angels were waiting for the words to come out of Joshua's mouth.

Michael, Natsar, and Milchamah were going to take care of the three strong spirits in Wade. Kientay was going to take care of the smaller demons inside him. The other warring angels assigned were going to stop any invading spirits that might answer the call to arms in the vicinity. Waiting in their positions assigned to them by the Holy Spirit, they were ready the instant he said the words.

Come on Joshua! Kientay spoke to his mind. *Say it.*

They couldn't do anything until Joshua said the word. The Word of God coming out of his mouth released their power . . .

. . . Joshua grabbed Mrs. Coyle's arm as she went by and yelled, "No! You are not going with him! You belong to Jesus not him!"

Fury released from Wade's heart causing his mouth to curse viciously. "The——she isn't! You————." He didn't look or sound drunk as he grabbed Sheila's arm and pulled her away from Joshua. Hurrying to his car and dragging her behind him, she tripped and fell.

Sheila was shocked, but instantly she knew in her spirit that Joshua was right. It wasn't Wade picking her up; it was a demon spirit kidnapping her. She pulled her arm away from Wade feeling a supernatural surge of power flowing through her.

Joshua screamed "*NO!* In Jesus' name release her!" With all his might and without thinking he ran and jumped on Wade's back before he could turn and go after Sheila.

Wade tripped and let out a yell as he fell on the concrete driveway. Joshua grabbed the back of his head, getting a fist full of hair. He slammed his forehead on the concrete. "In the Name of Jesus, demon, I command you to come out of him. Spirit of drunkenness! Come out! Spirit of rage! Come out of him! Spirit of murder! Come out of him!" With every command, he was hitting his forehead on the ground.

The men heard the screaming and wondered what was going on outside of the house. Sensing something was wrong, Dan ran out of the family room with the men close behind him to the foyer. They saw some of their kids blocking the front door.

"Stand aside!" Making his way through the kids, Dan saw Joshua beating a man's head on the driveway concrete. "What are you doing?" he yelled shocked at Joshua's actions. He ran over to pull him off of Wade.

Vicki tried to grab Dan's arm as he ran by her, but she missed.

"Joshua!" Dan locked his hands around Joshua's chest and tried to lift him off of Wade. He couldn't budge him.

"Dan!" Vicki screamed. "Joshua knows what he is doing!"

Dan couldn't believe his ears. "He's killing him!"

Abruptly, Joshua released Wade . . .

. . . Kientay helped Joshua tackle Wade. "yes!" He shouted. They both wrapped their hands around Wade as Joshua began to command the evil spirits to come out of Wade with the authority of Jesus' Name.

Chemah had great strength with the other spirits inside Wade to resist the commands of Joshua. Michael flew over and removed his sword to cut him out of Wade's heart.

"You can't do that!" demanded chemah.

Michael had his hand around chemah's throat with his blade sticking in his ribs. "I have the authority through the righteous one, Joshua. He used the name of the Lord and commanded you to leave. You have no choice but to leave *now*!" He used his sword to move faster than thought and cut out chemah's heart.

Immediately, chemah grabbed his heart out of Michael's hands and pushed it back in his spirit body. Blue blood started seeping around his hand and through his black shirt. He looked down at his chest in shock.

"Now you will have to face your master with proof of your defeat," declared Michael.

"You . . ." he couldn't finish his sentence. Losing his life force quickly, he disappeared.

Natsar went after shathah. The warring angel cornered the demon trying to sneak out of Wade's body by going down his pants leg as a snake slithering away on the floor. "Where do you think you're going . . . you devil of drunkenness? The sword of the Lord and the house of Knight comes against you. You're a dog that returns to your own vomit! Remember, Officer Natsar?"

Shathah recognized the eyes.

Natsar laughed at him. "You demons are so deceived. Truth will always prevail over lies!" He started hacking away at shathah.

"Look!" a warring angel cried out. "The wrath of God through the prayers of the saints has been released from heaven."

The prayers of the saints flowed in a covering stream giving great strength to the good spirits and taking strength away from the evil spirits. Natsar hacked shathah into pieces as an electrical current snapped around him and sulfuric acid ran with his green blood on the ground. A demon spirit like a blob appeared and vacuumed up the pieces of Shathah in his elephant-nozzle nose and then disappeared.

Meanwhile, Milchamah went after phonos. "How dare you try to kill a child of God."

The spirit of murder stopped dead in his tracks and cried out to Milchamah, "Which child of God did I try to kill? I only entered Wade Coyle. He had a heart of stone. I saw no heart of flesh!"

"You do not have the ability to know the humans who have been claimed for the Kingdom of God through intercession of the saints."

"No one told me that his wife claimed him for salvation."

"Ignorance is not an excuse in the eyes of God for any being in the kingdom of darkness. Wade is a child of God in the Almighty's sight. You have trespassed and there is no second chance for an android!"

Slowly, phonos backed away from the presence of the three angels surrounding him with their huge swords pointed at him. "You know," phonos continued backing up inch by inch, "since I wasn't aware of this little oversight, I don't think I should be punished. I just joined this assignment a few hours ago. Why don't I just go back to hell where I belong?" He was trying to bargain with them.

Phonos never finished his sentence. He turned around and screamed bloody murder as the swords started slashing his android body and green bloody-gunk spilled all over the ground as he tried to flee. His beautiful body shape-shifted between a male human, a bat and a grotesque gargoyle before it turned into ashes as it was trampled under the feet of the warring angels.

"He had no right to live because he was an alien on the planet earth and God did not create him," the warring angels shouted. "His body was a fake! God doesn't make any fakes!" . . .

. . . Vicki screamed at Dan, "Stop him! There is a gun in the car!"

Joshua again tackled Wade as he made it to the car door and brought him to his knees. Mose tackled the other side and brought him all the way down.

Dan ran over to his car and was shocked to see a gun in the front seat. He opened the car door and picked up the gun unloading all the bullets out of it, putting the bullets, and gun in his pocket.

"I command the rest of the spirits in Wade's body to come out of him!" shouted Joshua. This time he didn't bang his head on the ground.

Immediately, Wade ceased struggling and looked like a man that dropped dead.

Sheila came over and looked into his face. His countenance looked different. He seemed to be out like a light, but he looked peaceful. "I believe they are all gone," she declared as she looked up at everyone standing around Wade.

"Praise the Lord!" shouted Vicki and Ruth.

"Boys, help pick him up and take him into the living room," Pastor David told everyone as the team stood staring. Everything happened so fast, it was hard to believe what they all had witnessed with their own eyes.

"Is he dead?" Kellie asked.

"No. His body is in shock because of all the demons that left. He'll be fine," Joshua told them as he stood and brushed off his clothes.

Mose couldn't help himself. "That was so cool!" He finally got to see a manifesting demon with his own eyes.

"Awesome!" Kellie and Hannah shouted together.

‡ ‡ ‡

Laying Wade on the couch, Pastor David was the first to break the silence asking questions. "Will someone please tell me what is going on?"

Sheila was standing by Wade's head. "This is my husband; the one everyone was praying for." She was shaking so hard that it was difficult to speak. "He was an alcoholic until Joshua cast that devil out of him."

Vicki came into the living room with a cold washcloth and a bag of ice to put on his head.

"Should we call 911?" asked Ruth.

'No," Hannah pleaded, "will you pray now for my Daddy to get saved?"

"I think that is a good idea," Vicki said.

"Let's all gather around him and pray," Pastor David said motioning for everyone to get close. "Oh Lord, everything happened so fast, but I believe evil spirits have left this man's body. May he receive the Lord Jesus as his Savior when he awakes. We claim this soul as a member of Sheila's house. You said, 'You and your house will be saved.' We're asking for that to happen now, in Your Son's name and to Your glory! Amen."

"We remind you Lord, that it is our Covenant right for my Daddy to be saved," Hannah declared.

"I agree with the prophet of God. Thank you, Lord, for delivering my husband from all those evil spirits! I claim Wade, my husband, as the called of Jesus. Lord, fill him to overflowing with your precious Spirit!" prayed Sheila.

Kellie, Mose and Joshua were praying in the Spirit. Vicki, Ruth and Kathy laid their hands on the backs of the men praying for Wade. Hannah looked around at everyone praying and drew Joshua aside. "Are you sure every demon is gone?"

"Yes. The Lord told me the names of the demons that were inside your dad. And I heard Him say that they were all gone."

Hannah raised her hands and said, "Thank you, Jesus!"

After a few minutes of praying, Wade opened his eyes and sat up. "What . . . what's going on? Where am I?" Wade didn't recognize any of the people around him. His eyes went around the circle of people until he saw his wife. "Sheila . . . What am I doing here?"

"Wade, do you remember anything?"

"The last thing I remember was being at Joe's with Rick. How did I get here?"

"Wade, I'm Dan Knight. How is your head?" He was still concerned about Joshua banging his head on the hard cement.

"I must have tied one big one on. I don't even remember how I got here." Wade put his hand on the back of his neck and started rubbing it.

Dan noticed that he didn't touch his forehead.

"Hey! I know I got plastered, but why doesn't my head hurt? I should have a whopping hangover," wondered Wade.

"Your head doesn't hurt at all?" asked Vicki.

"No. Who are you?"

"I'm Joshua's mother, Vicki."

He stared at her and then stared at the boy standing next to her. "Who is Joshua?" He saw Sheila standing next to a lady that just spoke to him.

"I'm Joshua. Maybe we better explain some things to you."

"Wade, this is the group of people that I pray with. Ever since you told me I couldn't go to the prayer meeting . . ."

"Wait a minute, I told you that you couldn't come to some meeting?"

"Yes, and Vicki and I prayed for you and . . ."

"Wait, back up Sheila. Let's not go that far back. How did I get from the bar to this house?"

"Mr. Coyle, you were brought to this house by an evil spirit . . ."

"Uh . . . *oh boy*. An evil spirit brought me here?"

"Yes," replied Joshua. "He had you stop by your house and get your gun. I believe his intention was to kill Sheila."

"I don't believe you. I would never harm my wife!"

"You wouldn't, but an evil spirit of murder would!" Joshua said.

"This is crazy," Wade stood.

Dan took Wade's gun out of his pocket. "Is this yours?"

"Let me look at it." Wade turned it over and saw WC carved into the handle. "It's mine. Where did you find it?"

Dan handed him the bullets. "I found the gun on the front seat of your car. I removed the bullets."

"Okay, I admit that I have had big periods of time when I can't remember anything . . ." He was shaking his head. "But, I would never use this gun to kill my wife."

Vicki interrupted, "When was the last time you can remember talking to anyone with this much clarity?"

He had to stop and think. "It's been a long time!"

"Wade," Sheila spoke with a gentle love flowing out of the tone of her words. "I talked to one of the evil spirits in you."

"You've seen them haven't you, Mr. Coyle?" Joshua asked.

"Kid, when you're drunk you see a lot of things. It gets where you can't tell what is real and what is imaginary. You know, it's all in your head!"

"Demons have the ability to hide in your flesh and block your memory," Dan told him.

This was beginning to sound like a *Twilight Zone* adventure to Wade. "How do you know that they are real?" Wade sat down feeling his head spin. He was very weak from the deliverance and from the things they were telling him.

Joshua remembered what Jesus said after delivering a man. "Mr. Coyle would you like something to eat or drink?"

"I could use a drink." Wade noticed the shocked look on Sheila's face. "A glass of water, please."

Kellie indicated to Vicki that she would go into the kitchen to get it for him.

Joshua answered Wade's question. "I've seen demons before. The Lord opened my eyes twice to see into the spiritual realm. Demons are real. He gave Wade a description that exactly matched the ones that Wade had seen.

"Kid, I don't know how you did it, but that description of the octopuses with long tentacles stretching everywhere and the gross distorted monkeys and bears . . . those are the ones that I've seen countless times in the last year," he was shaking his head. "How in the world could they be real?"

"Listen to him Wade," Sheila pleaded with him. "I've never seen the demons in you, but I've talked to them. I knew when it was you, and when it was him!"

Wade looked into her pleading eyes. His brain went numb and nothing made any sense to him. But one thing was sure in his mind, the kid Joshua nailed him with the description of the ugly creatures he had been seeing lately. *Maybe there is something to what they are all saying*, he thought.

"I'm Pastor David Pearson. I would like to show you some scriptures and explain to you a little about demonic spirits, so you can get a picture of what was going on." He felt led by the spirit to open the Bible and read some scriptures to him. He sat down on the couch next to him. Everyone sat on the floor or in the chairs and they all began to silently pray in the spirit.

"Okay, I'm open," Wade confessed as he took the glass of water from a very pretty young lady.

Praise the Lord! Shouted Sheila in her spirit.

"First, I am going to turn to some scriptures to show you that people can have demon spirits in their bodies. Matthew 8:16 says, 'When evening had come, they brought to Him, Jesus, many who were demon-possessed. And He cast out the spirits with a word, and healed all who were sick.'"

"Okay Reverend, I believe you that the Bible talks about demon-possessed people, but that was in those days. We live in America, not some heathen country."

"Demons know no boundaries. They just have to hide themselves more cleverly in our nation," Pastor David told him straight as he could. "In third world countries, they can operate more openly. A lot of people in countries around the world know that demon entities exist."

"How did I get possessed?"

"Through your drinking," Sheila blurted out.

"I told you . . ." Wade shut his mouth quickly. "No, I can't lie to myself anymore. Okay, so they got into me through alcohol."

"When a person gets drunk, he opens the door for evil spirits to come into his body. You never knew when they entered you, because your natural senses were dulled and 'they that drink, drink in the night.' That means when you get drunk, it's like falling asleep. Many times you are not aware what is going on around you," revealed Pastor David.

"I know that feeling. I'm starting to lose long periods of time when I can't remember what I've done or where I've been."

"They replace your personality with their own and cause you to do things that you wouldn't do when you are sober."

Pastor David hit the nail right on the head with Wade. "I'm usually a mild-mannered man, but when I'm drinking," he shook his head, "I'm another person."

"When you were drinking, the spirit inside you made you act like a bully. He was trying to make you think you were more of a man and that's why you continued to drink even though you hated it." Joshua was operating in the gift of knowledge. "In fact you hated it so much you told yourself you would never drink again after your first experience with drinking and getting drunk. But then someone accused you of being a wimp, so to prove yourself to him you drank again and everyone accepted you. You then decided that if drinking helped you become more of a man, it wasn't so bad after all."

Wade's eyes widened, "How . . . how did you know that? I've never even told Sheila."

"Oh, Wade!" Sheila started crying.

"The Lord is revealing to me that a demon spirit told you that you weren't a man and that you would never receive love from a woman because you didn't act like a man," Wade embarrassingly confessed.

"I was so afraid of losing you. I thought the only time you would recognize me as a man, was when I was drinking."

Sheila put her hand over his mouth. "I've always hated drinking. I thought I would lose you if I didn't go to the bars with you or drink with you on our dates. I never thought I was good enough for you."

"You not good enough for me?" Wade made a grunting sound. "I always thought you were too good for me!"

"Both of you have been lied to by demons taught by the father of lies, the devil!" explained Pastor David.

"Wade, listen to Pastor Pearson, I know how we can make everything new again. Jesus can change our lives. He can give us a new start together. I love you so much. I want us to be a real family," Sheila pleaded.

Her words pierced his heart and then he realized that he was completely sober. "What do I have to do?" Wade asked as tears formed in his eyes.

"You need to repent of every sin that comes into your mind and ask the Holy Spirit to cleanse you and deliver you from any strongholds in your life," instructed Pastor David.

For the next hour or so, Wade confessed several transgressions in his past. Many were hidden from him as the Holy Spirit revealed things to his mind. He even confessed to an affair. Sheila realized that demons caused him to do several immoral sins; she forgave him.

"Sheila, I have stolen money from the company."

"What ever happens, Wade, I will stand by your side." Tears were falling from her eyes as she watched her husband become a new man.

"Jesus, forgive me for stealing company funds and stealing from my dad." The feeling of weights coming off his body followed everything he confessed. Finally, he looked up at the pastor, "Nothing else comes to my mind. Now what do I do?"

"Say this to the Lord, Lord Jesus, come into my heart and forgive me of my sins," directed Pastor David.

Wade looked at Sheila. He got on his knees and reached out his hand to Sheila. She got down on her knees next to Wade. Hannah followed them, positioning herself behind her parents and put her hands around their shoulders to pray with them.

"Lord Jesus, come into my heart and forgive me of my sins," Wade repeated everything every word from Pastor David.

"Wash me in Your Blood, and make me clean. I accept Your work of salvation and want to become a member of your body."

Wade cried as the Holy Spirit began a work on the inside of him. "I receive You by faith as my Savior and I am now worthy to be called a Son of God. I renounce satan and all his ways. Jesus, You are now the Lord of my life."

Pastor David looked at Wade and Sheila and said, "I now pronounce you, born again! You are a child of God. Sheila, kiss your new husband."

Everyone felt like they just witnessed at a wedding. There wasn't a dry eye in the living room. All were praising and thanking the Lord for the joyous event that had just taken place.

"Praise the Lord!" someone else said.

"Let's just take time to thank Him for Wade's salvation," Pastor David said.

Everyone raised their hands and started praising and rejoicing in the power of the Spirit. They all were feeling the powerful presence of the Lord in the house of Knight.

CHAPTER 42

Dan looked out his office window glad to see sunshine instead of rain. The trees seemed greener and perkier since the rain started falling, even though, they would soon lose their color. He turned around and looked at the folders sitting in front of him. It was Monday afternoon. He was finding it hard to concentrate on the work before him on his desk. The events of Friday night kept replaying over and over again in his mind. In his entire Christian walk with the Lord, he had never seen deliverance from a demon like he witnessed with Wade Coyle.

The rest of the weekend proceeded as originally planned.

Just a normal get together with four Christian families. He laughed out loud at that thought. *What is so normal about forming a devil-chasing ministry? Or what is so normal about seeing Jesus in His glorified body or going to the future with your guardian angel? What, if anything, is normal about angels, demons and God?* He wondered as these questions flooded his mind. He believed in the supernatural, but it was like he was living it now instead of after he died.

His thoughts centered on many of his former traditional beliefs that fell by the wayside after this weekend. He knew that most Christians believe in a place that is called heaven when they die, but very few believe that they can experience heaven on earth. In the last few days, he had experienced living and doing the supernatural personally. The pages of the Bible became reality at his house last weekend.

Joshua's calling transported them out of mere living into the supernatural experiences that he only used to read about. Life was becoming supernatural natural on a day-to-day basis and too many people experienced the past events to deny that it had happened. He had gone too far to reject that the supernatural experiences that he saw with his own eyes were real and not just a figment of his imagination. How could he ever be satisfied with normal living again?

Dan pondered the next steps that needed to be made. Whatever it meant or whatever the consequence, he told the Lord that the Knight family would stay loyal to visions from the Lord. No matter what anybody thought or believed about his family, they would not quit. That was the only conclusion Dan would consider.

He tried to concentrate on the work on his desk, but once again his thoughts carried him back to last Friday night. Dan couldn't deny how great it felt to know that Wade was delivered from demon spirits after Joshua more or less attacked him. Right before his eyes, Wade instantly changed. His face untwisted, his voice changed and his eyes cleared.

It was a miracle.

But the next day was even better. Wade and Sheila came over for a Bible study and a lesson on how to pray. Pastor Pearson got to spend all morning with Wade before he had to leave to seek the Lord for Sunday services. Of course, Wade and Sheila were invited to come to church on Sunday.

After everyone finally went to bed Sunday morning, Dan had a chance to talk to Joshua . . .

. . ."Son, tell me again about your visit on the timeline into the future with your guardian angel . . . Ken . . . what's his name?"

"Kientay. Did Mom tell you anything?"

"Uh . . . not really." At first he felt a little hurt that Joshua didn't confide in him, but he put that thought out of his head and bound it with the Name of Jesus.

"Dad, don't get offended. I barely even remembered to tell Mom. "

"I recognized my flesh was trying to take an offense, but I cast that thought down. That night, you tried to get me to stay in the living room, why?"

"At first I thought it would be better for you and Pastor Pearson to handle Mr. Coyle. But then the thought came into my mind that if you didn't know about the gun and the spirit of murder . . . well you might let her go like I saw Mom and I do."

"Did you change anything? Like the things you said?"

"Some of the conversations were almost exact words that I heard spoken, but the ending was different. It was because of my study on the law of repentance that I realized when you ask forgiveness for past sins, then you change the course of history. It helped me understand that we can change our life and those changes will effect other people."

"So, that morning you made up your mind what you were going to do?"

"Trust me Dad . . . I didn't know what I was going to do. When I saw Mrs. Coyle leaving, I knew in my heart that I had to do whatever it took to keep her from going with him. Evil had to be addressed and stopped." Joshua told his dad everything he could remember about his experience with Kientay in the future.

Dan still could remember the emotional shock when he saw Joshua pounding his head on the cement. He shook his head. "I couldn't believe my eyes. I saw you on top of this man beating his head on the concrete driveway."

Joshua started smiling. "I know what you mean. I saw myself grabbing his hair and pounding his head! I couldn't believe I was doing it either."

"Are you telling me that the Holy Spirit did that?"

"Believe me, Dad. It wasn't me!"

"You know, Joshua, if I hadn't seen it with my own eyes," he shook his head again, "I mean the fact Mr. Coyle didn't have a bruise or one mark on his forehead. And then he told your mom he didn't even have a headache, well, it was amazing."

"I'm glad you were there."

"Most Christians would argue with you about that being the Holy Spirit."

"Dad, I know how angry the Holy Spirit was at that devil in Mr. Coyle. I never want to tangle with the Holy Spirit. I felt like superman was inside me."

"When I realized that Wade wasn't hurt, that's when I understood that you were operating with the authority of the Holy Spirit."

"I was thinking the same thing. I just know that the Holy Spirit is awesome. It's like what James said, 'Be doers of the Word, and not hearers only, deceiving yourselves.' You know James says that if you don't put the Word of God into action you read it and go your way. Then when you're not reading the word, you forget what you read."

"I doubt if anyone who saw the Lord in action Friday night will ever forget what they saw."

"The biggest thing that I learned was to trust the Lord and not to lean on my own understanding. When it all came down, the Holy Spirit took over and I felt like a spectator in my own body seeing and hearing what the Lord was doing."

"Amazing."

"The Lord gave me a saying. He said, 'We are a spirit having a natural experience.'"

"Say that again . . ."

"We are a spirit having a natural experience."

Dan let those words sink deep into his spirit by saying it over and over. "We are a spirit having a natural experience. Joshua, that is a profound statement."

"It seems to me that Christians believe that they are natural trying to be spiritual."

"Hmm . . ."

"That's my desire, Dad, I want to teach and demonstrate that we are spiritual beings that have been ordained to live in this body on this earth, not according to satan's kingdom, but according to the Kingdom of God." . . .

. . . As Dan thought about his talk with Joshua, he made a decision. Joshua was right. *I am a spirit living in a natural body on a planet that is surrounded by the kingdom of darkness, but I am light.* He remembered that Jesus said that His body is the light of the world. It only made sense to him that Christians should live a supernatural life like Jesus did. Joshua was right they should expect to live a supernatural natural existence on earth and anything less was not acceptable any more.

Dan raised his eyes and hands up to heaven and said, "Lord, help me to understand that I am a spirit that has a soul and lives in a body. Lord, give me the Spirit of wisdom and discernment to be open to You in any situation that comes my way according to Your ways of doing things. I want to live as YOU live! Let me be a vessel that you can use for other people to know you!"

He continued to praise the Lord for a few minutes. "Lord, I surrender everything I have. I want to be putty in Your hands. I am committed to continue to see my family working your will on earth! Mold me and make me fit for Your use!"

Are you willing to pay the price? The Holy Spirit asked him.

"Yes, Lord. But I realize I might not know what the price is, but I trust you to help me to be willing to pay any price that you decide is necessary."

He lifted his hands and began to give praise and glory to the Lord. "I am willing to pay any price! Glory to God! Let the supernatural natural living begin today!" . . .

. . . Matthan was in the office with Dan. Area angels around the neighborhood had been rejoicing through the night over the wonderful victories the Lord had accomplished through the obedience of the house of Knight. Before they all went back to their assignments, Michael appeared before Matthan. He warned them about an attack that was coming through a human.

"Has the Lord someone to intercede for him?" asked Matthan.

Satan never gives up. He keeps coming and coming. An invisible spirit spoke to them.

"We are not surprised at the enemies' relentless pursuit," answered

Michael. "He never catches the Lord or His Spirit by surprise, and yes, a human long ago was led to intercede for him."

Matthan looked over at Dan at his desk. He knew that Dan had moments that his thoughts caused unrest, especially having knowledge that Joshua's revelations from the Lord over His Word would cause severe trials and tribulations. But it was imperative that he submit himself to the Lord no matter what storms come his way.

"Has he made up his mind?" Michael asked.

"Yes, Dan's natural thinking was trying to get him to desire Joshua's ministry to be less visible. You know something that the kingdom of darkness wouldn't want to attack all the time."

"What ministry was he thinking about? With Joshua's knowledge, a demon is never going to leave him alone."

"His flesh was fighting him hard with help from demon spirits, but in his heart he knew that wouldn't be possible. I think he is praying to follow the Lord without question and to settle his mind about counting the cost."

Both Michael and Matthan listened to Dan praying to the Lord. They heard his surrender. Two angels appeared behind him with a gold book and gold pen in their hands. They recorded the date and the time that Dan gave his will totally to the Lord in regards to the Devil Chasers ministry and his family.

They disappeared returning to heaven to record his words in his file.

"I knew he would surrender! It was just a matter of time," Matthan rejoiced. "It's not easy for humans to remove themselves from their comfort zones!"

"Another test is coming now," Michael informed them after receiving a communication from the graceline. "The kingdom of darkness will seize every opportunity to destroy this family. The Lord put it on the heart of the intercessor, Joan, and Dan's secretary to stand in the gap for him. Although they didn't know what they were praying for, they prayed through the situation with total victory for Dan. Praise the Lord! Because of Dan's surrender a door has been closed to demons that could have been used for great attacks against his family. Again the tempter has failed!" . . .

. . . Clearing his mind of all the events that happened last weekend, Dan focused on the work in front of him. He opened Mr. Gottman's file, because he was coming in to sign papers. Dan was very excited about his day in court last Friday. His summation was good. The jury was excused and all hoped they would come to their verdict by noon. They deliberated two hours. When everyone was called back into the courtroom, the jury voted unanimously that the

Mr. Gottman was not guilty of sexual harassment and discrimination toward the gay lifestyle.

Mr. Smith was furious as the spirit of rage took control over him. He cursed Mr. Gottman and then, he cursed the jury. His attorney had a hard time controlling him as he pointed his finger at Mr. Gottman and screamed, "This isn't over. Believe me. You will regret this!"

Dan recognized the demonic eyes staring at him. Mr. Smith's eyes looked a lot like Wade's eyes before the demon was cast out of him.

His telephone buzzed.

"Mr. Knight, Mr. Gottman is here to see you."

"Send him in."

Mr. Gottman walked through his office door with a huge smile and outstretched hands. He gave Dan a bear hug and kissed him on each cheek . . .

. . ."Are you saying that satan is going to attack Dan now? Matthan asked. "What about his secretary and Mr. Gottman?"

"Everyone in Dan's office is covered. Mr. Gottman will get his 'road to Damascus' experience he thinks he needs to accept Jesus of Nazareth as his Messiah," answered Michael.

"He is entering the building now." Natsar appeared drawing out his sword . . .

. . . Dark clouds of demons were flying over Mr. Smith, driving him toward a goal of destruction and death. The stench and sound of several thousand snake-like voices permeated the atmosphere. His heart was filled with violence and his eyes were blinded to the truth. He was a man fully possessed; spirit, soul and body by several hundred demons.

Several warring angels appeared with their swords illuminated from the light of the Holy Spirit's anointing. Matthan positioned himself in front of Dan with the shield of faith . . .

. . ."I have come to give you your New Testament and pay my bill," said Mr. Gottman as he walked through Dan's office door.

"You didn't have to do that, it was yours to keep," Dan stood to shake his hand. "Please, sit down."

"I am honored to have read Paul's letters."

Dan sat down at his desk. "What did you think about the Words of Jesus?"

"Quite frankly, I am not sure I understand all his words. I understand about the Jewish people living by tradition instead of the intent of the scriptures. But I do not understand about God being our Father the way Jesus teaches and this born again thing. That is a hard thing to understand."

"Your own prophets of the Old Testament prophesied about this new life. Ezekiel said it in chapter 11:19, 'Then I will give them one heart, and I will put a new spirit within them, and take the stony heart out of their flesh, and give them a heart of flesh.' The Hebrew in that passage for heart is spirit. If you get a new spirit, then God would have to take out the old spirit and give you a new one. That would be what being born again is."

Mr. Gottman started chuckling. "I feel like King Agrippa, when he said to Paul, 'You almost persuade me to become a Christian.' I am afraid I need a 'road to Damascus' experience."

"Welcome to the life of a completed Jew. If my wife prayed for you to have that experience, then . . ."

Unexpectedly, the door of Dan's office was kicked opened and a man holding a gun to the back of Gloria pushed her inside.

"I . . . I'm . . . sorry Mr. Knight!" Gloria squeaked out, her voice cracking.

Mr. Smith pushed her down into one of the chairs and shouted at her. "I told you to SHUT UP!"

Calmly, Dan stood. A supernatural peace came over him like he never felt before in his life. "What can I do for you?" Dan asked.

"Oh! That's a good one," he laughed sarcastically. "You could have lost the case. But no! You had to win. Well, what do you think now big lawyer? Who do you think is going to win now?" He came around and put the gun to Dan's head and cocked it.

A smile appeared on Dan's face. "I've already won. Haven't you read the end of the book?" . . .

. . . A host of demonic spirits filled the room and the office above them as the ceiling disappeared into the spirit realm.

The spirit of Lucifer appeared and stood behind Dan. "I predict that this human will crack and fear will be his greatest enemy!" He raised his hand and a bolt of lightning was released against Dan's head.

At that very moment, Mr. Smith pointed the gun at Dan. The helmet of salvation protected Dan's mind. Even though he cocked the gun, Dan did not waiver.

Matthan laughed at the spirit of Lucifer's pitiful attempt to break through the helmet of salvation. "You are deceived. He is wearing the armor of God.

No weapon formed against him will prosper in the name of Jesus Christ of Nazareth. The Word is proclaimed daily out of Dan's mouth. He knows who he is in the Anointed One!"

Chroni gave the orders as the Holy Spirit gave directions over the graceline. "Matthan, keep your shield over the left temple of Dan's brain. Milchamah, keep your shield over in front of Mr. Gottman. Natsar, keep your shield over the front of Gloria and a little to the right side of her."

Demon spirits could not hear the voice of the Lord, so they did not know what was going to happen next. They waited with worry and anxiety . . .

. . ."What are you talking about?" shouted Mr. Smith.

"I'm talking about God's book. Don't you know the devil loses and is cast into the bottomless pit for a thousand years? A seal is set on him, and he is bound by an angel who comes down from heaven."

"Shut up— you! Shut the —— up!" he began cursing.

"Hey you . . ." Mr. Gottman started to stand up.

He pointed the gun at him and screamed at him to shut up! "Hey! Old man! You're next! Imagine! You survived the holocaust to die at my hands!"

Dan felt a surge of boldness. "Mr. Smith, you can't harm me and you don't scare me. Jesus Christ has covered me with His Blood. No weapon formed against us will prosper. In the Name of Jesus I render you harmless and the Blood of Jesus covers Mr. Gottman and Gloria!"

Furious with the words Dan was speaking, he turned around and pointed the gun at Dan's head and pulled the trigger.

Gloria screamed.

Mr. Gottman closed his eyes . . .

. . ."Stand and see the salvation of the Lord!" Michael declared.

Instantly, the armor of God appeared over Gloria and Mr. Gottman.

The demons cursed.

"Foul play! The other humans do not put on the armor of God daily!" accused the spirit of Lucifer.

"Dan's Covenant is extended to them, because he is numbered among those called the Repairer of the Breach," Michael declared. He was there because he was the angel over the Jewish nation and Mr. Gottman was a direct descendant from Abraham.

The spirit of Lucifer cursed and dematerialized, fleeing from the inevitable outcome of this fight. He had no weapons that could penetrate the whole armor of God . . .

. . . Dan stood tall holding his ground. Around his waist, he was girded with truth. He should have fallen to the ground dead. Instead, he turned his head and looked at him with the fury of the Holy Spirit! The bullets could not break through the breastplate of righteousness.

The spirit inside of Mr. Smith quickly turned and tried to shoot Mr. Gottman and Gloria. He unloaded the gun. The shield of faith protected them.

Mr. Gottman put his hands up instinctively to ward off the bullets. He then looked at his hands and put his hands to his chest and rubbed himself all over. "I'm not shot!" He started laughing, "I'm not dead!" He stood up with a shout, rejoicing and dancing around and around in a circle in the back of the room.

Gloria screamed and almost fainted, but then she started laughing.

Mr. Smith cursed as he looked at the gun to see if it jammed or misfired. Banging the gun on the desk, he was stunned. *What is wrong with this stupid gun?* He looked at everyone with total disbelief. "No! No, this isn't possible!" He discovered his gun was empty of bullets.

"It is possible. You can't kill me because of the Blood of Jesus." The Holy Spirit illuminated from Dan and roared at the demons in Mr. Smith as they fled from the room.

He dropped the gun, petrified and started to run out of the office. .

. . . BANG! BANG! BANG! BANG! BANG! BANG!

When the bullets were released, the shields of faith protected Dan, Gloria and Mr. Gottman.

ZING! ZIP! ZING! ZIP!

Angels with white robes and wings flew around the room and intercepted the bullets that ricocheted off their shields. Faster than the speed of the bullets in the natural dimension, angels were catching the bullets in their hands and another caught a bullet in his teeth. It looked like they were having fun stopping the bullets as they snatched them out of the realm of the natural into the supernatural. To natural eyes the angels were invisible, but in the supernatural dimension it looked like the bullets were traveling at slow motion and the angels just picked them out of the air.

"No weapon formed against Dan Knight will prosper in the Name of Jesus Christ of Nazareth!" Chroni shouted.

Not one bullet went into a wall or a human. Not one hole could be found. It was like the bullets never existed. The demons were furious at the angelic intervention. Some materialized swords and tried to stop the angels from intercepting the bullets. Other angels appeared shouting with a voice of triumph and praise and fought the demonic spirits fiercely.

"The confessed Word of God out of the house of Knight has given us the authority and power to interfere with the natural outcome of events. Dan's words with the prayers of the intercessors have caused the angels to overcome the forces of the enemy in a mighty way." . . .

. . . Dan ran after Mr. Smith. Making a running jump to tackle him and stop him, Dan caught him before he could open the door and run. He was a big man. Grabbing his head, Dan started banging it up and down on the carpet of his office.

"Come out of him, you demon of lying and deceit! You devil of murder and revenge you can't stay in him either. Spirit of homosexuality come out of him and never try to enter him again. In the Name of Jesus all evil spirits in this man come out of him!" . . .

. . . Now the fun could begin. When Dan commanded the devils to come out of Mr. Smith, the angels surrounding him took their swords and pierced the demons hiding in his flesh. The demons screamed and took flight scrambling for their lives trying to escape.

"The Word of the Lord comes against you foul demons!" Kientay, who left Joshua at school to join in the fun, started whacking away at the demon spirits coming out of Mr. Smith.

The angels were shouting as they cut the evil spirits to pieces.

WHACK! An android head was severed.

BAM! An anointed lightning bolt released from a warring angel hit another android and he went spiraling out into space.

SPLAT! Natsar stepped on a spirit of fear and laughed as green blood sprayed the wall.

"I could get use to this," exclaimed Matthan.

"I've had a look into the future," announced Natsar as he cut off the head of another lying spirit. "You are going to get a lot of experience in warfare with Daniel and Joshua Knight!"

"Jesus is Lord over the house of Knight." Matthan raised his sword over his head and brought it down decisively to sever a spirit of rage. The android body fell to the ground and spilled out all his mechanical fluid. Instantly, the green blood caught on fire and the body burned to ashes.

"Dust to dust and ashes to ashes. You servants of hell are aliens on this earth. You have no right or authority to be here!" Kientay plunged his sword into the center of the android's life force. Instantly he was terminated.

"What about you?" A spirit of fear in the form of a bear dropped his sword and backed up against the wall and went through it with Chroni holding his sword at his throat. "You angels are alien beings on this planet with us. What gives you the right to be here and terminate us?"

"We are ministering angels to the heirs of salvation. You see that man praying over there?" He pointed to Dan leaning over Mr. Smith and commanding the demonic spirits to leave his body. "He is a member of the body of Christ. He gives us the authority to make you disappear!" Taking his sword, Chroni cut off the grotesque demonic bear's head. "All authority in heaven and earth and under earth belongs to the Lord Jesus Christ of Nazareth and His body!"

Natsar raised his sword over his head and shouted, "Jesus is Lord over the Devil Chasers!" . . .

. . . Mr. Smith went limp. He looked like he was dead, but Dan remembered what Wade looked like when the demons were cast out of him. Dan started to get up when he realized from the prompting of the Holy Spirit that more demons were inside him.

"NO! You cannot hide! Spirit of rejection and double mindedness, come out of him! You started this in him a long time ago when he was little, but you are exposed now. OUT!"

Mr. Smith started shaking and drooling. Green foam gurgled from his mouth as dog-like guttural sounds were coming from him. Dan continued taking authority over the demon spirits until the foam and the noises stopped coming from his mouth. He said, "Come out of him you dirty, filthy demons. Release him in the name of Jesus!"

When he sensed a release in his spirit, he stood up and rolled the sleeves up on his shirt. Casting out demons from the flesh of men was a messy business. Turning around he went over to Gloria and Mr. Gottman.

"Are you okay?" He put his arm around Gloria.

She looked up at Dan and grinned at him with a slow stupid grin. "That was the most awesome thing I've ever seen in my whole life!"

A white cloud hovered over the office. It was so thick, it seemed like it could be cut with a knife. Gloria started giggling. "I sound like a teenager."

An angel standing in front of Mr. Gottman took his sword and severed the veil of darkness that covered his eyes. Wide-eyed and free to see, he fell to his knees and said, "I believe that Jesus is the Messiah! I believe! Yes, yes, yes! I believe. God has given me my road to Damascus experience. I am so honored that He has chosen to reveal Himself to me. I see a bright light over there in the corner. Jesus is speaking to me."

Jesus appeared to him as He appeared to Saul, in the Bible. A bright light blinded him and Saul fell off his horse when he was on the road to Damascus. Being prepared by the Word of God beforehand, the glorious light of truth didn't blind Mr. Gottman like it blinded Saul.

Mr. Gottman folded his hands and bowed his head. "Yes, Lord! Yes! Lord, I want to know You like Paul knew You. I do believe that you are the Messiah. Please come into my heart, Lord Jesus, and forgive me of my sins. Forgive my family for following those who have rejected You. Thank You for opening my eyes so that I can see You. Open my family's eyes. Pour out Your Spirit on my household and me. You are that Prophet that was foretold in the Torah. Forgive me of my sins, cleanse me with Your Blood and baptize me in the Holy Spirit." Mr. Gottman continued to pour out words of thanks and gratitude to Jesus.

He was a man of many words.

Dan looked over at the corner of the room. He knew the Lord was there, but he couldn't see Him. He just witnessed the Holy Spirit in action in him. Not Joshua, his son, or Paul in the Bible, but him, Dan Knight.

Gloria was still laughing in the Spirit. "Do . . . you want me to . . . call 911?"

"Don't worry about it Gloria. You just continue to have a good time in the Lord," he laid his hand on her forehead and she fell down off the chair laughing and rolling on the floor. *A true holy roller!* At least that's what he heard from Vicki, since she was a third-generation Pentecostal.

He decided to call his family and tell them he would be late for dinner. Joshua answered, "The Devil Chasers, Jesus is coming soon, how may I help you?"

CHAPTER 43

Two enormous demonic bears entered one of the gates of hell holding a stretcher with chemah who was holding his heart inside him. His black shirt was soaked with his blue blood from the wound made with Michael's sword. Many evil spirits were limping behind him. One of the spirits picked up the pieces of shathah, carrying his remains in a bag. Immediately, an unseen force transported them to the center of hell where satan was waiting for them.

"Well, isn't this a lovely sight; my brave warriors coming home after a battle!" satan surveyed the miserable looking evil spirits facing him. Fury was building up inside him. Standing and raising his hands, lightning flashed all over the throne room. The demons in the center of hell, hit the ground and covered their faces.

Satan was tired of fools who let humans defeat them. "Bungling idiots!" He cursed them ferociously. "You can't take care of a simple boy and his parents? What am I to do with you?" He sat back down on his throne. "Where is chemah?"

Chemah tried to raise his head and body, but he was unsuccessful. He could barely talk. He was overcome with fear and lack of strength from the loss of blood. The demon bears carried him to the foot of satan's black throne and dropped him.

Chemah released a cry of pain. "Have mercy on me!?"

Satan couldn't believe his ears. He cursed him severely. Fire released from a finger pointed at chemah. "Mercy? How dare you ask for mercy! What in——has happened to you? What do we have here?" satan pointed his finger and chemah's heart appeared in the palm of his hand.

Instantly, chemah started choking and struggling to breathe. "My lord, my heart . . . please use your power and restore me."

Fire danced in satan's eyes. "Are you asking for mercy, chemah? Mercy and pity is an emotion for weak gods." He held up his heart and acted like he was going to crush it in front of the congregation of demons in hell. "Maybe you should go back to the Creator if its mercy you want."

"I need my heart repaired," he whispered.

"You need a new brain. It looks like you had the unfortunate meeting with an anointed sword of the Lord." He lowered his heart and started playing with it like a ball.

"Michael."

"Michael!" Satan released a wicked laugh as he grabbed his heart from mid air and held it to his black robed chest. "You fought with THE archangel Michael? What? Have you become a fool?"

Chemah closed his eyes. "I have already lost one body, my lord. Is it time to lose another?" He reminded satan that it was not time for the second death.

"Why should I have pity on you?" he said with a tone of disgust.

"I am not responsible for this failure!" chemah said through clenched teeth. He was trying to keep from screaming out in pain.

"Go ahead . . . I'm listening."

"It was shathah and phonos." He could not talk any more.

Satan waved his hand over chemah's wound to bind it. Chemah felt new strength course through his spirit body. Slowly, he got on his knees to stand up. "I wanted to wait and do more planning. Shathah wanted to attack immediately. I told him I thought his plan wouldn't work. He refused to listen to me." chemah was stronger but he could not stand straight until satan released him. "He wanted to impress you so that you would give him a greater commission."

"Where is shathah?"

An evil spirit who gathered most of the pieces of shathah that he could find stepped forward. "A warring angel sliced him to pieces with his sword." He dropped the bag on the floor before satan.

"Bring me a bottle!" shouted satan. Getting up from his throne he started shouting at every evil spirit in hell. "Listen to me all you sniveling, spineless, demons. This is what is going to happen to all that fail me!" Satan snapped his fingers and a bottle appeared before him. With a wave of his hand the pieces of shathah came out of the bag and swooshed into the bottle. He held the bottle up over his head and paraded around the circle of his throne to every demon so they could see. Green android blood was dripping everywhere and running down his arm.

"The next time you fail me with any assignment, you will live for an eternity dismembered and in a bottle." satan then pushed a cork in the top of the bottle that had appeared in his hand. "Never forget that this was once the famous spirit of drunkenness, shathah!"

He handed the bottle to one of his servants.

"Never, never, never forget what I am going to tell you. No one is to be spared my judgment and torture for failure of any assignment. I hate God, I hate humans, but most of all I hate failure from anyone in my army! I will not tolerate defeat!"

He sat back down on his throne. "Where is phonos?"

"He was terminated. Who was he lord satan?" chemah asked.

He shook his head and flipped his hand. "It's of no consequence."

The demons in the battle that were cast out of their human houses were flat on the floor shivering in their spirit bodies. The spirits that once had beautiful human bodies lost them as the fury in satan started boiling. He systematically took away their past rewards and treasured trophies. Ugly, slimy, grotesque beings were slithering quietly on the floor in front of satan's throne. No one spoke. Huge snakes and rodent creatures covered their eyes and waited for his fury to cease.

Satan sat in silence for a few minutes making chemah wait. If he didn't need this blasted angel so much, he would chain him in Tartarus with the other angels. He fixed his eyes on chemah who now laid flat on the floor with his face in the dirt. Grabbing his heart from mid air, Satan ordered him to stand.

Chemah stood with a supernatural power that held him up and hovered him in the air close to satan's outstretched hand. Satan looked at his chest and a hole opened up. Walking over to him, he placed the heart inside his chest cavity and the skin reformed over it and the hole disappeared as his blue blood dried up and strength returned to his spirit body.

"Now, I am your creator!"

Chemah fell to his feet and bowed himself before satan. "All hail, Master Jesus, King of kings and Lord of lords!"

A gasp of horror was released from the evil spirits and demons in the stands that surround the center of hell. They began ranting and raving for punishment. They waited to see what retribution satan would give chemah.

Satan whipped his head around and screamed at him. "What did you say?"

Chemah put his hand over his mouth. He fell to his face again.

"Thank you, Jesus!" He filled his mouth with dirt trying to choke out the words he was saying.

Satan thought maybe he heard wrong. He looked around his crowded throne and tried to use his special power to see if an enemy was cloaked among them. "It is fortunate for you that shathah was responsible for this failure." He couldn't discern if any angel of the Lord's was present among them. He slowly walked back to his throne to sit down. Satan stopped scanning the crowd of demons surrounding the fun arena and fastened his fiery eyes upon chemah.

It is fortunate that God created me, chemah thought. *My spirit came from God and I can never cease to exist like phonos.*

Satan heard his thought. Infuriated, he stood and raised his hands.

Lightning danced all around his throne, popping and cracking. "I may not be able to terminate you, chemah, but I can chain you in everlasting darkness until the time!"

"I'm sorry, my lord! I don't know what got into me?" Terror took hold of his heart.

Satan laughed as he realized what was going on. "Michael touched your heart didn't he?"

"Yes." chemah stood realizing that goodness touched his wicked evil heart.

Satan laughed again. "Your heart has been *hardened* by God."

"Is it permanent?"

"No. It will cease, eventually. Just like Pharaoh's." A frown came over satan's face. He hated it when he was reminded of the time of Moses. It was the first time that God revealed to the inhabitants on earth that His power was greater than his own power.

"You will have to work hard, but you can overcome. After all, where did Pharaoh go when he drowned? God didn't get him."

"Yes, but God's people escaped you!" Again, chemah put his hand over his mouth. *Forgive me lord! I cannot stop my mouth from saying these terrible words.*

"Away from me! I cannot bear a hardened heart toward evil!"

"My lord, it is not from my will that the Almighty's goodness has fastened upon my heart!"

Satan immediately transported himself at the speed of thought and touched chemah's heart. Electrical currents of blue and white light zapped his body and flowed into his heart.

"Pharaoh said the same thing when I confronted him." satan threw his head back and pushed more current of power into chemah's heart. When he withdrew his hand, he was exhausted from releasing much of his power into chemah trying to reverse the effect of one touch from an angel of God.

Chemah fell to the ground on his knees roaring like a lion at the pain of transference. He kept his head down. "I regret," he slowly spoke, "that I had to be the one to inform you about this defeat. If shathah hadn't been cut up in pieces, I would have already finished him myself."

"Are you back? Are you the evil, treacherous diabolical angel I once recruited?"

Chemah stood and breathed into his body the stench of hell and beat his hands on his chest showing his heart was now strong. "Yes! I have overcome the goodness of God!"

The evil imp guards that surrounded the failed androids started jumping up and down, laughing at his victory over the power of God. They were pounding their spears on the floor around their prisoners loudly causing a deafening noise rebating throughout hell.

Satan ran down toward him and put his arm around his shoulder. "Tell me. How did it feel to fight off the *goodness* of God?"

Chemah smiled deviously. "It feels great! The surge of power that I feel from releasing myself from His goodness is giving me the desire to kill several humans! I could crush them with my bare hands!"

"Oh I know! I know! Doesn't it feel like a rush of immense supremacy?" An insane laughter came from his mouth. "I love the flood of evil that flowed through my veins after each time I fought the goodness of God! With each victory evil grew inside me."

Satan raised his fist in the air and shouted! "Touch me God! I want to grow more evil!"

"I can't wait to go back to the surface of earth," chemah continually breathed stronger and stronger.

Sitting back on his throne, satan stopped laughing. "I am now giving you the full time assignment with the house of Knight and the Devil Chasers! Find a way to stop them, or you will be stripped of all commissions and disbarred from my elite group and I will chain you in the pit!"

At hearing the name of house of Knight, chemah felt a quick stab of pain in his heart. Once more he bowed to satan. "Your wish is my command."

As he started backing away from satan's throne, a thought entered his mind. *Why prolong the inevitable*? Where is that thought coming from? *You are no match for the house of Knight!* A new thought tormented him.

He screamed at the top of his lungs. "I WILL OVERCOME!"

"Is there something else?" satan asked him as he turned around to sit on his throne.

Turning around he bowed again, "Before I go and fulfill your will, could I ask for a brief stay on the dark planet to rejuvenate my spirit body and allow my heart to get stronger?" He looked down at the scar circling his heart. "My heart needs to be renewed to the evil and perverse ways of your kingdom once again."

The dark planet was filled with factories creating evil androids with training facilities like boot came. Evil fallen angels were devoted to training evil androids how to war against the Kingdom of God. It would be a good place for chemah to recuperate. A new hardened heart strengthened in evil works would be of greater pleasure to him and would accomplish more evil works.

"Permitted, but remember," satan's smile turned to a scowl. "I want the house of Knight destroyed! I can't believe that a stronghold and communication link was established in their name and now I am forced to recognize their legal status." He could feel his temperature rising. He couldn't believe that another link was established between heaven and earth and he was not notified. "I will not be satisfied until the Devil Chasers are disbanded, disgraced, and demolished!" He started to leave when he remembered something. He signaled for chemah to come to him.

Chemah walked up the steps to get closer, slowly. He wondered if satan remembered that he was responsible for the communication link that was established through the Knights to make them now the official house of Knight.

"Come closer," satan whispered as he looked from side-side of his throne.

He slowly walked closer.

Satan leaned over and whispered. "Tell my top engineers to work on another new android prototype. Phonos was our latest release. Another failure and I will fire all of them!" satan sneered. "And I do mean *fire* them!"

Thunder and lightning rolled over and over the throne room. A powerful gale of wind tore through hell. With a raised hand, satan disappeared. All that was left was a puff of smoke.

A sigh of relief could be heard throughout the throne room. Chemah turned around feeling the scar on his chest and the new skin that was soft as a newborn baby. Satan gave him a new enlarged heart to do more evil. He waited to get out of the center of hell before he released evil laughter. *No wonder satan couldn't afford to chain me! Who would run his kingdom since his latest line of androids was a complete failure!* Michael did him a favor.

‡ ‡ ‡

"The Devil Chasers, Jesus is coming soon, how may I help you?" asked Joshua.

"Young man, my son brought your card home today from school. I thought it was illegal for religion to be discussed at school"

"Ma'am, we are a club at school, but we have a phone line at home to pray and talk to students who need help. Can I help you?"

"I don't believe in the devil. I don't want my son to be involved in such nonsense."

"Ma'am, the cards are for those teens who need help. Your son does not have to talk to us. If it offends you, please accept my apology, and please give the card to someone else."

"Well, I think the principal should be notified of your little Devil Chasing club! And I am tearing up your card!"

The lady hung up on him. Joshua's ears were ringing from the phone being slammed so hard.

Hannah heard Joshua's call. She was in the cubicle next to him. "Are you having a hard day?"

"Actually, it's been a great day!" Joshua held up the different colored cards they had been collecting. "We have prayed for a dozen teens. Two teens accepted Jesus and we will be getting a harvest from all the seeds of God's Word that we have planted."

"That is so awesome, Joshua!" Kellie joined them from her desk. "I am getting a lot of calls about the angels and gold dust that so many saw when we passed out the cards."

Mose just got off the phone and stood with Kellie. "Hey, it's almost 6:30. My dad is coming to get me early."

"I think we should turn off the phone around 9:00." Joshua looked at his watch. "Before you guys leave, let's give God praise and glory for our first day." As it was their custom, they raised their hands in praise to the Lord.

"Thank You, Lord for Your protection. Thank You for sheltering us from all evil. No weapon formed against us will prosper," Hannah prayed.

"I agree with Hannah. We can do all things through Christ who strengthens us," Kellie quoted from the Bible.

"We are victors and overcomers of the world and the flesh!" shouted Joshua.

"Jesus is Lord over the Devil Chasers!" Hannah proclaimed.

A couple of phones began to ring. Joshua and Hannah went to their cubicle to answer them.

Their first day on the phones was not over yet.

It was 9:15. The phones had been quiet for 15 minutes.

"Joshua, why don't you turn off your line and get ready for bed. Remember, you still have school," Vicki said as she entered into the room to check on him. "Everyone left over an hour ago."

"I'm doing my homework."

"Are you getting it done?"

"Sure. I've only had one call since Kellie and Hannah left."

"I just want you to remember that you are a student."

"Sure." He started to turn off his line when he felt a check in his spirit. Fifteen minutes later, his line rang.

"The Devil Chasers, this is Joshua speaking how may I help you?" Joshua waited for a response. He could hear someone breathing. "Hello? Can I help you?"

"You're a kid," a raspy adult voice sounded surprised.

"I am a teenager," Joshua admitted.

"My kid brought your card home from school the other day . . ."

Joshua waited for him to continue talking.

"Are you being a wise-guy or are you serious?" the caller asked.

"I am very serious about Jesus and his defeat of satan."

"I see what you wrote on the back of your card . . ."

"Sir, would you like to talk to my dad?" Joshua thought that maybe the man would like to talk to an adult instead of a teenager.

"Never mind, kid, I'll talk to you."

Joshua waited.

"I don't know much about Jesus or demons, but I have a problem that I don't know how to handle. I have a son who has these epileptic seizures. The other day I asked God to tell me what was causing these attacks. I've never talked to Him before. I don't even know if He exists, but just in case He does, I thought it wouldn't hurt to ask. Many doctors have examined him and no one knows what is causing his seizures."

He paused.

"Less than 24 hours later, I find your card that says you chase demons. I don't know if you understand this or not, but it was like the word *demons* jumped out at me."

"Sir, I know exactly what you are saying. Many times the Lord shows me things from His Word and it's like a word magnifies or jumps out of the page at me," Joshua explained.

"Yeah, that's it! It was as if I couldn't put your card down."

"You asked the Lord to show you and He is."

"I don't know who this Lord is. Have you ever heard of an epileptic seizure caused by demons?"

"Yes. Do you have a Bible?"

"Uh, no."

"Let me tell you about a father who asked Jesus to help his son. The story is in the book of Matthew 17:14–18. 'And when they had come to the multitude, a man came to Him, kneeling down and saying, "Lord, have mercy on my son, for he is an epileptic and suffers severely; for he often falls into the fire and often into the water." And Jesus rebuked the demon, and it came out of him; and the child was cured that very hour.'"

"That sounds like my son."

"Jesus loves your son. He doesn't want your son to be tormented by the devil in any way. Even if a demon isn't responsible for the seizures, your son is suffering. Jesus died on the cross and took a beating for all sin, sickness and disease."

"How do you know that Jesus can still do this?" His voice had desperation mixed with doubts. "I mean, isn't He dead?"

Joshua's spirit leaped inside him. This was an open door to call on the name of the Lord and prove that He is Lord. "I will pray to the Father using the Name of Jesus Christ and your son will be healed."

There was silence on the other end.

"Will you agree with me?" Joshua asked him.

"Do I have to believe in Jesus?"

"Agree with me that when your son is healed, you will accept the Lord as Master of your life. I have the faith to believe for your son's healing."

"If Jesus can heal my son, then He can be my Master."

"Father, in the name of Jesus Christ, I claim the healing of . . ."

"Austin."

"I stand in the gap for Austin and declare that healing is his according to my Covenant in Jesus." Joshua directed his next statement at the enemy of God's Covenant. "Demon of epileptic seizures, I cast you out of Austin with the authority of Jesus name. Epileptic spirit be gone. Cease and desist in the seizures that have attacked this child."

Tears were forming in the eyes of the father as he listened to Joshua's words. A angel of hope was touching his heart.

"Father, I thank you that this father is agreeing with me for the total healing of his son. Thank you Lord that his eyes are being opened to Jesus, amen."

"Is that all . . . I mean are you finished?" asked the caller.

"A demon from the kingdom of darkness has been kicked out of your son. No matter what you see with your eyes, he is healed. Demons specialize in deception. He may make you see things that really don't exist."

"You really believe in this stuff?"

"Yes, I do. God is a good God. Believe me when I say God is hurting more than you because of the evil way they are treating your son."

"Why doesn't God just wipe the devil off earth if He really exists?"

"He will at an appointed time. Until then, He is giving man every chance to accept His Son. Jesus is the Son of God, and He was the first man that ever defeated the devil and his kingdom of darkness. With His army of saints He is coming back to wipe all evil off the face of earth and then we can live with Him forever to freely worship Him without interruption from demons."

The caller was silent again. "If He has done what you said . . ."

"You will call me and verify what I already know. Your son is healed in the Name of Jesus Christ."

"You know, I feel something I haven't felt in a long time."

"What?" Joshua asked.

"Hope."

Again, Joshua's heart leaped inside him. The Lord had fastened himself to the man's heart. Soon, he would be hardened to sin and his heart would melt to the goodness of the Lord Jesus Christ.

"God bless you and keep you. Remember Jesus is Lord and He is coming soon."

Joshua pushed the button on his phone pad and took off his head set. It was time to go to bed. In his heart he was rejoicing, because he listened to the Holy Spirit and waited for the last call. Several seeds had been planted today and this man's testimony was going to be awesome.

Jesus was right. Kicking the devil's butt was fun.

CHAPTER 44

A habit now formed, a week later the Devil Chasers team was together at the Hut during lunch celebrating the passing of the first week on the phone. Joshua talked about the last phone call he received on the first day that they officially turned on their phone line.

"I believe I will be hearing from the father soon," he told them. Joshua's belief in God's Word was so strong that the team realized it wasn't a question if the boy with epileptic seizures was healed, it was when.

"You're amazing," exclaimed Kellie.

"No, it's the Word of God that is amazing. Our job is to pray for people and lay hands on the sick. His job is to do the healing"

"But you never question or doubt when someone doesn't get healed," Kellie said.

"Kellie, healing always comes. God always does his part," Joshua stated.

"Then why are some people not healed?" Hannah asked.

"Think about it. If God always sends healing to those who ask Him for it and some people don't seem to be healed, who is responsible?"

"Of course you want us to say it's the people who are at fault," replied Kellie.

"No, I want you to see that healing always comes, but it isn't always received. We may not know why a person doesn't receive his healing because we need to remember that a very complicated evil system is coming against us in this world. But our faith is growing stronger everyday to overcome it."

"Wordman, I get it! If someone has prayed to be healed and they didn't get it, then their receivers were jammed for some reason," Mose said.

Kellie put down her hamburger. "Is this another one of those lunch hours where we don't eat our lunch and we are late for school? Because that will mean I will be very late, since my school is several miles away from yours."

"What if it is?" Mose questioned her. "You can leave anytime you want to."

Kellie replied, "I don't want to miss anything."

"Then stay," Mose picked up his hamburger and took a big bite out of it.

"Hey . . . yeah . . . wait a minute," Hannah picked up her napkin to wipe mustard that dripped on her chin. "That points the finger back at us." She was talking about not receiving healing.

Kellie pushed her finger away. "Point that finger at yourself."

"There is no condemnation to those who are in Christ Jesus, who do not walk according to the flesh, but according to the Spirit," Joshua quoted. "The key is to walk in the spirit."

"So, how do you walk in the spirit?" asked Kellie as she stuffed a fry into her mouth.

"Jesus said His Words are spirit and they are truth."

Mose said with a full mouth. "How?"

"When you meditate day and night in His Word and ask the Holy Spirit to teach you and give you understanding, that is walking in the spirit. It's not by my might or by my power, but it is by the power of the Holy Spirit."

"How does that help people to receive healing?" asked Hannah.

Scripture in 1 Corinthians chapter two came to Joshua's mind. He decided to read it from his Bible instead of quoting from memory. "God has revealed to us through His Spirit. For the Spirit searches all things, yes, and the deep things of God. For what man knows the things of a man except the spirit of the man which is in him? Even so no one knows the things of God except the Spirit of God. Now we have received not the spirit of the world, but the Spirit who is from God, that we might know the things that have been freely given to us by God."

He looked up to see if they were still listening to him. They were all eating, but listening intently to him with open ears.

"These things we also speak, not in words which man's wisdom teaches but which the Holy Spirit teaches, comparing spiritual things with spiritual. But the natural man does not receive the things of the Spirit of God, for they are foolishness to him; nor can he know, because they are spiritually discerned. But he who is spiritual judges all things, yet he himself is judged by no one. For who has known the mind of the Lord that he many instruct Him? But we have the mind of Christ."

Joshua closed his Bible. "Healing and walking in health is a spiritual thing. The more you saturate your life with spiritual things, the easier it is to receive those spiritual things from God. Healing is a spiritual gift manifested in the flesh. But you have to receive it before you see it."

"I don't understand," Hannah put down her drink. "I mean how can we be spiritual in this world?"

"That's just it Hannah, if you are born-again, then you are already spiritual. You just have to know that you are a new born-again spirit."

"You make it sound so easy Joshua," Kellie put her hand on her cheek and breathed in and out heavily.

"Joshua, I want to thank you for obeying the Lord last weekend." Hannah was referring to her dad getting saved and Joshua taking action against the devil and his plans.

"How is your dad?" asked Kellie.

Tears welled up in her eyes. "My dad is doing great! He hasn't had any withdrawals from the alcohol. My parents are reading the Bible everyday together. He can't get enough of the Word. He's listening to teaching tapes and he really liked Pastor Pearson's sermon last Sunday."

Joshua expected a good report. "This is only the beginning. The Lord God has ordained that the works of the devil be completely destroyed off our earth. The Devil Chasers are fulfilling the Lord's will by kicking the devil's butt!"

"Yeah! We are destroying the works of the devil through His Blood and the Word of His testimony," stated Mose.

Kellie looked around and realized the Hut was empty. "It's too late to go back to school, where do you want me to take you?" She stood and gathered their trash and went to pay for her lunch.

"In the name of Jesus I speak mercy over us," Mose proclaimed as they left the restaurant.

‡ ‡ ‡

Joshua was at his locker after school thanking the Lord for giving them mercy at the school office. They were almost a full class late from lunch and the secretary was busy. All they had to do was call their parents to get them excused. It was a good practical application of speaking the Word of God in faith and receiving the manifestation immediately.

Joshua closed his locker door and turned to go home.

"Knight! I want to talk to you!"

He turned around and looked into the angry face of Justin, his neighbor.

"What's this?" Justin was holding one of the Devil Chaser cards in his hand.

"It's a card."

"I know that stupid!" Justin read from card, "Have Bible will travel? What's this crap?"

Joshua didn't know whether to talk to Justin or just walk away, until he looked into his eyes. In them, he saw a spirit of anger daring him to say anything. Not wanting a confrontation with the devil at the moment, he decided to walk away from him.

"Hey, Knight!" Justin yelled at him and grabbed his arm. "Turn around! I'm talking to you! You aren't getting away from me this time."

Everyone in the hallway stopped and listened. Someone ran over yelling, "Fight! Fight!"

The demon of anger in Justin exposed himself to Joshua. He summoned other demons to come to his help through by yelling out to them. The demons stirred up the kids and caused them to run over so they could see a fight. Not knowing the root of their desire, they loved to see a fight.

Joshua was aware that everyone was starring at them. In his mind, he remembered Jesus' parable about the sower that sows seed. Demons come to steal the Word out of the heart of the hearers almost as soon as the Word is deposited into that person. The kingdom of darkness was using Justin to attack Joshua was coming after the great teaching session the Lord anointed during lunch. He knew he had to be careful with what he said, so he started praying in the Spirit quietly.

Justin flipped his card at him. "I'm waiting loser."

The card hit Joshua in the face. Justin moved close enough to Joshua to put his finger in his chest and blow his bad breath over his nose.

"Look, stupid! You're making all of us Christians look bad." Justin kept hitting his chest with his finger. "Don't you know what kids think of you around here?" he laughed.

"Yeah, Knight, you must be crazy if you think you can chase devils!" another kid yelled out from the crowd.

Justin thumped the side of his head hard with his finger. "We thought you were an idiot talking in those *tongues* that nobody can understand! After reading your card we know what a fool you are!" He mocked speaking in tongues.

"Yeah! Knight!" Someone yelled.

"Hit him!"

The crowd was beginning to chant again.

"Hit him! Hit him!"

Joshua wasn't sure what he was going to do. It was hard not to respond to him in the flesh. He knew he couldn't back away from the commitment to God's calling on his life by having a fit of carnality. But maybe just this once he could hit Justin and ask the Lord to forgive him afterwards.

It doesn't work that way Joshua, his spirit told him sternly.

Lord, I need some wisdom before I get creamed! He opened his mouth and heard himself say, "Go ahead and hit me Justin. You want to hit me more than anything, do it!"

"What?"

Joshua kept his eyes open the whole time as he lifted his chin and pointed to it. "Go ahead. Hit me!" His flesh started yelling at him. *Are you crazy! This guy is going to knock your block off. He's at least a head taller than you!*

Justin pulled his arm back to put his fist in Joshua's face. The desire to hurt him was driving him so hard he was hurting. He smiled thinking how long he had awaited this day and then his eyes narrowed. "Wait a minute, why do you want me to hit you?" He put his fist down by his side. "What's up with you now, Knight?"

"Just one hit and I will have you to thank," Joshua smiled. "Go ahead! Make my day! Hit me!"

The thought of hitting him made him draw back his arm like he was going to throw this grand punch. *Wait a minute! Something's wrong.* The demon in him relaxed his posture. "What in——are you talking about?" He relaxed his fist and put his arm down a second time.

"No! I'm not talking about hell, I'm talking about heaven. I will be a lifetime member of the martyr's club in heaven!" *Wow! How awesome!* Joshua was hearing his own voice say something that he never heard before.

Justin looked at Joshua with a puzzled look on his face. All the desire to hit Joshua left him like the air out of a busted balloon. "What did you say Knight?" Justin asked as he released his shirt. A look of astonishment came over his face.

"You know, martyred saints, those people who suffered for the cause of Jesus Christ." Joshua stuck out his chin. "Make me a member for eternity of that prestigious elite club." He pointed at his chin again. "Go ahead and hit me. The angels in heaven will add my name to the book of martyrs. I can just see it now when Paul calls roll, my name is on the list with some of the most famous Christians in the history of the church."

Justin couldn't believe what he was hearing. "You're crazy Knight."

"You are so right! I am crazy in love with Jesus. I am crazy enough to start the Devil Chasers ministry out of obedience. He gave me the idea and the name of this ministry. If you think that's crazy, then I am guilty and Jesus is crazy too."

Justin was stunned.

"Come on! Hit me!" He really wanted him to punch him after he heard the words coming out of his mouth. Until now he never knew that there was a book of martyrs in heaven.

No one said a word from the crowd. They couldn't believe what they were hearing. When they realized there probably wasn't going to be a fight, they lost interest.

One by one the kids started leaving.

"You're nuts. I'm not wasting my energy over a crazy!" Justin pushed him out of his face and thumped him on his head. "You're a loser!" He turned around and walked away from him. To hit him now would be a mistake.

What Justin didn't know was that the evil spirit using him stopped the signal that was driving him to hurt Joshua. The urgency to hit him totally left Justin. How could the demon allow Justin to hit Joshua knowing that he was going to receive another reward in heaven? That knowledge took away all his fun and the evil spirit left Justin frustrated.

Joshua got in the car rubbing his head. He was a little disappointed. Maybe he would get another chance to get his name recorded in that special club in heaven. Becoming a martyr for Jesus didn't seem such a big deal after all . . .

. . . Kientay reached for the card and it rose off the floor and went into Joshua's pocket. The Holy Spirit had decreed that not one card would be lost or destroyed. Sitting in the backseat of the car, he heard over the graceline that the Lord Jesus gave instructions to a recording angel to add Joshua's name to the book of martyrs.

After all, the Lord told Kientay, *he did get thumped in the head twice.*

Joshua ran inside his house wanting to answer the phone line and talk to teenagers about Jesus with a passion. The phone pad beeped as soon as he turned his line on. "The Devil Chasers," he was trying to get his breath. "How may I help you?"

"Are you the one I talked to?"

He recognized the caller as the father with the boy who had epileptic seizures. "Yes sir, I am."

"I want to tell you that my son is different. He . . ."

It sounded to Joshua like the man was trying to hold back tears.

"Ever since you prayed for him, he's been different. We took him to the clinic to get some testing done. The doctor compared these test to past tests and he said that the chemical imbalance he had is gone."

There was silence on the phone for a few seconds.

"Some of the tests showed a malfunction in his brain is no longer there." He choked out, "I believe he is healed!"

"Praise the Lord!" Joshua said. He never had a doubt.

"I do accept Jesus as the Son of God and so does my family. We believe He has great power to heal and save."

Praise the Lord! The Lord kept Justin from hitting me so that I wouldn't miss getting this call. God is so good!

Joshua prayed with them over the phone and gave them the name of Pastor Pearson to call. He looked up to heaven and gave the Lord special thanks. "Praise the Lord! Thank you Lord for teaching me how to kick the devil's butt and be an overcomer!"

As he waited for the next caller, Joshua heard the Lord speaking to him in his spirit.

This is the beginning of a new generation on earth. It is a new age, a new thing that I, the Lord God, am going to explode all over the whole earth. This is the Joshua Generation. As you have prostrated yourself before Me and cried out for the youth of this country, I tell you that I will bring them out of prisons and make them preachers. I will take them out of drugs and will cause them to be apostles. For the Lord says, I have seen you. I have taken those and thrust them to the ground, where they can go no further. I cry for you, says the Lord, because there are many that have said, How can it be possible for the Lord God to use this younger generation? Many have said that they are too bad, too rebellious, too far gone. They err in that they do not understand the power of My Word, says the Lord.

They are going to be raised up and when they are raised up, they will be raised as warriors. Even though you have been wounded, even though you may have fallen in the battle, I will take the wounded warriors and raise them up. You will see the very face of the snake. You will see the face of the serpent. While you are down, you will recognize him, but when you get up, you will put your foot on the serpent's head, says the Lord.

I, the Lord say that a harvest of souls is coming to the world. Many, many, many, souls will be saved. Many people will be healed and filled with the Holy Spirit. Many people will dance before me filled with laughter and many, many people will be come out of darkness and be saved. I, the Lord, have spoken and no weapon of the enemy can stop Me, says the Lord.

I declare and proclaim that this is the beginning of the Joshua Generation! This is a new beginning. I the Lord have declared that it will happen and My word will come to pass!

After he wrote down what the Lord said, his phone beeped. He pushed the button on the phone pad and answered.

"The Devil Chasers, this is Joshua speaking. Jesus is Lord and He is coming soon! How may I help you?"

Contact K.L. Hopkins at
www.devilchasers.com
or order more copies of this book at

TATE PUBLISHING, LLC

127 East Trade Center Terrace
Mustang, Oklahoma 73064

(888) 361 - 9473

Tate Publishing, LLC

www.tatepublishing.com